Lake of Blood
Book Two of the Discordia Series

John Alspaugh and Ken Daniels

Original cover art by Ashley Hart
https://www.twitch.tv/icehart92

ISBNs: 978-1-7344997-2-8 (paperback), 978-1-7344997-3-5 (ebook)

Table of Contents

Chapter 1

The sound of what could only be described as thunder echoed loudly throughout the night sky as Seth dove behind a nearby building, the cut across his back staining both his purple shirt and the wall behind him red. Fortunately for him it wasn't a deep cut, as it did not hinder his ability to move in any way, and it didn't feel fatal. Unfortunately for him, however, despite it not being fatal it seemingly refused to stop bleeding, which was more than a little annoying for him because due to an unfortunate series of circumstances, this was the only purple shirt he had left. He liked this shirt. Hell, he liked the color purple in general, and while it was not a hard color to find in the small town where he lived, it always frustrated him whenever he had to wait for the town's seamstress, Tabitha, to make him a new one. Even if the wait was never really that long.

None of that mattered at the current moment, however, as Seth took these brief few seconds of respite to catch his breath.

"Keep it together," he said quietly to himself through clenched teeth. "You can do this. You've done it before and it isn't hard. You know that." As he spoke he curled the fingers of his left hand inward, as if to grasp a ball that wasn't there. As he did the ground beneath his feet began to tremble slightly. "And it's not even that big, so it should be even easier, right?" The sudden sound of thunder rapidly approaching from behind him instantly shook him out of his momentary calm. "Only one way to find out!"

The next few seconds were tense as the sound of thunder grew louder and louder, the ground even began to shake slightly from the force of whatever was making that sound. Then, the instant the volume of the thunder seemed to reach its apex, Seth ran out from behind the building, and as he did so the earth beneath his feet suddenly tore a chunk of itself out from the ground beneath him and vaulted Seth into the air. His timing had been impeccable as the source of the thunderous noise sprinted past him while he was airborne.

Time almost seemed to freeze for Seth as he momentarily locked eyes with the monstrous entity before him. For all intents and purposes it resembled a horse, though with several notable differences. The most apparent of which was that its coat was jet black in color from its hooves all the way to its head. Its mane and tail were a color, somewhat similar to Seth's shirt, but more indigo than purple in color. The most glaring difference between it and a normal horse, however, was that jutting out from its forehead was a seventy centimeter long, forward facing, jagged, blade-like horn that dripped with blood. All of this culminated in a pair of blood red eyes, one of which stared directly back at Seth as he leapt through the air.

Time instantly returned to its normal pace as Seth landed on the horse-monster's back. As soon as he was able to, he grabbed onto the horse's mane for support as it galloped forward at its full speed down the main road through the small town of Canaan towards the southern gate, which was open. Walls made of fire leading all the way to the southern gate then suddenly sprang up on both sides of the horse as it galloped forward, preventing it from going anywhere else as Seth struggled to stay on its back. Not about to let go, Seth held out his right hand as, from a cloud of crimson smoke, a longsword appeared in his hand, which he then immediately thrust into the horse-monster where its shoulder met its neck and held onto it with all the strength he had. The horse monster in turn let out a loud, distorted, neigh like noise as it picked up speed and charged through the southern gate and out into the desert.

As soon as the horse-monster was through the southern gate it slammed closed behind it as two of Canaan's town watchmen quickly came out and barred the gate closed. The horse-monster, as if realizing where it was, and with the flames no longer directing its movement, slowed its gallop as it quickly shifted from sprinting forward to leaping up from the ground where it stood again and again in an attempt to buck Seth off of it. Seth, with one hand still on the horse monster's mane and the other on the hilt of his sword, held on for his life as the horse-monster repeatedly attempted to buck him off of it. Out of the corner of his eye, Seth noticed a flash of green light from the top of the southern gate. Glancing in that direction he saw the brown haired and green eyed visage of Raz, another citizen of the town of Canaan, though not a member of the town watch like he was.

"I've got this!" Seth shouted to him as he held onto the horse monster. "Get the other one!" Raz did not respond with words, but with another flash of green light as he teleported off of the southern gate back to somewhere within the town. With that out of his mind, Seth returned his full attention back to the horse-monster as it still relentlessly attempted to buck him off. Unable to do much of anything, as it took his full strength just to maintain his grip, Seth grit his teeth in frustration as the fingers of his left hand, the hand that held onto the horse's mane, danced with electrical sparks. Within seconds, the sparks went from mere sparks to a full on electrical surge as Seth, without letting go, ran an electrical strike up along the horse's mane, lighting it aflame instantly.

The horse monster let out another distorted neigh as it became wilder and tried to buck Seth off with much more vigor. Forced to let go of its mane, Seth instead aimed his open hand down towards the horse-monster's hooves, whereupon the earth beneath it suddenly opened up and swallowed all four of the horse-monster's hooves, burying them beneath the earth. However, this did nothing at all to impede the horse-monster's movement as it bucked one more time and pulled all four of its hooves up and out from the earth, kicking up sand and chunks of the earth with it. Some of which got into Seth's eyes. Momentarily distracted, and without both of his hands holding onto the horse monster, with one intense buck Seth was thrown forward off of the horse-monster. Seth still held onto his sword, however, as he hung limply from the horse-monster's thick neck like a human shaped necklace. The horse monster, in response, continued its bucking motion and with one more intense buck, Seth was thrown several meters into the air before landing on the desert sands and rolling away from the horse.

Blurry vision and a loud ringing in his ears washed over Seth, along with the fact that he was in a lot of pain both from the impact of hitting the ground and the sting from the sand that had decided to jump right into the open wound on his back. Despite this Seth managed to pull himself onto his knees as he cleared the sand from his eyes. His hearing returned before his vision, as he soon heard the thunderous sounds of the horse-monster's hooves behind him. Acting on instinct more than training, Seth instantly rolled over onto his knees properly and with another spontaneous cloud of crimson smoke, re-summoned his sword from the horse-monster's neck into his hands. The instant he felt the cold metal of his sword in his hand again he held it up and blocked the horse monster's bladed horn just as it was less than a meter away from his head. As Seth and the horse monster locked blades, Seth slowly stood back up onto his feet, never once breaking eye contact with the horse-monster as it silently stared back at him, its mane having long since burned away from the flames.

Seth grit his teeth and unconsciously let out a deep, growl like noise at the horse-monster as he pushed its bladed horn slightly farther away from him. The horse-monster in response, didn't make any noise at all, it simply bared its sharp, flesh ripping teeth while it stared back at him with its large, blood red eyes. Thinking quickly, and still furious at this thing for bucking him off, Seth pulled back his left hand as it crackled brightly with electricity. The horse-monster, seeing this, quickly drew its head back away from Seth as he thrust his left hand forward and shot a bolt of lighting from his fingertips, which only barely missed the horse-monster as it pulled away from Seth and spun itself around.

Seeing what was coming, Seth quickly threw his left hand upwards as a wall made from the earth shot up from the ground in front of him just as the horse-monster reared back and kicked at Seth with both of its rear legs. To Seth's utter shock and disbelief, the horse-monster actually kicked through his earth wall and hit him square in the chest as he was knocked several meters backwards from the force of the blow before landing on his back again. While the impact was mostly softened by the earth wall, Seth nevertheless needed to take a moment to get his breath back as he pulled himself back onto his feet, only to see the horse monster spin itself back around and charge directly towards him with its bladed horn forward. Seth in turn quickly rolled to his right before the horse monster could gore him with its bladed horn as it sprinted past him.

Without slowing down the horse-monster made a u-turn as it ran back in Seth's direction with its horn lowered. Seth prepared himself to dodge, but then stopped himself as an idea suddenly came to him and he realized that this horse-monster could easily change its tactics if he dodged again. He wasn't sure at all if this particular monster was smart enough to do that, but personal experience had taught him to never underestimate the intelligence of a monster. With that in mind, Seth dispelled his sword as it dissolved back into a crimson cloud of mist and stood his ground as the horse monster's hulking form galloped closer and closer towards him.

'*I hope this works!*' Seth mentally screamed at himself as what would be his impending doom if he messed this up galloped even faster towards him. At the last possible second Seth threw up both his arms as another, thicker wall of earth shot up from the ground in front of him. With no time at all to react, the horse-monster crashed head first into the earth wall, its bladed horn piercing through it as easily as a sword would pierce through flesh before fully embedding itself into the stone wall, with the tip of its horn only a few centimeters away from touching Seth's nose. Seth wanted to let out a sigh of relief, if only for the fact that his idea actually worked, but stopped himself when the horse-monster let out another loud, distorted, neigh-like noise. While Seth could not see behind the stone wall, he could see from the subtle movements of the horse-monster's horn and the frantic sounds of hooves on sand that it was attempting to pull itself out from his earthly trap.

With only seconds until the horse-monster inevitably pulled itself free and no better ideas of what to do, Seth held up both of his hands. At first nothing appeared to be happening, but then a series of cracks formed along the base of his stone wall. After a few more seconds of this, with a loud snap the large slab of earth was separated from the ground, held aloft by Seth's sheer willpower. The horse-monster, thinking that it was somehow closer to freeing its horn from the wall of earth, let out another, louder, distorted neigh as it began to thrash about more violently by hopping about and bucking its back legs. Sweat poured down Seth's forehead as he began to feel the effects of fighting a large monster like this with only a slab of earth held together only by his magical grip, that being a headache that felt more akin to being repeatedly bashed in the back of his head with a shovel. Eventually the horse monster began to jerk its head back and forth in another attempt to free itself from the earth wall. Seeing this, Seth waited for the horse monster to make one more quick jerk to his left. As soon as it did, with all of the strength and willpower that he could muster, Seth pulled the stone slab in the opposite direction. A sound akin to a tree branch snapping echoed through the night air, then shortly followed by the horse-monster letting out what sounded less like the distorted neigh sounds it usually made and more akin to a growl-like scream that Seth was certain was loud enough to be heard by everyone back in town.

With that done, Seth released his magical grip on the slab of earth, causing it, along with the horse-monster's severed horn still embedded into it, to fall. The earth wall cracked apart when it hit the sand, as it no longer had Seth's magic to hold it together. For a moment Seth let out the sigh of relief he had been holding in, as with that sound the fight seemed to be over. Those thoughts lasted for only a single second, however, as Seth once again found himself staring directly into the blood red eyes of the horse-monster before it quickly closed the distance between them and opened its mouth. While Seth was no expert on horses, in the few interactions he had had with them he had seen that their teeth were more or less flat, not unlike his own. In contrast to that, this creature's maw was filled with sharp, triangular shaped, flesh ripping teeth. Thinking as quickly as he could, Seth backed away, re-summoned his sword, then held it horizontally in front of him with both hands before the horse monster snapped its jaws down onto the blade. The monster's bite strength far exceeded what Seth had expected from it as with that single bite, Seth swore that he could hear the sound of the metal of his blade cracking.

'*No no no no no!*' Seth mentally screamed to himself as his eyes darted every which way they could in the seemingly vain hope that he could find something or someone to help him. A sudden wave or hot air rushed over Seth's face as the horse-monster pushed its face in closer towards him and exhaled through its nostrils. The smell of its breath reminded Seth of rotten meat. As that thought ran through his head, he looked down towards his feet and saw what he had been looking for in the pile of rocks left behind from his wall of stone. Without thinking twice about what he was about to do, Seth let go of his sword with his left hand and held it out in the direction of the rocks. Before he could do any more than this, however, the sound of metal snapping hit Seth's ears as the blade of his sword suddenly shattered into three pieces before turning back into red mist as they faded back into the nothingness from whence they had come.

With nothing to hold onto, Seth stumbled backwards and fell onto his back. Thankfully the desert sand was soft, so the impact did not hurt him as much as he knew it could have. Before Seth could even think of what he could do next his attention was taken by the sound of another distorted neigh as he looked up to see the horse-monster rear up on its hind legs, with its forelegs positioned directly over him. Seth did not even need to think about what he needed to do as he quickly rolled to his left before the horse-monster could bring its hooves down on him. As he rolled back onto his knees Seth threw his left arm out to his side in a sweeping motion. As he did so the horse monster's severed horn, as if on its own, lifted itself up from the sand, flew through the air, and straight through the horse-monster's throat as effortlessly as a hot knife would cut through butter.

At first nothing seemed to happen, but then after a few short seconds the horse-monster's jet black coat was suddenly stained red as blood sprayed from the freshly opened wound in its neck and covered the sand below it. The horse-monster gasped in vain again and again for air as it stumbled left and right in an attempt to keep its balance as more of its blood continued to pour from the open wound in its neck, covering its dark coat and the sand beneath its hooves in a crimson color that matched its eyes. Eyes that eventually found Seth as the horse-monster continued to stumble back and forth. There was a tense moment of silence between them as their eyes met, the horse-monster standing defiantly, as if the open wound in its neck was an inconvenience rather than fatal. Seth, in response, let out a low growl at the horse-monster before it lost the last ounce of its strength and collapsed onto its side.

With the monster finally defeated, Seth stood back onto his feet and wandered over towards its corpse. He found himself staring directly into its blood red eyes again as they in turn starred lifelessly up towards the sky. He could see his reflection in them like a kind of scarlet mirror, which allowed him to see exactly how disheveled he looked. He was covered in cuts, bruises, sand, and most of all sweat. His hair was an absolute mess as it went in all directions and his shirt desperately needed to get washed if not thrown out due to how damaged it was. The worst of which being the nice, clean cut across his back courtesy of the monster that was now a corpse in front of him. Needless to say, this was not his best look.

Before Seth could take in any more details regarding how he looked, the horse-monster's eye suddenly blinked. Startled, without thinking Seth let out another, louder growl as he re-summoned his sword and thrust it directly into the horse-monster's eye, which made a wet, squishing sound as the blade went right through the horse monster's head. Seth then let out several heavy breaths for almost a full minute as he grit his teeth, his breathing sounding more akin to growls rather than human breaths. Eventually, after the minute had passed, his breathing returned to normal and the growls had in turn subsided into normal, human sounding breaths as Seth let go of his sword before it dissolved back into red mist. With that the horse-monster ceased to move and Seth was now certain that it was dead as he took more than a few steps back away from it and sat down onto the sand.

The instant he felt himself relax, his attention was taken by a sudden flash of green light to his left. When he looked in that direction his eyes beheld the near two meter tall, brown haired and green eyed visage of Raz.

"Brutal," Raz said aloud before tossing something onto the sand beside the corpse of the horse-monster. While Seth could easily assume that what Raz had tossed onto the sand was the corpse of the other monster that had set foot in Canaan, the twisted, mangled corpse of the thing was burned to an absolute crisp, leaving no indication at all as to what it might have originally looked like. There was even still smoke coming off of it. After Seth had managed to tear his gaze away from the crispy corpse of the other monster he saw that Raz had walked over towards him and was holding his hand out towards him. As if by instinct more than actual thought, Seth began to reach out for Raz's hand, but then quickly stopped himself before he could actually touch him.

"I'm fine," Seth said as he recoiled his hand back. "I can get myself up." Seth followed that statement by quickly picking himself up off the sand and patting his legs a bit to shake any hitchhiking sand off of his pants.

"Looks like you didn't need us to save your scrawny ass this time!" a more than familiar female voice called out to them. Upon hearing it Seth turned his attention away from Raz and towards the owner of that voice as she walked out from the now open southern gate of Canaan. There he could see, walking towards them, was the red headed visage of the monster hunter, Vivian. She was making her way towards them at her own leisurely pace, obviously in no rush. That, however, did nothing to stop the mild feeling of dread that began to form in Seth's gut with each step that she took closer towards him. She stopped once she had reached the two of them, her eyes darting between the duo of deceased monsters in the sand. "So, fucking Raz pops in out of nowhere and roasts the one I was fighting and you somehow managed to take down the big one. Fucking great."

"Yeah, I-I got it," Seth replied without looking at her. There was an obvious coating of anxiety in his voice as he spoke to her. "Is everyone in Canaan okay?"

"Before I ran out here I saw Jacque and Ruben carrying Gene in the direction of Andrea's clinic," Vivian answered. "But that's about as far as I know."

"Is he okay?" Seth then immediately asked, actually bothering to make eye contact with Vivian as he did so. "He's not dead is he?"

"The fuck if I know," Vivian responded, seemingly ignoring how concerned Seth was for Gene despite having never met him. "He seemed like he was alive when they were taking him there. That's all I know."

"Well, I'm probably going to find out soon anyways," Seth said with a sigh as he turned himself around and began to make his way back towards the southern gate. "I'm headed that way myself." Once he was far enough away to be out of earshot of both Raz and Vivian Seth pulled on his shirt a little bit so that he could examine it more closely. "This is my favorite shirt."

"Fucking Solaris," Vivian let out once she was certain that Seth was far enough away that he would not hear her. "This being nice to him thing is more exhausting than my actual job."

"That was you being nice?" Raz asked her with a raised eyebrow.

"Fuck you," Vivian immediately respond to him.

"Sorry, you're not my type," Raz responded with a smirk, only to get an icy glare in response from Vivian.

"Well hopefully by the end of next week I won't have to deal with him or you anymore and I can stop pretending to be a fucking actress," Vivian then said as she began to make her way back towards the southern gate herself. Raz was quick to follow behind her.

As Seth made his way back within the town's walls towards Andrea's clinic, unbeknownst to him, in between two buildings, camouflaged within the shadows cast by them, a bat-like creature the size of a hawk sat perfectly still as it kept a careful watch on Seth as he made his way through the town past its hiding spot with both of its large, piercing, blood red eyes focused directly on him.

Chapter 2

Seth's walk to Andrea's clinic was surprisingly uneventful given all that had happened that night. He had been to her clinic enough times already to know exactly where it was, so there was no reason for him to deviate from what he knew was the quickest path there, and thankfully no one bothered to stop him to talk about what had just happened. When he entered the clinic, however, he found himself greeted by three other members of the town watch. The first two were Jacque and Ruben, which did not surprise Seth at all. The third, however, was a surprise to him. There with them was Kurt, who was currently speaking to Jacque and Ruben with his back to Seth. Well, speaking with Jacque was more accurate as Ruban now possessed a large patch of scar tissue covering the front of his neck. From what Seth was told, Ruban was almost killed in the monster attack a few months back and only barely managed to survive, but lost his ability to speak. While standing there, Seth took notice of the notebook and graphite stick that he now used to communicate in one of his front pockets.

"Very well, I'll report this to Charlie as soon as I'm done here," Kurt said to the two of them. "You two can leave if you want now. I don't need anything else from you guys." As soon as he finished speaking, without saying anything both Jacque and Ruben walked around him and past Seth. Neither one of them paid him any mind as they exited the clinic. As they did, Kurt spun around to follow them before he noticed Seth standing there. "Oh, Seth. What brings you here? That fucking horse thing didn't gore you too did it?" A look of genuine concern suddenly washed over Kurt's face as he asked that.

"I don't know what that means, so I'm going to say no," Seth answered as calmly as he could before turning around to show him the long, clean cut on his back. "I need Andrea to help me out with this."

"Oh, damn!" Kurt let out as he took a good look at Seth's injury. Despite how terrible they both knew it could have been, it was a completely clean cut, as if it had been made by a surgical instrument, not a simple blade. Not only that, but it continued to bleed while Seth stood in front of him, staining more of his now ruined purple shirt red. Despite this, Seth continued to act as if it was more of an inconvenience than anything worrying. It was almost as if the loss of that much blood didn't affect him at all, which worried Kurt somewhat. "Well, you might need to wait a while. She kind of has her hands full right now."

"Is it Gene?" Seth then asked as he turned back around to properly face Kurt. "Vivian told me that he got hurt."

"Hurt is putting it mildly, but yes," Kurt answered. "Poor bastard got gored... Sorry, stabbed all the way through by that Solaris damned horse."

"All the way through?" Seth asked in turn.

"Yeah, that's what gored means," Kurt responded. "To get stabbed through the front and have it come out the back. Or the back to the front, both are just as bad."

"Is he okay!" Seth then immediately asked. The concern in his voice was evident.

"For now, yes," Kurt answered. Hearing that put Seth somewhat at ease. "That's actually why I'm here. I need to get a full report of what exactly happened from the ones who were actually there."

"Well, the horse is dead," Seth said. "I killed it. So do you need to hear from me too?" Kurt's eyes went slightly wider upon hearing that.

"Really," he said, sounding more than a little surprised. "Well, if that's true then yeah, I actually do."

From there Seth proceeded to spend the next ten minutes explaining to Kurt everything that had happened from his point of view since the monster attack had started. Starting from when he had heard the alarm bell go off, to his initial fight with the horse-monster, to riding said horse-monster outside of the southern gate before finally finishing at the point where he sent the horse-monster's own severed horn through its neck. Kurt, for his part, simply stood in complete silence and took as many mental notes as he could of Seth's story.

"I have to say, I'm glad that I spent the time learning how to lift objects with magic," Seth said with a small chuckle as he finished his story. "Or else I would've had to come up with a completely different plan."

"Well, um..." Kurt responded as he quickly recomposed himself. "I'm not an expert on magic or anything, but isn't that like one of the simplest things a mage can do? I mean, Celene told me she figured out how to do that when she was I think... six or something."

"Maybe," Seth answered with a shrug. "But I only figured out how to do it recently. It's come in handy quite a few times actually... Wait, how do you know

Celene?"

"It's a small town, Seth. Most people here know each other," Kurt responded in a monotone voice. "And I've been dating her for the past three years, so yes, I know her very well." He emphasized that last part with a slightly smug tone. Seth, however, only blinked at him as a confused expression crossed his face.

"Okay…" Seth eventually said, the confusion in his voice now more than evident. "I didn't know that. Sorry."

"It's fine," Kurt replied with a wave of his hand. "It's not like we go screaming it from rooftops or anything."

"Well you are practically screaming it in my clinic," a stern female voice suddenly spoke up from seemingly nowhere. As soon as they both heard it Seth and Kurt turned their attention towards the source of the voice. There, walking out into the waiting room with them from the door to the clinic itself, was a woman with long, pale blonde hair that reached all the way to her knees wearing a white coat that both men immediately recognized as Andrea, who stared coldly at the two of them with her icy blue eyes. "This isn't a schoolyard playground, so unless you have a reason to be here then I suggest that you take your gossip elsewhere."

"I have this cut on my back," Seth then said as he turned around to show it to her.

"Of course you do," Andrea responded in that same, stern, yet emotionless voice of hers.

"It hurts a lot," Seth added.

"Of course it does."

"And it won't stop bleeding."

"I can see that," Andrea responded. The sound of Kurt letting out an abrupt cough, however, took their attention away from that awkward moment.

"Well, before I take my leave, may I ask if Gene is okay?" Kurt asked. The look of anticipation and concern on his face was obvious even to Seth.

"You just did, but he's stable," Andrea answered without any change in the tone of her voice. Kurt involuntarily let out a breath that he had been holding in for what seemed like a while before Andrea could continue. "For now. He's going to have to stay here for a while so that I can keep an eye on him for whe-… If he wakes up." The air in the room suddenly became heavier as the deliberate pause before the word "if" did not go unnoticed by either Seth or Kurt. It hit Seth particularly hard, though he did his best not to show it. The fact that monsters could do this kind of damage every time they came to this town, or anywhere from what he had heard, was more than Seth could stomach sometimes. Especially given his own history with them. After a few long moments of awkward silence, in what seemed like an attempt to lighten the mood, Kurt let out a rather loud chuckle before he spoke again.

"Well, I guess I'll have to tell the guys that tomorrow's poker night is off," he said before he then turned around to leave the clinic.

"What is poker night?" Seth then asked before Kurt could reach the door.

"How do you… Oh, right," Kurt responded before turning himself back around to face Seth properly, which wasn't too difficult since Seth still had his back to Andrea. "Once a month Gene, Joseph, Alvarez and I head to the pub and play poker, but without him… We could probably play with just the three of us, but then the game would be a lot less interesting."

"So poker is a game?" Seth then immediately asked, now curious.

"Yes," Kurt answered. "You play it with a deck of cards. You do know what a card is, right?"

"Yes," Seth answered plainly. At his answer a sudden light went off in Kurt's head like a candle being lit with magic as a smile slowly spread across his lips.

"Hey, Seth," he began. "Since Gene can't make it, do you wanna join us?"

"But I have no idea how to play," Seth answered without thinking.

"Don't worry," Kurt quickly responded with a wave of his hand. "If you come along with us we can show you. Besides, after tonight I'm sure you could use a drink like the rest of us."

"I don't like the taste of ale," Seth said as soon as Kurt had finished speaking.

"Or don't, that's fine too," Kurt responded. "You can still play poker with us. Come on, it will be fun."

"If all of this is just a thinly veiled excuse to take all of Seth's money then I am going to put a stop to this right now," Andrea interjected as she looked past Seth and narrowed her eyes directly on Kurt.

"Oh no, it's fine, it's fine!" Kurt responded rather suddenly to her as he threw both of his hands up. "We don't have to play for money. I mean the guy doesn't even know how to play, so that would just be mean."

"You guys play for money?" Seth couldn't help but ask, now slightly worried as well as confused.

"Not always," Kurt answered. The smile on his face had quickly changed from sinister to guilty in the time it had taken him to direct his attention back to Seth.

"Well maybe the two of you can talk about this after we're done here so that you can stop wasting my time," Andrea interjected again. "Or did you already forget that I have a patient that's much worse off than you are, Seth?"

"Oh, umm… Yes, sorry," Seth quickly responded as he turned back around and approached the doctor.

"Just think about it!" Kurt called back to him as he left the clinic and closed the door behind him.

Roughly ten minutes after talking to Kurt, Seth was sitting on a stool with his shirt off while Andrea sat behind him with a bucket of water, a washcloth, and a first aid kit by her side. After dipping the washcloth into the bucket and wringing out the extra water, Andrea placed the cold and wet cloth against Seth's wound. Seth winced as he felt a slight sting of pain from the sudden contact of the cloth, but he did his best to keep still so that Andrea could do her job. As Andrea cleaned the blood and sand from Seth's back, her free hand began to glow with a slight teal colored light as she ran the hand gently over Seth's wound close enough so that her magic could be effective, but far enough so that she was not physically touching him. As she slowly ran her free hand over Seth's wound, it slowly stopped bleeding and some of the redness that surrounded the wound began to recede. It was slow, but it was effective enough as she could see Seth's blood beginning to coagulate around the wound.

"Tell me, Seth, how long have you been here?" Andrea then suddenly asked him while she worked.

"I don't know," Seth answered. "Twenty minutes maybe."

"I mean in Canaan," Andrea clarified. "How long has it been since you started living here?" Seth needed to take more than a few seconds to do some math in his head before he could come up with an answer.

"Seven months," he eventually answered.

"So in seven months you've ended up in my clinic four times," Andrea then said as she continued to clean more of Seth's wound. "Though I will give you some credit. At least you were conscious this time." Seth did not know at all how to respond to that. Mostly because he was unsure of whether or not she was scolding him for that.

"I'm sorry," was all he could think of to say.

"At least you don't hold the record for the most visits in the shortest amount of time," Andrea said to him after that. "Take a wild guess who holds said record." Seth did not even need to take a single second to think about who that might have been.

"Vivian," he blurted out.

"I can see why you would think that, but surprisingly no," Andrea responded as she continued to run her hand down Seth's back. "She's in second place actually, with you in third. No, the one who holds that record is actually Ash's hired hand, Dean."

"Really?" Seth couldn't help but let out, as he was more than a little surprised to hear that.

"As I said, surprisingly yes," Andrea answered. "The first two months he was here he ended up in my clinic at least once a week. I'm still unsure whether or not he was just really, really clumsy or if he had a crush on me. If that was the case though then apparently he was even more nervous than you were when you first arrived since he didn't have the stones to ask me out."

"Would you have said yes if he did?" Seth asked, genuinely curious. From a conversation he had had with Lydia and Bethany roughly two months back, Seth had attained the knowledge of what a 'date' was. Though he was still unsure why only outings with one's significant other were considered dates when they did the same things that everybody else did.

"Solaris no," Andrea responded much quicker than Seth had expected her to, sounding almost offended at the mere suggestion of that. "For one thing, he's an absolute moron. For another, he's much too lanky for my tastes, and for yet another, he smells like dirt and sweat all the time. I mean seriously, I don't think he even knows what a bath is." As she finished her rant her hands reached the end of Seth's wound. "Okay, now that I can actually see the wound it doesn't look as bad as I initially thought it did. It's a good thing you came straight to me as well. A wound like this is prone to all kinds of infections, especially if it keeps bleeding. Ordinarily I would suggest stitches, but knowing you, you'll probably be mostly healed by the end of the week."

"That's good to hear," Seth said as he let out a sigh.

"Don't sell yourself short," Andrea then said as she walked over to another nearby wash basin and cleansed her hands of Seth's blood. "You still can't let anything touch it, at least for a while, and I would avoid leaning on things. In fact I'm going to suggest that you don't let your back touch anything for at least a few days, and when you sleep, sleep on your stomach and try not to roll over." As she cleaned her hands Seth began to stand up from the stool. "I never said that I was done with you," Andrea suddenly said without turning around before Seth could even properly lift his knees into a standing position. The instant he heard her speak, Seth sat back down on the stool. At this point he knew better than to argue with her. Especially when it came to healing him.

After Andrea had finished cleaning her hands she grabbed a small bottle from a nearby shelf and walked back over to Seth. As soon as she sat back down behind Seth she removed the cap from the bottle and set it aside. She then lifted up her index finger, and as she did, a clear, viscous liquid floated up and out from the bottle, as if by its own accord. This continued until there was enough to cover the wound on Seth's back, after which Andrea set the bottle aside. That done, Andrea then held up both of her index fingers and began to move them both in identical figure eight patterns. As she did this, what was once a perfect sphere of liquid began to elongate until it was the exact length of the wound on Seth's back. Much like a serpent under the spell of a charmer, with direction from Andrea's fingers the rope of viscous liquid slithered closer towards Seth's wound.

"Warning you now, this might sting a bit," Andrea warned just before one end of the rope of viscous liquid touched the top of Seth's wound. Seth could not help himself as he immediately tensed up and let out a scream of pain as he felt what felt like thousands of tiny needles stabbing into his wound. "Don't be so dramatic. I'm sure getting cut was worse."

"No! It wasn't!" Seth responded, still in agony but doing his best not to yell. "What even is that stuff anyway!"

"An extra bit of added protection," Andrea explained as she applied more of the viscous liquid to Seth's wound, which again immediately caused him to tense up in agony. "It'll help keep you from getting an infection in the near future and it will also help the healing process."

"If it hurts that much, why do you even use it!" Seth asked her without thinking through gritted teeth.

"Do you want me to help you or not?" Andrea then immediately asked in response as she stopped applying the liquid to his wound, the remainder of it hanging in the air as if waiting for a command. While Seth could not see her face, he did not need to in order to imagine the look in her eyes when she had said that, and he knew better than to argue with her. With no other words to say. Seth did his best to relax and took a few long, deep breaths. Taking his silence as a cue to continue, Andrea continued to apply the rest of the liquid to his wound. It took all of Seth's willpower not to squirm from the sheer amount of stinging that he was feeling.

After spending another hour in Andrea's clinic getting bandaged up and making absolutely certain that he would be okay, Seth was finally able to return to his home in Canaan's library. His torso had been wrapped in bandages that covered the whole distance of the wound on his back from one end to the other. The cut itself had multiple pieces of cotton along it as well. While this did not restrict his movement too much, the repeated itchiness from the cotton was a constant reminder that the bandages were there. Andrea had insisted that he keep the bandages on for at least a week, which frustrated him because he kept wanting to take them off even though he knew that would not be a smart thing to do at all. Especially since, according to Andrea at least, the cotton was there to prevent any more bleeding.

He had since stopped noticing any pain in his back after Andrea had finished with him as well. Because of that he assumed that he did not have anything to worry about afterwards, and perhaps he would even be able to return to work. Andrea had responded to this by rather forcefully poking him in the back, which hurt so much more than Seth had anticipated. It was so much in fact that he nearly fell over. After having proved her point, Andrea insisted that he take it easy for at least a week, and that if he insisted on going back to work then she herself would walk over to speak to the watch commander, Charlie and have him tell Seth to take it easy. Seth stopped assuming anything after that and agreed that it would be best to do as Andrea said.

Regardless, he was more than okay to walk as he made his way to the front door of Canaan's library. After unlocking the front door with his key, upon stepping inside he was greeted by a very familiar sight.

"Seth!" The long, dark haired and blue eyed visage of Tara, his caretaker for the past seven months, shouted at the top of her lungs as she ran towards him and threw her arms arounds him in a great big hug.

"Ow!" Seth immediately exclaimed as both of Tara's arms slapped him across his back.

"I'm sorry!" Tara responded as she let go of Seth and stepped away from him as quickly as she physically could. "I'm so sorry, Seth! I-"

"It's okay, you didn't know," Seth interrupted her as he took a moment to regain his composure.

"Do you need anything?" Tara then asked with obvious concern in her voice. "Is there anything I can do for you?"

"Sleep," Seth answered as plainly as ever. "I think that's about it."

"Okay…" Tara replied. "Come on, let's go. I can help you up the stairs."

"That's okay," Seth responded as he walked past her. "I can walk just fine." And with that, Seth walked ahead of her up the stairs and before long was out of her sight. Tara could only stare after him for several long seconds of silence before following him up.

The following morning, after getting some much needed rest, Seth left the library with a new destination in mind. Much to his chagrin, the itching from the cotton was still there, which left him unable to fully remove the fact that he had recently been injured from his mind. Though upon reflection the thought occurred to him that perhaps that was intentional on Andrea's part. Whatever the reason, he did his best to ignore it for now as he made his way towards the next person he needed to talk to as he approached a building not too far from the library with the words "Fashion from the Sun" emblazoned above the door in bright orange letters. Seth reached for the doorknob in order to enter the establishment, only to find that it didn't budge a millimeter. Wondering if he had shown up too early he leaned over to look through the large window next to the front door. Past the two mannequins dressed in what Seth could only guess were fancy, and likely very expensive clothes, he spotted the slender, curvaceous figure of Tabitha, who in turn could also see him.

Tabitha initially looked surprised when she saw Seth through the window, but the look on her face quickly morphed into one of absolute delight as she suddenly darted out of Seth's view. Once she was certain that she was out of his line of sight, Tabitha set to work on adjusting the dark gray skirt she was wearing as she smoothed out any wrinkles that were obvious before adjusting it to hug as much of her form as possible. That done, she then set about undoing two of the buttons on her blouse, exposing roughly five centimeters of her cleavage. That done, she then made her way towards the front door, but then stopped herself.

'*Wait, what am I doing?*' Tabitha thought to herself. '*This isn't just anyone, this is Seth. This isn't going to work on him.*' After taking a second to contemplate exactly what she should do, she reached back up and undid one more button on her blouse. '*There, perfect.*'

Back outside Seth began to wonder exactly what was taking Tabitha as long as it was for her to just open the door. When he saw her, she wasn't even two meters from it, so there was no reason, at least in his mind, why it would take someone so long to do something so simple. In the end he settled for simply knocking. He was about to hold up his hand to do so before the front door to Fashion from the Sun suddenly swung open on its own, revealing the town's local tailor herself on the other side.

"Why hello, Seth," Tabitha said to him with a velvet-like smoothness to her voice. "What brings you to my humble little boutique this fine morning?"

"I need clothes," Seth stated as if that should have been obvious. Had it been anyone else who had said that, Tabitha might have been a little offended. However, she knew who Seth was, and by extension knew what he was like.

"Well if that is the case, then come on in," Tabitha then said to him as she moved over and held her arm out as if to invite Seth in. While Seth knew he could have walked in anyways, he took her up on her invitation, if only to be polite. After closing the door, Tabitha turned back around to properly face him, only to treat herself to a full view of Seth's back from the clean cut across his now ruined shirt to the bandaged wound underneath, and most importantly, at least to her, the immense amount of dried blood that was still all over it. It was only then that the smell of said dried blood hit her nose. "Ugh, Seth… Did that… happen last night?"

"Yes," Seth answered plainly as he turned himself around to properly face her. "That's why I need more shirts."

"Well, why aren't you wearing one of the other ones I made for you?" Tabitha then asked. "It's been a day, surely you must have had a chance to change your clothes at least once."

"I don't have any more purple shirts," Seth answered, again plainly and without much emotion behind his voice. "This was my last one."

"What happened to the others?" Tabitha couldn't help but ask, now more than curious herself.

"Other monsters, Florence, and I don't even know what happened to one of them," Seth answered as he looked directly into her eyes. Her eyes, and nothing else. "I hung it out to dry one day, but then when I came back it was gone. The wind must have taken it." As good of an answer as that was, Tabitha couldn't help but feel somewhat disappointed due to the lack of a more exciting answer. Still, she knew that this was Seth she was talking to. She had always known him to be direct.

"Well, let me see what I can do for you right now," Tabitha said as she walked away from him and began to browse through her selection of her available purple shirts, making sure to give Seth a full view of her backside as she did. "You don't want to spend all day wearing that ruined thing if you don't have to, do you?"

"I would prefer not to," Seth answered. While he could not see it, Tabitha couldn't help but smile at that response. Though she kept those thoughts to herself as she browsed one of the other nearby clothing racks.

"You're lucky that purple is a popular color," she said as she very closely examined one particular selection of purple clothes. "Especially at this time of year." As Tabitha looked through her selection as closely as she could, Seth took a moment to scan around the room himself for anything purple. While there were many items of clothing that he could see that were purple, very few of them were the particular shade of royal purple that he liked, and of those few, fewer of them were things that he could see himself wearing. In fact, he could not imagine at all why anyone would want to wear clothing as strange as the ones he was seeing. From just his one cursory glance at them they seemed uncomfortable and constricting, especially the ones that he knew were for women. That aside, many of the purple items of clothing that he saw were matched with garments that were orange and white. In fact, those three colors seemed to be the most prominent out of everything that Tabitha currently had in her store. Almost every major suit, dress, or other important article of clothing that Tabitha currently had on display were some combination of purple, orange, and white.

It was while perusing through every article of purple clothing he could see that Seth caught something at the far end of the room out of the corner of his eye. At the opposite end of the room from Seth, on a lone side table sat a tea set. While this particular tea set did not appear special in any way, Seth actually recognized one of the cups as the one he had thrown against a wall the first time he had come to Tabitha's boutique for new clothes. While Tara had managed to repair the teacup and apologies were thrown about and graciously accepted, Seth could not help but still feel guilty for throwing it in the first place. Interestingly enough, along with the kettle there were actually three teacups. While Seth couldn't tell at all which teacup he had thrown against the wall, as they all looked exactly the same, the fact that there were three of them caused him to remember something.

"Tabitha," he eventually said.

"Yes, darling," Tabitha responded without looking up from the one selection of clothing she had been looking through.

"How are you doing?" Seth then asked.

"I'm sorry?" Tabitha responded as she suddenly stood back up and returned her full attention back to him. It was easy enough for Seth to see that she was confused by his question, as he had become considerably more adept at reading facial expressions since he had first come to this town.

"You and Clementine," Seth clarified. "Are the two of you okay? I mean, there was a monster attack last night, but you don't seem that bothered by it. I know your store wasn't touched but other people were still hurt. Are you not at least a little concerned?" As he spoke another realization dawned on him as he scanned around the room one more time. "Actually, where is Clementine? Is she okay?"

"Oh, she's fine, darling," Tabitha answered as she took a few steps closer towards Seth. "She's upstairs with Pollyanna right now. She is actually going to be staying with us while her sister and those two farmhands of her's are going to Dis. So they are, in their own words, 'planning the best slumber party ever.'" She then paused for a few awkward seconds and placed her hand on Seth's shoulder. "To answer your other question. I suppose I should tell you first that in certain situations, that is a very rude question to ask, but since it's you, darling, I forgive you. Don't worry." Upon hearing that Seth immediately opened his mouth to speak again, but Tabitha held up her other index finger and silenced him before he could. "And you don't have to apologize. You do that quite often, and while it certainly is an endearing trait, I already said that you were forgiven. So you don't need to worry about it. As for an actual answer…" Tabitha then paused again as she lowered her free hand back to her side. As she did Seth noticed for the first time since she had placed her hand on his shoulder that she was trembling. He felt it first before he could see it, but as soon as he did he looked over to Tabitha to see that her whole body was very subtly trembling. It was almost as if she wasn't merely touching his shoulder, but holding onto it for support.

"I am worried, Seth…" Tabitha continued, doing her best to maintain her composure. "More than you know." While it had been difficult for him at first, Seth had since gained enough understanding of body language to know what may have been going through Tabitha's mind.

"I'm… sorry," Seth let out. Unsure of what else to say.

"It's fine," Tabitha quickly replied as she removed her hand from Seth's shoulder and seemingly instantaneously regained her former composure. "It's just that… when you've lived in a world like this for so long you become used to certain things. Whether you want to or not. Sometimes things just happen, and when they do you have to go and keep on living. Because that is the only thing we can do." Despite how calm she seemed to be, Seth could see that the hand that had previously been on his shoulder was now firmly grasping her other arm, as it still was trembling. A few more long, awkward moments of silence passed between them. Seth, seeing her like this, felt that he should say something, but nothing came to mind other than something she had explicitly told him not to say.

"I'm sor-"

"No, no!" Tabitha quickly interrupted as she instantly let go of her arm and held up an index finger again. "Don't say it." Seth immediately fell silent upon seeing that reaction. Tabitha couldn't help but let out a giggle at his quick response. "I did say that your constant apologizing was an endearing trait, but that doesn't mean it can't become annoying sometimes. Just a little something to keep in mind whenever you talk to other people, darling."

"Okay…" Seth eventually responded, unsure of what else he could say. "It's just-"

"It's just what, darling?" Tabitha interrupted again, though she did seem genuinely interested in what he had to say.

"I just realized that the whole time I've been in this town, I don't think I've ever seen the two of you in the same room," Seth answered with a completely straight face.

"Oh..." Tabitha let out before taking a moment to process what Seth had just said. "Do... Do you want me to go and get her or-"

"No, it's fine," Seth responded before she could finish. "If she's with Polly I don't want to take that from her, and I still need a new shirt."

"Oh, of course, darling!" Tabitha exclaimed with an eccentric clap of her hands before folding them behind her back. "But um... about that..."

"Is something wrong?" Seth asked as a growing look of concern crossed his face.

"No, no," Tabitha quickly answered before momentarily averting her eyes from his. "It's just... I must apologize, Seth, darling, but I am afraid that I have at least one short-sleeved shirt of every other color except for the shade of purple that you are so fond of."

"Oh," Seth responded, more than a little disappointed, but he did his best not to show it. "Well... I guess I can wear something that is purple as long as it's not too different or weird."

"Does it absolutely have to be purple?" Tabitha couldn't help but ask.

"Yes," Seth responded much quicker than Tabitha had expected. "I like that color." Tabitha needed to take another moment to process what he had just said before she could speak again, though she could very easily pick up on his disappointment.

"Very well," she eventually said before bringing a hand to her chin and ran a few quick numbers through her head. "I might be busy this week, and maybe next week as well, but I believe that I can work on at least one new short sleeved shirt for you in the time that I do have."

"Really?" Seth let out, seeming hopeful.

"Assuming of course that I don't suddenly get any orders that are much bigger than what I currently have, or any that would be more important to my career as a designer, of course," Tabitha answered rather plainly. "Once I finish those I should be able to make a few more for you as well."

"Thank you, Tabitha," Seth said with a smile, as he couldn't help but smile at her kindness and generosity. "You're the greatest."

"Oh, no need for flattery," Tabitha responded with a giggle. "Though it is appreciated." She then turned around and with a purposefully enticing, "come hither" motion with her index finger, beckoned Seth to follow her. She then led him over towards one of the clothing racks towards the front of the store, whereupon she pulled out a royal purple long sleeved collared shirt and presented it to Seth. "In the meantime I hope that something like this will suffice."

Seth carefully examined the shirt that she had presented to him, though there was not much to glean from it at a first glance. It certainly was the color he wanted, though it seemed to be made of a much thinner material and aside from the aforementioned long sleeves and collar, Seth could also see a series of buttons along the front which held it closed. While the color was correct, this was certainly not at all what he had wanted. Given his options, however, he supposed that it could have been much worse. At least this shirt wasn't torn or drenched in blood and sweat.

"How many of these do you have?" Seth asked with a rather obnoxiously loud sigh.

"Currently three," Tabitha answered after a brief glance behind her to check. "Is that alright?"

"I suppose so," Seth answered with obvious disappointment in his voice. Despite his reaction, Tabitha could not help but find it somewhat endearing as she pulled the remaining two shirts off of the clothing rack.

"Very well," she then said in response. She then, with practiced hands, neatly folded all three of the shirts before leading Seth towards a desk situated near the entrance, whereupon she pulled out some twine from one of the drawers and carefully tied all three of the shirts together before handing the bundle to Seth. "Here you are, darling. Sorry it isn't exactly what you were looking for."

"It's alright," Seth answered in what he hoped was a reassuring tone. "It isn't your fault. If anything it's that monster's fault. Though it's dead now, so I don't think blaming it is going to make me feel any better." Despite the morbid implications of that comment, Tabitha could not help but let out a giggle at the seemingly innocent way Seth had said it.

"Now lets see," Tabitha said as she brought a hand to her chin. "Each one of those is ten coppers, so your total is going to be thirty coppers."

"Thirty!" Seth exclaimed.

"That's not going to be a problem, is it?" Tabitha asked, a look of genuine concern adorning her face as she did.

"No," Seth quickly responded. "I just never realized how expensive clothes shopping is."

"The price comes from the cost of the materials and the time I had to spend making them," Tabitha explained before a rather devious thought popped into her head. While still facing Seth, she leaned backwards slightly and placed both of her hands on the desk in a manner that fully accentuated her figure, which was helped by the purposefully tight clothing she wore. "Although, Seth, darling, if it is too much for you, I am certain we can figure something out." To top off her words she also shot Seth a very unsubtle wink.

"No, it's fine," Seth responded as plainly as possible as soon as she had finished speaking. "I can afford it." With that Seth, while still holding onto the bundle of shirts, reached into one of his pockets for some copper coins. Tabitha couldn't help but quietly curse to herself as her sultry spectacle soared over his skull like a swift swallow in spite of her obvious shortage of subtlety. Again. Before long Seth had dug his coin purse out of his pocket, and with his newfound shirts under one arm he quickly counted out not thirty copper coins, but three silver coins. "Here you are."

"Thank you, Seth," Tabitha replied as she took the coins from him in a vain attempt to hide her disappointment. Thankfully, for her at least, Seth showed no reaction at all to that. "Your patronage and your company are always greatly appreciated."

"No, thank you," Seth replied as he put his coin purse back into his pocket. "You didn't have what I wanted but you still tried to help. So thank you for that." Seth then turned and headed for the door. Before he left, however, he turned back to face her one more time. "I'll see you when those other shirts are ready." With that said, Seth then walked out the door and was gone.

As soon as he was out the door Tabitha let out an extremely loud groan as she stood up from her desk and faced the door, dumbfounded by Seth's completely innocent rejection of her. Again.

"D... Did he seriously not get that?" Tabitha began to mutter to herself.

"What in Solaris' name am I supposed to do? Bring him to my room, put on my sexiest lingerie and beg him to take me like a stallion claiming a mare in heat." As she spoke her face began to grow somewhat red as she brought a finger to her chin and actually began to consider that as a possible course of action. At least for a few seconds before her own internal logic stopped that train of thought. "Would that even work though? He shows no reaction at all to anything I do. So would wearing lingerie be any different? Should I skip the lingerie and just present myself to him? For Solaris sake does he even know what-"

"Couldn't you just tell him that you like him?" a high pitched voice suddenly spoke up from somewhere behind her. The sudden appearance of that particular voice caused Tabitha to instantly jump in surprise before turning around to see her younger sister Clementine standing behind her holding a glass of water.

"C-Clem…" Tabitha let out before she coughed into her hand and very quickly recomposed herself. "Well… Um… How much did you hear?"

"Around when you started asking yourself what you were supposed to do and then you started talking about your room and horses," Clementine answered before taking a long, drawn out sip of water. "And you didn't answer my question." Tabitha needed to take more than a few seconds to think of a proper way to answer her younger sister's question, lest she shatter her precious innocence.

"Clementine," she eventually began after taking a deep breath. "When you get older… Things become… More complicated than that. Sometimes romance isn't always the way you want it to be and it may not be exactly what you want. You'll understand as you get older."

"Is that why I've never seen you go on more than one date with the same guy?" Clementine then asked almost instantly with a raised eyebrow and a quizzical look upon her face. The instant those words left her younger sister's mouth, Tabitha's face lit up like a fire as she turned as red as a beet. Partially out of embarrassment, but mostly it was out of anger. So much anger in fact that an intense battle within herself had erupted in order to keep it contained as she balled both of her hands into fists.

"Go to your room, please," Tabitha then ordered her younger sister in the calmest possible voice she could manage. As much as Clementine wanted to ask why, she had seen her sister mad enough times to know that that was probably a really bad idea, and with Pollyanna over it wasn't worth risking being grounded. So without saying anything, Clementine simply and quietly turned around and headed back upstairs with her water.

Seth went straight back to the library after he had acquired his new shirts, as thankfully he had no other errands to run that day. It was a good thing too, as his back still stung quite a bit whenever he had to do any movement more complicated than walking. Thankfully most of the initial pain had long since faded. Upon entering the library, however, Seth stumbled upon a rather unusual sight. In the library speaking with Tara was a woman whom Seth did not immediately recognize. She had dark brown hair with only a few strands of gray sprinkled here and there, which while she clearly did not look as old as either Missus Chevrolet or Marynen, the mayor of Canaan, was still enough of an indicator for Seth to know that she was slightly older than most of the women he usually saw around Canaan. That, however, was only going off of what little Seth knew about aging. Her clothing consisted of a white buttoned shirt, much like the ones that Seth had just bought, and a long, dark green skirt that seemed to fit perfectly to her slightly plump figure. She also wore a pair of glasses that had a bright red frame.

It took him a few seconds to recall who she was, as while Canaan was a small town, this was still someone he had hardly ever spoken to. As far as Seth was aware, her name was Liliana, and from what Seth could recall about her, she was the local school teacher. More specifically, she taught in that bright red building that Seth had seen Pollyanna and Clementine enter and leave on an almost daily basis. As Seth approached her and Tara he began to overhear their conversation, which was not the easiest thing to do in a library as they were both whispering.

"Dis, really?" Liliana said in what sounded like a surprised tone. "I never saw you as the type of person who would travel for a festival."

"Well, you are actually right about that. I am not," Tara answered her. "I am not going there for the festival. I have official business that I need to take care of there. Though hopefully I will have a chance to enjoy it while I am in the city."

"I see," Liliana said in understanding. "Well I hope that you do get to. I've never been myself, but I hear that it's something to behold. Especially in Dis. My week off is more than likely going to be me spending as much time as I can reading this while wrapped in a warm blanket with a nice cup of tea and having a cat cuddled on my lap."

"Honestly, I think you are getting the better deal here," Tara responded. Liliana could not help but giggle.

"Well, I won't keep you from packing any more," Liliana then said to Tara as she turned around. "I'll see you soon, hopefully." Then with that she began walking towards the door that Seth had just entered through. As she passed him, while she did not say anything to him, she did give him a polite smile. As she did Seth managed to see the title of the book she was carrying, which was titled, '*An Unexpected Flame*'. As Liliana left the library, Tara unconsciously followed her with her eyes, and it was only then that she noticed that Seth was there.

"Oh, Seth!" she let out before coughing into her hand and went back to whispering. "Did… Did Tabitha have what you wanted?"

"Not exactly," Seth responded quietly as he held up the bundle of shirts he had. "But it's close enough. They will do for now until she gets a chance to make more of the kind I like."

"Oh, well if that is the case, then how about you head upstairs and change," Tara said to him. "I am sure you must be dying to get out of that old one so we can get rid of it." Despite how simple and logical her request had sounded, Seth couldn't help but feel more than a little disappointed upon hearing it. He knew that there was a very good chance, in fact he was sure it would be a ninety percent chance, that he would have to throw away his last purple shirt once he was done with it. So he couldn't help but hold onto the last little bit of hope that it could somehow be salvaged. A fool's hope he knew, but he still could not help but hope. Still, it was a trivial thing, so he did his best not to show his sadness as he made his way up the stairs of the library towards Tara's loft.

Once he was upstairs and alone, Seth wasted no time as he dropped his newfound bundle of shirts onto the couch before proceeding to remove the one he was wearing. Despite how slight his movements were, some of his arm movements tugged at the bandages he still had to wear, which in turn tugged at his wound somewhat. It did not hurt nearly as much as it had before, but it was still noticeable. More than waiting for a proper shirt, he could not wait for the day when he could stop wearing these accursed bandages and get back to moving around without worrying about them. Once he had removed his last remaining purple t-shirt, he held it out in front of him so that he could get one last good look at it.

The front wasn't too bad, more than a little dirty maybe, but nothing that could not be cleaned. The back, however, was a completely different story altogether. Seth had assumed that when the horse-monster sliced him across his back that a similar cut would have been on his shirt. One that could perhaps have been easily fixed by Tabitha. It was, however, much worse than that. While there was indeed a long cut across the back of the shirt that matched Seth's wound, the cut on the shirt was much longer than the wound, so long in fact that it went all the way to the end of the shirt so that it actually flapped open. Worse still, while it was a clean cut, there were many loose threads dangling from various parts of the shirt. Seth had pulled on enough loose threads on his older shirts to know that many of them were very bad. None of that was even counting the incredibly large bloodstain that covered almost the whole back side. While most of his shirt was still the same, royal purple color that Seth normally associated himself with, the vast majority of it was covered in a large bloodstain that had long since dried into a cristy black color.

Seth couldn't help but be shocked as he saw the ruined state of his shirt. He had never realized before just how much he bled when he had received that wound. Then again, thinking the night over, he never really stopped to pay attention to anything. Still, Andrea had told him before that losing so much blood was very, very bad, but there was so much blood on the back of his shirt that he couldn't help but wonder exactly how much he had lost, as well as how much more he could have lost before it became as bad as Andrea had said. Along with the blood, the smell that came off of the shirt, which Seth had only noticed for the first time just now, assaulted his nostrils. The combination of all the blood and sweat made Seth wonder why he never noticed the smell before, or why Tara didn't make him go out and replace the shirt the second he had returned home last night, or why Tabitha hadn't said anything when he was in her boutique. He also paused to wonder why he had never felt the wind on his back in the time since the monster attack, or felt the open flap that was the bottom of the shirt moving around as he walked. With that thought, however, he looked down at his torso and saw that it was still covered in bandages, along with his wound, which did indeed take up most of his back.

Even after seeing the exact state that one of his favorite colored shirts was in, however, he couldn't help but let out a loud sigh of disappointment as he, as neatly as he could, folded up the ruined shirt in such a way so that it covered up the large bloodstain and set it aside. That done, he turned his attention to his new shirts as he undid the twine that held them all together and picked up one of them. He slipped it on easily without needing to unbutton it first, which was good because he did not understand why shirts even needed buttons in the first place. The idea of an extra step that needed to be taken just to put on a shirt made no sense to him at all. Then again, most of the clothing he had seen in Tabitha's boutique made no sense to him at all, which was why he always asked for normal clothes. Regardless, with the shirt on, Seth walked over towards a nearby mirror so that he could see what he looked like while wearing it.

Despite it being a very different style than what he was used to, it did not look too bad, and he supposed that he would get used to it in time. Especially since he had no choice at the moment. There was one thing about it, however, that he had not considered until he actually saw himself wearing it. Its longer sleeves. It wasn't that he was uncomfortable with wearing a longer sleeved shirt, far from that, the issue lay more in the color. Seth liked the color purple, he always had. It was the only color he would willingly wear on his shirt, but this, as strange as it seemed, felt like too much purple. With this in mind he wandered back over towards the couch as he pondered a solution. It did not take him long to come up with one, however, as before he could even sit down he remembered the only other time he wore something with longer sleeves.

Knowing exactly what to look for, Seth walked over towards a nearby dresser. As he stepped in front of it, however, he suddenly heard the sound of wood hitting wood. Not only that, but he felt as if one of his feet was somehow out of place. When he looked down he saw that one of the floorboards that ran underneath the dresser had come loose, as when he accidently stepped on it he had kicked it up so that it hit the underside of the dresser. Seeing that, Seth slowly and carefully removed his foot from the board and allowed it to fall back into place as he did so. That done, he committed to memory exactly which board on the floor that was and resolved to tell Tara about it after he had fixed his shirt issue.

With that out of the way Seth then opened the bottom drawer of the dresser, the one that normally held what little clothing he had. Thanks to his newfound lack of purple shirts, the drawer was mostly empty. However, that allowed him to easily find what he was looking for as he pulled out a single tan jacket. The last time he had worn this was when he had accompanied Vivian and Agatha out into the desert three months ago. Before he could make any motion to put it on, however, he froze as he saw his own hands trembling while they held onto the jacket. For a split second Seth worried that something might have been wrong with him, but then he remembered, Vivian had given him this jacket and it was the last genuinely nice thing she had done for him before he had told her the truth about himself. Before she had started only acting like they still were friends. He wasn't sure at all how long he stood there holding the jacket, nor was he aware of exactly when his hands had relaxed, but the next thing he was aware of, he had just finished putting it on.

Now that he actually had it on and was aware of it, he walked back over towards the mirror. Along with solving the 'too much purple' conundrum, the jacket actually felt somewhat nice on him. Surprisingly, the long sleeves under the jacket made it feel a bit more comfortable to wear. Then again, that probably could have been because it had been getting colder recently due to the change of the seasons. Especially at night. Tara had explained to him before that this was because it was now Felize, the thirteenth and final month of the year, and this was simply something that happened during Felize. Still, he could not deny that it was a nice jacket.

Chapter 3

It had been more than a few hours since Seth's change of shirts, and in that time he had since returned to helping Tara in the library by putting away some newly returned books. Interestingly enough, rather than put his new shirts away, Tara had told him to set them, as well as any other clothes he would want to take, aside for their eventual trip to Dis. As he put away more books, Seth noticed that there were quite a few more returns now than there would be on a normal day. This made Seth curious, but he soon realized that it likely had something to do with the fact that he and Tara were not going to be around for roughly two weeks. People were most likely returning and checking out books while they still could, something that was more or less confirmed for Seth by the fact that there were still quite a few residents of Canaan browsing through the library as Seth was doing his job.

Of their eventual trip to Dis, Seth knew very little. He knew that Dis was a city, and he knew that they were traveling there because Tara had some type of business that she needed to take care of there. Business that she would not discuss with him. That was, however, all he knew. The nature of this 'festival' that everyone kept talking about was something that still eluded him. Tara had tried to explain it to him before, but after repeatedly failing to understand some of the things she had been saying, Tara had decided that it would be better if Seth had seen exactly what a 'festival' was for himself.

As Seth was about to put away one more book onto its proper shelf, he noticed the title on its gray cover, "*The Wanderer and the Mystical Hostages,*" along with the author's name, R.A. Fernandez. Seeing that, Seth looked back towards the shelf and saw that next to where this book was supposed to go there were more books of the same series. Seth didn't bother to remember all of their titles, but they all followed the naming convention of "*The Wanderer and the-*" followed by two to four words that Seth could only assume alluded to the adventure described within. He could also see that there were currently five books in the series, at least from what he could see on the shelf. It seemed that the one that was supposed to go next to the one that Seth had in his hands, however, had been checked out. Most likely by the same person who had just returned the book Seth was currently holding. Based on that, Seth guessed that that book was next in the order. Not only that, but following that idea Seth saw that the book in his hands belonged on the farthest left of the self from all the rest, indiciating, to him at least, that this book must have been the first of the series.

Seth then remembered that Tara had recommended to him that he bring a book or two along for their trip to Dis so that he would have something to do along the way. From what Seth understood, it took three to four days of travel by horse to get to Dis, depending on if conditions favored them. Not only that, but Seth was reasonably certain that this was the series of books that Vivian really liked. With all of that in mind, something else occured to Seth. Something that he had never thought of before until now. In his previous outing into the desert, he had only traveled for two days, one day to get to their destination and one day to get back, and it was the single most boring thing he had ever done in his life. With all of that in mind, rather than putting the book away, Seth decided that he would check it out himself so that he would have something to take to Dis. If Vivian liked it then it couldn't have been that bad.

Eventually night had come, and with it the library had closed once the sun had disappeared from the sky. While this was not by any stretch of the imagination unusual, the fact that the library would not be open again for at least another two weeks was an interesting change of pace for all involved. With the sun gone and the library closed Seth sat across from Tara at her kitchen table with a plate of chicken salad in front of him. While Seth still had absolutely no idea what a chicken even was, it tasted absolutely delicious.

"So, do you have everything that you want to take with you for the trip?" Tara asked as she ate her dinner.

"Yes," Seth answered after running through a mental checklist of everything that Tara had told him he would need. "I believe so."

"Good," Tara responded before stabbing her fork through another piece of chicken and some lettuce.

"What about Florence?" Seth then asked without thinking. Not that Seth cared about that needlessly aggressive cat, but he knew that Tara did. To his surprise, however, Tara only responded to him with only a confused look. "Are you going to take him with us or-"

"I thought I told you that I had dropped him off at Lydia and Bethany's already?" Tara answered before he could finish.

"If you did, I have no memory of it," Seth responded to her. "I'm sorry."

"It is okay, Seth," Tara said in understanding as she brought her attention back to her dinner. "It is kind of funny actually. Lydia was actually the one who came to me volunteering to catsit for me. Apparently those two have been thinking about getting a cat and want to use Florence as sort of a trial run to see if they are up for it."

"Why?" Seth asked, absolutely baffled. "Why would anyone want one of those things? If Florence is anything to go by, they're nothing but angry balls of spite and anger that think they're better than everyone else." Tara needed to take a long, deep breath so that she could properly ignore the insult that Seth had just thrown at her pet before she could properly respond.

"Well, first of all," Tara began. "The phrase 'angry balls of spite and anger' is redundant, and second, does that not sound like someone you know? Perhaps a certain red-headed monster hunter?" As soon as she had brought her up Seth opened his mouth to respond, but no words came out. For the life of him he could not come up with anything to say at all to counter what Tara had just said to him. After a few awkward seconds of sitting at the table with his mouth open, Seth eventually closed his mouth and recomposed himself as he accepted that Tara may have had a point. From there the two of them ate in relative silence for the next several minutes until they were both finished. After which Tara stood up and collected both of their plates.

"Do you need any help with those?" Seth automatically asked as he stood up from his chair as well.

"I think I can handle washing two plates," Tara responded in a monotone voice. "But I appreciate your offer to help." Without saying any more Tara then took both plates over towards her wash basin.

"So what are you going to do?" Seth asked as he watched her set the plates aside before she could actually start washing them.

"I am sorry?" Tara responded as she turned her head to face Seth. The look of confusion on her face was obvious enough.

"You said that we're leaving early tomorrow morning, but it's still a few hours before we normally go to sleep," Seth clarified. "So do we still need to do anything else to prepare or is everything taken care of?"

"Well…" Tara began as she brought a hand to her chin in thought. "You said that you were all packed when I asked you earlier."

"I am," Seth answered plainly. "Are you?"

"I am."

"If you are all packed too, does that mean you aren't going to need me around?" Seth then proceeded to ask. Upon hearing that question, Tara, as if knowing what was coming, closed her eyes and took a very long, very deep breath before speaking again.

"Where are you planning to go?" she asked before opening her eyes.

"Last night while I was in Andrea's clinic I ran into Kurt," Seth began to explain. "We talked for a while and he invited me to go to The Empty Barrel with him for something he called 'poker night'."

"So you are asking me for permission to gamble?" Tara then asked, again in a completely monotone voice as she spun around to face him properly.

"I don't know what gamble means," Seth answered. "But if that is what people do at 'poker night' then I'm going to assume that the answer is yes."

"Considering that the last time I said no to you going to the Empty Barrel, you went anyway, does my opinion even matter?" Tara asked, the tone of her voice shifting from monotone to something that sounded more akin to frustration as she spoke. Seth, more than a little taken aback by Tara's sudden change in mood, and feeling somewhat hurt by it, needed to take a few seconds to recompose himself before answering.

"Of course it does," he began. "The reason I'm thinking about going is so that I can get to know some of the other town watch members better. I've been working with them for a few months now and I still can't tell you anything about any of them. For example, I only just found out last night that Kurt is dating Celene."

"Wait, they are!" Tara exclaimed, now sounding more surprised than frustrated.

"For the past three years, apparently," Seth answered her.

"Well, this is news to me," Tara then said. "Honestly, Celene always came across as the type of woman who is more married to her work than anything else."

"Wait, someone can marry their work?" Seth couldn't help but ask, now more than a little curious himself. Though to be fair to him, he still didn't have that great of an understanding of exactly what marriage was. Even after Lydia and

Bethanay had tried to explain it to him.

"It's an expression, Seth," Tara answered as her voice returned to her previous tone of frustration.

"Oh, okay," Seth responded. "But anyways, I don't even care about whatever a 'gamble' is. I just want to get to know the people I am supposed to be working with better."

"Are you going to drink?" Tara then asked the instant he had finished speaking.

"No," Seth answered just as quickly.

"No?" Tara responded as she raised both of her eyebrows.

"I don't like the taste of ale," Seth answered before she could say anything else. "I am pretty sure I told you that."

"You did?"

"Yes," Seth responded. Tara actually had to take a few seconds herself to think of a way to respond to this seemingly sudden new development.

"Well, you have never gone back to the Empty Barrel after that first time," Tara began. "So how could you expect me to know that?"

"Of course I've never gone back," Seth responded. "I don't like the taste of ale. Why would I ever go back there?" That response actually caused Tara's mouth to fall open as she realized exactly how obvious Seth's response should have been before she had even asked him anything. Worse still, she had no one to blame in this instance but herself for walking directly into that one. "If it makes you feel any better," Seth then began in an attempt to break the tension he felt in the room. "I have no plans to tell any of them about my secret."

"Why would you feel the need to add that?" Tara eventually responded as she lowered her eyes towards the floor and brought a hand to her forehead.

"Because I felt like that would be something you might be worried about," Seth answered as honestly as he could. He also shrugged as he spoke, however, that only served to make his back pinch a little, as if to remind him that his injury was still there.

"You know what, fine," Tara eventually said as she shook her head and brought her eyes back up to meet Seth's. "You can go. I don't care anymore."

"Really?" Seth exclaimed as his eyes went wide from shock.

"Yes," Tara repeated. "But if you do play for money, please at least try to be responsible. If you come home and tell me that you lost all of your money and do not have any left for the festival, then you will have only yourself to blame."

"Okay…" Seth said in response. While he did not want to ask any more questions for fear of making her actually angry, he couldn't understand why Tara would be worried about him losing money. However, if that was a legitimate concern that she had, then he saw no reason why he shouldn't be concerned about it either. So before anything else could happen, without saying anything he promised himself right then and there that he would not lose any money.

Night had long since fallen by the time Seth had arrived at the pub known as The Empty Barrel. The last and only time he had set foot in this place was a few months ago, and it looked relatively unchanged since then. Since this place had opened Seth had seen numerous people enter and leave on a nightly basis, and the general consensus he had heard was that apparently it was the best pub in town. Seth himself could not for the life of him understand why this was though. He also wasn't entirely sure whether or not there even were other pubs in Canaan.

As he stepped inside he saw that the inside had remained as unchanged as the outside. The iron chandelier still hung from the ceiling, behind the bar the giant mirror that was there remained spotless, and the wall with the sign 'Memories of the Empty Barrel Coming Soon' was still as vacant as it was before. As it was still relatively early, Seth saw many vacant tables and chairs throughout the pub.

"Ey, Seth!" a familiar voice suddenly called from across the pub, snatching Seth's attention away from the vacant memories wall. Towards the far end of the pub from where he stood, Seth saw Kurt stand up from the table he was sitting at and enthusiastically wave him over. Having found whom he had been intending to meet, Seth approached the table, whereupon he could easily make out the faces of Joseph and Alvarez.

"What's he doing here?" Joseph asked with a thick layer of scorn in his voice as soon as he saw Seth approaching the table.

"Well, since Gene is currently out of commission," Kurt began to explain as he sat back down. "I figured why not invite him to keep Gene's seat warm in the meantime. Besides, he did kill that monster horse that gored Gene, so I think he at least deserves a drink or two for that."

"Heh. I could have killed that monster easily," Joseph said as he crossed his arms.

"Why didn't you then?" Seth then immediately asked as he took the open seat next to Kurt. Despite Seth's genuine curiosity, which was evident enough to Kurt and Alvarez, the response Seth got from Joseph was a dagger-like glare that suggested that he wanted to strangle Seth where he sat. It reminded him of the looks Vivian often gave him, though it wasn't the same at all when it came from Joseph. A few moments of awkward and tense silence passed before Joseph's expression slowly changed into a smug grin.

"You know what, fuck it, why not," Joseph eventually said as he uncrossed his arms and visibly relaxed again. "It'll be nice to take someone else's money for a change."

"I'm just glad not to be the new guy anymore," Alvarez suddenly cut in. "Maybe I'll even win something this time because of that." Both Kurt and Joseph responded to that with identical sounding snorts. Kurt even had to cover his mouth to keep himself from laughing. Joseph, however, made no such attempt to hide his amusement. "Hey! It can happen!"

"I still don't know how to play this game," Seth suddenly interjected amidst all of their noise. The second those words had left his mouth, however, both Joseph and Alvarez's eyes instantly fell on him. The smug grin that Joseph had been wearing then began to quickly grow until it stretched from ear to ear.

"Why don't I explain it to you over at another table," Kurt then spoke up as he put a hand on Seth's shoulder. "If only so that these two assholes don't fill your head with false information." As he spoke that last part he pointed with his thumb over towards his two friends and co-workers. The instant he finished speaking the smug grin that Joseph had been wearing instantly dropped and he returned to his dagger-like glare, only this time it was directed at Kurt instead of Seth.

"Alright," Seth responded as he and Kurt stood up before Kurt led him away towards another table far away from earshot of either Joseph or Alvarez.

"If he doesn't even know how to play then maybe you do actually have a chance," Joseph whispered to Alvarez as soon as Seth and Kurt were far enough away from their table.

"Maybe," Alvarez responded. "Assuming he doesn't have beginner's luck or anything like that."

"Oh please," Joseph said with a wave of his hand. "That's just an excuse that loser's make whenever they get their asses handed to them by a newbie. If that really was a thing then you wouldn't be zero to five right now."

"Fuck off," Alvarez spat back at him.

"Hey, don't get mad at me," Joseph quickly responded as he peeked over his shoulder towards the table where Seth and Kurt were sitting. "And I wouldn't worry if I were you. Who knows if he'll even retain any of the information Kurt tells him. That moron seems like the type of person who doesn't even know his own asshole from a hole in the ground." Alvarez opened his mouth so that he could say something nice about Seth in response, if only to give him the benefit of the doubt, but before he could he suddenly remembered the first time he had met Seth. That being when Ash was taking him to her home so that her little sister, Polly, could teach him math.

"You might have a point," Alvarez said when he eventually spoke.

"Hey guys!" a distinctly feminie voice suddenly rang out, much to the surprise of both Joseph and Alvarez. Both of them turned to see the braided haired, smiling face of Lydia standing in front of their table. "I couldn't help but overhear that you guys were going to play some cards. You got room for one more?"

"Yeah, we do this once a month," Alvarez began to explain. "In fact, I'm pretty certain you've seen us play before?"

"Yeah, I have," Lydia answered. "That's why I came over here."

"Don't you have anything better to do?" Joseph asked, his scowl returning to his face as he did so.

"Well I did," Lydia began. "But apparently another bard is passing through here from Taurus on his way to Dis for the festival and he needed some extra coppers. So Barry's giving him a chance to play instead. Said it would be a nice change of pace. Anyways, with that in mind I'm now suddenly finding myself without a way to make any money unless that guy sucks and they kick him out, but I don't wanna be a cunt and pray for that to happen just so I can make a few coppers instead of him. That's when I remembered you guys. So… You got room for one more?" Both Joseph and Alvaerz looked at each other for a moment in quiet contemplation before either of them spoke.

"I don't see why not," Alvarez eventually said after a few short seconds.

Joseph's only response was to let out an obnoxiously loud sigh. Alvarez ignored him for the moment as he looked over towards the direction of Kurt and Seth. "Ey Kurt! You mind if Lydia plays with us too!" Kurt, without looking up from his explanation of what the different cards were to Seth, simply held up his hand and gave the thumbs up sign before returning to his explanation.

"Perfect!" Lydia instantly exclaimed before she ran over to a nearby table and took another chair from it, which she promptly set down in front of the table. "So are we getting some drinks too or what?"

"Oh, you're buying for us?" Joseph asked as his smirk returned.

"When did I ever say that?" Lydia responded with a smirk of her own.

Eventually both Kurt and Seth returned to the table to see that Joseph, Alvarez and Lydia each had a pint of ale in front of them.

"So do the two of you have everything sorted out?" Lydia asked, clearly aware of the situation.

"I think so," Seth responded with an obvious lack of confidence in his voice.

"Great!" Lydia exclaimed as she clapped her hands together. "So how much are we playing for?"

"The buy-in is usually two-hundred coppers," Joseph answered.

"Two-hundred!" Seth exclaimed just as he had pulled out his chair.

"Well, if you don't have that much we can lower the amount," Kurt tried to reassure him as he took his seat next to Seth and began to shuffle a deck of cards.

"No, I do have that much but-"

"So it's no problem then," Joseph interrupted, the same wide grin still adorning his face. He then reached below the table and pulled out the leather coin purse he had attached to his belt, which he promptly plopped onto the table. Alvarez, Lydia, and finally Kurt all followed suit as they dropped their coin purses onto the table as well.

It was only at this moment that Seth understood the full implications of what was really going on here. While he did indeed have two hundred coppers on his person at that exact moment, that was almost all of the money he had, barring fifty or so coppers that he kept aside in case of emergencies, as Tara had insisted. The other problem was that that was all of the money he had set aside for the festival in Dis, and as that thought occurred to him Tara's warning echoed through his head again, '*If you come home and tell me that you don't have any money left for the festival, you'll only have yourself to blame*'.

"Is there a problem, newcomer," Joseph's voice broke Seth out of his thoughts as his attention returned to Joseph's smug grin. It was only then that he noticed that everyone else at the table had been staring at him, and as he realized that a foreboding sense of nervousness spread through him. It was as if each of their gazes were adding ten kilograms of weight to his shoulders. Unsure of what else to do given the circumstances, and the fact that he had willingly agreed to come here tonight, Seth reached down and removed his own coin purse from his belt as well before setting it on the table.

Chapter 4

No more words were said as all five players took a few moments to count out exactly two-hundred coppers, after which Kurt wasted no time as he dealt out two cards for everyone. Alvarez and Lydia wasted no time either as they put in four and eight coppers respectively for the blinds. Seth on the other hand, took a moment to look at his cards and saw that he had the two of clubs and the ace of hearts.

Both Joseph and Kurt immediately folded as they dropped their cards onto the table. However, Seth noticed something as they did. Just before Joseph had dropped out of the round he had made a small frown towards his cards.

"Call..." Seth spoke up as he pushed eight of his coppers forward. "That's the right word, right?" Kurt only nodded in response to that.

"Call," Alvarez also said as he placed four more of his coppers forward. After he did that Seth saw Lydia tap two of her fingers onto the table.

"Check," she said.

After that had happened, Kurt drew the five of hearts, the king of spades, and the two of diamonds from the deck. Seeing those cards, Seth tapped his fingers and checked as well, as did Alvarez and Lydia. With that done Kurt then drew the two of hearts.

"I'm betting eighty-eight," Alvarez said with a grin as he pushed nine stacks of his coins forward.

"I got nothing," Lydia then said as she placed her cards onto the table. Seth took a moment longer to look at his cards and try to remember what Kurt had told him about what cards went with what. He saw that he had three twos, so keeping in mind what Kurt had told him he felt as if he had a chance, at least for this round.

"Call," Seth said as he added a large chunk of his coppers to the pot as well. His eyes on Alvarez the whole time. Kurt then drew the last card of the round, which was the queen of clubs. Alvarez, seeing Seth's stare down as a challenge, took a long drink from his pint of ale before pushing the rest of his coppers forward.

"All in!" he said with enthusiasm. The look on his face was similar to the smug grin Joseph wore.

"Um... All in," Seth echoed as he pushed the rest of his coins forward as well. With that done both he and Alvarez revealed their cards, showing that Alvarez had the two of spades and the four of clubs.

"You both have three of a kind," Kurt said, looking towards Alvarez. "But Seth has an ace kicker. Seth takes pot and since you bet everything… Sorry Alvarez, you're out." Alvarez did not say anything in response. Instead he simply sat there with a dumbfounded expression plastered across his face while also making noises that sounded like they were attempts at words, but none of them could even remotely be considered a language.

"Did you seriously bust out in the first round?" Joseph spoke up, doing his best not to laugh.

"Sorry," Seth sheepishly said as the realization dawned on him that he had in fact taken all of Alvarez's money.

"Don't be sorry," Lydia said as she clapped Seth on the shoulder. "You won. So take what's yours." Without any other idea of what to do, Seth took her advice and pulled the pot over towards him.

"Well, as long as you're out, you mind taking over as the dealer?" Kurt then asked. In place of a proper response, Alvarez let out a loud groan in defeat as he took the cards from Kurt and began to reshuffle them.

Once that was done he dealt everyone their cards much quicker than Kurt had done. This time Seth got the jack of clubs and the two of spades. As he was looking over them Joseph and Kurt both put in their blinds.

"Call," both Lydia and Seth said almost in unison.

"So, Seth," Lydia spoke up after that happened. "I heard from Bethany that you and Tara are heading out to Dis tomorrow."

"Yes," Seth responded. "We are."

"Are you excited?" Lydia asked with what seemed like genuine interest. "I mean it's gonna be an amazing new experience for you."

"I suppose so," Seth answered. "I mean… this will be the first time I've been to a town other than Canaan." After he finished speaking he suddenly remembered that everyone at the table was still under the impression that he had amnesia. "That I know of." As Seth had been speaking, Joseph placed four coppers into the pot. Kurt checked immediately after he did so.

Alvarez then drew out the three of hearts as well as the six and nine of spades. Seeing that Joseph quickly checked, and Kurt, with his own smug grin on his face, bet twelve coppers. Seth, upon seeing the cards on the table and the cards in his hands, grew worried as he thought that he would not be able to win this round. With no other idea of what to do, without saying anything he folded for the first time as he placed his cards down on the table.

"I'll call that," Lydia declared as she added to the pot, an action that Joseph mimicked, as if to mock her. The fourth card that Alvarez drew ended up being the four of clubs. After the card was drawn Seth noticed Joseph take a very deep breath before checking.

"Come on," Kurt then spoke up as he added in twenty eight coppers. "It's not fun if you don't play."

"Maybe you should take your own advice," Lydia taunted as she raised the bet by fifty-four coppers.

"Yeah, um, no," Joseph then suddenly said as he violently threw his cards down onto the table.

"It's just a game," Kurt quietly mumbled to himself before he then pushed all of his coins in. "All in."

"Alright, if you say so," Lydia responded as she went all in as well, though since Kurt had eight more coppers than her at the start of the round, those went back to him. Once that was all said and done they both revealed their cards. Lydia had the five of clubs and seven of hearts while Kurt showed the six and ace of clubs. Seeing this Lydia grinned wickedly at Kurt as Alvarez revealed the river card, the jack of diamonds.

"Lydia has a straight and Kurt has a pair of sixes," Alvarez announced half-heartedly. "Lydia wins the pot."

"Thanks for the tip," Lydia said with a smug grin as she dragged this round's winnings over towards her.

With that it was now Seth and Kurt's turn to place in the blinds. Kurt did so half-heartedly. Unsurprising considering it was half of what he had left. Alvarez, with even less enthusiasm than Kurt, dealt out everyone's cards again. This time Seth saw that he had ended up with the ace and seven of hearts.

"So… any of you have any plans for the new year?" Kurt asked as he looked over his two cards.

"I already said what I'm doing," Seth answered with a straight face.

"Well…" Lydia began as she held her cards over her mouth. "Bethany and I still haven't decided if we're gonna head out or if she's going to cook, but either way we're gonna have a nice dinner. Call by the way." As Lydia spoke she added to the pot.

"Nope," Joseph scoffed. "It's just another day. I mean so what, we got to survive another thirteen months. Big fucking deal." As he finished speaking Joseph silently called as well. With his only other option being to fold, Kurt pushed in the last four coppers he had in order to call as well.

"Alright, I was just wondering," Kurt said as he did so.

"What about you?" Seth then asked. "Do you have any plans?" Upon hearing that Kurt's mood seemed to instantly improve.

"Well I'm glad that at least one of you cared enough to ask," he said as his own smug grin returned to his face. "Yeah, I have a few plans. Mostly one that's gonna prevent me from coming to poker night for… a while." Alvarez was just about to reveal the next three cards when that last part stopped him dead in his tracks.

"And why is that?" Alvarez asked, suddenly sounding much more invested in what was happening than before.

"Well…" Kurt began as the grin on his face grew even wider. "I've decided that it's finally time. New year's day… I'm going to ask Celene to marry me, and assuming she says yes, I'm going to have to save up for the actual wedding."

"Oooh! Congratulations!" Lydia exclaimed with a soft smile. Alvarez was about to do the same before Kurt suddenly held up his hand and stopped him.

"Don't congratulate me yet," Kurt said. "She can still say no. I mean, I pray to Solaris that she doesn't, but there's always the possibility." Seth wanted to say something, but the fact that he still did not fully understand the concept of marriage kept him from having any idea of what the right thing to say would be. Especially since Kurt had already said not to congratulate him. With all of that said, Alvarez then finally revealed the next few cards. The specific cards he drew ended up being the four of spades, the three of hearts, and the two of diamonds. Seeing that, Seth tapped his fingers on the table to check.

"Someone doesn't look too confident," Lydia taunted as she bet eighteen coppers.

Seth then noticed Joseph suddenly shoot an icy glare to what appeared to be everyone at the table before he then pushed all of his coins forward.

"I'm going all in," he said as he did so. Seth took that as a sign to bow out for the round, so he folded, as did Lydia, which in turn made one hundred and fifty-four of Joseph's coppers go back to him. It took a little while for him to count all of it out, but once that was done both Joseph and Kurt flipped their cards. Joseph had the four of hearts and the six of diamonds.

"Damnit," Kurt whispered as he saw that. Alvarez then revealed the last two cards, which were the seven and queen of clubs. "Damnit!" Kurt then shouted loud enough for everyone in the pub to hear.

"Joseph has a pair of fours and Kurt has king high," Alvarez announced to the group as opposed to the whole pub. "Joseph wins the pot and Kurt is out."

"Well, there goes my plan to get a head start on the wedding fund," Kurt said before letting out a very loud, tired sigh.

"Well, as long as you're out too," Alvarez then said before taking all of the cards back and reassembling them into the deck before holding it out to Kurt. "You wanna go back to dealing?" Several long moments passed as Kurt just stared at him with an icy glare of his own before saying anything.

"Ugh, fine," Kurt eventually responded as he took the deck back from Alvarez.

"How do you not last as long as the guy you literally just taught how to play?" Joseph asked with an air of smugness as he collected the pot.

"Shitty luck," Kurt answered as he began to shuffle the cards before returning his attention back to Alvarez, who was taking another long drink from his pint of ale. At least he was before it ran out. "As long as you're not doing anything then. You mind getting me one too?" Alvarez's only response to that was to stare blankly back at Kurt and not say anything, as if doing so would somehow allow him to escape that responsibility. As if holding it as a threat, Kurt stopped shuffling and refused to deal the cards until Alvarez answered him.

"You know what, sure," Alvarez said as he stood up from the table. "Mr. Groom." Before Kurt had a chance to respond to that, Alvarez was already gone. With all of that finally said, done, and out of the way, Kurt finally dealt out the cards.

The next round began with Lydia and Joseph placing in the blinds while Seth looked at his cards. This time he had ended up with the ace of spades and the jack of clubs.

"Call," Seth said as he added some coppers to the pot. Seeing him do that, Lydia called as well as she added four. Seth then saw Joseph shoot him that same icy glare again before he pushed in fifty-four copper coins.

"I raise," Joseph said as he did so. As he spoke, Seth remembered that when

Joseph shot that icy cold glare at everyone during the last round, he went all in, which made both him and Lydia fold. In the end Joseph's hand didn't turn out to be that great, even if he did end up winning. It was at that moment that a sudden realization dawned on Seth.

'*He's trying to scare me,*' Seth quietly thought to himself. With that hypothesis in mind, Seth called his bet.

"I'm just going to let you two meatheads fight this one out," Lydia suddenly interjected as she folded.

"What's a meathead?" Seth immediately asked almost as soon as her cards had hit the table. Lydia, in place of a response, shot him a rather quizzical look before Kurt revealed the first three cards. The cards in order were shown to be the king of diamonds, the four of hearts, and the six of clubs.

Seeing this, Joseph pushed in thirty more coins. Seth, who believed that he had a relatively good idea of what was going on in Joseph's head, did the same. Kurt then drew out the eight of clubs. Joseph checked as soon as he saw that, and Seth did as well. With both of their checks confirmed Kurt drew the last card of the round, which was revealed to be the two of clubs. Both Seth and Joseph instantly checked again upon seeing that card. Before he revealed his cards, Joseph shot his icy glare directly at Seth. This time it was more focused, as if he were silently threatening Seth with his gaze. Seth, however, remained undeterred. He had killed things that were bigger than Joseph, after all. Both Seth and Joseph then flipped their cards over at nearly the same time, with Joseph revealing that he had the queen and nine of diamonds.

"Seth has ace high and Joseph has king high," Kurt announced as he saw this. "Seth wins the pot."

"Do you always do that?" Seth asked as he pulled the pot over towards himself before pushing back eight coins for this round's blinds.

"Do what?" Kurt asked as he began to shuffle the cards again.

"You always announce what the result is," Seth clarified. "Do you always do that?"

"No," Kurt answered as he began to deal the cards. "That's actually entirely for your benefit. You know, so you know what's going on."

"But Alvarez was doing it too," Seth said.

"Probably because he saw me doing it," Kurt answered as he dealt out the last of the cards to Joseph and Lydia. "I mean, everyone in the usual group have all been doing this for a while, so we know how this game is played, but since you don't I figured I would say what's happening to help you along."

"Oh, okay," Seth then said in understanding before he looked at his cards. "Thank you, but I think I got the idea." Looking at his new cards, Seth saw that he now had the ace of spades again, though this time it was accompanied by the six of diamonds.

"I'll call that," Lydia said aloud as she slid some of her coins forward. Joseph silently called as well. After Seth tapped his fingers to check, Kurt drew out the ten and seven of hearts, along with the six of clubs. Seeing those cards, Joseph scratched his chin for a few seconds before betting thirty-four coppers. Seth, upon seeing that he now had a pair, called.

"If that's how we're going to play, then how about we make this a little more interesting?" Lydia suddenly spoke up as a wide smirk began to grow across her face.

"What, strip poker?" Joseph responded with a laugh.

"Haha, nice try," Lydia shot back. "But one. You got something I don't want and never have. And two, what's hidden under this outfit is for the eyes of one Missus Bethany Swithin-Harquin only." After she had finished speaking Lydia pushed eighty coppers forward. "This is what I meant."

"Alright, I'm in," Joseph said, calling her bet.

Seeing what was happening, Seth began to lose confidence in his hand and thus, decided to fold. After he did so, Kurt drew the three of diamonds.

"Well then if that's the case, time to separate the men from the women," Joseph said as he once again gave Lydia that same icy glare, while pushing all of his coins forward. Lydia in turn shot her own icy glare at Joseph in response.

"You know, I'm not entirely sure if that was meant to be sexist or not," Lydia then said before adding forty-two coins into the pot to match his bet. They then both flipped their cards over, with Lydia having the seven of diamonds and the queen of hearts. Joseph on the other hand, had the two of clubs and the six of spades. A wide grin swept across Lydia's face as she saw this. "Well, I guess lady luck doesn't appreciate any potentially sexist comments either." Lydia's confidence, however, disappeared the instant Kurt drew the last card. Which turned out to be the six of hearts. "Okay that's not fair!"

Joseph, wearing his own smug grin as he did so, grabbed all of his winnings and pulled them back towards him. As he did that Seth mentally kicked himself as he realized that if he had stayed in that round, not only would he have won, but he would have kicked Joseph out of the game. It was because of those thoughts that Seth did not notice Alvarez returning to their table with five full tankards.

"Ah, good," Joseph said before downing the last of whatever was in his current tankard. "I was running low." Without acknowledging him Alvarez handed out the tankards to everyone at the table, including one for Seth.

"Thank you, but I don't like the taste of ale," Seth said to Alvarez as he tore his eyes, and his thoughts, away from all of the copper coins that Joseph had just taken from him.

"I know," Alvarez replied before scooting past Joseph and returning to his own seat. "Kurt mentioned that before you got here. Originally I wasn't going to get you anything, but then I remembered Ash once saying something to me about you liking lemons a lot. So I had Burt make you a hard lemonade." It was only after he had finished speaking that Seth looked down to actually see what was in the tankard that had been placed in front of him. It wasn't the brownish color that he normally associated with ale, and unlike ale it wasn't foamy at all. Instead, his drink was bright yellow in color, which immediately set off a warning bell in Seth's head as its appearance reminded him of a certain other liquid. It did not smell like that other liquid at all though, which reassured Seth somewhat. Despite all of that, however, one key part of Alvarez's explanation made no sense to Seth whatsoever as he lightly sloshed the contents of his tankard around to confirm it.

"This isn't hard," Seth stated with the same amount of confusion in his voice that he likely would have possessed if anyone at the table had suddenly sprouted an extra pair of arms. "This is a liquid." The instant those words had left his mouth, the eyes of everyone at the table were on him. That only lasted for a second, however, before Kurt, Lydia, and Alvarez all suddenly burst out laughing.

"That means it has alcohol in it, you moron!" Joseph shouted over the laughter of the others.

"Oh…" Seth responded before waiting for Kurt, Alvarez and Lydia to all stop laughing. "I didn't know that was what that meant. Also the insult wasn't necessary."

"You hang out with Vivian all the time," Joseph responded without skipping a beat. "I figured you would be used to it by now." Seth was going to stay quiet, but then his eyes drifted down towards the sleeve of the jacket he was currently wearing. The one that Vivian had given him.

"Yes, she does insult me a lot," Seth calmly responded as he brought his eyes back up to meet Joseph's. "But she's my friend. She can get away with it because she doesn't mean it." It was only after those words had left his mouth that images of very recent events flashed through Seth's mind. "At least… I think she doesn't mean it… anymore."

"Whatever, let's just get back to the damn game," Joseph then said with an obvious roll of his eyes.

"Fine by me," Seth responded before taking his first sip of the hard lemonade. The second the drink touched his lips, however, his eyes shot open. While he had some idea of what lemonade would taste like based on the name, it was slightly different from what he had expected. The tangy flavor of the lemon danced on his tongue with the liquid, but there was also a sweetness to it as well. It was similar to the lemon bars that he usually got from the bakery, only as a drink instead of a pastry. There was also a slight sting to the drink as well that was similar to ale, which Seth supposed was the alcohol. With all of this in mind, Seth quickly took a large swig of the hard lemonade before chugging down at least half of what was in the tankard.

"I think it's about time to raise the blinds to six and twelve," Kurt piped up as Seth was enjoying his lemonade before dealing out the cards. After setting his tankard back down Seth put in six copper coins while Lydia put in twelve. After that Seth took a look at his cards, which he saw were the five of clubs and the five of diamonds.

"Call," Joseph spoke up rather quickly as he added in a few coppers to the pot, which Seth did as well.

"Check," Lydia said as she tapped her fingers on the table. It was after she spoke that the first three cards were drawn, revealing them to be the four of diamonds, the two of clubs, and the seven of hearts.

"I raise," Joseph then muttered as he pushed in fifty coins. As he did Seth took notice of him giving his familiar frigid glare towards both him and Lydia. It was getting to the point that Seth was beginning to wonder if that and his smug grin were the only two expressions he was capable of. Despite that, however, between the glare and the exchange the two of them had just had over the lemonade, Seth decided that he was not going to let Joseph scare him. So with that in mind he added fifty coppers to the pot as well. Lydia, on the other hand, quietly folded as she found Joseph's icy glare too intimidating.

The next card was then shown to be the jack of diamonds. Both Seth and Joseph checked upon seeing it, resulting in the fifth card being drawn. That card was quickly revealed to be the ace of clubs. Seeing that card, Joseph chuckled loudly as he decided to raise his bet to sixty coppers. Seth briefly paused upon seeing this. He thought for a moment about whether or not it would be wise to put his faith in the pair of fives he had in his hand. However, he also knew that all he had to do was look at the mild smugness on Joseph's face to decide if it was really worth it or not. Seeing that it was, Seth called the bet. The two of them then flipped their cards. Joseph had the three of hearts and the eight of spades.

Seeing that he won the round, Seth dragged the coins over towards him and his growing pile of coppers.

The next round then began with Lydia and Joseph putting in their blinds while Seth looked over his new cards. This time he had gotten the king of diamonds and the ace of hearts, both of which he knew to be good cards. Seth decided to call, as did Lydia. This was then followed by Joseph checking. After that was done Kurt drew out the six of clubs, the king of clubs, and the three of diamonds.

"Try to keep up," Lydia said with a smirk as she bet thirty-eight coppers.

"Nah," Joseph responded as he dropped his cards onto the table. Seth, however, chose not to back down as he put in the same amount as Lydia. The next card that was shown was the seven of spades. Both Seth and Lydia checked upon seeing that card, after which the final card of the round was revealed to be the king of hearts. Lydia tapped her fingers to check, but Seth, seeing what he had, decided to add twelve more coppers to the pot.

"Oh, so you're gonna play like that, eh? Alrighty then," Lydia then said as she pushed the rest of her coppers forward. Seth did not even wait a single second as he wordlessly added the same amount to the pot. As she watched him do that, Lydia's face began to grow red. After only a few very tense seconds, the two of them finally revealed their cards. Lydia had both the ace and jack of spades.

"Sorry Lydia, you're out." Kurt said to the bard.

"That was not smart," Joseph mocked her with a smirk of his own.

"Oh you can go fuck yourself," Lydia responded. She was about to say more, but then stopped herself before taking an incredibly deep breath. After repeating that same gesture a few more times, as if with each breath she took she slowly grew to accept her loss more and more, she eventually stood up. "Well, that was fun while it lasted. Maybe I'll play with you guys again in the future when nights are slow for me like this. Unless any of you have a problem with that." As she said that last part she cast a cold glare at Joseph.

"No problems here," Kurt responded rather quickly.

"Yeah, I don't see anything wrong with it," Alvarez added before taking a drink from his tankard. Joseph responded with only a shrug instead of words.

"Well then, I think I'm gonna take my leave here," Lydia then said as she grabbed her things and what was left of her money. "You boys enjoy the rest of your game. Oh, and Seth."

"Yes," Seth responded as he instantly turned his gaze towards her. Once she had his attention, Seth saw a very visible, wide smirk scitter across her face.

"Kick this meathead's ass," was all she said before turning around and strutting away from the table. This lasted for only a few steps, however, before her shoulders suddenly slumped over. Before she left Seth barely heard her say, "Now I just need to figure out how to explain to Bethany how I somehow lost money instead of making any tonight." She was out the door before Seth could hear her say any more.

"You beat her, yet she's mad at me? Whatever," Joseph said as he refocused his attention back to Seth with a beast-like grin on his face. He then proceeded to tilt his head from side to side as a duo of loud cracking noises expelled from his neck. "I'm going to enjoy this."

"If you say so," Seth responded as he met Joseph's gaze, unintimidated. Seth did not even need to look to know that his pile of money was at least five times larger than what Joseph currently had.

That said, they both put in their blinds before receiving their new cards. This time Seth had been handed the seven of diamonds and the eight of hearts. Seeming satisfied with his hand, Joseph decided to call before adding six more coppers to the pot. Seth followed this by tapping his fingers on the table to check.

Kurt then revealed the three new cards for the round, which ended up being the two of spades, the six of clubs, and the queen of clubs. After both Seth and

Joseph checked, the next card was revealed to be the ten of hearts. Seth tapped to check again, but then Joseph suddenly decided that he was done playing around and pushed in thirty-two coppers.

Seth instantly got a dubious feeling in his gut as he saw that, but decided to call the bet anyways. The final card was then drawn, and it ended up being the ten of clubs. A repeat of last time happened as Seth checked again only for Joseph to bet thirty-six more coppers this time around. With the cards that were on the table, Seth saw that he had a pair of tens, though that did not inspire much confidence in him. Unsure of what else to do, Seth grabbed his drink and let the rest of the sweet, lemony flavored liquid slide down his gullet before gently placing his tankard back onto the table and matching Joseph's bet.

They then both flipped their cards over. Joseph had the jack of diamonds and the eight of spades.

Joseph laughed rather loudly as he pulled this round's winning's towards him. Seth only watched him wordlessly in response. As that was happening Kurt handed the deck to Alvarez.

"You mind taking over as the dealer again?" Kurt asked. "I need to take a piss."

"Sure, why not," Alvarez responded before he took the deck from Kurt and began to shuffle it. Kurt then stood up from the table and left without a word. The next round then began with Seth placing in six coppers for the blinds while Joseph put in twelve.

The cards that Seth got this round were the king of diamonds and the six of spades. With that kind of hand Seth decided to add six more coppers to the pot in order to call Joseph. He expected Joseph to check in response, but he didn't. Instead, Joseph pushed forward eight stacks of ten coppers to the pot. Seth instantly thought that move was strange, considering that they had not even seen the first three cards of the round yet. Despite this, Seth called the bet anyways. The first three cards were then revealed to be the ace of hearts, the five of clubs, and the four of diamonds.

Joseph then, yet-again, shot Seth an icy glare as he bet thirty-six more coppers. At this point Seth was beginning to grow tired of Joseph attempting to scare him like he was. So, Seth did his best to mimic Joseph's ice like glare as he raised the bet by seventy-two.

"Ugh, fine!" Joseph growled before literally throwing his cards onto the table. "Fucking take it."

The next round then started and Alvarez then dealt out the cards. This time Seth had received the seven and the ace of clubs. Both players quickly checked as the eight of clubs, the five of hearts, and the jack of spades were all drawn. Both Seth and Joseph quickly checked again as the next card was drawn, the five of diamonds. Seth once again tapped his fingers to check upon seeing that card, but after he did, Joseph began to smile again.

"You know what, all this checking is getting boring," Joseph said as he slid all of the coins he had left forward. "How about we go all in?"

Seth sat there for a few seconds mulling over what to do. He had a pair of fives, but he could tell that Joseph also had the same pair. Although, he did have an ace, so perhaps he could win with it as a kicker. Not only that, but Seth was beginning to get tired. Not physically tired, but tired of staring at Joseph's face, a face that kept bouncing back and forth between smug and angry, and it was becoming more and more boring for him to look at the longer this game went on. So Seth decided to take the risk in order to end the game here with a call.

Then they both flipped their cards. Joseph had the four of spades along with the four of clubs.

"You best start praying now, boy," Joseph then said with a smirk. The fifth card was then shown. The four of hearts. Joseph began to loudly laugh at this, which annoyed Seth more than he wanted it to.

"The blinds are now eight and sixteen," Alvarez announced while Joseph was collecting his coppers.

Seth put in eight coppers for the blinds while Joseph put in sixteen. The cards that Seth had gotten this round, like the last, were from the same suit, with them being the queen and the two of spades.

Seth then put in eight more coppers, expecting Joseph to check, but he didn't, much like last time. Instead the smug faced watchman added one-hundred more coppers to the pot. Seth didn't say anything at all in response to this. Instead, he shot his own version of Joseph's ice-like glare back at him, as if silently saying *'I'm not going to play your game'* before folding.

"Looks like I'm on a roll," Joseph said with a chuckle. Seth did not say anything in response to that. Instead he kept up his icy glare. It was at this time that Kurt had returned from the bathroom, but Seth hardly noticed him as he sat back down. Before the next round even officially began Seth silently put in sixteen coppers for the blinds while Joseph put in eight.

Seth only took a quick glance downwards to look at his cards when he received them and saw that they were yet another duo from the same suit. The ace and the ten of clubs.

"Call," Joseph said aloud. Seth, however, tapped his fingers on the table to check without taking his glare off of Joseph. Out then came the two of spades, the nine of spades, and the seven of clubs. Seeing those cards, Seth once again checked, but this time Joseph matched Seth's imitation of his glare with his own original. As Seth had expected, Joseph then bet one hundred and eight coppers. While he found the number rather strange, Seth decided to call it as well.

Alvarez then revealed the fourth card, the ten of spades. Seth tried to check again, but Joseph kept his glare up and acted before he could.

"You know what, let's go all in," Joseph then said, though it came out as more of a growl than a sentence. Joseph's attempt to be intimidating, however, did not phase Seth in the slightest. In fact, seeing him do that inspired all the confidence that Seth needed. Slowly, as if to both mock and imitate him, Seth's lips slowly formed into a smirk of his own as he, without any words or ceremony, called the bet.

Both of them then flipped their cards, revealing Joseph's hand to be the four of diamonds and the queen of clubs. Time around the table appeared to move ten times slower as Alvarez drew the last, and hopefully final, card from the deck. After moving his hand away from it, both players could see that it was the four of spades. No words were said, at least at first. However, there was no longer any sort of glare or even remotely intimidating look on Joseph's face, nor was there his usual smugness. The only thing that was there was pure disbelief.

"Joseph has a pair of fours, and Seth has a pair of tens," Alvarez eventually said as his eyes darted between the two players. "Which, if I am not mistaken means-"

"Seth wins the game!" Kurt interrupted loud enough for everyone in the pub to hear as he, without warning, grabbed Seth by his right wrist and held it up in the air in victory. That was the only thing that pulled Seth out of the moment as the smirk he wore instantly dropped from his face. By instinct he looked around the pub, as he was more than aware of how loud Kurt was. Thankfully, no one else in the pub seemed to notice, much less care, what was happening with them.

"This is bullshit!" Joseph suddenly shouted as he slammed both of his hands onto the table and stood up. "He must have been lying about never playing before! Or he cheated using his freaky fucking magic or-"

"No, I could just tell what you were going to do," Seth interrupted as Kurt let go of his wrist.

"What?" was the only response Joseph could muster.

"Almost every time you had a bad hand, but you wanted us to think it was a good one, you glare at everyone," Seth explained with a completely straight face.

"Wait!" Alvarez cut in as he looked between Seth and Joseph. "Are you saying that Joseph has a tell?"

"I don't know what that is," Seth answered. Before any one of them could say any more, Joseph, without saying another word, walked away from the table and stormed out of the pub before any of them could stop him. Seeing that reaction, Seth just watched him go before slowly turning his attention back to Kurt. "Is he going to be okay or-"

"Oh, just ignore him," Kurt answered as he pushed all of the copper coins on the table over towards Seth. "He always gets like that whenever he loses a game. He'll probably come back in later and take that stick out of his ass after he's had a few more drinks at home."

"Alright," Seth responded, though internally he still felt uneasy about the whole thing. He had seen Vivian act like that before, but whenever she did she was usually much calmer by the next time Seth had seen her. Joseph wasn't Vivian though, so he had no idea how he would react the next time he saw him, and that worried him somewhat. Seth did his best to push those thoughts from his head as he looked around for something else to distract him. It was then that his eyes fell upon all of his winnings.

Without thinking he reached under the table for his coin purse, but then stopped once he realized something. If his math was correct, with five players and a two hundred copper buy-in for each of them, that meant that there were exactly one thousand copper coins in front of him right now. While this was not a bad thing by any stretch of the imagination, it became a problem once Seth realized that his coin purse could only hold at most three hundred coppers, and even that was pushing it.

With that in mind Seth brought his hand to his chin, as he had seen Tara do sometimes whenever she needed to think. He then let out a hum to himself as he mentally sorted out all of the ways he could carry this many copper coins home. The most obvious solution, at least to him, was to take off his jacket and use that to carry all of the coins. If he did that, however, then that would mean that everyone in the pub would see him with a long sleeved shirt on, and he wasn't sure if he wanted that.

Alvarez, however, seeing Seth's reaction to the obvious conundrum that was in front of him, thought of a solution before Seth could as he stood up from the table and walked directly towards the bar.

"Ey, Burt," Alvarez spoke up as he approached the bartender.

"Yeah, that's me," Burt replied without looking up as he wiped down a glass.

"You wouldn't happen to have one hundred silvers on you would you?" Alvarez then asked without thinking. "Or perhaps ten gold?"

"Does this place look like a bank to you?" Burt responded with a deadpan stare as he finally stopped what he was doing so that he could properly look at who he was talking to.

"So that's a no, then?" Alvarez then asked. Burt began to narrow his eyes at Alvarez, but then he looked past him and over towards the table where the card game had been held and saw the particular situation that Seth was in.

"Hold on," he then said before he suddenly walked off and disappeared into the back room. After almost a full minute he returned with an empty burlap sack in his hands. "Will this work?"

"I don't see why it wouldn't," Alvarez answered before he took the sack from him. "Thank you, Burt."

"Don't mention it," Burt quickly responded as he picked the now clean glass back up and set it back where it was supposed to go. "Just pay your tab and we'll be square." Without saying anything else Alvarez quickly turned around and headed back towards the table.

"Here you go," Alvarez said to Seth as he handed him the sack. Momentarily startled, Seth blinked a few times and frantically searched around the table before his eyes eventually found Alvarez.

"Oh, thank you," Seth answered as he took the bag from him and began to gradually pour all of his newly acquired winnings into it. It was only after he started doing that that he realized exactly how heavy one thousand copper coins actually were.

"So," Kurt spoke up after taking a long swig of ale from his tankard. "Any idea what you're gonna do with all that money?"

"I don't know," Seth responded before placing the sack back onto the table, as he was unsure of where else to put it. "I don't know what to do with one hundred coins. So I have no idea at all what I'm going to do with one thousand." After saying that, however, a thought popped into his head. "Although, maybe I could get some more of that lemonade."

"While you're at it, you wanna buy drinks for everyone in the bar?" Alvarez then suggested before taking his own long swig from his tankard. Seth was about to seriously consider that proposal, but before he could Kurt suddenly started laughing and slapped Seth rather hard on his back.

"Don't let this cheapskate fool you," Kurt said before taking another drink. "I did that once. So trust me when I say that whenever alcohol is involved people will always be more than willing to take advantage of your kindness. Especially when one of those people is Vivian."

"Wait, is she here!" Seth immediately asked as he instantly stood up from his seat and began to frantically search around the pub for anyone with red hair. Seeing that kind of reaction, Alvarez leaned in closer towards Kurt.

"Is something going on between them?" Alvarez whispered.

"I have no idea," Kurt whispered back. "Probably best not to ask."

The night passed from there with the three of them drinking and telling each other stories. While most of it was Kurt and Alvarez telling Seth about things that happened before Seth had arrived in Canaan, Seth was not without his own stories. The only one he had that really stood out, however, was the time he had accompanied Vivian and Agatha out into the desert and had his first taste of combat. That is to say, his first real taste of combat where he didn't get his ass handed to him. Of course, there were certain details of that story that Seth kept to himself, mostly those concerning a certain two and a half meter tall woman. In fact, to this day he had still never told anyone about her.

"And that was when Joseph tripped over a loose rock and tore his quad," Kurt finished explaining rather loudly before taking yet another drink from what

Seth guessed was his third or fourth tankard of the night. "He was out of the fight at that point."

"Is that injury really that bad?" Seth asked, still as placid as ever. "Also what is a quad?"

"It's a muscle in your legs," Kurt answered. "And it's certainly not fun, but that beast broke Charlie's arm and he still managed to load his crossbow and send a bolt right into the center of that thing's head. So make of that what you will."

"Impressive," was all Seth could say in response to that.

"Yeah, that motherfucker's the sheriff for a reason," Alvarez cut in. "You know, aside from being the oldest member of the watch."

"But the fact that he can still fight at his age says a lot," Kurt then added before taking yet another drink.

"How old is he?" Seth couldn't help but ask, now genuinely curious.

"You guys gonna wrap this up soon!" the voice of Burt suddenly hit their ears before anyone could give an answer. All of them in unison turned to look in his direction only to see that he wasn't at the bar, but was instead standing at their table.

"What do you-" Kurt began before he then looked past Burt and noticed that they were the only ones left in the pub. "Oh... I guess we all lost track of time. Sorry."

"Yeah, I gotta close up for the night," Burt said before heading back towards the bar. "So finish any drinks you have left and then scram."

"Yeah, we probably should get going," Alvarez managed to say without slurring. "After all, doesn't this one have to get up bright and early to head to Dis tomorrow?" As he spoke he gestured towards Seth. It looked as if he was attempting to point at him, but he seemed barely able to hold his hand straight let alone his finger. Before saying anything Seth took one last look into his tankard, only to see that it was empty. He took that as his cue to leave.

"It's alright," Seth said as he stood up from the table. "I'm used to getting up early for watch duty. So I'm not worried. This was fun by the way. Thank you for inviting me."

"Yeah no problem," Kurt replied as he stood up, though he seemed only barely able to. "Maybe we can do this again when you get back."

"Maybe," Seth answered as he picked up his large burlap sack of money from the table. In what felt like the short amount of time since he had put it there he had already forgotten how heavy it was. "I guess I'll see you guys when I do get back from Dis."

"Yeah… See you when you get back," Alvarez responded as he held up his still half-full tankard before bringing it to his lips to finish it.

"Have fun!" Kurt then shouted before finishing whatever ale he had left. After which he then began to collect all of the tankards from the table, including Alvarez's, who stubbornly refused to let go of it until he had actually finished.

Seth was a little more than half way back to the library before the sound of someone's footsteps behind him made him stop in his tracks.

"Hey, you!" the aggressive voice of Joseph then suddenly rang out. Hearing that, Seth turned around to see Joseph step out from behind a nearby building. Seth was more than familiar with the layout of Canaan by this point, so he knew that that building could not have possibly been where he lived.

"What do you want?" Seth asked him, his voice carrying both his annoyance as well as signs of how tired he was. Joseph didn't say anything at first as he approached Seth, and within moments stood less than a meter from him. The look on Joseph's face was the same, familiar, icy glare that he had frequently shown during the poker game, only this time there was something more intense about it. One look was all it took for Seth to understand. There was rage behind those eyes.

"I want my fucking money back," Joseph eventually said.

"No," Seth responded, completely unfazed by Joseph's glare. "You lost."

"You cheated," Joseph immediately shot back.

"No, I didn't," Seth responded. "I told you how I won. If reading your face was cheating then Kurt or Alvarez would have told me s-" Seth was interrupted by Joseph's hands suddenly grabbing his jacket collar.

"I said give me back my fucking money," Joseph repeated to him. It took Seth a moment for the full gravity of his new situation to dawn on him, but when it did, his face slowly morphed from his usual, blank stare, into a cold glare that matched Joseph's in intensity.

"Please take your hands off of my jacket," Seth said to Joseph, trying his hardest to do so without raising his voice. "Vivian gave it to me." Joseph immediately shoved Seth backwards as soon as those words left his mouth. As a result Seth stumbled backwards for a little bit before he fell onto his backside. His sack of coins fell beside him with a loud clanging sound that echoed throughout the empty streets of the town.

"Don't you dare bring up that bitch in front of me," Joseph said as he glared down at Seth's prone form. "If she did her fucking job then Aiden would still be alive. I'm glad I left that fucking cunt for dead. Of course you had to come along and fuck that up too." That last part triggered something within Seth as his eyes shot back open. However after a moment, and one very deep breath, he relaxed and the look in his eyes returned to the glare that they held before.

"Wait..." Seth began as he pulled himself up from the ground. "Are you saying that you let her fight that monster by herself?"

"And what if I did?" Joseph responded. "She-"

"You're no better!" Seth interrupted before Joseph could get another word out. The tone of his voice, however, had something of a deep growl to it, not unlike the sort of sound a wolf would make. It was so jarring from his normal speaking voice that Joseph's eyes instantly shot open and he had to mentally fight himself to keep from taking a step back.

"What?" Joseph let out in an attempt to maintain his intimidating presence, though Seth could see through it as easily as he did Joseph's face during the poker game.

"You keep talking about how it's her fault that Aiden is dead," Seth then began in a much calmer manner as he took a few steps closer towards Joseph so that he was back where he stood before. "She blames herself for it more than anyone, but you just admitted that you were fine with that monster killing her."

"What are you getting at?" Joseph asked as he attempted to match Seth's glare with his own.

"At least with her it was a mistake," Seth continued. "A mistake that she continues to blame herself for every day, but at least she still tried to do her job. You just admitted to me that you refused to do yours and almost let her get killed on purpose." Seth then took one more step forward so that he and Joseph stood face to face. They were so close in fact that Seth could feel Joseph's breath. It reeked of alcohol. "Like I said. You're no better than her. In fact, you're worse."

"Do you honestly think I give a shit about what you think," Joseph responded to him. "Hell, I bet the only reason you're defending her is because you're probably fucking her."

"I don't know what that word means," Seth responded without any hesitation. "No one has ever explained it to me."

"Don't play dumb with me you fucking prick," Joseph shot back, seeming unintimidated, but Seth could see his eyes twitching. "I've seen how often you two were together when you were training." Joseph then paused for a moment as his now familiar smirk slowly crept across his face again. "Though I've been seeing less of that now. What happened? Did your girlfriend put you in the doghouse? Is that why you showed up tonight to steal my money?"

"I have no idea what you're talking about," Seth responded without skipping a beat. "I don't even know what some of those words mean."

"You know what, fine," Joseph said. "Deny it all you want. I don't give a shit." Joseph then shoved his way past Seth and went directly for the burlap sack full of money that was still on the ground. Before he could move even one meter away from Seth, however, he suddenly found himself unable to move his legs. Immediately he looked down, and while it was initially hard for him to see with the only illumination being the moonlight, he could tell that he was now buried up to his shins in the earth. Without even looking at him, Seth then turned around and walked past him towards the sack of money. "Oh, so you can't even fight me without your magic. Is that it?"

"No," Seth answered with a calm voice as he picked up his sack of money. "And I'm not going to fight you, Joseph."

"Oh, what are you scared or-" Joseph tried to say before Seth suddenly spun his head back around and shot Joseph that same cold, yet intense glare.

"If I fought you, you would lose, possibly even die," Seth answered without any hesitation. "I've fought monsters that were three, no, five times bigger than you. I helped Raz fight six people at once. I've taken hits that would kill most people. There are at least five different ways I can think of right now that I could defeat you without using magic. You don't scare me, Joseph." Silence reigned in the night air for several long moments as Joseph took in every word Seth had said. With the way Seth was staring at him, he almost seemed like an entirely different person than the unsure moron who didn't even know how to play poker before tonight. "I came out here tonight to have some fun and get to know the people I work with better. I don't want to fight you and I didn't come here to steal your money. In fact, I'm honestly still surprised I won that poker game. Though I can say that I was successful when it came to learning about all of you. Do you want to know what I learned about you, Joseph?" Joseph didn't say anything in response as he kept trying to pull his feet out from the ground. "I learned that the wrong town watch member died that night."

With that said, Seth flung the burlap sack over his shoulder and with a quick flick of his wrist, he released Joseph from the earth, which caused him to fall forward and smash his face into the dirt as he had attempted to pull himself free at the same time that Seth had released him. As soon as he was out of sight from Joseph, however, Seth took the opportunity to run as if his life depended on it as he broke into a full sprint and did not stop until he had reached what he hoped was the safety of the library. By the time Joseph had gotten himself back onto his feet Seth was already long gone. In the silence of the night he stared down the road that he knew led towards the library as if in contemplation for almost a full minute. While he debated chasing after Seth, he felt both his legs and fists begin to shake, though he was uncertain as to why. At least that was what he told himself.

"Bastard's not worth it," Joseph eventually muttered to himself before turning around and stomping in the other direction back towards his home.

Unbeknownst to both of them, however, on the roof of one of the nearby buildings, with a perfect view of the shouting match between Seth and Joseph sat a bat-like creature, obscured by the darkness. As Seth and Joseph left for their respective homes, a wide grin began to slowly crawl across its face, showing off its sharp, pointy teeth before it let out a small, sniveling giggle. With the two of them long gone, the bat-like creature then extended its wings and with a single flap, launched itself into the air before flying up and out of the town of Canaan.

Chapter 5

As quickly as his reflexes would allow him to, Seth threw open the front door to the library before sprinting inside, slamming it shut behind him, and locking it tight. He didn't even care if Tara had heard him or not. As he stood there with his back to the door, a painful sting ran along his entire back as his still not entirely healed wound reminded him that it was still there, and that it did not appreciate all of the running he had just done. Not only that, but every breath he took seemed much harder to take than the last with each inhale and exhale. It felt to him as if someone were squeezing his lungs like one would squeeze the juice from a lemon. As he stood there breathing heavily, he eventually pulled himself away from the door and held his free hand out towards it. Despite the fact that his hand could not stop shaking, sparks of electricity began to flow between his fingers.

'*Please please please tell me he stayed put!*' Seth screamed in his thoughts as he stared at the door as if it led to some kind of endless abyss. '*Please don't leave me with no choice! I don't want to give them all another reason to hate me! Not again! Please Solaris not again!*'

Eventually, after enough time had passed, though Seth was unsure of how much, he realized that if Joseph had indeed followed him home, even if he had been taking his sweet time, he would have arrived at the library by now. After that realization circulated through his head enough times, the sparks faded from his fingers as he lowered his arm. Whatever imaginary grip that had been suffocating him also seemed to disappear with it as he was more easily able to catch his breath. With the possibility of Joseph hiding on the other side of the library's front door out of his mind, Seth felt secure enough to go to sleep.

Slowly, Seth trudged his way up the stairs as he did his best to make as little noise as possible. Between the occasional squeak from some of the wooden steps and the jingle of over one thousand copper coins though, it was not the easiest thing to do. Eventually, however, he had reached the top floor and made his way over towards the couch. Still with the intention of being silent, Seth slowly and gently placed the bag of coins onto the floor near the couch. While Seth could not see Tara sleeping up in her loft, the sound of gentle breathing he heard assured him that she was indeed there.

'*If trouble comes, please don't let her get hurt,*' Seth thought to himself as

he let out a rather long breath before collapsing face down onto the couch.
'*Please...*'

Seth's eyes shot open to see that the library was suddenly filled with light. With nothing else to go on, Seth had to assume that it was now morning. This momentarily threw him off as the incredibly abrupt transition between the two made it seem as if all he did was blink and then suddenly it was daytime again. The fact that he did not feel entirely rested despite his dreamless sleep did not help matters either.

Slowly, Seth flipped over onto his back and sat up from the couch. After rubbing the last bit of sleep from his eyes he looked down towards the floor next to the couch to see that the burlap sack filled with his winnings from the previous night was still there. Seeing it still there, Seth couldn't help but let out a breath he hadn't even realized that he had been holding in as he relaxed his muscles for what felt like the first time in hours. If his money was still here, then there was no reason for him at all to believe that Joseph had come into the library while he was sleeping. If Joseph had come in, Seth was more than certain that he would have made sure to take the money. With those thoughts out of the way Seth stretched out his legs for a little bit before standing up, his knees cracking slightly as he did so. His attention was momentarily stolen when he suddenly heard the hum of Tara's voice. Instantaneously he spun himself around to see her up in her loft making sure her bed was in order and humming a soft tune to herself.

"Good morning," Seth called up to her. The sound of his voice momentarily startled Tara as she suddenly jumped and let go of the bedsheets in her hand. As quickly as she could, however, she straightened them out again before turning her full attention to Seth.

"Oh, morning, Seth," Tara replied back to him as she stopped what she was doing and descended the steps from her loft to properly meet him. "I didn't hear you come in last night. You didn't get back too late I hope."

"No, it wasn't too late," Seth answered in what he hoped was a truthful tone. While he did return much later than he had initially planned, he knew that it was not any later than he was used to with his job as a member of the town watch. So while it did not bother him, he wasn't sure of whether or not it would bother Tara since she usually liked to keep everything running as orderly as possible. Especially in recent days. As Tara walked around the couch to stand in front of Seth she stopped once she saw the burlap sack at his feet.

"Seth, what do you have there?" she immediately asked.

"Money," Seth answered plainly, as he was clearly able to see where her eyes were. Upon receiving that answer, however, Tara instantly got a suspicious look on her face.

"And where did you get it?" Tara asked warily with a raised eyebrow. In response Seth raised both of his eyebrows in confusion, as he knew for a fact that he and Tara had talked about this before he left last night.

"I won it," Seth answered, his confusion prominent in his tone of voice. "Don't you remember? I said that I was going to a poker game with Kurt and the others at The Empty Barrel last night?"

"Wait, you actually won!" Tara then exclaimed as the expression on her face instantly changed from suspicious to surprised.

"Yes," Seth answered, again plainly. While he was content to simply leave it at that, the surprised look on Tara's face raised many red flags for him. "Wait, were you expecting me to lose everything?"

"Well..." Tara began, but then quickly stopped herself before she could say any more. She then diverted her eyes from Seth's as she looked about the room seemingly everywhere at once. The look on her face was the look of someone who realized that they had been caught stealing from someone else's coin purse. If Seth didn't know any better, he would have guessed that Tara was thinking very, very carefully about what to say next. The fact that she was not looking at him while she did this did not reassure him in the slightest. She was silent for a full twenty seconds before she eventually spoke again. "It is just that.... Well... You have never gambled before and you were playing against three other-"

"Four actually," Seth interrupted. "Lydia joined in after she saw that someone else was playing that night."

"Okay, four other people," Tara let out with an exasperated sigh as she dragged her gaze back up to make proper eye contact with Seth. "Anyway. The point I am trying to make is that with your inexperience, the twenty percent chance statistically of an average player winning, and the fact that you were playing against four other people who had been playing for much, much longer than you have. The odds of you actually winning anything seemed very, very low."

Seth initially felt hurt as he heard those words from Tara. The implication that she would assume that he would simply lose dug up too many bad memories for him. As he opened his mouth to respond to her, however, he thought really, really about the specific words that she had used. When he thought about it like she had, the odds really did seem stacked against him, so a losing conclusion really was the safest one. That realization instantly switched his mood from feeling hurt to a feeling of understanding.

"Well, when you put it like that..." Seth began after he took a moment to recompose himself. "You're actually right. I guess I really did just get lucky." He saw Tara's mood soften upon hearing those words, which he took as his cue to ask her the one question he really needed an answer to. "So what should I do with all these coins?" He asked as he held up the bag, which made a loud jingling noise as he lifted it up. "I thought about taking it to Dis with me, but I don't know what to do with this much money and I don't want to carry this sack with me everywhere I go."

"Well, how much money is in that bag?" Tara asked, now more than curious after hearing what had happened.

"Over one thousand copper coins," Seth responded without skipping a beat. Tara did not respond to him for several seconds after that, at least not with words, as she needed to use that time to mentally process exactly what Seth had just told her. Once she became aware of how she must have appeared to him, however, she quickly shook her head and recomposed herself. An action that did not go unnoticed by Seth.

"Well, um..." Tara began as she looked around the room one last time before bringing her attention fully back onto Seth. "In this case you are actually right. Taking that much money with you to Dis would be an extremely bad idea. Dis is not like Canaan, it is a big city. Between pickpockets, shady merchants, and all the other unsavory characters there, there are far too many people who will want to take advantage of the fact that you have a lot of money if not outright steal it."

"So what should I do with it?" Seth then asked.

"How about you only take however much you are comfortable with to Dis and leave the bag with the rest of it here so that nothing happens to it," Tara suggested with a smile.

"But where should I put it?" Seth then immediately asked, as he was still to this day unsure of exactly where in the library Tara kept her money. With that in mind he had absolutely no idea where he should keep his.

"Wherever you think is safe," Tara answered. "Just at least make sure that it is out of sight and somewhere that cannot easily be found. Those are the safest places." With that said Tara then turned herself around and began to head back up towards her loft. "If you need help I will help you brainstorm after I do one last check through everything that we need to take to Dis."

With her gone, Seth took a moment to think about what she had said as he sat back down on the couch. He then spent the next several minutes transferring some of the copper coins from the burlap sack to his coin purse. He wasn't sure at all exactly how much money he would need in a big city like Dis, but most of the things he bought here in Canaan typically cost anywhere from three to fifteen coppers at most. So with that in mind, for a week in a big city that he knew nothing about, he settled for three hundred copper coins to take with him.

Once that was done, Seth took a moment to think about places in the library that were safe. A few places came to mind, but then he thought back to last night and his confrontation with Joseph, and as he did the realization dawned on him that Joseph might still try to take his money. Not only that, but Seth knew that Joseph knew that he was going to Dis. They had only talked about it several times during their poker game. So with that in mind, Seth adjusted his thought process to think about a safe place in the library where Joseph specifically wouldn't find his money. A few spots still came to mind, but after thinking about them for more than a few seconds, Seth realized that if he were Joseph, he probably still would have been able to find it if he looked hard enough.

Just as he was about to give up any hope of hiding his money, however, he suddenly remembered the loose floorboard underneath the dresser, which gave him an idea. As quickly as he could he walked back over towards the dresser, being mindful of exactly which floorboard it was, and knelt down next to it. As carefully as he could without making too much noise, Seth lifted up the floorboard and set it aside. He then carefully set the burlap sack full of money underneath the floor and moved it so that it was directly underneath where he was kneeling as opposed to underneath the dresser, as Seth realized that if Joseph did find this loose floorboard, the most obvious place to look would have been under the dresser. Once that was done, Seth carefully set the floorboard back, and it was only after he had done so that he mentally slapped himself in the head as he realized that he had completely forgotten to tell Tara about it.

"Did you find a hiding place!" Tara suddenly shouted down from her loft.

"I did!" Seth shouted back without looking up at her.

"Great, now that that is taken care of..." Tara then shouted as she came back down from her loft carrying a rather large suitcase, which she set on the floor beside the couch. "Give me ten minutes to get myself dressed and we will get going. I will take the bathroom. You can get changed out here."

"What about breakfast?" Seth asked.

"We can stop by the Chevrolet's bakery on the way," Tara answered. "They told me before that they were going to open extra early today so that they had a chance to hopefully catch everyone before they left. Don't worry, this will be my treat."

"No," Seth responded quickly.

"No?" Tara repeated, more than a little bewildered by that response.

"You saw how much money I have," Seth clarified. "I'll pay this time." Tara was about to say something in response to that, if only to insist that it would indeed be fine if she paid for whatever they bought, but stopped herself once she saw the look on Seth's face. Despite the fact that Seth rarely, if ever, changed his facial expression, Tara had over time managed to pick up on the subtle hints he gave out here and there, and she could tell that he genuinely wanted to be generous. With that in mind, Tara gave him a soft smile.

"Thank you," she said to him. "Speaking of money, where did you-"

"Oh, there's a loose floorboard under the dresser," Seth quickly interrupted before he had a chance to forget to tell her about it. Again.

"What, where?" Tara immediately asked, now suddenly worried.

"Underneath the dresser, like I just said," Seth responded as he pointed towards the dresser in question. When Tara looked that way, however, Seth could tell that she saw nothing out of the ordinary. He had after all, made a point to put that floorboard back exactly the way it was when he put it back.

"Well I do not see it," Tara began. "But if what you say is true then we should get that fixed as soon as we get back."

"That's where I hid my money," Seth quickly said before she had a chance to say any more. "If you fix it then I won't be able to get it back." Tara shot Seth a quizzical look as she adjusted her gaze back onto him.

"That is…" Tara began, but then stopped herself as she thought through exactly what Seth had said. "Actually somewhat clever."

"Thank you," was the only response Seth could think of to give to that.

After picking up some breakfast from the bakery, Tara and Seth made their way through town towards the open market. While Tara had been content with a single cinnamon bun, Seth took advantage of the fact that he now had a lot of extra money and bought himself a dozen lemon bars. Two of which he ate in the bakery while the rest were in a small bag that he had neatly set inside of his suitcase.

"Are you really planning to eat all of those lemon bars?" Tara asked as they walked down the road.

"Not all at once," Seth responded defensively. "Just when I get hungry. You said that it takes three days to get there, so I'm bound to get hungry along the way, right? Also if anyone else wants one I'd be willing to share… Depending on how many I have left."

As Seth spoke the two of them passed by the wealthier district of Canaan, and as they did so the open market came into view. As opposed to being packed to the brim with different stands and merchants selling their wares, as it usually was, today it was completely free of any stands or wares to buy, which gave the appearance of it being more than a little barren. Instead the open market was lined with what must have been at least thirty different carriages, all of which were being loaded up with different crates, suitcases, and passengers of many different shapes and sizes while the horses were being seen to in preparation for the long journey.

"Seeeeeettttthhh!" A very familiar, high pitched voice suddenly hit both Seth and Tara's ears as the two of them walked into the barren marketplace. Following it both Seth and Tara were greeted with the short, curly haired visage of Agatha Schaal as she raced towards the two of them at a speed that only she would think was appropriate for this situation. Seth braced himself for a sudden impact, but it never came as Agatha somehow managed to stop herself directly in front of him with an incredibly wide grin on her face. "How's it going? I haven't seen you in a while."

"I saw you last week," Seth responded.

"Well that's still seven whole days I didn't get to see you," Agatha then responded with an obvious air of fake sarcasm. "Besides, I spent most of my time lately locked in my house looking over my collection, checking to see what I have multiples of, digging out the few good things that I know I had, and determining the values of all of them with my expert appraisal skills. So I haven't had time to see anyone lately, much less you." As she spoke her voice gradually shifted in tone until by the end she sounded more like Tabitha than herself.

"What are ap-"

"And now the carriage is so stocked full of your shit that it doesn't have room for any passengers!" a very familiar, raspy sounding voice shouted before Seth could finish speaking. The sound of that voice snapped Seth to attention like the crack of a whip, as it was a voice he knew all too well. Looking past Agatha, Seth saw the familiar red haired visage of Vivian as she hopped down from one of the carriages. "You don't really think you're going to sell any of this garbage do you!"

"Considering how I usually leave Dis with more money than I come in with, yes!" Agatha shouted back. As she was doing this Seth's eyes met Vivian's, and the look on Vivian's face instantly changed to a hate filled glare the instant her eyes connected with his. It was a look that Seth had seen Vivian give before, usually to monsters.

"How… many things are you bringing?" Tara couldn't help but ask as she saw the number of not just suitcases, but trunks that had been loaded onto the carriage in question.

"Only the essentials," Agatha quickly responded as she returned her attention back to them. "Only one suitcase is full of clothes. The rest are filled with some of the things I had lying around my house. You know, things that the archeological guild might want to see, things that I'm going to sell when I get there… Ooh, and one suitcase full of… provisions for the trip." Seth would have commented on the awkward and suspicious sounding pauses in the last part that she had said, but was too fixated on Vivian's death glare to really focus on what Agatha was saying. Every time Seth had seen Vivian recently she had always shot him some variation of that look, and given what had recently transpired in their shared history, it worried him immensely. Every time he saw her now he worried that it might be the day, or night, that she decided to end his life where he stood. It was that thought process that caused Seth to remember that they would all be traveling in the empty desert far away from Canaan for days, and suddenly that was not a comforting thought.

"Right..." Tara eventually said, effectively breaking the lingering tension that was in the air. "Well, if there is not any room with you, then I am certain someone else can accommodate us."

"Or we could tie one of you to a fucking rope and drag you the whole way!" Vivian shouted back before she walked around the carriage and out of sight. Seth did not need to ask to know whom she was referring to.

"Just ignore her," Agatha said after she had gone. "I'm sure her tone will change once we're on the road." Despite how optimistic she sounded, Seth very much doubted that would be the case. "I think a few of the carriages over that way are available if you still need someone to take you." As Agatha spoke she pointed off to her left, upon which Seth looked deeper into the open market area and saw even more carriages. Many of them looked similar, but a few of them were somewhat unique, and at least one of them did not have a roof.

"Thank you, Agatha," Tara quickly responded as she suddenly grabbed Seth by the arm. "We should probably get one before it is too late. We would not want to be stuck here, would we?" With that said she then pulled Seth along with her as she walked off towards the rest of the carriages.

"Oh yeah, I can totally understand that," Agatha spoke up before they had taken more than a few steps away. "I wouldn't want to be left here either at a time like this..." By the time she had finished her next sentence Seth and Tara were already more than a few meters away from her. "Good luck you two! See you out on the road!" Then with that as quickly as she had come, Agatha spun back around and ran back towards her carriage.

"Huh... That was easy," Tara said aloud once Agatha was out of earshot.

"What was easy?" Seth then immediately asked without any hesitation.

"Oh, um...." Tara began, but then stopped herself in a manner that Seth had long since learned to recognize as 'trying to think of the right words to say', which was not always a good thing. "You know how she always likes to talk a lot... Like way too much a lot... I was... worried... that she would keep us there forever and we would never get a carriage."

"I like talking to her," Seth stated.

"I know you do," Tara replied with a soft smile. "However, we really are on a time crunch here. There will certainly be time for the two of you to talk later." Somehow, Seth was sure that she wasn't telling him everything, as she would not look him directly in the eyes when she had told him that. He did not want to ask her any more questions, however. If he did then he was certain that she would not give him a straight answer, again.

Despite what Tara had said, however, it did not take either of them long to find an available carriage. While there were many that were still being loaded up for the long trip, very few of them had anyone nearby other than what Seth assumed would be their drivers and any hired hands they had to help them load all of the crates of things they were taking with them.

"Excuse me, sir," Tara spoke up as the two of them approached a carriage that was currently being loaded up by only a single person. "Is this carriage available to take passengers?" The man in question looked to be a somewhat older gentleman, maybe around the same age as Charlie. His skin was very tanned, almost looking like leather. Though it was difficult to tell if that was his natural skin tone or if it was like that because of frequent sun exposure due to the nature of his profession. He also kept his semi-long, straight, graying brown hair tied behind him into a ponytail. As far as his clothing was concerned, he actually dressed in a similar manner to Seth with a thick, tan jacket and matching pants. Despite that, however, he wore sandals instead of shoes.

"For passengers?" the man answered as he directed his full attention towards Seth and Tara. "Sure. If you can make it worth my time."

"Oh, of course," Tara responded as she reached into her pocket and pulled out a small bag, which she then handed to him. As she did Seth heard the telltale sound of the jingling of coins. After taking it from her, the man took a quick look inside.

"Hmm, I suppose this will do for the trip there," he then said before quickly pocketing the bag of coins. "How much luggage do you have?"

"Just these," Seth interjected as he held up the two suitcases. Instead of responding with words, however, the man just stared directly at Seth with narrow, unblinking eyes.

"Alright," he eventually said. "Well get it loaded up. We set off in an hour."

"Thank you," Tara responded as Seth set their suitcases into the carriage. He didn't immediately find space for them, but after looking inside for more than a few seconds he found some space in between two crates that were off to the side. "Well, since we are going to be traveling together I suppose I should introduce myself." Tara then continued as she held out her hand. "I am Tara. Tara Schäfer."

"Schäfer..." the carriage driver said as he eyed her a little more closely. "That name sounds familiar. Have we met before?"

"Have you been to Sol recently?" Tara then asked with wide eyes, now more than interested. The instant she finished asking her question, however, the man's eyes shot wide open. Several long, awkward moments passed as Seth climbed back down from the carriage and stood behind him. "Is... there a problem?"

"No, no problem at all?" the carriage driver answered as he suddenly snapped back to reality and shook her hand. "You can call me Jorge."

"Well, it is very nice to meet you Jorge," Tara replied as she shook his hand. "The one behind you is Seth, by the way." At those words Jorge spun around to see Seth staring him in the face with the same, empty stare that he usually gave to everyone.

"Pleasure to meet you," Jorge said to Seth as he held his hand out to him.

"It's nice to meet you too," Seth replied in turn as he took Jorge's hand. "I'm Seth."

"I know," Jorge said. "She just told me."

"Oi, Seth!" another voice, this one also familiar to Seth, suddenly called out from somewhere behind him. The second he had let go of Jorge's hand Seth spun around to see Nicky and Dean off in the distance loading several large crates onto another carriage. "If you're not doin' anythin' care to lend us a hand!"

"Go ahead," Tara quickly said before Seth could say anything to her. "We have time."

"Thank you," was all Seth said in response before he spun back around and ran off in the direction of Nicky and Dean. "I'll be right back!"

"He's an odd one," Jorge said as he watched Seth run off.

"Yes, unfortunately he is," Tara responded without looking at him.

"Right," Jorge then said before walking around the carriage towards the front. "Just make sure you're both back here within the hour." As he said that last part he hit the side of his carriage with his fist. As he did, some of the contents that were already loaded shifted around slightly, including one smaller crate that was positioned directly above Tara's head as it shifted uncomfortably close to the edge of the larger crate it was stacked on top of. Tara did not see it at first, as her eyes were still focused on Seth as he ran towards the other carriage. The sound of someone else's hand abruptly hitting wood from behind her, however, instantly snapped her out of her concentration as she spun around to see who was there.

It was then that Tara's eyes fell directly on Raz, who stood only a few centimeters behind her with his arm held up. She followed the length of his arm to see that he was holding up a small crate that had fallen from the carriage directly above her head. Had he not been there, that crate would have certainly hit her head.

"Oh, um... Raz..." Tara stammered as she awkwardly backed away from both him and the offending crate. "Th... Thank you."

"It's alright," Raz replied as he slowly and carefully dropped the crate into his arms before setting it onto the floor of the carriage. "Some people just need to learn how to pack their shit better."

"Are you going to Dis too?" Tara then asked now that the awkward air between them had been cleared.

"Of course," Raz answered with a smirk as he readjusted himself. "This time of year, why wouldn't I be there?"

"I suppose there is some merit to that," Tara responded as she held both of her hands behind her back. "If you have the option to be there, then of course you would go. Wouldn't you..." Raz didn't say anything to her for several long moments as the two of them simply stood still and held eye contact, both with different types of smiles on their faces.

"Well, it was nice seeing you again," Raz eventually said before he turned around and began to walk away from her. "Maybe we'll run into each other again when we get there." Then as quickly as he had appeared, Raz was gone as he walked around the carriage towards one of the others in the distance. Tara watched him go for a moment before she turned back around. There were other things on her mind.

"That was a short conversation," a voice that was all too familiar to Raz spoke up as he approached his carriage. Leaning against it, Raz beheld the tall, dark skinned, and well dressed visage of Daedalus.

"What about it," Raz replied as he, with one precise leap, hopped into the back of the carriage and lay on the floor with his legs hanging out the back and his hands behind his head.

"Usually all of your conversations with women are filled with ill fated attempts to get into their pants," Daedalus then said as he walked around the carriage so that he could stare directly into Raz's face, which between his great height and the fact that Raz was laying against the floor of the carriage, was easy for him. "And Ms. Schäfer has never been an exception. So what happened? Did she reject you before you even had the chance to speak?" Raz couldn't help but let out an incredibly loud groan at that comment.

"No, that didn't happen," Raz responded without looking at him. "And you won't ever have to worry about it happening because it never will. I'm done with her Daedalus. I have been for months."

"Forgive me if I don't believe you," Daedalus said almost as soon as Raz had finished speaking. Raz, in turn, let out another, even louder groan as he deliberately looked away from Daedalus.

"Daedalus, whatever you might think of me, I know when enough is enough," Raz responded as he closed his eyes. "So believe me when I say that that ship has sailed, wrecked, and sunk to the bottom of the ocean." Daedalus didn't say anything to Raz for several long seconds as he stared down at his prone form. Eventually, after what seemed like enough time had passed, Daedalus stepped into the carriage himself and took a seat on the edge next to Raz's feet.

"Raz," Daedalus then began. "How long have we known each other?"

"Since we were five," Raz answered without any hesitation.

"Correct," Daedalus spoke. "So you can believe me when I say that I know bullshit coming from you when I hear it."

"Maybe I've suddenly grown more mature," Raz responded without opening his eyes.

"Now I know that is bullshit," Daedalus immediately shot back. When Raz didn't say anything immediately back to him, Daedalus let out a sigh loud enough that he was certain Raz could hear it. "Raz, I understand that after what happened the two of them needed their space, and I respect you for giving them that. But it is going to take a lot to convince me that any of this has changed you. I know you, Raz.

You've been through worse, much worse. That didn't change you, so there is no reason that I can see why any of this would have. I know you too well, Raz, much as I am ashamed to admit it." Several long seconds of silence passed wherein Raz did not respond. When Daedalus looked back, he saw that Raz's eyes were still closed. Seeing that, Daedalus let out another loud sigh before he hopped off the carriage and walked away. It was only after he had gone that Raz opened his eyes again.

When Seth got to where Nicky and Dean were he saw the same familiar cart he had seen the two of them pull from Canaan to Ash's farm. Now there were still quite a few crates left in it, only a third of which had already been loaded onto the carriage in question. When Seth arrived he saw that Nicky was already in the carriage organizing the crates that were already in there while Dean was busy moving crates from the cart to the carriage.

"Oi, how's it goin', Seth?" Nicky asked once Seth was close enough. "Been awhile since we've seen ya."

"Hello, Nicky," Seth responded as he ran up to greet them. "Hello, Dean."

"Oh, hey, Seth," Dean let out, sounding more than a little surprised as he turned around from picking up another crate and saw him standing there. "When did you get here?"

"Just now," Seth answered plainly.

"Did ya' not hear me call for 'im, dumbass?" Nicky said to Dean with a glare that was not at all intimidating.

"Are the two of you going to Dis too?" Seth then asked before Dean could say anything.

"Sure are," Nicky quickly responded. "Boss lady has some business there, and someone's gotta move all these damned things."

"Is that what you need my help with?" Seth asked as he looked over what they were doing more carefully. "To move crates again?"

"Essentially yea'," Nicky responded. "Just hand 'em to me and I'll set 'em where they need to go. This'll go faster with three people."

"Okay, sure," Seth said as he walked around Dean and picked up a crate from the cart. To his surprise, despite their size they were not as heavy as he had expected them to be.

"Oi, careful with those!" Nicky shouted at him as he did so. "Some of those 'ave fragile contents. So handle 'em with care will ya!"

"What does fragile mean?" Seth immediately asked as he stood behind Dean waiting for a chance to hand his crate to Nicky.

"It means they break very easily," Dean responded before Nicky could as he handed him his crate.

"Wow, you actually remembered that," Nicky spoke up, sounding surprised. "Color me impressed."

"Impressed isn't a color," Seth interjected as soon as he heard that. Nicky almost dropped the crate he had in his hands as his attention immediately shifted in Seth's direction. A few more seconds went by before he remembered what he was supposed to be doing and set the crate down.

"How do I always forget..." Nicky mumbled to himself. "How do I always forget that both of ya' have the same level of intelligence?"

"By the way," Seth interjected as he picked up another crate. "You mentioned Ash. Is she going to Dis too?"

"Yeah," Dean answered in place of Nicky. "That's why we're loading all this stuff for her."

"Where is she?" Seth then asked.

"She's around," Dean answered, though didn't sound exactly sure of himself. "Somewhere..."

It was only after he had said that Seth looked off in the direction opposite of the carriages and saw Ash more than a few meters away on one knee with both of her arms wrapped around what was obviously her younger sister, Pollyanna, in a tight, loving hug. Tabitha and Clementine stood nearby. Much to Seth's surprise, as this was actually the first time he had actually seen the Bellamy sisters in the same place at the same time. Despite how far away they were, from where he stood Seth could still hear their conversation.

"Now ya betta' be good for Tabitha while I'm gone," Ash said to her younger sister as she pulled out from their hug. "Cause when I get back she's gonna tell me everythin' that you did while I was away. Yah hear?"

"Yeah, yeah, I know," Polly responded with a roll of her eyes that went unnoticed by her older sister. "Yah told me this the other night."

"And I'll repeat it a third time if I think it's necessary," Ash then said in turn as she finally let go of Polly and stood back up.

"Are you sure that you're gonna be okay though?" Polly asked with genuine concern in her voice.

"What do ya mean?" Ash asked with obvious concern in her own voice now.

"I mean…" Polly began, but paused for a moment as she averted her eyes from her sister's. "This is the first time you're goin' on this trip instead of Mal-"

"Polly," Ash quickly cut in before Polly could finish. The seemingly instantaneous change in her tone and eyes as she did so was enough to make Pollyanna stop talking. "I'm goin' to be fine. Everything is goin' to be just fine. So you don't have anythin' to worry about. Yah hear."

"It's a shame that you need to travel in the first place," Tabitha quickly interjected as if to intentionally break up the tension in the air. "While living in a small town like Canaan has its perks, I do sometimes wish that we were important enough for people to want to travel here instead of through here. It might lead to more business."

"I wish I could go to Dis, or anywhere that did anything actually interesting," Clementine then added once her sister had finished talking. "Last week our class was talking about ideas for what we could do to celebrate the new year."

"Didn't that boy Mitch suggest puttin' on a play of Solaris killin' Chaos?" Polly asked.

"Yes, he did," Clementine answered as her eyes dropped towards her feet. "I'm still a little disappointed that Miss Chávez shot that idea down. I really wanted to play Chaos." Tabitha could only barely suppress a giggle as she heard this.

"I don't think you could have done such a role justice," Tabitha said through her giggles. "You're too cute to be Chaos."

"No I'm not!" Clementine shouted as her face instantly became red. However, the squeakiness of her young voice only served to prove Tabitha's point as Polly, Ash, and even Tabitha herself all burst out laughing the second they heard that come out of her, which unfortunately also made Clementine's face turn even redder from the embarrassment.

"W… Well…" Ash eventually spoke up after the laughter at Clementine's expense had died down. "I suppose I should be goin' now. I'm almost certain those two meatheads messed somethin' up without me there to watch 'em." She then paused for a brief second before she returned her full attention back to Polly. "Just remember what I said, okay?"

"Okay," Polly answered with another roll of her eyes. From where he was Seth wasn't sure if Ash saw it or not, but if she had, she showed no reaction.

"Okay, perfect," Ash said as she suddenly enveloped her sister in another great, big hug. "I'll see you in two weeks. Ah love you."

"I love you too," Polly responded to her older sister as they both slowly let go of each other. With all of that said and done, Tabitha took Clementine by the hand as the two of them and Polly all turned and began to walk back in what Seth knew was the general direction of Tabitha's boutique. Ash watched them all go for a few moments before turning back around, only to instantly meet Seth's gaze. Without saying anything she walked directly towards him.

"Seth…" Ash said as she approached him. "What are you doin' here?"

"Nicky said that he and Dean needed some help loading these crates into your carriage," Seth answered as he gestured towards the crate that was currently in his hands. "So he asked me to help them."

"Yeah, I did!" the voice of Nicky suddenly rang out from behind him. Immediately Seth turned around to see him still standing in the carriage with his eyes trained on him in glower that he probably thought was intimidating. "So are ya' gonna help or are ya' gonna keep standin' there starin' at the boss, ya creep!"

"I don't know what that last word means!" Seth shouted back.

"Just ignore him," Ash said with a roll of her eyes. "He only wishes you were a creep so that he can feel betta' about himself."

"I still don't know what that word means," Seth repeated as he handed a crate to Nicky, who had suddenly stopped talking the second Ash had arrived. Ash seemed to notice this as she looked back at Nicky with a devilish smirk on her face. At her gaze Nicky instantly averted his eyes as he picked up another crate from Dean.

"If ya' really wanna know, ask Tara," Ash then said to Seth as she slapped him on the arm. "But trust me when I say you don't need to worry about it."

"If you say so," Seth replied as he took another crate from the cart.

"I do say so," Ash responded to Seth before turning her attention back to her two employees. "Alright you useless sacks of meat!" As she shouted at them she picked up a crate herself. "Let's get these things loaded up! Sooner we get this done the sooner we can get our asses movin'!"

With Seth's help it only took them a little over fifteen minutes before the last crate had been loaded onto the carriage.

"Alright, I think that's everything," Dean said as he handed Nicky the last crate.

"You think that's everything?" Nicky responded to him. "Key word there is think. You wanna check again there dumbass?"

"No," Dean responded in a surprisingly calm tone. "That was the last one when I looked in there. I know it is."

"Oh, so now you know," Nicky then said in what Seth guessed was supposed to be a sarcastic tone of voice. "Which is it then? Do ya' think or do ya' know that's the last one."

"Ah shut your trap," Ash interjected as she walked around Dean and with a discerning eye, carefully examined the stacks of crates that had been loaded into the carriage.

"I stacked 'em exactly to your specifications, boss," Nicky spoke up as if he had instantly forgotten about Dean.

"Did you now?" Ash then asked as she shifted her gaze from the crates to his eyes. "I don't want any of 'em movin' around on the way there, you know that, right?"

"Of course," Nicky quickly responded, seeming proud of himself. "In fact I-"

"Then check 'em again," Ash quickly interrupted before he could get another word in. "If any of these fall off at any point then it's your ass."

"Yes ma'am!" Nicky just as quickly responded as he spun around and began to carefully examine one of the stacks of crates himself. Or at least he acted as if he was. Ash watched him for a few moments before she turned towards Dean, her mood softening noticeably as she did so.

"You can take the cart back to the guy in the warehouse," Ash said to him. "We won't be needin' it till we get back."

"Yes ma'am," Dean responded, exactly as Nicky had, before walking over towards the cart, stood in the spot where a horse normally would, and then with nothing but his own muscles, pushed the cart forward. Seth was well aware of how heavy those carts were, but the way Dean was pushing it, he made it look easy.

"Was that all you needed me for?" Seth asked as soon as Dean was away.

"I reckon so," Ash responded as she turned back to face Seth. "All we gotta' do now is double check everythin' before we head out. Besides I'm sure Tara's waitin' for ya. Speakin' of which is she around, or are you by yourself again?"

"She's probably still by that carriage over there," Seth answered as he pointed towards the carriage that he and Tara had paid to take them. He did not see her there, but he was sure that she could not have gone far. "We still had an hour to wait when we got here, so I figured that I would have time to help you."

"She's out here too?" Ash then asked as she turned her head to look for her, but did not see her either. "I'm actually surprised. Didn't-" Ash suddenly ceased talking as she slowly turned back to give Seth her full attention. A look of realization slowly spread across her face as she did so. "Wait, are you goin' to Dis too?"

"Yes," Seth answered. "Tara said that I need to experience new things, and since I've never seen a city before she said that it would be good for me." A few long, somewhat awkward seconds of silence passed after he finished speaking, and all Ash did in response was stare at him with wide eyes. Something that Seth felt was more than a little worrying. "Is that a bad thing?"

"No, no," Ash quickly reassured Seth once she realized what she must have looked like to him. "I'm just... sort of surprised is all. Ah mean, you haven't even been here a full year and you're gettin' to go out and see the wider world. You should consider yourself lucky. Most people never get that chance." There was a look of longing on Ash's face as she looked away from Seth off in the distance somewhere. Seth, knowing the layout of this town as well as he did, did not need to look to see that she was looking in the general direction of Tabitha's boutique. This only lasted for a second, however, before Ash suddenly recomposed herself as if nothing had happened. "Well if that's the case then you should probably head back. Don't wanna keep your driver waitin' cause knowing this lot they won't wait for you. Now go on, git. I'll see you on the road."

"Alright, thank you," Seth politely said to her before walking past her towards the carriage that he and Tara had paid for.

"Oi, Seth," Ash called out to him before he had gotten too far. "Thanks for the help."

"It was no problem," Seth replied to her. "And you don't need to thank me."

"No, no, I do," Ash responded with a flick of her hair. "Momma didn't raise no goat." Then with that said she turned her attention back to Nicky. She didn't say anything, but she did keep a close eye on him. While Seth could not think of any reason why goats had anything to do with what she had just said to him, he did acknowledge that she was right. Probably more right than she knew with the way Jorge had acted towards them.

With that in mind Seth set off towards Jorge's carriage. Before he could take more than ten steps in that direction, however, two people pulling a chestnut colored horse behind them suddenly walked directly in front of him. The instant one of the horse's eyes fell upon Seth it let out a loud 'neigh' noise, as if panicked, and pulled back on its reins as hard as it could. Momentarily startled, one of the men pulling the horse immediately let go of the reins while the other one was pulled backwards by the horse's strength before falling onto the ground. Now freed, the horse let out another loud 'neigh' as it reared back on both of its hind legs.

Seth, who had since become accustomed to this type of response from animals, knew immediately what to do as he backed away from the horse as quickly as he could. Unfortunately for him, however, he backed away too quickly and did not pay attention to where he was going as he tripped and fell over backwards onto his back. A sting of pain traveled through his back as he instinctively looked up to see the bottom of the horses' front hooves above him. Immediately he rolled away from the horse just before its hooves hit the dirt where he previously lay.

"Seth!" Ash's voice suddenly rang out as she rushed up behind him and quickly helped him to his feet. "Are ya alright?"

"I'm fine," Seth quickly responded as he stood back up. In front of him the horse let out another 'neigh' as it reared up on its hind legs again and attempted to move backwards. Before it could get very far, however, the man who hadn't been knocked down bravely ran up and grabbed the reins again as the other man pulled himself back up onto his feet.

"Woah, woah, easy there!" the first man shouted at the horse as he attempted to get it under control. The second man, seeing what was happening, ran up and took hold of the reins just as the first one did. As he did the horse attempted to rear up on its hind legs again, as if in a deliberate attempt to pull away from the two men, but the both of them pulling back made it difficult for the horse.

"The fuck is wrong with her!" the second man shouted as he held onto the horse for dear life.

"I have no idea!" the first man responded as the horse began to back up and pull the two of them with it.

Seth, still aware of what was going on, pulled himself away from Ash's grasp and continued to back up, still quickly, but more carefully and controlled than before. The farther back he went the less aggressive the horse became as Seth watched it fight with the two pulling on it less and less. It still made several loud 'neigh' noises, but its attempts to fight back lessened the farther back Seth went. Eventually Seth was forced to stop as he suddenly ran into something behind him. A quick glance told him that it was another carriage.

"Hey man, what are you doing?" Someone nearby asked him. For the moment Seth ignored him as he kept his full attention on the horse. A few more 'neigh' noises followed along with one great shake of its head, which despite the force, neither of the two men let go of the reins when it did that. Seth could only imagine how hard that must have been considering the horse was strong enough to pull one of them back.

"The hell you doin'?" Ash asked almost in an echo of the previous person who asked him that as she ran up to where Seth was. For the moment Seth ignored her too. After a few more long, very tense seconds of watching the horse fight the two men, with Seth as far away from it as he was, the horse eventually calmed down.

"There, there, easy now," Seth heard one of the two men say to the horse as he petted its head.

"What even happened to her?" The other one asked as he began to pull the horse in the direction they had been trying to go before. At first it wouldn't go, but after the first man began to pull as well it followed them.

"I don't know," the first man answered as they walked out of sight. "She's never done anything like that before. Something must have really spooked her." As he closed out that last thought the two of them and the horse walked out of sight. It was only after they were gone that Seth realized the exact position he was in.

"I'm sorry," Seth quickly said to the man that he could only assume was this carriage's driver as he pulled himself away from it. After that he turned his attention to Ash. "I'm sorry." After repeating that to her Seth very quickly walked away from the carriage and the two of them before either of them had a chance to ask him any more questions.

As he made his way as quickly as he could back towards the carriage that was supposed to be his, out of the corner of his eye Seth saw in the distance the postwoman Grey helping what looked, to him at least, like a smaller version of herself into one of the carriages. Seth remembered that Grey had said that she had a daughter, but he had never seen her before. Those stray thoughts were pushed from his mind, however, as he quickly made his way back towards Jorge's carriage.

Unbeknownst to Seth, however, the entire incident with the horse had been seen by both Tara and Jorge, who stood next to each other by Jorge's carriage as they watched Seth quickly walk back towards them.

"So…" Jorge began. "Does that sort of thing-"

"Unfortunately it does," Tara quickly responded before Jorge could say anything else. "For whatever reason animals have never seemed to like him. At all." As Tara spoke she nervously rubbed the back of her head. Something that did not go unnoticed by Jorge.

"Who is he?" Jorge asked, his eyes narrowing on Tara's as he did so.

"Someone who lost his memory," Tara answered, mostly honestly. "Two of the residents of this town found him in the desert out west seven months ago. He's been living with us here ever since."

"Who was he before?" Jorge then asked, now more than a little curious, if only for his own safety.

"Nobody knows, not even him. He didn't even remember his own name when they found him."

"But whoever he was before, animals don't like him?"

"Yes, unfortunately," Tara answered as she did her best to keep eye contact with him. Several long, awkward seconds of silence passed wherein Jorge kept his narrow gaze on Tara, as if in an attempt to see through her before he eventually spoke again.

"He's not going to be any trouble, is he?" Jorge then asked without any hesitation.

"What, no, no," Tara answered quicker than she probably should have. "Not at all. He is actually the nicest person you will ever meet. Truly."

"But animals don't like him?" Jorge immediately followed up with.

"Yes," Tara responded, again quicker than she probably should have. "Not to be rude, but I feel that we are going in circles here." Jorge fell silent again as he looked back over towards Seth and saw that he was now close enough to hear what they were saying. With that in mind Jorge let out an incredibly loud sigh without any care for whether or not Seth heard it.

"Do you want me to stick towards the back," Jorge then asked Tara. "You know, so he doesn't freak out any of the horses behind us."

"If that is an option then that would be perfect," Tara answered as her expression instantly seemed to brighten. Unfortunately for her, Seth had reached them by that point and heard what she had said.

"You... saw that?" Seth asked as he looked between Tara and Jorge.

"Unfortunately, yes," Tara answered.

"I'm sorry," Seth then said as he dropped his eyes towards the ground.

"No, no, it is okay," Tara replied with what she hoped was a reassuring smile before Jorge had the chance to say anything. "It was not your fault. You do not have anything to apologize for." Despite her words, Jorge, with an obvious roll of his eyes, let out another obnoxiously loud sigh and turned away from them.

"If either of you have anything else you need to take care of before we leave I suggest you do it now," he said to them as he walked back towards the front of his carriage.

"So what do we do now?" Seth asked once Jorge was out of their line of sight.

"I suppose we just wait," Tara answered with a shrug of her shoulders as she recomposed herself. "I do not think there is anything else that we can do."

Before Seth knew it he found himself sitting in the back of Jorge's carriage waiting for all of the other carriages to slowly make their way out of the small town now that its gate had been opened to them. Because Jorge had promised to wait until all of the other carriages had gone before he set on his way, Seth sat there doing nothing but waiting for what felt like a really, really long time. While it was not the longest amount of time Seth had to sit and wait for anything, it was long enough for him to realize that with a three day trip, if conditions were favorable, that he would essentially be stuck in this position for that entire time. Before he could think any harder about that realization, however, the sound of Jorge snapping the reins of his horse hit Seth's ears. Not even a second after that sound had rung out the carriage suddenly lurched forward as it began to move. It was slow at first, but after a few quick moments they had picked up a decent pace.

Seth could only watch as they made their way through the town gates and past the four town watch members stationed outside, two of which Seth recognized as Ed and Jacque. After what Seth guessed was six meters away from the gate, he watched as the four watch members all suddenly turned around and darted back into the town as the gate was slowly shut behind them. A loud 'clang' rang out as the two large wooden doors of Canaan's southern gate came together and the town was cut off from Seth's view.

With nothing else to do, Seth simply stared out of the back of the carriage at the tall, wooden walls of Canaan. An odd feeling came over him as he watched the town that he had called home for the past seven months slowly become smaller and smaller the farther away they went. He likened it to sadness, but didn't entirely understand himself why this was making him sad at all. He didn't feel anything like this the last time he had left Canaan to go into the desert, so for the life of him he could not understand why he was feeling it now. The only reason he could come up with was that maybe it was because he knew that he would not see Canaan again for another two weeks at least. He pushed those thoughts and feelings down the second they started taking him to places that he did not want to go, and did his best not to think about them again. Thankfully for him, that became easier once the walls of Canaan were far enough away that they began to disappear into nothing but a spec amongst the seemingly endless desert.

Night had long since fallen in Canaan since the carriages had left for Dis. Despite this, the Empty Barrel was still open, though its number of patrons had greatly diminished. At this late hour, just before the pub had begun to close, Joseph stumbled out of its doors and onto the dirt road. With the moonlight being the only thing to light his way, Joseph made his way through the dark streets of the town towards his home. The sound of a giggle, however, stopped him dead in his tracks before he had even gotten two thirds of the way back to his home.

"Hello?" Joseph said aloud as he looked behind him. All that was there, however, was darkness and silence. "Punk kids."

"Hm Hmhm Hmhmhmhmhm Hm Hmhm Hmhmhm..." Joseph instantly spun back around the second he had heard something. However, the only things that were behind him were still darkness and silence. Stranger still, the pattern of the humming was one that he recognized. It was to the tune of a nursery rhyme he had heard as a child called 'Pop goes the weasel'.

"Look kid!" Joseph shouted into the darkness. "Don't waste my time, you little shit! It's late, I'm tired and I want to go the fuck home! You better do the same before I drag you by the nose back to your parents!" The only response he received was an eerie silence. Undeterred, Joseph stayed still and waited for the telltale sounds of footsteps to signal to him that his threat had not fallen on deaf ears, but none came. Even after a full minute of waiting for a response, the only thing that he received was more silence.

"Fuck it," Joseph muttered to himself before turning back around. The instant his back was turned, however, something scratched him across his right cheek. "Ah! What the fuck!" he shouted as he instinctively reached up to feel what had happened, only to feel a stinging pain that came from a trio of fresh claw marks. Unseen by Joseph, in the air above him hovered a large, bat-like creature that despite its size, was able to remain completely silent as it flapped its wings. It let out another giggle as it watched Joseph's reaction.

"Where the fuck are you!" Joseph shouted as he pulled a large hunting knife from his belt. The thought occurred to him as he did so that if he had brought his knife with him the other night, then maybe he would have gotten his money back from Seth, but he pushed that thought aside as it only served to distract him from what was happening right now. That momentary lapse in thought, however, proved to be his undoing as the bat-creature landed on Joseph's left shoulder like a trained parrot. Before it could even register in Joseph's head that something had touched him, the bat-creature sunk its teeth into the side of Joseph's head where his ear was. Joseph in turn let out a loud scream as the pain from the bat-creature's bite ran through him. Before he could do anything about it, however, with one powerful flap of its wings the bat-creature took off from Joseph's shoulder and with a bloody tear, ripped Joseph's ear from the side of his head.

Joseph let out another, louder scream in pain as he switched hands with his knife so that he could put a hand over the freshly opened wound on his head. Without thinking Joseph swung the knife blindly around him. After several seconds of failing to hit anything he finally looked up and saw the bat-creature perched on the roof of a nearby building illuminated by the moonlight. Joseph could only shoot a wrath filled scowl at the creature as he watched it chew on his ear like a piece of steak before swallowing it right in front of him.

"You picked the wrong guy to fuck with," Joseph said to it as he took a few steps in its direction. "I'm going to skin you and turn you into a pair of gloves." The bat-creature only giggled at him in response before its lips curled into a wide smile that perfectly framed its blood coated, serrated teeth.

Before Joseph could take one more step towards it, however, he was suddenly blindsided by something that was much larger than the bat-creature. He couldn't see what it was. All he knew was that one moment he was on the ground glaring up at the bat-creature with his knife in hand, and the next, he had dropped his knife, felt something violently pierce the front of both his shoulders as well as the center of his back, and then not even two seconds later his feet were no longer touching the ground. When he looked down he saw the town of Canaan below him become smaller and smaller as whatever was carrying him soared, without making any sound, out into the seemingly endless desert, followed by the bat-creature.

Joseph screamed at the top of his lungs for help, but by then it was too late. Any night watchmen who would have heard his cries were too far away by the time any of them had noticed the large, flying creature that was carrying him. All Joseph could do was watch as the town of Canaan became smaller and smaller as he was carried farther away from it until he could no longer see it.

Joseph wasn't sure at all how long this thing, whatever it was, had carried him for. Minutes? Hours? Not that he paid that much attention as he spent the whole trip shouting and squirming in desperate attempts to shake himself free from the creature's grasp. All of this was in vain, however, as the creature barely even acknowledged his presence and its grip was too tight for him to budge even a centimeter.

Eventually he noticed the creature begin to slowly descend. Exactly where they were descending towards still eluded him, however, as everywhere in this Solaris forsaken desert looked exactly the same to him, especially at night. Once they were three meters from the ground the creature suddenly opened its talons and let go of him. Joseph let out a scream as he fell for only a few seconds before hitting the ground hard and rolling a few meters before finally stopping.

Dazed and still somewhat drunk, Joseph attempted to push himself up, only to receive a sudden surge of pain from his right wrist as he fell face first back into the sand. With his mouth full of sand he rolled over onto his back and spit it out as he held his right wrist out in front of him. It was difficult for him to see in the darkness, but he was certain that he had broken something. Looking up at the night sky above him, neither the large creature that had carried him nor the small bat-like creature were anywhere to be seen. As the realization that they might still be around hit him, he sat up as quickly as he could and looked all around him, but they were nowhere to be seen. This greatly confused him, as he knew perfectly well what they were, but the fact that they weren't trying to finish him off was more than a little disconcerting. As he slowly stood back up onto his feet he turned around again and saw something that he did not expect to see at all.

Standing a little over a meter away from him was a woman with shoulder length, astonishingly messy black hair wearing a tattered and somewhat skimpy black dress that only barely conformed to her figure. For a brief second, Joseph felt that he had scored a bit of luck after the barrage of unfortunate events that had just happened to him. As quickly as they had come, however, those thoughts were dashed away the instant he noticed a few more details about this woman. First, she was much taller than him. While not a deal breaker, the fact that she stood over two and a half meters tall and bore an incredibly slender figure was more than a little off putting. Second, despite them being in a desert, her skin was paler than a glass of milk. Neither of those held a candle to the last and most important detail, however, the one that made Joseph's tanned skin turn as white as her's. Her eyes were a piercing blood red color, something that he had seen on only one type of creature.

"Hi," the woman said to him with a gentle smile.

Chapter 6

After a long, long day of traveling, the sun eventually began to set on the caravan of carriages. Seth fell out of his concentration on his book when he felt the carriage that he and Tara were traveling in come to a sudden and complete stop. Without thinking he looked around towards Tara, who seemed lost in thought herself and thus showed no reaction to him at all. He then shifted his attention towards the carriage's owner, Jorge, but he only saw his back. With no reaction from him either, Seth looked past Jorge to see if any of the carriages ahead of them were still moving. As ridiculous as it seemed, the past few days had seemed longer to Seth than any night spent in a watch tower or the days he had spent walking the last time he had been out in the desert. It was bad enough for him that he would not have been surprised if time had somehow come to a total standstill and he did not notice.

"Alright," Jorge eventually said to him and Tara before turning around to face them. "We're setting up camp for the night. Assuming nothing goes wrong, we should arrive in Dis before midday tomorrow."

"Oh… okay. Very well… Thank you," Tara responded to him with a layer of anxiety in her voice that did not go unnoticed by Seth. As much as he wanted to, he chose not to call attention to it, as he wasn't sure of how he could do so without sounding accusatory.

There were a few other questions Seth wanted to ask, such as what would happen if something did go wrong, but given the apparent tension in the carriage, he chose instead to return his attention back to his book only to see that he was not only in the middle of the chapter, but in the middle of the page as well. This slightly annoyed him, but he also knew that it was far from the worst thing that could have happened as he placed his bookmark back into the book, stood up, and then slid the book into one of his jacket pockets.

"I'm going to help keep watch," he said, though he was unsure if either Tara or Jorge had actually heard him, before jumping out the back of the carriage.

Once his feet had hit the ground Seth took a few steps away from his carriage so that he could get a better view of the others. With only a glance he saw all of the other merchants and everyone accompanying them trying to set up camp as quickly as possible so as to take advantage of whatever sunlight remained for the day. As Seth watched all of these people a rather strange thought crossed his mind.

There were thirty carriages in this caravan, and each one had at least one person on it. However, some of them had upwards of four people stepping off of them now that they had stopped. With that in mind he couldn't help but wonder if there were more people here than the entire population of Canaan. Seth was well aware by now that there were very few people who actually lived in Canaan, and most of the people that were there were either passing traders or people who did business that Seth could not understand that were on their way to either Taurus or Dis. However, even with that knowledge it still felt as if there were more people here than in Canaan. If that was indeed the case, then why did it not feel like it? Even if there were a good handful of people here that he knew, it did not help to shake the feeling of isolation that had been welling up in him since this trip began.

It was then that Seth remembered that he said he would keep watch, so he quickly turned away from all of the people and faced out towards the desert. Looking at it did not help his feelings of loneliness at all. Instead of a group of people all he saw was a long stretch of sand that seemed to go on forever, as it always did. While the desert here was slightly more rocky than the area surrounding Canaan, it was still a familiar sight to him. The sight of absolutely nothing. Eventually Seth began to linger past the carriages, hoping not to spook the horses. Luckily for him, by this time most of them were either currently being fed or provided with water, so they were all too distracted to notice that he was there.

Seth stopped once he was roughly halfway through the row of carriages. The reason for this was due to the other person currently on watch, Vivian. She did not say anything to him, she did not look at him, she only walked past him and continued to patrol the area around the carriages with her hand on the hilt of her sword. While most would take this as a sign of professionalism, Seth knew that there was a much colder reason for it. His eyes followed her for a few moments as she continued on past him and towards where he had just come from. He wanted to call her name out, he wanted to talk to her like they did months ago, but he couldn't. The sight of a certain ovallar scar on the base of her neck kept his feet from moving. While it was hard to see from where he stood, he knew it was there. He knew exactly where it was.

"Yeah, I got two," Seth heard the familiar voice of Jorge say from somewhere ahead of him. Thankful that he had something to take his mind off of Vivian, Seth turned his attention back to what was in front of him and kept walking.

The sound of Jorge's voice became clearer as he walked. "A man and a woman."

"Couple?" a female voice then asked. Sadly Seth could not see who the voice belonged to, as both its owner and Jorge were on the opposite side of the carriages from him.

"No idea," Jorge responded. "If they are then they sure as hell don't act like it."

"What, do you expect them to start making out in the back of your carriage while you're still there?" The woman asked. "People do have restraint."

"You say that, but remember Marcus?" Jorge shot back.

"Who?"

"Marcus Carmen. Skinny, sold wine, retired a few years back."

"Oh, right, now I remember. What about him?"

"He literally had that happen to him. Two young kids. Couldn't have been much older than sixteen or seventeen. Apparently they got into one of his crates of wine and well… he got a free show." The woman suddenly burst out laughing as she heard that. "Anyways, the woman I'm transporting. She's apparently from Sol."

"Oh, I'm so sorry. I feel your pain," the woman responded, much to Seth's confusion. "I've had to deal with those pompous pricks myself on occasion. Just because you happen to live in the same city as the queen doesn't make you fucking royalty too. At least they usually pay well enough to make it almost worth it."

The two of them had another hearty laugh at that. Seth, having felt that he had listened to enough, continued on with his patrol. While he still had little to no idea what some of the words they had used meant, from their tone he could tell that they were clearly meant to be insulting towards Tara, which made absolutely no sense to him. As far as he was aware, Tara had acted as kind as she usually was towards Jorge in the few times that the two of them had talked. So this perspective that Jorge and his other trader friends apparently had seemed completely unfounded to him.

As much as he wanted to, he chose not to say anything about it to Jorge. He knew that doing so would cause a scene, especially when it was his carriage they were riding in, and despite whatever opinions may have had, he still agreed to take them.

As Seth continued on forward towards the front of the caravan, not too far away in the distance he saw the blonde haired, one eyed visage of Grey Dressler as she knelt down next to her daughter. A few meters away from them three extra planks of wood were stuck upright into the sand while the young girl held her mother's crossbow in her hands.

"Okay, now, relax," Seth heard Grey say as she adjusted her daughter's aim slightly. "Take a deep breath. Don't think about what's going on around you. Just keep your eye on where you want to go and don't look away." After a few silent moments Grey's daughter had seemingly steadied her aim with the crossbow. The thing that was interesting, to Seth at least, was that Grey appeared to be encouraging her daughter to aim out of the same eye that Grey herself usually kept covered with an eyepatch. "That's it, don't rush. You got all the time in the world right now. Can you see where you want to go?"

"Yeah," Grey's daughter responded without dropping her aim.

"Good," Grey replied as she released her hands from the crossbow and stepped away from her daughter. "Now pull the trigger." The instant those words had left Grey's mouth her daughter did as she was instructed, and as she did a bolt flew from the crossbow and stuck itself into the plank on the left, which fell over backwards as soon as it was hit.

"I did-!" Grey's daughter shouted, though before she could say any more Grey suddenly threw her arms around her and scooped her up into a great big hug.

"That was amazing!" Grey shouted at her daughter as she squeezed her tight before snuggling her face into her daughter's. After a few moments of this, Grey eventually let her daughter go and set her back down. "Okay, now hit the next one." Her daughter then enthusiastically took aim with the crossbow again. This time without her mother's help.

Seth couldn't help but find the sight endearing, as it reminded him of how he was when he was still learning how to use a sword. As soon as those thoughts came to him, however, he immediately pushed them away. As endearing as those memories were for him, they also brought many painful memories with them. Memories that he would rather not think about.

"Ey, you there! Purple shirt!" someone suddenly shouted from the second carriage from the front. Without thinking Seth tore his attention away from the mother and child and looked around him to see if maybe the voice was directed at someone else, but from what he saw, no one else in this caravan was a fan of the color purple. With that in mind Seth directed his attention towards the source of the voice and saw an older man attempting to pull a large crate from the back of his carriage, but he seemed to be struggling with it. "Mind helping me out here!"

"Sure," Seth answered before quickly making his way over towards the man. Once he was there he grabbed hold of one end of the wooden crate and helped the man carry it over towards where a few of the other people were stocking up a pile of sticks and logs for a campfire.

Once they had set the crate onto the sand Seth got a better look at the man he was helping. At first he thought that he was an older man, maybe around the same age as Maryen, the mayor of Canaan, though Seth only assumed that from his wrinkled skin and graying hair. The tone of his skin and the shape of his eyes, however, were more similar to those of Rose, the woman who worked in the town watch station.

"Thank you," the man said to Seth as he took a quick breath. "I don't believe we've met. You can call me Makoto." As he spoke he held out his hand towards Seth.

"It's nice to meet you. I'm Seth," Seth replied as he shook the man's hand. "If you don't mind me asking, why were you trying to carry this box by yourself if you couldn't lift it."

"Well, my son Hoshi was supposed to help me with it," Makoto answered. "But he went to take a piss after we stopped. That was a while ago. If you ask me he probably used that as an excuse to gawk at that red-headed monster hunter that was riding in front of us. I thought that maybe I could handle it myself, but I'm not as young as I once was and well... well, you saw." That last part he said with a chuckle.

"How long have you been doing this?" Seth asked with obvious curiosity in his voice.

"Well let's see..." Makoto answered as he momentarily looked up towards the sky. "I took over for my father when I turned twenty-four and I'm fifty-six now so... thirty-two years."

"Really, that long?" Seth then said, surprised. "What's that like?"

"Honestly, pretty much like this trip, just, you know, over and over and over again," Makoto answered. "Though I'll tell you, this route used to be much harder to take before that Canaan town was built. Though long travel is in my blood since my grandparents traveled all the way to this country from our homeland in Cheondung."

"I've never heard of that place."

"Eh, I'm not surprised. It's a small country thousands of kilometers to the east. I've never been there myself. Come to think of it, last I heard they had gone to war with the kingdom of Vladishire, and that was about five years ago. So for all I know it might not even exist anymore."

"Oh... I'm sorry."

"Ah, don't be. It's not like you had anything to do with it."

"Okay..." Seth responded hesitantly. He did not know what a few of the words that Makoto had chosen to use meant, but he chose not to ask about them. Past experience had taught him that questions like that tended to annoy people, especially when he asked a lot of them. "So, what's in this crate? If you don't mind me asking."

"Everyone's dinner," Makoto answered as he smacked the top of the crate. "Since I'm the merchant here with the most experience, they thought it best to put me towards the front and carry all the rations. Of course some people still bring their own, which if you ask me, it would be easier if everyone did that, but then you have the people who don't properly plan well and that's a whole headache in and of itself if and when they start whining about it."

"Oh, I understand," Seth said in response, if only because in this instance he actually did understand perfectly well what Makoto was talking about. "That's what I've been doing with the lemon bars I bought."

"Lemon bars?" Makoto questioned as he raised an eyebrow.

"I've eaten nothing but lemon bars for the past three days," Seth answered with a completely straight face.

"That... doesn't sound healthy," Makoto then said as he stared at Seth like he had suddenly sprouted two additional heads.

"Why not?" Seth asked, now genuinely curious. "Lemons are fruit."

"Well, yes, lemons are fruit," Makoto answered. "But lemon bars are not. Yes they do use lemons to make them, but most of the bar is more like bread. Not only that, but there's probably more sugar in it than actual le-" Before he could say any more Makoto suddenly stopped in the middle of his rant. Looking at his eyes, Seth saw that he wasn't looking at him anymore, but rather past him. "Oh, there you are!"

Immediately Seth looked over his shoulder to see a younger man running towards them, young enough to probably still be a teenager. As he grew closer Seth saw that he resembled a younger version of Makoto.

"You done flirting with that monster hunter?" Makoto snapped at his son as he stopped next to Seth and took a moment to catch his breath. "How about you do at least one part of your job and bring the crowbar over." Hoshi let out an obnoxiously loud groan before turning around and running back to the carriage that Seth and Makoto had just come from. A few seconds later he returned with the tool that his father had asked for.

"I wasn't flirting with her, dad," Hoshi said to his father as he jammed the crowbar into the top of the crate so that he could open it. "I just… appreciate monster hunters." As he spoke he popped open one side of the crate. "They're all just so awesome, you know. What they do, training every day to become the strongest so that they can put down those hellish beasts that plague the world for the sake of everyone else. If you ask me, it's a much cooler job than this." As he finished speaking he popped off the other side of the crate, which caused the wooden top to fall to the ground in between Seth and Makoto.

"If you like monster hunters so much, why not become one?" Seth then asked without thinking. To his surprise Hoshi let out a laugh as he heard that.

"You're kidding right?" he responded to Seth. "If I tried that then I would probably die instantly. It's safer to admire them from a distance." Given his own experience with monsters Seth was unsure of how to respond to that. Upon closer inspection of the teen, however, while he wasn't entirely skin and bones, he did look like someone that even Tabithia could break in half over her knee. A monster would tear him apart like freshly ground beef.

"Fair enough," Seth eventually responded. "Well, I should get back to keeping watch. Vivian will probably get angrier if she thinks I'm not helping out."

"Oh, so you know her?" Hoshi then suddenly asked in a tone of voice that reminded Seth of Raz when he had been asking him all those weird questions about Tara. Makoto, however, shot his son a stern look the instant he had finished talking.

"Yes I do," Seth answered before going back to his route without another word.

"What the hell was that?" Makoto then asked his son once he thought Seth was out of earshot from them.

"What the hell was what?" Hoshi responded.

"Your attitude there. What's with the jealousy?"

"I don't know what you're talking about."

"You sure? Cause it sure looked like jealousy to me. You really think you can fool me, boy?"

"Whatever you say," Hoshi responded with an obvious roll of his eyes as he walked away from his father and back towards their carriage.

Not too far from the bickering father and son, on top of one of the many carriages was Raz, who lay on his back with his arms behind his head and his eyes closed as he soaked up whatever sun was left for the day.

"What do you think you're doing?" Daedalus then suddenly asked from the ground next to the carriage.

"Relaxing," Raz responded without opening his eyes.

"And you didn't do enough of that when the carriage was moving?" Daedalus shot back. "Unless you want to convince me that you were using that time to do something productive like writing letters to your family." To Daedalus' surprise, Raz did not respond to that at all. He didn't even acknowledge whether or not he had heard him, which Daedalus knew he had. "Look, just because you are an arrogant prick doesn't mean you get to act like one. Now get your lazy ass down from there before the carriage's owner kicks you off, and if he doesn't I will."

With the sound of a deep, guttural breath that sounded more akin to a growl than a sigh, Raz stood up where he was, and without even looking walked to the side of the carriage's roof before jumping off of it, doing a flip in the air, and then landing behind Daedalus.

"There, happy?" Raz asked without turning around.

"No, because I shouldn't have to remind you to act like an adult."

"Come the fuck on man," Raz then said as he slowly turned himself around to look Daedalus in the eyes. "We're heading to Dis for a new years festival. Take a load off your shoulders, enjoy yourself for once."

"No, you're going to the festival," Daedalus responded. "Unlike you, I have actual business in Dis."

"Festival lasts a week," Raz responded calmly as a smirk began to crawl across his face. "So unless this 'business' of yours is actually code for a secret rendezvous, which I wouldn't blame you for by the way, Solaris knows you could use it more than me, then that excuse isn't going to work. Certainly you could take at least one or two nights to grab a few drinks and have some fun. Or if that 'business' of yours doesn't work out I'm sure there's somewhere in Dis where we can find you some company." Raz emphasized that last part with a click of his tongue. Daedalus, however, only responded to him with a very threatening, dagger-like glare, seemingly offended that Raz would even suggest that. "Or we could find you something with chocolate in it if that's what you're into."

"Do I look like I'm eight?" Daedalus responded without dropping his dagger-like glare. Before Raz could even open his mouth to respond with what Daedalus was certain would be another smart-ass remark, Daedalus cut him off. "The others are setting up a bonfire for the night. How about you do something useful and help them." As Daedalus spoke he pointed behind him over towards the other side of the carriages where a fire pit had already been dug up and whatever bits of dried wood that could be spared were being thrown in.

"What am I, a box of matches?" Raz asked with a shrug.

"No," Daedalus responded without skipping a beat. "Unlike you, a box of matches is more useful because it doesn't talk." At those words Raz dropped his smirk and shot Daedalus a threatening glare that rivaled the one he had been giving him in intensity. Daedalus, however, did not back down as he stood firm, as if no force on this earth could move him and kept his eyes locked onto Raz's own. This staredown continued on for only a few, silent moments before Raz gave in and with a loud, exasperated sigh, Raz walked around Daedalus towards where the bonfire had been set up.

One of the merchants had just approached the bonfire with a tinderbox and some flint before Raz walked right past him and touched the pile of wood.

"You can save that," Raz said to the merchant. "I got this." Before any one of the merchants there could say anything to him, Raz's hand suddenly lit itself aflame. The resulting fire then quickly spread throughout the bonfire and set it ablaze, surprising the surrounding merchants and passengers as they all quickly backed away. Once the initial burst of flame had passed the bonfire settled onto a more manageable flame as Raz pulled his hand away.

"Could... could you do that the whole time?" The merchant with the flint and tinder then asked Raz.

"Yes," Raz answered without even looking at him.

"Why the hell then didn't you ever do it before then!" one of the other merchants then shouted at him. "Solaris knows it could have made the past few days that much easier!"

"None of you ever asked," Raz responded with a shrug before turning around and walking back over towards Daedalus.

The end of the day drew ever closer as the sun crept slowly down the horizon. Vincent had placed the sack of gold that was his payment into one of his horse's saddlebags. Though stopped once he heard the sound of someone approaching. He quickly turned around, ready to draw his blade if need be. He relaxed the second he saw the gentle face of Stella.

"So you're heading out?" Stella asked.

"Job's done. No need to stick around." Vincent answered, starting to turn back around, planning to mount his horse, but was stopped once again by Stella.

"I get you're trying to be dramatic with the whole 'riding off into the sunset' thing, but isn't that a stupid idea? You're going to be in the desert at night. A desert full of monsters."

"That's no problem. It's my job isn't it? Besides, you saw how I handled that Chaos cult. I can handle a monster or two."

"Oh yes, how could I forget that you and only you fought those cultists." Stella said sarcastically, "How can I think that Vincent Hornbill the legendary monster hunter got help from anyone? Especially not a local mage."

"That's not what I meant." Vincent said with a tired sigh, "What are you complaining about anyways? Is it about the money, because if I remember correctly you're the one who hired me in the first place?"

"It's not about the Solaris damn money!" Stella shouted, surprising Vincent, but also causing a smirk to grow across his face.

"So what is it about?" He asked as he slowly approached her, "Is it just that you don't want me to leave?" Stella didn't say anything in response, but the reddish tint that was forming on her face as she looked away from him told Vincent everything that he needed to know. Now directly in front of her, he placed a hand on her cheek and lightly pushed in forward, bringing her gaze back to him. "I might be

willing to stay a little longer, if you can convince me to." he said to her with a
velvety smoothness to his voice.

Stella's face was now as red as the eyes of a monster as she exclaimed, "W-
W-What are you implying? What? Were you after more than money this whole time?
Besides I'm a noble woman and I'm already betrothed to the son of Lord Alcross. I-"

"Oh yes, the same man that you described as 'boring' and 'who's family tree
probably looks like a ladder'."

"T-That's not what I... I mean yes, I did say that, but..." She then let out an
annoyed grunt while forcibly removing his hand from her face, "You are irritating,
egotistical, and are probably closer than anyone I have ever met to the bottom of the
social hierarchy!"

"And yet when we made camp for the night when we were going off to save
your father and all the other mages I made you laugh. If I didn't know any better I'd
say I actually saw you truly happy. To me at least you seemed like you were free to
be yourself for once."

Stella stood there silently for several silent seconds, then suddenly grabbed
Vincent by his coat and pulled him in for a deep, passionate kiss which Vincent
gladly returned. After nearly a full minute of passion the two broke the kiss, Stella
breathing heavily before saying, "My bedroom is the last one down the hallway on
the left. Be there within the next ten minutes. If you get caught I'm going to deny
everything." Before quickly walking off.

Vincent simply watched her go, admiring the womanly curves she possessed
as she disappeared back into her home. Vincent simply smirked and said, "You
wouldn't be the first woman to do so."

"Isn't it a bit too dark to be reading?" the raspy voice of Vivian suddenly
spoke up, the sound of which instantly snapped Seth out of the world of his book and
back into reality. Seth had been sitting by what was left of the now dimming bonfire
using the little light that it was still producing to read through what was printed on
the pages. Now that his concentration had been ruined, however, he looked over his
shoulder to see Vivian standing a few meters away from him. The fact that she had
willingly spoken to him surprised him a great deal, and it also put him on edge.

"When we stopped for the night I was in the middle of the chapter," Seth answered as he again placed his bookmark into the book where he left off. "So I wanted to see if I could finish it up before bed. Also you read one of these books when we were trapped in that desert cave and it was much darker in there."

"I was just being a smartass, but whatever you say," Vivian responded with a shrug. "Wait, what do you mean by one of-" Before Vivian could finish her sentence, with one glance downward she noticed the word "Wanderer" on the book's front cover, partially obscured by one of Seth's fingers. "Oh, you're reading the Wanderer series? Which one is that?" As Vivian spoke she walked over towards Seth before squatting down next to him.

"The first one," Seth answered without looking at her.

"Do you like it?" Vivian then asked, appearing at least to be genuinely interested.

"I don't know," Seth responded, still without looking at her. "It's kind of… bad."

"Bad?" Vivian in turn responded, sounding somehow offended as she narrowed her eyes at him. "How is it bad? I'll admit that the first one is the weakest of the series but-"

"Well, Vincent is kind of rude to everyone he meets," Seth interrupted once he realized that Vivian was beginning to shout. "Yet he just gets away with it. There were at least four times where he made a problem worse because of this. Before you started talking to me I got to a part where Stella just kissed him, which seemed to come out of nowhere considering that they just argued for most of their conversations. Also, I don't see how there could be a group of people who worship Chaos like most people do Solaris considering that humans hate monsters and want nothing more than to kill them on sight." As Seth spoke that last part there was an air of venom-filled bitterness to his voice, which did not go unnoticed by Vivian. The monster hunter opened her mouth to issue a rebuttal towards Seth's criticisms of her favorite book series, but then at the last second chose to bite her tongue. She was thankful that Seth was not looking at her when she did that.

"Well, one," Vivian began as she tore her eyes away from Seth and over towards what remained of the bonfire. "A character needs flaws or they're gonna be boring. Hence Vincent's attitude and how it gets him into trouble. And I wouldn't say he just 'gets away with it', Stella calls him out on it all the time. That's literally what causes all of their arguments. As for the romance, well in this one it's just…" She stopped there as she tried to think of a way to describe what happened in a way that would hopefully preserve whatever innocence that Seth may have still had. However, this train of thought suddenly ceased when Vivian realized that if Seth had mentioned that he had just gotten to the part where Vincent and Stella kissed then that meant that he had long since passed the chapter with the barmaid. In that instant Vivian knew that unless either Tara had forced him to skip that chapter or he simply didn't understand what was happening in that scene, which she knew for Seth was very probable, then whatever remained of Seth's innocence was already completely gone. With that in mind she resolved not to beat around the bush with her answer. "Yeah, at that point Vincent just treats her like all the other women who throw themselves at him. They develop more of an actual romance with decent chemistry when she comes back in book four, which if you ask me that's one of the best ones. Granted it's more of a murder mustery than an adventure, but it's still fun. As for the Chaos cult… Yeah, that's actually a thing sometimes. It makes no sense to me either, but some people are insane and sometimes groups of insane people get together."

During Vivian's rant Seth slowly shifted his eyes over towards her direction. As he watched her talk about Vincent and the other books in the Wanderer series he saw her slowly start to smile the more she explained these things to him. It was as if she were talking about an old friend that she had not seen in a long time, yet it clearly filled her with joy just to remember that person. It was nice to see her smiling at him again like she used to.

"Okay," Seth said once Vivian had finished speaking. "Maybe I'll give the others a chance."

"You should," Vivian responded as she unconsciously looked into his eyes. "Like I said, they do get better and the first one is by far the weakest of the series." Once those last few words had left her lips a long, drawn out silence fell between the two of them. Neither Seth nor Vivian were sure of how long it lasted, but neither of them said anything to each other as they held eye contact, as they were both unsure of what to say. Eventually, however, it was Vivian who broke that silence.

"Well, I'm getting tired so I'm gonna hit the sack," Vivian said to Seth as she stood back up. "Since you're the only one still awake you take the first watch." Having said that, without another word Vivian turned away and headed back towards the carriages.

"Who do I wake up to take over when I get tired?" Seth asked as he watched her leave.

"That's your problem," Vivian answered without turning around. "You figure it out."

While Seth had other questions he wanted to ask her, he chose to stay silent and accept his fate, as he did not want to start an argument with her. Knowing that reading would keep him distracted from what he was supposed to keep his eyes on, he slipped the book back into his jacket pocket. He hoped at the very least that he would get to finish the chapter tomorrow.

Seth quietly walked around the perimeter of the caravan as he did his best to keep both an eye and an ear on everything, which wasn't the easiest job in the world considering that it was nearly pitch black out here and there were a lot of sleeping people to keep an eye on. Thankfully the darkness did not bother him too much, as he found that he could actually see fairly well in it if he focused on something, but the fact that he was alone made the whole experience more worrying. When he went on nighttime patrols in Canaan he usually had the comfort of knowing there was at least one other person out there doing it as well. Doing a full patrol by himself left him with too many things to worry about. The thought crossed his mind that this would be easier if there were one, or preferably two other people up with him, but he was unsure of who to ask.

"Maybe Raz…" he muttered to himself, as he had first hand knowledge of what Raz could do to a monster if one decided to show up. He started to heavily consider this when he suddenly heard something that sounded like the flapping of wings. It was faint, but it was there. The instant that sound hit his ears Seth spun around and looked up, but he did not see anything.

"Psst," someone whispered out from the darkness with a voice that Seth did not recognize. Immediately he turned his head back around towards the source of the noise, which seemed to come from the top of one of the carriages directly behind him. When he looked in that direction, however, he saw nothing. "Over here." The instant Seth heard that voice again he looked around for the source of the voice, which this time seemed to be the top of the carriage next to him. What Seth saw, however, made absolutely no sense to him at all. On top of the carriage was not a person, but instead a creature that had the shape of a bat, but was the size of an eagle, or perhaps a large hawk. The most defining feature about this creature, however, were its large, piercing, blood red eyes that even in the darkness Seth could see perfectly well as they stared directly at him. Without even needing to think twice about it sparks of electricity began to run through Seth's left hand.

"Wait wait wait!" The bat-creature suddenly spoke in a strangely high pitched, nasally sounding voice as it held up both of its wings in a gesture that, were it a human, could be seen as surrendering. "I'm just here to talk. That's all. Our mistress, you call her Lilim, she sent me."

An almost painful chill ran down Seth's spine the instant that name reached his ears. The image of her smiling, red eyed face flashed in front of his eyes as all of the memories that involved that name and face flooded back into him all at once. Despite being confused for many, many reasons, not the least of which was the fact that this was the first time he had heard a monster other than himself and the aforementioned Lilim actually speak, he couldn't help himself as he lowered his hand back to his side. The sparks that had begun to appear before slowly faded as he did so.

"Wha… What does she want?" Seth couldn't help but ask.

"Speak quietly," the bat-creature whispered. "Lest you wake the humans."

"Okay…" Seth then said much more quietly. "What does she want?"

"With you. Nothing," the bat responded. "Not yet anyway. She is busy. Busy with a plan. Big plan. She sent me to keep an eye on you."

"Why? And what plan?"

"I can't say as to why, but I'm sure it's because you're like her. Being one of us yet having the misfortune of being born looking like one of these sad humans. As for mistress' plan… It's not my place to tell. Mistress wishes to explain it to you herself."

"Okay…" Seth responded, more than a little annoyed by the lack of a real answer from this thing. "What's stopping me from killing you right now?"

"You could," the bat responded with a nasally chuckle. "But mistress also wanted me to inform you that she has quite a few of us waiting outside of that little town of yours. What was it called?" The bat-creature then paused for a moment as it brought the tip of one of its wings towards its snout in a manner that Seth had seen

Tara as well as some other people do when they were trying to think. "Eh, doesn't matter. Mist-"

"Canaan," Seth cut in as he narrowed his eyes at the bat-creature, which was now really beginning to irritate him.

"Yes, that's it, Canaan," the bat-creature piped up again. "As I was saying. Mistress has them set to rip that town and everyone in it to pieces if she doesn't hear back from me on a regular basis. And with you, the hunter, and the fire wizard gone, do you really think they can protect themselves from us?" As the bat-creature finished speaking it's lips curled into a wide smile that showed off its full set of razor sharp teeth.

"They were able to before any of us showed up," Seth shot back.

"Really?" The bat-creature retorted before with one great flap of its wings it took off from the carriage and landed on the sand at Seth's feet. With it directly in front of him now, Seth almost had to take a step back as he saw that this bat-creature was tall enough for its head to nearly reach his stomach. As it stood in front of him the bat-creature held out both of its wings in a manner similar to someone holding their arms out. With its wings spread out Seth was shocked to see that this thing's wingspan was nearly three meters long from one end to the other. "If you're that confident in them, then do it. Kill me and send an entire town of humans to their deaths. Nothing would please us more, but you know that, don't you?" The bat-creature emphasized its point with another wide, sharp toothed grin as it finished speaking.

Seth wanted to call this creature's bluff, he desperately did. He wanted to slice the thing in half, and he knew it would be easy, but he couldn't. While he may not have known this creature, he knew Lilim, and he knew how she felt about humans. With that in mind he was more than certain that she would live up to a threat like that. Without realizing it Seth's hands had begun to tremble at his sides as all of this ran through his head, something that did not go unnoticed by the bat-creature.

"That's what I thought," the bat-creature then said before it flapped its wings again and hopped up from the sand and onto Seth's shoulder. Seth almost fell over from the sudden shift in weight, but he managed to keep himself on his feet. Despite its size, the bat-creature was not as heavy as Seth had assumed it was. "There there, why the long face, friend? You don't have anything to worry about.

They're not gonna attack the town. They're only there just in case. You can trust me. I'm not your enemy, I'm your friend… Although mistress did say that you would not believe that."

"I don't," Seth interrupted before the bat-creature could say anything else.

"Mistress said you would say that too," the bat-creature continued with a smile. "But the truth is, Seth, that mistress and I are the only real friends that you have in this world. You may not believe us now, but you will soon enough. That's why I'm here. My task is to make sure that nothing bad happens to you, like mistress promised. Not a single one of these humans will harm a hair on your head while mistress has anything to say about it." Those words caused another painful chill to run down Seth's spine as he remembered Lilim saying more or less those exact words to him all those months ago. Seeing a reaction like that from him, the bat-creature smiled wider. "Don't worry. When you want to see her again, just say so. I can take you to her. Mistress told me to. Whenever you want to." Seth couldn't help but notice the bat's use of "when" instead of "if" when it came to whether or not he would willingly want to see Lilim again, but despite wanting to call him out for it, he kept his mouth shut.

"How…" Seth began, but hesitated for a moment, which did not go unnoticed by the bat-creature either as it leaned its snout closer to Seth's head in anticipation. "How am I supposed to call out to you? What do I call you? Do you even have a name?"

"A name?" The bat-creature exclaimed as its eyes went wide, seeming surprised to even hear that type of question. "I… I've never had one. Never needed one." It then paused for another moment as it brought one of its wings up to its snout in thought again. "Yes. You do need to call me something if you need to call out to me, don't you. What would I like my name to be?" The bat-creature then paused again as it silently pondered that thought for several long, long seconds. "Maybe something with a 'Ka' sound. I've always liked that. Something like…"

"Cain," Seth suggested without even thinking about it as he remembered the name of one of the chaos cultists from the book he had been reading.

"Ooh, I like the sound of that," The bat-creature then exclaimed, seeming as excited as one could be while still whispering. "That settles it then. If you ever need me for any reason just call out to your very good friend, Cain. Don't worry if you don't see me." The bat-creature then paused for another moment to deliberately twitch both of its large ears, as if to show them off. "No matter where you are, I'll hear you." Before Seth could say anything to it in response to that Cain suddenly spread his wings and took off from Seth's shoulder.

"Wait!" Seth tried to call out while still keeping quiet, but he was too late as Cain disappeared into the dark of the night. No matter where he looked, Cain was nowhere to be seen. Unsure of what else to do, Seth simply stood still where he was. The only thing that he knew for certain was that he no longer needed to worry about who to ask to take over the watch for him. He knew that he would not get any sleep at all even if he did.

Chapter 7

When Seth opened his eyes the first thing he saw was the color of wood. It wasn't the same as the wood that made up the ceiling of Andrea's clinic or the ceiling of the library, both of which he could almost perfectly recall every detail of as he had seen both on a regular basis. After blinking a few times his vision slowly became clearer, and it was with that clarity that he realized that what he was staring at was in fact the roof of Jorge's carriage. As the rest of his senses came to him he also realized that they were moving. He couldn't see it, but he could hear the telltale sounds of horses' hooves hitting sand and of wooden wheels turning not too far away from him, sounds that he had become accustomed to hearing over the course of the past few days.

Despite all of that the space underneath his head did not feel hard, like he knew wood should be. With that in mind Seth suddenly got the sense that he should probably sit up. When he did he found himself staring out the back of the carriage and into the endless sea of sand that it was leaving behind.

"Morning sleepyhead." The instant Seth heard someone else talk he spun to his left towards the source of the noise, which turned out to be Tara. Despite seeming as bright and cheerful as she usually was when Seth heard her speak, when he turned to look at her she was backed all the way to the wall of the carriage with her hands and knees held tightly against her chest, as if she had backed away very suddenly. At her side Seth saw an open book, which signaled to him that perhaps she had been reading it at one point, but then quickly dropped it. Seeing her like that, Seth began to look around for whatever had spooked her, but then stopped once he realized the position he was in.

It had all happened too fast for him to notice, but when he looked into Tara's eyes he saw that they were looking directly at him. It was at that moment that Seth realized that he was on his hands and knees, a position wherein he could be ready to move in an instant. Not only that, but his right hand was held out in preparation to either summon his sword or throw lightning at something. With all of this in mind he did not want to imagine what the look on his face was. Once he realized all of this, Seth slowly pulled himself back into a sitting position as he backed away from Tara towards the opposite wall of the carriage. Once he was there he leaned back against it and tried to make himself look as relaxed and unintimidating as possible.

"Sorry," he said to her as he propped one hand onto his knee. "I... I didn't mean to do that."

"It is okay," Tara responded as she began to visibly relax herself. Despite this, she ignored the open book at her side. "You... You were up quite late last night."

"I know," Seth said as he turned his attention back towards the ocean of sand. "I'm sorry." Seth then suddenly realized that he had just woken up, and as such there was something that he needed to do now before anyone who didn't already know about his secret saw. With that in mind he quickly brought his hand up to his eyes, completely covering them. After only a second of this he dropped his hand from his face to reveal a pair of normal looking brown eyes.

"You do not need to apologize," Tara quickly replied to him. "It is good that you take your work so seriously, but..." Tara then paused for a moment to see if Seth would turn his attention back to her, but he never did. "If... If you do not mind me asking. Why did you stay out as late as you did? You do know that there are other people here who could have taken over the watch for you, right? People who are just as diligent as you are."

"I know," Seth answered without looking at her. "I just-" Seth froze before he could say any more, as it dawned on him that in all of the time he spent awake with his eyes and ears open last night looking out for more monsters, he never once thought of exactly what to say when someone inevitably asked him why he had stayed up that late. That thought made him suddenly feel foolish because he knew that they would, but he was so preoccupied at the time with what could have happened that he never spared anything else even a single second's thought. Sweat began to pour from his brow as he knew he would have to think of something to say quickly, but it was Tara he was speaking to. After everything that had happened between them he still was unsure of exactly what he could and couldn't tell her. Eventually it came to him speaking without thinking. "I was just worried, okay."

"Really?" Tara responded after a few silent moments. "You were... that worried?"

"Yes," Seth quickly answered. "I know monsters usually come out at night, and during my watch I thought I heard something. So I got worried and didn't want to go back to sleep after that." Seth felt strangely proud of himself for that answer. In a way it wasn't a lie. Despite that, however, Tara did not respond to him. Instead she simply kept silently staring at him. It got to the point where Seth had to turn to look at her to see if she was even still there, and indeed she was, having not moved a single centimeter since she had relaxed in the carriage. With that sight all of the pride that Seth felt for himself melted away, as he knew that Tara would likely not let this go if he didn't. "What time is it?"

Rather than respond immediately, Tara instead partially stood back up and moved towards the back of the carriage. Once there she poked her head out for a moment and looked up at the sun.

"I would say a little after one," Tara answered before pulling her head back into the carriage and crawling back over to where she was sitting before. At first Seth thought nothing of her answer. Sure it was later in the afternoon than he would have preferred to wake up, and he knew that he could wake up early after staying up late, as he found himself having to do so often in service of Canaan's town watch. However, that feeling of easiness instantly shattered like glass once Seth remembered something else that was important.

"One? You said one right?" Seth quickly asked as he locked eyes with Tara.

"Yes?" Tara answered as she sat back down, a look of confusion and uneasiness adorned her face as she did so.

"As in one in the afternoon?" Seth clarified.

"Yes," Tara answered. "Why, is that-" Before she could say any more, as quickly as he could Seth moved towards the back of the carriage, stuck his head out, and looked up at the sun himself. By his own estimations, which he admitted were not as accurate as Tara's, with his own eyes he saw that the position of the sun was some time in the early afternoon, just as Tara had told him it was.

"Where is Dis?" Seth then suddenly asked, though before Tara could answer him he climbed out from the back of the carriage slightly so that he could look around the side. With a clearer view around the caravan Seth directed his eyes forward towards the front, but beyond the front of the caravan he saw nothing except more desert. "Why aren't we there yet?" As Seth spoke, as quickly as he could he climbed back into the carriage before frantically moving past Tara towards the front. "You said that we would be there by noon."

"No I didn't," Jorge responded to Seth without turning around. "I said that we might be there by noon."

"No you didn't?" Seth frantically said back to him. "I remember exactly what you said. You-"

"Seth, it is all right," Tara quickly interrupted Seth as he felt her hand touch his shoulder. The instant he felt something touch him he spun his head back around and locked eyes with her again. Instinctively Tara backed away from him again due to the quickness of his movements, but her hand remained where it was. After a few eerie moments of silence between all three of them Tara eventually spoke again. "Relax. Nothing is wrong. Just sit back down, please. I will explain everything." Seth did not answer Tara immediately, and for a few more, long, eerie moments of silence Seth simply kept his eyes locked on her's. As he did he saw that the look on her face had changed from confused to worried. It was a look he had become more than familiar with coming from Tara.

Unsure of what else to do at the current moment, Seth gave in to her advice and slowly backed away from Jorge and over to where he had originally been sitting.

"I'm sorry," Seth said to her as he sat back down.

"You do not need to be sorry," Tara replied as calmly as she could. "You were asleep, so you did not know." After saying that to him Tara turned her attention back towards Jorge. "I am so sorry about that."

"What do you need to apologize for?" Jorge responded to her without turning around. "You ask me, you should take your own advice and stop apologizing so much. I swear to Solaris that was maybe the twelfth time you've said 'sorry' to me in the past three days." Tara was about to open her mouth to let out what Seth knew would be another apology, but then stopped herself once she realized what she was about to do. Tara then silently crawled back over to where she had been sitting as well and took her former place against the wall. She kept silent for a few moments longer before she eventually spoke to Seth again. "We got something of a late start this morning."

"Why?" Seth asked as soon as Tara had finished speaking.

"It took a little longer than we would have preferred to put back all of the crates that were unloaded last night," Tara explained. "But that did not cause too much of a delay, and we got going quickly once everything was loaded and taken care of. So there is no reason to worry."

"We also had to make a slight deviation from our usual route," Jorge cut in once Tara had finished speaking.

"Why?" Seth immediately asked, his full attention having shifted from Tara to Jorge. "Did something happen?"

"No," Jorge responded. "We just ran into another, smaller caravan traveling the way opposite us towards Tarus and they told us that they had spotted something suspicious looking out in the direction we were heading, so we're just being careful. An extra hour or two of travel time ain't nothing to us."

"Did they see any monsters?" Seth then immediately asked.

"No," Jorge repeated. "Like I said, it was just something suspicious. If it were monsters they would have told us."

"No one in this caravan saw any monsters, did they?" Seth asked even more quickly than his last question the instant Jorge had finished speaking. A few moments of silence passed as Jorge finally turned his head back to look directly at Seth for the first time since he had woken up. The look in his eyes was disconcerting to Seth, as he seemed more annoyed than cautious, and that in turn made Seth even more worried than he was before. Jorge only stared at him for a few seconds, however, before turning back and directing his eyes towards the caravan in front of him.

"Again, no," Jorge answered Seth without looking at him. "If we had then we would have woken you up. Some of the other people here have told me a few things about you, kid. I'm aware that you're a mage and that you've killed monsters. So don't worry. If something did happen or we did run into a monster I would have woken you up myself. So quit that needless worrying of yours and sit back down, kid. If my estimations are correct, and they usually are, we should be arriving in Dis in the next hour or so."

While Seth was unsure of how he should take the fact that Jorge kept referring to him as 'kid', as everything else he had said made sense to him. Sure if there was an actual problem then Tara at the very least would have woken him up. If not that then he knew that he would have at least woken up from the sound of explosions from Raz or the sound of monsters screaming their lungs out because Vivian had gutted them. With that in mind Seth saw little reason to keep worrying about any of these things. So, with nothing else to say, Seth sank back into the place where he had been sitting before and directed his eyes back out towards the ocean of sand behind him.

"Are..." Seth heard Tara's voice say to him. "Are you alright, Seth?"

"Yes," Seth lied. "I'm fine." While the answers that Tara and Jorge had given him had managed to alleviate his current fears, they did nothing at all to alleviate the fears that were really causing him to worry as much as he was. Even with his eyes on the desert behind them, in his mind's eye he could still see Lilim's smiling face in front of him.

Seth was unsure of exactly how much time had passed since he had woken up. He hadn't spoken to either Tara nor Jorge since then, as he had never diverted his attention from the seemingly endless wasteland behind them. For whatever reason that seemed infinitely more interesting to him than anything in the carriage or anything else that either Tara or Jorge had to say. Tara had long since returned to the book she had been reading and Jorge had not moved from his position at the front at all. The only sounds that were to be heard were the sounds of horses hooves on the desert sand and the turning of carriage wheels. That was how Seth preferred it right now.

Without any warning, however, with a sudden lurch their carriage ceased to move. The sudden lack of movement instantly snapped Seth out of his daze as he turned his attention back around towards Jorge. The view in front of the carriage, at least from what Seth could see, had not changed.

"Why did we stop?" Seth asked.

"We're here," Jorge responded as he fully turned around to properly look at both him and Tara. "Told you we'd be there within the hour."

The instant Seth heard that answer, as quickly as he could he scrambled out the back of the carriage and looked around the side, as he had before. What he saw froze him to his core as his eyes went wider than dinner plates and he nearly fell onto the sand from losing his grip on the carriage. In front of the caravan, which Seth knew to be thirty carriages long, Seth's eyes beheld a wall that was unlike anything he had seen in Canaan, or indeed anything he had ever seen in his entire life. His brain nearly shut down where he stood as it struggled to process all of the new information it had received all at once.

For starters, this wall was absolutely massive. Even from thirty carriages away Seth could not even begin to figure out just how tall and how wide the wall surrounding Dis actually was. The wall surrounding Canaan was only slightly taller than most of the houses, with only some of the taller buildings like the mayor's office and the hotel being taller than it. This wall by comparison was so tall that Seth could scarcely see the top. If he had to guess, this wall had to be at least four, maybe five times taller than the one in Canaan. At least from what he could see. Secondly, whereas the wall surrounding Canaan was made of wood, this one was made of solid stone, with hundreds upon hundreds of stone blocks so perfectly inlaid with each other that they almost seemed to be one solid piece. The fact that it was made of stone also caused Seth to wonder exactly how thick the wall was, and with that in mind he couldn't help but wonder whether or not this wall could be broken down at all.

Lastly, and this was the thing that astounded Seth more than anything else, he could not for the life of him tell where this wall began or ended. The wall surrounding Canaan was rectangular shaped to match the town, and was only as big around as the town itself. With that in mind, looking at this wall, Seth could not see any corners, which gave the impression that this wall was circular rather than rectangular, but Seth could not see where the curve of this wall actually began. On both the left and right sides of the wall it simply seemed to go on forever. If the size of a wall was meant to give a sense of scale to how large a town, or in this case city, was behind it, then Seth was completely unsure whether or not he could even imagine what lay beyond this enormous edifice.

Directly in front of the first carriage Seth could see a closed wooden door which, while taller than the carriage, was dwarfed by the size of the wall it was attached to. To the left of it was a smaller building that looked to be a wooden shack with no windows. To the right Seth saw an open area surrounded by a simple wooden fence. At present there was nothing in it except for sand. At the very front of the caravan Seth also saw someone that looked like a guard speaking with someone in the carriage up front, though they were unfortunately too far away for him to hear what either of them were saying.

"Amazing, is it not?" Seth heard Tara's voice say. While he would usually turn to look at whomever was talking to him, in this instance he felt himself unable to take his eyes away from what was in front of him. Tara on the other hand, did not even need to look to imagine the expression on Seth's face. "And to think that across the Solaran empire cities like this one have stood for hundreds of years." As interesting as that fact was to Seth, there was one part of it that stuck out to him more than the rest.

"There are…" Seth began, though he found his words caught somewhere in his throat. "There are more cities like this?"

"Of course," Tara answered with a giggle. "You did not think that the entire population of the world was in Canaan, did you?" As much as he wanted to, Seth could not come up with a response to that. In truth, he knew that there were other places in the world besides Canaan. He had read about them in the books in Tara's library and the traders who passed through Canaan talked of them often, but he had never once thought to imagine what any of those places might have looked like. More than that, he never once contemplated the idea that Canaan would be that small by comparison to them.

After roughly ten minutes or so the caravan began to move again. Seth had long since pulled himself back into the carriage, as he had gotten tired of hanging off of the side. As soon as he felt the carriage begin to move again, however, he immediately scrambled out the back and took his former place again. Towards the front of the caravan Seth could see that one by one the carriages were beginning to pull themselves into the fenced in area to the right of the door, whereupon they began to organize themselves into rows of what Seth could only guess would be six judging from the size of the fenced in area. With that in mind it seemed that there would be plenty of room for each carriage.

"What's happening now?" Seth asked as he crawled back into the carriage again, as he could tell that this was likely going to take a while.

"Inspection," Jorge answered. "They're just going to check to see what we're bringing in and make sure everything is on the up and up. Don't worry. Unless you're hiding anything you got nothing to worry about."

"Why do they need to do that?" Seth then immediately asked, now curious. "Do people often bring things into the city that they're not supposed to?"

"Oh yeah," Jorge responded. "More often than you'd think. Don't worry, they're not gonna dig through everything in every carriage. They're just gonna ask us a few questions and they might ask to see inside your suitcases. Just do what they say and everything'll be fine." Hearing all of that made Seth nervous, as Canaan had never done anything of the sort to anyone who came into the town. Sure Charlie kept a tight watch, but not like this.

"Is this… normal?" Seth asked Tara once Jorge had finished speaking.

"Unfortunately, yes," Tara answered. "But it is not anything you need to worry about. We do not have anything that we are not supposed to have and we have not done anything wrong, so everything will be okay." While Seth was not at all satisfied with that answer, he was forced to resound himself to the fact that in this situation, he was forced to trust them. For whatever reason that fact did not make him feel even the slightest bit at ease.

Due to the number of carriages it took quite a while for Jorge to eventually pull into the fenced off area and get himself settled. Considering that they were the last carriage in the caravan, Seth knew that there really was no way this could have been avoided. Once they were there, Seth looked around outside and saw that many of the other traders and passengers had disembarked. Seeing that, Seth hopped out the back the first chance he got. He immediately regretted doing so, however, as the instant he looked to his right he saw the massive stone wall surrounding the city up close. A sense of vertigo hit him as he couldn't help but look directly up towards the top. He only stopped after his eyes drifted too far up and he found himself looking directly into the sun.

"Everybody please do not wander too far!" Seth heard a voice he did not recognize shout out. Looking in the direction it came from, Seth caught sight of someone who was unmistakably a city guard by the entrance to the fenced off area. Looking around further, over by the gate to the city, which Seth could now see was four meters tall, stood two more guards. Not only that, but amongst the crowd that made up the caravan Seth saw three more guards moving from carriage to carriage as they questioned the people traveling in said carriages.

Unlike the town watch in Canaan, who all wore mostly normal clothes or basic leathers for armor if they could get them, and were distinguishable only by an iron badge that they all carried somewhere on their person, all of these guards were dressed identically. Not only that, but some of their clothing appeared to be made out of metal. Over what appeared to be a very basic, featureless dark brown fabric uniform, they all wore steel breastplates as well as metal coverings over their forearms and shins. At their sides all of these guards wore longswords, and on their backs Seth could see that most of them carried crossbows. The two standing by the door also carried long spears, which they simply held up at attention. All of this was completed with the addition of wide brimmed, simple, circular hats that matched the dark brown color of their uniforms.

The fact that they all wore metal clothing confused Seth greatly, as he saw it as unnecessary. The idea, to him at least, obviously seemed to be that the metal clothes would protect them from monsters, but Vivian, Raz, nor he himself ever wore anything like that. While Seth did not have an exact idea of how much the sword he created with his magic weighed, he remembered what it felt like to carry a real sword on his person from the first time he was out in the desert, and just that was heavy enough to be noticed. With that in mind, metal clothes must have weighed much more than a sword, so the idea of wearing those all the time meant that they were probably slower because of it. Not only that, but given his own encounters with monsters, Seth severely doubted whether or not those metal breastplates would actually protect them from anything. The ability to quickly move out of the way had saved his life more times than he could count, and he wasn't sure he could do that while wearing metal clothes.

Throughout all of this Seth wasn't sure how long he stood there thinking about all of that, all he knew was that when he looked back up at the guard's face, he saw him glaring back at him, as if the mere act of staring at him was offensive. Unsure of what else to do, Seth simply held his gaze, and it was then that he saw the guard's hand move over towards his sword. While Seth recognized the gesture as one getting ready for a fight, as he had seen Vivian do it enough times, he was unsure of what he had done to warrant that kind of response as he raised his eyebrow. This, however, seemed to evoke the opposite kind of response he expected from the guard as he narrowed his gaze directly on Seth. Unfortunately for Seth, however, he did not get much more of a chance to think about it as he felt himself suddenly get pulled away by his left arm.

"Sorry!" Tara shouted in the guard's direction as she pulled Seth around to the side of their carriage. Once they were there Tara immediately let go of him. "Seth, what have I told you about staring at people?" Surprisingly, the tone of her voice evoked more concern than disappointment.

"I know that it's rude," Seth answered plainly enough. "You, Agatha, and

Daedalus have all told me that before."

"Then why were you blatantly staring at that guardsman?" Tara then asked.

"Was that making him angry?" Seth asked in turn. "He had a hand on his sword, but that couldn't have been from me staring at him? Was it?"

"I do not know," Tara answered. "Probably?"

"Why, though?" Seth then immediately asked, now concerned for himself. "Why would staring at someone make them angry enough to want to fight? It just seems like a bit of an overreaction."

"Because…" Tara began, but then stopped herself. Instead of continuing whatever it was she was going to say, she instead stared at him with a look on her face that Seth could easily read as someone who knew the answer, but had no idea how they wanted to phrase it. It was a look he had since become very, very familiar with. After a few moments of staring at him silently, during which Seth noticed that Tara was having a hard time focusing directly on him, Tara looked to her right first, then to her left. While there were people on both sides, they were far enough away that none of them would likely hear them. "We were going to have to have this conversation at some point." When Tara spoke again she did so very quietly, as if she were deliberately trying to hide her words from others. "Seth… You need to understand. This place. It is not Canaan. The people here will not be as kind or understanding to anything you might say or do, and the amnesia excuse will not always resolve everything. In fact it might make things even worse here. I am sure you want to know why, but the truth is that there are so many reasons for this and I cannot tell you all of them because I do not know them. Seth, you… The most important thing that you need to know right now is that you need to be very, very careful. Even more careful than you usually are." While Seth had a response for what she was saying, the look of grave concern on her face gave him pause.

"So all those lessons about how to interact with people…" Seth began.

"Yes," Tara quickly spoke up before Seth could finish. "You do remember everything I taught you, right?"

"I was going to ask if they were meant for here more than Canaan," Seth then said before he looked away from her and in the general direction of the guardsman he was staring at before. He couldn't see him anymore, but somehow he knew he was there. "You always told me to be careful of what I say or do because I might offend someone. In Canaan everyone is nice so if I accidentally do that they usually tell me, but you always said that people won't ever do that. So is Canaan different from everywhere else?" Tara actually had to think for a few moments about how best to answer that question before she could.

"Well, umm…" Tara eventually spoke. "Yes and no. I know that does not make much sense as an answer, but the truth is that the world does not often provide simple answers. I suppose the best way to explain it to you would be that there are some places, like Canaan, where people are really nice, and there are other places, like here, where people are not so nice."

"So while we're here I should be even more careful than I usually am," Seth said without taking his eyes away from the direction of the guardsman.

"Yes," Tara answered. "And please, Seth. If you cannot remember everything I taught you, then at least remember to always be polite. Within reason of course."

"How am I supposed to know which places are nice and which ones are not?" Seth then immediately asked Tara as he directed his full attention back towards her. Before Tara could even open her mouth to answer his question the sound of someone being struck and then hitting the sand hit both of their ears.

"You lying little bi-!"

"Stay down!"

The instant those noises hit their ears both Seth and Tara ran around the front of their carriage towards the source of the noise, whereupon they found themselves standing in the row of carriages directly in front of theirs. Roughly three carriages away from where they stood towards the opposite edge of the row, the two of them beheld what was, at least to Seth, a very unusual sight. Face down on the sand with two guardsmen on top of him was one of the merchants that Seth and Tara had been traveling with. Neither of them knew his name, but Seth at least had distinctly remembered seeing him on multiple occasions in the past three days, even if they never talked. Not only that, but a sizable crowd had begun to gather around this apparent spectacle.

"Will you just listen for one fucking second you mo-!" Before the merchant could say any more one of the guards put a hand on the back of his head and shoved his mouth into the sand.

"By order of the crown," the other guard calmly spoke as he pulled a set of manacles off of his belt and began to affix them to the merchant's wrists. "You are under arrest for possession and transportation of illicit substances."

"I told you they're not mine!" the merchant shouted after blowing a handful of sand out of his mouth. "None of it is mine! It all belongs to that bi-" Before he could say any more one of the guards reached over and turned his face so that he was face down in the sand again, and thus unable to speak. Looking up from that commotion, not too far behind the two guards and the merchant was another sight that made Seth's eyes go wide.

A few meters behind where the merchant was being arrested, at least from Seth's point of view, stood a very familiar looking shorter woman with incredibly curly brown hair and both of her hands raised high above her head. In front of her stood another guardsman with his sword drawn and held at her throat.

"I'll say it as many times as you need me to," Agatha spoke quickly. "I do not know this man. I have never seen him before in my life. I just paid him to take me to Dis."

"How much did you pay him?" The guard then asked her.

"Sixty coppers," Agatha answered.

"Where did you come from?"

"Canaan."

"Where's that?"

"A little over three hundred and fifty kilometers to the southwest of here."

"If we were to search your-"

"Mine are the large, lightish brown leather trunk and the backpack on top of it," Agatha answered before the guard could even finish asking. "Search them both. Search them all you want. You can even search me if you want. Fucking hell I'll let you strip search me even. I don't mind. I've got nothing to hide."

"You fucking lying bitch!" the merchant shouted at her as the two guardsmen hoisted him back onto his feet. "You know it's yours! Stop playing-"

"What's my fucking name!" Agatha shouted at the top of her lungs directly into his face as the two guardsmen pushed him past her. Seth could only barely see the dumbfounded expression on the merchant's face as he mentally processed that question. He only saw it for a second, however, as one of the guardsmen pushed him forward as they started walking in the direction of the wall. "Yeah, that's what I thought!"

"Send a few more guardsmen out here," the guard with the sword at

Agatha's throat said to one of the other two guards as they passed him. "We're going to need to search this one a bit more thoroughly."

"Aye," the guard responded before he and his partner took the bound merchant towards the edge of the caravan line before turning left and vanishing from sight.

"You, come with me," the remaining guardsman said to Agatha as he returned his sword to its sheath.

"Aye aye sir!" Agatha responded rather loudly. "Lead the way." The guardsman then walked up to her, put his hand on her arm, then spun her around so that she faced the wall as well. Without saying anything, Agatha complied as she walked forward towards the wall a few steps ahead of the guardsman. All the while she never lowered her arms.

Without thinking Seth unconsciously took a step forward to follow Agatha and the guardsman, but the second he did so he felt Tara's hand touch his shoulder.

"No," Tara said to him. "I know it might seem wrong, but please, no. You will only make things worse for her." It took all of Seth's willpower not to take another step forward. Every coherent thought in his mind kept screaming that Agatha was his friend and that he needed to do something to help her, but his common sense also reminded him that these people were this place's equivalent to Canaan's town watch. While Seth had never witnessed such a thing himself, he had heard from the other members about times they had to bring people in like this. The conflicting sides, both of which seemed to be screaming at him, left him entirely unsure of what to do.

"What will…" Seth began, but he felt the words get caught in his throat as he tried to say them. "What will happen to her?"

"If she does what they tell her, then nothing," Tara answered. "As long as she complies then she has nothing to worry about."

"What if she doesn't do what they say?" Seth couldn't help but ask.

"Then…" Tara responded as she squeezed Seth's shoulder tighter. "Then that is when we will have to worry about her." After she finished speaking Seth felt Tara squeeze his shoulder even harder still. There was something else to it, however, and it took him a second to realize it with everything else that was happening. Her hand was shaking. "I know you are worried for her, Seth. Believe me, I am too, but there is nothing we can do to help her right now. The best we can do right now is to wait for her. If Agatha really has done nothing wrong then they will let her come right back. So please, Seth. Please. I know it is hard, but please listen to what I am saying this time." While Seth could tell that she clearly meant what she had said, it was the trembling of her hand that convinced him more than any of her words.

Without saying anything, Seth broke away from Tara and walked back around towards the other side of their carriage. Once he was there Seth found that all he could really do at that point was lean against the side of the carriage and wait for their turn to be searched. It was only once he was there that he realized that in the past three days, this was actually the first time he had seen Agatha. With how active and chatty he knew she was, it was hard for him to imagine any situation where she wouldn't talk everyone's ears off, let alone a gathering of thirty carriages for a caravan to Dis. He knew that there must have been some part of this story that he was missing, but something did not feel right about her.

Seth had not moved from his spot at the side of the carriage by the time the city guardsmen had showed up to search their carriage. He wasn't sure at all of how long it had been, but he knew that it couldn't have been that long after Agatha and that other merchant had been taken away.

"Alright, this is the last one, sir," a younger sounding guardsman said as Seth looked up and saw a trio of them approach the carriage. Without thinking he pulled himself off of the side of the carriage and walked over to meet them.

"Ruff ruff ruff! Ruff ruff ruff!" Seth's attention was immediately stolen by an unusual sound as he immediately lowered his eyes towards one of the guardsman's feet, only to see a pair of unusual looking animals that reminded Seth of Tara's cat, Florence, only these animals were much, much larger, had longer snouts, and possessed much sharper looking teeth, which they were all too eager to show to Seth as they both kept making those barking noises in his direction. He could tell that these creatures weren't monsters, as they lacked the characteristic red eyes or black color. Instead, their eyes were much darker in color and both of them possessed short, lightish brown fur. He could have picked out more details about them were it not for the fact that the literal second that both of those creatures had started making those barking noises at him, two of the city guardsmen had drawn their swords and were holding them at his throat. The third stood roughly two meters behind the other two as he pulled back on a pair of leashes that Seth could see were affixed to collars around both of these creature's necks as they both tried their damndest to pull away from the guardsman's grasp. Had he not been doing that, Seth was more than certain that these creatures would sink their teeth into him without a second thought.

Unsure of exactly what to do in this situation, Seth immediately held up his arms in the same manner that he had seen Agatha do earlier.

"Ruff ruff ruff! Ruff ruff ruff!" the creatures continued to bark.

"You," one of the guardsmen with the sword at Seth's neck calmly spoke. "Start by giving us your name. Now."

"What's going on!" Seth heard Tara shout before he could answer the guardsman's question. That sound was followed by the sound of footsteps as Tara walked around the carriage to see what was happening, only for one of the two guardsmen to take his sword away from Seth's neck and point it in Tara's direction. Exactly like Seth had done, as soon as Tara saw the sword she held up both of her hands. Behind her Seth saw Jorge climb out from the back of the carriage.

"I asked you a question, boy," the guardsman with his sword still at Seth's throat then said. Seth could plainly see from the look in his eyes that he almost certainly would cut him with that sword if given the chance.

"Seth," Seth answered the guardsman as calmly as he could.

"Please, you have to understand!" Tara suddenly shouted. "He's not a criminal! Animals just don't like him for-"

"Shut up!" the guardsman with the sword pointed at her interrupted her.

"She ain't lying," Jorge then said as he walked over next to Tara, only for the guardsman to move his sword from Tara's neck over to his the instant he was close enough. Just like Seth and Tara before, he held up his hands.

"Who are you?" the guardsman asked.

"Edmond Jorge," Jorge responded. "This is my carriage, and what she's saying is true. Animals just don't like that guy for whatever reason. I've seen a horse have the same reaction to him."

"You see!" Tara began to shout again. "He-"

"Did I say you could talk?" The guardsman interrupted as he moved his sword back to Tara's neck the instant she spoke.

"Ruff ruff ruff! Ruff ruff ruff!" the creatures continued to bark at Seth.

Several long, long moments of silence passed wherein no one said anything. All three of the guardsmen, however, despite none of them moving nor taking their weapons away from any of them, visually sized up Seth, Tara, and Jorge. All the while the strange creatures continued to bark at Seth non-stop. Seth was unsure what they would have been looking for, but he imagined that it would be the same sorts of things he would have to look for if he found someone suspicious in Canaan.

"You," the guardsman in front of Seth eventually spoke up as he pushed his blade slightly close to Seth's throat. "You're coming with us." Completely unsure of what he was supposed to say or do to something like that, Seth glanced over towards Tara, who only nodded at him.

"Alright," Seth responded to the guardsman. As soon as that response was heard the guardsman with his sword at Tara's neck pulled his sword away and put it back in its sheath. As soon as he did that, however, he walked away from the two of them and over towards the guardsman with the two leashes.

"You stay here," he said to him. "We'll send two more to search the carriage as soon as we're able. If either of them try to run you have our permission to release the dogs." Seth wasn't sure whether or not knowing the names of these barking creatures was a good thing at this point. As he contemplated that, however, the guardsman in front of him nudged his head in the direction of the wall, the same direction that Agatha had been taken earlier.

"Start walking," the guardsman then said to Seth. With only a nod in response, Seth did as he was told as he, with his arms still held high, began to walk in the direction of the wall. With a quick glance behind him Seth saw the look on Tara's face as he walked away from her. He had never seen her look more worried than she was at that moment, "Eyes forward." That last sentence was emphasized by the same guardsman poking Seth in the back of the neck with his sword. Immediately Seth did as he was told and directed his eyes back towards the large wall in front of him. He dared not look back again.

All the while, as Seth was led away by the two guardsmen, the dogs, as the one guardsman had called them, relentlessly continued to bark in Seth's direction as they pulled harder and harder against the leashes the third guardsman held. Thankfully he did not let either of them go.

Chapter 8

After a few minutes of silent and awkward walking Seth found himself back in front of the gate to the city, which seemed even larger now that he was this close to it, and being led in the direction of the windowless wooden building on the other side of the gate. Rather than walk directly towards the door, however, the two guardsmen led Seth around the side of the building and back out towards the desert. It was only once they were there that they stopped. During the entire walk there Seth had not once put down his arms.

"Face the desert," one of the guardsmen said, to which Seth complied. Much to his confusion, however, both of the guardsmen remained behind him. "Jacket. Off." While Seth still found it slightly embarrassing to show other people that he was still wearing a long sleeved purple shirt with a collar, he knew that there was nothing he could do to argue in this situation as he lowered his arms and did what the guardsman had commanded. Once his jacket was off one of the guardsmen walked up behind him and snatched it from his hand. "Boots. Off." Again without arguing Seth complied as he bent down to remove his boots, and again, once they were off, one of the guardsmen came up behind him and snatched them away.

As Seth's bare feet touched the hot sand beneath them, he couldn't help but wince in pain slightly. To him it felt as if it had been eons since he had woken up in the desert, and in all that time he had long since forgotten exactly how hot the sand was thanks to the sun. It was more of an annoyance than anything else, but he still couldn't help but silently wince to himself as he was forced to endure it. Behind him, neither of the guardsmen said anything else to him and he dared not turn to look at them, though he had a fairly good idea of what they both were doing. He knew that at least one of them still had his sword out and was pointing it at him, and while it was subtle he could hear the telltale sounds of the other guardsman rifling through his jacket pockets as well as his boots. He wasn't sure at all what he expected them to find in his boots, but he wasn't about to ask either.

"Arms to your sides," one of the guardsmen then said after a few minutes of this, to which Seth again complied as he lowered both of his arms and held them out at his sides. As soon as he had done so, however, he felt one of the guardsmen come up behind him and with both of his hands, started patting down his right arm before moving on to his left. Seth wasn't surprised by this, in fact he had expected them to do this first. While no one in the Canaan town watch had ever instructed him to do anything like this, it was what he would have done if he needed to find something hidden on someone. The guardsman quickly followed up with his legs after both of his arms had been searched, though the guardsman in question did get closer to Seth's crotch than he would have preferred. His waist and torso followed after his legs, and were quickly searched as well. After all of that was done he felt the guardsman step away from him.

"Are you a mage?" the same guardsman as before asked. That question surprised Seth, but only for a moment as he realized that with the word he lived in, it was a fair question.

"Yes," Seth answered without turning around.

"Prove it," the guardsman then said. Despite the fact that Seth knew that the guardsman wanted a quick response, he hesitated, as he wasn't sure of exactly what he could do to prove that he was a mage that wasn't, in a word, destructive. Only one thing came to mind as he summoned his sword into his right hand. He then held it there for only a few seconds before he let it disappear back into nothing. A few, long moments of silence passed before either of the guardsmen said anything else after that.

"Turn around," the same guardsman eventually said, to which Seth complied, still with his arms held out. Once he had done so Seth saw that he was indeed correct as one of the guardsmen stood a few steps away from him and still had his sword pointed in his direction while the other tossed both his boots and jacket at his feet without any care for whether or not any sand got in them. "Put those back on. Boots first." Like before, Seth compiled without looking back up at either of the guardsmen, though he did have to admit it was incredibly awkward to do so while someone was pointing a sword at him.

"Hands back up," the guardsman with the sword out then said once Seth had finished redressing himself, to which Seth again complied as he raised his hands. "Come with us." The guardsman who had searched Seth walked ahead of them back around to the front of the wooden building. The guardsman with the sword out in turn glared at Seth, as if expecting him to follow him, which Seth did as he took the hint. The guardsman with the sword then followed behind him.

Moments later, after the guardsman in front of him had opened the door to the wooden shack, Seth found himself being escorted into something that reminded him of the town watch office in Canaan, only much smaller and with no windows. The first room that he saw looked to be a small waiting area with a few chairs set up, but no reception desk. He didn't get a chance to see much else, however, as the two guardsmen then led him into a short hallway before reaching a door on the left, which the guardsman in front of him opened, but did not enter as he took a few steps forward and turned around. Seth, in understanding, walked forward and into the room. To his surprise neither of the guardsmen followed him.

"Wait here," the guardsman that was in front of Seth said before he then suddenly slammed the door shut. That sound was then followed by the sound of the door being locked. Unsure of what else to do but wait, as the guardsman had instructed, Seth looked around at the room he now found himself in as he walked around in it. It was a very basic and featureless rectangular room, with nothing on the walls except for the wood that made them up. The only things that were in the room were a long, rectangular wooden table that ran almost the length of the room, but not quite, and three wooden chairs, two of which were on one side of the table and one on the other. Both the table and the chairs had definitely seen better days just from a glance, but more than that, Seth couldn't help but find the number and placement of the chairs odd.

Why were there only three? The table was clearly long enough to seat more than that, so why the small number? Not only that, but the fact that the door locked confused him even more. This wasn't a prison cell, he knew that much from the ones he had seen in the watch office in Canaan. So if he wasn't in a cell, clearly he wasn't being arrested, but if he wasn't being arrested then why was he being locked in here? It also occurred to him that if he wanted he could very easily escape this room, and indeed this building, but it also occurred to him that if he figured that out, then the city guardsmen must have already known that. With that in mind he couldn't help but wonder why they would lock him in here in the first place.

Thankfully he did not have to wait long for answers as the door soon opened up again and two guardsmen entered. One of them was the one that had been holding his sword at Seth this entire time. The other he did not recognize.

"So sorry about all of this, but we do appreciate you being cooperative," the new guardsman said to Set as he entered. "Sit down, please."

"Thank you," Seth responded as he walked over towards the side with two chairs. As soon as he took a step forward, however, the guardsman he recognized immediately put his hand back onto the hilt of his sword.

"Other side, please. If you don't mind," that guardsman then said to Seth, and that answer told Seth everything he needed to know about why there were two chairs on one side of the table and one on the other. Without saying anything or taking his eyes off of the guardsman in question, Seth backed away from him and took a seat on the other side of the table where there was only one chair. Once he had sat down the guardsman removed his hand from his sword as they both took their own seats across from him.

"You don't need to worry," the new guardsman said to him as he took his seat. "I can assure you that we will not have a need for you much longer. We're just going to ask a few very basic questions and then that will be it. Is that alright?" While the new guardsman spoke, the other guardsman, the one whom Seth recognized, remained silent and glared at him with the same look in his eyes that he had kept on Seth since he had taken him away. As intimidating as it may have been, it also left Seth unsure of exactly whose eyes he should be staring into when he answered these questions. While the new guardsman seemed polite, Seth also was unsure what would happen if he took his eyes off of the other guardsman.

"Sounds fair," Seth answered as his eyes shifted back and forth between the two guardsmen. It was only after he spoke did he realize that answering that question at all was pointless. After all, if he was comparing these guardsmen to the Canaan town watch, then he knew that they would not let him leave until they said that he could. So it really did not matter if Seth answered any of their questions or not.

"Now, for starters," the new guardsman began. "Tell us your name."

"Seth," Seth answered plainly.

"Surname?"

"I don't have one," Seth answered without thinking.

"Really?" The new guardsman let out, seeming genuinely surprised to hear an answer like that. At least his face gave Seth that impression. Out of the corner of his eye, Seth thought he could see the edges of the familiar guardsman's mouth curl up into the beginnings of a smirk. "You have no surname?"

"I don't, sir, no."

"Well then," the new guardsman began as he placed both of his hands onto the table. "If that is indeed the case then would you care to enlighten us as to why that is." There were at least three ways that Seth could think of at that moment that would let him pick apart that question, but he held himself from doing so as he had the feeling that asking questions here would only give him more trouble. Especially with the way the familiar guardsman was staring at him.

"If I do have a surname I don't know it."

"Why?"

"I have amnesia," Seth answered, as he had been expecting that question. "I was found in the desert outside of Canaan with no memory."

"Canaan..." As the new guardsman spoke he brought a hand to his chin and fell silent for a moment. "That's that small trading town between us and Taurus, correct? If I remember correctly it's roughly..."

"Three hundred and fifty kilometers to the southwest," the familiar guardsman spoke up without taking his eyes off of Seth. Inwardly Seth couldn't help but wonder exactly where they had gotten that very specific bit of information, though he felt that he already knew.

"Thank you," the newer guardsman responded to him before turning his attention back to Seth. "So with that being the case, are we safe in assuming that Seth is not your real name?"

"It was the name I was given," Seth answered.

"By who?"

"By the people who found me, Tara, and-?"

"Who is Tara?"

"She's the one I traveled from Canaan with. She is probably still by the carriage you guys took me from if you want to talk to her."

"No, I don't think that will be necessary," the unfamiliar guardsman answered almost as soon as Seth had finished speaking. Him saying that gave Seth the impression that they didn't feel the need to question her. While that was certainly good for her, Seth wasn't sure how good that fact might have been for him. "But we are getting off topic here. You said that you were found outside of Canaan. Do you live there now?"

"Yes."

"What exactly is it that you do there?"

"I'm a member of the town watch."

"What is that?"

"Well, umm..." Seth began as he quickly tried to think of the best possible way to explain that to them. "I guess... You all enforce the law here in Dis, correct?"

"That would be our profession, yes," the unfamiliar guardsman responded.

"Well then, much like you do here, we enforce the law in Canaan," Seth answered. "Only we don't all wear matching clothes."

"What rank are you?"

"Rank?" That word, and by extension the question confused Seth more than anything he had heard since coming here. He had never heard it before, and no one in the Canaan town watch, nor Tara, had ever used it around him.

"What position in Canaan's town watch do you hold?" the unfamiliar guardsman clarified for him. Beneath the table, while Seth could not actually see it, he could tell by the placement of the familiar guardsman's arm that he was slowly moving his hand towards the hilt of his sword. It was at that sight that Seth became instantly worried. Even with that clarification he still did not understand the question, yet he knew that he had to come up with an answer quickly.

"I'm..." Seth spoke, but he couldn't help but hesitate. "I'm a newer member of the town watch if that is what you are asking."

"Ah, so a trainee then?" the unfamiliar guardsman then asked.

"No, I've had training," Seth responded, as he understood that question. At least he believed he did.

"Duly noted," the guardsman said. "How long have you been with the Canaan town watch?"

"I joined five months ago," Seth answered.

"Who is your superior officer?"

"Charlie Russel," Seth answered. While he had never heard that exact term before, he was easily able to infer what it meant, and for that he couldn't help but inwardly thank Tara.

"And if we were to say... send an inquiry to mister Russel, he would be able to confirm everything you've said?"

"Yes, of course he would." As soon as he had finished speaking Seth instantly became worried again as he remembered that it took him and the entire caravan three days to get here. That meant that if they were going to indeed contact Charlie, that it would take their message three days to get there and then three days to get back, meaning that Seth would have to spend six days in here at least before they would let him go. It didn't help that the unfamiliar guardsman fell silent and nodded his head a few times. After he did that, however, he leaned over towards the familiar guardsman and whispered something in his ear. As much as he tried to, Seth could not hear what he had said, though he did see the familiar guardsman nod in response.

"I understand that you're a mage," the unfamiliar guardsmen then said. "Tell me, are you registered with the academy in Sol?"

"I don't know," Seth quickly answered.

"You don't know?" The unfamiliar guardsman repeated. "How could you not-"

"I have amnesia, remember?" Seth interrupted before the guardsman could finish. "I told you that earlier."

"Oh, right. You did," the guardsman then said as he brought one of his hands to his face. "I am terribly sorry. That should have been obvious." The guardsman then fell silent again for a few long seconds as he kept his hand over his face. Seth's gaze then drifted over towards the more familiar guardsman, who continued to glare at him, though the smirk on his lips had long since faded. However, Seth could see from the placement of his left arm that the guardsman did still have a hand on the hilt of his sword.

"Tell me, Seth," the unfamiliar guardsman eventually spoke again as he removed his hand from his face. "Are you familiar with a substance known as pox?"

"No," Seth answered. "I've never even heard that word. So I don't know what it means."

"It-" before the unfamiliar guardsman could get any more words in, however, the door behind the two of them suddenly opened and in stepped a third guardsman that Seth didn't recognize. Unlike the other two this newer guardsman was lacking a hat. As quickly as he had entered, this newer guardsman walked over towards the guardsman that had been questioning Seth and whispered something into his ear.

Seth tried to listen in to what he was saying, but as he did he unconsciously leaned forward in his chair to do so. The instant he did that he heard the sound of what was unmistakably a metal glove grabbing the hilt of a sword. Instantly Seth's eyes switched back over towards the one guardsman he recognized, and on his face was a familiar looking glare that he had seen Vivian give him more than enough times. Getting the hint, Seth leaned back in his chair and gave up listening to the other two. As quickly as all of this had happened, unfortunately, the guardsman without the hat had finished speaking and left the room as quickly as he had entered.

"Well, I don't think there's much of a point in wasting any more of our time here," the guardsman who had been questioning Seth then said as he stood up from his chair. "Sorry we took up so much of your time. You're free to go. Enjoy the festival."

"Wait, really?" Seth responded, shocked. Despite how good this was for him, he couldn't help but remain confused as to why this was happening in the first place. There was too much information that he didn't know for him to feel comfortable with any of this. "But you didn't-" Before Seth could finish, however, both the guardsman who had been questioning him and the familiar guardsmen had left the room. Even stranger still, after leaving, they left the door open for him. Despite the obvious cue to leave, Seth kept still and listened for a few more moments as he heard the sounds of their metal boots walking in the direction of the front door before being followed by the sound of the door opening, then closing as they both left.

Despite the comforting feeling of knowing that he could leave, Seth was hesitant to. There were still too many things that he did not know, and even more still that he knew had to be going on, but knew nothing about. This left him in a strange state of mind as he felt comfortable again for not getting arrested, but uncomfortable at the same time due to all of the unknowns. With no other idea what to do, and with no idea how long he actually sat there contemplating all of this, Seth eventually stood up and left the guard station.

When Seth had returned to the lot where all of the carriages had gathered the first person to greet him upon his return was not Tara, nor Jorge, nor even Agatha, but Vivian.

"Did..." Vivian began to speak, and it was only then that Seth noticed the completely dumbfounded expression on her face, as if she had seen something that she could not comprehend. "Did you just get fucking searched?"

"Yes," Seth answered plainly as he walked towards her.

"Why?" Vivian then blatantly asked. "What the actual fuck did you do to piss off the city guard?"

"Nothing," Seth answered. "At least I don't think so. They came up to search the carriage with two of these weird animal things that kept making noises at me."

"You mean dogs?"

"I think that was what they called them, yes."

"That was you!" Vivian exclaimed as her eyes suddenly became wider than they already were. "I heard that shit all the way from where I was. What the hell did someone like you do to piss off a bunch of dogs?"

"I just said that I didn't do anything," Seth answered, sounding more than a little annoyed. "They came up to the carriage and started making those noises at me. The next thing I knew, two of the guards had their swords pointed at me and told me to go with them, and after seeing what happened with Agatha, I didn't want to argue." Vivian remained silent for several long seconds as she stared at Seth with an expression on her face that reminded him of how he used to stare at people when he first came to Canaan. It actually creeped Seth out somewhat to see that look on Vivian.

"That..." Vivian eventually said. "That was probably the smartest thing you could have done. I know joining the town watch seemed like hot shit to you way back when, but trust me, the Canaan town watch has nothing on these guys. Charlie's boys are cool and all, but they've always been not much more than a ragtag team of weirdos that work with whatever weapons and equipment they can get their hands on. By comparison the guys here in Dis are like an army. They would eat up all of you for breakfast and then shit you out before you even had time to register what the fuck had happened."

"What's an army?" Seth asked the second Vivian had finished talking.

"That..." Vivian began, but then stopped herself. "Well, ask Tara for the details, but the best way to explain it to you would be... Imagine a lot of people with weapons and magic."

"Okay," Seth responded in understanding.

"A lot a lot," Vivian emphasized as the look on her face suddenly grew serious. "Like, take the entire population of Canaan and times it by thirty, and even that would still be considered small for an army."

"How many people is that?" Seth couldn't help but ask. Vivian remained silent for several long seconds as she simply stared at Seth with that serious look still on her face. To Seth's surprise, however, after those long seconds had passed she suddenly burst out laughing.

"Ah, Seth you fucking dumbass," she said as she slapped her hand on his shoulder. Immediately Seth felt himself tense up as that happened and by reflex he opened up his right hand to summon his sword in case he needed to. "I know you've gotten a lot better at that fancy mathematics stuff since we met and all, but I don't think even in your dreams you could count that high." That answer did not make Seth feel any better about the idea of what an army was. Seth remained silent in thought following that as he returned Vivian's gaze. She had kept laughing as if she had just heard him tell a very funny joke. A few more awkward moments passed as Seth debated with himself whether or not he should ask her any more questions about what an army was. In the end he decided not to, as there was another question that she appeared to know the answer to that he wanted to know more than that.

"What about those animal things?" Seth asked as he pushed Vivian's hand away from his shoulder. "Are they part of an army as well? Actually, what are they for?"

"You mean the dogs?" Vivian asked in turn as she calmed herself down from her laughter.

"Yes, those," Seth responded with an air of annoyance in his voice. Inwardly he couldn't help but wonder if Vivian was drunk right now, which would explain why she was even talking to him in the first place. He didn't smell it on her breath, but he still couldn't help but wonder.

"Well for one thing," Vivian began. "They're vicious little fuckers, so they're good for if you need backup. The real reason they keep 'em around though is because they're loyal, they make good pets, and they have a sense of smell like you wouldn't believe. Seriously I've seen one track a guy all the way through a city and out into the desert once. They can also sniff out-" Before the next word could even escape her mouth Vivian suddenly stopped talking as her eyes became even wider than they were before. All the while she never broke eye contact with Seth. A few more moments like this passed where she didn't continue her explanation, and with the way she was looking at him, it gave Seth an uneasy feeling.

"What?" Seth eventually asked. "They can sniff out what?" Vivian, however, remained silent for a few moments longer before answering.

"Just… She began, but hesitated. "Just stay away from dogs while you're here. Trust me. You'll be better off for it." Before Seth could ask her what she meant by that or what specifically dogs could sniff out she had already turned herself around and was walking quickly away from him.

The entire experience left Seth with an air of uncertainty. In Canaan, while it took him a while to understand all of it, everything made sense and usually there was always someone around who could fill in the blanks for him whenever he needed something to be explained to him. Here, he hadn't even gone through the front gate yet and already several things had happened that he could not understand. What was worse, the people who usually helped him understand such things were strangely unwilling to do so. It gave him the sense that perhaps, for the first time in a long time, he was well and truly on his own. He did his best to push those thoughts from his head as he walked back over in the direction of Jorge's carriage. He hoped at least that Tara would still be there.

Thankfully he didn't have to wait very long to see her, as the moment he was within visual distance of the carriage he saw her standing nearby nervously rubbing her hands together. After a few seconds her eyes drifted over in his direction and she saw him too, and the instant she did she suddenly dropped all pretense and ran over towards him as quickly as her legs allowed her too.

"Oh thank Solaris you're alright!" Tara shouted as she ran up to Seth and threw her arms around him in a great big hug. Given how easily he had gotten through that whole ordeal with the city guard, Seth wasn't sure at all if the hug was necessary, but he returned it regardless. As he did, he felt Tara squeeze him tighter. She held onto him for almost a full minute without saying anything as she buried her face into his chest. Her silence gave Seth the impression that he should say something, but with everything that had happened he wasn't sure at all of what to say. There was so much that he didn't know now, and given her reaction, he was reasonably certain that she didn't want to hear him asking her a thousand questions right now.

Eventually, after what seemed like a long time, Tara finally pulled away from him.

"They did not do anything to you, did they?" Tara immediately asked as soon as her eyes locked with Seth's.

"I don't know," Seth responded. "What sorts of things do you think they did?"

"They did not hurt you, did they?" Tara then quickly asked as soon as Seth finished speaking. That question caused Seth to raise an eyebrow, as the answer to that seemed obvious enough to him. Surely if he were hurt Tara would have at least been able to tell that from a glance. He certainly knew that she was smart enough to.

"No," Seth answered anyway. "Why would they do that?"

"Oh thank Solaris!" Tara exclaimed again. "You were gone for quite a while though. What did they do to you?"

"Nothing, really," Seth answered, unsure of exactly what Tara had been expecting from him. "First, they patted me down like they taught me to do in the town watch, then after that they took me into this building with no windows and asked me a bunch of questions."

"What sorts of questions did they ask?" Tara quickly asked as soon as she had heard that part. "What did you tell them?"

"Just very simple things," Seth answered, unsure of why Tara was so worried. "They wanted to know what my name was and what I did in the town watch. They also asked whether or not I was registered with the academy in Sol since I'm a mage."

"Oh," Tara let out as the look on her face instantly switched from one who appeared gravely concerned to one who seemed gravely interested in what the other person had to say. Seth could tell this because she didn't say anything else after that.

"That's not something we need to worry about, is it?" Seth then asked, taking the silence as his cue to speak. "I wasn't really sure what to tell them."

"Not at the moment, no," Tara answered. "I am just surprised they brought it up." That actually did make Seth feel better somewhat.

Before the conversation could progress any further, however, a low rumbling sound caught the both of them off guard. Both of them immediately turned their attention towards the source of the sound, which turned out to be the city gate opening, albeit very slowly, as Seth imagined that a gate that big must have been difficult to move. Once the gate was open wide enough, Seth saw a single member of the city guard step through it as the gate continued to open behind him. Seth then saw the guardsman walk over towards the windowless building that he had been in earlier, and it was then that he saw two other guardsmen that he had not noticed before because he hadn't been paying attention while he had been standing in front of it. It was difficult for him to see from this distance, but Seth could make out the features of the two guardsmen that the one from the gate was approaching, and they happened to be the two guardsmen that had been questioning him earlier.

That sight instantly made Seth nervous, as the fact that those two specifically were talking to this new guardsman made him incredibly uneasy as to what they could have been discussing. They didn't speak for very long, however, as the guardsman from the gate soon broke away from them and started heading towards the open lot where they all were. Seth instantly tensed up as he saw that and by reflex he felt his hand open up in preparation to summon his sword. Given what he now knew about the city guard here, he wasn't sure at all why he did that, but he couldn't help himself. As much as he knew that drawing a weapon would only make things worse for him, he could not close his hand. He dared not look to see if Tara had noticed this either, as he didn't want to see the look on her face if she had.

"Alright then!" the guardsman from the gate shouted at the top of his lungs as he reached where the fence was. To Seth's surprise, he stopped there and didn't come any further. "The city of Dis would like to thank all of you for your patience and cooperation! It is my pleasure to inform you all that our business here is concluded and you all may enter at your leisure!" At the sound of that Seth relaxed his hand and let out a breath that he didn't even realize he had been holding in. "Traveling merchants, we would ask that you please allow any passengers traveling with you to enter first! Once they are all inside city representatives will help get you and your wares into the city in an orderly fashion! We would ask that you remain patient while doing so! We know that there are a lot of you so the sooner we get through this the sooner we can get you all inside! Enjoy the new years festival!" Then with that, as soon as he had finished speaking the guardsman turned around and headed back inside the gate, though it remained open.

A series of cheers and yelps could be heard throughout the lot as people began to take their things from the carriages. Hearing this, and seeing that none of the guardsmen that worried him seemed to be around anymore, Seth turned his attention back to Tara.

"Should we-"

"Yes, I suppose we should," Tara interrupted before Seth could finish. With that said the two of them silently turned around and walked back to Jorge's carriage. They caught sight of him just as he was walking around from the front.

"Oh, there you are," he said to the two of them, but more so to Seth, as they walked towards him. "You were gone for quite a while. What'd you do, call one of their mothers a harlot or something?"

"What's a harlot?" Seth immediately asked. Out of the corner of his eye he saw Tara's face instantly go red as soon as he asked that.

"How do you…" Jorge began, but then immediately stopped himself. "Oh, right. Why do I keep forgetting about that? Anyway, I suppose you'll be wanting your stuff."

"Yes, actually," Tara responded once she had fully recomposed herself.

"Very well then," Jorge then said as he climbed into the back of his carriage.

"No, no, that is alright!" Tara exclaimed as she quickly walked over to the carriage herself. "We can-"

"Don't worry about it!" Jorge shouted back before she could say any more. "I'm already in here. So let me get your bags. It's the least I can do." As he spoke he found both Tara and Seth's luggage, which he then picked up one by one and set them on the edge of the carriage. Afterwards he hopped back out onto the sand and with seemingly no effort, picked up both suitcases from the carriage and set them gently onto the sand. "See, there. Done. Don't know why you were so uptight about it." Tara opened her mouth to speak again, but no words came out. Taking her silence as a cue to act, Seth walked over and picked up both suitcases.

"Oh, no, Seth. You do not-"

"It's okay. I can carry both of them. They're not heavy," Seth responded before she could finish. As he did though, it dawned on him just how out of character Tara had been acting since they had left Canaan. She was usually one to worry about things, but since this whole trip began she seemed to worry about every little detail, including things that made no sense for her to worry about at all. Sure, getting pulled away by the city guard was cause enough to worry about him, so he gave her a pass on that one, but everything else she had been worrying about seemed unnecessary. At this point it was starting to make Seth worry too.

"Well, I suppose this is goodbye then," Jorge then said to the two of them as he read the situation.

"Yes, I suppose it is," Tara replied as she recomposed herself. Again. "Thank you, Jorge. Thank you so much for taking us here. And again. I am so sorry for any trouble that we may have caused for you." As she spoke she held out her hand to him.

"Ey, no need to apologize for anything," Jorge said to her as he shook her hand. "It's not like any of it was your fault." As he finished speaking his eyes slowly drifted over towards Seth. "If anything it's this guy's fault for being like monster blood to animals. Seriously, though, you don't have any idea why that is?" In an instant, with that one sentence, Seth understood everything that had happened with the dogs and why they would not stop barking at him.

"No," Seth answered as quickly as he could to avoid suspicion. "I really have no idea."

"Huh…" Jorge let out as he stared at Seth quizzically. "Well, whatever it is. You won't have to worry about it for a while. At least until you have to get back. Anyway, I'm sure the two of you have better places to be than here. So you two get going, and if you happen to see my shop during the festival don't hesitate to say hi."

"We will," Tara responded with a smile. "And again, thank you so much. You enjoy the festival as well."

"Heh, well I'll try in between trying to sell all of this stuff," Jorge responded with a smirk. "See ya."

"Bye, and thank you," Seth said to him as he and Tara turned back around and started heading towards the gate. During their conversation, it seemed that most of the other passengers in the caravan had gotten the jump on them and were already walking towards the gate themselves. Among them Seth could see Raz and Daedalus, who were lost deep in their own conversation. As usual, Seth couldn't tell at all if Daedalus actually cared about what Raz was saying or not. In any case, with all of the difficulties of the past few days, as well as the past few hours, behind them, Tara and Seth soon set off with everyone else to enter the city of Dis.

Chapter 9

Prior to coming here Seth had been told many things about the city of Dis. He had been told that it was essentially like Canaan, but bigger. He had been told that it was the largest center of trade in this region, which was why many of the people who passed through Canaan were trying to get there. He had been told that there were so many people in Dis that selling things there was as easy as cake. He had even been told that out here Dis was the center of the world, which made absolutely no sense to him. None of that, however, could have prepared him for what his eyes beheld when he saw what lay beyond that large wooden gate.

Directly in front of him he beheld a street that seemed to go on forever, or at least it went on for longer than he could see, which said quite a lot to him since in Canaan it was relatively easy to stand on one end of the town and see the other. The street itself wasn't like any of the dirt roads in Canaan either, as it was made up of what seemed to be an almost infinite number of gray stones. While Seth was certain that such a thing might have been certainly preferable to walking on sand, he couldn't help but wonder where all of the stones they had used had come from. Not only that, but this one street seemed to go on forever, and he knew that there must have been other streets in this city. So with that in mind he couldn't even begin to fathom just how many stones made up the streets of this city.

That wasn't even getting into the buildings surrounding the streets. Even at the entrance to this city Seth could see that he was surrounded by many different buildings, and every single one of them looked to be made of the same, stone like material that matched the color of the sand outside the city. Not only that, but paradoxically, every building looked to be somehow unique while also looking the exact same in a way that was difficult for Seth to wrap his head around. The fact that many of these buildings were situated so close together that it made it incredibly difficult for him to tell where one building ended and another began didn't help matters at all for him either. What's more, Seth didn't see a single building that was shorter than three stories, and this was just at the entrance to this city. Even from where he stood he could see other buildings in the distance that looked to be much, much taller.

Neither of those, however, were as much of a metaphorical gut punch to Seth as the one aspect of this city that caused his feet to instantly freeze in place where they stood, and that was the sheer number of people that this city contained. They were only at the entrance to this city and already Seth could see more people here than the entire population of Canaan on a full market day. Even with this many people in front of him, however, these were only the ones that he could see. Even from where they stood Seth could hear distant conversations, people coming and going from the main street that he was looking at, and bunches of people in the far, far distance doing who knew what.

All of these were just the things he could see. Aside from the many, many, many conversations he could hear of people going about their merry business in this city, many of which contained words that he did not know, this place also contained so much noise that it was difficult to parse through all of it. Off in the distance somewhere Seth could hear the distinct sound of a horse's hooves clopping on the stone road, and off in the distance in some other direction was the sound of some sort of string instrument that sounded similar to the one that Seth had seen Lydia play, only with a higher pitch. Then there was the clanking of metal clothing as members of the city guard patrolled the streets, some of which were even walking in their direction due to the number of people entering the city.

All of this at once proved to be too much for Seth as he stood in the entrance to Dis, eyes wider than dinner plates and unable to move no matter how much he attempted to will himself to. Around him the other passengers from the caravan passed right by him and Tara without even batting an eye, as if this was something that they were so used to seeing that they didn't even notice the sheer contrast between this and where they had just come from. As Seth stood there gawking at everything that was in front of him, a strange scent hit his nose. It was not in any way pleasant, as it reminded him of the results of eating, but it didn't smell exactly like that and was too far away for him to tell exactly what it was. Once the smell hit him though, it didn't go away, as if the city itself was somehow generating it.

"Come on, Seth," Tara eventually said to him as she gently pushed his back. "We need to get going." While Seth only barely acknowledged Tara's words through the sensory overload that he was experiencing, her light touch was all it took to remind him that there were other things he could do than stand and stare. In fact, her touch caused him to involuntarily take an abrupt step forward away from her in an instinctual attempt to get away from whatever was touching him, which was then followed by another as he fully stepped onto the stone streets of Dis.

As soon as he had done that, however, Seth realized his error as he quickly spun around to look at Tara. As he had expected, Tara had backed away from where he had been standing and was holding up both of her hands. For a moment he was thankful that she had not been carrying either of their suitcases, because he felt that she would have dropped them if she had.

"Sorry," Seth apologized much quicker than he had intended to. "I ju-"

"It is alright," Tara interrupted him before lowering her hands and stepping onto the stone streets of Dis so that she was next to him. "I understand that it can be more than a little overwhelming at first glance, but it is not going to hurt you. I know Canaan must have been scary for you when you first saw it, but you gave it a chance, and look how that turned out. All you need to do is give this place a chance too." As she spoke Tara slowly reached up and gently grabbed Seth by the arm. "Come on. If not for you then for me. Please." There were many, many holes in Tara's logic that Seth wanted to point out to her, not the least of which was that Canaan did not scare him the first time he had seen it, not like this place did anyway. Not only that, but when Seth had given Canaan a chance, not everything about it had turned out so well for him in the end. It actually made Seth feel a little insulted and more than a little confused as to why she had said that at all, as he felt as if she should have known all of this. She was there when it all happened after all.

Strangely, however, Seth felt no desire to argue as his brain began to work properly again, and in turn several realizations hit him at once. For one, they had traveled three days through the desert and he himself had almost been thrown into a cell, all in the effort to simply get here. For another, Tara had seemed incredibly determined to come here, and she would not tell him why. Lastly, he was already here, and if he wanted to back out now then he would have to take another three day trip back to Canaan, and he had absolutely no idea how to go about arranging that himself, which meant that he was essentially stuck here for the time being. So, with all of those thoughts in place, Seth let out a long sigh, relaxed, and consented himself to his inevitable fate. He didn't even need to say anything either as Tara could both see and feel him relax.

"Just stay close and follow me," she said to him. "I know where we are going." Tara then took a step forward and, with her hand still on Seth's arm, pulled him with her as Seth followed her into the city of Dis proper.

As the two of them walked down the stone street towards whatever destination Tara had planned for them, Seth couldn't keep his eyes from wandering as his head and eyes frequently shifted in a new direction every second in an attempt to take in everything that surrounded him all at once without actually paying any attention to where he was going. Thankfully, Tara held onto him firmly enough that he felt he could get away with it for now. Every direction he looked, however, all he saw was more of the same things.

Everywhere he looked he saw more tall buildings, and all of them looked the same no matter which direction he looked in. He saw more streets as well, all of which were covered in the same gray stone, so they all looked the same to him as well. No matter which direction he looked, everywhere had the exact same appearance in this city. It actually made him somewhat dizzy as he felt as if he were spinning in circles. In his head all of this made him seriously start to question exactly how Tara knew where she was going in a place like this. At least in the open desert it was completely clear, so if you saw something in the distance you could head towards it. Here there was no such way at all, at least from what he could see, to tell where or in which direction they were going.

That wasn't even touching on the vast number of people that were absolutely everywhere. When they had entered the city Seth had assumed that the large number of people he had seen were also more people coming from other places for this festival that everyone had kept talking about, and that once they had made their way further in their numbers would thin out. That, however, turned out not to be the case at all. No matter which direction Tara led him in, the number of people surrounding them had not diminished at all. In fact, the opposite seemed to be happening as the further into the city they went, the more people he saw.

"Come on, I know you have it," Seth heard someone they passed by say. He unfortunately did not get to hear the rest of their conversation as he lost them as quickly as he had seen them.

"Spare copper, anyone?"

"By Solaris, is that you!"

"Hey, which way are you going!"

"Excuse me sir, but you can't be here."

"Thief! Thief!"

"You ready to get drunk!"

"I know you got what I'm looking for. You gonna give it to me?"

He also heard the sound of that string instrument in the distance become louder for a moment, but before he could find the source of it Tara had led him onwards and it faded into the distance behind them.

"Out of the way, bitch!"

"Sorry!" Seth suddenly heard Tara say as she moved behind him and out of the way of a larger man that was walking in the direction opposite of them. After a few seconds the man disappeared into the crowd behind them and Seth could no longer see where he was.

It was at that point that Seth remembered all of the people he and Tara knew that had come to this city with them, and with that the realization dawned on him that he had no idea where any of them were nor did he have any idea of how to find them in this city where everything looked the same. He had assumed that they had all walked ahead of the two of them at different points. He hadn't seen Vivian since she had last spoken to him after the incident with the city guard, he saw Raz and Daedalus walk into the city on their own ahead of them, and he hadn't seen or heard from Agatha at all since she had been taken by the city guard herself. Then there were Ash, Nicky, and Dean, whom he assumed had to stay behind with the carriages because they had many things to unload from theirs. Grey and her daughter also came to mind, but he didn't know them as well as any of the others so he wouldn't have even begun to guess how to find them. With all of them in mind and all of the people surrounding him no matter where he looked, Seth began to doubt whether or not he would see any of them in this city at all, or ever again. The guy who had almost walked into them was a big man, and even he had become lost in the immense crowd of the city as soon as he had passed by them. All of this gave Seth a sinking feeling in his gut that eventually Tara would be gone too, and then he would be all alone in this place.

"Excuse me! You there! Sir and madam!" At first Seth ignored that statement like he did all of the other voices of the people that had passed him by. At least he did until he looked directly in front of him and found himself staring directly into the face of a pale looking man with long, red hair wearing a long, brown coat that went all the way down to his knees. The thing that stood out the most about him to Seth, however, was the fact that his face was not exactly clean. The fact that this man was staring directly at him at Tara with a wide, toothy grin on his face, however, meant that he was definitely talking to them. "I dare say, the two of you look relatively new to this city. Are you perhaps in need of-"

"No thank you," Tara interrupted as the two of them kept walking. "We are perfectly fine. Thank you."

"Is that so?" the strange man responded as he kept pace with the two of them. "Well then, why don't you tell me where it is you're going. I know this city quite well. If you are in need of a guide, I am more than-"

"No, that is okay," Tara interrupted again as she did her best to avoid direct eye contact with this man. That reaction told Seth everything he needed to know about this situation. "I have been to this city before, and I know where I am going."

"Really?" The man then said, appearing somewhat surprised, though Seth was sure he was faking it. "Well then do you at least need to know where something is? I-"

"She said we're fine," Seth interrupted without thinking as he locked eyes with the man and shot the most intimidating glare he could muster at him. The man's expression instantly changed as his smile dropped and his eyes went wide in what Seth recognized as fear.

"I... I see..." the man bumbled as he took a few steps back away from them. "Well I will be on my way then!" Then with that said he turned around and walked away from them as quickly as he could. Within seconds he too had disappeared into the crowd and was far away from them.

Seth dropped his glare the second he was gone and looked back over to Tara, who only stared back up at him with a look of grave concern on her face. It was a look that Seth was all too familiar with, and it was also only at that point that Seth realized that they had stopped walking.

"I'm... sorry," Seth said to her. "I just-"

"No, no, it is okay," Tara interjected before Seth could say any more. "Actually, thank you for that. I was worried that he was not going to stop bothering us until we gave him what he wanted." That reaction caused Seth to raise both of his eyebrows in confusion. In Canaan, a glare like that directed at anybody would have never gotten a pass from Tara, at least not without a very good reason. Here, however, the fact that she was okay with it at all raised all kinds of questions in Seth's head. He actually had to fight the urge to ask Tara a hundred questions where they stood, as he had gotten out of the habit of doing that long ago and she had been

all the more thankful for it. "Come on. We should get going." Then, before Seth had
a chance to think any more, they started walking yet again.

Seth wasn't sure at all how much longer they had walked, though he knew
that it couldn't have possibly been any longer than fifteen minutes. It was difficult
for him to tell since all of the buildings and streets here looked the same and as a
result he felt as if he and Tara had been walking along the same road forever. That
was, at least, until they rounded one more corner and, after walking down a new
street for a few minutes, finally emerged from the endless maze of buildings into an
area that Seth could finally see was different from everywhere else he had seen in
this city. In fact, the contrast between it and everywhere else here was so jarring that
it almost felt like another punch to the lungs for Seth.

Before his eyes was an absolutely massive open area that reminded him of
the crossroads in Canaan, only much, much larger and with more roads connecting to
it. In the center of it was a large, completely circular pool of water that looked to be
at least twelve meters across which acted as the lynchpin for all of the roads. To
Seth's surprise there wasn't much of a divide at all between the walkways and the
pool. Conceivably one could easily walk forwards and step in it if they felt so
inclined, which after days in the desert Seth was sure many people would want to.
Surrounding it at various points in no logical order or pattern that Seth could
recognize were trees of varying heights and sizes, all with lush, bright green leaves.
The presence of these trees confused Seth more than anything, as while he knew
perfectly well what a tree was thanks to Ash, he had never actually seen one before
aside from the ones on her farm, and he knew that they couldn't grow out in the
desert. Not normally anyway.

Surrounding the pool and trees were all kinds of tents and wooden stalls of
varying sizes, shapes, and colors, some of which looked to be incomplete as they
were still being set up. Many of the wooden stalls Seth recognized as merchant
stands, only they all had rolls of cloth set up on sticks above them to provide shade.
That, however, was only what was surrounding the pool. All of the buildings that
surrounded this central space, nearly all of which Seth recognized as shops of some
kind, all looked to be exceedingly well put together, more so than in Canaan by a
large margin. The amount of detail in all of the signs these stores had, the
professional demeanor of those who appeared to run them, even the stone designs of
the buildings themselves all screamed to Seth that these were shops that had been

here a long time, knew how to keep themselves in business, and would continue to be here long after he had gone.

Some of the shops Seth recognized as places that sold food even had fenced in, outdoor seating areas by the entrances. These were all protected from the sun by large, light green colored awnings that spanned the entire length of the fenced in areas. As soon as Seth saw the awnings, something clicked in his head as he looked back around at all of the other shops and saw that above their entrances nearly all of them also had awnings. Most of them appeared to be the same light green color as the trees, but some were different colors, more elaborate, or in some cases custom made to fit the theme of the shop. While not every shop in this area had an awning over its entrance, the vast majority of them did. It was so much that just from the amount of awnings present, Seth had to assume that in an open area like this shade was something akin to prime real estate. It was enough to make him wonder why they did not have them in Canaan.

That was not all, however, as along the roofs of nearly every building, in their windows, or in some cases nailed to the sides of walls, Seth could see all sorts of decorations being set up. Much of what he saw on the roofs appeared to be banners bearing the colors purple, orange, and white in that order from left to right. It was a pattern that Seth recognized, as he had seen it before on a flag in the mayor's office in Canaan. It had never actually occurred to him to ask anyone what that flag was about since he had never seen it anywhere else, but now that question had shot straight to the top of the long list of questions he wanted to ask Tara when he had the chance. Within the shop windows and on the walls there were also things like signs denoting sales or special offers, smaller tapestries, flags, one shop even had something that looked like a long pole with many, many, many thin ribbons tied to it that all blew with the wind like a flag set up in front of it. Nearly all of these decorations bore the colors purple, orange, and white in that order from left to right, or in some cases, from top to bottom.

Decorations and repeating colors aside, as with everywhere else in this city that he had seen, this place was absolutely packed with people. In fact, there were easily more people here than Seth had seen in the entire rest of the city. That fact did not surprise him at all, as he was easily able to gleam that this area was likely this city's equivalent to Canaan's market district, but what did surprise him was the sheer number of children running about. Children of all ages, ranging from toddlers to teens, some with parents and some without, ran absolutely everywhere around the pool of water. Some of them were even trying their hand, or feet, at dipping them in the water only to be stopped by their parents or a nearby city guardsman. It was that sight that made Seth realize that there must have been so many more city guardsmen here in this city than there were town watchmen in the entirety of Canaan. Again, because this was a larger city, that fact did not surprise Seth, but the fact that every single one of them was outfitted equally well with identical looking weapons and armor made Seth question whether the Canaan town watch was under-equipped or these people were over-equipped.

It was as those thoughts ran through Seth's head that a cacophony of different scents all assaulted his nose at once. He wasn't sure if they were always there and he hadn't been paying attention or if the wind had somehow only blown them in his direction now, but he did know that all of them smelled absolutely delicious. It didn't take long for him to figure out that what he was smelling must have been some of the different food items that were being sold here. Some of the smells he recognized as different forms of meats being cooked and even some that vaguely reminded him of the smells inside of the Chevrolet's bakery. Many of them, however, he did not recognize at all, as in his entire time in Canaan he had never once smelled anything even close to what they all smelled like, even in the open market. It was enough to make him want to wander around here, if only to find out what sorts of animal, plant, or mixture of the two was enough to create these delicious smells.

That was as far as Seth got, however, before he felt Tara pull on his arm again and before he knew it he was more or less dragged into the square. As the two of them walked through what Seth assumed was the center of this city they had to make more of an effort to avoid bumping into people, as there were more people packed into this space than any of the roads. Thankfully for them most of the people were polite enough to get out of their way, but a few of them weren't and at least one insisted that Seth get out of his way instead. Before Seth could respond to him Tara pulled him aside and that person passed them by without another word.

The scents of many more different kinds of things, Seth wasn't even sure if some of them were food or not, continued to pass by Seth's nose as they walked on. Most of them still smelled like different kinds of meats, but mixed in with them there were other scents that he had never smelled in Canaan before, as if the unusual smell itself was part of the meat smell. As much as he wanted to ask what many of them were, he was unsure of exactly how to go about asking what a smell was. He was, however, able to gleam that many of them were also coming from the trading stalls, not just the shops that he saw.

Eventually the two of them walked a ways around the pool before turning down onto another street where to Seth's surprise, the decorations and merchant stands actually continued onto the street. This, of course, meant that there were lots of people here as well, and all were packed into a much smaller area, which made it more difficult to navigate through. While it wasn't too bad, it was bad enough that Seth was forced to take his attention off of everything around him in order to make sure that he kept close to Tara.

At some point, however, Tara suddenly and abruptly pulled Seth to their right as the two of them escaped the crowd and ducked into a nearby building that Seth had not noticed at first since he was no longer paying attention. As such, he did not get much of a chance to see the outside of it. The inside, however, had enough to keep both his eyes and attention occupied.

The building they had found themselves in, whatever it was, opened into a large foyer that was covered in a light green carpet that spanned almost the length of the room. Directly opposite of where they stood was a long desk where a single young woman with long, dark hair which she kept tied behind her in a ponytail stood watch. At the sides of the desk were four entrances, two on each side. Two of which Seth could see led to staircases while the other two led into the room immediately beyond the foyer. Mounted on the wall behind the desk, as if made to be the centerpiece of the room, was another, larger flag that from left to right bore the colors purple, orange, and white in that order. Between the colors of the flag and all of the green that Seth had seen, he was beginning to think that there was a theme that the people in this city were keeping up with, and at this point it was really bothering him that he didn't know what it was supposed to be or represent.

"Ah, hello hello," the young woman behind the desk said the second she saw the two of them enter. "Welcome to the Hearth of Dis. How may we be of service to you?" With the amount of enthusiasm she had put into her words, Seth was unsure of whether or not she was faking it.

"Umm... thank you," Tara responded as she finally let go of Seth's arm and walked over towards the desk. With no crowd of people to get lost in, Seth followed suit. "I have a reservation under the name Schäfer. I made it months ago so it should be alright."

"Let me check the registry," the woman responded before pulling a large, leather bound book out from somewhere beneath the desk. It hit the desk with a loud "thud" as she practically dropped it before opening it up to one of the pages. She remained silent for a few moments as she scanned through what Seth saw was a very long list of names and dates. There didn't appear to be any order to them that he could recognize, so the idea that she could find anyone in that long, seemingly endless list of names seemed impossible to him. "Ah, here you are. Thank Solaris that I happened to open it up to the correct page."

"Yes, thank Solaris," Tara nervously responded. Apparently, much to Seth's relief, she found this girl's forced enthusiasm a little off putting as well.

"You're lucky you made the reservation when you did," the woman then said as she closed the book and put it back beneath the desk. "Otherwise we might have had to turn you away. Rooms always become something of pain to obtain whenever the festival is on. Not just here, but everywhere."

"Oh believe me, I know," Tara replied with a dismissive hand wave. "My father made a similar mistake back when he and my mother got married. I heard that story countless times growing up." In response to that the receptionist let out a giggle that, even to Seth, didn't sound even remotely genuine. It was enough to make him wonder if her seemingly chipper personality was somehow mandatory for her job. That thought led him to wonder whether or not she wouldn't get paid if she didn't at least try to humor the guests like she did.

Those thoughts were quickly pushed aside when, after a few quick moments of rifling through drawers, the receptionist pulled out two identical iron keys, which she then handed to Tara.

"Here are two room keys for you, Miss Schäfer," the receptionist said as Tara took the keys from her. Both keys had small green tags hanging off the end of them which appeared to have some sort of number written on them, but before Seth had a chance to clearly see what either of the numbers were Tara had already taken them and put them both in her pocket. "Please be sure to return them when you check out. We have had incidents in the past and we would very much appreciate it if we didn't have to add you to that list too. Enjoy your stay and have a good time at the festival."

"Thank you," Tara quickly responded before she just as quickly turned and walked away from the receptionist desk. Seth, not in the mood to hang around this woman any longer than he had to, quickly followed suit, though he did see her beam an obviously fake looking smile at them as they left. Seth tore his eyes away from her as quickly as he could the instant he saw that, lest he be forced to keep looking at her and the creepy looking expression she wore as a result of holding up her fake smile. With that behind him Seth instead returned his full attention back to Tara.

After ascending more flights of stairs than Seth was comfortable with, not because he had been walking for what felt like hours and was carrying two heavy suitcases, but because any building that was taller than two stories seemed unnecessarily excessive to him, the two of them found themselves in a long hallway. Thankfully they did not need to travel much farther to find their room, as it was only a few meters away from the staircase. Nailed to the door was a simple wooden sign with the numbers "406" painted on it. The walk to the room, however, did give Seth a chance to see that the interior of this building was the exact same as the buildings he had seen outside, with almost the entirety of the hallway being made up of that same, sand colored stone surface. He hadn't had a chance to notice it before since there were actually things to look at in the reception area, but everywhere he looked the walls of the building were the same inside as outside. While it may not have been much of an observation, it was enough to make Seth begin to question whether or not he would go insane if he was forced to keep looking at that same color the entire time he was here.

In the time it took him to process that thought, Tara had already unlocked the door and Seth saw for the first time where the two of them would be staying for the next week. It was not much to look at, however, as it was mostly a simple, rectangular space with two identical beds bearing matching white sheets and leaf green blankets separated only by a small nightstand that had a single fresh candlestick on it. The only other pieces of furniture in the room were a wooden writing desk and a single wooden chair to go along with it. At the very back of the room directly opposite the door was a window, though at a first glance it didn't offer much of a view. There was also a small section of the wall that was extended further into the room and had a door on it. From its size Seth assumed that it had to be some sort of closet. Sadly, like the hallway and the buildings outside, all of the walls and even the ceiling of this room were the exact same sandy brown color. While Seth had hoped that his concern that he would go insane from seeing the same color all the time was nothing more than a childish one, as he sometimes still got those due to his lack of common knowledge, after seeing the room that concern began to grow to a more legitimate one.

Pushing those thoughts aside, Seth walked over and placed the two suitcases on the floor between the two beds as Tara closed the door behind him. His arms instantly felt lighter as he did so. Seth then walked over to the mysterious door and upon opening it saw that it wasn't a closet, but in fact was a lavatory that was the size of a closet. Not only that, but it wasn't even that clean. Seth instantly closed the door once he saw what it was.

"Finally," Tara exclaimed as she fell backwards onto the bed that was closer to the door and stretched herself out. She then let out a loud sigh of relief as she stared directly up at the ceiling. Seeing that, Seth followed suit as he walked over towards the other bed and lay down on top of the covers. The bed was indeed comfortable, and after three days on the road and carrying two semi-heavy suitcases through a crowded city, Seth had to admit that it felt extremely good to lay down on something soft and not have to worry about anything. Except of course for the fact that the ceiling was the same sandy brown color as everywhere else he had looked.

The two of them lay there in relative silence for what felt like an hour, but Seth wasn't sure exactly how long it had been. There were at least a hundred questions that Seth wanted to ask Tara about everything he had seen since they had first stepped into this city, but he refrained from doing so right now, as he could clearly see she was exhausted. Despite that, however, the long silence still bothered him.

"Tara, can I ask you something?" Seth asked, if only to break the silence.

"Of course," Tara replied without looking at him.

"I'm just curious," Seth began. "You mentioned a story that your dad told you all the time. How did it go?" To Seth's surprise Tara actually began to chuckle upon hearing that.

"Well, it is funnier when he tells it," Tara answered through her laughter. "And he probably would tell you if you ever meet him."

"He's still alive?" Seth couldn't help but immediately ask as he turned his head towards her.

"Yes, of course he is," Tara answered as she sat back up. "As is my mother.

Whatever gave you the impression that they were not?"

"You've never said anything about them," Seth answered. "You've told me about your brother, but you've never said anything about your parents. So I thought that they were dead and you just didn't want to talk about them like Ash does whenever people mention her brother. If they were alive I assumed that they would have come up by now. I'm sorry if I did something wrong by thinking that."

That response actually caused Tara to freeze where she sat as she began to ponder whether or not she had ever actually mentioned her parents to Seth in the seven months that she had known him. While she was certain that she must have at some point, the fact that she knew that Seth's memory was like a steel trap told her otherwise. This in turn made her feel like a terrible daughter. However, with this in mind, she shook her head free of any shame and fell back onto the bed with a smile on her face. To her it felt like the first genuine smile she had worn in days.

"Well, how about I fix that mistake," Tara began. "As I said though, my father tells the story better than I ever could, but I will do my best. My family never had much in the way of money, even when my parents first got married. Despite that, however, my father endeavored to give my mother a honeymoon she would never forget." She paused there for a moment as she began to chuckle to herself again. "To his credit, he did accomplish exactly what he had set out to do, just not in the way he had been hoping for."

Chapter 10

"So where are you going exactly?" Seth asked as he stared out the window. To his surprise the view that the window in their room offered was not that bad, as he could see the street outside of the hotel below as well as a good majority of the city's skyline, including the wall in the distance. As nice as the view was, however, all it did for him was further reinforce how much everything in this city looked the same to him and how easily one could get lost in it.

"I told you," Tara answered as she finished tying her remaining shoe. "I have some important errands that I need to run before we do anything else. I should be back around midday. After that I will show you around as much of the city as you want. I know it looks big and intimidating at first glance, but trust me, it is actually not that bad once you actually start walking around in it." After she had finished speaking and her shoes were good and tied, Tara stood up from her bed and looked over towards Seth, who was still looking out the window. "You can turn around now, by the way."

"I know all of that," Seth responded to her as he turned around to properly face her. "What I'm asking is where specifically in this city do you have to go to run your errands."

"Seth, that-" Tara began before she suddenly cut herself off and diverted her eyes away from him, as if suddenly the wall behind their beds seemed to be more interesting to her. That reaction did not go unnoticed by Seth, as he also saw that Tara's face had turned slightly red as she looked away from him. "Seth. You... You do understand how some things can be... personal... to some people, do you?"

"Yes," Seth answered with a raised eyebrow.

"And you understand that sometimes things of a personal nature..." Tara continued as her eyes drifted down towards the floor. "People... sometimes do not wish to talk about them."

"Yes," Seth repeated, though he was still unsure of where exactly this was going.

"Well..." Tara began as her eyes drifted back up to look at Seth, but then immediately blinked and looked towards the wall to her right, opposite the beds, instead. "The errands that I need to run... are of a personal nature... So as such... I... I do not-"

"What kind of personal errands do you need to run that you had to come all the way to Dis to do them?" Seth interrupted, as he was becoming more and more unsure of whether or not Tara would actually tell him anything unless he pressed the issue. Tara then blinked again and her eyes looked directly into Seth's. While he knew that they appeared brown now, from the look on Tara's face Seth was unsure if that was what she saw when she looked at them.

"I..." Tara began as her eyes drifted away from Seth again. Seth was about to interrupt her again, if only to attempt to force an answer out of her, but before he could Tara suddenly walked right up to him and took hold of his right hand. "Seth..." Despite her speaking again she still would not look him in the eyes. "You trust me, do you not?" Her actions, followed by that specific question actually forced Seth to do a double take, as it took him a few seconds to answer.

"Yes," he repeated again, though he did not sound convincing, even to himself.

"Then please," Tara continued as she finally looked directly into his eyes. "Please trust that I will be back. I... I... I cannot say where I need to go or why, but at least trust that for me. Please. Please at least trust that I will come back." From the look in her eyes, at least from what Seth could see, Tara seemed to be somehow desperate. That fact only made this whole situation that much more confusing to him, as it left him unsure of exactly what the right thing to do in this situation even was.

"Y... yes," Seth eventually answered, though he himself struggled somewhat to look back into Tara's eyes while he did so.

"Thank you!" Tara all but shouted as she let go of Seth's hand and very quickly stepped away from him. "Thank you, thank you so much Seth. That is all I ask. So will you please wait until I return?"

"Doesn't trusting you imply that I will?" Seth couldn't help but ask as he raised both eyebrows.

"Yes," Tara replied as she struggled to contain a giggle within herself. "I suppose it does. Well, now that that is out of the way, I am going now. I will return around midday. I promise." Then as quickly as she could, almost suspiciously quickly, Tara darted away from Seth and was out the door before he could even process his next thought.

The entire exchange between the two of them raised so many questions in Seth's mind. Not the least of which was why Tara was being so secretive with him about all of this. She had seemed nervous when the trip here began and had been unusually quiet the entire way, and now that they were here she was dodging all of his questions. That, and there was the simple fact that despite what Seth had just said to her, the truth was that he didn't trust her.

After everything that had happened between them, it seemed like so long ago now, Seth wasn't sure at all who he could trust anymore. Vivian and Raz were a given, he knew that both of them would turn around and gut him without blinking if he did anything they didn't like, and Tara, despite apologizing to Seth and continuing to let him live with her had remained more or less the same as she always had been ever since, and that was what worried Seth. He believed he could trust her before, but it was that belief as it turned out, that blinded him to the fact that she had been keeping secrets from him. So if she had remained the same, and was obviously still keeping secrets from him, then Seth saw little reason to trust her with anything she said.

It was this thought process that led Seth to decide to ignore what she had told him to do as he followed her out the door. She was no longer visible in the hallway, but Seth knew that there was only one way she could go if she wanted to leave here, so without slowing his pace he hurried down the stairs towards the lobby. Once he was there he caught sight of Tara just as she walked outside the door. Undeterred, and without thinking he followed her outside, and it was only once he was out in the street did he freeze in place.

Like yesterday, people were absolutely everywhere, as the sheer number of them combined with all of the identical looking buildings and the seemingly never ending streets caused all of the blood to rush from Seth's head as he suddenly felt dizzy and his vision went white for a split second. That split second loss of control, however, was all it took for someone to bump into him before Seth had managed to pull himself back together.

"Oh, Solaris I am so sorry," the man who ran into Seth said as he awkwardly pushed himself away from him.

"No, no, it's okay," Seth quickly replied to him. "It was my fault. I didn't see you. I'm sorry."

"Alright, if you say so," the man then said as he continued on his way past Seth. Once he was gone Seth began to frantically look around the street for some sign of Tara. With all of the people surrounding him, however, Seth soon began to worry that he wouldn't ever find her, as it became increasingly difficult for him to pick out any individual in this massive crowd that despite their obvious differences all began to look the same the more he looked around. His fears turned out to be for naught, however, as he soon looked down the direction they had come from to get to this hotel and saw her walking back towards the square with the large pool in it.

When Seth tried to move his feet to follow her, however, he found that they refused to move. Out here in the street again, Seth quickly began to realize that with this city's immense scale compared to Canaan, if he left on his own he may never find his way back. While this place may not have been the desert, between all of the identical looking buildings, the endless streets, and the immense crowds wherever he looked, it may as well have been. If his past experiences were any indication, he might not return anywhere if he didn't have someone to guide him. That thought made his stomach suddenly sink as he then thought of all the people he knew who were in this city, but then quickly realized he had absolutely no idea where any of them were, much less how to find them. That thought in turn led Seth to believe that Tara had somehow outplayed him as he watched her move farther and farther away from him.

"You know you should be more careful with your things," a very recognizable voice suddenly spoke up from behind him. Momentarily startled, Seth quickly spun around to see none other than Raz standing there. Once he had Seth's attention Raz suddenly tossed Seth a small brown pouch that jingled when he threw it. Seth caught it without any issue. When he looked at it, however, he saw that it was a familiar looking coin purse. A very, very familiar looking coin purse.

Seth's eyes then instantly shot open as he checked the side of his belt, but felt nothing there. Unable to believe what he was seeing, he then opened the coin purse only to see that in it was what looked to be about forty copper pieces, the exact amount of money he had put into his own coin purse this morning. As Seth was more or less forced to accept that he was indeed holding his own coin purse in his hand, his eyes drifted back up to Raz.

"How...?" Seth began, as he was unable to figure out how to form exactly what he wanted to say into a question. "When...?"

"That guy who bumped into you," Raz answered as he walked up next to him. "You're lucky I was around." Seth played back the encounter with that man in his head the moment Raz mentioned him. He played it over again and again, but no matter how many times he did he could not fathom how someone could have removed his coin purse from his belt that quickly. The coin purse in his hand, however, told him a vastly different story. With that in mind, however, another question soon presented itself.

"Wait…" Seth began. "Then how did you-"

"The same way he took it from you," Raz answered before Seth could finish with a smirk as he held up his right hand and wiggled his fingers a little bit. While Seth still found it incredibly difficult to believe that what Raz had said could have actually happened, a sudden, more important realization crossed his mind as he instantly spun back around. To his relief he could still see Tara, though now she was much farther away than he was comfortable with. The only thing he could spot of her at this distance and with this crowd was her hair, though he was uncertain how much longer he could keep his eyes on it with all these people around. "So, what are you doing out here?" As Raz spoke he dropped his smirk and put both of his hands in his pockets.

Initially Seth was going to ignore Raz, as he had little reason to talk to him of all people, but then he instantly remembered what had been on his mind earlier. He needed someone who knew their way around this city, and while he would have preferred it to be anyone other than Raz, his timetable for finding that sort of person was walking farther and farther away from him by the second. This left him with little choice as Seth bit his lip and felt his stomach turn uncomfortably in anticipation of what he was about to do.

"Can… Can you help me?" he asked Raz without looking at him.

"Help you?" Raz responded with a raised eyebrow. "I suppose I could. What with?"

"I…" Seth began, but the words died in his mouth as he struggled to think of exactly how to tell him what he wanted. Had it been literally any other person, even Vivian, he knew it would have been so much easier. At his lack of response, however, Raz leaned in and noticed the direction in which Seth was looking. Upon which Raz looked in that direction as well, and it did not take him long to spot the familiar long, brown hair of Tara walking away from them.

"Oh…" Raz let out as his more than familiar smirk crawled across his face. "You wanna follow her?"

"Yes," Seth quickly answered without thinking as he watched Tara's head become smaller and smaller the longer this went on, but then realized what he had said. "No. I mean-"

"Let me guess," Raz interrupted him. "You do want to follow her, but you've never been to a city before and you're worried that if you do you're going to get lost and won't be able to find your way back." Seth, to his surprise, actually felt his mouth drop open and hang there for a moment before he recomposed himself and tore his attention away from Tara and back to Raz, as he could see that Raz was looking in her direction too.

"How did-"

"Seth, it's you," Raz again interrupted. "It's incredibly easy to believe that you've never been to a city before." Despite trying his hardest, Seth for the life of him couldn't come up with a proper response to that comment. Before he could, however, Raz suddenly rolled his neck around and let out an obnoxiously loud sigh. "Ah, why not. I need to kill some time anyway." Raz then shifted his attention back to Seth so that he was now looking into his eyes. "Lead the way. I'll stick close by." Seth's breath then suddenly left him and eyes instantly went wide as he, again, could not for the life of him come up with any kind of proper response to what Raz had just said. In his mind he imagined that this would be a lot harder, but Raz had agreed to help him without even hearing his explanation first. To say that this was not what he had expected would have been a massive understatement. "You know you're going to lose her if you keep staring at me like that, right?"

The instant Seth heard those words he snapped himself out of his surprised daze and moved his attention back over to Tara, only to see that her head was almost a mere spec among the seemingly endless ocean of people in this city. With nothing more to say and his target far enough away from him that it was actually making him scared, Seth took off down the street with Raz following close behind.

The two of them had to run for a short ways to make up the distance they had lost with their conversation, but eventually they had gotten close enough to where Seth was easily able to pick Tara out amongst the crowd easily enough again. To Seth's surprise Raz never asked him any questions or even said anything to him at all the entire way. Eventually they reached the square with the pool of water in it again, and once again the smell of all the different meats and fresh foods hit Seth's nose as they wandered through it. At one point they had to duck behind a tree when Tara stopped and turned around, and again to Seth's surprise, Raz hid with him without a word. Thankfully that moment passed quickly enough as they were able to continue on when Tara turned back around. There were many questions that Seth wanted to ask Raz about why he was helping him right now, but none of them came to mind as he focused on the task at hand. If anything he figured that there would be time to ask him later.

From there the two of them proceeded to follow Tara through much more of the city than Seth was able to see yesterday. It was difficult for him at times to keep his eyes on Tara, as everywhere he looked there were more different buildings and shops to see, but unfortunately for him all of them were the same sandy brown color as all of the other buildings he had seen so they all blended together the more he saw of them. Throughout the entire way Tara never went into any of the shops he saw, nor did she ever make any stops of any kind. She seemed to be going forward with a singular objective in mind.

While she never did make any stops, on occasion she did look behind her. Whenever that happened Seth instantly grew nervous as he ducked out of the street as quickly as he could. At one point when this happened Seth momentarily froze as he was unsure where he should move to, but before he could make a decision Raz suddenly grabbed him by the shoulder and quickly pulled him over towards the windows of one of the nearby shops so that they could pretend to look inside. This seemed to work well enough as out of the corner of Seth's eye he saw Tara turn back around and continue onwards.

Eventually the two of them came upon, much to Seth's surprise, another wall. Much like the one that stood between the city and the surrounding sands, this one was incredibly tall, even taller than some of the surrounding buildings. It was constructed from gray stone and was clearly made with the idea of separating one thing from the other. The fact that it ran directly through the city, however, greatly confused Seth, as he could not for the life of him figure out why the people here would want to separate one part of the city from another. The outside elements he could understand, but anything else seemed unnecessary and excessive. Directly ahead of them in the wall, however, was an at least five meter tall archway, which was where they both saw Tara heading directly towards.

Beyond the archway, in contrast to all of the identically colored buildings currently surrounding him, all of the buildings that Seth could see had quite a bit more color to them, with white and gray being the most prominent that he could see thus far. There was also quite a bit more plant life beyond the archway, as many of the buildings had either rows of trees that surrounded them, short fields of grass, or, again to Seth's surprise, flower beds. Not only that, but all of the buildings were a lot more spaced out and had more room to breathe than the buildings on this side of the archway, many of which were built so close together they could easily have been mistaken for one building. Stationed on opposite sides of the archway, however, were two city guardsmen, one of whom stopped Tara as soon as she approached.

Tara then spent the next several minutes talking with the guardsman, though much to Seth's disappointment he couldn't hear a single word either of them were saying. While he could have moved closer towards them to listen better, Seth did not want to risk it, as there was hardly any cover between the building he and Raz were currently next to and the archway. Eventually, however, Seth saw Tara make a bunch of motions that he recognized as her profusely thanking the guardsman before she then walked right around him and through the archway. It was only as she did that that Seth finally noticed that beyond the archway there were not nearly as many people, though the few that he could see were much more finely dressed. While the path ahead was just as visible to Seth now as it ever had been, there were a few obstacles in his way that at this moment he was unsure of how to get past.

The main obstacles were the two city guardsmen at the archway. While Seth couldn't see any more, with the amount of them he had seen in this city thus far he knew that more could not have been far if they were needed. The next obstacle wasn't so much an obstacle in and of itself and more of a lack of understanding of the rules of this city. Beyond the archway Seth could not see many people apart from Tara, and no one else he saw was going through the archway or coming out of it. So he had to assume that there were rules governing who could go in or out. If there were then Seth certainly did not know them, and after his previous encounter with the city guard he certainly wasn't looking to potentially draw their ire again. Those thoughts occupied his mind, but in his eyes he watched Tara slowly move farther and farther away from him again, close enough to run to, but far enough that he hesitated to take another step forward. It was enough to make Seth wonder if he really had been better off staying in the hotel.

"What're you stopping for now?" Raz then suddenly asked. The sound of his voice broke Seth out of his inner turmoil as he quickly spun around to see Raz leaning on the wall behind him as if nothing at all was out of the ordinary. While he appeared calm, the look on his face screamed to Seth confusion and impatience.

"I don't..." Seth began before he quickly turned back around to see if he could still see Tara. Much to his relief, he could. "She's gone through there." As Seth spoke he pointed towards the archway.

"Yeah, and?" Raz responded as he peeked around Seth and saw the archway for himself. While normally Seth would have been hesitant to answer that question, watching Tara walk farther and farther away from him was enough to force him to put his anxiety aside.

"I don't know if we're allowed to go that way," Seth answered without looking at Raz.

"Why wouldn't we be?" Raz then asked as he took in the sight of the archway on his own. At first he didn't see anything that Seth didn't, but then he noticed where Seth's eyes were looking. It took a moment for him to trace exactly where that was, but once he got it, a smirk quickly crept back across his face. "Wait? You're not scared of the guards are you?"

"No!" Seth quickly answered, but one look back at Tara instantly made him regret saying that. "Okay, yes. I am." Much to Seth's ire, that answer caused Raz to laugh a little bit.

"Seth, you're a guardsman," Raz then said to him. "Why the bloody hell would you be scared of other guardsmen?" That question actually confused Seth, as he wasn't immediately sure why he was scared of them himself. Surely he and them had essentially the same jobs, just in different places, and it wasn't as if he didn't understand the reasons why they had taken him aside and questioned him yesterday. With all of that in mind it dawned on him that he didn't actually know why he was hesitant to approach them. "You know what, nevermind." Before Seth could mentally comprehend that Raz had said something else to him, Raz had already stepped out from behind him and was walking towards the archway himself.

"Raz!" Seth called out, though he did his best to keep himself from shouting. "What are you-"

"You wanna follow her or not?" Raz asked before he could finish, his face still bearing that same smirk. When Seth didn't immediately answer Raz took that as a cue to continue on his way as his smirk grew even wider. "Just stay cool then and stick close to me. I've got this." With that said Raz turned back around and resumed his pace towards the archway.

For the second time that day Seth felt his stomach turn as his only guide through this city was walking away from him. Towards Tara yes, but still away from him. Without thinking he tried to take a step out to follow him, but his legs wouldn't move, as if his feet were somehow stuck to where they were by the same earth based ability he had used on others. Seth's eyes then drifted back over towards the two guardsmen, who didn't seem to have noticed either of them yet, though they undoubtedly would soon if Raz kept up his pace. With all of these things happening at once, the reality of the situation hit Seth like a hammer to his head as he saw the two paths laid out before him. On one path he would get where he wanted to go, but be forced to confront the city guards again, and on the other he would have to make his own way back to the hotel through this city where everything looked alike to him. Neither prospect was appealing to him, and every second that he hesitated both Raz and Tara grew farther and farther away from him still.

Without much of a choice, and forced into the metaphorical corner that he was, Seth bit down as hard as he could as he struggled to comprehend exactly what decisions had led him to where he currently was. Despite everything that was in front of him he forced his legs to move as he stepped out from behind the building and fell in step behind Raz. Raz, for his part, didn't appear to have even noticed that Seth had hesitated as he kept on walking forward.

Despite what seemed like a long distance between the buildings and the archway at first glance, the two of them made it there in relatively little time. As soon as they approached the archway, however, one of the two guardsmen stepped out in front of them.

"Halt," the guardsman said to them.

"What's up," Raz responded without skipping a beat.

"What business do you have in the Suntop district?"

"I got some friends that way that I'd like to visit while I'm here."

"What friends?"

"Does it matter?" It was at that point that Seth began to internally debate with himself whether or not he should subtly hide behind Raz so that the two city guardsmen could not see him. In the end he decided not to, as he quickly realized that would look more suspicious than simply staying where he was. He did, however, resolve then and there not to say a word and let Raz continue with whatever insane plan he had.

"Ordinarily no, it wouldn't," the guardsman responded plainly enough. "But as you can see, we have a lot more people in the city for the upcoming festival, most of which are visitors. So you know, we can never be too careful."

"You mean there's a lot more poor people in the city right now," Raz countered. While Seth wasn't sure of the exact meaning of the word "poor", at least in the way Raz had used it, the look on the guardsman's face upon hearing it told him enough. "And I'm sure the riff raff who live that way are very much aware of this, given that this happens every year, and your boss gave you all very specific instructions about what to do should any of them try to come this way." The guardsman that Raz was speaking to remained silent for several long seconds as he narrowed his eyes at him.

"Sir, what are you implying?" the guardsman then asked. It was at that point that Seth began to believe that trusting Raz may have been a mistake.

"Oh, I'm not implying anything," Raz responded as casually as ever. "I know you all have your orders and you have to follow them. Believe me, I know, but seriously is there an actual reason you're keeping us from going this way?" What followed was several long, silent seconds wherein Raz and the city guardsman just stared at each other. The guardsman kept up his knife-like glare while Raz simply looked the same as ever, as if the glare from someone who could arrest him where he stood didn't bother him in the slightest. Next to him, Seth had to fight to keep himself from shaking, which was not easy for him as he couldn't help himself from doing so, but he knew that showing it would only make him look more suspicious. Eventually the silence went on for long enough that the other guardsman began to walk over towards them with his hand on the hilt of his sword. To Seth's utter relief, however, the first guardsman held up a hand and stopped him.

"Sir," the guardsman began. "If you-"

"Look," Raz quickly interrupted. "If it will really make a difference I'll tell you what my family name is, who I'm going this way to see, and what they could do to you for keeping me from them, but I'm not going to bother because we both know that one, you wouldn't believe me anyway, and two, that you haven't been given any actual orders to prevent anyone from going this way. If you had then either there would be more guards here or the gates would be closed." There was another, even longer pause wherein again, neither Raz nor the city guardsman said anything. To Seth's continued surprise, however, it was Raz who broke the silence this time with an obnoxiously loud sigh. "Look, if it will really make you feel any better. I will assure you right now that neither of us are criminals, and that we have no plans of either stealing anything or wrecking anyone's shit. If we did then we wouldn't be talking to you right now."

The guardsman that Raz was talking to remained silent for several, much longer seconds as he simply glared at him. This began to worry Seth as he looked past Raz and the guardsman to see if he could still see Tara. To his relief he could, but she was only a dot in the far distance at this point. Before he could worry any more about that, however, the guardsman suddenly stepped out of their way.

"Welcome to the Suntop district," the guardsman then said in an uncaring, monotone voice.

"Thank you," Raz responded as he walked past him and past the archway. While there were many, many, many questions Seth wanted to ask right now, he wasn't one to let an opportunity like this go to waste as he followed Raz through the archway and the two of them stepped into what the guardsman referred to as the "Suntop District".

What Seth beheld once the two of them had actually passed through the archway and there was no longer a wall in his way was, to say the least, not what he was expecting at all. As opposed to the many identical looking tall buildings that the rest of the city sported, this place was like walking into almost a completely different city. While there were indeed many tall buildings here, they were all widely spaced apart from each other enough that Seth could easily see the sky without having to look straight up. Not only that, but while some of them bore the same, sandy brown color as the buildings outside of the wall, many of them didn't, with white and stone gray being the most common colors. What's more, every single building here was unique and had distinctly different designs from one another.

There was also a lot more vegetation here than Seth initially saw through the archway. There wasn't that much to see due to the type of urban environment they were in, but around the edges of nearly every single building there was either a row of trees, a small field of grass, or a bed of flowers, though those were few and far between. To Seth's complete disbelief, off in the distance he saw what appeared to be a perfectly flat, open field of grass that acted as its own public square much like the pool of water he had seen earlier. The contrast between the two sides of the city was more than a little jarring to Seth. While he had seen a clear view of it before, actually walking around in it was something else entirely, like he had somehow walked hundreds of miles without actually doing so.

The one downside to this district, to Seth at least, was that there were drastically fewer people here than there were outside of the archway. The few that he did see also wore much nicer and more elegant clothing than the people outside of the archway. That fact did not bother Seth at all, what did though was that the vast majority of them traveled in groups of two or three, sometimes four, and were as spread out as the buildings in this district were. This of course, meant that if Tara happened to turn around at any point then she would easily be able to see both Seth and Raz, as their outfits made them stand out from everyone else that he could see here. There was a trade off to this, however, and that was that Tara stood out just as much as they did, and the fact that she was walking alone with that much fewer people in this district made her that much easier to track, even at longer distances.

This resulted in Seth having to adopt a new strategy for following her wherein he kept as far back from her as his vision would allow and only approached when she was far enough away that Seth was confident that she wouldn't see them even if she did turn around. Several times they did have to duck behind a building when they got too close to her, but this turned out not to be nearly as stress inducing for Seth as he initially believed it would be. It actually instilled in him a nearly overwhelming feeling of wonder as he really, really wanted to ask Raz about what all of these buildings were and what people did in them, but he refrained from doing so, as he wasn't sure how far their voices would be carried in this place. In the far distance, however, Seth did spot a collection of buildings that even he could tell were houses, albeit much larger than any of the houses in Canaan.

Their tailing of Tara eventually ended when they saw her approach an incredibly tall, rectangular building with a wide, stone staircase leading up to the entrance. The building itself was completely white in color, with everything except for the windows, the roof, and the stairs at the entrance being uniformly the same color. The interesting thing about the roof, however, was that while most of it was the same sandy brown color that most of the buildings outside of the wall were, in the center of the roof was a large, almost completely spherical domed structure that looked to be made of a reflective gold or bronze surface, as in contrast to literally every other building that Seth had seen the surface of this was actually shiny and reflected the light from the sun easily. It actually hurt Seth's eyes a little bit when he attempted to look directly at it. When his vision cleared he saw Tara walking up the steps to this building.

"Well, looks as if we found out where she's going," Raz then said to him. "This good enough for you or do you wanna take this whole 'stalking your parental guardian' thing a step further?" While Seth had his own choice response for what Raz had just said, there was one question on his mind that was much more prevalent at the moment.

"What is that building?" Seth asked without taking his eyes off of Tara.

"That, my ignorant friend," Raz began as he moved his head back and forth to stretch out his neck. "Is… I suppose the best way to explain it to you would be that that's the mayor's office." Seth's eyes immediately went wide upon hearing that.

"That's the mayor's office?" Seth exclaimed as he did his best to keep himself from shouting.

"Yeah," Raz responded as he leaned against the nearby building. "Needlessly excessive I know. Though really it's not just the mayor that works there. The regional governor, the minister of trade, this region's treasurer, nearly everyone who's somehow important in the government around here works in that building."

"So who's Tara going in there to see?" Seth then asked. While he did not understand at all what those titles that Raz had mentioned were, he did get the general idea of what he was saying.

"Damned if I know," Raz responded with a shrug. "Your guess is as good as mine. The only way to find out would be to follow her inside." It was at that moment that Seth watched Tara open up the needlessly tall front door of the building and step inside. Upon seeing that Seth stepped out from behind the building and made his way towards it as quickly as he could. "And there he goes." As Raz spoke he stepped out from behind the building as well and followed Seth.

To Seth's surprise there were no guards around the building, which struck him as odd since if this building had as many important people in it as Raz said it did, then certainly there would be a few guards around it. Even if there were guards walking around everywhere he would have expected at least a few of them to be stationed outside of this building. His confusion about that was immediately relieved when he stepped inside and saw three city guardsmen in three different corners of the foyer. Their uniforms were the same, though being inside, they were lacking their hats, though one addition they all shared was an orange armband that looked like it had words written on it. However, Seth could not make out what they said.

The room that he and Raz now found themselves in was nice and open, though sparse of details as the only things that Seth could really see were the simple stone walls and floors that lacked intricate designs in them, as if they were all one smooth surface. There weren't any paintings on the walls or decorations placed about the room of any kind, almost as if this room was designed with function first in mind. At both ends of the back of the room Seth could see four different exits, though two of them were clearly staircases, as the guard rails extended a little bit beyond the wall and into the room itself. It was at one of these staircases that Seth saw what he could only assume was Tara's foot disappear from view as she ascended the staircase.

Before Seth could give chase, however, Raz suddenly held his hand out in front of him and walked forwards. It was only then that Seth looked directly ahead of him and saw the main thing that took up most of this room that he initially didn't notice, as his full attention was on looking for city guardsmen and Tara. Directly across from the door was a long, long wooden desk that spanned three meters from one end to the other. It was also a tall desk as well, tall enough that one had to stand rather than sit to be able to comfortably do anything at it. Despite its enormity, however, only one person was working at it, a young woman with long dark hair. On the wall behind the desk, taking up nearly the entirety of the space that the wall offered, was another one of those purple, orange and white flags. Seth right then made a point in his mind to ask someone, at this point it didn't matter who, what that flag was about.

Without waiting for him Raz walked directly towards the woman at the desk and leaned against it.

"Excuse me, miss," Raz said to the woman with a charming smile. "The brunette that was just here a second ago. Would it be alright if I asked where you sent her?"

"That would depend," the woman answered with her own smile. "Who wants to know."

"We're friends of her's from Canaan," Raz responded as he motioned towards Seth behind him. "We're all staying in the same hotel you see, and she was in such a rush to leave this morning that she forgot something important to her." Seth's eyes went wide as that statement hit his ears. The incident back at the archway was bad enough for him, but now Raz was straight up not telling the truth anymore, and with three city guardsmen watching him as well. Seth actually had to fight himself to keep himself from saying anything or looking too suspicious as he froze where he stood. He desperately wanted to say something, he really did, but the implications of what Raz was doing sent so many different thoughts spiraling through his head, all of them bad. It was bad enough that he actually felt himself begin to sweat.

"And what exactly, if you don't mind me asking, did she forget?" the woman, with the smile still on her face, then asked.

"Oh, just this," Raz immediately answered before reaching into his pocket and pulling out a folded up piece of paper. "She tends to panic over little things and minute details, so she often forgets things. Sometimes important, sometimes not. So she writes down the things that she needs to remember on pieces of paper like this so that she won't forget them, but like I said, she was in such a hurry this morning that she ran off without it." Silence hung in the air between the two of them for a long time. Long enough that Seth without thinking looked over towards each of the three city guardsmen, who much to his horror were all indeed staring directly at them.

"You know, now that you mention it," the woman behind the desk eventually said. "She did seem quite anxious." Raz let out a light chuckle as he heard that.

"Trust me, you have no idea," he said to her. "So if it's alright with you, we just wanna drop this off with her and we'll be back down here and out of your hair before you can even think, 'Hey, those guys are back.'" That last remark actually caused the young woman to let out her own light chuckle.

"Alright," she said after she had finished. "But only if you come right back down once you find her."

"Of course," Raz responded.

"She inquired about the postmaster's office when she walked in," the woman finally answered him. "So I sent her up to him. His office is on the third floor, room number 306."

"Thank you so very much for your help," Raz then said to her as he pulled away from the desk. "We'll be out of your hair before you know it." Then with that said he walked away from the desk towards the staircase on their left. As he did Seth saw him wink at the young woman at the desk. While she did not respond Seth did see her face go red for a moment before she recomposed herself and set herself back to work.

Seth remained silent as he followed Raz towards the stairs and remained so once they had begun to ascend them as he did notice that the three guardsmen in the room still had their eyes on them. Once they had ascended far enough that Seth was certain they were out of earshot from them the first thing he resolved to do was ask Raz the question that he desperately needed to know the answer to first.

"Raz-"

"Talk quietly," Raz interrupted Seth with a quiet voice as they ascended the staircase. "People are trying to work here." While Seth had no doubts at all that that was true, he was also certain that wasn't the only reason Raz wanted him to talk quietly.

"Why did you do that?" Seth asked as quietly as he could. For the moment he was thankful that working in a library had taught him the value of indoor speaking voices.

"Do what?" Raz responded.

"What you did downstairs," Seth answered. "To that woman?"

"What did I do to her?"

"You didn't tell her the truth."

"Oh, that," Raz responded as if he had only realized what he had done just now. "You wanted to get in here to see what Tara was doing. So I got you in. Do you have a problem with that?" Despite how obvious the answer to that question seemed initially, Seth needed to take a moment to think about exactly how he wanted to answer that.

"No, but... Why didn't you just tell her the truth?" To Seth's surprise, Raz's initial answer was to laugh at him. It was a quiet laugh, but a laugh nonetheless.

"Seth, if I had told her the truth she would have told us to get the hell out of here as soon as I was done talking, and if we tried to press the issue then she would have sicked those three guards on us and they would have made us leave. That, or she more likely would have thought that we were stalking her and would have had those guards throw us out anyway." That answer actually caused Seth to rethink the incident downstairs. He was perfectly aware that stalking was illegal, but it never occurred to him to think that right now he was stalking Tara. That thought led him to rethink the entire day, and it was only now that he realized that their actions could have indeed been seen as stalking.

"Would she have really done that?" Seth asked after a few moments of silence.

"Oh yeah, easily," Raz answered immediately. There was another question that Seth wanted to ask, but it died in his throat as the recent revelations of the day's activities played out in his head. Instead he decided to ask about something else that was on his mind.

"What was on that piece of paper though?"

"Oh, this," Raz replied as he pulled out the piece of paper in question and handed it to Seth. "Here. Take a look for yourself." Immediately Seth took the paper from him and unfolded it. To his complete and utter shock and disbelief, it was blank.

"Wh… wha…" was all Seth could get out. At the sound of those noises Raz began to quietly laugh again.

"Seth, while I would love to explain to you why I keep a blank piece of paper with me," Raz began as he took the paper back from him. "If I did then I would never hear the end of it from Tara and Daedalus would probably punch me in the face." After putting the paper back into his pocket he brought his hand up to his chin. "Actually no, Daedalus would definitely punch me in the face and Tara would probably kick me in the nuts."

"But what if the woman downstairs asked if she could see what was on the paper?" Seth then asked as the implications of what could have happened ran through his head. To his confusion Raz turned to look at him with the same sinister looking, yet oddly optimistic smirk he always wore.

"Then we would have been fucked," was all Raz said to him before he exited the staircase onto the third floor. With absolutely no idea how to respond to that, Seth followed him in silence.

The two of them then emerged from the staircase into a long hallway that for better or for worse, looked mostly the same as downstairs. Doors lined both sides of the hallway for what appeared to be the entire length of it, which for a moment caused Seth to worry that they would never find the specific office they were looking for. That was at least until he saw that all of the doors had signs with numbers on the front of all of them, all of which began with the number three. Remembering what the woman downstairs had said, all they needed to do now was find the room labeled

"306". Unfortunately, however, the first room that Seth could see was labeled "321", meaning that they still had to search for it.

That task turned out to be much easier than Seth had anticipated, as all they needed to do was follow the numbers on the doors, as they strangely went in descending order rather than ascending. This greatly confused Seth, though he supposed that this ordering of offices made sense to someone. What did make sense to him, however, was that all of the odd numbered offices were on one side of the hallway while all of the even numbered ones were on the other. Eventually the two of them saw in the distance the office labeled "306". To the surprise of both of them, however, the door was slightly ajar, which allowed them to hear voices inside. Unfortunately, they were still too far away to hear anything.

With this in mind, Raz quickly stopped and held up his hand. Unsure of what was going on exactly, Seth immediately stopped. Raz then turned around and quietly motioned Seth towards the wall. Seth, who figured at this point that Raz hadn't led him wrong thus far, did as he was told and moved up against the far wall where all of the even numbered doors were. Raz did so as well before he then looked at Seth and held a finger over his lips, an indication that Seth knew to be silent. Seth simply nodded to show that he understood. Having seen that Raz then quietly moved ahead of Seth towards the open office. Seth took notice of the way Raz moved, careful that his feet would make as little sound as possible. Seeing that, Seth followed suit and kept as quiet as he could.

It took them a few moments, but eventually the two of them, moving silently, got close enough to the office to where they could actually hear the voices coming from inside. Surely enough, one of the voices belonged to Tara. While Seth was content to stop where he stood after hearing that, Raz continued forwards, so with some hesitation he did as well. After a few more long, incredibly tense moments of this, Raz eventually stopped uncomfortably close to the office door. While being this close made Seth nervous, it did allow him to clearly hear everything that was being said in the office.

"Th... Thank you so much for seeing me, mister Guilloux," Tara's voice said.

"Oh, it's no issue at all, miss Schäfer," a not very deep, almost mumbly sounding voice responded to her. "After all, you made the appointment, and you arrived on time. So for now my time is yours. Now, how can this humble civil servant be of assistance to you?" Tara paused for almost a full minute after he had asked that question. If Seth didn't know any better, he would assume that she was trying to gather her thoughts and think of how best to respond. In this situation, however, he did not know what to think.

"Well… Umm…" Tara eventually began. "I… I used to get regular parcels from my brother in Sol once a month."

"Sol, yes," the other voice in the room chimed in. "That is quite a ways away."

"Yes, it is," Tara replied before continuing. "And I know that for shipments of that distance all mail is sent directly to Dis first before being redistributed and properly shipped throughout the frontier."

"Yes, that is our official policy," the male voice then said to her. "Times may not be as trying as they once were, but the roads throughout the frontier have never been exactly safe. Chaos, as I'm sure you know, is everywhere ma'am."

"I understand. Believe me I do," Tara chimed back in. "That is not what I am here for, however. Three months ago I stopped receiving parcels from Sol."

"Really?" The male voice chimed back in, now seeming interested. "Well if that is the case then I'm sure something simply happened along the road. Between monsters and bandits it always seems like someone is trying to take something from someone. If you file a proper complaint with us, however, we will have it looked into for you. The postal service out here does employ mercenaries specifically for that purpose."

"No no no, that is not exactly it," Tara then quickly stammered out before the other man could say any more. "I did think that was what it was at first. So I filed a complaint, as you said, and the nice people at the post office here wrote back to me saying that it would be looked into. I also wrote to my brother and told him what had happened. In his reply he was… honestly shocked to hear that such a thing could happen out here, but nonetheless he sent another parcel. However, I never received that parcel either." There was a long pause after Tara had said that. As Seth listened to her speak he tried his best to recall any time where she had talked about receiving mail, specifically packages, from Dis. However, he could not recall a single memory where that had happened, at least not in his presence. In his own mind this more or less confirmed to him that Tara had indeed been hiding things from him, as he had feared. "When that happened I thought it was just my bad luck. Maybe the bandits you were talking about got to me twice. However, I never did get any replies from the post office here about either of my parcels from being found. What's more, a few weeks later, around the time when I was supposed to receive yet another parcel from my brother, it never arrived."

"I see," the man in the room responded, though he seemed to have lost his previously jovial outlook as he did so. Outside, Seth began to believe that he had a good idea of where this conversation was headed now.

"So I did the same thing again," Tara continued. "But I got the same result. No parcels were recovered. Then another month passed and I still received nothing. So I had a friend of mine who travels between Dis and Canaan frequently make some inquiries for me and well…"

"Go on," the man in the room said after Tara had stopped speaking again. Despite that it took a few moments for Tara to eventually continue.

"The information I received was…" Tara hesitantly continued. "She told me that all of the parcels that were addressed to me did in fact arrive in Dis, but that someone higher up had ordered them not to be shipped. To my knowledge they are all still in the post office here."

"I see…" the man's voice repeated. This time slower.

"So that is why I am here," Tara then said. "I made my own inquiries of course, but no one ever gave me any answers when I asked. They would not even tell me why none of my parcels were allowed to be shipped. The closest thing I received to an answer was that if this was indeed something ordered by someone higher up, then you would be the one to talk to, mister Guilloux. You are the postmaster here in Dis, so not a thing happens in the post offices here without you knowing about it."

"That is indeed correct," the man's voice responded.

"So…" Tara continued. "Beyond that, I must admit that my knowledge as to the exact nature of this problem is limited, but whatever it is I am hoping that you and I can work out some sort of solution today so that I might have what is rightfully mine returned to me before I leave the city." Both Tara and the other person in the room fell silent after she had finished speaking. Despite hearing all of that, Seth could still not help but feel that something was missing. If what Tara was saying was the only problem then why keep it a secret from him?

"If I may ask, miss Schäfer," the man in the room then began. "What exactly is it that these parcels contain that you are hoping to reacquire?"

"I…" Tara stammered. "I do not feel comfortable saying what they are out loud."

"For the sake of helping you resolve this issue," the man responded. "I am afraid I am going to have to insist." Despite his insistence Tara remained silent for several long seconds before answering. Outside of the office Seth made sure to pay careful attention to whatever she was about to say next. Whatever was in those packages, he was sure that it would somehow explain everything.

"It…" Tara stammered again. "It is actually money. I work in the local library in Canaan, and unfortunately, because Canaan is a small town it does not pay much. Between my own expenses, the rent that the town's owner used to charge me every month, and one other person I promised to help support, on average I only barely make enough to get by. So my brother sends me some extra money each month to help out."

"What exactly does your brother do that he can afford to send you money each month?" the man in the room then asked Tara.

"He works at the university in Sol," Tara answered.

"I see," the man replied before he then fell silent. Despite the answer seeming clear enough, it still confused Seth. If Tara really was having issues with money, why would she keep that a secret from him? Surely the money he made working for the town watch would have at least helped her out a little, and he would have lent her some if she had asked. So if that was really all the issue was then why didn't she say anything to him? "The good news, Miss Schäfer," the man eventually continued. "Is that I am indeed familiar with the type of problem you are having, and I have a solution."

"Really!" Tara instantly exclaimed upon hearing that. "What do I have to do? Just tell me where to go, who to talk to, and what to sign. I will-"

"Miss Schäfer, I said that was the good news," the man interrupted her. "Usually when people say that it means that there is bad news too." Tara instantly fell silent upon hearing that and listened, as did Seth and Raz. "The bad news is that there are people that I report to as well, and this particular issue goes a little bit above me." While Seth could only imagine the expression on this man's face as he was explaining that, he could see Raz's, and what he saw surprised him more than anything else he had done today. The look on Raz's face was one that he was innately familiar with, if only because he himself wore it frequently. It was the look of someone who was confused beyond all belief. "There is a way, however, that I can make this problem go away and have your belongings returned to you, but-"

"What do I have to do?" Tara immediately asked before the man could even finish. Surprisingly, however, the man did not give her an answer immediately. Instead he remained silent for almost a full minute, during which Seth noticed the expression on Raz's face slowly change. He was no longer confused, instead his eyes were like daggers and were aimed directly at the crack in the slightly ajar door. While he didn't make a fist, Seth did see his hand begin to twitch as well.

"Well, miss Schäfer," the man eventually spoke again, though this time in a more hushed tone. "There isn't necessarily anyone else you need to speak to or anything you need to sign per se. Despite what I said this is something that I can take care of for you myself. However, I will need something from you in return." As he spoke, it was subtle, but Seth could hear that his breathing was slightly heavier than it had been before, though without actually seeing him it was difficult to discern why. Despite how simple what he had said seemed, Tara kept silent for several long seconds before she answered him.

"How much do you need?" Tara eventually asked in a hushed tone as well. "I did not bring much with me from Canaan, but-"

"Oh no, no, miss Schäfer," the man cut her off before she could finish again. "You can keep your money. Money is the entire reason you are here. I understand. No, what I require from you is but a single simple favor." There was another long pause again as Seth could only guess that Tara was contemplating what this man had just said. Nearby, however, Seth suddenly heard something that to him, sounded like a small scratching noise. Momentarily startled by it, Seth instantly traced where the sound had come from only to find himself staring at Raz's other hand. Before that hand had been touching the wall in their, seemingly minimal, effort to conceal themselves, but now Raz seemed to be trying his damndest to dig his fingernails as far into the wall as possible. A vain attempt, as Seth noted before, that all of the walls here were made of stone, but nevertheless Raz kept doing it, even to the point that Seth began to worry that he would break his fingernails off. Seeing that reaction however, caused Seth to suddenly grow concerned, as he could clearly tell that Raz did not like what he was hearing.

"What do you want me to do?" Tara eventually asked in an incredibly quiet voice. To Seth it didn't even sound as if she were trying to speak quietly, more as if she were ashamed to even ask.

"Well…" the man then spoke again in a hushed tone, though his heavy breathing was more noticeable now. "I understand that this is your money, and you very much want it back, miss Schäfer, but let me ask you. What are you willi-"

Before he could speak any more words, and before Seth could even comprehend himself everything that was being said, Seth watched as Raz suddenly pushed himself off of the wall before casually walking over towards the slightly ajar door and pushing it open. As Seth watched him do that he momentarily froze as he neither expected this to happen, nor did he have any idea what to do if or when they actually decided to confront Tara. He had planned to think of how to do this later once they had snuck back to the hotel, at least that was what he thought they would do. Now, however, all of that had been thrown out the window as he felt his heart momentarily stop and his stomach sink further into his gut than before. Raz, however, seemed to have forgotten that he was there as he casually strolled into the office.

"I'm sorry, but who are you," the man in the office said in a more normal, indoor speaking voice once Raz had entered the room.

"Raz!" Tara immediately shouted upon seeing him. Hearing that, Seth realized now that all of his attempts to hide from her had been for nothing as he took a deep breath, steeled his nerves, and then pushed himself off of the wall as well and walked into the room himself.

Beyond the door the inside of the office was about what Seth had expected to see. A simple, square room with a window at the back and a single wooden desk in the middle of it. It actually reminded him somewhat of Celene's office in the building where Canaan's mayor worked, though here the walls and floor were clearly stone as opposed to wood. At the desk sat two people with one empty chair, one of whom was Tara. The other one, the man whom Tara had been speaking to this whole time, this mister Guilloux, was one of the most unusual looking people Seth had ever seen in his short life.

While nearly every person that Seth had seen, male or female, possessed a similar, vertical build, mister Guilloux was nothing like that. As opposed to being vertical, mister Guilloux was more round, almost like a sphere. His body type actually reminded Seth of missus Chevrolet from Canaan's bakery somewhat, although he was more spherically shaped than she was. The clothes he wore seemed to only barely fit him, and actually reminded Seth of the clothes Daedalus typically wore, consisting mainly of a plain white shirt and a necktie. On his face he wore a pair of spectacles and underneath his nose was a relatively thin looking brown mustache that matched his short, combed hair. Even with all of that this man reeked of salt and sweat, something that Seth first thought was due to the heat, but then he quickly realized that neither he, nor Raz, nor Tara were sweating in any way, so the cause had to be something else. Nearly everything about this man confused Seth, as he kept racking his brain in an attempt to come up with some sort of explanation for how a man could look like this.

"Seth!" Tara shouted even louder upon seeing him, which instantly snapped him out of his confused state.

"I'm sorry," Seth responded to her in a quiet voice, as he didn't know what else to say to her at this point.

"I am terribly sorry, but this is a private conversation we are having," Mister Guilloux politely said to both Seth and Raz. "So I am afraid I am going to have to ask you to step outside if you don't mind. I will speak with the two of you as soon as I am finished here. Of that you have my word."

"Oh no, don't mind me," Raz then responded in a calm and collected voice, much to Seth's continued surprise. When he looked over in his direction he saw Raz calmly walk over towards the wall next to the door and lean against it. He then crossed his arms and locked his eyes directly on mister Guilloux. "Please, continue." As he finished speaking his lips twisted into his wide, familiar looking smirk. Seemingly as surprised as Seth was, mister Guilloux actually remained silent for a few moments before he could even think of a response.

"That…" mister Guilloux eventually spoke, though hesitantly, as Seth noted. "That is, I'm sorry to say, for the ears of Miss Schäfer only. If you would-"

"Oh don't even worry about it," Raz interpreted him. "Go ahead. Continue with your conversation. Just pretend that I'm not here. You were saying something about a favor that you wanted from her." Seth watched as mister Guilloux began to sweat more visibly and again, he hesitated to answer. Tara's eyes frantically shifted between all three of them as she tried to put the pieces together regarding what exactly was going on here, something that Seth himself was trying to do as well.

"A… As I said," mister Guilloux hesitantly continued. "That is a part of a private conversation between myself and-"

"I only barely know this woman," Raz interrupted him again. "I could care less what happens to her or anything she owns and she is a grown woman, free to make her own choices and all. So I'm not gonna get between you and whatever conversation the two of you are having. So go ahead. Really. Tell her this favor that you want from her." As he finished speaking Raz's smirk grew slightly wider.

Raz's choice of words greatly confused Seth, enough that he desperately wanted to say something to take control of the situation, as it seemed that Raz wasn't helping at all. Mister Guilloux's reaction, however, told him a different story, as he seemed to grow more and more tense the more Raz spoke. That, and Seth was very much aware that there were aspects of this whole situation that he knew nothing about, such as why Tara had never told him about her missing packages in the first place or why asking for a simple favor was making Raz act the way he was. All of that actually made Seth more afraid to say anything for fear of making things somehow worse, as he had unknowingly done in the past.

"If you would be quiet and simply listen to what I am trying to tell you, sir," mister Guilloux eventually continued. "That-"

"I'm sorry, help me understand," Raz interrupted yet again. "You're just trying to ask her for a favor, right. Why is that so difficult to do while I'm in the room with you? You're a civil servant and she's just a librarian from a small town in the middle of nowhere. What kind of favor could you possibly ask of her that requires such secrecy? Hell, you're supposed to be the postmaster of this region, right? What about anything in your job requires you to be so damn secretive?" Raz then paused for a few seconds as he stared directly at mister Guilloux. As he did his smirk slowly grew across his face until it nearly reached his ears. "Unless of course, you were going to ask her to do something illegal." Before anyone else had a chance to speak Raz pushed himself off of the wall and started walking towards mister Guilloux's desk.

"S- Sir!" mister Guilloux exclaimed as he watched Raz walk towards him. "T- This is getting out of hand now. I am afraid-"

"You see I would have left if you had just asked miss Schäfer here for that favor," Raz interrupted yet again as he reached the desk. "But now you've gone and gotten me curious." Raz then placed his hand on mister Guilloux's desk as he spoke. "So tell me, mister postmaster. What exactly is this favor you were going to ask of her?"

"Raz, you don't have to-" Tara tried to speak.

"You can relax, Tara," Raz interrupted her as he glanced in her direction. "If everything really is on the up and up here then we'll be out of your hair as quickly as we came in." There was a moment of pause when Raz stopped speaking, as if to reassure her. However, it did not appear to work on either her or Seth, who still didn't understand at all what was happening. "That said. I wouldn't be quick to trust mister postmaster here cause from the evidence I've seen he's apparently shit at his job. For one, withholding someone's mail for any reason is illegal unless he was specifically ordered to do so, and even if he was he would be required to tell you that when you asked, as well as who gave that order and for what reason. Things which I am certain mister postmaster here knows very well. Otherwise he wouldn't be the postmaster. For two, assuming all of that did happen, why would mister postmaster here not tell you any of that if he was required to by his job."

"I'll have you know I have a name," mister Guilloux spoke up. "It's-"

"Lucien Guilloux, I know, it's on the door to your office, but I really don't care" Raz interrupted yet again. "And I would appreciate it if you shut your doughy ass up because I wasn't finished." That remark caused mister Guilloux's eyes to suddenly widen in what Seth could only assume was sheer shock at what Raz had just said to him. "As I was saying, you chose not to inform Miss Schäfer here of any reason why her mail was being withheld, nor did you say on whose order that came from. Instead you told her that this was a problem that you could solve yourself. Why is that? Surely if this really was a problem that you could solve yourself you would do so without being asked or requiring any favors because you know, it's your job. For three, in return for this you asked her for a 'favor', a very unusual request for someone whose job it's supposed to be to take care of shit like this anyway. And finally, for four, the fact that you said all of this, out loud, with your door open." Both mister Guilloux as well as Tara's eyes instantly went wider than dinner plates as the reality of that statement hit them. Not only that, but Seth could see that mister Guilloux was beginning to sweat even more now upon that realization.

"And there it is," Raz continued as the smirk adorning his face showed some teeth upon seeing mister Guilloux's reaction. "So that leaves a few possibilities open, none of them good. However, the way I see it, there's a very easy way we can all tell what's really going on here." Raz then paused for a moment and took in a deep breath. He was still smiling, but Seth could see that his eyes held the same dagger-like glare that they had earlier when they were hiding outside of the office. "So, Lucien, I am going to ask you one very simple question, and if you answer it honestly I will leave right now and let you get back to your conversation with miss Schäfer. If Tara had done that favor for you, would you really have been able to get her mail back? Would you really?"

Silence fell across the room as if all sound had suddenly been killed, and no one dared move except for mister Guilloux, who despite sweating like a pig shivered uncontrollably as if the room was colder than ice. Seth, for his part, felt as if he was finally beginning to understand what was going on here. As he understood it, the man at the desk, mister Guilloux, was not doing his job the way he should have been and may have been breaking several rules that came with his job, and as part of that he was somehow taking advantage of Tara. Raz, who saw through this, had interceded on Tara's behalf, and as Seth understood the situation, was trying to get mister Guilloux to confess what he was doing to them. The only thing that he still couldn't understand was Tara's part in all of this. Sure, she had problems with her mail, but she had always been smart, so surely she must have known what was going on as well. If she did, then why hadn't she said anything yet?

"S-sir," mister Guilloux eventually spoke. "This business is not necessarily-" Before he could say any more Raz suddenly slammed his hand onto his desk.

"I'm sorry, what?" Raz uttered before he could finish. "I just asked you a simple question, one that you should be able to answer easily. Why aren't you?" A few more seconds of silence passed before Raz continued. "Come on, either you're a scumbag who's shit at their job or you're into something illegal. One of those will get you thrown in a cell, the other will just get you demoted! So which is it!"

Before Raz, mister Guillox, Tara, or Seth could say or even think anything more they were all suddenly cut off by the sounds of footsteps coming from the door. Like lightning they all turned their heads to see who was there and the sight they beheld caused every single one of them to instantly freeze where they stood, or sat in the case of Tara and mister Guilloux. To Seth, the person he saw seemed largely out of place compared to literally every single person Seth had seen in this city. At least every single person he had seen thus far.

Chapter 11

Vivian's eyes slowly creeped open as a single strand of sunlight broke through the exceedingly faded curtains of her cheap hotel room with its oddly specific target being her face. Unable to fall back to sleep, she instead let out a loud, almost growl-like groan as she sat up from the old, worn mattress that served as her bed. It made a loud creaking noise whenever she shifted her weight on it, though since renting out this room she had learned to ignore it. She sat there for several long seconds doing nothing but blinking as her eyes adjusted to the light of the room, which even with the thick curtains pulled over the window was still too much light for her tastes. If there was anything at all to see in this room then perhaps things would have been different, but alas, the space that beheld Vivian's eyes once her vision had cleared was less than half of the space that her shack in Canaan had offered, and all that was in it were four walls and the old mattress. A scurrying sound echoed from somewhere in the ceiling above her, a sound that she had also become accustomed to hearing after her multiple attempts to quickly fall asleep the previous night, as she stood up from her mattress.

With the only pieces of cloth covering her being the loose tank top and shorts that she had fallen asleep in, Vivian reached as high as she could towards the ceiling and stretched out her back as she let out another loud groan. After a few not so subtle cracks echoed through the room she let her arms fall back to her sides before smacking herself in the face a few times in an attempt to fully wake herself up.

"So this is how you wanna start out your last fucking day of the fucking year, eh," Vivian spoke aloud to no one as her eyes fell on the only suitcase she had brought with her to this city. "Almost naked in a fucking cheap hotel room without having booze as an excuse." As she spoke she sat back down onto the old mattress before reaching over to grab her suitcase and pulling it towards her. "And fucking Ingrid demanding that I 'look professional'. Let's see how professional you'll look when I have one of those fucking rings." As she ranted Vivian opened up her suitcase and without taking much time to look, took out a few articles of clothing and threw them onto the mattress next to her before diving right back in, seemingly in the hopes of finding something specific. "Hopefully that bitch doesn't drop dead before that happens. I need to rub it in her face when it does." As she finished speaking her fingers found something in her suitcase that was colder than cloth.

Feeling that, a confident smile slowly grew across her face as she pulled out the bronze bracelet of her guild. The symbol of the shield with the hourglass on the front and the two crossed swords behind it seemed to stare back up at her despite its obvious lack of eyes as simply holding it invigorated Vivian more than any cup of coffee could.

"Because I am motherfucking Vivian Beatrice Hawks," Vivian then said to herself as she slipped the metal bracelet onto her wrist. "Third generation monster hunter, and you can't take that from me. No matter how hard you try you fucking bitch. This year will be better than the last. Just need to get through today. Then after that it'll only be uphill from here."

After a cold bath, a change of clothes, and running a hand through her hair using the reflection in the blade of her sword as a mirror because the cheap as sin hotel room she had decided to stay in didn't have one, Vivian set out into the city of Dis. While the task of making one's way through Dis would have been annoying at any other time of the year, with the New Year's Festival going on and all of the tourists and merchants that now packed the streets, even the simple act of trying to get anywhere in this city had gone from annoying to frustrating. The festival had not even technically begun yet, but already Vivian saw plenty of people celebrating the fact that tomorrow would be the year Three-Hundred and Fifty-Seven After Solaris with food, drink, and music. The only solace that Vivian could take from this as she made her way through the city was that she didn't have to suffer a hangover along with it. She could hardly blame or judge any of them, however, as she knew perfectly well that she was more than likely going to be joining them the instant her business had concluded.

After several long, long minutes of walking Vivian finally found the building she had been looking for. It was made of stone, like every single other building in Dis was. However, this one in particular was much larger and had its own, more unique look compared to the buildings surrounding it. Standing fifteen meters across and three stories in height, the stone that composed this building's surface was not completely smooth, but rather was carved and molded to resemble pillars, each one while initially appearing smooth, bore the image of a different type of monstrous creature crawling up it only for it to meet its end before it could even reach the second story. Some of the images portrayed were of a large wolf with a spear shoved through its head, a long serpent riddled with arrows, and a gigantic, aquatic creature with many tentacled limbs being blasted through by what looked like a ray from the sun. Each of these pillars were separated by windows, and the two closest to the center of the building framed the over three meters tall, dark wood double doors that made up the building's entrance. Above the tall doors, carved into the stone itself, was the symbol of a shield with an hourglass on the front and two crossed swords behind it, and framing that, also carved into the stone were the words "Futura Collegium Aureum".

With that sight in front of her, Vivian closed her eyes and took in a long, deep breath before she then spurned herself forward and pushed the doors open. Inside Vivian was overjoyed to see that the inside of this place had not changed at all since the last time she had set foot in it. The sight that greeted her upon entering was that of a single, large, open room that spanned almost the entire length and width of the building. Spread out amongst the room were many tables, some long and rectangular, some shorter and round, but nearly all of them were filled up with many different people of varying builds, skin tones, and creeds. At first glance the majority of the people here looked as if they wouldn't have been caught dead in the same building as each other, let alone room, as some were roguishly handsome and wore armor, some wore simple leathers and looked little different from common street thugs, and others wore simple clothes much like Vivian and looked more or less like normal people. The one feature that they all shared, however, was that on their wrists they all wore the same metal bracelet that Vivian had. Some were bronze like her's, many more of them were silver, and a small handful of them were gold, but all of them had the same design and all bore the symbol of the guild.

Some of them looked to be getting an early start on the upcoming festivities as a few of the assembled groups all had tankards of ale either nearby or were in the process of drinking them while their brothers in arms either cheered them on or simply watched in merriment. Two people at one of the far tables even looked to be having a drinking contest. Even with that the torrent of noise from the near constant chatter between all of the assembled groups made it difficult to pick up on anything that was actually happening. Vivian didn't blame any of them for their early start, in fact she fully intended on joining some of them after her business here had concluded, but only after.

Vivian did her best not to pay anyone any mind as she walked past everybody towards the back, though a few interesting characters and stories did catch her attention. There was one man who looked skinny enough to be able to run through a thunderstorm without getting wet and had a mustache that was so thick that it looked more like a caterpillar the size of a croissant. He seemed to be recounting to his friends about how he had recently taken down a large, bird-like monster before he chugged down what looked to be his third tankard of ale. There was also another man who sat at one of the tables in the far corner of the room eating what looked to be a breakfast steak and some eggs, his only companions being a large falcon that sat on his shoulder and a dog that was laying on the floor next to him. He was one of the few in the room who wore a gold bracelet. Then there was a gigantic, stone wall of a man who was covered in so many scars that his arms and face resembled reptilian scales more than human skin. He was one of the people having the drinking contest with what looked to be a young, blonde woman who was less than half his size in both height and girth. Despite her disadvantage in size, however, the number of empty tankards next to her vastly outnumbered his. Vivian couldn't help but smirk at that woman's impending victory.

Vivian passed by the drinking contest without a second thought as she made her way towards the back of the room where an incredibly long wooden desk took up almost the entire length of the room. To the left of it on one end of the room stood a door to what Vivian knew to be the back room while to the right was a staircase leading to the upper floors, where Vivian also knew that the private meeting rooms and offices were. On the wall behind the desk, as if framed by the room itself, was an actual shield bearing the symbol of an hourglass with two crossed swords behind it. The guild's emblem, made real.

Vivian then turned her attention to the only man currently at the desk, a skinny man with brown hair who looked to be a bit younger than Vivian herself. By comparison to some of the others in the guild hall, his clothes were much nicer, consisting mainly of a collared shirt and a dark red vest that had a badge of the guild's logo stitched onto the right breast. Vivian didn't need to see his clothes, however, to know that he clearly wasn't a monster hunter. He didn't seem to notice Vivian as she approached, as his attention was currently focused on a stack of papers next to him while he muttered incoherently to himself and scribbled down notes on a separate piece of paper with a quill that he appeared to be grasping a little too tightly to be comfortable.

Vivian stood by and waited for a few moments for him to notice her. After a full minute of him not even bothering to look up, however, Vivian decided to take a more direct approach as she let out a loud cough. The sudden noise caused the man at the desk to nearly jump out of his chair in shock as he almost knocked over the bottle of ink onto his papers. Thankfully, by only the hair on the back of his hand, he missed and his papers remained unscathed. That did not stop him from looking up at Vivian with a dagger-like glare of self contained rage, however.

"Can I help you?" the man asked in a voice that was surprisingly deep for his build. He didn't even bother to raise his voice over the rowdy patrons of the guild hall, as if he did so in some vain attempt to avoid being heard by her.

"Nice to see you again too, Omar," Vivian responded, ignoring his glaring eyes and obvious frustration. "I'm here for my meeting with the big three." Despite how straightforward her words had seemed, the guild receptionist, Omar, raised a quizzical eyebrow at her. After a few moments of silently staring at her like this Omar turned around to look at something, and it was only then that Vivian noticed the tall, fancy looking grandfather clock pressed up against the wall by the staircase.

"Wow," he said with obvious sarcasm in his voice. "You're actually early. Looks like Ingrid owes your uncle ten silver." Vivian wanted to say something in response to that, she really, really did, but in the end decided not to just in case one of them happened to be listening in. She knew from past experience that they had done that sometimes.

"So what then?" Vivian then asked. "Am I supposed to just sit here and twiddle my thumbs until it's my turn?"

"Yes," was all Omar said in response before returning to his paperwork. Knowing that she would get nothing else out of him, Vivian took that as a sign to turn around and find a spot to patiently wait her turn, but not before her eyes fell upon the grandfather clock again. Curious, as she didn't remember it being there the last time she had been here, Vivian left Omar and walked over towards it to get a closer look. Its sleek, shiny silver color and unstained glass that was as clear as day and showed the pendulum swinging within it betrayed the signs of a recent addition to the guild.

"I recommend that you don't touch that," Omar's voice echoed from where he sat as Vivian quickly looked over to see that he hadn't even looked up from his paperwork.

"I wasn't planning to," Vivian responded, more than a little irritated at the fact that he didn't even look at her when he spoke.

"Good," Omar responded in kind, still not bothering to look up from his paperwork. "Because that clock is worth more than everything you own. Including yourself."

"The fuck's that supposed to mean?" Vivian then asked, now more offended than irritated.

"It means that we spent far too much money on that Solaris damned clock when we could have bought a simpler one that could have been mounted to the wall," Omar responded, still not looking up from his paperwork. "But as I'm sure you know, nobody listens to Omar. You know, the person who manages practically everything in this place because everyone whose actual job it is says they have better things to do." Even from where she stood Vivian could feel the annoyance of everything he had just said radiating off of him. As much as she wanted to hit back at him with a clever comeback, she still knew that doing so here would be a bad idea. So she instead ducked away from the desk without saying another word.

Vivian then quickly found an empty seat at the first empty table she saw, which fortunately for her was at the end of one of the long dining tables at the end of the guild hall. Hopefully nobody would bother her here while she waited. Hopefully. She contemplated grabbing something to drink herself, since she knew that she might have to wait awhile given Omar's words, but then thought better about it as she realized that she probably was being watched. As she sat there her eyes wandered about the guild hall a bit more, which allowed her to pick up on updates and recent happenings from those around her. News that interested her, unfortunately, did not travel to Canaan as often as she would have liked.

Caterpillar-stache had never stopped talking and while Vivian was too far away from him to have even the slightest idea of what he was saying, she was able to easily see how the people around him were reacting. Most of them seemed to not be as interested as they were before and some of them were even rolling their eyes before walking away. The only thing that Vivian could guess had happened was that whatever tale Caterpillar-stache had been spinning about his adventures must have been too outlandish for any of them to believe.

She then drew her attention over towards the beastmaster. However, the only thing that he was doing was placing his plate, which still had roughly a third of his breakfast steak left on it, onto the floor next to him. Within seconds of him doing so the dog scarfed it down.

'*I wonder if the falcon got any,*' Vivian couldn't help but wonder. '*Wait, do falcons even eat steak? I mean they eat rats, snakes, and smaller birds, right? It's not like a falcon could pick up a cow and eat it but if it could it probably would. Steak is fucking delicious after all.*'

With those thoughts wrapped up Vivian then diverted her eyes in the direction of the day-drinking contest, and it seemed that the man with all of the scars had long since passed out. Either that or he was crying and wasn't man enough to show it. The only thing that Vivian could tell from what she was able to see was that his face was pressed down onto the table with only four empty tankards nearby. The smaller woman, however, had seven empty tankards next to her along with an eighth in hand and was standing on her chair so that she could reach over the table and pat the man with all of the scars on the head with her free hand. The bronze guild bracelet that she wore was very visible to Vivian as she did so. Seeing this woman stand on the chair like she was made Vivian realize exactly how small this woman actually was. While before it was easy to see that she was simply shorter than the man with all the scars, now Vivian could see that she was only about a meter tall, give or take a few centimeters. If Vivian didn't know any better she would have easily assumed that she was a child.

'*She has to be a newbie,*' Vivian thought to herself. '*I've never seen her around here before and I think I would remember someone as tiny as her. Even while drunk. I wonder what she can do?*' Vivian took a few silent moments to contemplate that before she reached what she thought was a conclusion. '*Gotta be a mage or some shit like that. I mean being towered over by Agatha doesn't make you seem like any kind of fighter and we don't just let any fucker with a weapon in. Unless they've softened up the membership requirements since I was last here. That'll be fucking bullshit if they did. Then again maybe she uses a bow, or knives, or some kind of light weapon. Being that small she's probably pretty quick.*' Vivian couldn't help but laugh to herself as a humorous thought, to her at least, entered her mind. '*Fuck it, if she's part of a team then she's probably bait for the monsters so the other, bigger guys can take it out. Hit and run. Actually now that I think about it that's not-'*

"Well, I'm surprised to see you here. It's been a while, Hawks," a nasally voice that was higher pitched than anything that could sound natural broke Vivian out of her thoughts. She, unfortunately, recognized it immediately and on instinct couldn't help but close her eyes, if only to delay actually having to acknowledge its owner for a few brief moments longer. "Ah, what's the matter? Monster rip your tongue out or something?" Vivian couldn't help but let out a loud groan in response to that as she opened her eyes back up to behold the sight that she knew was waiting for her.

Standing across from her at the long dining table was a tall, thin, yet still well built dark-skinned man with very nicely groomed, slicked back black hair, cold brown eyes, and the kind of smirk someone would wear if they had just gotten laid and wanted to brag about it. His obnoxious clothing consisted of a long, mustard yellow coat, a pair of tan cargo pants with a lot of pockets, a matching pair of leather gloves, and a shiny pair of boots that looked as if they had only recently been acquired. What's more, Vivian could also see that he wore at least a dozen knives on his person, with six strapped to his chest, two on his belt, two on his arms, and two on his legs. Knowing him, however, Vivian was certain that he had many more on his person somewhere. The last thing that Vivian noticed about him, however, was the gold guild bracelet attached to his wrist, as with the color of his coat it almost blended into it. Were it not so shiny, Vivian might not have even noticed it at all.

"What the fuck do you want, Arthur?" Vivian said as she blinked and diverted her eyes away from him. The mere act of looking at him made her cringe on the inside.

"Ah, what's with the attitude?" the obnoxiously dressed man, Arthur, replied. "Is it a crime to say hello to an old friend?" There was an obvious layer of sarcasm in how he used the word 'friend' when he said it. Before Vivian could say anything about it, however, Arthur suddenly took the empty seat directly across from her. "So what are you in town for? Are you finally being promoted to gold or... Wait a second, what's that?" While he sounded surprised, Vivian could easily tell that he was faking it as he pointed to her bronze bracelet. "That's weird. I could've sworn that we were both silver the last time we spoke. What happened there?"

"You know damned fucking well what happened," Vivian responded with a glare. Inside of her head, however, the words in her thoughts were very different.

'Give me an excuse. Please, Solaris, give me a fucking excuse and I'll strangle this motherfucker right here!'

"Oh that's right!" Arthur spoke as if he had suddenly remembered. "That giant flying lizard. The one that could shoot lightning out of its mouth. The one that burned down the city of Eden because you failed to kill it. Remind me because I forgot…" He then paused for a moment as he rested his head in his hand, his smug grin widening as he did. "How many people died that night?" The instant those words hit her ears, whatever had been holding Vivian back shattered as she quickly stood up from her seat, more than eager to wipe that smug grin off of his face. However, he was faster than her, as before she could make even a single move he simply held up a single finger with his opposite hand. "I can see that you're getting aggressive Hawks. So unnecessary. If you don't want to fill me in on all the juicy details about how you ended up in that boony town you're currently in, I can tell you what I've been up to instead." Before Vivian could say anything he dropped his finger as his smug grin widened enough to show his pearly white teeth. "Unless you really do wanna find out right here if you've gotten quicker than me since the last time we spoke. If that's what you really want then by all means, go ahead. I'm not stopping you."

Several painfully long moments of silence passed as Vivian and Arthur stayed where they were with their eyes locked on each other. Vivian really did want more than anything to grab that smug bastard by his hair and slam his head into the table until he stopped talking. She really, really did, but her common sense got the better of her as two very important realizations dawned on her. Firstly, because she knew Arthur she knew for a fact that she was a better fighter than he was, but only a better fighter. She knew how he fought and knew there was a reason he mainly used knives, and as such she also knew that he was right. While she was better than him, she wasn't faster than him, and on the draw a knife was always quicker than a sword, especially this close. Secondly, and more importantly, she knew from experience that trying anything here, especially against a fellow guild member would incur extremely heavy consequences. Especially with what she had come here to do. So, knowing fully well that she had been defeated before the battle had even started, Vivian slumped her shoulders, looked down at the table in front of her, and fell back into her chair.

"That's what I thought," Arthur said as he picked his head up off of his hand

and leaned back in his chair. "Anyway, as I was saying…"

"Do I look like I give a fuck, you turd with a mouth?" Vivian snapped back with venom in her words as she reluctantly looked back up at him.

"Well, as you can see. I got promoted to gold six months ago," Arthur continued, ignoring Vivian's insult. "Got quite a few jobs since then. Built up quite a reputation for myself. I've even gotten my own apprentice."

"Good for you," Vivian snarled back at him as her eyes fell back onto the table in front of her.

"It is good for me," Arthur responded. "If I can show how good of a leader I am then at this rate I'm sure to be first in line for the position of guild leader. Once the position becomes available of course. Hell, who knows. I might even end up replacing that uncle of yours." Vivian's only response to that was to instantly look back up at him with another death fueled glare before another voice caught her attention.

"Vivian! You're up!" Omar's voice suddenly called out very loudly from the reception desk. Across from her, Arthur simply sat where he was with that smug grin still on his face, as if waiting to see what she would do.

"We're done here," was all Vivian said before she stood up from her chair and walked as quickly as she could towards the staircase.

"Good luck!" Arthur shouted with a wave of his hand. Vivian responded in kind by sticking up her middle finger at him as she stormed off to her meeting.

The room wherein the three leaders of the Futura Collegium Aureum monster hunting guild sat and judged all aspiring guild members who were up for promotion was more than familiar to Vivian, as she had been in it many times before. That fact, however, did nothing at all to wash away any of the nerves that she was doing her damndest to hide. Dull and gray cobblestone lined the floor and walls. The same stone was used for the three steps that lead up to the elevated, horseshoe shaped platform that ran roughly two thirds the circumference of the round room. A long, desk-like, dark wooden table that was made specifically for that platform lined the entire length of it. The only decoration in the room was a painting that was hung on the far wall by a custom frame made specifically for the round stone walls of the room.

  The painting itself depicted three people standing outside of the guild hall the day it had been completed. Vivian, of course, knew who each of those three people were. They were none other than the founders of the Futura Collegium Aureum guild and its original leaders. In the center with his arms crossed was a tan, muscular man with long brown hair that he kept tied back into a ponytail. He wore a full suit of armor, minus the helmet of course to show off his powerful, chiseled features, including his strong chin. This man was Alejandro Ortiz. To his left stood a dark skinned woman with frizzy hair, glasses, and more freckles on her face than Vivian had ever bothered to count. The expression she wore was of a soft smile as she pointed her right index finger upwards to show off a green light that emanated from it. This woman's name was Dominique Mambwe. However, Vivian also knew that was only the name she went by when this painting had been commissioned, as a year and a half later she would be known by all those that knew the history of the guild, and indeed all of the Solaran Empire, as Dominique Ortiz. To the right of Alejandro stood the third and final founding member of the guild, a shorter man, or at least he appeared short next to Alejandro. He was pale skinned, possessed bright, but shaggy red hair, and wore a jubilant, toothy smile on his face. The painting did an amazing job of hiding it, but Vivian knew for a fact that he bore a large burn scar that ran the entire length of his right arm. The reason for that could be seen in the fact that much more detail and prominence was given to the unsheathed sword that he had resting up against his left shoulder. The very same sword that currently hung at Vivian's side. This man was none other than Lance Campanelli, but to Vivian, for the handful of times she got to see him before he passed away, he had been known as something else, "grandpa".

  While Vivian did admire this painting and all of the people in it, the guild leaders of the past were not what concerned her right now. No, the source of her anxiety was in fact the three other people in the room with her. The guild's current leaders.

  The first two were the ones she had expected to see. To the right of where she currently sat, which happened to be the center of the horseshoe shaped platform so that the eyes of all three guild leaders were on her, was a large man who at first glance looked to be overweight, but Vivian knew for a fact that anyone who dared to attack him would quickly find out that there wasn't an ounce of fat on him, only muscle. He also possessed long hair as well as a beard that was equally as long, which gave him a lion-like appearance. Vivian also noticed that while his great mane of hair and beard were still mostly red, the scars of the never ending battle against time were beginning to show as many gray hairs were beginning to sneak in amongst the jungle of red. The last noticeable thing about him were the spotted burn scars from years working in the forge that were along his hands and forearms. This man was none other than Leonardo Campanelli, but to Vivian he had always been "Uncle Lee".

Directly in front of her, however, was someone who, to Vivian at least, stood for the opposite of everything that her uncle did. She was a pale and slender woman, but her eyes portrayed the appearance of a snake about to bite down on an unsuspecting mouse as she stared, unblinking, at Vivian, as if waiting for her to twitch first like she knew she would. She sat silently as she waited with her elbows resting on the table and her fingers interlocked with each other, and because of that Vivian couldn't see much of her wrinkled face. Despite that, however, Vivian knew that she had to be grimacing at her, as it was next to impossible for her to imagine this woman with any other expression. This, Vivian knew, was none other than Ingrid Braunstein.

The thing about her that threw Vivian off, however, was the fact that she was sitting in the horseshoe shaped desk's center chair. As far back as Vivian could remember Ingrid had always sat in the chair to the left. This time, however, that chair was occupied by a man who, unlike the other two, wore full plate armor as opposed to any type of normal clothing. He also looked to be quite a bit younger than the other two. By Vivian's best guess he looked to either be in his very late thirties or early forties, which didn't sound young, but by comparison Vivian knew that her uncle Lee was pushing fifty and Ingrid had long since passed that. His face didn't look that special, as he possessed plainly styled, short, black hair and possessed dark tan skin. However, it was the combination of those two features that led Vivian to realize exactly who this man was, as she had done her share of jobs with him when she had first joined the guild.

"Piers!" Vivian couldn't help but exclaim. "What are you doing there? Wait, did Ale-"

"Oh, don't worry," Piers interrupted her as he held up a hand to prevent her from saying any more. "My father is still with us. He simply chose to retire when he turned eighty last month and I was chosen to take his place."

"Eighty?" Vivian could scarcely believe it. "Shit, he stuck around for that long? Well, if you get the chance, tell him I said hi."

"I'll be sure to do so," was all Piers said in response before a sudden cough from Ingrid diverted everyone's attention.

"It would seem that you've already forgotten why you're here, Miss Hawks," Ingrid said to Vivian with a particular bitterness in her voice. Especially when she spoke her last name.

"Of course I haven't," Vivian answered as she did her best to match Ingrid's glare with her own. Unfortunately for her, however, Ingrid didn't even blink as she, with agonizing slowness, opened up a leather bound folder on the table in front of her.

"We sent you to the town of Canaan two years ago," Ingrid began without looking back up at her. "And in that time we have received six confirmed minor incidents involving monsters that you took care of, one of them being questionable at best, and two major monster attacks." As Ingrid finished speaking her eyes slowly rose back up to meet Vivian's. As she did Vivian also saw a twisted grimace begin to appear on her face, something that proved to Vivian that her theory about Ingrid had been correct.

"The second of which we only received the report for yesterday," Leonardo chimed in. "And while the report states that the two monsters that attacked the town were killed with no casualties and only a few notable injuries to the town's civilian population, it also states that both monsters were killed by members of Canaan's town watch. One full time member and one volunteer." At the sound of those words Vivian watched as the grimace Ingrid wore grew into a very sinister looking smirk.

"Care to explain to us why you weren't the one to protect the people of Canaan in that particular incident?" Ingrid asked, making no effort at all to hide the smile that was now plastered on her face.

"Those two simply managed to kill them first," Vivian responded with a shrug. "It's not like I wasn't there doing my part."

"It is, however, your job to kill any monsters that enter the town or city you are stationed in," Ingrid said as soon as Vivian had finished speaking.

"It's also part of the town watch's job isn't it?" Vivian spat back. "That's why they're there. Personally I think that incident shows that Canaan is in good hands and that they don't need me or any one of us there. They seem like they can easily take care of themselves." Piers simply nodded at that statement, which caused Ingird's smile to drop almost immediately as she returned to the scowl that she had been wearing before.

"Very well," Ingrid hissed. "However, that being said, the incident last week is not a subject of any concern to us. Miss Hawks, as the subject of this meeting is your prospective return to the rank of silver, would you care to enlighten us as to what exactly happened earlier this year on the Tenth of Promethuit?" A feeling of cold dread and regret instantly filled the pit of Vivian's stomach as Ingrid read out that date. "The report that we received states that on that night Canaan was attacked by one large monster and many smaller ones. While each of them were confirmed killed, that wasn't until after the deaths of one town watch member and five civilians." Ingird then paused for a moment as she glanced over towards Leonardo. "Leo, if you wouldn't mind. Please read to your darling niece the names of exactly who she failed."

Leonardo's only response to that was to let out a small sigh before he opened an identical leather bound folder in front of him, pulled out one of the pages and began to read from it.

"Aiden McCarthy," Leonardo began, and Vivian couldn't help but shiver as his face instantly flashed in front of her eyes the instant his name had been said. "Eaten by a large, bipedal monster with a face like a deer. Carol Trout, torn apart by spined wolf-like monsters. Richard Robins, torn apart by spined, wolf-like monsters in front of his wife and child… unnecessary detail."

"Keep reading," Ingrid spoke up once he had hesitated.

Vivian only barely heard her uncle as she sat in her chair and listened to him read out the rest of the names of the people who died that night as well as the incessantly brutal ways in which they had met their ends. The thing that bothered her the most, however, was that with the exception of Aiden, she didn't recognize any of them. It was only now, as she was hearing their names spoken aloud, that she realized how five other people had died that night and it didn't change anything at all about her daily life, and that thought disturbed her greatly. She'd never heard the end of Aiden's death from Maryen, Charlie, and especially Joseph, but none of the other names had been mentioned to her even once. It made her wonder. Did the people of Canaan not blame her for any of those deaths? Did they blame her, but nobody ever said anything to her face? Did they simply accept that they were gone and moved on? Did they just happen to be the five most hated people in that town? Vivian didn't know, and it only dawned upon her as that realization washed over her that now she might never know.

"Well, Miss Hawks," Ingrid spoke up once Leonardo had finished reading out the list of victims from that incident. "What's your excuse?" Vivian could not help but lower her head in shame. She still remembered that day, she remembered every detail, she knew that everything they were saying was true, and because of all of that she also knew that she had no good excuse to give them.

"If you want to blame me for Aiden's death, that's fine," Vivian eventually said to break the silence. "I'll admit it. I fucked up. Trust me, I know I fucked up. You're not the first people who I've said this to. I still have to say it to nearly everyone in Canaan because they won't let me forget it. Everyone else though..." There was a long pause before Vivian could continue. "At the time I didn't even know there were any other monsters in the fucking town, and even if I did, I had my hands full with the big guy."

"A monster hunter shouldn't let anyone die," Ingrid spat back as soon as Vivian had finished speaking. The words pierced through her like the spear that Vivian knew Ingrid had wielded in her youth.

"I'm only one woman!" Vivian shouted at the top of her lungs as she lifted her head back up, which took the guild leaders aback. "What do you expect from me! To be able to run around the entire fucking town and kill several monsters at once without a single person dying! Maybe if I was a mage and could teleport, sure I would understand, but even then that is a bit too much to ask! I shouldn't be punished or chastised for not being able to do something that fucking none of you could have done!" Vivian then directed her full attention towards Ingrid, the contempt in her eyes was obvious to everyone. "None of you could have done it! Not one of the people outside in the main hall could have done it! None of the founders even in their prime could have done it! Fucking Solaris, my mother couldn't have even fucking done it!"

"Amanda has nothing to do with this!" Ingrid shouted back as she slapped her hands on the desk and shot up from her chair. Her outburst was loud enough that there was little doubt that everyone in the main hall downstairs could have heard it.

"You're right, she doesn't!" Vivian shouted back at her. "But I know that if she were in my position all you would have done was give her a slap on the wrist at worst!"

"If she were here she would be the one in that chair instead of Piers!" Ingrid then shouted as she pointed directly at him. The instant those words left his mouth, however, Pier's head snapped over in her direction. The contempt in his eyes was enough to match Vivian's.

"And what's that supposed to mean?" He asked Ingrid as calmly as he could manage. "Do you think I didn't earn this position?" As soon as Pier's words reached her ears Ingrid instantly realized her mistake as she dropped her eyes back down towards the desk in front of her and pinched the bridge of her nose.

"You're reading too much into this," she responded to what Piers had said.

"I don't think I am," Piers continued. "Do you want to tell us all what you really think, Ingrid? Do you think my father played favorites with me or something? You know him better than that, you know that he never did that with anyone. Especially his own children. Oh, and I seem to recall that all three of you had a say in-"

"Enough!" Leonardo roared as he slammed his fist onto the desk as hard as he could. This not only effectively silenced the other two guild leaders, but made it clear that he would absolutely win any shouting matches that they got into. "Whatever squabbles the two of you have can wait. We're not here to discuss either of you." As soon as he had finished speaking Piers took a deep breath to calm himself as Ingrid slowly fell back into her chair with her face in her hands, evidently too embarrassed to look at either of them. "As you so eloquently said, Ingrid, my late sister is irrelevant to our current topic of conversation. However, with the intent of getting us all back on track I feel the need to ask if someone else is." Vivian, who still had not fully recovered from her previous emotional outburst, could only raise an eyebrow at that.

"Who?" She couldn't help but ask.

"In Sheriff Russel's reports," Leonardo continued. "I noticed that someone by the name of Seth comes up quite consistently. Would you please explain to us who he is and how he is relevant to any of this?" The image of Seth's face flashed in Vivian's mind the instant his name was brought up, particularly the image of him showing her and Agatha his red eyes. That then quickly transitioned into how the rest of that meeting played out, particularly with her pinning him to the floor and then him biting her neck in retaliation. A searing, boiling rage began to bubble up inside of Vivian's mind as those memories came flooding back to her. Nevertheless, however, she did her best to remain calm.

"He was a civilian who decided to play hero and attempted to help me fight that giant deer headed monster," Vivian answered. "Dumb bastard nearly got himself killed. He was lucky that I was there to save his dumb ass. After that night he decided to join the town watch and Charlie forced me to teach him to fight as punishment for my mistake."

"I don't think he has the authority to make you train one of his watchmen," Piers commended with his own raised eyebrow.

"Maybe not," Vivian responded. "But if he didn't then I'm certain that all three of you would be bitching about how I didn't receive any form punishment for my fuck up. Anyways, I trained him, like Charlie asked, and now he's part of the town watch. He was actually one of the two that killed one of the monsters in the attack last week. So to answer your question, Uncle Lee, he's not important."

"Very well," Leonardo then said as he returned his attention to his two colleagues. "Unless either of you have any other grievances you would like to make known to my niece, I think we've discussed everything important that is relevant to the topic at hand." As he spoke that last part his eyes shot directly to Ingrid, who dared not look back at him. "Agreed?" Piers only nodded while Ingrid went back to staring daggers at Vivian.

"Agreed," Ingrid muttered.

"Good," Leonardo spoke up. "Vivian, is there anything at all you wish to add before we move on?" Vivian opened her mouth to respond, but after thinking through everything that had been said to her since she had walked into this room she realized that nothing she could say would change any of their minds, for she could see that they were already made up. With that in mind she simply took in a deep breath before responding.

"No," was all she said to them.

"Very well then," Leonardo said to his niece. "If you really do have nothing else to say then would you please step outside so that we might discuss all of the information relevant to the topic at hand amongst ourselves." As he said those words Vivian could see Leonardo shoot his own death fueled glare towards Ingrid, which she could clearly see, but did not react to. "We will send for you when you are needed again. So we would ask that you please do not wander too far." Vivian didn't say anything more to any of them as she stood up from her chair and walked out of the room as quickly as she could.

The second the large, wooden door was shut behind her Vivian could hear the three guild leaders begin to speak amongst themselves, though it was nearly impossible to make out any of their exact words. As much as Vivian really, really wanted to know what the three of them could possibly have to discuss that they couldn't say in front of her, she knew better than to ask. She already knew before coming here that she wouldn't get Ingrid's vote, so the last thing she wanted was to piss off her uncle or Piers. The fact that he was the one sitting in that chair now instead of his father was still something of a shock to her, though after thinking about it for a while she supposed that it had to happen at some point. She just didn't expect it to happen so soon.

The rest of the guild hall was little more than a blur to Vivian as she threaded through the halls and down the stairs before she ended back in the main hall on the first floor.

"So how did it go?" Omar asked from the front desk. At the sound of his voice Vivian looked over to see that he had apparently finished his paperwork and was instead leaning on the desk and staring directly at her, apparently bored.

"Not sure," was the only thing Vivian could bring herself to say to him.

"I'll give you credit for making Ingrid scream loud enough for us to hear down here," Omar then said to her with a shrug as he pulled out a book from beneath the desk and opened it. "I mean, it only happens eighty-seven times a day." Despite the obvious ill intentions of that comment Vivian couldn't help but smirk to herself at it. At least she could take solace in that one little thing, even if it wasn't much.

Vivian wasn't sure at all how much time had passed since she had been asked to leave the room, but it felt like it had been longer than an hour. She had considered waiting in the main hall of the guild where she had before, but in the end decided not to as she didn't want to deal with anyone in there right now, especially Arthur. Instead she had opted to leave the guild hall and walk around into the alley to her left. There wasn't anything there to see except for the wall of the building next to the guild hall. When she was younger, however, the building next to the guild hall hadn't been there, instead the space was occupied by an open area that served as a park, but many of the younger monster hunters and recruits used the space for sparring or exercise grounds, and many of the children who came by to play in that park did so so that they might watch and admire them. That included Vivian herself as there used to be a bench in the exact spot where she stood where she would take breaks in between sparring sessions when she was a recruit herself.

That was years ago now, and that bench had long since been removed as it served no purpose anymore. Instead all there was was the two buildings and the shade they provided. So, with nothing else to do, Vivian leaned back against the wall where the bench used to be and then slid down it until she was sitting on the dirt. As she sat there with only the sound of the passing civilians to keep her occupied she thought over the words that each of the three guild leaders had said to her, and about all of the events of the past year that they had brought up to her. As she did a feeling of boiling rage began to build up in her gut as she grit her teeth harder and harder. She wasn't angry at what had happened, or at anyone else, for she didn't blame any of them. No, the reason she was angry was because deep down she knew that everything they had said to her was true, and that there was nothing she could say or do to change any of it now, and that she had no one to blame for them but herself. Herself and her own fuck up.

As she sat there grinding her teeth together the events of the night of the tenth of Promethuit played out in her mind again. Her arrival, her fight with the large deer skulled monster, seeing Aiden die, the realization that five more people she didn't even know about had died that night with him, and how the only thing that had saved her from getting herself crushed to death was the intervention of that dumbass, Seth, when he decided to play hero and fight the thing for her. That last thought led in turn to all of the events that had happened afterwards. Getting chewed out by Charlie for her fuck up, getting chewed out by the mayor and all of the town watchmen, and being ordered to train Seth to replace Aiden. Vivian couldn't help but grind her teeth together even harder as his face appeared in her head again. All of the training sessions they had, all of the mistakes he had made and all that she had taught him, she remembered it all, and every last thought filled her with more and more boiling rage. All of it culminated in the image of her pinning Seth to the floor with his red eyes staring in confused desperation back up at her. A stare that then shifted into a mixture of sadness, betrayal and then ultimately rage before he sunk his teeth into her neck.

"Fuck!" Vivian couldn't help but scream at the top of her lungs as she picked up something solid, she didn't even look to see what it was, and without standing back up threw it as hard as she could against the wall in front of her. Unfortunately, the thing she had picked up and thrown turned out to be a chip from one of the buildings that had weathered away with time, and upon hitting the wall opposite her it didn't shatter, as she had hoped it would, but instead bounced off of the wall as hard as it was thrown and hit her directly on her forehead. "Ow!" Vivian screamed as she held her head with both of her hands. "Motherfuck... fucker! Ow!"

"I thought I would find you here," Omar's voice suddenly rang out as Vivian looked up to see him standing there in the alleyway with her. "I'm only here to tell you that the big three are asking for you again. I wouldn't keep them waiting." Then, having said that, as soon as he had appeared Omar turned around and walked towards the front of the building and back into the guild hall. As much as Vivian dreaded what she knew was coming for her should she walk back through those doors, especially after her little incident just now, she knew that Omar was also right. Keeping the three of them waiting would be worse for her than staying here. So with great reluctance, she stood up from the dirt, dusted herself off and followed Omar's steps back into the guild hall.

The inside of the guild hall was again little more than a blur to Vivian as she walked directly past everyone in the main hall and up the stairs. She didn't even see if Arthur was still there, but if he was he hadn't said anything, or perhaps he did and Vivian had automatically ignored him. Either way it didn't matter to her, not now. Eventually when she reached the door to the meeting room on the third floor it seemingly opened by itself as she approached. Upon inspection, however, that wasn't the case at all as she could clearly see Piers on the inside as he had just finished a hand waving motion.

Without saying a single word Vivian stepped back into the meeting room and took her seat, and as she did with another wave of Pier's hand the door closed by itself behind her. Now that she was back in here Vivian could feel her heartbeat steadily increase with every second that passed as the three guild leaders silently stared down at her. Outwardly she did her best to maintain her composure, but given who these people were Vivian couldn't help but worry if one of them, especially

Ingrid, saw through it.

"Miss Hawks," Ingrid then began, appearing much calmer than she had been before. "After much deliberation and further reviewing of your past year's performance, we, the three heads of the Futura Collegium Aureum monster hunting guild have reached a decision regarding your candidacy for promotion within the guild." Vivian's heart began to beat faster, for she knew that this was the moment she had been simultaneously looking forward to and dreading since long before coming to this city. "I would also like to stress, Miss Hawks, for I feel that in your case this needs to be said, that this was a decision reached after lengthy discussion and was unanimously agreed upon by the three of us. So there is no one person in this room who should be deserving of any blame for what you are about to hear." Vivian's heart nearly instantly stopped at those words. "Given your past year's performance according to the reports that we have received as well as your own words spoken in your defense. We have decided not to promote you to silver." The instant those words reached Vivian's ears her heart rate had returned to normal, only for it to steadily begin to slow as the meanings of all of those words sank in.

"Wh... what?" was all Vivian could say in a voice that was only barely above a whisper.

"Furthermore," Ingrid continued. "You will also remain assigned to the town of Canaan for another year. Our hope is that you spend the coming year reflecting on and in turn avoiding any more of the mistakes that led you to where you are now. And of course, we expect to see you back here for another review on the first of Solarun next year."

"Mistakes!" Vivian then shouted at the top of her lungs as she shot up from her chair. "Mistakes! I only made one fucking mistake in my time in Canaan, and I fucking owned up to it! Shouldn't I-"

"No, you shouldn't," Ingrid interrupted coldly and without raising her voice. "If that had been the first and only mistake you had made in your career as a monster hunter then we would have been more lenient towards you. After all, what you said was indeed correct. You were caught in a situation you were not prepared for and there was little you could have done. However, we all know that wasn't your first mistake. Need I remind you of what happened in Eden-"

"You fucking know damn well that I tried!" Vivian shot back as soon as that name was spoken aloud.

"Trying isn't good enough," Ingrid spoke, still coldly. "Three-hundred and eighty-nine people died three years ago because of your failure to kill one monster. You were lucky enough to not be expelled from the guild then and there. The only reason you were even allowed to stay at all was because your uncle here was able to pull all of the right strings to get Alejandro's vote on that decision." Vivian fell silent as her eyes drifted over towards her uncle. Upon meeting his gaze all he did was let out a sigh as he let his eyes fall down towards the table in front of him, as if he didn't even have the will to look at her anymore. "Even if we were to ignore the people whom you claim that you could not have saved. A member of Canaan's town watch still died because of your incompetence due to, according to the report that we received, the fact that you were intoxicated at the time of the attack."

"Oh what!" Vivian shouted back at Ingrid as she threw her arms up in disbelief. "Do you expect me to be able to somehow predict whenever a monster is going to attack before I decide to go out and grab some drinks!"

"No," Ingrid responded. "It is simply something to take note of. Many of the members of this guild drink, including the three of us from time to time. We will not deny it. However, unlike you, the other members of this guild are able to maintain themselves and control their impulses in the event that the worst should happen. If it were up to me I would ban you from having any alcohol for at least this next year until we see improvements from you. However, we both know that the only way to properly enforce that would be if we were to assign one of the other guild members to be your probation officer, but nobody here deserves that." Having heard enough, Vivian shot a hate fueled, dagger like glare towards Ingrid.

"You know if you think that I'm a lost cause you can say it to my face," Vivian said, making sure that the spite in her voice was obvious to anyone who listened.

"Well, I can't speak for Piers or you uncle but…"

'*What the fuck are you even on?*' Vivian said to herself in her thoughts. '*You've had pretty much the run of this meeting haven't you? Aren't you all supposed to be equals?*' She actually had to mentally fight herself in order to keep herself from saying any of that out loud. However, after everything that had been said already she knew that doing so would only make things worse for her, and at this point she was drained enough from all the shouting she had already done.

"I don't think it's too late for you," Ingrid then continued. "That being said, you make it very difficult for us to give you chances to redeem yourself, and after everything that has happened since Eden can you honestly say that you have?" Vivian wanted to respond to that, she really did, but no words came to mind. She already knew that she had been defeated. "That's what I thought. I'm sure that you are trying, but at this point trying isn't good enough anymore. You need to be better. If you keep going on like this you won't be able to get a job as a monster hunter anywhere. I'd even go as far as to say that the only job you will be able to get is selling yourself on the streets, and nobody here, not even me, wants to see that happen to you."

Vivian could only stand in silence as she took all of those words in. If either her uncle or Piers had said them to her, she would have believed them. However, it was Ingrid, not either of them, who was speaking to her right now. Ingrid, the woman who for reasons that were beyond her, had been spiteful and bitter towards her even when she was a child. Before she had joined the monster hunting guild even. As far as she knew and was concerned Ingrid's heart didn't exist, and she was probably trying to save face after her previous comments in front of the others.

"Now miss Hawks," Ingrid continued. "Unless you have anything else to add, I do believe this meeting is concluded." With all of that said, Vivian looked back over towards her uncle, who still refused to look at her. With nothing from him she then glanced over towards Piers, who didn't appear to be ashamed of anything. He was, however, still apparently perturbed by Ingrid's earlier comments as he kept shooting her occasional dagger-like glares. Everything that had happened with Vivian didn't seem to bother him at all, as he seemed more concerned with his own insulted pride than her's. This, unfortunately, gave Vivian no insight at all as to how exactly the voting between the three of them must have gone.

"No," was the only Vivian could say, though it came out in a much weaker voice than she had intended as her eyes fell towards the floor beneath her feet.

"Very well," Ingrid then said with a sigh. "You are dismissed then, miss Hawks."

No sooner had those words been said that Vivian turned around, marched her way out of the door that had seemingly opened on its own again, and then kept marching. She didn't look at or say anything to anyone, though she knew that all of their eyes were on her. Whether or not that was actually the case, however, she did not care as she continued to march straight out the doors of the guild hall. She did not want to be there any more. Now that she found herself outside in the blazing sun of Dis again, she simply turned herself in a direction away from the guild hall and kept walking. Which direction had she turned and where was she going, she did not care. All she knew was that she wanted to be somewhere else.

Chapter 12

The person that stood in the doorway was a young woman. Very young, possibly younger than all of them except for Seth, given her height and build. To Seth's best guess she had to be around one hundred and seventy centimeters tall, which would have made her slightly shorter than Tara, whom he knew to be the shortest person in the room with them. She was also incredibly thin, as there barely seemed to be any mass at all around her arms and waist. Long, smooth, almost shiny red hair that was so bright in color it almost appeared orange fell down her back almost reaching to her waist. Lastly, staring at all of them were a pair of clear, striking, almost sapphire like blue eyes that seemed to pull Seth into them the longer he looked. The part about her that confused him the most, however, was her skin. She was pale, like him, which made no sense to him given the type of environment they all lived in. Not only that, but her skin was completely flawless, with no visible blemishes or imperfections of any kind.

Her clothes, however, were what set her apart from everyone more than any of her physical features. She wore a long, long bright orange dress that reached all the way down to her feet. In fact, Seth could only barely see her feet at all, which were covered by perfectly smooth, laceless shoes that matched the dress. The bottom and the neckline of her dress were lined with a somewhat frilly looking fabric and the corset she wore with the dress was tied together by a shiny, almost obnoxiously white ribbon. Around her neck she wore what Seth could only guess was an incredibly well crafted, gold chained necklace with its centerpiece being taken up by a very shiny, clear rock that reflected the sunlight. It was only because of that necklace that Seth noticed that dangling from the lobes of her ears were well made, golden earrings that also had similar clear rocks placed in them, albeit much, much smaller.

This strange, well dressed woman didn't do anything but stand completely still at the entrance to the office with a wide eyed expression on her face as if she, for whatever reason, found it impossible to believe what she was seeing despite it being in front of her. At first Seth worried that it might be because she was clearly able to see everything that was happening and no doubt heard Raz's long winded rant to mister Guilloux. Perhaps, he thought, she knew mister Guilloux and found herself unable to believe that someone would throw accusations like the ones Raz had said at him. Because of that Seth worried that the next thing she was going to do was turn and run away to get the city guard. As those thoughts seemed more and more likely, Seth found it suddenly difficult to breathe as he desperately tried to come up with some way to save himself, and if he could Raz and Tara as well, should she decide to run. That, unfortunately, was something that he found incredibly difficult to do as he still did not entirely understand the situation himself. The only thing he could think to do was to brace himself in case he had to suddenly run the second she did. However, she did not run.

Instead the young woman stayed perfectly still where she was and just stared into the office, the look of shock and disbelief on her face never wavering as if it were incapable of changing. A full ten seconds passed and she had not moved a centimeter, which only added to Seth's worries as he tried to control his breathing. However, as he stood there with his eyes fixated on her, he noticed something. Despite the fact that she had a clear view of the entire office as well as all of them, she wasn't looking at any of them, as like the rest of her her eyes seemingly remained frozen in the direction they were looking. With this in mind Seth followed her gaze and saw that her eyes were firmly locked onto only one of them, Raz. Raz in turn simply stared back at her as if nothing was wrong, something that Seth did not find reassuring at all.

Then, suddenly, without saying anything, Raz seemingly completely forgot about mister Guilloux as he pushed himself off of the desk and walked slowly over towards the young woman. It was only then that the young woman herself began to move as she, her expression still completely uncharged and her eyes still completely fixated on him, matched Raz's pace as she stepped into the office with all of them. Before long the two of them stood in front of each other, but neither one of them said anything. Throughout the office not even the sounds of breathing could be heard as Seth, Tara, and mister Guilloux all watched both Raz and the young woman to see what they would do.

"Raz?" the young woman eventually spoke in a soft voice. At the sound of it, however, Raz's lips curled into a smile, but it wasn't like the overconfident smirk he usually wore. The only real way that Seth could describe it was genuine.

"Hey, Filly," Raz responded to her without skipping a beat. At the sound of his voice the young woman's blue eyes suddenly grew wider than they already were and her mouth slowly opened as wide as it possibly could. Before Seth or anyone else in the room could possibly comprehend exactly what was happening the young woman suddenly let out an incredibly high pitched squeal as she leapt forward and threw her arms around Raz in a great big hug. Seemingly expecting it, Raz caught her just as she leapt into his arms and enveloped her in his own big hug before he then picked her up and spun her around the small office. As they did this they both burst out laughing hysterically as if they both were children.

Now even more confused than before due to the sudden radical shift in tone, the only thing that Seth could think to do was look to Tara for help as he subconsciously relaxed his breathing. Tara, however, only responded to him with a shrug before drawing her attention back towards Raz and the young woman. With nothing from her, Seth instead looked back to mister Guilloux, but he was no help either as he appeared to be even more confused than either of them.

"What are you doing here!" the young woman practically shouted at Raz in an elated voice as he put her down.

"I should be asking you that!" Raz responded to her in a surprisingly upbeat manner despite his choice of words. "The frontier's no place for someone like you, what are you doing here!"

"I'm here with my mom!"

"Oh, well what's that bitch doing here then!"

"We came for the festival!"

"A-fucking-scuse me!"

"I know, right!" At that the both of them threw themselves back into their hugs and continued laughing as if no one else in the room was there with them. Before Seth could ask what was going on and who this woman was the sound of metal boots hitting a stone floor caught his ears as he instantly shifted his attention towards the office door. The sound of metal grew louder and louder until the owners of those boots soon appeared in the doorway. Seth had expected to see the city guard, but that wasn't what he saw at all.

Instead of the city guard, standing at the office door were two people wearing what Seth could only describe as completely metal clothing. Unlike the members of the city guard who only wore metal on their forearms, boots, and chests, every part of the clothing that these two wore, that Seth could see anyway, was made of metal. From the bottom of their boots to the top of their helmets, all of it was metal. It all looked to be made of steel, the metal that Seth eventually discovered was what most swords were made out of it, but was much shiner and more well kept than anything Seth had ever seen in Canaan or even the city guard here in Dis, whose metal clothing despite looking functional bore scuffs and scars from frequent use. The helmets that they wore also obscured their faces, as the only parts of them that Seth could see were their eyes and mouths through a small, T shaped design carved out of the front of them, which Seth assumed allowed them to see and breathe at all. As impressive as all of that was, none of it mattered as much as the large, metal shields that both of them carried on their backs and the finely crafted swords that both of them wore on their hips. Just from one glance their swords appeared to be so well made that Seth momentarily began to wonder exactly what he would have to do to get a sword like that.

Despite the sudden appearance of these two, neither Raz nor the young woman seemed to pay any attention to them as they continued to laugh and spin around the room. Their appearance, however, caused both Tara and mister Guilloux to instantly stiffen. Tara in particular instantly sat up straighter than she had been before as her eyes went incredibly wide with what appeared to be fright. Not only that, but Seth watched, and also smelled, as mister Guilloux began to sweat much, much more than he had been before. The radical difference in reactions to the appearance of these two metal wearing people forced Seth to wonder if he should be worried or not. Certainly Tara was worried, and that was usually cause for concern, but Raz wasn't. Then again, Seth knew that Raz was not the best judge of character.

Eventually both Raz and the young woman ceased their incessant laughing once the two of them had seemingly run out of breath, and it was only then that Raz turned towards the door and saw the two people wearing metal.

"At ease, gents," Raz calmly said to the two of them as if he were speaking to Seth, Tara, or anyone else he knew. "Nothing to see here, just a small reunion."

"Small?" The young woman cut in with a chuckle. "Raz, when, if ever, have you done anything small?"

"When I have to," Raz responded with his usual, overconfident smirk. It was only at that moment that Seth decided he was done with not knowing what was going on anymore.

"Um, Raz," Seth suddenly piped up. "What is going on? Who is she?"

"I... I would very much like to know the answer to this as well," Tara chimed in afterwards.

"A-As would I," mister Guilloux spoke up as well, though with some obvious hesitation.

"Oh…" Raz responded as his face suddenly went a little red. "Sorry about that. Got lost in the moment there." Raz then paused for a moment to recompose himself before he, much to Seth's surprise, stood up perfectly straight and coughed into his fist. "Seth, Tara, this is-" Before he could say anymore, however, the young woman suddenly stepped out in front of him so that she stood between him, Seth and Tara. She stared directly at the two of them for a moment with a genuinely pleasant looking smile on her face before she then, with what Seth could see was a delicate touch, hiked up both sides of her long dress and did a short bow towards them.

"It is an absolute pleasure to meet you," the young woman said to the two of them. "I am princess Filia Solara of the Solaran royal family."

"It's nice to meet you too," Seth politely responded, just as Tara had taught him, as he held out his hand to her. "My name is Seth."

"Seth…" Filia replied as she looked him up and down. To Seth's confusion, again, she actually took a few longer than usual moments to do that before she eventually took his hand. "What an interesting name. If you don't mind me asking, where are you from?"

"Canaan," Seth answered honestly, as he saw no reason to be dishonest with this woman. It was only after he answered, however, that he glanced over in Tara's direction and saw that her mouth was hanging open and that a look of complete and utter shock was plastered on her face as her eyes were stretched open as far as they could go and seemingly refused to blink. Seeing that Seth couldn't help but worry for a moment whether or not this young woman saw her.

"Canaan…" Filia repeated as she raised an eyebrow. "That's also an interesting name. I've never heard of it before."

"You wouldn't have," Raz chimed in before either she or Seth could say any more. "It's a small, podunk town roughly three hundred and fifty kilometers to the southwest of here. Including me and Seth I'd say… maybe three hundred people at most living there. Maybe." At those words Filia instantly spun around and diverted her full attention back to Raz.

"Wait, so you live there too!" she practically shouted at him.

"Yeah," Raz responded calmly with his usual overconfident, toothy smirk adorning his face. "I said I wanted to get away, didn't I? Can't get much farther than

John Alspaugh and Ken Daniels

the edge of the frontier." Filia couldn't help but laugh at that.

"No, I suppose you can't," she said as her laughter died down. "Is Daedalus out here with you?"

"Oh yeah," Raz responded with a wave of his hand. "He's around. Somewhere." Seeming satisfied with that answer, Filia returned her attention back to Seth, only for her eyes to fall on Tara next to him with her mouth still hanging open.

"Oh, forgive me I am so sorry," Filia said as she quickly covered her mouth with her hand, but then dropped it back down to her side as she finished speaking. "I didn't mean to startle you. I know my family and I have that effect on people sometimes. It's a pleasure to meet you as well." Despite the seemingly polite greeting Tara remained silent for a few long, long seconds before she could actually respond.

"Th... Th... The pleasure is all mine, really," Tara barely uttered out as she quickly stood up, dusted herself off and attempted to make herself appear as professional looking as possible. All of which drew a slight giggle from Filia. "Tara... Tara Schäfer. That is my name." As she spoke, much to Seth's surprise and confusion, she actually bowed her head a great deal, so much so that she seemed to be looking at the floor more than at Filia, something that struck Seth as very impolite given how Tara always emphasized looking people in the eyes when you were talking to them.

"You don't need to do that, really," Filia said to her as she held both of her hands out in front of her. "I'm not my grandmother, or my mother, so you're fine."

"I am sorry! I am sorry!" Tara then quickly responded as she picked her head back up. "I... It is just-"

"Ah come on, Tara," Raz spoke up as he walked up and put his arm around Filia, something that she seemed to very much enjoy. "Ain't no need to be shy. It's just Filia. She's not going to bite, or make you explode with her mind."

"Can people actually do that?" Seth immediately asked after Raz had finished speaking. Filia, however, couldn't hold herself back as she broke out laughing out loud. To say that this person greatly confused Seth would have been an understatement. It wasn't her appearance or the way she acted that confused him, it was more people's reactions to her. Raz spoke to her as if he had always known her, which he likely had given her reaction to him, and she seemed kind to Seth when he spoke to her. Tara, however, just by being in the same room as her appeared incredibly nervous. It actually reminded Seth of when the two of them had gone to see Vito Smeraldo all those months ago back in Canaan and she had been afraid to speak to him. Unlike Vito, however, Filia was incredibly kind, so Tara's apparent fear of her seemed unjustified in his eyes. Mister Guilloux appeared to have a similar reaction to Filia as well as he remained perfectly frozen at his desk and dared not speak.

"Filia, is that you!" a new, heavily accented voice called out from somewhere down the hallway outside of the office before Seth could wonder any more. "I know your voice! So I know you are here somewhere!" The voice grew louder as it grew closer. "Though I can only speculate what in the name of Solaris would interest you on this-" Before the voice could continue any further its owner stepped into view as the two men in metal clothing stepped back away from the door and positioned themselves along the opposite wall so as to give him room to walk through.

The man who owned the heavily accented, yet incredibly smooth sounding voice was one of the most unique looking people Seth had ever beheld, and that included Filia. He was a tall man, though not that much taller than Seth and Raz, and appeared to be extremely well built. He was also much older than all of them as Seth could see that his slicked back hair was almost completely gray, and his tan, almost bronze colored skin was littered with a few wrinkles despite obvious attempts to maintain it. He also walked with an air of pride and dignity as he stood completely straight up at all times and carried himself with a certain poise and grace that Seth had only seen before in men like Daedalus and Vito.

Like Filia, this man wore extremely fancy clothes, though unlike her he appeared to prefer the color white to orange. His clothing mainly consisted of a very finely made, almost completely white suit jacket with a gold trim and matching trousers that looked like something Tabitha would make, though Seth couldn't help but wonder if something this well made would be a challenge even for her. Especially with the gold trimming that almost seemed to shine like real metal. The only part of his clothing that wasn't white was the shirt he wore underneath his suit jacket, which was orange, though it was a much darker shade of orange than Filia's dress. The white ascot that he wore around his neck, however, made his shirt very difficult to notice as it only added more white to his ensemble. Also, while it was difficult to see at first due to the limited angle that Seth could see outside of the door to the office, behind him Seth could also see that he was being followed by two more people wearing completely metal clothing.

As this new man stood in the doorway his dark eyes instantly fell upon Raz, and while his expression had at first appeared pleasant enough, at the sight of him Seth watched as his lips slowly formed into a scowl. Raz seemed to notice this as well, though he appeared unconcerned as he took his arm off of Filia's neck and turned to properly face the man, who took a few steps into the office so that he could stand in front of him. The room fell completely silent once again as Raz and this strange, new man in white stared each other down, though Raz remained completely unfazed as he still wore that same smirk on his face. Then, before anyone could say anything at all, Raz suddenly, but gracefully, held out his right arm, touched his left hand to his chest, extended his left leg out behind him, and then bowed his head.

"Isaac," Raz said to the man.

"Michael," the man, now identified as Isaac, responded to him. As he did Raz straightened himself back up. As much as Seth wanted to ask who Michael was, he got the feeling that this was neither the time nor the place to do so. "It is interesting how you choose to bow before me, yet not to address me by my full title." As Isaac spoke he crossed his arms in front of him.

""Would you prefer it if I didn't bow?" Raz replied to him in an obviously mocking tone. "And I think 'Lord Isaac De La Rosa, personal advisor to the queen of the Solaran empire' is a bit of a mouthful, don't you think?" Filia seemed to enjoy that type of response from Raz as she stifled a giggle, though Isaac appeared to be less amused.

"I was…" Isaac began, but then paused for a moment as he directed his gaze over towards Filia. "Tasked to retrieve princess Filia Solara at the request of her mother. It did not occur to me to look for her in this particular section of the capitol building, as I did not believe that she would have any reason to come here. I see now that I was mistaken."

"Tell me," Raz chimed back in. "Is Faust here too or is it just Filly and Nicole?" It was Isaac's turn to smirk as the last of Raz's words reached his ears. For some reason that sight worried Seth a great deal, though he was unsure why.

"If you wish to know," Isaac answered. "Perhaps you could come upstairs with us and see for yourself. I am sure they would love to see you again."

"I'm sure they would," Raz responded to him without skipping a beat.

"Um... Excuse me," the voice of mister Guilloux suddenly piped up. At the sound of it every pair of eyes in the room instantly turned and fell upon him. At the sight of that, however, mister Guilloux appeared to suddenly find it difficult to speak, as he hesitated for a moment and then coughed into his hand before he said anything else. "As much as I... love a good reunion. It..." He hesitated to speak again for a moment as his eyes fell upon Isaac, who stared back at him like a hawk would a snake. "It is very good that you brought some security... good sir. This man." He then pointed his finger at Raz, though it was shaking quite a bit. "J... Just before you arrived... was accosting me... He was threatening me with violent retribution... He-"

"Perhaps you'd like to explain then to the personal advisor to queen Faust why you were unlawfully withholding this woman's mail," Raz cut him off again just as easily as he had before as he motioned towards Tara. "As well as what 'favors' you were going to request of her in order to get it back." Isaac's expression then appeared to suddenly perk up a bit with obvious interest.

"Interesting..." Isaac said as he pushed past Raz and stood in front of mister Guilloux's desk with his hands behind his back. On his face was a smile, though Seth sincerely doubted that he was actually happy in any way. "I would very much like to hear about this. Please. Tell me everything." Mister Guilloux then instantly fell silent as Seth saw the sweat beginning to drip from his forehead.

"A... as I said... Sir..." Mister Guilloux only barely managed to mumble out. "This man-"

"I know what this man did," Isaac interrupted as he motioned towards Raz. "Now I want you to tell me what you were doing." Again, mister Guilloux instantly fell silent as his eyes darted between every single person in, and out of the room in a vain attempt to look for any kind of safe haven. When he didn't get an answer from him Isaac instead shifted his attention over towards Tara.

"You there..." Isaac said to her. "I am terribly sorry. I did not catch your name." Tara, as if on instinct, immediately straightened herself up as soon as he had finished speaking.

"My... My name is Tara," she answered him. "Tara Schäfer." At the sound of her name Isaac raised an eyebrow in what appeared to be interest.

"Tell me, miss Schäfer," Isaac then said to her. "You are the subject around which this issue is centered, are you not?"

"Y... Yes," Tara hesitantly answered. "I am."

"Since our dear postmaster seems, for the moment, unable to respond," Isaac began. "Perhaps you would care to enlighten me as to the reason you are here as well as what issues you are having with the postal service here in Dis." Despite the seemingly simple question, Tara was hesitant to respond, at least until her eyes found Raz, who only nodded at her in response.

"I…" Tara hesitantly began, but then shook her head and recomposed herself. After which she looked directly into Isaac's eyes. "I used to receive regular parcels of money every month from my brother in Sol. However, three months ago they stopped coming. After making some inquiries I found that they had all reached as far as Dis before someone had ordered them not to be shipped to me. I came here today to find out why."

"And what did the postmaster here tell you?" Isaac then asked.

"He said that he was aware of the issue and was more than capable of fixing it," Tara answered. "However, in return he asked for a certain… favor."

"And what was this favor that he asked of you?" Isaac asked.

"He never got a chance to say," Tara answered. "Before he could, all of you arrived."

"I see," Isaac said as he returned his attention back to mister Guilloux. "Well then, mister postmaster. As the gentleman here so eloquently said." He motioned towards Raz as he spoke. "Would you care to explain to me the exact reason you are withholding Miss Schäfer's mail as well as the exact nature of this favor you were going to request from her?" Mister Guillox began to visibly shake as his eyes darted between everyone, including the men in metal clothing, again before eventually falling back onto Raz.

"S… Sir… If you would only listen to my side…" Mister Guilloux eventually spoke "Th… That man-"

"You keep coming back to that," Isaac interrupted again. "The disadvantage you have, however, is that I know this man." As Isaac spoke he pointed towards Raz himself. "And while it is absolutely true that he is both aggressive and a fool, he is not without a sense of justice. So while I believe what you have been saying about him accosting you and threatening you, the fact remains that you still did not answer my question. So let us try this again." As he finished speaking Isaac put both of his hands on mister Guilloux's desk and slowly leaned forwards towards him. "What exactly is the reason you are withholding Miss Schäfer's mail and what was the exact nature of this favor you were going to ask of her as payment for returning it?" At that, mister Guilloux suddenly stopped shaking, he stopped blinking, he even stopped sweating as all he could do was stare back into Isaac's dark eyes. When he didn't receive an answer, Isaac smiled wickedly as he stood back up from the desk. "That was what I thought." Before anyone had a chance to say anything more Isaac suddenly turned around, snapped his fingers, and pointed at the two men wearing metal clothing who had first arrived with Filia. "You two. Get him out of here."

At his command, without saying a word or making any other motions the two men wearing metal clothing walked into the room, went around to opposite sides of mister Guilloux's desk, and then grabbed him by his arms.

"What are you doing?" Mister Guilloux frantically asked as they were doing this. No one, however, gave him an answer as the two metal men with great effort lifted him out of his chair and began to lead him out of the office. "What are you doing!" Mister Guilloux screamed as he fought them the whole way. "You can't do this!"

"Actually I can," Isaac responded to him as the two metal men led mister Guilloux out of the room. "If you have an issue with that then I suggest you file a complaint with the city guard." Before mister Guilloux could in any way respond to that comment he was already out of the room and being dragged away by the two metal men. Though his screams were no doubt heard across the whole floor, Seth, Tara, Raz, Filia, and even Isaac all silently watched him go for a few moments until his screams eventually went silent.

"Now that that issue has been resolved," Isaac then said as he turned back to address Filia. "My lady. Your mother requests your presence upstairs." As he spoke to her he gave her a look that seemed akin to a parent scolding a child, though Seth was unsure if he was Filia's father given what they had said earlier. Filia only responded with an obnoxiously loud sigh as she visibly rolled her eyes, which fell back on Raz as she finished. Seeing that, Isaac's eyes drifted over towards Raz as well. "If Michael wishes to join us then he may." Isaac then smiled again as he finished speaking, though Seth could tell that it wasn't a pleasant smile. It was a type of smile that Seth actually recognized, as he had seen it numerous times by this point. That smile screamed to him of deception and trickery, as well as overconfidence in believing that one had another person exactly where they wanted them.

Raz, however, was unintimidated by this as his eyes drifted back over towards Filia, who stared back at him with an almost pleading expression on her face. Seeing that, Raz's familiar, overconfident smirk began to readorn his face.

"You know what, sure, why not," Raz responded with a shrug. "I'm sure Nicole would love to see me again." Filia's face appeared to immediately brighten as those words hit her ears.

"Yes, I am sure she would," Isaac responded coldly.

"One condition though," Raz then said as he pointed to both Seth and Tara. "They're coming too."

"What?" Seth spoke up, confused.

"What!" Tara shouted at the same time and at the top of her lungs, unable to contain herself any longer. It was at that moment that Seth's eyes finally met Isaac's as his smiling face turned to look in their direction. He found it strange staring into this man's eyes. It was like looking down a hole, only he couldn't see the bottom. Because of that Seth found Isaac incredibly difficult to read as Isaac seemed to stare through him rather than at him.

"And who are they?" Isaac asked without taking his eyes away from Seth.

"To answer that question, they're friends of mine," Raz immediately answered. "And to answer the question you're no doubt going to ask next. They're no one you need to worry about. Tara here is from Sol so she knows proper etiquette as well as how to properly address a lady of the royal family and Seth here is very polite. So I'm sure they'll be fine." Isaac did not appear to accept that answer at first as he never took his eyes off of Seth. Before he could open his mouth to speak, however, Raz cut him off. "And don't worry. Neither of them have any secret agendas or any intention of harming and/or kidnapping any members of the royal family. If they did then they're stupider than horses." Isaac seemed to contemplate this for a moment before he finally tore his eyes away from Seth and directed them back over towards Raz.

"Because if there is one thing that you have always excelled at, Michael," Isaac said to Raz. "It is being an excellent judge of character." As he spoke those words the smile on Isaac's face began to darken somewhat as it slowly formed itself into a scowl.

"Haven't I always," Raz responded with a smirk. There was another, longer moment of silence between them as neither Raz nor Isaac blinked.

"Very well," Isaac eventually said. "If they lady wishes-"

"I wish it," Filia interrupted before Isaac could finish, much to Isaac's obvious disapproval, even if he did a very good job of not showing it.

"Very well," Isaac then said. "Then they may come with us." With those words having been spoken Isaac turned around and began to walk out of the office. As soon as his back was turned, as quickly as she could Filia rushed over to Raz.

"Thank you," she whispered to him, though she was close enough for both Tara and Seth to hear her.

"Hey, you know me," Raz responded to her as he put his hand on top of her head and ruffled her very nicely combed hair, which only messed it up slightly. Filia, however, seemed to greatly enjoy that as she let out another giggle. "I wouldn't leave you hanging like that. Go on ahead. I'll be right behind you."

"You better be," she said back to him with a smile as she left the office. The second she was out the door the remaining two men in metal clothing flanked her and followed her every step. With them gone Raz let out a very loud sigh and returned his attention back to Seth and Tara, both of whom wore looks of obvious confusion on their faces, Tara more so than Seth.

"I know you guys have a lot of questions," he said to them. "Believe me, I know, and I'll answer all of them, but not right now. Later. For now just play along. Trust me, it'll all work out fine. Hell, you might even have some fun." Then, with all of that said, Raz casually walked out of the room as quickly as he could so that he could catch up with Filia.

That left Seth and Tara alone in the office together as their eyes finally met. Seth had absolutely no idea what was going on nor what to do, but he also had a strong suspicion that Tara didn't either, and the look of absolute bafflement that was still on her face confirmed that for him. With that in mind Seth knew that there was no way that Tara could answer any of the questions that he had right now, and at this point he still wasn't entirely sure if he could trust her. Especially since she hadn't told him about any of this business with the postmaster. With no other idea what to do, without saying anything Seth began to walk out of the office in order to catch up with Raz.

"Seth!" Tara tried to call out to him, but he didn't stop for her. Not this time. With no other recourse, Tara let out a loud groan as she quickly fell in step behind Seth. Before either of them knew it they had already caught up to Raz and Filia and were following Isaac and the four people wearing metal clothing to wherever they were leading them.

It was only after Seth had left the office and fell in step behind Raz and Filia that Seth's eyes fell back on Isaac again. When they did he beheld the back of his suit jacket, and at the sight of it his eyes nearly went wide enough to burst out of his skull, not because anything was wrong with the jacket in any way, but because he could scarcely believe that what he was looking at was possible with clothing. Emblazoned on the back of Isaac's white suit jacket was an incredibly detailed image of, to Seth, what looked like a dog-like creature with a spotted pattern from a side view as it stalked through its hunting ground. Instead of sand or grass, however, the dog-like creature walked upon a field of a very specific type of flower. Seth had seen that type of flower before, but only once when a passing trader brought some through Canaan. Tara had told him that they were called roses. Despite how intricately detailed the image was, the entirety of it was a singular color, a dark purple much like the shirts that Seth usually wore. It was only then that Seth realized that the colors of Isaac's clothing, white, orange and purple, matched the colors of that flag that he had been seeing everywhere lately.

It took a few moments after getting over the initial shock that pictures could be put onto clothes that Seth realized that Raz and Filia had fallen eerily silent. While before the two of them were uncontrollably excited to see each other, and could only barely keep their mouths shut when they were in the same room together, now they had both fallen as silent as the grave. It was actually more than a little disturbing to him.

"Is something wrong?" Seth asked as the group found the stairs and had begun to ascend them.

"Hmm?" Raz grunted in confusion as he turned his head to look back at Seth, and only realized after he had done so why Seth would ask that question in the first place. "Oh. Sorry. No, nothings wrong at all. Talking's just not really a good idea around Isaac. Ever. At all."

"Why's that?" Seth couldn't help but ask despite what Raz had just said.

"Because the man has a memory like a Solaris damned steel trap and remembers everything everyone says," Raz responded plainly as he returned his attention back to where he was going. "I wish I was kidding." Despite him being the subject of their conversation, Seth saw no visible reaction from Isaac, though he was certain that he heard them. This, to Seth, meant that Isaac was either ignoring them or he didn't care, neither of which were ideas that fared well for him. Unsure of what else to do, much less say, Seth remained silent as well as he continued to ascend the staircase with them, as did Tara. However, Seth was given the impression that unlike him, her silence was more due to disbelief than confusion. It was an experience that felt surreal to him, like it was his first time seeing Canaan again and he had to ask what absolutely everything was because he legitimately did not know. That in turn led Seth to wonder exactly how much about the world he really did know.

After a few short, silent minutes of walking up the stairs to what felt like the top floor and navigating some more, identical looking hallways, the group found themselves standing in a large room that reminded Seth of a strange mix between mayor Maryen's office in Canaan and her secretary, Selene's office in front of that. In that respect it was a very open, and very well put together room with a carpeted floor, thick drapes over the windows, and tapestries hanging on the opposite wall that all bore the same white, orange and purple colors. The comparison to Selene came from the fact that to the right of them not too far from the entrance sat a large receptionist desk, though no one was sitting at it at the moment. Last, and most important, at the opposite end of the room from where they stood was a set of large, thick double doors. Behind the double doors, however, Seth could hear the distinct sound of multiple people talking. He couldn't make out their exact words, but they sounded as if they were just finishing a long conversation and were only just now saying their goodbyes.

Isaac, to Seth's surprise, didn't bother to wait until anyone had returned to let them in or even knock as he walked straight to the other end of the room and pushed the doors open for them. With them now open Seth beheld another office that almost perfectly resembled mayor Maryen's office in Cannan, except on a much grander scale. In fact the layout of the room was almost the exact same, with the only real difference being that the room itself was larger and more spacious. So much so that as they entered Seth saw two couches sitting at opposite ends of the office, presumably so that whomever's office this was could meet with more people aside from whomever could occupy the pair of chairs that sat across from their desk, again much like mayor Maryen's office.

In the room stood a bunch of people, but only two of them stood out to Seth as the majority of them were all wearing the same metal clothing that the people following them were, and one of the few that wasn't was another young woman wearing the same kind of outfit that Seth had seen the receptionist wearing downstairs. The two central figures, however, who stood in the center of the room shaking hands as Seth's group all walked in, appeared to be making every effort to stand out, which Seth supposed likely came with the nature of their professions. The one on the left was a tall, lithe looking man wearing a finely crafted back suit similar to the one that Isaac wore except for the fact that he did not have an ascot and possessed very well combed dark hair with a matching mustache.

"My lady," Isaac said to the other apparently important person as he gracefully made a bowing gesture similar to the one that Raz had performed earlier. As he did the four men in metal clothing who had come with them all touched their right fists to their chests and bowed their heads to her as well. "You will be pleased to know that I have returned with the runaway princess." At the sound of his voice both figures turned to address him and saw the assembled group. At the sight of them the man with the mustache turned back to face the other figure.

"I am afraid duty calls me to oversee the matters we have just discussed," he said to her before he made his own, identical bowing gesture towards her. "So I shall take my leave now, your grace. You are free to use the room for as long as you wish. My assistant will show you to the exit when you are done."

"That will not be necessary," the other figure responded to him as her eyes fell on Filia and did not leave her. "I am certain at least one of our royal guards remembers the way out." As she finished speaking she blinked and suddenly her eyes fell upon the collection of men in metal clothing with her. None of them responded, not with words anyway, but they all touched their right fists to their chests and bowed their heads as she looked at them. With all of that said the man with the mustache and his secretary walked past Isaac and the assembled group and left the office, which left Seth's group alone in the room with the other figure and all of the men in metal clothing with her, whom Seth now knew were called 'royal guards'. While he had guessed before that they were guards for someone due to the weapons they carried, this confirmed it for him.

With the man with the mustache gone the remaining figure's eyes began to pick apart everyone in the assembled group. This left Seth with a moment to take in what he was seeing as well, because this woman was different in so many ways from literally everyone that Seth had ever seen before that it almost made him go dizzy for a moment.

For starters, this woman was tall, at least just under two meters if Seth had to guess. Despite her height, however, she was not thin, as her more than generous womanly curves filled out the elegant dress she wore that only barely seemed able to contain her assets. Long, smooth, elegant, pale blonde hair flowed freely from her scalp all the way down past her waist. Like Filia her smooth, clear skin was much paler than the majority of people that lived out here and lacked imperfections of any kind, as if this woman made an absolute effort to maintain it and by extension her beauty. Her eyes, blue like Filia's, but more of an icy blue as opposed to the sapphire-like blue of Filia's, scanned over the assembled group one by one before her eyes eventually met Seth's. Despite her obvious beauty, the expression she wore on her face was as cold as iron, as her slightly smaller than normal lips appeared to be perpetually frozen into a scowl and her eyes cast a dagger-like glare directly at Seth as if she were attempting to stare through him rather than at him, much like Isaac had earlier.

Like Filia, the dress this woman wore was very extravagant and reminded Seth of something that Tabitha would make, though even with that comparison this dress seemed to push the limits of what someone like Tabitha could accomplish. Completely white in color except for some slight gold trimming along the edges, the dress itself almost seemed to sparkle in the light as the sun reflected off of it and hugged her generous womanly curves so perfectly that it appeared to leave nothing at all to the imagination. Like Filia this woman wore jewelry, though considerably more so than Filia as around her neck hung a beautiful golden necklace bearing a sun motif, and in the center of which was another one of those shiny white rocks that reflected the light of the sun, though hers was much larger than the one that Filia wore. Also interesting, to Seth at least, the necklace was held to her neck by five small golden chains as opposed to one larger one like the one that Filia wore. Dangling from her ears were earrings bearing three of those shining rocks as opposed to one like on Filia's and a multitude of rings bearing other shiny stones of various colors adorned her fingers. Completing the ensemble was a golden band that she wore on her head that also bore a large, shiny, white rock in the center of it. To Seth, the amount of shiny things that this woman wore almost made her appear as if she was somehow producing her own light rather than reflecting it from every which way.

The woman's scornful gaze was taken away from Seth by the sound of someone frantically moving. Both she and Seth looked over next to him to see Tara as she frantically made the same bowing gesture that Isaac had performed earlier.

"My lady Nicole," Tara said to her as eyes focused on the floor in front of her. "It is the greatest of honors to be in your presence." While she did not say anything else, Seth could tell that behind her eyes Tara was panicking. Confused, Seth returned his attention back to the woman, whom he now knew was named Nicole. She appeared to only barely acknowledge Tara as her dagger-like glare found Seth again, which began to make him more than a little worried. Unsure of what exactly to do in this situation, Seth looked over to Raz and Filia, but neither of them were bowing, and none of the royal guards had bowed like Tara or Isaac had, so he was completely unsure of what to do.

"And who is this boor who doesn't bow before royalty?" Nicole then spoke before Seth even had a chance to decide what to do. While he had never heard the term 'boor' before, the context in which she had used it was more than enough for him to discern its possible meaning.

"He's with me," Raz spoke up before either Seth or Tara could say anything as he stepped out from behind Isaac and walked in front of him as if he did not matter. As soon as he did Nicole seemed to completely forget about Seth as her scornful gaze found him, though again, Raz was completely unfazed by it. Next to Seth, Tara had stood back up again, though Seth could see that her hands were shaking as she held them together in front of her as tight as she could.

"Michael," Nicole spoke, though her lips seemed to drip with venom as she said it. "I should have known."

"Ah, and I thought you would be glad to see me," Raz responded to her as he crossed his arms. "Isaac said that you would be." Despite the obvious jab at him Isaac also appeared completely unfazed by any of this as he watched the conversation play out in front of him.

"I see that your disposition towards us has not changed," Nicole then said as she narrowed her gaze at him.

"And I see that you're just as much of a bleeding cunt as ever," Raz responded with a completely straight face. The instant those words left his mouth Seth watched as Tara suddenly gripped her hands together so tight that her knuckles began to turn white. Not only that, but she suddenly found herself no longer able to control her shivering as she began to visibly shake next to Seth. Seeing that, Seth began to worry as well as he saw that behind Nicole's eyes she was only barely able to contain her rage.

"You should be careful what you say," Nicole spoke slowly to him.

"To who, you?" Raz responded without a care. "What can you do to me? You're not the queen."

"I will be," Nicole responded without skipping a beat.

"And if you're still a bleeding cunt when that happens," Raz responded in turn, still without a care. "You may find that your reign will be much shorter than you would have preferred." A long, drawn out silence followed as Seth could see that the only thing keeping Nicole from hitting Raz was her own common decency.

"I should have your tongue cut out," she said to him.

"Awh," Raz responded with an obvious air of sarcasm. "I thought that the crown and the colors you represented were better than that. How do you think all of the boors as you call them would feel if word reached them that you did something like that to someone of your own blood. You do want to live up to your mother's example, don't you?"

"Enough!" Isaac suddenly shouted louder than Seth had expected from him as he walked over and stood in between Raz and Nicole. "That is enough bickering from the two of you! You are not children and you are not common street thugs! You are of royal blood and you should remember the stations you occupy!" Isaac then paused for a moment and turned his full attention to Nicole. "Especially you, my lady. Such behavior I would expect from Michael, but not from you. You should be above such things. You after all, will be queen yourself one day, as you so eloquently said. So you should act like it." While Seth didn't hear anything from her, he got the distinct impression that under her breath Nicole was growling as she glared back at him. If Isaac had heard it, he didn't say or do anything to acknowledge it as he took a few steps back from the two of them and crossed his arms. "Now I want the both of you to apologize to each other. I did not bring Michael here so that the two of you could yell at each other. You are family. So start acting like it." Tension hung in the air for several long seconds as Nicole continued to glare at Raz in silence. To Seth's surprise, however, it was Raz who broke that silence first as he let out a loud sigh.

"Isaac's right," Raz then said as he dropped his smirk and visibly relaxed. "It was wrong of me to call you a bleeding cunt and I'm sorry. I was out of line and I should not have said that in the first place. The fault is my own, not yours and I hope you can forgive me." Then, as he finished speaking, Raz held out his hand towards her. Tension hung in the air again as Nicole looked down at Raz's hand, then back up into his eyes. Seth wasn't sure at all what would happen as he watched the exchange play out before him, though next to him Tara seemed more terrified of whatever would result from this than he was.

"What repercussions would I receive for not apologizing to someone like you? Oh that's right, none," Nicole responded as she turned away from him and made her way towards the exit. The second she had started walking all of the royal guards in the room except for four of them followed in her step. "Come, Filia. We are leaving."

"No!" Filia shouted angrily as Nicole had just walked past the threshold of the office doors. The instant that word had reached her ears, however, she stopped, and as she did all of the royal guards stopped with her.

"I'm sorry?" Nicole said to Filia as she only barely turned her head to acknowledge her. Filia, in response, angrily stared back at Nicole as she folded her arms across her chest.

"I haven't seen Raz in three years," Filia answered. "I want to stay with him."

"Perhaps you did not hear me," Nicole then said as she fully turned around to face her. "I said we are leaving."

"And perhaps you did not hear me," Filia responded to her. "I said that I want to stay with Raz." Nicole, in response, could only barely suppress a groan as she leveled her dagger like glare on Filia.

"Filia," Nicole spoke softly, but with purpose. "As your mother I am ordering you to return with me." At that, much to Seth's immense surprise, Filia actually smiled.

"Then I refuse," Filia responded calmly. It only lasted for a split second and Seth wasn't sure whether he actually saw it or not, but at the sound of those words he could swear that he saw Nicole's eye twitch.

"I am sorry, what did you say?" Nicole said with all the fury of a monster despite her calm tone.

"Did I stutter?" Filia responded with an obvious air of sarcasm. "Oh wait, no I didn't, you taught me better than that." Nicole opened her mouth to respond to that, but like Raz, Filia beat her to the punch. "And before you say anything. You and I are both princesses, so you can't give me any orders that I would be forced to obey and any orders you give me as my mother I can refuse because they aren't bound by royal decree. So yes, your move, mother." As she finished speaking Filia shot Nicole a look that was strikingly similar to the smug, overconfident smirk that Raz always put on.

Tension hung in the air like a hammer waiting to drop as Nicole glared angrily at Filia while Filia, in turn, shot her a look that Seth had only seen before on Raz. One that Seth knew tended to have mixed results. While she wasn't saying or doing anything, Seth could tell that behind Nicole's eyes was now a raging inferno of emotions, but mostly anger, and that it may have been taking all of her willpower to not shout at all of them or punch a nearby wall. While Seth would usually turn to Tara for advice of what to do in situations that he didn't understand, now she looked even more confused than he did, so he knew that any help from her was beyond her current capabilities.

"There will be consequences for this, young lady," Nicole eventually said to Filia as she turned back around and began to walk away from the office.

"Oh I'm so scared," Filia responded as she waved her hands in front of her with an obvious air of sarcasm. "What's the worst you can do to me! Lock me in a room that I can easily get out of!" Nicole did not respond as she and her procession of royal guards reached the door, upon which one of them opened it for her and she stepped through with them in tow. With her and most of the royal guards gone, that just left Seth, Tara, Raz, Filia, Isaac, and four royal guards all in the office of someone that Seth did not know, and because of that Seth felt like even more of a stranger than he usually did.

"Se supone que eres mejor que esta, princesa," Isaac muttered in obvious frustration as he pinched his brow. To Seth, what he said sounded like gibberish, but Isaac did not seem to notice or care that no one could understand him.

"Filly I don't know if I should be disappointed or impressed with your behavior," Raz said to Filia as he walked up next to her, seemingly ignoring Isaac.

"I learned from the best," Filia replied as she shot her smirk in his direction.

"Yeah well I wouldn't go around bragging about that," Raz then said as he put his hand on top of her head and ruffled her beautifully smooth red hair again.

"Stop it," Filia replied as she playfully pushed him away.

"I'm sorry but I can't take this anymore!" Tara suddenly shouted at the absolute top of her lungs, which caused all eyes in the room to instantly fall on her. "You're princess Filia Solara! That was princess Nicole Solara! You just called her a bleeding cunt! He said you were of royal blood! You know him! He knows all of you! All of you know him! They all keep calling you Michael! Who! What! How!... What in the name of everything that Solaris has blessed us with is going on!" After she had finished shouting Seth hesitantly raised his hand.

"I would actually like to know this as well," Seth spoke up in a very quiet voice compared to Tara's. In response to what they had both said, however, Filia's expression changed to one of absolute confusion as she looked back at Raz.

"They don't know?" she said to him. Raz in turn, let out a rather loud sigh as he rubbed the back of his head.

"Everyone out here only knows me as Raz," he answered her. "So no, they really don't." Filia's eyes instantly went wide as she appeared genuinely shocked. Seeing that, Raz let out another loud sigh as he rolled his eyes. "Well, I guess there's no running away from it now." Before saying anything else he then suddenly reached his arm around Filia, grabbed her by her opposite shoulder and pulled her close to him. A gesture that she seemed to very much appreciate. "I suppose a reintroduction is in order. Seth, Tara, allow me to introduce to you my little cousin, princess Filia Solara."

"What!" Tara shouted at the top of her lungs again, her mouth hanging open after she did so.

"What's a cousin?" Seth immediately asked the second he was given a chance to speak. Before anyone could answer him, however, Tara spun around as quickly as she could to face Isaac.

"Isaac!" she shouted again before she realized what she was doing and recomposed herself. "My lord Isaac. You are the personal advisor to Queen Faust of the Solaran Empire, so more than anyone you would know. Is he telling the truth? Is that man really of royal blood?" As she spoke she pointed behind her directly at Raz. Isaac, for his part, appeared completely composed as if nothing out of the ordinary had happened, though Seth supposed that nothing out of the ordinary had happened for him. Before he answered her he unsubtly looked over to Raz, then back to her as if to confirm that she was really asking that question.

"As difficult as it may be to believe," Isaac began as he crossed his arms.

"Yes. That man there is of royal blood." Tara's eyes instantly widend in obvious disbelief at that, but Isaac ignored that as he continued. "He is the son of Mara Dagon, the cousin of Nicole Solara by way of the late King Helios' sister Philomena. So effectively he is, as he says he is, second cousin to princess Filia Solara." As soon as he had finished speaking, and before Seth had the chance to ask what a cousin was again, Tara, with her eyes wider than dinner plates, spun back around and stomped directly over to Raz.

For several long moments Tara appeared to have forgotten about everyone else in the room as she stared directly at Raz. Seth, Isaac, Filia, the other royal guards, as far as she was concerned, none of them mattered or even existed at that moment as she and Raz held eye contact for several long, drawn out, silent moments. Raz meanwhile, just politely stared back at her as he waited for the inevitable next words to leave her mouth. As much as Seth wanted to interrupt he got the feeling that it would end better for him if he waited patiently.

"You!" Tara eventually yelled at the top of her lungs again as she pointed at Raz.

"No need to get all dramatic about it," Raz responded as if nothing at all was different. "I'm just royalty, not a psychopathic madman."

"I still would like my question to be answered," Seth then spoke up as he raised his hand. "Also I don't know what royalty is, so it would be nice if someone would explain that to me too."

"How do you not know what either of those are?" Filia asked him, seeming more confused than anyone as to why someone would ask those types of questions at all.

"Because I have amnesia," Seth answered without any hesitation. No sooner had Seth's answer left his lips that all attention was on him. Well, almost all attention as Tara had suddenly buried her head into her hands and was mumbling to herself and all of the royal guards looked more or less the same as ever. So much so in fact that Seth had begun to wonder if they were even capable of speaking or showing emotions, as they had done neither in the entire time Seth had spent with them. While Filia's reaction was more predictable to Seth, being a wide eyed mixture of shock, confusion, and curiosity, it was Isaac's reaction that actually gave Seth pause as he saw Isaac blink, then afterwards both of his eyes were completely focused on Seth, unmoving and unwavering. It was subtle, but Seth could tell that Isaac was at the very least intent on paying attention to him.

"No… no no…" Seth barely heard Tara mumble to herself. "Please Solaris no. Why did I not prepare you for something like this? Why why why…"

"Are you serious?" Filia then asked in a disbelieving tone.

"Yes," Seth responded as plain as day. "Why would I not be serious about that?" Filia opened her mouth to say something in response to that, but then stopped herself when it became evident that she really had nothing to say. With this in mind Filia turned her attention to the one person whom she assumed at least could give her all the answers she wanted, Raz. When Raz saw this he began to chuckle loudly to himself.

"Sadly, Filly," Raz began. "This man here speaks the truth. He was found collapsed in the desert all by himself about a day or so southwest of that town Canaan I told you about. When he came to, he didn't remember anything, not even his own name. So Tara here, being the kind, caring woman that she is, took him in and that's how it's been for the past seven months." Filia, not seeming satisfied with that answer, looked over to Tara, but when it became evident that Tara was so far buried into her hands that she didn't notice her, Filia returned her attention back to Seth and took a few tentative steps forwards towards him.

"Is…" she began with some apprehension. "Is that true?"

"Yes," Seth answered plainly enough. As soon as that answer reached her ears Filia gasped as her eyes became even wider and she brought both of her hands to her lips. Before Seth could say anything to her, however, her hands suddenly shot from her lips to Seth's right hand as she grabbed onto it and held it tightly between them.

"By everything that Solaris has given us I am so sorry!" she practically shouted at him.

"Why?" Seth asked as soon as she had finished speaking. "What do you have to be sorry about?"

"Because…" Filia responded with some confusion, but mostly empathy as she squeezed his hand tighter. "That… That just sounds… so sad."

"Why does it sound sad?" Seth immediately asked, making no effort at all to hide his confusion at that statement, something that actually visibly shook Filia.

"Why?" she almost spat out, but managed to keep herself in check. "Because… because… I… Solaris I can't even imagine what it's like. If I woke up tomorrow and didn't know who I was I... I don't know what I'd do." The amount of emotion that she was showing for something that Seth for the longest time had used as the most convenient of all excuses drew his curiosity towards her somewhat. It had never occurred to him before exactly how terrible a situation like his would be if it had happened to another person. After seeing how Filia reacted to him he began to actually think more about it. Before Seth could say anything more to Filia, however, she suddenly pulled her hands away from him. "Wait a second. If you have amnesia then..." Before she said anything else Filia suddenly grabbed her head with both of her hands. "Oh Solaris my mom called you a boor didn't she. Which means that my mom insulted a cripple. Oh Solaris, Seth, I am so so sorry."

"I don't know what 'boor' means," Seth replied before she could say anything else. "So it doesn't bother me."

"Well it doesn't mean anything good," Filia responded. Before Seth could respond to her in turn, however, she suddenly grabbed Seth's hand again. "Seth, on behalf of my family I am so so sorry."

"You said that already," Seth couldn't help but point out as soon as she finished speaking.

"Ah, I wouldn't worry about it," Raz spoke up as he walked up and put his hand on Filia's shoulder. "Seth isn't the type of person who gets bothered by things that people say about him. Besides, your mom is still a bitch so I'm certain that even if she did know she would have some other insult that she thinks is clever for him."

"In light of this revelation," Isaac then suddenly began as he walked up to the assembled group. "Know that for her words she will be severely reprimanded and this incident will not be forgotten. Especially by her mother." As Isaac spoke that last part his eyes fell on Filia, who smiled again upon hearing it.

"Thank you, Isaac," she said to him.

"There is no need for thanks," Isaac replied to her. "Everything I do I do in service of the Solaran Empire. How the representatives of the empire present themselves to those beneath them is simply another facet of the station I hold." After finishing he then turned to face Seth. "Seth of Canaan, on behalf of the Solaran royal family I would also like to apologize to you. Know that in all future interactions with you we will strive to be better."

"You don't have to apologize," Seth responded to Isaac. "I'm not insulted. Really. So you don't need to worry." That response actually made Isaac smile himself.

"Be that as it may," Isaac began as he folded his hands behind his back. "An apology is still warranted. You do not need to accept it, but know that the royal family is sorry for the words that were issued to you today."

"Thank you," Seth responded politely, though in truth that was the only thing he could think of to say that would get them to stop apologizing to him. What followed then was several long seconds of silence as both Seth and Isaac held eye contact with each other. Despite how he presented himself to them, something bothered Seth a great deal about Isaac, and his eyes betrayed that to him. Part of it was that while Seth was certain that he must have blinked a few times, he never saw Isaac blink even once. The more important part of it, however, was that despite the smile Isaac wore and how the rest of his face appeared to reflect it, something was off about his eyes, as if they were not the eyes of a smiling person. That was the only way Seth could think of to describe it anyway.

"So... now that that awkwardness is out of the way," Raz eventually spoke up again, effectively breaking the silence. "What happens now?" Immediately after he had finished speaking Filia's mood appeared to instantly brighten as she, while still standing next to Seth, turned to face Isaac.

"Isaac," Filia then began in an extremely polite manner. "Might this humble princess request that she spend the rest of the day with her favorite cousin?" Despite how simple the request she made had sounded, Isaac brought a hand to his chin and was silent for a few quick seconds while he thought about it.

"Hmm," he began. "An interesting request you have made, my lady. One that I am certain you know that your mother would not approve."

"My mother wouldn't approve of me going out to buy bread," Filia shot back. "So her opinions are moot, and it's not like I won't be protected. I'll have Raz with me, and who in the Solaran army was ever badass enough to take him down?"

"Language, my lady," Isaac politely shot back as soon as Filia had finished speaking. "And as compelling as your argument may be, I am afraid that it still may not be enough to convince me."

"Just let her go," Raz chimed in as soon as Isaac had finished speaking. "You more than anyone know that it'll only be more of a headache for you later if you don't. Even if you were to say no and forcibly drag her back to wherever you guys are staying she's liable to sneak out and come looking for me. Which of course would mean that I would have to drag her kicking and screaming back to you guys, which would then mean that I would never hear the end of it from Nicole, which admittedly doesn't amount to much at all, but then I would never hear the end of it from Faust, which unlike the bleeding cunt would actually mean something. So yeah, for the sake of all of our collective sanities just let her hang out with us for the day."

"And what, pray tell," Isaac responded as he shifted his gaze over towards Raz. "Am I to tell Nicole when I do not return to the regional governor's estate with her daughter."

"Tell her whatever you want," Raz answered with a shrug. "Tell her that Filia would have gone anyway even if you had said no. Tell her that she was so much of a bitch to my friend that you took it upon yourself to make the decision for her. Tell her that I came and kidnapped her, I'm sure she'll believe that one more than anything else. Hell, she'll probably think that no matter what you tell her. Besides, Filly's right." Raz then stopped talking for a moment as he walked over next to Filia and put his arm back around her. "I'll be there with her. Anyone lays a finger on her I'll knock their teeth out, and the best part about that is that you don't have to feel bad about it since I'm not a royal guardsman and I don't associate with you assholes anymore. I'll just be a guy who saw his princess being harassed so I stepped in and did the right thing. Win for you, win for us, win for Filia since she gets what she wants. So what do you say, Isaac? Your move."

Both Raz and Filia then stared up at Isaac with identical looking smirks on their faces. Isaac, for his part, appeared to take this all in stride as he matched their smirks with a polite, yet stern gaze of his own. For the next several long, long seconds silence reigned throughout the room as Raz and Filia engaged in a battle of wills against Isaac, each side waiting to see who would break first. To Seth's utter shock, confusion, and disbelief, he saw Isaac blink once, and then when he opened his eyes again he had locked eyes with him once again. For a moment Seth felt himself unable to breathe as he was unsure of what that look may have meant. As soon as it had come, however, Isaac blinked again and his gaze returned to Raz and Filia.

"I can see that the two of you really do intend to make this difficult for me," Isaac eventually responded. "So in the spirit of that, I suppose choosing the lesser of two evils would not be the worst thing that I could do." As those words left his mouth both Raz and Filia broke eye contact with him as they turned to look at each other. Raz looked the same as ever. Filia, however, looked as if she could barely contain her glee as she stared wide eyed, and mouth agape at Raz. This lasted for all of a single second, however, before she suddenly let out another high pitched squeal and leapt into Raz's arms again for another great big hug. "However. I will only allow this under one condition." The sound of his voice caused both Raz and Filia to break their hug as their attention fell back onto Isaac. Isaac, however, ignored their antics as he turned his attention to two of the royal guardsmen who had followed them into the room, upon which he snapped his fingers and pointed at them. "You two. You will accompany them. Stay with Princess Filia wherever she goes and under absolutely no circumstances are you to let her out of your sight." At his order both of the royal guardsmen touched their right fists to their chests and bowed their heads to him in acknowledgement.

"Oh come on, really!" Filia cried out as soon as Isaac had finished speaking. "It-"

"Just accept it, Filly," Raz interrupted her. "You aren't going to get a better deal so it's better to quit while you're ahead." Filia opened her mouth to respond to that, but before she could Raz suddenly shot her his own stern looking gaze, something that Seth had never seen Raz do to anyone, not even him. So the idea of him doing that to Filia of all people was more than a little shocking to him. With that sort of look from her biggest supporter, Filia let out an obnoxiously loud sigh and slumped her shoulders in defeat.

"Fine," she eventually said after the majority of the air had left her lungs. "I suppose you're right. You always are."

"I wouldn't say always," Raz replied to her as he rustled her hair again, which instantly put the smile back onto her face as she quickly straightened it out again before walking directly to Isaac.

"Isaac, thank you so much for doing this for me," Filia said to him as she held both of her hands together in front of her and bowed her head. "I promise I will not make you regret it."

"Do not thank me yet, my lady," Isaac responded to her with his own smile. "Your mother, after all, has yet to be informed of any of this and will most likely have words for you upon your return." Filia, seemingly ignoring that last part, let her smile encompass her whole face as she spun back around and walked back over towards Raz.

"So, what are we still doing here then?" Filia asked him.

"Your guess is as good as mine," Raz answered with a shrug. Filia retorted in turn with a short giggle before she suddenly hugged him again, though it wasn't as abrupt or as energetic as any of the other times she had hugged him. It was only a regular hug, which lasted only a single second before Raz put his arm around Filia again and led her towards the exit. They only got three steps towards it, however, before they stopped and Raz turned to look towards Seth and Tara. "So are you coming or what?"

"I'm sorry," Tara let out as if she had suddenly been hit in the chest with a hammer. "Wha-"

"You guys are part of this too, obviously," Raz interrupted before Tara could say any more. "And besides, there's still so much of Dis to see and only so much daylight left, and I know Seth here needs to see more of it so that he won't instantly get lost the next time he leaves his hotel room. So what do you say, are you coming or what?"

"We umm-"

"Oh won't you please come with us," Filia suddenly interrupted before Tara could say anything more. "It's not like you have anything to worry about. Royal blood or no, any friend of Raz's is a friend of mine, and I would very much like to meet Raz's friends. So please, if only to indulge me." At her words Tara fell instantly silent, as any words she could have spoken died in her throat. With no answer from her Filia's eyes then turned to Seth. Seth, while he still had many, many, many questions about what was going on, such as exactly who Filia was and what all of this royal family nonsense was about, Filia had been nice to him in the short time he had known her. In that respect he found little reason to say no, especially since what Raz had said about him was correct. He did legitimately want to see more of Dis so that he would not get lost in it again.

"Sure," Seth answered. "I'll go with you." Tara's mouth fell open again as her eyes instantly turned towards Seth. In that instant Tara tried to say something to him, but all of her words continued to die in her throat.

"Great!" Filia practically shouted with enthusiasm. "Onwards then!" Then with that decided Filia led Raz out of the office with Seth not far behind. Tara, even as she continued to make pathetic, gibberish sounding noises, quickly recognized defeat as she watched the three of them walk towards the office exit. Before they were able to cross the threshold she quickly fell in step with them.

The two royal guardsmen whom Isaac had told to follow them, as if on some sort of cue, fell in step behind the group of four the second they crossed that threshold with the loud, clanking sound of their metal boots constantly reminding all of them that they were there as they followed them towards the stairs. The instant they were gone and the door to the office had closed behind them, however, with a wave of his index finger Isaac called one of the remaining royal guardsmen over to him.

"You. Change out of your armor as quickly as you can," Isaac said to the royal guardsman. "Follow them. Watch them closely. Tell me everything that they do, and pay special attention to that Seth character."

"Of course, my lord," the royal guardsman answered. "B… But if I may ask, my lord… Why him specifically?"

"Something about him does not sit right with me," Isaac answered without looking at the royal guardsman. "Call it a hunch if you must."

"V- Very well sir," the royal guardsman answered. "B… But-"

"Speak, guardsman," Isaac interrupted before he could finish. "You only have so much time."

"If I may ask another question, my lord," the guardsman continued, undeterred. "Why are you asking me to do this? You sent two guards with them, can't you just ask one of them what happened?"

"Because I did not ask either of them, I asked you." The instant Isaac had finished speaking he suddenly blinked and when he opened his eyes again he was looking directly into the royal guardsman's eyes. The look in Isaac's eyes could only have been described as hate fueled glare with all of the intent to kill where he stood behind them. "Does that satisfy your curiosity?"

"Y- Yes my lord!" The guardsman quickly answered as he suddenly stood up straighter and slapped his right fist to his chest. "It does my lord!"

"Good," Isaac then responded as he turned to face the guardsman properly. While the glare in his eyes remained, his lips had curled into his familiar, friendly looking smile. "Then you had better get going. You only have so much time before you run the risk of losing them." Before the guardsman could respond to or even acknowledge that order, Isaac quickly silenced him by raising his hand. "Oh, and this goes without saying, but under no circumstances are you to let them see you. After all, we do not want them to know that they are being followed, do they?"

"N- No my lord!" the royal guardsman responded. "No we do not, my lord!"

"Good, I am glad you understand," Isaac said as the expression on his face suddenly returned to the calm, complacent one he had previously worn. "Now if I were you. I would stop asking questions and start running."

At those words the royal guardsman quickly slapped his fist to his chest again and bowed his head to Isaac in acknowledgement of the order before he turned and walked as quickly as he could in heavy armor out of the office, past the reception area, and out the door that Seth, Raz, Tara and Filia had just used. This left Isaac alone in the office with the remaining royal guardsmen as he glared out of the office doors, past the reception area, and directly at the door in question.

Chapter 13

Seth, Raz, Tara and Filia all felt as if a weight had been lifted off of all of their shoulders as they walked down the steps of Dis' capitol building, even with the two royal guards following them. Filia had kept close to Raz the entire way out of the building as she peppered him with questions about where he had been and what he had been doing since she had last seen him. All of which he answered honestly, and Seth knew he was being honest because most of the questions that Filia was asking him he knew the answers to as well, as Raz had been strangely reluctant to talk about anything that had happened to him before he had arrived in Canaan. Thankfully Raz had omitted certain details regarding Seth.

"So you sure you don't wanna stop by whenever you're staying and grab something else to wear?" Raz asked her as they reached the bottom of the steps. "That dress kind of looks a little too fancy for most of Dis."

"Oh it's alright," Filia answered with a wave of her hand. "I hate this dress. So I don't really care what happens to it. Besides…" Filia then paused for a second as she motioned back to the two royal guards following them. "These two are gonna be with us wherever we go so I don't think it really matters what I'm wearing. People will still probably figure out who I am."

"Yeah, that's probably true," Raz responded before he glanced back towards the two royal guardsmen and gave them a nod. Neither of them appeared to acknowledge him, however.

"Hell," Filia then continued. "Even if something does happen to this dress it'll still be alright since it'll piss mom right the fuck off."

"Yeah, well I wouldn't make pissing your mother off a regular habit," Raz replied in turn. "Also where did you learn that word?"

"From you of course," Filia answered with a giggle.

"I still do not even know how I ended up here," Tara said to herself louder than she would have likely preferred.

"Tara," Raz answered even though what she had said wasn't directed at him in any way. "You're here because you were being so incredibly cryptic on the way here that it was obvious to everyone, including Daedalus and I, and it made Seth worried. So naturally I, being a nice person, stepped in and helped him figure out what was going on." Tara looked as if she wanted to say something to that, but before she could Raz turned to face her properly. The look on his face was one that by all accounts appeared to be sincere, at least to Seth. "And I'm sorry for interrupting. I really am, but there are a few things in this world that I can't for the life of me stand and one of those is seeing a woman being taken advantage of. So for whatever it's worth. I'm sorry."

"Y- You do not have to apologize," Tara awkwardly answered as she waved her hands in front of her. "If... If anything you actually helped me. So really I should be thanking you." As she finished speaking Seth noticed her face begin to grow a little red. Raz's only response to her, however, was just to smile back.

"Oh, I am so so sorry," Filia quickly spoke up as she turned her attention to Tara as well. "I didn't mean to ignore the two of you. Really, I didn't. It's just that I haven't seen Raz in so long and-"

"It's okay," Seth interrupted, which caused Filia to immediately turn her attention towards him. "You wanted to talk to him first. So you don't have to apologize. It's okay. I understand." To Seth's continued surprise, as well as slight confusion, as ke spoke he saw Filia's face become a little red as well.

"Okay," Raz then suddenly spoke up before anyone else could say anything. "Before anyone says anything else. How about we all promise each other right now that we won't apologize to each other anymore for anything that happened or may have happened today. Otherwise we're all going to keep apologizing to each other every time one of us opens our mouths and nothing will get said or done. That sound fair?"

"Does to me," Filia answered almost immediately. "Even if I really am sorry, in the spirit of meeting new people and making a good first impression, I'm willing to drop the apologies and talk about something more meaningful." As soon as she had finished speaking she very quickly returned her attention back to Seth, which caught him off guard somewhat. "You agree with me, don't you Seth?" In truth Seth had no idea what to even make of what Raz had just said, and he still needed to apologize to Tara because he still felt bad about disobeying her. However, since he was being put on the spot by Filia.

"Sure," Seth answered, unsure of what else to say.

"Good," Filia replied, seeming satisfied with his answer before turning back to Tara. "What about you, Tara?" As she was suddenly put on the spot herself, Tara frantically looked between Filia and Raz, both of whom stared back at her with what appeared to be genuinely good natured smiles on their faces. Unsure of where else to look, Tara turned her eyes to Seth, who only stared back at her with the same blank stare he always wore. With the full realization of the situation that she was now in upon her, however, only one seemingly acceptable answer came to her as she took in a very deep breath and then exhaled before speaking.

"Yes," Tara replied to them with a genuine looking smile on her face. "You are right. We will not get anywhere if we do nothing but apologize to each other. There is, after all, still so much to see and do."

"Spoken like someone who means it," Raz declared as he took a few exaggerated steps in front of Filia. "Onwards then!" Despite what Tara had said, however, while still wearing her smile Tara locked eyes with Seth. Seth did not need to read her face to know what she was thinking as he silently nodded at her. He wanted to talk to her about all of this later as well, and he had already accepted what he knew was coming.

"So…" Filia then began, effectively breaking the awkward tension between Seth and Tara. "How do the two of you know my cousin?" The second she finished asking that question, all of the previous encounters Seth had had with Raz, including the… incident between the two of them in the desert played through Seth's mind. It didn't take long for it to become instantly clear to him that he had absolutely no idea how to even begin to answer that question in an honest way.

"Canaan is a small town," Tara answered as she came to his rescue. "So everybody there pretty much knows everybody. So we know Raz by virtue of having that privilege rather than simply being friends. Though he is friendly, do not get me wrong."

"And what do the two of you do in Canaan exactly?" Filia then asked.

"I work in Canaan's library," Tara answered first. "I am actually from Sol originally. I studied at the mage academy there."

"Really!" Filia let out, appearing to be very interested in that. "You're a mage!"

"I am," Tara replied as she held up a hand and wiggled her fingers. As she did, a few bright sparkles of light danced between each of her fingers. "My speciality was light based magic. Though I must admit I am not like Raz or other mages. I was never trained to fight."

"If you're from Sol," Filia spoke up as soon as she was given the chance.

"What made you decide to move all the way out here to the edge of the frontier?"

"I…" Tara began, but then paused as her eyes drifted back over towards Seth. She remained silent for a few short seconds longer as Seth could tell that she was trying to think of exactly how to say what she wanted to. Thankfully, however, she did not let the silence linger too much longer. "I came out here because I wanted to study monsters."

"You couldn't do that in Sol?" Filia then asked with genuine confusion in her voice. "Or in the northern forests? There are plenty of research stations out there made for that purpose that are much safer than anything out here."

"I wanted to see if I could study them while they were alive," Tara answered honestly. "And all of the different varieties of monsters in the north are well documented so I wanted to see what the frontier had to offer. Dangerous, I know, but if we are to learn anything we must sometimes be willing to take risks, and I… well…" Tara then paused again as her eyes fell on Seth, though Filia didn't appear to notice. "I was more than willing to take those risks. I know enough magic to keep myself alive, if only that much." Seth could tell that Tara was obviously hiding some crucial pieces of information from her, though Filia appeared to accept that answer and asked no more questions.

"And what about you?" Filia then asked Seth as she returned her attention back to him. "What exactly do you do in Canaan, Seth?" As she asked him that question Filia leaned in rather close to Seth. Not uncomfortably close, but close enough.

"When I'm not helping Tara in the library I'm part of the Canaan town watch," Seth answered honestly, as unlike Tara he had no reason to hide anything this time. "I guess the best way to explain it is that I'm like the city guards here, except in Canaan."

"Oh, so you're a guardsman?" Filia immediately asked, seeming a little more interested in what he had to say than Tara.

"We don't use that term in town watch," Seth answered. "But now that I think about it I suppose you could call us guardsmen."

As soon as Seth had finished speaking he returned his attention to what was in front of him and saw the same archway in the wall. He knew that it was the same archway because the same two guardsmen were still standing at it.

"What's up," Raz said to the two of them again as he approached the gate ahead of the group. When the two guardsmen saw him one of them rolled his eyes and took a few steps closer to the edge of the archway so that he could lean against it. The other, the one whom Raz had spoken to before, simply let out a loud sigh before he let Raz approach him.

"You've returned," he spoke with all the air of a man who had no motivation at all to deal with whatever Raz was.

"Indeed I have," Raz answered him as politely as he could. "Nice to see that you're still doing your job." Initially the guardsman didn't say anything to Raz in response, though the look on his face told Seth that he was about to tell Raz to get out of his sight. When his vision shifted past Raz and he saw who he was with, however, the look in his eyes, and subsequently his face, changed in an instant.

"S... Sir," the guardsman then began, though he seemed hesitant to continue immediately after he had begun speaking, at least for a few seconds. Seth, however, knew from the look on his face that he was trying to figure out what to say. "Might I... ask you to please explain your present company?"

"What, her?" Raz answered as if he didn't know who they were talking about. When neither of the two guardsmen responded to him, Raz's smirk widened considerably. "She's the friend I said I was coming here to see." After he said that Raz pretended to notice how confused the two guardsmen looked as his smirk widened even more. "Oh come on. You're not going to tell me that you didn't believe me are you?" To the surprise of no one, least of all Raz, neither of the two guardsmen responded as the two of them looked to each other for answers, but found that neither had any. With no other idea of what to do, the guardsman who had been speaking to Raz instead turned his attention past him towards Filia.

"M... My lady," he hesitantly spoke to her. "I... If you would please-"

"You're going to ask me if my cousin speaks the truth," Filia answered before the guardsman could even finish speaking. Before the guardsman could even open his mouth again to properly respond to her she beat him to it. "The answer is yes. Everything he is and has been saying is absolutely true and both of you should feel ashamed of yourselves for doubting him. Now are you going to keep stuttering or are you going to let us through?" At her words the two guardsmen instantly shut their mouths and moved to opposite sides of the archway where they stood at attention.

"Please enjoy your day, my lady," the guardsman said to her once the way had been cleared. "And please, on behalf of the Dis city guard please accept our sincerest apology for any transgressions we may have caused."

"You are forgiven," Filia responded without even looking at him as she and her two royal guardsmen walked past Raz and ahead of the assembled group as they crossed the threshold of the archway. "Just don't let it happen again." With her and her royal guardsmen having gone through, Raz swiftly followed, as did Tara and Seth, as neither of them felt any need to ask questions or even dare speak after a display like that. Just before Raz had crossed the threshold, however, he stopped in front of the guardsman he had been talking to.

"Don't worry about any of it, man," Raz said to the city guardsman as he put his hand on his shoulder. "Everyone makes mistakes. It's just part of being human. You enjoy your day too." He then patted the guardsman's shoulder twice, much to his annoyance, before following after the assembled group.

Once they were all far enough away that they were out of earshot of the two city guardsmen Filia let out a loud sigh as she looked towards the ground.

"Wow, that actually felt kind of good," she said to herself as Seth and Tara caught up with her. Before either of them could say anything to her, however, a look of horrific realization crossed her face as she looked back up and stared forward. "Is... Is this how mother feels all the time?"

"Probably," Raz answered from behind them as he finally caught up with them. "I wouldn't get too used to it though. It stops being fun when no one likes you." Filia's response to that was to burst out laughing for a few quick seconds before actually saying anything.

"Yeah, I suppose you're right," she eventually replied to Raz.

"So, where are we going?" Seth immediately asked the instant he saw that the opportunity to ask that question had come, if only because he had wanted an answer to that question for some time.

"That's an excellent question," Filia responded before she shifted her attention back to her cousin. "So, where exactly are we going, Raz?"

"Well, considering that there's a lot to see, only so much daylight in a day, and the fact that Seth here really, really does need a tour of this city more than you do," Raz answered as he took his former spot next to Filia. "I say we just start walking in a random direction and see what happens."

"Sounds good to me," Filia quickly agreed. "Let's do that." The two of them then quickly looked to Seth, who only responded with a shrug since Raz had said exactly what he would have if they had asked him where to go. With what appeared to be approval from him, the group then looked to Tara, who still looked more than a little nervous, and all of the attention on her only seemed to make it worse, at least at first. She started by darting between all of their eyes, hoping that one of them would speak for her, but when none of them did she instead closed her eyes and took in a very deep breath. When she let it out and reopened her eyes she appeared much, much more relaxed and more like her usual self.

"Why not," Tara answered with a genuine smile on her face. "It is not like any other plans I may have had today were more important. Besides, I did want to show Seth around the city anyway, and this way might be more fun."

"Well then, what are we still wasting time talking about this for?" Raz then asked as he walked slightly ahead of the group before turning around so that he could address them all while still walking backwards. "Fortune favors the bold, not those who stand around and talk. So I say less talking, more walking." Then, before any one of the group could say anything more he spun back around on his heel and obnoxiously pointed forwards. "Onwards!" That outburst made Filia laugh rather loudly as her eyes fell on Seth and Tara, particularly Seth. Neither of them said anything, however, as they resigned themselves to their fates. Which they knew that considering all that had happened, could have turned out so much worse for them.

From there the assembled group then proceeded to walk back down the same street that Raz had led Seth through to get to the Suntop District, so there wasn't really anything that was new for him to see that way. Not only that, but he actually did remember the way back to his hotel through this way. So at the very least now these streets were somewhat familiar to him. Filia, however, couldn't keep her eyes off of anything nor her mouth shut as she bombard Raz with question after question about what he had been doing since she had last seen him. Much more so than before now that her mother and Isaac were no longer present. Raz, of course, answered every single question he could. None of his answers surprised Seth in the slightest, as he already knew most of what he was telling her, though there were few new details Seth caught in the midst of the answers he gave such as how Raz and Daedalus had apparently known each other for years before moving out to Canaan and how quickly they had left for the frontier once they had decided to.

"So, Seth," Filia eventually said to him after she had finished peppering Raz with questions. "Is it really true that you have amnesia?"

"Yes," Seth answered quickly.

"And you really don't remember anything?" Filia then immediately asked.

"No."

"Nothing at all?"

"No."

"Not even little details?"

"No," Seth answered as he shook his head. "I don't remember anything at all."

"That's…" Filia began, but then stopped herself. "I am so sorry."

"You said that already," Seth responded as soon as those words had left her mouth. "And I said last time that it's alright. It's not like it was your fault."

"I know," Filia said in response. "But I…" Filia then looked as if she really, really wanted to say something, but then at the last second turned away from him and shook her head. "No, you're right. I shouldn't repeat things like that, especially after you've already said it was okay, and I don't want to come across as annoying."

"You're not annoying," Seth quickly said, as in his eyes she appeared to be getting worried. Filia didn't respond immediately to that either, as instead she simply returned her attention back to Seth and locked eyes with him as they walked. They stayed like that for a few long moments, though for Seth it felt like a few moments longer than necessary. He also saw a hint of a shade of red on Filia's face, though that only lasted for less than a second before she suddenly looked away from him and shook her head again.

"Alright," Filia then said as she returned her attention fully back to Seth. "Since you really don't know anything, I bet all the stuff that we've been talking about has been very confusing to you."

"Very," Seth responded plainly and quickly, which caused Filia to let out another giggle.

"I love your honesty," she said to him as she recomposed herself. "And let it not be said that Princess Filia Solara of Sol isn't the kind of person who does not care for her subjects. So, since I'm sure you must have a ton of questions. Feel free to ask me anything you wish and I'll answer it for you to the best of my ability."

Tara's eyes instantly widened the instant those words hit her ears as she was well aware of what floodgates the princess had unknowingly opened.

"Um, my lady Filia," Tara attempted to cut in. "I do not think that is-"

"What is a princess?" Seth quickly asked before Tara could even finish speaking.

"Wow, that was fast," Filia responded, somewhat shocked. "Well, the simplest answer to that question is that a princess is the daughter of a king and a queen. Though I'm sure your next question is going it be-"

"What is a king and queen?" Seth then asked before Filia could finish.

"And here we go," Tara quietly mumbled to herself as she let her head fall into one of her hands.

"And there it is," Filia responded, somewhat annoyed that she had been interrupted, but she did not appear to let it bother her. "Well, to answer that…" Filia then paused for a moment as she looked towards the sky in thought. "You said that you were from Canaan, right? I'm sure Canaan has someone who's in charge of it, doesn't it?"

"You mean Mayor Maryen?" Seth answered for her.

"Yes, exactly," Filia responded as she snapped her fingers and pointed back towards Seth. "Like a mayor. So, you know how in Canaan the mayor is in charge and everyone has to do what he says."

"Maryen is a woman," Seth corrected her. "But yes, I know what you're talking about."

"Oh, sorry," Filia quickly apologized once she realized her obvious mistake. "Anyway. Just like how everyone has to do what the mayor says, above the mayor there is someone called the regional governor, and all of the mayors of every town across this part of the world have to do what the regional governor says. Basically a regional governor is the mayor's boss. Then above the regional governors, at the very top are the king, who is always a man, and the queen, who is always a woman. They are pretty much the regional governor's bosses, and as such they get to tell them what to do. Not only that, but because the king and queen are the bosses of your boss's boss, this pretty much makes them the boss of everyone in their country. So they can pretty much tell everyone what to do. It is pretty sweet I will admit."

"And a princess is the daughter of the bosses of everyone?" Seth then asked for clarification.

"Mmhmm," Filia answered with a nod. "And when the king and queen eventually die, the princess will become the new queen. Or in the case of a man, who is called a prince, he will become the new king. That's kind of why my mother acts the way she does. She thinks that she is going to be able to tell everyone in the country what to do one day."

"But she can't right now?" Seth asked.

"Nope," Filia quickly answered with both a nod and a smile. "Because princesses can't really tell anyone to do anything, or at least not when it comes to actually running the country. All they have the power to do is just be the daughters of kings and queens. So as long as grandma Faust is still kicking the country is safe from her."

"What's a country," Seth then asked as soon as he was certain that it was his turn to speak again. Filia's eyes went somewhat wide at the sudden, new question.

"Wow, you fire off questions like most mages fire off spells don't you," Filia playfully said to him with a laugh.

"I'm a mage and I don't think I use spells that often," Seth responded, unsure of what else to say. Before either he or Filia could say anything else, however, Tara suddenly cut in in between them.

"H-His curiosity does get the better of him sometimes," Tara answered for him. "So whenever he feels that he is allowed to ask questions he tends to ask as many as he can. I am sorry for putting this on you, my lady Filia."

"What are you apologizing for?" Filia responded to Tara with a skeptical look on her face. "I don't mind answering questions for him. The man has amnesia, so he has the right to ask as many questions as he wants to as far as I'm concerned. And you don't have to put 'my lady' in front of my name every time you wanna say something to me. I think we're more than past that now. So Filia is just fine." Tara looked as if she wanted to say something particular in response to that, but one glance at Seth told her that responding in the way she wanted to might not have been the best idea. So with that in mind she simply smiled and took a step back.

"Of course," she said. "I am sorry my... Filia."

"That's better," Filia responded to Tara with a smile before turning back to Seth. "So, anyway, Seth. To answer your question from before, a country is..."

Throughout the early afternoon the assembled group made their way throughout the city as Raz had turned out to be right. There was a lot to see of it, though much to Seth's disappointment most of it did look the same to him. They did get quite a few stares from various people walking about due to the presence of Filia and the royal guards with them, but thankfully nobody bothered them about it. Initially it was just Raz who was leading the charge and showing off as much as he could of Dis. At some point, however, Tara overcame her initial shyness around Filia and had taken up explaining things where Raz could not. Tara, as it turned out, was much more knowledgeable than Raz about pretty much everything. So while Raz explained the basics of whatever they came across, Tara filled in the details. In this regard they actually made a pretty good team.

To Seth, however, he could not deny that at times he preferred Canaan or even the open desert to this place. They had started by returning to that pool of water in the middle of that large city square, which Raz had explained was called the Moon Pool because supposedly at midnight the moon was reflected in the exact center of the pool. While Seth had accepted that explanation, in his own head he thought that that was a stupid reason to name a pool of water. From there they had walked down several different streets, nearly all of which were lined with identical looking buildings on both sides. That was at least until they reached where the wall was, then there were simply buildings on one side and a wall on the other. It was also annoying to Seth because for the longest time everything in Dis looked so similar with their sand colored buildings that he kept forgetting where he was. At least that was the case until Filia had pointed out to him the names of the streets written on the corners of the buildings, which saved him from ever getting lost again.

Filia, all the while, was very receptive to Seth and true to her word, she did answer every single question that he had asked her, at least all of the ones that she was capable of answering. From her Seth learned what a country was, that the name of the country they all lived in was called the Solaran Empire, that said Solaran Empire was actually much, much larger than he had imagined, that area that Dis and Canaan were part of was only a small part of it called the Frontier, and that Sol, where Filia, Raz and Tara were all from was nothing at all like the desert. That last one Seth had the most difficulty imagining as some of the things that Filia had described to him, such as forests and beaches, seemed impossible to exist given his relatively small world view.

Filia also, much to Seth's surprise, seemed to greatly enjoy talking to him and in between answering his questions she bombarded him with a few of her own questions about him. Seth answered her to the best of his ability of course, even if at times he purposely left out many details. Thankfully Filia accepted his answers and didn't ever press for more. Tara, of course, was there to fill in any details that Seth was not able to, but for whatever reason Filia seemed less interested whenever it was her explaining anything. She was polite and friendly of course, but she just appeared to pay more attention whenever it was Seth answering her questions rather than Tara.

As they walked on Seth noticed that hanging from many of the buildings they saw banners and flags with the same purple, orange and white color scheme that Seth had since learned from Filia were the colors of the Solaran Empire. While most of the assembled group took them for granted, for Seth, seeing them all was a relief, as they added some much needed color variety to a city that looked the same no matter where he looked. Not only that, but lining the majority of the major streets that they passed through were stands, carts, and various small shops that were being set up for the upcoming festival. It reminded Seth of the market district in Canaan, only this was seemingly everywhere and had much more variety of goods and color to them. Unfortunately few, if any, of the stands were selling anything due to the fact that the annual festival they were all eagerly awaiting had not officially begun yet. However, that didn't stop one stand in particular down one of the streets leading back to the Moon Pool from catching Seth's eye.

"Ah keep tellin' ya it ain't hangin' straight!" a very familiar feminne, yet heavily accented voice shouted out amongst the crowd.

"Looks fine ta' me!" a similarly accented male voice responded back to her.

"That's cause you ain't lookin' at it from down here!" the female voice shouted back. "Your end is too low!"

"Well maybe that's cause I ain't as tall as the other guy here!" the male voice shouted back. At the sound of that Seth turned to see a very familiar looking blonde woman as well as a very familiar skinny man with dark hair and a larger, muscular man. At the sight of them Seth broke off from the group and began walking towards them as their argument continued.

"Seth, where are you going?" Filia asked as soon as he began to walk away, which drew the attention of both Raz and Tara. As soon as they noticed where he was headed, however, they both smiled.

"Oh, nowhere," Raz responded before Tara could. "He's just saying hi to a friend of ours from Canaan." Before Filia could say anything in response Raz suddenly nudged her forward. "Come on."

"Ah come on boss, it looks just fine!" Nicky said to Ash as he stepped down from the box he had been standing on and walked over next to her. In front of both of them was a simple wooden table with red cloth draped over it while slightly behind it, held up by two posts, was a bright orange banner with the words "Allen's Apple Pies" emblazoned on it in bold letters. Behind the table were some unopened boxes and some, at the moment, unused cooking equipment.

"Yeah and who's payin' ya," Ash responded to him. "Oh that's right I am and I say it ain't level."

"My side can't possibly be too low," Nicky responded. "What just cause Dean's taller-"

"It ain't that your side is too low!" Ash shouted back in his face before he could say any more. "It's that it's too damn high! You were standin' on a box so you probably weren't even thinkin' about it when you-"

"Ash?" Seth suddenly interrupted as he walked up behind the two of them. At the sound of his voice both Ash and Nicky instantly fell silent as they quickly spun around to see him standing there. Dean, by comparison, who was busy using a crowbar to open one of the boxes behind the table, simply raised his head and looked over towards him.

"Oh, hey, Seth," Dean then said to him with a slight wave of his hand.

"Hello, Dean," Seth replied politely. "What's going on here?" Before Nicky could answer him Ash shot him a glare which instantly made him close his mouth before walking back around the table to assist Dean.

"Oh notin' much," Ash responded to Seth before pointing with her thumb back to the table behind her. "We're just tryin' to set up this here stand before this whole festival shindig blows up and everyone starts goin' crazy."

"Doesn't look too difficult," Seth then said as he quickly glanced behind her at the stand. It appeared to look functional enough to him.

"It ain't," Ash responded. "The problem is gettin' it to look nice enough. You see how many stands are here on just this street." As she spoke she motioned with her arm to pretty much everywhere around her. She didn't need to do that, however, for Seth to see that the whole street was packed with identical looking stands. He had seen them all on the way here. "So what we gotta do is make ourselves look as nice and presentable as possible so that everyone will wanna' come and spend their coppas here instead of over there."

"Oh, I understand what you're saying," Seth answered as he quickly worked out in his head why all of that mattered. If the entire point of making a stand was to sell things then it wouldn't matter if no one bought anything from them. At least that was the conclusion he came to.

"What's up, Ash," Raz suddenly spoke up as he approached before Ash could say anything more to Seth.

"Ah, so you're here too," Ash responded to him as politely as she could. She was about to say something to Tara when she saw her, but before she could her eyes fell on Filia and two royal guards behind her and a look of genuine confusion crossed her face.

"So…" Ash spoke to Tara, as she knew that she would be more capable of answering the questions she wanted to ask than either Raz or Seth. "What's with tha fancy escort?"

"Oh, um," Tara quickly responded, as she had since become so accustomed to Filia following them around that she had momentarily forgotten how strange it was to see. "Ash, this is-" Before Tara could even finish her sentence, however, Filia stepped out from between Raz and Seth.

"Nice to meet you," Filia said to Ash as she held out her hand. "Princess Filia Solara of the Solaran Empire, at your service." The instant those words hit her ears Ash's eyes suddenly became as wide as dinner plates as she suddenly lowered her head and quickly made the same bowing gesture that Seth had seen Raz and Tara do earlier, though she lacked the fluidity and grace that they had possessed when they did it.

"P- Princess Filia," Ash spouted out as she stood back up. Much like Tara had been earlier, the sudden appearance of royalty made her more than a little nervous. Given what Seth had seen from most people's reactions to their group over the course of the day, however, her reaction no longer surprised him. "Ah'm so sorry I didn't recognize you immediately. Ah should have-"

"No, no, it's fine," Filia quickly interrupted before Ash could go on for too long. "You didn't know, and it's not like I was advertising who I was to everyone in this city."

"Well…" Raz suddenly interjected. "You are wearing a dress that a good majority of the people here would never be able to afford even if they had saved an entire year's worth of wages." As soon as Raz had finished speaking Filia's own eyes went wide as she looked down at her clothes, as if she had seemingly forgotten what she had been wearing all day. That reaction confused Seth more than anything Filia had done over the course of the day, as throughout his entire short life Seth had never once forgotten what he was wearing, so the idea that someone would was impossibly outrageous to him.

"Oh…" was the only thing that left Filia's mouth as she returned her attention back to Ash. "Okay, maybe I am advertising it a little, but you don't need to worry about my unexpected presence. You didn't do anything to offend me. Honest."

"T- Thank you very kindly, m- my lady," Ash responded as she recomposed herself. Nicky looked as if he was about to say something, but one glance in Ash's direction told him otherwise as he instantly shut his mouth and went back to what he was doing.

"So," Filia began once the situation had calmed down. ""Raz tells me that you all are friends from Canaan."

"We are," Ash answered. "Although Canaan is a fairly small town so if I'm bein' honest we're more of…" Before Ash could even think of finishing her sentence a look of sudden realization crossed her face as she mentally ran through Filia's exact words. "Wait, Raz?"

"Yeah, short version," Raz cut in. "Princess Filia and I have known each other for-"

"He's my cousin," Filia interjected before Raz could finish, and as she did upon Ash's face appeared an expression identical to the one that Tara had worn when she first learned that fact. Namely shock and immense confusion.

"I'm sorry wha-"

"Yeah," Tara cut Ash off before she could say anymore. "I… did not believe it either."

"It's okay," Raz cut in after Tara had finished speaking. "It's not really something I ever talk about so there's no reason you would know." As he finished speaking Seth watched as a rather unusual expression took hold of his face as he looked towards Ash. It was similar to his usual, overconfident smirk, but something about his eyes was different, as if there was intent behind them. "And it's not really something I would want other people talking about. If you catch my meaning." After he finished speaking Raz then winked and clicked his tongue at Ash. Despite Seth having absolutely no idea what he meant by that, Ash appeared to as she simply nodded at him before recomposing herself.

"Yeah, I can imagine some folks would try to take advantage of that," Ash then said. "Unless you want ta come home one day and find that Tabitha has broken in and is layin' on ya bed dressed like a common streetwalker."

"How can that possibly be a bad thing?" Nicky piped up with a level of excitement that made it clear he was now picturing that exact scenario in his head, "I mean that woman's a Solaris damn eleven out of ten."

"Eh, I disagree." Dean then spoke up with a shrug.

"Well of course you would say that because you would much prefer it if it was Andrea instead wouldn't ya." Nicky responded with a cheeky grin.

"Well... uh... umm... shut up Nicky!" was the only thing Dean managed to respond with as a red tint washed over his face.

"Both of you shut up!" Was all that Ash said to her employees before Seth spoke up with his own question.

"What did you mean by 'common streetwalker'?" Seth then asked. "Everyone walks down the street. Unless you can't walk I guess."

Everyone within earshot instantly looked at Seth and just stared at him, unblinking and dumbfounded by his level of innocence that, while it shouldn't have been a surprise to anyone who knew him by now, they still found themselves flabbergasted by the fact that he had even asked that question.

"Well if ya wanna find out," Nicky began as a sly grin grew across his face. "After I'm off work I'm sure I can help ya find a nice lady to-"

"You do not want to finish that sentence," Tara interjected as she glared at the farm hand like she was about to throw him through the closest wall with her magic. Nicky, unsure if Tara could actually do that or not, for the first time in his life found himself intimidated by the tiny librarian and promptly shut his mouth.

"So..." Ash then began as she returned her attention back to Filia. "I'm sorry to say my lady Filia, but we don't have anythin' to sell at tha current moment. We're still tryin' to get set up here... As I'm sure you can see."

"Oh, it's alright," Filia responded with a genuine smile. "I just came out here to see the city before the festival started. I wasn't expecting anything special so you don't have to worry about it. I'm just happy that I got to meet some of Raz's friends."

"Well that's mighty kind of ya," Ash replied. "Very mighty kind."

"Just out of curiosity though," Filia began as she took a closer look at Ash's stand. "What are you going to be selling here? If I get the chance I'll make the effort to stop by. You know, assuming of course certain people will let me." As Filia finished speaking she pointed behind her towards her two royal guard companions, which drew a laugh out of Ash, though Seth wasn't sure if it was genuine or not.

"I can't say that I understand," Ash responded as she finished laughing. "But I do sympathize, and we certainly would appreciate it if ya did stop by. Then we'd be able to tell everyone that Princess Filia Solara shops here." That response drew a laugh from Filia as well. "But to answer your question we're sellin' apple turnovers. Using our own ingredients fresh from our own Allen family orchard. Somethin' we're quite proud of if I do say so myself."

"What's a turnover?" Filia then asked with genuine curiosity. "I've never heard of that before." While Seth himself was genuinely curious what a turnover was, when he saw the look of dumbfounded shock and surprise suddenly fall upon Ash's face he instantly decided against saying anything since Filia had already asked.

"You really don't know what a turnover is?" Ash couldn't help but ask. "Well, ah guess the best way to describe it is that it's kind o' like a pie ya can fit in your hand."

"Kinda like a jelly doughnut in a way." Nicky added.

"Oh," Filia responded rather quickly with a pinch of giddiness in her voice. "You sir just sold me on this. Mostly since anytime any of us in the palace want a pie they just make us a full one. So a small personal one that's like a doughnut sounds quite interesting, quaint even." As she finished speaking she turned back to Raz. "Okay, Raz, we have got to come back here once the festival starts! Whatever it takes! Make it happen! Please! I'm counting on-" Before she could finish Raz suddenly burst out laughing as he put his arm around her.

"Alright, alright," he said to her. "I'll see what I can manage. Though I'm not promising anything."

"It's okay, that is enough!" Filia responded as she suddenly hugged Raz. "Thank you, Raz! Thank you thank you thank you so much!"

During that whole conversation, however, while Seth had heard every word that they had said, his attention was somewhere else. Far down the road they had just come from, but not too far, Seth spotted a very familiar looking redheaded woman walking in the opposite direction of him. Based on what he could see of her gait and posture, she looked absolutely pissed.

"Tara," Seth said to her as Filia, Raz and Ash all kept talking. Once her attention was his Seth pointed down the street at the redheaded woman so that she could see her. "Isn't that Vivian?" Tara held her hand over her eyes as she leaned forwards a little bit to get a better look, but that only lasted for a single second.

"I think so," Tara answered. "It certainly does look like her. If only because of the hair and clothes."

"Where do you think she's going?" Seth then asked.

"I cannot say," Tara answered. "Though given what I know she usually does, it is kind of early for that, but to be honest I would not put it past her." That remark made Seth suddenly feel worried as his mind flashed back to the time he and Vivian went out for drinks at The Empty Barrel back in Canaan. While the night had started fine, things took a downward spiral towards the later half of the evening, and that was when she was in a good mood.

Since then Seth had learned more about what the effects of alcohol actually were and why people willingly choose to drink it. Being a member of the town watch had given him insight into new areas of knowledge that Tara either hadn't or wouldn't teach him. With that in mind, if Vivian drank as much as she did on a good night, then what would she do when she was more than a little upset? That thought was something that Seth would rather not have contemplated.

"I'll be right back," Seth then quickly said as he suddenly took off running in Vivian's direction. His sudden departure drew the attention of Filia, Raz and Ash, who all turned to look in his direction.

"Seth, where are you going!" Filia called out to him, but to no avail as he didn't respond to her at all. Raz, however, looked past Seth and saw the redheaded woman down the street, and when he did he immediately understood what was going on.

"Seth wait-"

"Let him go," Raz spoke up before Tara could take off after him. The instant he did Tara stopped where she stood and spun around to face him. The look on her face was an odd mixture of shock, confusion, and anger.

"Are you insane!" she shouted back at him. "What if-"

"He'll be fine," Raz responded calmly before Tara could say any more. "We've been through most of this city already, so he should be able to find his own way back no problem. Or at least to the moon pool, and your hotel isn't far from there so if he makes it there then he should be fine."

"But he-"

"Tara," Raz interrupted again as he suddenly dropped his smirk and focused his eyes on her. The look he was giving her was almost a glare. "He can't rely on you forever." Tara opened her mouth to respond, but stopped herself after Raz's words echoed in her head a few times. That knife-like glare he was giving her also brought back to her mind their past encounters, which did not end in the best of ways. Seeing that she was still apprehensive, however, Raz let out a loud sigh. "Look, if you're really that worried about him. If he doesn't show up by the time it gets dark I'll go looking for him myself. Does that make you feel better?" Tara did not respond to him with words, but rather by letting out a loud sigh of her own before she suddenly slumped her shoulders and dropped her eyes towards the ground.

"Where is he going though?" Filia suddenly cut in, completely oblivious to the context of Raz's words.

"Oh, nowhere, just to talk to one of our other friends from Canaan who came with us," Raz answered her as he instantly regained his former composure and put his friendly smile back on.

"Oh, really," Filia responded, appearing interested. "Can I meet her too?"

"I think you might wanna hold off on this one," Raz answered with a laugh. "She... has issues that she sometimes needs help getting through, and more than likely this is one of those times. So Seth's just going to talk to her to see if he can help her out is all."

"Oh... Alright then," Filia responded. The disappointment in her voice was obvious to anyone who could hear her. With that in mind Raz simply put on his best smile again as he put his hand on top of her head.

"Ah, don't worry," Raz said to her as he rustled her hair again, which again drew a giggle out of Filia. "I'm more than certain we'll run into 'em again somewhere down the line."

"Yeah, you're probably right, as always," Filia responded as she playfully pushed Raz's hand away from her. "I need to learn to be more like you. More optimistic." That response drew a hearty laugh out of Raz.

"Trust me," he said to her. "I know it sounds cool, but you really, really don't want that. Though a little optimism never hurts." With that Raz returned his attention back to Ash. "Sorry Ash. It was nice talking to you and all, but I'm afraid we need to get going. It-"

"Is okay, I get it," Ash responded before Raz could finish. "It ain't like there's much to see here anyways, and Ah'm sure you all have better thin's you wanna be gettin' to than this. So go on. Off with ya's. Go have fun. We still need to finish settin' up this here stand anyway."

"I'll come by and see you again when the festival actually starts," Filia was quick to cut in once she heard the direction the conversation was going. "I promise I will."

"I'll hold you to it," Ash responded with a laugh of her own. "Now git goin'." With that the assembled group then turned and headed in another direction away from the turnover stand.

"Bye!" Filia shouted as she waved back at Ash. "It was nice meeting you!"

"Nice meetin' ya too!" Ash shouted back as she responded with her own wave. Once they were all far enough out of earshot, however, Ash suddenly returned her death fueled glare to Nicky. "And what are you standin' around for now!"

"I liked her voice," Filia said to Raz as they walked. "It was so... so..."

"Sexy," Raz finished for her with his wide, toothy smirk on full display. Filia's cheeks instantly went red upon hearing that response.

"Raz!" she shouted, trying her best not to let out a laugh.

"What, it's alright," Raz responded with a shrug. "I'm not your mother. You don't need to hold back with me." That response caused Filia to suddenly burst out laughing, and then continue laughing for several long, long seconds as they walked before she finally calmed down. Tara, while still apprehensive about Seth's sudden departure, couldn't help but let her eyes fall back upon Raz. The way he acted around Filia, it wasn't how she was used to seeing him. Yet, in this new light it felt strangely uplifting to see. She couldn't help but smile herself as Filia's laughter filled her ears. Even with that, however, there was still something about Raz that would not let her relax.

"Solaris, they have these things out here!" Filia suddenly exclaimed as she suddenly took off running ahead of Raz, her two royal guardsmen diligently keeping pace with her. "Come on, Raz! You up for a little taste of home!"

"Why would I want that?" Raz replied calmly. "We're on the frontier. Why not-" Before he could say any more or take another step, however, he suddenly felt someone tug firmly on his shirt sleeve. Upon inspection Raz was unsurprised to see that it was none other than Tara. He was surprised, however, to see that the seemingly cheerful smile that she had been wearing before had completely vanished and was now replaced by a downhearted frown. She wasn't even looking directly at him, as her eyes were more focused on the ground in front of her rather than at him. Seeing that made Raz drop his own smile.

"Raz!" Filia called out to him again.

"Go on ahead!" Raz shouted back. "I'll be right with you! Give me a second!" Filia didn't respond with words, but rather with a confused expression and a raised eyebrow as she turned back and continued on her way. With her gone Raz turned to face Tara. "What's up?" Tara didn't respond to him immediately, however. Instead she took a deep breath and steadied herself as she finally looked up at him. The look in her eyes was almost pleading.

"Okay, no one else is around now," Tara began. "So I want you to tell me the truth. Raz, are you really a member of the royal family? Is Filia really your cousin?" While Raz did have a response for that, the look in Tara's eyes caused him to rethink his words as he stared deep into them. This close, looking at them made him recall past events, as well as how he used to think of her. More important than either of those, however, in her eyes he could plainly see that she was more or less begging him to tell the truth, even if she wasn't willing to admit that. With all of that in mind Raz let out a loud sigh himself as he put on the most genuine smile that he could.

"It's not something that I shout from rooftops or anything, but yeah," Raz answered. "My grandmother was King Helio's younger sister. She had a daughter, and that daughter is my mother."

"And your father?" Tara then asked.

"My father was a soldier in the Solaran army," Raz answered. "He's..." Before he could say any more Raz's expression suddenly changed as he dropped his smile and looked away from Tara. His use of the word 'was' did not escape Tara's attention as a wave of guilt suddenly washed over her.

"Raz, I'm so-"

"Don't be," Raz quickly interrupted before she could say that one word.

"He died when I was very young. I've had time to make my peace with it. And before you ask he wasn't anyone important and he wasn't of noble birth. He was just a regular guy. It's only by my mother's blood that I'm considered royalty." Having received the answer that she wanted, Tara returned to the former composure that she had been wearing before.

"And if I were to ask Daedalus about all of this?" she then asked with quite a bit more of an air of seriousness.

"Daedalus will say whatever he wants. I mean he has his own strong opinions of the crown," Raz answered. "But he isn't a liar. You know that." Tara remained silent for several long seconds after that. Despite how serious she appeared now, she still seemed to have trouble finding any words to say.

"So…" she hesitantly began. "So you really are royalty."

"Yep," Raz answered. "That is what I just said, isn't it?" Despite his answer, Raz could tell that Tara was still uneasy. "Does that bother you?"

"What, me!" Tara exclaimed louder than before as her face suddenly went red. "No. No, no of course not. I… It is fine. It really is. It is just…" Tara then suddenly fell silent again as she averted her eyes from Raz. Raz, however, could tell what was happening with her as he couldn't help but quietly laugh to himself. "I have never really… been friends with anyone who was a member of the Solaran royal family before. I am of common birth myself, so most nobles will not even look at, much less speak to me. So this is just… How… How should I address you? How am I supposed to speak to you? How-"

"How about we just pretend that we've known each other for a long time already and that nothing at all has changed," Raz interrupted with a very genuine smile on his face before Tara could say any more. Tara fell quiet in an instant as those words hit her ears. For what seemed like a long time the two of them simply remained silent as they stared into each other's eyes. For Tara it was as if simply staring into them was like staring into a world she wasn't aware of before, with all kinds of new concepts and ideas she thought she understood, but didn't. For Raz he was simply happy to see her eyes at all as he took in every detail of them. More than that though, he was just happy that she wasn't angry at him for what had happened before.

The sound of a crashing noise broke the two of them out of their moment as they both turned to look back down the way they had come.

"What the fuck," Raz said to no one in particular as he saw what was happening.

Nearby, laying on the ground was a man dressed in armor that was similar to the ones worn by the local town guardsmen, though it appeared to have less shine to it, as if it was either older or was made of a different material. Possibly even both. His hat had fallen off and landed about a meter away from where he had fallen. Standing over him with his fist clenched and looking down at him with the glare of an enraged bull was, to both Raz and Tara's surprise, Dean. Dean by contrast looked as if he was just waiting for the man to do something, practically daring him to retaliate, and it appeared that he was about to get what he asked for as the guardsman stood back up and sized him up.

That was as long as their fight was allowed to go on, however, as before either one of them could do anything else eight different guardsmen rushed in from different directions and tackled the two of them to the ground.

"Stay here with Filia," Raz said to Tara before with a flash of green light he had suddenly teleported away.

He reappeared not far from where the fight had been happening. However, as he did he saw that he was already too late as the city guardsmen were already beginning to put manacles on both of them.

"What's going on here?" Raz asked aloud as he took a few steps closer to the scene.

"Kindly keep back, citizen," one of the city guardsmen responded as he stepped in front of him. "This doesn't concern you."

"You fucking lowborn son of a bitch!" the city guardsmen who had been punched by Dean shouted in his direction. "Attacking a member of the city guard! I'll see that your head is cut off!"

"Oh I sincerely doubt that," one of the other city guardsmen said as he walked up next to the guardsman on the ground, put his metal clad boot on top of his head, and then pushed his face down into the cobblestone road with it. Not hard enough to hurt him, but hard enough to make his point. "Did you really think that none of us would recognize you, Roland? If you did then you're stupider than we thought."

"I'm tellin' ya he came at us!" Ash shouted at one of the other city guardsmen who appeared to be speaking to her. "We was mindin' our own business 'ere tryin' to get this stand set up! Then suddenly he comes around and starts demandin' some kind of tax for the 'privilege' of lettin' us sell our stuff here in the city in the first place!" To his credit the city guardsmen that she was talking to appeared to be silently and patiently listening to every word she said. "And I don't want none o' you all tellin' me there is a tax! I know bullshit when I hear it and that man was definitely spewing bullshit from his mouth! So when I refused he started demandin' 'favors' from me in order to make up for it! So of course I refused that too! Then when I did he grabbed me and that's when my employee there socked him right in the face! He was defendin' me! He did the right thing 'ere! That's my story and I'm stickin' to it! Arrest me too if you dont' believe me!"

"No one here is saying that we don't believe you, ma'am," the guardsman then responded to her. "In fact, we've actually had dealings with this particular individual before. He used to be a city guardsman, but was let go under…" The guardsman then paused for a moment to look back as the apparently fake guardsman was hoisted to his feet, as was Dean. "Not exactly the best of terms."

"Great," Ash then spoke up again, seemingly having calmed down, but she did not appear to be any less angry. "So you know it was self defense. Then would you kindly see fit to get those there manacles off of my employee so that we can get back to work." The guardsman in question remained silent for a few more moments as another guardsman came up and whispered something into his ear. After he had finished the guardsman speaking with Ash simply nodded at him. Then with that having been said the other guardsmen began to escort Dean and the fake guardsman away.

"Unfortunately, ma'am," the guardsman then said to Ash. "I'm sorry to say that we can't do that. Even by your own testimony your employee attacked him first. Which means that he initiated the confrontation, so we need to take him in for questioning too."

"Are you fuckin' kidding me!" Ash then shouted at the top of her lungs at him. "That's real bullshit and you know it! Why in the actual fuckin' hell would you arrest someone for doin' the right thin' like I said he was!"

"Be that as it may, ma'am," the guardsman replied to her, as calm as ever. "The law is the law, and since he did initiate the confrontation he is technically at fault as well so we need to take him in for questioning." Before Ash could say anything more to him the guardsman slowly turned and began to leave with the rest of his fellow guardsmen. "I wouldn't worry," he said to her as he began to walk away. "The situation being what it is, I'm sure he'll be out in no time at all. If you have any further questions or just want someone to yell at then please come by the guard station." Then with that having been said he and the other real guardsmen began to walk away.

"You fuckin'-"

"Ash, don't!" Nicky yelled as he ran up behind Ash and grabbed her by both of her arms before she could take off running after the guardsmen. Ash struggled fervently in his grasp as she tried her damndest to break free, but Nicky surprisingly held true as he kept her from going anywhere. "It ain't worth it! Goin' after 'em will only make things worse! You know that! So calm the fuck down and actually think this time instead of runnin' off barin' your teeth like a damn rabid monster before you get arrested too! You wanna help him! Then calm the fuck down!" Ash still struggled in his grasp, but only for a few seconds longer as she didn't say anything to him.

"Don't worry Dean!" Nicky shouted towards his friend as he was being escorted away. "I'll git you out! Don't worry!"

"What happened here?" Filia's voice suddenly spoke up from behind Raz as he turned to see that she, Tara, and the two royal guardsmen had all ran back to catch up with him.

Chapter 14

Vivian trudged her way through the streets of Dis in something of a sullen daze, barely paying any attention at all to where she was, what was around her, or where she was going. All of the people surrounding her might as well have not existed at all. They were just vague peach and brown shapes that made noise and got out of her way whenever she approached. In the state she was in she could have likely walked directly over the side of a cliff and not have noticed until it was too late.

Even she, however, couldn't walk forever and eventually she had to stop once she felt her legs beginning to get tired. Only now did she bother to take the time to look around and see where she had ended up. A quick glance told her that she was in one of the non-residential areas of the city, made apparent by the abundance of shops, restaurants, and other businesses. She didn't spare any of them more than a single second glance at most, with the exception of the building she happened to stop directly in front of. Directly to her left stood a beige building that probably wouldn't have stood out at all were it not for the wooden sign that was hanging over its wooden double doors. Said sign displayed in white, cursive letters similar to that of Tabitha's boutique in Canaan, the words, "The Tipsy Rabbit". Next to the establishment's name was a painted image of a white rabbit with its front legs, acting in place of arms, wrapped around a bottle of wine as if it were hugging it. Vivian couldn't help but find that image a little cute, though her attention was more drawn to the word "Tipsy", which made it easy for her to assume what type of establishment this was, and right now it was exactly what she felt like she needed.

Seth saw the disgruntled redhead that he knew to be Vivian stop in her tracks several meters away from him as she looked around, though thankfully not in his direction. Part of him wanted to run directly over to her and see if she was okay, but he stopped himself and like his former mentor, found himself standing still in the middle of a busy street. Were it three months ago, before he had told her the truth about what he was, he would have chased after her in a heartbeat. Now he wasn't sure at all how to approach her.

In the time it took him to think through all of that he watched as Vivian suddenly took a sharp left turn before going straight into the beige building to her left. The second she was inside Seth began to move again as he walked forward until he stood in the same spot she had not even a moment ago. Like Vivian his eyes were drawn to the wooden sign that was hanging above the doors to this building, though unlike Vivian, both the name and the image next to it confused him immensely. The word "Rabbit" was unfamiliar to him, and the strange, white creature with long ears that was holding a bottle was unlike any animal or monster he had ever seen in life or in any of Tara's books. While he assumed that the white creature on the establishment's sign was a rabbit, he still couldn't help but wonder exactly what a rabbit was or why a place would be named after one. These were all questions that he knew wouldn't be answered if he stayed standing here, so he made a mental note to find out what a rabbit was later and walked on into the Tipsy Rabbit.

As he pushed open the pair of wooden doors that led inside he was reminded of the entrance to The Empty Barrel back in Canaan, which he found interesting but not at all surprising as his suspicions about what sort of establishment this was were confirmed the instant he saw the inside. Tables, booths in the corners and against the walls, a long bar with a mirror behind it that ran the exact length of the bar, and the dozens of bottles that rested on the shelf behind the bar told Seth everything he needed to know about this place. The only thing about this tavern that surprised Seth was how strikingly similar it looked to the Empty Barrel save for the fact that it was a much larger building, nearly twice the size of Burt's establishment in fact. One other minor difference though was that on the wall directly opposite of where Seth stood were a number of plaques, though nearly all of them read the same thing, "Best Ale in Dis", along with the year in which the plaque must have been placed there. On the wall surrounded by the plaques, however, was a painted portrait of a well dressed man with dark tan skin that wore a very well made set of dark grey clothes that looked like something Tabitha would make and bearing a large mustache that reminded Seth of Charlie's. Next to him stood a woman with very light skin, to the point that even Seth looked as if his skin possessed some color by comparison, long blonde hair that was tied into a braid, and was wearing a pure white dress. Not only that, but in the arms of the woman was a much more detailed version of the creature from the tavern's sign outside, a white rabbit that almost perfectly blended into the woman's dress.

With that image now burned into his memory, Seth glanced over the rest of the tavern to see only two patrons other than the huntress he had followed inside. One was face down in one of the booths in the back corner opposite of where Seth stood while the other one was being given a plate of what looked like eggs by someone whom Seth assumed must have worked here. He didn't pay any more attention to either of them, however, as he made his way directly towards the bar where he found an obviously distraught Vivian sitting on one of the barstools with her head in her hands.

Seth stood awkwardly beside her for a few prolonged seconds, as he was unsure of exactly how to make his presence known to her, assuming of course she hadn't noticed him already. Eventually he decided that the best course of action was the simplest, and the one that made him instantly cease to look like a weirdo as he quietly took a seat on the barstool to her left.

"Um… hi?" Seth said to her, unsure of what else to say. The instant his voice reached her ears Vivian leaned over in his direction.

"What the fuck do you want?" she hissed at him.

"I…" Seth began, but then stopped himself as he tried to find the right words to say, though to him that felt as if he were trying to tiptoe through a den of sleeping wolves. "I saw that you looked upset and… I just thought I would see if you wanted someone to talk to."

"So what, you're stalking me now?" Vivian then asked as she lifted her head from her hands to look at him more directly.

"What? No, of course not," Seth quickly answered. "Tara told me that's illegal." Vivian couldn't help but roll her eyes at that.

"Whatever," Vivian said to him as she leaned against the bar and rested her head in her hand. "I'd tell you to fuck off, but you're not going to, are you?"

"That depends," Seth answered with a completely straight face and a tone that was one hundred percent serious. "How do I do that?"

"Is this man bothering you, miss?" a third voice interrupted before Vivian had a chance to respond to what Seth had just said. Almost at the exact same time the two of them looked over to see that the source of the voice was none other than the bartender, a tall, surprisingly muscular woman with tan skin and wearing a white collared shirt. While Seth had seen muscular women before, especially considering who was currently sitting next to him, this woman's muscle mass was so much that to Seth it looked as if Vivian and Ash had somehow been fused together into one person. The fact that she was also giving a look that he was more than familiar with thanks to Vivian, a look that gave him the feeling that she was less than a second away from grabbing him by the scruff of his neck and throwing him out of the tavern with one hand if need be, was also something that instantly drew his attention. With that in mind Seth made a mental note that it would most likely be a very bad idea to cross this woman.

Vivian, in response, looked over to Seth and for the next few seconds contemplated exactly what she wanted to say to the bartender. She would have contemplated longer were it not for the sudden interruption of her stomach growling. Instinctively she looked down in slight embarrassment, but when she did she noticed the coin purse hanging off of Seth's belt.

"In the sense that he's annoying, yes," Vivian eventually answered the bartender. "But I know him, he's just like this. So don't worry about it." After hearing that the bartender looked back over to Seth, her expression only softening up a little bit.

"If you say so," she then said. "Can I get the two of you anything?"

"Ale," Vivian immediately responded as soon as the bartender had asked that. "In the biggest cup you have." She then paused for a moment to look back at Seth. "You hungry?"

"Umm... sure," Seth hesitantly responded.

"What do you have here for food?" Vivian then immediately asked the bartender before Seth had a chance to say any more or change his mind.

"Eggs, pork, chicken, steak-"

"A steak for each of us," Vivian said before the bartender could list out anything more.

"Very well," the bartender acknowledged. "And how would you like them cooked?"

"With fire?" Seth responded with a raised eyebrow. That answer caused both Vivian and the bartender to shoot Seth rather scornful looking scowls, which only added to his confusion.

"Just ignore him, he's a dumbass," Vivian spoke up with a loud sigh before Seth could. "Just make them both medium rare."

"Alright," the bartender responded slowly without taking her eyes off of

Seth. "And what about you? You want anything to drink?" Seth was about to say that he wasn't thirsty, but then he remembered something he had drank no more than a week ago.

"Do you have any hard lemonade?" he asked the bartender, which in turn caused her to raise an eyebrow.

"I'm going to have to check the back for sugar," she answered. "But if we have some then I can probably make it."

"Just bring him water," Vivian spoke up before Seth could tell the bartender to do that. "He doesn't really drink anyway." As she finished speaking the bartender shot Vivian her own scornful glance before slowly returning her attention back to Seth.

"Water's fine," Seth said to her, if only to be polite and hopefully to get her to stop looking at him like that. "If it's too much trouble."

With that the bartender got to the task at hand as she reached underneath the bar and pulled out a particularly large tankard, which she then proceeded to fill with the familiar foamy, brown liquid that Seth recognized as ale before setting it in front of Vivian. Once that was done she then grabbed a more regular sized tankard as well as a pitcher filled with clean water, which she set in front of Seth. With both of those things done she left the pair and walked over towards a door that led to somewhere that Seth could not see from where he was sitting.

"Hey, honey!" she shouted. "Two medium rare steaks!"

"Got it!" an unseen feminine voice replied.

Vivian, meanwhile, had begun chugging down her ale the instant it had been placed in front of her. Before the bartender had even returned, which took several long seconds, Vivian had already finished her drink as she violently slammed the tankard down onto the bar.

"A... Are you okay, Vivian?" Seth couldn't help but ask after seeing her do that.

"Peachy-fucking-keen!" Vivian shouted rather loudly as she glared back at him.

"Vivian I..." Seth stammered out, unsure of exactly what he could say here in this place that wouldn't make her yell at him. "I'm serious. I'm worried about you."

"And what?" Vivian shot back. "You expect me to just tell you everything?"

"I would appreciate it," Seth responded with a completely straight face. For several long seconds Vivian said nothing as she narrowed her glare in an attempt to see if he actually was being serious or not with that statement. Before Seth could react, however, Vivian let out an obnoxiously loud sigh and broke eye contact with him.

"Fine," she said as she pushed her now empty tankard away from her. "But you're paying for the steaks."

"What, why?" Seth responded.

"You want me to talk, that's the price," Vivian answered without looking at him. "Besides, you got one too. So one way or another you'd be paying for one of them anyways." As much as Seth wanted to protest, the more rational side of his mind kicked in and reminded him that the person he was currently talking to wasn't exactly the easiest person to deal with. After thinking it through he actually felt lucky that given the circumstances she was actually letting him talk to her at all.

"Fine…" Seth responded with a loud sigh of his own. "I'll pay for the steaks. Whatever a steak is." Vivian's only response to that was to stare at him as if she were a priestess that had just witnessed an entire village commit heresy against the church of Solaris. As the two of them sat there in silence, with Vivian continuing her unblinking, priestess-like judgemental stare at Seth, the older gentlemen stood up from his table and began to make his way towards the door.

"Great eggs as always, Joshilyn!" he shouted as he passed by Seth and Vivian. "Tell Margo that I left the money on the table!"

"Will do!" the same, unseen feminine voice shouted back to him. That whole exchange snapped Vivian out of her steak-fueled disbelief as she turned her eyes towards the older gentleman as he exited the tavern.

"With no staff around he could've easily stiffed the bill and walked out," Vivian muttered to herself, but was unfortunately loud enough that Seth could hear it.

"Why would-" Seth began, but then remembered that there sadly was such a thing as untrustworthy people who would do something like that. He had encountered more than his fair share of them even in a small town like Canaan. "Well… I wouldn't want to make that tough looking lady angry."

"Fair enough," Vivian responded as her eyes went back to her empty tankard. As she did the bartender, whom the both of them now knew to be "Margo", returned to the bar with a large sack over her shoulder.

"Your lemonade will be ready in a minute, sir. Don't worry," she said to Seth as she gently set the sack down onto the floor behind the bar.

"Oh, um… Thank you," was all Seth could say in response, as he was honestly surprised that she would even bother to make that for him at all after Vivian had ordered him water.

"And when you get a chance can I get topped off?" Vivian then spoke up as she pushed her empty tankard towards Margo, apparently not caring that she was in the middle of something else. Without saying a word Margo looked down at the larger than usual tankard, then at Vivian, who only glared back at her in response. Still silent, Margo snatched the tankard from the bar and quickly refilled it before handing it back to Vivian. After which she returned to the task at hand, which Seth could now see was making his, admittedly more complex than he believed, drink.

As Margo began to squeeze some lemons for their sour juices in front of them, which she made easy with her large, muscular hands, another woman stepped out from the doorway that Margo had yelled into earlier holding two plates. This woman was much, much smaller than Margo in both height and build, and her face was much more soft and gentle looking, helped all the more by the bright looking smile she wore. Like Margo she also possessed lightly tanned skin similar in tone to Seth's jacket, as well as short, dark hair that didn't fall that far past her ears. Also like Margo her clothes weren't much to look at, consisting only of a simple, daffodil colored dress with a white apron over it.

"Looking good, hot stuff," the new woman said with a whistle as her eyes fell over the display of Margo squeezing the juice out of lemons with her bare hands. Margo didn't say anything in response or even turn her head, though Seth could see a faint smile appear on her face as that remark hit her ears. "Alright I got two steaks here, and since no one else is here that looks like they want to eat I'm assuming that they're for the two of you." As she spoke, without even asking she set the plates down in front of Seth and Vivian.

"Thank you," Seth politely responded to her before he then looked down at his plate to see exactly what a steak was. To his mild disappointment it appeared to be little more than a slab of meat with nothing else that made it special. Though he did notice the smokey and savory aroma that came from it and it made his mouth instantly begin to water. However this slab of meat was prepared, he could tell just from looking at it that it was prepared well.

"You look familiar," the woman from the kitchen then said before either Seth or Vivian could take a single bite out of their steaks as she looked Vivian over. "Have we met?"

"Maybe," Vivian responded with a shrug. "I don't recognize you." Much to Vivian's annoyance the woman from the kitchen didn't leave after getting that response as she instead let out a hum and tapped her chin. To Vivian's further annoyance she stayed that way for a few very long moments until her eyes fell on Vivian's guild bracelet.

"Oh, you're part of Futura Collegium Aureum!" the woman from the kitchen let out with a jovial smile, apparently excited at that prospect. "That may be where I've seen you. I'm sure you know my Uncle Piers." Vivian had only just picked up her silverware when that name hit her ears. Instantly her eyes went wide and she began to panic, though she tried her best to hide it.

'*Don't freak out, Vivian,*' she thought to herself. '*It can easily be another Piers, right?*'

"Piers Ortiz?" Vivian then spoke up as her mouth moved quicker than her brain.

"Yup!" the woman from the kitchen cheerfully responded almost instantly.

'*Fuck!*' Vivian screamed in her own thoughts as she spent the next several seconds attempting to keep herself from screaming that out loud. '*What are you doing, you bitch! Do or say something!*' Then before either Seth or the woman from the kitchen could speak or even process what was happening Vivian suddenly grabbed her plate, stood up as quickly as she could, and then proceeded to rush over towards one of the booths that was as far away from the bar as possible. Seth, Margo, and the woman from the kitchen could only exchange confused looks as they all watched that happen.

"D-Did I say something wrong?" the woman from the kitchen asked Seth, as he was the only person there other than Margo that she could ask.

"I don't know," Seth responded as he stood up more slowly than Vivian had. He was about to go over and join her when he realized that he had forgotten his steak. When he looked over at it again, however, something else occurred to him. "Um, before I go, I have two questions."

"Okay," Margo responded first as she placed a glass of yellow liquid onto the bar. "Here's your hard lemonade by the way."

"How much were the steaks and what's a rabbit?" were all Seth asked.

As Vivian sat alone in her booth eating her steak the first thing she did was mentally smack herself in the head for rushing over here without grabbing her second tankard of ale. The second thing she did was glance over towards the bar where she saw that Seth was still in a conversation with Margo the bartender and the woman from the kitchen, whom she assumed to be Joshilyn based on what that old man from earlier had said. She couldn't make out at all what they were talking about or how long they had been talking, but she occasionally heard laughter from the two women and saw the more than familiar confused expression on Seth's face before speaking what was no doubt another question. At one point Margo's face turned beat red after Joshilyn had said something and winked at her.

'*Typical Seth,*' Vivian thought to herself. '*Being able to make friends with practically every-fucking-one. He's probably told them that bullshit amnesia story he keeps sticking to and now they're probably telling him that they're so so sorry and that they can't imagine how much that must fucking suck. Yeah, I'd like to see you act all casual and friendly when you find out he's lying to your face and what's behind that eye illusion mask thing he always wears. I mean, fuck, that bartender chick could probably crush your skull with one hand. She'd probably do it if I told her too. Maybe I shou-*'

Before she could finish that thought Seth, who had apparently wrapped up his conversation with Margo and Joshilyn, had suddenly walked over to her booth and set his plate down across from her. Once he had he then walked back over to the bar, grabbed his glass of hard lemonade and Vivian's tankard of ale and brought them both over to the booth as well.

"They were nice," Seth said as he set Vivian's tankard of ale down in front of her before taking a seat himself. "Apparently they met at your guild h-"

"Don't care," Vivian interpreted him as she grabbed her tankard and took in several large gulps of ale before returning to her steak.

"Sorry," Seth responded before another long, sullen moment of silence dominated the space between the two of them. In the midst of it Seth finally looked back down at his steak and began to cut into it. "So... what happened that made you so upset?"

"Like you actually fucking care," Vivian responded without even looking at him.

"I do. That's why I asked," Seth then said in a deadpan tone of voice before taking his first bite of his steak. To his surprise it was actually incredibly tasty, and while he wanted to savor the flavor of this juicy slab of meat, he tried his damndest to maintain a straight face in front of Vivian. With her he felt that that mattered more than the taste of the steak. Vivian in response grabbed her tankard of ale one more time and took several more long, long gulps.

"You really wanna know?" Vivian said before slamming her tankard down onto the table. "Fucking fine. I'll tell you. The reason I came to this fucking city in the first place is because my guild's headquarters is here. Every year everyone in the bronze and silver ranks gets called in and each of them gets a meeting to see if we got what it takes to get promoted. If I was then I could finally leave Canaan." While Seth was certain that he hadn't been touched, he suddenly felt as if he had been punched in the stomach when she said that. While he now had an idea of where this story was going to go, the idea of Vivian suddenly leaving one day was something he had never considered, and despite everything he knew that had happened between them he felt his heart suddenly sink further into his chest. "I thought that maybe I'd done enough, you know. Maybe they'd understand. Okay, that bitch and a half Ingrid was going to vote against me even if I'd killed a thousand monsters right in front of her, but I mean fucking shit, the second I saw that Alejandro had retired and that fucking Piers had taken his place I thought for certain that I had at least two votes between him and my Uncle Lee. You wanna know how many votes I got in my favor in the end though?" Seth was about to respond to that, but before he could Vivian slammed her elbow onto the table and made a circle with her hand. "Fucking zero!" As she screamed, tears suddenly began to stream down her face. "My own Solaris damned uncle voted against me! All because of that night! That fucking night! The tenth of Promethuit! That date is going to haunt me until the day I die! Along with the seventh of Ninix and the twenty-first of Camisix!"

"The seventh of Ninix?" Seth repeated once he finally got the chance to speak. Hearing that date surprised him, if only because it was important to him as well. "Isn't that the day that I..." He didn't want to say it out loud, but as he spoke he motioned to a particular spot on his neck. The same place where Vivian now bore a scar that resembled a bite mark. To his great surprise, however, she suddenly burst out laughing once she realized what he was getting at.

"No no no," she continued. "That's not the shittiest thing to happen to me on that date." Seth sat in silence as he expected Vivian to continue, but she never did as her expression suddenly turned more somber and her eyes fell onto what was left of her steak. For a while all she did was sit in silence and stare down at it as tears continued to stream from her eyes and down her face.

"If you don't mind me asking..." Seth spoke up when it became obvious that Vivian wasn't going to say anything more. "What happened?"

"I do mind," Vivian spat back bitterly as her tear filled eyes slowly glared back up at him. "But I just know that you're going to insist on me telling you anyways and you're not going to let it fucking go until I do, so here it is shitlord." Vivian then paused for another long moment of silence as she looked directly at Seth with what little composure she had left. "The seventh of Ninix, three-hundered and thirty-nine AS. My ninth birthday to be exact, was the day I got my mom killed."

While Seth was certain that one, nothing had happened in the length of time that they had been talking and two, that Vivian wasn't a mage, he suddenly felt the air around them both turn cold as ice as those words left her mouth. Seth opened his mouth to speak, but no words would leave his mouth. He tried desperately to think of something to say, some way of telling her that everything was alright, but he couldn't. Worse still, he knew that he couldn't. He himself had seen and heard of enough people dying of monster attacks to know what that did to people, and knowing Vivian like he did, anything he said to her would no doubt be taken the wrong way.

"I'm... so sorry..." was the only thing he could think of to say as he lowered his head and looked down towards his own, barely touched steak. "I didn't know... I... What about the other date?" Vivian didn't respond to that immediately, as she took in a deep breath and held it for several long seconds before slowly letting it out.

"I..." Vivian hesitantly began. "I don't know if I even wanna talk about it. Because that... that Seth... was the worst day of my fucking life."

"You don't have to if you don't want to. I understand," Seth quickly said once he saw how Vivian was reacting to this line of questioning.

"No, you don't!" Vivian shouted the instant Seth had finished speaking. "I know for a fact that most normal people could never understand! Especially someo… something like you! So unless you find out that you somehow managed to get nearly four-hundred people killed because you weren't strong enough then don't give me that bullshit!" The longer Vivian continued to talk the more she slowly began to raise her voice again. To Seth, the air around the two of them began to grow even colder as he still couldn't find any words to help.

"Viv-"

"You know what, fuck it!" Vivian quickly let out with an obnoxiously loud groan before she then picked up her tankard again and with a few more long, large gulps, drained it completely dry before violently slamming it onto the table again. "Three years ago I was hired to take out some monster that was plaguing a city not far from here called Eden... Seemed simple enough, I mean it was just one fucking monster. I was there for a few days before the fucker finally showed up. I mean sure, it was big, had wings and shot fucking lighting out of its mouth, but I was Vivian fucking Hawks. Doing this shit is in my blood. So with a spear in hand and my sword at my side I ran up to the thing, only for it to fly at me and pick me up off of the fucking ground. I was barely able to move, with my only free hand being the one that was holding the spear. Then the fucker held me in front of its face and just stared at me as electricity bounced between the spaces in its teeth. I knew what was happening. Fucker was gonna blast me until there was nothing left of me but dust. So I did the only thing I could do. I threw my fucking spear at it. I hoped that would be enough to take it down, but hope isn't worth anything. The spear lodged itself in the fucker's right eye and I swear to Solaris the thing screamed so fucking loud I thought I was gonna loose my hearing. Then it did something I wasn't ready for... It dropped me. I don't know how far I fell, but the next thing I knew my head hit something and I was knocked the fuck out. To this day I'm still surprised that bullshit didn't kill me. Worst I got was a concussion... When I came to though, it turned out that fucking hours had passed and the entire city of Eden was up in flames." Silence fell again as Vivian, without thinking, reached for her tankard again and took another drink. Upon finding out that it was already empty, however, she suddenly let out a scream and threw the empty tankard towards the wall next to the booth they sat in. "Three-hundred and eighty nine people! That's how many people that fucking thing slaughtered because I wasn't good enough to kill it! If you want to count my mom and Aiden that makes three-hundred and ninety one! Or at this rate, fuck, throw the corpses of the other five people who died the night Aiden did onto the pile! Ingrid sure as hell was ready to do that!"

At this point Vivian had completely broken down into tears and her eyes had turned as red as Seth's. All Seth could do was sit there and try his best to process what Vivian had just told him. He searched through his mind space for something, anything, any way of telling her that all of this was okay and that none of it was her fault. A search that he knew would be futile, but he didn't know what else to do. However, all that he got from all of that was that he now knew that he had more context for the drunken rant she had dumped onto him after he had helped her back home from The Empty Barrel all those months ago.

"Whether you want to count them or not it doesn't matter," Vivian eventually continued after regaining some of her former composure. "There's still an entire fucking lake's worth of blood on my hands. I keep thinking that maybe if I get better, maybe if I get promoted and live up to the legacy of my mother and grandfather then maybe the blood will wash away, but I'm not getting better. No matter how hard I try, no matter how much time passes, I'm still the same as I was back then. I'm still in the middle of that lake and… I'm drowning. I'm drowning and I have nothing else to fall back on. I have no other skills. What the fuck am I supposed to do if the big three decide that they've given me enough chances! I don't want to go back to my dad's farm! I know if I do he's probably going to try to get me to marry one of his farmhands! I don't want that! I'm not a fucking housewife!" It was at that point that Seth had stepped out from his side of the booth and walked around to Vivian's, whereupon he put a hand on her shoulder.

"Vivian…" he began, still unsure of what exactly he was supposed to say, but he knew that he had to say something at the very least. "I wish I could tell you that it's all okay. That I could provide you with some sort of solution to your problems, but I would be lying if I did, and I don't want to lie to you." Seth then paused for a moment to see Vivian's reaction. She didn't even look up at him. "That being said, I don't like seeing you like this. So if you want me to do anything to help you, even if it's just for a short while. Please let me know."

Vivian only sat there silently for several long, long moments, and for a while it seemed to Seth that she was genuinely thinking about his offer. Eventually, after some of her tears had cleared up she finally turned her head to look up at him. As she did she placed her own hand on top of Seth's. At first, to Seth this seemed like a sign that everything might be okay, if only for right now, but then he felt her grip on his hand suddenly become tighter and tighter. Before long the telltale signs of pain washed through his hand as Vivian began to squeeze it more and more, almost to the point that Seth feared she might actually break something if she kept it up. When he looked back into her eyes he saw her shoot that same, dagger-like glare at him that she had been giving him the entire night.

"Fuck off," was all she said to him. A feeling of dread washed over Seth as Vivian slid out from the booth and stood up next to him, all the while she kept tightening her grip on his hand as if she were fully intending to break it.

"Vivian, I-"

"Shut the fuck up and stop with this 'I care about you' bullshit!" Vivian then shouted in Seth's face as she finally let go of his hand. Out of instinct he pulled it away from her as quickly as he could and rubbed it a little in an attempt to massage the pain away. "I don't know why you're so obsessed with me, but fucking stop it!"

"I... I-I'm not obsessed," was all Seth could respond. "I'm your friend and I-"

"We're not friends!" Vivian cut him off again. "Maybe at some point we were, but not anymore, and you know why!" Those words hit Seth like another punch to the gut. He stood there silent for what, to him, seemed like a long time before his brain was finally coherent enough to form words.

"Fine..." he began. "You know I-"

"I said shut u-"

"No! You shut up!" Seth shouted back at her in a voice so loud and so unlike him that hearing it shocked Vivian so much that she instinctively took a step back away from him. It was also enough to grab the attention of everyone else in the tavern, which had gained a few more patrons in the time that the two of them had been having this conversation. "I've tried to be nice to you! I tried to be your friend! I even tried to pretend that nothing was wrong because everyone else asked me to! All because the night I took you home from The Empty Barrel you broke down exactly like you did today! You told me then that everybody hated you! So to make you stop crying I made a promise that I would never hate you! No matter what you did! Though you've been making it really, really hard for me to keep that promise! I understand why, believe me I do, but don't stand there and pretend that I betrayed your trust and that was all that happened! We both know it's just as true the other way around!"

"Where do you get off acting like I'm the asshole here!" Vivian shouted back at him as soon as he was done. "I-" She would have said more, but her attention was suddenly taken from her by one of the patrons who had been there originally as he drunkenly wandered into her in an attempt to leave. In her blind rage Vivian spun around and punched the man square in the face the instant he had touched her, which knocked him to the floor almost instantly.

"Hey!" Margo yelled the second she saw that, but Vivian ignored her.

"What the fuck, you bitch!" The man exclaimed as he pulled himself up into a sitting position. Once he did, however, and saw who was in front of him, his eyes snapped open as they focused directly upon not Vivian, but Seth. "You!"

"Me?" Seth responded, genuinely surprised. Almost enough to make him forget that he was angry too.

"Yeah!" the man shouted as he pulled himself back onto his feet. The instant he did he seemed to completely forget about Vivian as his attention was focused solely on Seth. "You're one of those two motherfuckers that cost me my job!" With that having been said Seth quickly looked over this man with his long blonde hair, wide brimmed brown hat and matching duster, but as hard as he tried, nothing about this man appeared familiar to him at all.

"I'm sorry, who are you?" Seth felt that he had to ask that point, though when he did the man's face suddenly turned red with fury and rage.

"Julian!" the man then shouted at the top of his lungs. "Julian Plantier! I had a sweet and easy job watching over Mister Smeraldo's daughter until you and that other bastard fucked it up!" The instant the name "Smeraldo" hit his ears a wave of memories flashed through Seth, and this man was in them.

"Oh, you were one of those people that worked for Vito," Seth then said without an ounce of compassion in his voice. "Okay then."

"If the two of you are going to continue with this sudden and unexpected reunion then take it somewhere else so that I can drink in fucking peace," Vivian then interjected with a scowl on her face before Julian could properly respond to what Seth had said.

"Oh no bitch!" Julian growled as he brought his attention back to her. "You attacked me!"

"And you bumped into me!" Vivian shouted back at him. "And don't say it was an accident, there's plenty of room in this tavern so I wasn't even remotely in your way!"

"So it's my fault that I didn't notice you!" Julian in turn shouted back at Vivian. "Sorry that I was in too much of a daze to notice a screaming bitch!" Vivian, at that point, seemed to completely forget about Seth as she walked right up to Julian and got so close to him that her face might as well have been touching his.

"Call me a bitch one more time and I swear I'll-"

"You'll what," Julian responded before Vivian could finish, appearing unintimidated.

"Alright break it up!" Margo suddenly shouted in a commanding tone of voice as she put her beefy arms between Vivian and Julian and easily separated them. "Now I want all three of you to leave. Now. I've already sent my wife to get the city guard so if you're smart you'll do what I say. Got it?" As she finished speaking she turned her wrathful eyes towards Vivian. "You leave first."

"Fuck that!" Vivian shouted uncaringly at the bartender. "I've had a really shitty day and none of this is helping."

"Not my problem," Margo responded without blinking.

"I think we should listen to her," Seth attempted to interject.

"You don't get a say in this!" Vivian snapped back at him before he could say another word. As the situation began to escalate in front of him, and now denied the right to even speak, Seth couldn't help himself as he began to grind his teeth together and a subtle, almost inhuman sounding growl escaped his lips.

'Vivian…' Seth began to think to himself. 'Why must you be so difficult? You could have just apologized and then maybe we wouldn't be in this situation. I tried to be nice to you, but you didn't want it. Margo gave you the chance to walk away, but you didn't take it. Do you want things to be difficult? Do you not want anybody to like you? Why would you want that?' As those thoughts ran through his head he watched as Vivian kept shouting at Margo. Seth didn't bother to listen to what Vivian was saying anymore, but he could see Margo's eyes beginning to twitch. Given his past experience, he knew what that usually led to. 'I need to do something to make her leave. If she was going to leave on her own she would have by now. I can't just ask her to, she won't listen to me. I can't drag her out of here either, she'd fight me the whole way. Though maybe that might be the only way she would listen…' As the idea of physically dragging Vivian out of the tavern became more and more appealing to Seth, another idea suddenly popped into his head as he remembered a fight he had recently been in. *'Wait a second... I suppose I could try it. I've never done it with anything as big as her, but there's no reason it shouldn't work... right? Right?'*

With neither Vivian, Margo, nor even Julian paying any attention to him anymore Seth took a few steps back away from Vivian so that he would be out of her range of punching him. Assuming of course that what he was about to attempt actually worked, and if it didn't he would at least be far enough away to see an incoming strike from her. With all of the noise still going on around him Seth took in a deep breath and held out his right hand towards Vivian. Vivian, who was still screaming at Margo, didn't even notice him move much less see what he was actually doing, and Julian wasn't there anymore. A quick glance around told Seth that he wasn't even in the tavern anymore, so Seth assumed that he must have snuck out while Vivian was distracting Margo. Seth put that thought out of his head quickly as he returned to concentrating.

At first nothing happened, but then, in the midst of Vivian's ranting she suddenly began to float up into the air until she was roughly thirty centimeters off of the ground. It took her a few seconds to notice this, but once she did she began to flail around helplessly as Margo took a step back from her.

"What the fuck!" Vivian shouted as the full reality of the situation hit her. Knowing that there was only one person she knew who was capable of something like this she turned her head to barely see Seth standing behind her. "Seth you fucking dumbass! Put me right the fuck down now or I'm going to kick your ass into next year!"

"So only for a few hours then," Margo interjected with a smirk.

"Shut up!" Vivian shouted back at her without looking.

"If I let you down will you listen to her and leave?" Seth asked as he, taking some inspiration from her, shot her the most determined, dagger like glare he could muster given the circumstance. Vivian attempted to resist as she let out a growl of her own, but one look into Seth's eyes told her what would happen if she did. While Seth's eyes appeared brown to everyone else, in her eyes they appeared to be a very different color. Several long, long moments of silence followed as both Seth and Vivian held their gaze, seeming waiting for the other to break first. In the end, however, it was Vivian who lost that fight as she let out a groan.

"Fine," she eventually said. "But you fucking better not follow me this time."

"Okay, fine," Seth quickly agreed before he dropped his arm. As he did, Vivian in turn dropped back down to the wooden floor. She landed on her feet, though she did stumble for a bit. With her feet back on solid ground again she focused her attention directly on Seth, who hadn't budged an inch.

"Never do that again," she said to him before walking past him and straight out of the tavern doors. As Seth watched Vivian leave a sudden feeling of cold, empty sadness began to well up within him, as if a part of him had somehow been severed and he now had to adjust to the idea that it wasn't there anymore. It was so much that the impact of the tavern doors slamming shut behind Vivian felt to him as if they had hit him directly in his head as, with her no longer there to see him do this, he suddenly fell to his knees and brought both of his hands to his face to hold back a scream. In reality he knew that the pain he was now feeling was because lifting Vivian off of the ground like that took so much more effort, concentration, and willpower than he had initially thought it would when the truth of the matter was that this wasn't that much different than when he had attempted to move vast amounts of sand out in the desert, but it certainly didn't feel like just that to him. Regardless of whatever the source of his pain was, he still made a mental note to himself to never, ever attempt something like that ever again. Lifting small, inanimate objects with his mind had been easy, but trying to lift a living person that was actively resisting him the whole time turned out to be a completely different type of experience, one that he hadn't been prepared for at all.

The drops of blood that could have only come from his nose that he saw in his right palm as he lifted his head from his hands only confirmed all of this for him. Before he could contemplate any of that, or anything that had happened, however, the sudden feeling of someone's hand touching his shoulder made him instinctively pull away as he pulled himself back onto his feet and spun around to see whomever it was that had touched him. It turned out to be none other than Margo, who upon seeing his reaction kept her hand raised, but was slowly beginning to close it into a fist in case anything else were to happen. Seeing that Seth instantly made himself look more visibly relaxed.

"I'm sorry," Seth quickly said the instant he was able to as he attempted to regain his former composure and look like the least threatening person possible, a process that turned out to be quite hard for him to do at the moment because while he was sure that he looked as kind and unthreatening as possible, he still didn't feel like that at all on the inside.

"Don't worry about it," Margo slowly responded as she lowered her fist back down to her side. "If anything I should be thanking you. If you hadn't done that then... well, then she probably would have tried to hit me." Seth wanted to respond to that, but when he opened his mouth to do so the feeling and taste of blood on his lips reminded him that he was still bleeding from his nose. Instinctively he brought a hand up to his nose to touch it, and the sight of fresh blood on that hand told him all that he needed to know. Before he could say anything about it Margo, with a disgusted look suddenly springing up on her face at the sight of Seth's blood reached into one of her pockets and pulled out a handkerchief, which she then held out to Seth.

"Thank you," Seth said to her as politely as he could as he held the handkerchief up to his nose.

"Don't worry about it," Margo responded to him. "So... sorry about your... whatever your relationship is with that woman, but-"

"You want me to leave too?" Seth interjected before she could finish.

"I was going to ask you to pay for her drinks," Margo answered. "But yes, that too. If you don't mind. I don't-"

"No, it's okay," Seth interrupted her again. "I understand." As he spoke he reached into his coin purse, but as he did his eyes drifted back over towards the table where he and Vivian were sitting and his still barely touched steak on it. "Is it possible for me to finish my steak before I leave, or can I take it with me?"

"We don't do doggie bags," Margo responded as she scratched the back of her head. "But if you give me an extra two coppers I can give you two slices of bread and a piece of cheese to make it into a sandwich."

"That's fine," Seth responded with a sigh, which unfortunately made more blood drip from his nose.

With all of that said and done Seth walked through the city streets eating his steak sandwich, something that he found slightly harder to do than he had expected due to the steak being tougher than the bread it was on. Despite that, however, he finished the thing in hardly any time and he did have to admit that it tasted really, really good for being little more than a slab of meat. With that no longer on his mind Seth's thoughts began to drift as he made his way through the streets of Dis back the way he came. At least that was the direction he hoped he was going.

With nothing but the sounds of the city and people surrounding him, Seth's thoughts, despite his best efforts, eventually returned to Vivian and what had just transpired in The Tipsy Rabbit. Part of him wanted to believe that Vivian didn't mean anything she had said before she was obviously drunk. At the same time, however, the part of him that knew better reminded him that Vivian wasn't the kind of person who said things she didn't mean. She had always been very blunt, very aggressive, and whenever she said something she meant it. Especially when she had declared her intentions to hurt something or someone. Knowing that, Seth couldn't help but clench both of his fists as the close call that almost broke out into a fight played out in his head again. Specifically the part when she screamed in his face that they were no longer friends.

Despite how he had been when she first found him out in the desert, Seth liked to believe that at least now he wasn't a fool. He had known that Vivian had felt that way about him since the incident where he gave her that scar on her neck. He knew that she was only pretending to be his friend because Tara had asked her to. He knew that she hated monsters for a multitude of viable reasons, all of which he could understand. He knew all of this, and yet, actually hearing those words from her own mouth felt like more of a betrayal and a knife to the side than anything else he had ever felt from anyone, including Tara. He knew all of that, but what he didn't know was why he felt the way he did now despite knowing all of that.

Before he could contemplate that any further, however, the sight of a very familiar woman with curly brown hair standing behind a table caught his attention. As he walked closer he saw that it was none other than Agatha standing behind a table that was covered from one end to the other in a gaggle of seemingly random items that made it appear as if she had scooped up all of the junk from a random corner in her house and dropped it all onto the table. Behind her was a slightly askew sign that read 'Schaal's Treasures From The Past' that possessed absolutely no artistic flair to the letters of any kind. If anything it looked as if she had just grabbed a paintbrush and a bucket of whatever paint she could find and quickly painted the name onto a wooden board she had found. Knowing her, Seth would not have been surprised at all if it turned out that the paint was still wet.

"Come on! Come on! Come one! Come all! Feast your eyes on these wonderful pieces of lost technology from the time before Chaos!" Agatha called out to the ocean of people passing her by, most of which ignored her. Those that didn't merely gave her a quick passing glance before moving on. Agatha, however, kept it up with a smile and continued to shout despite all of that. If anything the fact that she never, ever stopped talking seemed to actually be helping her out here. "While you're at it not only can you look, but you can take these beauties home with you! Oh? Hi Seth! I haven't seen you since we left Canaan!"

"Hi... Agatha," Seth replied as he walked up to her. Part of him wondered how, if Ash couldn't get her stand set up before the new year had started, how could Agatha. His curiosity about that was quickly dashed when he saw that all her "stand" consisted of was an obviously cheap wooden table and her makeshift sign, which he now saw wasn't so much part of the stand as it was a hastily made sign that was leaning against the building behind her to keep it up rather than being part of the table. "Yeah... where were you exactly? I mean on the trip here. I don't think I ever saw you."

"Oh, I spent most of the trip writing," she immediately answered him. "Yeah, mostly just writing, scrapping, and then rewriting a letter to my parents. I figured that if they won't write back to me then the least I can do is write to them to remind them that I exist."

"I'm sure they didn't forget that you exist," Seth did his best to reassure her. "You're... unforgettable?"

"Aww, that's sweet of you to say," Agatha responded with a wide smile. "But you haven't met my folks. Trust me, it wouldn't be the first time the fact that they have a daughter slipped their minds. Anyways, it took me a while to make one that I was satisfied with. I was going to drop it off, but then the city guard pulled me away because that bottomfeeder I was traveling with turned out to be a smuggler and he tried to pin it on me. So that took a while. Mostly because they had to look over all of my stuff so that they could be absolutely certain that I wasn't hiding anything illegal in them. By the time they let me go I was just tired. Then I tried to drop it off again today, but then they told me that it might be awhile before they could actually send it because apparently the postmaster had been arrested for some reason. I mean they still took it and said that they absolutely would send it at the first available opportunity, but still. What the actual hell? Maybe Grey knows something about it. I'll try to remember to ask her if she happens to walk by." Somehow, to Seth's utter shock and amazement, Agatha had expelled all of that in such quick succession that Seth wasn't sure if she had taken a breath at any point during it. "So that's how I've been, how about you?"

"I… I'm not having a good time," Seth answered her as his eyes drifted towards his feet.

"What happened?" Agatha then immediately asked, appearing to be genuinely concerned.

"Well…" Seth began. "The first thing that happened when I got here was that I also got pulled aside by the city guard because those dog things wouldn't stop making noises at me. You know, like all animals do. Then Tara wouldn't stop being all nervous and secretive about why we came here. Someone tried to steal my coin purse, but then I ran into Raz when he stole it back from the guy that stole it from me. Then we followed Tara to the postmaster's office where he was being all creepy and weird with her about getting her missing packages back-"

"Wait," Agatha interrupted as she held up a hand to stop him. "The postmaster?"

"Yes," Seth answered.

"The same postmaster that got arrested this afternoon?" Agatha then said. Seth only realized the implications of where she was going with this after those words had left her mouth, upon which Seth's eyes instantly went wide.

"Oh…" Seth eventually responded. "Yeah um… Raz and I were there when it happened."

"What happened?" Agatha then immediately asked, now really, really curious as she leaned in a bit closer towards him.

"I was actually getting to that," Seth continued. "Like I said, he was being all weird and creepy with Tara and said that he wanted special favors from her or something to get her packages back." While she didn't say anything, Seth saw a look of realization cross Agatha's face as he told that part of the story. As if she knew exactly what he was talking about even if he himself didn't. "Then Raz walked in and started threatening him. I was actually worried that it was going to turn into a fight, but then suddenly this girl I'd never seen before came in and she turned out to be Raz's cousin. Though everyone kept calling her a princess-"

"Wait!" Agatha suddenly interrupted again, this time with much more volume to her voice. "That Raz guy is actually royalty!"

"I guess…" Seth answered with a shrug of his shoulders. "I'm still not entirely sure what royalty even is though." Agatha then opened her mouth again, supposedly to interrupt Seth one more time, but after a second she stopped herself. Seth took her continued silence as a sign that he should continue. "Anyways. After that happened this old man showed up, and after Raz explained to him what had happened he had the postmaster arrested. We left after that, so I don't know what happened to him."

"Then what happened?" Agatha asked.

"Well…" Seth continued after a few long seconds in an attempt to find the right words for what he wanted to say. "Then Filia took us-"

"Who's Filia?" Agatha interrupted him yet again, though Seth didn't blame her that time as he only realized his mistake after she had spoken.

"Raz's cousin," Seth answered her. "The prin-"

"Wait, Princess Filia Solara!" Agatha shouted as loud as she could.

"Yes," Seth answered plainly.

"Princess Filia Solara is Raz's cousin!"

"Yes…" Despite the answer she had been given Agatha remained silent for several long seconds as she just stared wide eyed at Seth. She was silent for so long that it actually began to worry him somewhat. "Is… that a problem?"

"No," Agatha quickly answered as she recomposed herself and relaxed somewhat. "Anyway, please, continue. I promise I won't interrupt you again." Somehow Seth doubted that would be true, but he decided to continue anyway.

"Filia took us upstairs to meet her mom, who wasn't all that nice really," Seth continued without any interruptions from Agatha. "Then Filia asked her if she could spend the day with Raz since she hadn't seen him in a long time. I think. Her mom said no, but the old man allowed it as long as some guards went with her. Then we all left so that Raz could show her around the city, and while we were out I saw Vivian and she looked really, really upset. So I followed her because I wanted to talk to her about what was going on, but now I'm pretty sure she hates me more than she already did." As he finished his story, Seth couldn't help himself as his head suddenly felt too heavy for his neck, so he let it fall into his hands in a vain attempt to hide his face from Agatha. "Why... Why am I even here?"

"Because Tara had business here and took you along..." Agatha attempted to answer.

"No, I don't mean this city, though I already want to go home," Seth answered as he lifted his head from his hands. The beginnings of tears were forming in his eyes as he did so. "I mean why are all of you still trying to be friends with me, or at least pretending to?"

"I don't understand what you're asking, Seth," Agatha then said to him in as calm a tone as she could muster.

"Like I said, Vivian hates me," Seth sort of answered.

"She doesn't-"

"I'm not that much of an idiot!" Seth shouted without thinking. The look he shot at Agatha as he did so was a type of a glare that rivaled only Vivian's in intensity, so much so that Agatha felt a shiver crawl down her spine upon seeing it. "I know I don't understand everything. I know there's still a lot about the world that I don't know and probably never will. I still ask questions every now and then that, from the looks I get, I can tell were apparently stupid, but that doesn't mean that I can't see that Tara's afraid of me, and that she has been for who knows how long now. Raz and Vivian are just waiting for me to snap again. I know they are. It's not an if to them, it's a when, and all of you want me to act as if nothing happened. How can I do that? I bit Vivian in the neck. I caused an incident where many townsfolk had to get involved. I almost killed Raz with my bare hands, and when you showed up I was no less than two seconds away from attacking you too. If Raz hadn't knocked me out I know that I would have easily killed you and not hesitated. Then I got dragged back to town where all the people who know about my secret are afraid of me and those that don't look down on me. So I'll ask again..." As he spoke his eyes began to tear up more and more with each word that left his mouth. It took all of the willpower he had to keep himself from outright sobbing where he stood. "Why am I here? Why didn't you just take Raz and leave me in the desert? Why am I being forced to be paranoid and miserable because I thought that I could trust you and Vivian?" As that name left his lips Seth unconsciously looked away from Agatha towards the sky. "Maybe she was right..."

"Maybe who was right?" Agatha couldn't help but ask. As impressed as she was that all of this was the most intellectual thing she had ever heard him say, her concern for his well being took precedence. The instant Seth heard Agatha's voice, however, the image of Lilim's smiling face sitting across from him at the campfire flashed through his head.

"No one," he quickly answered as he just as quickly wiped his tears away.

"Okay then…" Agatha responded as calmly as she could, though in her own mind she wasn't convinced. "As for everything else you said… Seth, I can't speak for Vivian or Tara, or anyone other than myself. So I'll do that. Seth, the reason I brought you back to Canaan wasn't just because I was the one that organized the search party to find you, but because I've gotten to know you. Hell, if I was scared of every person that could easily kill me I'd never be able to leave my house. I'm no fighter. There's a reason why whenever I go out digging I hire Vivian to keep me from being gobbled up like the snack that I am. Do you understand what I'm getting at?"

"Not really," Seth quickly answered, which made Agatha let out a loud sigh.

"What I'm trying to say," Agatha continued after suddenly adopting a very serious look on her face, which shocked Seth because he didn't believe that she could be serious. "Is that people do like you, but everyone needs to come to terms with your… relation to certain 'people' at their own pace." Despite her use of the word "people" Seth knew full well what she was really talking about and why she had phrased it like that. "You just need to be patient. I'm sure they'll all come around eventually. Though if it really bothers you that much maybe it would be best if you tried talking to some of them about this. Start with Tara. She's around you the most and she's very understanding. So if anyone will listen it will most likely be her." Seth wasn't sure at all if he even wanted to do what Agatha was suggesting, but it was the first real piece of advice anyone had given him since the incident in question had taken place.

"I… guess…" was the only thing he could respond with.

"Great!" Agatha exclaimed as her familiar smile adorned her face again. "Now are you planning on buying something and giving me extra ale money for later or are you just going to keep standing there and using me as a free therapist?"

"What's a therapist?" Seth immediately asked without thinking.

'And there's the Seth I know,' Agatha thought as her smile widened a little bit.

Chapter 15

The sun was only just beginning to set over the frontier city of Dis. However, due to the soul rending heat that was offered by the region, even at this time of year, very few people took notice of it right away. Least of all not Filia, Raz, Tara or either of the two royal guardsmen that accompanied them, as they were all much too focused on Filia's current distraction to care about little things like that. Said distraction was another merchant stand that had miraculously managed to get itself set up and selling its wares before the new year had even begun. Any discussion about whether this particular merchant was giving himself an unfair advantage over the others by selling his wares early was quickly dropped once Filia had taken an interest in said wares and was already discussing exactly what she wanted from him.

Raz and Tara simply watched as Filia finished paying the man, as neither of them had any interest in something as childish as what he was selling.

"So…" Tara eventually began. "Has she… always been like this?"

"What, Filia?" Raz responded, though not nearly as subtly. "No, actually. Way back, when she was younger, she used to be the shyest thing you would ever meet. A bird would make her jump up and run away, and I know what you're thinking and no, I am not kidding."

"Okay then," Tara then said, not wanting to admit that she did in fact want to ask that question if only because it was Raz explaining this to her. "So what changed?"

"A bunch of different things really," Raz answered as he directed his attention back towards the princess in question. "Since you're from Sol like us, it might not surprise you to learn that being a princess isn't exactly a life of relaxation and luxury. People might say that they don't care about their image, but when the eyes of everyone in the country they rule over are on them every single second of every single day, then what they say isn't worth any more than the sand beneath our boots. Believe it or not, her mother actually preferred her when she was shy, because then she could at least be controlled."

"Controlled?" Tara replied, confused. "Surely you do not mean like actual control, do you?"

"Would you believe me if I said that I did," Raz answered in a drastically different tone of voice as he blinked and suddenly Tara found him staring directly at her again. Between his sudden lack of a smile and the severity in his eyes, one look was all Tara needed to tell her that Raz was indeed being serious. "Like I said, people only say they don't care about their image. Someone who's insecure and so concerned with what everybody thinks of them is easy to mold. Like clay, only you're shaping the inside, not the outside. Her mother used her insecurities to make her into, what she considered at least, to be the perfect princess. A quick lesson on the proper ways to do one's hair one day, an explanation of which outfits would make people judge her the least another day, and regular lessons in proper manners and what specifically to do to avoid people saying bad things about you all other days. It wasn't just for her public image either, though that was certainly part of it. Her mother also had a public image that she was desperately trying to maintain. Especially after the circumstances surrounding Filia's birth."

"Oh, I see..." Tara said before falling into silence. She stayed that way for several long seconds before returning her attention to Raz. "You still have not answered my question though. What changed about her?"

"Well, like I said, a bunch of different things really," Raz repeated as another smile broke out on his face and he regained his former composure with it. "On her end, if I had to guess I'd say that at some point she realized that she wasn't making any of her own decisions doing anything her mother said, and that can be disheartening in any circumstance. Other than that... Well, I'm not going to say I had anything to do with it-"

"But you did. That is what you were going to say," Tara interrupted as she narrowed her eyes at him.

"What, no!" Raz responded quickly as he saw the look she was giving him. "No, no I really didn't. At least it couldn't have been only me." Though unconvinced, Tara relaxed her glare at him, if only because she did genuinely want to hear the rest of this story. "Speaking only for myself though, since, you know, I'm not her and I'm not other people. I'd say it started when she saw me talk back to her mother and suffer absolutely no repercussions for it whatsoever. You see, due largely in part to her mother's influence over her shyness she didn't really know anyone. The only people she saw on a regular basis were servants and family members like myself, most of whom like her, were trained from the youngest age possible to show respect for her and her mother because they were princesses, lest they suffer grave consequences. So seeing me… Well, I won't lie to you. I wasn't much different when I was younger than I am now. So when she saw me talk back to her mother and not get punished, it might have… broken her entire world view."

"And then you took her under your wing?" Tara didn't so much ask but rather state as she narrowed her eyes at him again.

"Oh fuck Solaris no," Raz responded with a laugh and a shrug. "I would say that I'm awesome at many things, Tara, there's no doubting that, but I'm no role model. I know that for a fact. All I did was encourage her to talk more and to start thinking about what she wanted, not what her mother wanted. Years later, well, here we are. That's all there is to it really. Sorry if that story was less epic than you were expecting, but it's the truth." Tara simply stared at him in silence as she narrowed her gaze even further on his eyes. Raz, for his part, appeared to take her glare in stride as he smirked back at her.

"And in all that time did it ever occur to you that perhaps you may have influenced her more than you realized?" Tara asked, making sure that it was blatantly obvious how serious she was being with that question.

"What?" Raz replied, looking genuinely confused. "I… What are you-"

"I'm done!" Filia's voice suddenly rang out before Raz could say anymore. The instant that sound hit their ears Tara dropped her glare and returned her expression to her usual, pleasant smile while Raz made no attempt to change how he looked at all. "Sorry about that, but the guy there made me a special offer since I was a princess and well, he actually had to make it on the spot. It was fascinating to watch actually, but look." As she finished speaking Filia held out her hand and showed them the pair of bracelets that she had bought from the merchant. They didn't appear too special on their own, as they were made from simple, colored cords that were tied together at the end with a black string that had a bead dangling from it. What made this pair of bracelets special, however, was that rather than being made out of one single cord they were actually made from three different colored cords wrapped together to form a spiral pattern. The colors that made up both bracelets were, of course, purple, orange, and white, while the bead on the end of one of the black strings was blue and the other red.

"Ooh, nice," Raz said as he looked them over. When he noticed that there were two, however, without moving his head he slowly looked upwards so that he could make eye contact with Filia while a sly smile spread across his lips. "So who's the other one for then?" The literal instant he had finished speaking Filia, as if she had only just then realized what she had shown to him, immediately closed her hand and spun around so that neither Raz nor Tara could see her face.

"N- No one you need to know about," Filia answered quickly and defensively.

"Aha!" Raz shouted as he straightened himself back up. "So the other one is for someone!" Filia didn't respond to what he said, at least not with words. Despite her best efforts, however, both Raz and Tara saw that she instantly tensed up as soon as those words had left Raz's mouth. While Tara felt embarrassed for her, Raz couldn't help but laugh. "You know you can't hide anything from me, Filly, and you don't have to be ashamed. Really, you don't. Only chumps feel ashamed of things like that. Come on, I'll let you whisper it to me. You know I'm not gonna tell your mother or Isaac. So come on, who is it? Someone back in Sol finally become worthy of your attention?"

"N... No," Filia responded without turning around.

"I'm gone for only a day and who should I happen to see you with upon my return," a very familiar, very deep sounding voice said seemingly out of the ether. Immediately both Raz and Tara looked to their left to see Daedalus standing there in the street with them.

"Well of course he's with me," Filia responded as she quickly put the pair of bracelets into the small satchel bag she had slung over her shoulder, another thing that she had happened to see and want while they were out and about. As Filia spoke she walked over to stand directly in front of Daedalus, although the vast difference in height between the two of them made the scene more than a little comical. "Who else would he be with when I'm around?" Daedalus' only response was to stare down at her with the same, very familiar scowl on his face. Even for royalty it appeared that he wouldn't drop it. "It's good to see you again by the way, Daedalus." Even with Filia's last words, however, Daedalus remained silent for several long seconds as he stared down at Filia. Filia, to Tara's surprise, did not blink at all or seem intimidated by Daedalus in any way as she stared back up at him.

"It's rather presumptuous don't you think," Daedalus eventually began. "To think that I would find it good to see you or to assume that I was talking about you in the first place, or that I would want to speak to you at all." While Tara at this point knew that she should have expected such a response from him, she still could not help but bury her face into her hands as another person she knew acted disrespectfully towards royalty. As she did this Filia, confused by Daedalus' words, turned her attention towards Tara, though she could tell immediately that she wasn't going to get any answers from her. "Nevertheless, within the menagerie of morons that is your family you are a welcome sight. It is good to see you, Filia." At his words Filia could not help but burst out laughing.

"Menagerie of morons," she let out. "What, did you come up with that one on the spot?"

"Yes," Daedalus answered plainly.

"Well," Filia began as she calmed herself back down. "It's nice to see that you still have that same spear stuck up your ass. Since you're here would you care to join us? Unless of course, you have somewhere that you would rather be?" Daedalus, at her question, didn't respond immediately but instead directed his eyes back up towards Raz, who only responded to him with a shrug.

"Given the circumstances," Daedalus answered. "It would seem that that decision has already been made for me."

"Or, you know," Raz responded as his smirk returned to his face. "You could just pretend to ignore us and run off to meet with another 'client' of yours. I'm sure you would have way more fun with that." As Raz finished speaking he clicked his tongue and raised his eyebrows at Daedalus. Daedalus, however, only stared back at Raz with a death fueled glare in his eyes, as he usually did when speaking to him.

"I am not going to dignify what you just said with a response," was all Daedalus said to him. Tara, at that point, could no longer hold herself back as she let out an obnoxiously loud sigh. So loud in fact that quite a few people on the street turned to look at her as she did. Once she realized that, however, Tara quickly dropped her gaze towards her feet again.

"Sorry!" she quickly let out. "I-"

"Ah, don't worry about it," Filia said as she slapped Tara on the arm. "We all know that Daedalus is a hard ass. It's nothing to get worked up over."

"And there you go again speaking based on assumptions," Daedalus said in turn, though it didn't appear as if Filia had heard him, or if she had she was purposefully ignoring him. In the spirit of that it seemed, she had begun to lead the group down another street as they all began walking again.

"So," Filia began as she walked over next to Raz. "What else is there to see out here? Don't hold anything out on me now. With a city this big there's bound to be at least ten things left we could do."

"Actually..." Raz responded as he glanced up towards the sky and saw that it was beginning to take on an orange-ish hue. "I think it's about time we saw you back to... wherever you're staying." Immediately after those words left his mouth Raz turned to one of the two royal guardsmen accompanying them. "Ey, where is Nicole staying while she's here again?"

"Princesses Nicole and Filia Solara are the honored guests of the regional governor and are staying in his home for the duration of their stay in Dis," the guardsmen politely responded.

"Thanks," was all Raz responded with. Before he could say anymore, however, Filia ran out in front of him in order to stop him in his tracks as she attempted to get herself as close to him as possible without actually touching him. The look on her face was one of intense disbelief.

"Raz, come on," she said as she got into his face. "You can't be serious?" When Raz didn't respond to her, however, Filia's eyes went wide with shock. "Solaris you're serious aren't you?"

"Deadly," was all Raz responded with.

"Oh come the fuck on, Raz!" Filia then shouted at him as loud as she could. "You can't do this to me! I haven't seen you in... I don't even know how long! Fuck, I didn't even know you were here until I saw you! So why would you-"

"Because you're a princess in the common area of a city with only two guards and one reject to watch over you," Raz answered calmly and without a smile. "And because regardless of whatever you might think I do care enough about you that I don't want to see you hurt, or worse. This city isn't a kind place, Filia, you know that."

"But you're here with me!" Filia shouted back at him. "That's got to count for something, doesn't it!"

"To your mother and Isaac," Raz responded calmly. "No, not really. Not even a little bit. You know that they think less than a monster carcass of me, right?"

While Raz and Filia were arguing Daedalus suddenly felt a tug on his sleeve as he noticed Tara attempting to pull him away from the rest of the group. He complied, and before long he and Tara were a few steps behind Raz, Filia and the two royal guards.

"Daedalus," Tara said quietly to him. "I... I have something that I need to ask you."

"Why are you whispering?" Daedalus asked in his normal speaking voice.

"Because I do not want them to hear us," Tara responded, still quietly. "Obviously."

"What could you possibly have to say that is so secret that you had to wait for them to be distracted to ask me?" Daedalus then asked, still in a normal speaking voice. That, combined with his near permanent glare caused Tara to let out another loud sigh in frustration.

"Alright," Tara then said without whispering, but still somewhat quiet. "Princess Filia... she claims that Raz is her cousin and-"

"Let me guess," Daedalus interrupted her. "You want me to confirm whether or not he is indeed who they say he is."

"Y... Yes," Tara responded quickly, as she could see that Raz and Filia's argument was beginning to wind down. "Ordinarily I would not have cause to doubt someone so much, but-"

"But it's Raz," Daedalus interrupted again. "And there is no possible way that someone like him could ever be of noble blood because he is uncouth, undisciplined, and lacks any and all of the qualities that someone like you would associate with being royalty, correct?" Tara instantly fell silent as Daedalus' words rang in her ears. The particular way he had phrased all of that made her feel more than a little terrible for even asking him in the first place. "I will save you the trouble. Yes. He is who she claims him to be. His full name and title is Prince Michael Frederick Dagon of the royal house of Solara and fourth in line to the throne of the Solaran Empire after Nicole, Filia, and his mother. Though honestly, miss Schäfer, I don't see at all why you felt the need to ask me this. If you've met Filia then you must have also met her mother. Not only that but I heard Raz mention the name Isaac, and the only Isaac I know of who is associated with the royal family is Isaac De La Rosa, the personal advisor to Queen Faust. So if both of them are here in Dis then they must have confirmed his identity for you already. So really, tell me the truth, Miss Schäfer. Even after having your suspicions confirmed by two very reputable sources, why did you still feel the need to ask me to confirm his identity for you?"

Tara was silent for quite a while after Daedalus had finished speaking, as in truth she did not have a real answer for him. Next to them, both Raz and Filia continued to argue with each other and seemed oblivious to the fact that she and Daedalus were talking to each other privately. However, she knew that that would not last for very much longer, so she had to say something now while she had the chance.

"Because..." Tara began, but stopped herself.

"Miss Schäfer," Daedalus interrupted, as if he could see what was going on inside of Tara's mind. "You need to accept that the world doesn't always work the way you think it does. You made that mistake once already and look what it nearly cost you. I would even go as far as to say that the only reason you got out of that with as much as you did was because of the generosity of both myself and Raz. So before you run off to ask ten more people the exact same question you just asked me in a vain attempt to fix what you no doubt see as some sort of mistake in the world, take a single second, that's all, just one second, and ask yourself. Is what I'm trying to fix really a mistake?"

Tara felt her breath instantly leave her as her mind flashed back to the night both Seth and Raz were carried back to Canaan by the search party that went out to look for Seth. She remembered the gut wrenching horror she felt seeing the broken and beaten forms of both of them, the denial she felt when she first heard the fabricated story of what had happened out in the desert as it was repeated over and over again to Vivian, Charlie, and all of the others who had asked what had happened. The more she heard it, the more she was forced to convince herself that it was the truth. Most of all, however, she remembered how all of it started, and how all of it was essentially her fault and that there was no changing that.

"You are right," she eventually said to Daedalus after a few long seconds. "And I am sorry, Daedalus."

"Don't apologize to me," Daedalus replied to her, though because his facial expression never changed throughout their entire conversation Tara was unsure if he was being condescending or not with that statement. All Tara could do was let out another sigh as she seemingly felt a weight lifted off of her shoulders. Again.

"And again you are right," she said. "Perhaps I should... Hey, wait a second!"

"What is it now?" Daedalus replied with obvious frustration in his voice.

"You said that Raz's full name was Michael Frederick Dagon?" Tara then asked.

"Yes," Daedalus repeated.

"Then where does the name 'Raz' come from?" Tara asked as she made no attempt to keep silent, as she knew now that doing so would be pointless.

"It's a nickname," Daedalus answered with a completely straight face. "That's all there is to it. There's no grand story behind it or anything if that's what you were wondering. It was just a nickname he insisted everyone call him when he was younger and it stuck."

"Really?"

"Yes."

"So it is not short for anything?"

"What would it be short for?"

"Rasputin."

"Why would you think that?"

"Because that makes the most sense."

"Why does it have to make sense?"

"I do not know," Tara answered, but then quickly realized that she had no real answer to that question either. "Becau-"

"Miss Schäfer," Daedalus interrupted again. "Do I need to repeat what I just said?" At his words Tara instantly fell silent again as she realized that he was indeed right, again. She was about to open her mouth to apologize to him again, but then stopped herself as she realized that doing so one more time would be pointless. He had already said after all that it was not him that she needed to apologize to.

"Can I at least stay until midnight!" Filia then pleaded to Raz loud enough for most of the people passing by on the street to hear.

"Why do you want that?" Raz asked in turn. "If you're staying up for the new year it won't really matter if you're with me or in the regional governor's house, right?"

"But it'll be more fun if I'm with you!" Filia whined. "If I'm over there all I'll get to do is sit somewhere bored out of my skull while my mom and the other nobles sip wine and go on and on about how awesome they all think they are. If I'm with you then I know at least I'll have fun."

"My idea of fun isn't something that I would feel comfortable having you around for," Raz responded with a completely straight face. "Like, at all, and I know that you know that both Isaac and your mother would agree with me on that one."

"If this is about me drinking you don't have to worry about that," Filia then said in a normal speaking voice. "I've tasted ale before. It tasted like shit. So I'm never touching that stuff again."

"When did you try ale?" Raz then asked, concerned.

"That's not the point!" Filia shouted again. Before saying anything else she then stepped closer to Raz and grabbed his shirt with both of her hands. "Please, Raz! I'm begging you! Please don't send me back there yet! I'll do whatever you want! I'll stay quiet! I won't say who I am to anyone! I'll pretend I don't exist! I'll buy you and Daedalus a spot of land somewhere closer to Sol! I don't know how but I will! Just please please please don't make me go back there yet! I hated being cooped up in that house enough as it is and you're the only good thing that's happened to me since I came to this city! I didn't even want to come here in the first place but now that I know you're here everything's different! Please, Raz! You know what life with my mother is like! You can't send me back to that! Not yet! Not after you've given me this! So please! Please Raz…" Filia had stopped shouting at that point, and due to how close she was to him Raz could see the beginnings of tears forming in her eyes.

Raz did not immediately respond to Filia's long winded rant, as he silently kept staring down at her with what was unusual for him, a completely, deathly serious look on his face. After a few silent moments of this, however, Raz suddenly took in a deep breath and closed his eyes. When he opened them again they beheld a much softer look to them and his usual smirk had returned.

"If I say yes," Raz began. "Would you promise to-"

"Yes!" Filia instantly shouted before Raz could finish, which only caused his smirk to widen.

"To accept all of the blame for whatever your mother throws at us afterwards," Raz continued and clarified. "Whatever punishment, whatever penance you are forced to endure after this will all be on you and only you. Even if they tell you you can't see me again for the rest of the week. Whatever they say, whatever happens is all on you. You are the one making the decision to stay out later than you're supposed to, not me, you're the one who is defying the orders that they were given. I am blameless in this situation, so whatever blame is going to get thrown at me, you are going to stand in front of me and accept it and tell your mother that I did nothing at all to influence your decision. It was all you and as such, whatever punishment that befalls any of us is yours to bear, not ours." Raz then paused for another moment to cross his arms across his chest in a sort of mock intimidation fashion as he continued to stare down Filia. "So if you can accept that, then sure. I'll let you stay out here with me, cause then it will be you deciding to do that, not me. I can't be held responsible for every decision you make."

Filia, to no one's surprise, stayed silent for several long, long seconds as she contemplated Raz's words. However, to the surprise of Tara, something like a light went off in Filia's head as she stared up at Raz with a smirk that was very reminiscent of his, as if she had spent time in the mirror attempting to copy it.

"I see what you're trying to do," Filia said to Raz. "And unfortunately for you, I know how you think and I know what you would do in this situation." At that, Filia then stood up straighter than she had been before, made a fist with her right hand, and then touched her fist to where her heart was in a mock salute. "I, Princess Filia of house Solara, swear upon my honor as a princess of the Solaran Empire that I will accept any and all punishments that may be bestowed upon any member of this group as my own. For it was my decision that led us here, and I shall bear full responsibility for it. There, does that satisfy you?"

"Wow," Raz responded surprisingly calmly. "You actually agreed to that a lot quicker than I thought you would. I thought that at least you'd want to think about it for a few minutes or-"

"Raz, it's me," Filia interrupted. "Who do you think I am and what do you take me for?"

"If you say so," Raz responded with a shrug before regaining his former composure. "Well, if we're gonna be staying up past midnight then we're gonna need something of a pick me up." Then, having finished that thought, Raz began walking again. "As you would say, onwards everyone. We have other places to be than here." Filia didn't really have any kind of response for that as she walked around next to him and leaned against his arm. She didn't hold it, just leaned against it.

"Oh, and what exactly do you mean by 'pick me up'?" Filia then asked as the two of them walked together. Without any other ideas of what to do, Tara began to follow them with Daedalus in tow. True to his nature, after their conversation he remained completely and utterly silent, though for whatever reason Tara found that comforting right now.

"Oh, nothing special," Raz responded while pretending to look in a different direction than Filia. "You'll see."

"Nothing special..." Filia repeated. "Sounds like the exact sort of thing I would want." As Filia spoke Tara directed her attention back towards the two of them, but more specifically on Raz. In light of all of the new revelations she had only recently learned about him, Tara wasn't sure at all what to think of Raz anymore. He put on this air of childish impulsivity, yet at times, especially now, he frequently surprised her by breaking that persona and doing something responsible. What's more, his cousin Filia appeared to admire him a great deal, even if she did know fully well what he was like. All of this greatly confused Tara more than anything else, and in that confusion she realized that this must be how Seth felt all of the time. That last thought made her feel incredibly uncomfortable.

The 'nothing special' turned out to be little more than a quick stop at a very cheap restaurant built into the side of a building that thankfully had outdoor seating. The food they served there was little more than assorted meats wrapped in a thick flatbread, but despite its simplicity it was very delicious. Filia appeared to enjoy it more than any of them, however, as she reveled in the idea of eating something that wasn't prepared by hundreds of servants or came with their own sets of cutlery. She enjoyed it so much in fact, that she even joked about deliberately letting some of it fall onto her dress so that she could ruin it in her mother's eyes. Thankfully Raz was quickly able to dissuade her from that.

As quickly as they had arrived there, however, they had soon left with Filia seemingly gaining more from the experience than any of them. Once they had left they all collectively began to make their way back through the city towards the Moon Pool. The sky had begun to darken significantly in the time it took for them to walk to that restaurant, eat a quick dinner, and then walk all the way back to the Moon Pool, but thankfully nothing happened nor did they attract too much attention. Something that Tara was more worried about than any of them. What worried her more, however, was the continuing absence of Seth from all of this.

She had not seen nor heard anything of him since he had left, and it was beginning to worry her. The thought occurred to her that she should go out looking for him, but in a city as big as Dis even without the festival going on she knew that the chances of actually running into him were slim at best. Not only that, but even after all the time that had passed Daedalus' words about the mistake she had made still repeated through her head, and in that light she began to wonder whether or not she should worry about him at all. Not out of a lack of concern for him, that was the farthest thing from her mind, but more out of the revelation that she needed to trust him. She knew he wasn't a child, that he was more than reasonably intelligent despite his lack of common knowledge, that he had enough common sense not to do anything that was obviously against the law, and that once he had acquired a piece of knowledge he seemingly retained it forever. That last bit of knowledge led Tara to remember that Seth knew where and what the Moon Pool was, and if he did get lost he could always ask where that was, and from there their hotel wasn't that far of a walk. If anything she knew he was intelligent enough to figure that out at least.

With that Tara took in an incredibly deep breath and, against what she had previously believed was her better nature, stuck with the rest of the group as they made their way back to the Moon Pool. At least there if Seth was going to return she would be able to hopefully see him. That was of course, assuming that Seth had not already returned to their hotel room prior to midnight.

Above the group the sky had taken on a much darker color, and slowly but surely all of the stars began to light up the night sky one by one. Due to all of the surrounding light from the city's street lanterns and buildings, however, the night sky wasn't nearly as visibly beautiful here as it was in Canaan. However, that was a minor concern within the city's walls as no one was here to admire the night sky, as beautiful as it was. Perhaps at any other time of the year, when the city was truly dark, it would have been beautiful, but the night of a celebrated holiday was a different story.

By the time the assembled group had returned to where the Moon Pool was, a crowd of people had already begun to form in the surrounding area. Not a large crowd by any stretch of the imagination, as it was still a few hours from midnight, but a crowd nonetheless.

"Hey, wait a second, Raz, what are we doing here now?" Filia asked as soon as they arrived, as if she could read Tara's mind and saw that she wanted to ask that same question. "Midnight isn't for another couple hours."

"That may be true," Raz responded without looking at her. "But this is the commoner's district, remember. There's no reserved seating or special boxed-in areas for important people here. Within the next couple of hours this place is going to get so packed full of people you aren't going to be able to walk around or even sit much less enjoy the night. So-"

"So we're here now so that we can beat the crowd," Filia interrupted with a smirk that matched Raz's. "I'm not a moron or my mother, Raz. I know how stuff like that works."

"That may be true," Raz responded. "But you still asked, so as such it is my obligation to answer." Filia couldn't help but laugh a little bit at that answer.

"Yeah, you got me there," she said to him. "So what are we going to do then while we wait?"

"That," Raz began. "Is something that you are no doubt going to find incredibly boring, but it's what you get for insisting on staying out so late with me." That remark confused Filia to no end as she gave Raz a look that reminded Tara of Seth somewhat, which further reminded her that he wasn't here with them.

She put that thought away as Raz led the assembled group towards what, to Tara at least, appeared at first to be a cafe on one of the opposite street corners from where they stood, as it had outdoor seating with well put together tables. The cafe itself didn't look too much different from any of the other buildings and cafes around the city of Dis, save for the wooden fence that surrounded the outdoor seating area. However, as they walked closer towards it the name above the building's wooden double doors made itself known to her, as above the doors was a wooden plaque bearing the image of a long, yellowish-green snake that slithered underneath the words "The Sloshed Snake" as if underlining it. The literal instant Tara saw those words she knew where Raz was leading them and instantly became nervous. Not for herself, but for Filia.

As they approached, however, rather than walk inside Raz led them around the fence as they took the first available table with the best view of the Moon Pool. The table Raz chose even had seats available for the two royal guards, though they did not immediately take a seat as the rest of them had. Daedalus, oddly enough, chose not to sit down either, much to Tara's initial confusion. That confusion was immediately dispelled once Raz was comfortably seated.

"Daedalus," Raz said to his friend. "If you would be so kind." Daedalus, however, only stared at him for several long, hard seconds before speaking.

"Kindness and mistrust are not necessarily complementary to each other," Daedalus responded before turning his attention to Tara. "Miss Schäfer, do you have a preference?"

"Oh, um…" Tara answered, as she needed to take a moment to think of exactly what she wanted once she realized what she was being asked. "Just some red wine, please, if they have it."

"Very well," Daedalus replied before turning his attention over towards the two royal guards. "And for you two gentlemen?" As soon as they realized that he was indeed talking to them, both of the royal guardsmen looked surprised, but only for a single second before they returned to their usual composure.

"Nothing for us," one of them said. "We are knights of her royal majesty Qu-"

"Oh come the fuck on," Raz interupted as he put his feet up on the table. "It's the new year, live a little. Besides, the only reason you're out here right now is because of us and I honestly feel bad about it. So come on, take a load off. I know that the two of you have a duty that you've sworn to uphold but take it from a guy who used to do what you do. It is possible to do both." Both of the royal guardsmen remained silent for several long seconds as they exchanged looks before answering.

"While we thank you for your generosity," one of them began. "We are still sworn to our duty and were given the explicit command to watch over princess Filia Solara, and unlike you we would prefer not to risk inebriation while carrying out that command."

"Alright alright," Raz responded as he leaned back. "But don't let it be said that we didn't offer, and that offer is still on the table if either of you change your mind."

"Nothing for me, please," Filia spoke up as soon as Raz had finished speaking. "I don't like the taste of alcohol. So I'm good."

"I know," Daedalus responded to her. "But even if you did I still wouldn't give you any. No matter what you promised or threatened me with, and take it from someone who knows your beloved cousin better than you do. No matter how inebriated he may get he'll still have enough mental capacity to not let you have any either." With that said Daedalus then turned around and headed inside of the Sloshed Snake.

"Okay fine, be like that," she said to no one in particular as she put on a pouting expression.

"So…" Tara then finally spoke up. "What do we do while we wait?"

"So wait!" Filia exclaimed as she slammed her tankard full of water onto the table. "You're really telling me that you beat up six of them!"

"Hell the fuck yeah I did!" Raz responded before taking several long gulps from his tankard of ale. "Limp dick amateurs couldn't even touch me. Though if I'm being honest it wasn't just me. Seth helped too."

"Wait, Seth is as good as you are?" Filia then asked, seemingly astonished, which in turn caused Raz to burst out laughing.

"I wouldn't say that," Raz answered. "But the guy is good enough to hold his own."

"I… I can actually confirm his story," Tara spoke up as she had finished taking a sip of the wine she had been drinking. "I was t… there. I saw the whole thing."

"As did I," Daedalus piped up, but that was all he said before taking another drink from his own tankard of ale.

"Ooh…" was all Filia let out as a look of astonishment took over her face. "So what happened after that? I bet that Vito guy must have been pissed."

"Oh you have no idea," Raz responded. Before he could continue with the rest of his story, however, he was interrupted by the sound of Tara as she suddenly burst out laughing. This uncharacteristic outburst caused all of the attention at the table to instantly fall on her.

"Hey… Hey… Raz…" Tara began, though while she certainly appeared to be able to keep herself sitting upright, she seemed to have some trouble looking at any of them as her eyes kept darting between all of them as if in some desperate attempt to look at all of them at once. "You… You should tell her what Vito did to all of us after that. How he… You know… invited all of us to his home and-"

"If I am not mistaken it was not his home," Daedalus interrupted. "No, he invited us to his office in Canaan's only luxury hotel because his home had been destroyed in the previous monster attack. And I suppose he also thought that it would somehow intimidate us."

"Yes, sure, whatever," Tara responded rather quickly before returning her full attention back to Raz. "So, Raz… Tell her about that-"

"Are you alright, Tara?" Filia interrupted before Tara could finish speaking. She appeared to be genuinely worried, as Tara nearly fell out of her chair when Filia leaned in closer towards her. Momentarily startled, Tara suddenly sat up much straighter and seemingly regained the composure that she had barely managed to maintain throughout the day. However, between the fact that her eyes were still darting between everyone at the table and that the skin on her face had within the last few seconds suddenly turned a few shades redder, everyone could tell that something was going on with her.

"O-Of course I'm alright," Tara quickly responded, though the sound of her free hand continually tapping the table next to her did not help in convincing anyone of that. "Why would you not think I was alright? I am perfectly fine. Nothing at all is wrong with me. In fact, I think I'm the most alright person here, if I do say so myself. I even-"

"Tara," Filia interrupted as she narrowed her eyes at Tara. "How much wine have you had?"

"Hardly any," Daedalus answered before Tara even had the chance to speak. "And I would know because I've been the one refilling all of your drinks throughout the evening and in that time she's never once asked me to replace the first wine glass I got for her." As the sound of that answer reached her ears Filia's gaze softened. Her smirk, however, only grew wider by contrast.

"Oh really," Filia then said directly to Tara. "So you should be alright then, right?"

"Of course I'm alright," Tara quickly responded. "I just told you I was alright, didn't I?" Despite her answer, hearing Tara use contractions made Filia's smirk widen even more.

"So then if you were to take one more sip of wine," Filia began as she leaned back in her chair. "Then you should still be alright, right?"

"Of course!" Tara quickly answered, though in her mind she knew exactly where this was going.

"Well then," Filia continued as she leaned forward and rested her head in her hands. "Go right ahead. No one here is going to judge you. Hell, look who your company is. But of course if you don't want to I can't force-" Before Filia could even finish her next thought, much less her sentence, all those assembled watched as Tara suddenly emptied her glass of wine with one great big, long gulp. Contrary to how she usually acted, the way in which she drank the wine was very undignified. Even Filia, who had known Tara for the least amount of time, was shocked to see her spontaneously do that.

Silence reigned for the next full minute and a half as both Raz and Filia stared at Tara with near identical looks of shock on their faces. Daedalus by contrast, completely ignored all of them as he sat there in the silence enjoying his drink. The two royal guardsmen likewise, remained silent and kept whatever opinions they may have had to themselves. Even Tara herself remained silent as she sat completely still and stared back at Raz and Filia, though it was unclear to either of them which of the two she was supposed to be staring at, as her eyes appeared to focus on the space between the two of them rather than directly at either of them.

"Um... Tara," Filia eventually broke the silence. "Are... you okay? I didn't mean to-"

"I'm completely alright!" Tara shouted at the top of her lungs before Filia could finish speaking, again. This sudden outburst of her's nearly caused Raz and Filia to fall back over in their chairs as they both simultaneously leaned back.

"Wow," Raz finally spoke up. "I've got no words. I mean, really, I don't have any words at all."

"Heeey Raz," Tara then spoke up as she leaned in his direction across the table. She wore her own smirk on her face as she did so, as if she were poorly attempting to emulate the smirk that Raz and Filia put on, only it didn't look nearly as intimidating on her. Not only that, but while her face may have been red from embarrassment before, now after finishing her drink her face had become as red as a cherry. "W... weren't you about to tell Filia about what you said to Vito to... to... get him off our backs."

"Well I was," Raz responded as he took another sip of ale from his tankard. "But I don't think I got quite that far yet."

"Come ooon," Tara practically whined as she leaned farther across the table towards him. "Tell her what you said to him. Tell her every word. I bet she really, really, really wants to hear what you said." As if on cue as soon as she had finished speaking Daedalus suddenly stood up.

"Does anyone else want or need any more?" he asked as he took Raz's tankard from him, as if he didn't even need to ask to know what his answer would be.

"Oh yes please!" Tara practically sang in response as she handed her wine glass to him. Daedalus took it without saying anything more, though he did shoot Raz a rather intense glare the instant it was in his hand. Raz only answered by staring back at him with a rather serious look on his face as he matched Daedalus' glare. That seemed to be the only communication that the two of them needed as Daedalus turned away from the group and walked back inside of the Sloshed Snake without saying anything more to anyone.

"Sooo…" Tara then cooed as she returned her full attention back to Raz. "You were saying Raz, about what you were saying to Vito…"

"Why are you trying so hard to get him to tell this story?" Filia cut in. "Weren't you there?" In response to that question Tara suddenly burst out laughing. She didn't say any actual words, she just laughed and laughed and laughed. It was enough for Filia to shoot Raz a perplexed look, though all Raz could do in response was shrug his shoulders. Her laughter did eventually die down around the time Daedalus returned with two fresh tankards full of ale, though he was curiously missing a wine glass.

"Sooo Raz," Tara repeated after she had taken a few deep breaths, though even after she did so her face was still as red as a cherry. "What-" Tara's words were then suddenly cut off by the very loud and intense sound of many, many cheering people coming from right next to them. Looking over, the assembled group could now see that in the time they had spent at the Sloshed Snake drinking and talking a rather large crowd had formed in the area surrounding the Moon Pool. As soon as they saw it both Raz and Filia turned to look at each other, and when they did their lips, seemingly in unison, both curled into identical looking smirks again as if they both knew what was coming.

"Say, Tara," Raz said as he stood up from his chair and began to walk over towards the wooden fence that separated the outdoor drinking area of the Sloshed Snake from the Moon Pool. "You asked me once exactly what someone like me does for a living in Canaan, didn't you? And I don't think I ever gave you an answer."

"Aaactually," Tara began with a noticeable slur to her words. "I don't think I recall ever asking you tha-" Before she could finish speaking she was again cut off by Raz when he, as swift and as gracefully as an acrobat, and without even touching it, jumped over the wooden fence with a flip before landing perfectly on both of his feet. Once there, without turning around he took a few steps away from the fence toward the edge of the crowd. "Raaaz!" Tara practically wailed as she stood up from her seat and walked over towards the fence, though she made no attempt to jump over it. "Where you going? You-"

"Just let it go," Filia said to her as she also stood up from her chair, walked over, and then leaned against the fence next to Tara. "Trust us, you're going to love this." As she spoke Daedalus stood up as well and, with his tankard still in hand, walked over and stood on the opposite side of Tara. Greatly confused, Tara could only return her attention to Raz, and when she did she was nearly blown back when she saw him perfectly spin around on his heel to face them and point upwards towards the sky. He held that pose for a few quick seconds before he relaxed and put his hands into his pockets.

"Well!" Raz spoke up louder than before so that he could be heard over the crowd. "Since you wanted to know! Here's your answer!" Before Tara could shout back to ask what exactly he was talking about, she was suddenly cut off again by the sound of the whole crowd erupting into a great chorus of cheers.

Above the heads of all of the assembled people, on the opposite side of the Moon Pool from where they stood, on what appeared to be a hastily constructed stage, Tara thought she saw someone small walk up onto it before that person then began to speak to the assembled crowd.

"People of Dis! Hear me!" the small person began to shout. As difficult as it was to hear what he was saying between him being on the complete opposite side of the square from them and all of the people still cheering, once the crowd had begun to quiet down Tara, Filia and Daedalus could more or less hear what he was saying. "Allow me to be the first to congratulate all of you! Yes you! For it is because of all of you that we are here today! I know to some that may sound like hollow praise! But believe me when I tell you that it isn't! It is true! Over this past year we all have lost many. Some to the spawn of chaos, others to the harsh reality of the world in which we live, and we each in our own way remember them! But while we remember and honor our fallen, we must never forget that we also do so as a celebration of life! For we all stand here today to celebrate not just the passage of time, not just the lives of those who came before us, but the lives of those who will come after us!" There was a short pause as the surrounding audience took in this man's words, and only now could Tara see that while this man's short stature made it difficult to see exactly what he was wearing over the heads of all of the people in front of her, with the movement of one person's head Tara was able to see the white and orange vestments of a priest of the church of Solaris. "Tonight marks the three-hundred and fifty-seventh year of the Solaran calendar! A day in which we all gather in remembrance! When we remember all of those who were taken from us by the spawn of the Chaos! We remember those who fell to their claws, teeth, and poisoned blood! Those who in their own ways fought bravely knowing that while harm may befall them, that none shall befall anyone else! Those here on the western frontier, in the northern forests, and on the eastern front, who give their lives every single day to ensure that we can enjoy the gift given to us by Solaris that we call life! And after three-hundred and fifty-seven years of this, we all must remember that which matters most!" Silence fell over the crowd again as everyone, including Tara and Filia, listened intently for whatever came next. "We are still here!"

At those words the crowd surrounding the Moon Pool erupted into a cacophony of cheers, shouts, and screams. So much so that Tara actually lost sight of Raz as some of them began to move and toss their arms up into the air. His sudden disappearance worried her, but her fears were cut short as the priest of the church of Solaris began to speak again.

"Tonight!" the priest began again. "Let us light up the sky! Shake the stone beneath our feet! Shout so loud that the winds will carry our voices to the ends of the world! Tonight! Let us send a message to those vile beasts who desire nothing more than to take Solaris' gift of life from us! We are the children of Solaris! We are humanity! And we will endure!" The cacophony of cheers then erupted even louder than it had the last time, so much so in fact that it almost began to hurt Tara's ears a little bit. In all of this, however, she couldn't help but smile as the words of the priest rang true in her ears. Yes, a lot had happened this year, especially with her, but in the end she, like all those gathered here in this square, was still here, and that in and of itself was a comforting thought. Filia seemed to notice this too, as she suddenly put her arm around Tara and smiled along with her. For that brief moment Tara actually forgot who Filia was, and in her mind the person next to her wasn't royalty, but simply a friend.

Amidst the cheering crowd, however, silence then began to fall again, but only for a brief moment as everyone knew what was coming next.

"Ten!" Filia then shouted at the top of her lungs along with the crowd!

"Nine!" Tara at that point could not help but join in as well.

"Eight!" Daedalus and the two royal guardsmen, however, seemed relatively content to remain silent and simply watch.

"Seven!"

"Six!"

"Five!"

"Four!"

"Three!"

"Two!"

"One!"

While Tara, Filia, nor Daedalus or the royal guardsmen could hear it over the sound of the assembled crowd counting down. Somewhere nearby, the sound of snapping fingers was heard and was quickly followed by the sound of Raz's voice.

"Boom."

Chapter 16

As Vincent quietly slipped on his coat he looked back down at the still sleeping form of Stella in her large bed. Her long, silky raven black hair spread about behind her head like a finely woven tapestry. Her soft, pillowy lips still formed a smile from the previous night's experiences. The pièce de résistance though, was that due to the covers having slid down to her waist he was treated to a full view of her lovely, peach-tipped breasts, who's size and shape were so perfect that he was certain that even the most talented of artists wouldn't be able to recreate them in any artform. Even if they had unlimited time and resources at their fingertips.

It was a sight that, if time had somehow ceased to move then and there, Vincent wouldn't have minded staring at for the rest of eternity. Alas, Vincent knew that he couldn't stare forever as dawn was breaking. With the sight of the sun he knew that he would be racing against the clock before any of the servants woke up for the day.

After taking a few more moments to forever burn Stella's beauty into his mind, Vincent slid out from the bedroom, tiptoeing through the hallway of her family's manor and eventually making it to the main hall. Everything seemed to be clear, but then he noticed someone coming out from the hallway across from him. With no time or place to hide he stood still as the familiar, gray haired and only slightly wrinkled form of Ursa looked at him with a mop in one hand and a bucket of water in the other. The smirk on her face told Vincent that the elderly maid knew exactly which room he was walking away from. Sweat began to pour from his forehead as he worried that this would incur the wrath of Lord Dupont.

Ursa, much to his surprise, however, winked at him.

"Lucky girl," she quietly said before walking off with the mop and bucket.

Vincent let out a breath that he hadn't even realized he was holding in as his forehead ceased its current production of sweat. Without any more haste Vincent made his way out of the manor and over towards the sables where he left Zinc.

Quickly and quietly he untied and led Zinc away from the sables before hopping onto his back as the two of them rode off away from the sunrise. Where exactly were the monster hunter and his gray steed going? Vincent didn't know, but he had a feeling in his gut that it wouldn't be long until he found his next job. Or to be more accurate, until his next job found him.

With that Seth finally finished the first book in the *Wanderer* series as he closed it before placing it onto the table in front of him. He then stood up from the chair he had been sitting in for what seemed like hours now and stretched out his back and arms. A low cracking sound expelled from his spine and elbows as he did.

As he stretched he took a few moments to reflect on the last thirty pages of the book he had just finished reading. For reasons that he still couldn't understand, almost the entirety of those thirty pages were spent in Stella's bedroom doing absolutely bizarre things. It wasn't as if those scenes suddenly made the book bad, but it was enough to make him question why exactly, despite her insistence that the series got better as it went on, that Vivian would call this her favorite book series. That thought, unfortunately, also caused him to remember the brief conversation the two of them had about the series on the way here. That in turn led Seth to realize that that was probably the only pleasant conversation he had had with her in the past three months. After the argument the two of them had today, that night by the campfire felt like it had happened a long, long time ago, despite Seth knowing full well that it was merely two days ago.

Before he could contemplate that any further, however, the sound of a sudden and very loud explosion rocked the room. To his best guess, the sound appeared to have come from outside, so without thinking Seth rushed over to the window and violently threw the curtains open to see what had happened. What he saw, however, was something that he wasn't even sure he could describe even if someone had given him all of the words he would ever need to do so.

All at once, as if Solaris himself had appeared, the dark, cold, quiet night sky above them all lit up with light, warmth and earth shaking explosions as a multitude of fireworks went off all at once and lit up the night sky so much that one could swear it had suddenly become daytime again. The cacophony of cheers erupted once again with the fireworks, but it was next to impossible to hear them over all of the explosions going off in the sky. Like their namesake, the fireworks themselves bore the colors of fire, with multitudes or red, orange, yellow, and even whites pushing back the darkness so effectively that it might as well have really become daytime. Not only that, but with what Tara could only assume was the aid of magic, some of them followed distinct paths where they crashed into each other and then exploded, or avoided others altogether at the last minute, or sometimes another explosion of a different color was hidden within another firework. Some of them even lit up and danced like real fire, and oftentimes in multiple colors.

"Beautiful isn't it!" Filia shouted next to Tara. She could only nod in response as she was unable to take her eyes away from the spectacle above her. "Not just anyone can make something like that you know!"

Amidst the fireworks and shouting of the people, music began to play all around them as a multitude of strings, wind instruments, drums, and even singing began to fill the brief voids of silence that lasted in between the explosions and the cheers. With them Tara felt the earth beneath her feet begin to shake slightly. With supreme willpower she managed to pull her eyes away from the fireworks long enough to see that in front of her, nearly everybody in the square surrounding the Moon Pool had begun to dance. Like a wave people began to move this way, that way, all ways. It was so much that it was difficult, nay, nearly impossible to tell where one person ended and another began.

Within the ocean of moving people Tara finally caught sight of the distinctly familiar, brown haired, lean build of Raz, though his movements caught her attention before his face. When she saw him Raz was spinning around on his feet so fast that one could swear the ground beneath him was spinning rather than him. When he stopped spinning only his legs appeared to move as he kicked them both out one after the other before bringing them back in. His arms seemed to move independently of his legs, yet they both moved perfectly in sync as he danced in place for a few seconds before kicking his right leg out and spinning around one more time. When he stopped he inadvertently faced in her direction as he pointed to his right, then kicked out to his left before he spun around once more, put his wrists to his waist, and from there his legs appeared to move on their own to the beat of the music while his upper torso remained perfectly still. That only lasted for a few short seconds, however, before he suddenly took a step to his left, though when he did so it appeared as if he had slid across the ground as if it were ice rather than taking a simple step before throwing up both of his hands, then quickly dropping them back

to his sides before spinning around again. That finished, he then threw his arms out
to his sides, stood still for only a brief second, then kicked out to his left before
turning to face his right. Tara then watched as he placed a hand on his crotch and did
a few pelvic thrusts to the beat of the music. As he did so, however, he appeared to
move forward each time he did it without moving his feet at all, again as if the
ground were slippery and he was simply sliding across it.

Tara could only watch dumbstruck as she beheld this man, who for the
longest time she saw as little more than a dullard and a thug, dance to the beat of the
music like he had been doing it his whole life while above them all the sky was being
lit up again and again with fireworks that she could only assume based on what he
had said earlier, he had made himself. Not only that, but the revelation that he wasn't
a simple plebeian like her, but was in fact both of royal blood and directly related to
Princess Filia Solara, to whom he had shown a sense of maturity that she had never
seen him do with anyone else, shook her very understanding of him to its
foundations. Ever since she had learned that Daedalus was of the very influential
Olympus family she had always wondered to herself exactly what sort of person Raz
was, even with the volumes of flaws that he possessed, that someone as sophisticated
as Daedalus would still call someone like him his friend. Now she knew, and it didn't
just break her view of him, it pulverized it again and again with a hammer until all
that was left of it was dust.

Her thoughts were interrupted when next to her, Filia suddenly jumped over
the fence that separated them from the dancing crowd and ran as quickly as her feet
could carry her over towards her cousin. Raz's reaction to her was as instantaneous
as it was smooth as the instant he saw her he took a few steps backwards, though like
before he appeared to slide along the ground rather than walk on it. What's more,
Raz didn't even appear to take any proper steps at all. All he did was move his ankles
up one after the other and he seemingly slid backwards like the ground was made of
ice.

Filia, however, didn't appear to go for that as she ran straight into Raz's
arms. Arm in arm the two of them proceeded to dance around in a circle for the next
few moments before Raz suddenly spun away from her while still holding onto her
hand, then twirled her underneath his arm before dipping her very, very low to the
ground. The instant they pulled themselves back up Filia then spun away from Raz
and let go of him, whereupon she continued her spin to properly face him, threw her

hands up, and then quickly brought them back down to her waist like Raz had done earlier as her feet moved to the beat of the music. Across from her Raz made the same movements, though it was clear which of the two was leading the other as Raz's feet were quicker. To Tara's surprise the crowd of dancers began to open up slightly to give the two of them space as if to marvel at the spectacle of this strange man who had moves like none of them did and this very, very well dressed young woman copying his movements to near perfection, even including the pelvic thrusts.

The light of the fireworks, the beat of the music, and watching the two royals dance soon became infectious as Tara began to tap her feet to the rhythm of the music. Next to her, Daedalus still held onto his drink as he took another long sip from it. When he finished, the fact that Tara was tapping her foot did not escape his attention.

"What's stopping you!" he said to her over all of the noise.

"Um um, what!" Tara responded back as she instantly stopped tapping. Daedalus, however, even with all that was going on around him his face remained stern and his glare was as intimidating as ever. With said glare focused directly on her, he didn't give her the time to say anything else or come up with any kind of clever response before he spoke again.

"You clearly want to be out there with the rest of them, so what's stopping you!" Daedalus clarified for her. Tara's face instantly became redder than it was before as she tried to come up with something, anything to say to that.

"Well well well… What about you!" she shouted back at him over the fireworks and the music. "I don't see you out there!"

"Me!" Daedalus shouted back without looking at her. "I don't dance! Well, I mean I do, but not like this! But you clearly want to so what's stopping you!"

"I… I… I-"

"You what!" Daedalus interrupted her before taking another sip of his ale. "You're afraid I'll judge you! Afraid that they will judge you! Tara you should know by now! I don't care, and neither do they! None of us care whether or not you can dance! And if it's not us you're worried about then what is it! Everyone else! Come on! Are you a child!" Those last few words hit Tara harder than she initially realized as she instantly froze up, her eyes staring directly into Daedalus' cold glare as she did. In his eyes all of the words he had spoken to her that day came rushing back to her at once. It wasn't only his words though, it was also the way he treated her, the

way he made her feel like a fool, even more of a fool than she thought Raz was.
Perhaps it was the alcohol, but something in her refused to accept any of it.

Her ability to feel returned to her again as she steeled herself, matched
Daedalus' glare with her own, and then ungracefully leapt over the fence to join the
crowd of dancers.

"That's what I thought," Daedalus said to himself as he took another sip of
his ale.

Once among the crowd of dancing people Tara's attempts at dancing were
not nearly as graceful or elegant as anything Raz, Filia, or even some of the people
around her were doing, but she didn't care. She shook her hips, tapped her feet, and
got her body moving, and that was all that she needed. One movement soon bled into
the next for her as she began to lose track of what she was even doing, and not long
after that lost herself completely in the dance as she felt the beat of the music and the
explosions of the fireworks above move through her. The fact that some of the
people around her were not any better dancers than she was helped with her
confidence somewhat as well.

In front of her Raz and Filia were arm in arm again as they moved around
the circle that had been created for them before moving back towards the center,
upon which Raz spun Filia away from him. Filia then let go of his hand and spun on
her own for a moment before instantly stopping to face him. She and Raz then both
moved their feet almost in perfect synchrony with kicks, taps, and even slides as they
moved their way around the circle.

The more they danced, however, the more it became clear to everyone
watching that Raz was beginning to outpace Filia, and as a result the majority of the
attention from the people surrounding them began to focus more on him. With one
more perfect spin and a pelvic thrust Raz managed to completely capture everyone's
attention. Filia copied his moves closely enough to make it seem like she was still
keeping pace with him, but then used the momentary distraction to perform one more
slide away from him and then took a few steps towards the edge of the circle near
where Tara was. Once there Filia immediately hunched over and rested her hands on
her knees before taking in several deep, deep breaths. Because of how inadvertently
close she had gotten to her, Tara could actually see sweat beginning to pour down
Filia's forehead.

Back inside of the circle, without Filia there with him Raz's moves began to gradually increase in pace while still remaining in step with the music. To Tara, it was simply amazing how despite moving as fast as he was, Raz was still able to somehow make the upper and lower halves of his body move independently of each other while still moving them both as fluidly as water when he needed to. An example of this was when both Tara and Filia watched as he threw out his right hand, snapped his fingers, then turned to face his left and took a few sliding steps back before he then clapped his hands together and thrust his chest out forward. Once he had done that he followed it up with another pelvic thrust which caused him to slide only slightly forward, and like before his feet appeared to slide along the ground as he did this. He then spun on his heels one more time to face forward, at least what forward was to Tara and Filia, performed the snapping motion again, and then took a single, larger sliding step in the opposite direction before following the beat of the music with his feet as he moved back to the center again.

"Fucking hell," Filia spoke up in between pants as she watched her cousin move. "I always forget that the man has stamina for days." Tara did not respond to her at all as like all of the others surrounding the circle, she too was entranced by Raz's moves. As skilled as Raz was, however, Tara couldn't help but wonder if all of the attention he was getting was because he actually was a skilled dancer or because of some of the utterly bizarre moves he was making, as even in the capital at the few celebrations she had gone to, she had never seen anyone, anyone at all dance like Raz was now. The fact that there were more than a few suggestive undertones to his moves only added to this as she found them utterly bizarre to watch, yet for some reason she could not bring herself to look away. What's worse, she wasn't sure if she could blame the alcohol for it later.

With her attention focused so thoroughly on Raz, Tara didn't notice at all as Filia looked up at her to say something, but then saw where her eyes were looking as she followed Tara's gaze. A sly, mischievous smile then slowly crept across Filia's face as she watched Tara continually tap her foot to the beat of the music. After Raz made another sliding step in their direction followed by another spin, Filia saw her chance as without warning she suddenly moved behind Tara and pushed her forward towards Raz. Tara, between the alcohol and her not paying any attention to what was happening around her, practically ran into the circle as she stumbled forward and flailed her arms about as she nearly lost her balance several times. She would have fallen over on her face had someone not caught her just before she could. Without thinking Tara looked up to thank whomever it was that did that, only for her to instantly freeze up as she found herself staring into the wide, glistening, green eyes of Raz.

For several long, long moments all Raz and Tara could do was stare at each other as the both of them realized that the awkward position in which Raz had caught her left the two of them arm in arm as if still in the middle of the dance. Almost as if Raz were waiting for something like this to happen, but expected to catch anyone other than Tara. Inwardly Tara remained frozen as the full implications of the position she was in hit her, and her mind raced with all sorts of wild, often provocative images of what something like this could lead to. The majority of which she didn't want to even think about. It was enough to make her face instantly turn red again just from picturing it. When she looked into Raz's eyes, however, the look he gave her betrayed all of her thoughts as she beheld something that she would never have expected at all from him. Focusing her attention away from just his eyes for a moment, Tara was able to see that the look on Raz's face was little different than her's, as he stared down at her with a face as red as an apple and a thousand meter stare as if despite who he was he didn't know what to do at all. It was only then that Tara realized that Raz wasn't moving at all, and in fact had stopped dancing altogether despite the near constant cheering of the crowd surrounding them. That was enough to make Tara wonder if the person she was staring at, nay, the person in whose arms she found herself in, really was the same person who had been dancing up a storm not more than a few seconds ago or just someone else who looked exactly like him.

The sound of the music and the cheering onlookers surrounding them slowly brought the two of them back to reality as the feeling in all of their limbs slowly began to return to them. Raz was the first to act as he closed his eyes, took in a very deep breath, and when he opened his eyes again he smiled at her. Much to Tara's continued shock and amazement, it wasn't his usual, smug-looking smirk or the lecherous smile of someone who was expecting something after this, but instead a calm, gentle smile that evoked in her mind the image of a child who was trying to reassure someone that everything would be alright, yet might not have believed it himself if his still red face was any indication. Tara wasn't sure at all if it was her own feelings or the alcohol, but seeing that type of smile on him practically made her melt in his arms as she literally felt herself fully relax and return his smile. To her further surprise, it was actually her who made the first move as she began to tap her foot to the beat of the music again.

Raz picked up on this instantly as he took her by the hands and danced with her from the center of the circle to the edge before moving all the way around it and then moving back towards the center. Once they were there again the two of them separated as Tara grabbed the edge of her skirt and began to dance on her own in front of him. To her continued surprise yet again, Raz actually changed his style of dancing to suit her, as gone were the sliding movements across the ground, the pelvic thrusts, and all of the spins he had been doing as he simply stayed in front of her and moved his feet to the rhythm of the music. To Tara's slight embarrassment, however, he was still a much, much better dancer than she was as his feet appeared to move with minds of their own while she was barely struggling to keep up with everyone around her. What was worse, she knew that everyone watching her could see it too.

Before Tara could even comprehend what was even happening next, with a sudden spin Raz slid across the ground again as he moved in behind her. Tara spun around to meet him, but Raz seemed to have expected that as he held out his arms for her. Without thinking she immediately grabbed onto them as the two of them danced together back towards the center of the circle and once there, simply spun in place over and over again before abruptly stopping, whereupon Raz leaned her down towards his right. When they picked themselves back up they spun in place again to let go of each other before returning to what they were doing before.

Tara was more than content to let Raz lead her, as she had little idea what to do herself and likely would have embarrassed herself if she hadn't. As the two of them kept on dancing the noise of the cheering crowd surrounding them began to fade from Tara's mind, and with them went all of her previous reservations about jumping out here in the first place. She couldn't even see any of the people surrounding them anymore, not even Filia or Daedalus, as she realized that when she kept her attention on Raz's beautiful green eyes everything around her simply ceased to exist. This unfortunately had the side effect of the longer she stared into Raz's eyes, the more she became lost in them. Before she knew it she was so caught up in the moment and the seemingly endless green ocean of Raz's eyes, that the music, the fireworks, everything she had learned over the past few hours, the fact that she may have been drunk, all of those things began to completely fade from Tara's mind along with the still cheering crowd surrounding them. Before long she wasn't even aware of what she herself was doing anymore, as all there was to her was the moment, the dance, and the joyous feelings that they were bringing her.

The next thing Tara knew, Raz and her were arm in arm in the center of the circle again, upon which Raz twirled her around him one more time before bringing her back in close and dipping her in his arms, much to the delight of the surrounding crowd as they began to cheer even louder than they had been before. Tara could barely hold in her breath at this point, as it had taken everything she had to even keep up with anything Raz was doing. To her surprise yet again, however, when she looked up at Raz she saw that he was breathing hard as well, and was sweating profusely, as if doing all of those moves really had taken a tremendous amount of energy out of him. Considering how long he had been dancing, Tara could easily guess that that may have been the case.

"Th... Thank you," was all Tara could say in between pants as she continued to stare into Raz's glistening green eyes.

"No," Raz responded in between his own pants before pulling her back up so that she was on her feet again. The look on his face was something that Tara could only describe as pure, unadulterated elation. "Thank you. Thank you so much."

"I got it, I got it," the sound of a very familiar, very feminine voice echoed from the other side of Seth's hotel room door, which snapped his attention away from the window. The explosions in the sky had long since stopped, but the near constant shouting of people outside and the fact that Tara still had yet to return kept Seth from falling asleep. That and the day's other recent experiences of course.

"Are you sure about that?" an equally familiar masculine voice echoed in answer.

"O-of course... W-who do you think you're talking to?" At that the door handle began to shake a little bit in an obvious attempt to open it. An attempt which failed as the door did not yield. "Wha... What is this? Why won't it open? This is my room... I know it is..."

"You need help?"

"I said I got it..."

"If you say so." That last comment was followed by a few more attempts to open the door. All of which failed. Seth could only let out a sigh as he stood up from the chair that he had dragged over towards the window so that he could watch the explosions in the sky and walked on over towards the door.

"You need this?" the masculine voice then suddenly spoke up, upon which the feminine one let out a very audible gasp that could be heard even through the door.

"Wh- wh- where? Ho-"

"You dropped it the first time you tried to open the door," the masculine voice interrupted, upon which the feminine voice instantly fell silent. "It was quite funny to watch, actually." At those words, before Seth could even reach out his hand to open the door for them, with an audible clicking noise the door handle turned properly and the door to his hotel room opened. On the other side of it Seth was not surprised at all to see Raz and Tara standing there. What did surprise him, however, was that Tara was limply hanging onto Raz with one arm around his neck as if she wasn't able to stand on her own. It was a look that Seth was more than familiar with.

"Oh! Heeya Seeeeeeth…" Tara sputtered out upon seeing him in the doorway. While her extremely flushed face would have given it away, Seth only needed to smell her breath to know what was going on with her. "Th… There you are… Wa… wa… Why are you still awake, eh? It's tomorrow… Isn't it?" She didn't need to say any more for Seth to realize that he wasn't going to get anything meaningful out of her, so he turned his attention instead to Raz, who only smiled dumbly back at him.

"Yeah um…" Raz began, and like Tara Seth could smell on his breath what he had been up to. "Care to give me a hand?"

"What!" Tara exclaimed as she shot what she probably thought was an annoyed look in Raz's direction. "Who… who needs a hand? I don't. I'm perfectly fine. I can-" Before she could say anything more Seth stepped out into the hallway and wrapped Tara's other arm around his neck in order to help support her. "Ey ey ey Seth… What're you doin? I said I was-"

"Tara, if you were fine you wouldn't have dropped your key and then immediately forgotten about it when you tried to open the door," Raz interrupted her as he and Seth carried her into the room.

"What're you talkin' about?" Tara then asked him. "I didn't drop my key… I don't drop keys… I never drop anything."

"Which bed is her's?" Raz then asked Seth, ignoring Tara. Rather than give him an answer, Seth instead left her to Raz as he walked around and removed the covers from one of them. Following his lead, Raz walked Tara towards the open bed before gently placing her onto the mattress back first, then followed by her legs, which for some reason she seemingly refused to move on her own. "There you go."

"What's going on?" Tara then asked, and then immediately after doing so rolled her head over and saw that she was laying on a pillow, as if she had only just now become aware of that. "Oh... are we going to bed now?" Raz couldn't help but laugh at that.

"After the night you had," Raz said as he began to undo the laces on her boots. "I'm honestly surprised that you haven't passed out yet. Not many people can keep up with me like the way you did." It was then Tara's turn to laugh as she suddenly burst out cackling even louder than Raz had earlier.

"And you..." she began, but then stopped as her eyes rolled back up towards the ceiling and she let out a loud sigh. "You..."

"Yes, me," Raz replied to her as he took off one of her boots and then began to work on the other. Tara could only sigh and shake her head back and forth on her pillow before looking directly at him.

"I still can't believe that you're a prince," Tara said to him in a type of voice that, to Seth at least, sounded more than a little strange coming from her. She sounded as if she were lost in thought, but he wasn't sure which kind of thought. Raz, however, only laughed again.

"Oh believe me," he responded as he removed her other boot. "I have trouble believing it myself most days." Seth then watched as Raz stood back up and pulled the covers back over Tara, all the while she had kept laughing.

"You... You..." Tara said, her eyes on Raz the entire time as he proceeded to tuck her in. "You know you're not so..." Unfortunately for her she did not get to finish that sentence as the words that followed were little more than mumbles as her eyes began to close. The only sounds that came out of her after that were the sounds of snoring as sleep took her.

The entire scenario brought to Seth's mind the aftermath of Vivian and Ash's drinking contest all those months ago in The Empty Barrel, and how after drinking as much ale as she had he needed to carry her home because she could barely stand. Not only that, but every time she spoke to him immediately after that drinking contest she slurred nearly all of her words and spoke as if she didn't realize what she was saying, much like Tara was now. At the very least Seth was thankful that Tara hadn't thrown up numerous times like Vivian had, at least from what he could see it didn't appear as if she had thrown up.

"How much did she have?" Seth asked as he turned his attention to Raz, who while he could tell was also drunk, he was at least still coherent enough to answer his questions. Instead of giving him a direct answer, however, Raz instead simply held up a single finger.

"Really?" Seth let out, surprised, but still with a soft voice, as he did not want to potentially wake their neighbors any more than Tara may have already.

"Really," Raz responded before turning to properly face him. "All she had was one glass of wine, and I know because Daedalus and I bought her drinks and we didn't let her have any more after that." Despite knowing fully well that while Raz may have omitted certain truths, he was not really one to lie. Despite that, however, Seth still had an incredibly difficult time believing him.

"How… How is that possible?" Seth couldn't help but ask. "Literally every single person I have ever seen drinking alcohol has been able to take at least two or three full tankards of ale before getting drunk. So how can she be like this after only one glass of wine?"

"Well…" Raz began as he let out a yawn and then rubbed his eyes. "Aside from the fact that different drinks have different amounts of alcohol in them, the easiest way to answer that is that everyone has their own level of tolerance for the amount that they can drink. Some people, like Daedalus and I, as I'm sure you know, can drink a lot because we have a high tolerance for alcohol. Others, like Tara here, unfortunately, are extremely weak to alcohol. So it doesn't take much at all for them to get plastered drunk. If you or I had drank it it probably wouldn't have affected us much, and before you ask, she probably wouldn't have reacted much differently to ale."

"That… makes sense," Seth responded. "I guess." In truth it didn't make any sense to him at all. While he would never say so out loud, he had always suspected that Tara was physically weak, but he had no idea that would somehow translate into being able to drink a lot or a little alcohol. There was one part of Raz's explanation, however, that made even less sense to him. "What about me then? I've drank a lot of ale before, and I don't think I've ever gotten drunk at all." Raz couldn't help but burst out laughing at that, though he quickly attempted to calm himself.

"You…" Raz answered as he slowed his laughter. "You, my friend, are an anomaly. In all my life I have never, ever, seen anyone or anything drink as much as you without getting drunk."

"So you're saying that I'm not normal?" Seth then asked, as he felt that he had to.

"Well…" Raz began as he finally stopped laughing. "Maybe not normal for most of us." Seth, upon hearing that answer, immediately knew what Raz was getting at even if he knew that he would never say it out loud. As if Raz were reading his mind, however, before Seth could respond to what he had said Raz suddenly put a hand on his shoulder. To Seth's surprise there was what appeared to be a genuine smile on his face as he did so. "Hey man, don't worry about it. It's not anything to be ashamed of and you don't need to hide it. You should be proud of it and everyone who isn't you is going to be jealous as fuck because of it. In fact, not only will people sing you praises, but they will come from far and wide and all over to see if they can outdrink the great Seth. The man who can hold more liquor than a fifty liter barrel."

"Thanks… I guess," Seth responded, if only to be polite. In truth none of what Raz had said sounded appealing to him in the slightest, but he did understand what he was trying to tell him. That didn't keep him from noticing, however, and perhaps it was because of that fact that Raz was also drunk, but he kept his hand on Seth's shoulder for a few seconds longer than Seth was comfortable with. Before Seth could say anything about it, however, as suddenly as he had put it there Raz removed his hand.

"Well, I'm gonna head off," Raz then said as he turned around and headed towards the still open door to their room. "I need to catch a few z's myself. See the two of you later." Before Seth could even say goodbye Raz had already shut the door behind him and was gone.

Now alone, or at least the only one awake in the room, Seth could only stand still where he was for several long seconds. He wasn't sure at all why, maybe it was in case Tara suddenly woke up for whatever reason, but Seth still couldn't bring himself to fall asleep immediately. It would be well over another hour before he finally decided to blow out the room's only candle and crawl into his own bed. Sleep did eventually take him, but only after he had stopped thinking about everything that had happened to him that day.

Shortly after the fireworks had ended a seemingly unimportant man wandered across the city until he found himself in one of the more densely populated areas of the Suntop district. While most in this area of the city were either already making their way back to their manors and fancy hotel rooms in order to find their way into their more than comfortable beds, this man instead walked into a dark alleyway between two of the taller buildings. While the fireworks had lit up the night as if it were daytime before, now it was so dark that he could barely see at all. A chill ran up his spine as the realization that wandering into a place like this would make him an easy target for any mugger or psychopath that happened to be nearby hit him. While the Suntop district was heavily patrolled, he knew that even on major holidays such as this things did still happen.

"My lord…" the man whispered into the darkness. "Are you there?" The only response he received was silence. "Is he seriously not here? Solaris damned noble makes me stalk some kids and doesn't even bother to meet me here when he's supposed to. Fucking usele-"

"If you are intent on keeping your job after tonight I would strongly advise against finishing that sentence," a soft, velvety sounding voice suddenly spoke out from behind him. Instinctively the man spun around quickly to see who the voice belonged to. Even in the near pitch black darkness of the alley the man could easily recognize the frame of Lord Isaac De La Rosa, the one he had come here to meet. "Now if you are done insulting the people you work for behind their backs, would you mind giving me your full detailed report?" Both Isaac's ice cold stare and the tone in which he spoke made his request sound like less of a simple request and more of a demand caused another chill to run up the man's spine.

"I… I don't really know what you want me to tell you, sir?" the man spoke up once he was able to find his voice again.

"Then tell me your report," Isaac responded coldly to him. "Like I asked you to."

"They…" the man then began hesitantly. "They just sort of… hung out. You know, like normal people. They spent the entire day walking through the city and checking out whatever festival stands were open. Nothing unusual or out of the ordinary happened, and Prince Michael and the two guards you sent with her did an admirable job of keeping Princess Filia safe. Nobody even got close to her."

"¿Eso es?" Isaac muttered to himself before returning his attention to the spy. "And what of that associate of Michael Dagon? The one that called himself Seth?"

"He left them," the man answered rather quickly, but despite that Isaac narrowed his cold gaze upon him.

"He left them?"

"Yes," the spy responded immediately. "At some point he left Michael and Filia to go chase someone else and never returned. Even when the fireworks went off and everyone started dancing, he still didn't return." Isaac, in response to that, let out a hum, which was then followed by several long moments of silence. A feeling of cold dread began to wash over the spy as Isaac's ice-like glare moved away from him.

"Very well," Isaac eventually spoke again. "You are dismissed, mister…"

"Dubost," the spy quickly responded.

"Mister Dubost," Isaac continued as he slowly turned around and began to walk away from him. "A piece of advice to take to bed with you, Mister Dubost. It is best to keep your thoughts in your head. Most of us, as you call us, 'Solaris damned nobles', are less forgiving than I was tonight." Isaac then walked further into the darkness until the spy could no longer hear his footsteps. For reasons unknown to even the spy, he found himself shaking in his boots as his feet for some reason refused to move no matter how much he willed them to, as if he had just finished speaking not with a man, but a devil.

Chapter 17

The rumbling of his stomach woke Seth up before he even considered opening up his eyes. At first it confused him why he would wake up like this, but then he realized exactly how many hours it had been since he last ate, along with how late he had stayed up last night. He ceased those thoughts as soon as they had appeared. After everything that had happened yesterday he didn't want to think about any of it any more.

Slowly but surely he eventually opened his eyes to see the beige ceiling of his hotel room and stretched out his limbs, if only so that he could get them moving. He then looked to his left to see Tara still in her bed with her eyes closed and in exactly the same position he and Raz had left her the night before. Not wanting to disturb her, as quietly as he could Seth slid out from his bed and put on his pants and shirt before doing anything else. As much as Tara had stressed the importance of privacy to him, the small room they had found themselves in here in Dis unfortunately did not allow for much of that, so he had to take it when he could get it.

Seth then walked over towards the curtains and, without thinking, pulled them open to let in the sunlight. The sun shone brightly over the city of Dis, very brightly, and with it came the new year that was so incredibly important to everyone. It was also the only means Seth had to tell what time it was, as there wasn't any type of clock in the hotel room. Given where the sun currently was, Seth guessed that it was a little after ten, which meant that he had slept in far later than he usually did. As much as he was used to waking up bright and early for his duties as a member of the town watch in Canaan, that didn't appear to make him immune from occasionally sleeping in it seemed.

While the light of the sun illuminated the city and told Seth what time it was, it also lit up the hotel room brighter than any candle ever could, and by extension shone past Seth directly onto Tara's face. The sudden appearance of the light caused Tara to let out a loud groan as she began to move in her bed. The sudden noise startled Seth and made him instantly turn his head to see who else was in the room with him, but once he saw that it was only Tara he immediately calmed down. Tara then let out several more loud groans before slowly sitting up in her own bed and covering her eyes with one of her hands.

"Where..." she began softly and with a dry voice. "Where am I?"

"In our hotel room," Seth answered.

"When did we-" Before Tara could even finish that sentence, Seth could see from between her fingers as her eyes suddenly shot open as if a pair of bells had been suddenly and violently rung right next to both of her ears. They were a little red and bloodshot, but they were open at the very least. Despite that, however, Tara remained silent as she blankly stared forward at the wall in front of her.

"Tara..." Seth eventually said after a few long moments of this. "Are you alright?"

"I'm sorry," Tara immediately responded as she blinked once, removed her hand from her face, and then looked over directly at Seth. "I mea... Of course. Of course I'm-" Before she could say any more Tara suddenly ceased talking for a few seconds and coughed into her hand, which somehow made her regain her usual composure instantly. "Of course I am alright, Seth. Why would you think I was not alright?" Despite how simple her question was Seth wasn't sure he could answer it.

"Because..." Seth began, but then stopped himself as he needed to take a few seconds to think of what exactly was the best way to say what he wanted to without making it seem obvious. "Is it enough to say that I'm just worried about you. Especially after the way you came back here last night. I mean, you're already not acting like your usual self."

"Oh..." Tara replied, more than a little embarrassed, though she did her best not to show it. "I... No, no, you are right. It is enough, and..." Before continuing she suddenly let out a loud groan as her head fell back into her hands. "I am sorry Seth, it is just that..." In the middle of speaking she suddenly stopped herself again, as if another realization had suddenly just come to her, but before Seth could say anything she let out another, louder groan. "Sometimes after people drink a lot, Seth, they get this thing called a hang-"

"I know what a hangover is," Seth interrupted before she could get too far into her explanation. "I've spent enough time with Vivian to know."

"Oh thank Solaris!" Tara very nearly shouted as she pulled her head back up out of her hands before falling backwards back onto her pillow.

"Do you need some water?" Seth then asked, remembering what he was supposed to do with people that had hangovers. Tara began to raise a hand at first in order to respond without words, but rather than do that she instead remained silent for a few quick seconds before dropping it.

"Actually, yes. I would love some," Tara eventually responded without looking at him. "Thank you, Seth."

"Alright," Seth replied as he walked past the two beds and towards the door. "I'll go get some from downstairs. I'll be right back." Tara was about to open her mouth to say something else to him, but before she even had the chance he was already out the door and gone.

Much to his own surprise, it took Seth hardly any time at all to get some fresh water in this hotel. He had intended to head downstairs and ask the lady at the front desk where the nearest well or water tower was so that he could get some himself, but after asking her that question she instead smiled and insisted that she get the water for him. Even after Seth had insisted that she didn't need to trouble herself, she did so anyway, claiming that it was one of the many services provided by the hotel. As a result Seth had returned to the hotel room he shared with Tara bearing a full pitcher of water and a cup within a little over ten minutes.

When he handed her said cup Tara practically snatched it from him with both hands and drank from it greedily. Seeing where this would no doubt go, Seth set the pitcher on the nightstand next to her bed before taking a seat on his own bed. After a few minutes of Tara refilling the cup multiple times she appeared content enough to let out what to Seth sounded like an exhale of satisfaction.

"Thank you," she said to him after she had finished.

"You're welcome," Seth politely responded, unsure of what else to say. Much to Seth's disappointment, however, while he didn't expect Tara to immediately return to how she usually was after she had drunk some water, he had expected her to at least say something in order to give him some direction. More than ever now, Seth needed it, as he didn't know what to do at all in this city that he already didn't want to be in any longer than he needed to. Instead of saying anything, however, Tara instead stared down at the empty cup for what seemed like a long time. Long enough that Seth wasn't sure if disturbing her would be a good idea.

"Seth…" She eventually said, and he could tell from her tone of voice that something was amiss.

"Yes," he responded.

"Can I ask you something?"

"Of course."

"If I um… told you that because of my hangover I cannot remember much of anything that happened last night, would you be able to answer some questions for me to help fill in the gaps?" That question caused Seth to raise an eyebrow, but he saw no reason why he couldn't do what she was asking.

"I can try."

"Good, that is all I ask. So um… I know that some of these might sound odd, so please bear with me. I suppose to start with… How… How did I get here?"

"You mean this hotel room?"

"Yes, exactly."

"Raz brought you."

"Right… Raz… and… when was this? I mean what time?"

"I don't know. It wasn't that long after those explosions in the sky had stopped though."

"You mean the fireworks?"

"Is that what those are called?" Tara let out a groan as Seth asked that question. Fortunately for her he was easily able to understand why this time, so he immediately stopped that line of questioning.

"Yes, but let us not get into that right now, please."

"Okay."

"So it wasn't that long after midnight… Did… Did Raz say anything about what we may or may not have been doing before?"

"You mean before he brought you here?"

"Yes." Seth actually needed to take a moment to think about what specifically Raz had said to him before he could answer that question. In this instance it was much harder to do than he believed it would be.

"Not really…" he began. "He said something about being surprised that you could keep up with him because not many people could." The instant he finished that sentence Tara's face immediately became red, and she knew that Seth could see it. "Then he told me that you only drank one glass of wine the entire night. Then after that he called me an anomaly because I can drink a lot more than most people and not get drunk. I still have no idea what that word means though." To Seth's surprise,

Tara did not respond to him when he finished speaking, in fact she seemed to be making an effort not to look at him now. "Tara…"

"Yes!" She very nearly jumped when she heard him say her name.

"Are you sure you're alright?"

"Yes, yes," she very quickly responded before suddenly regaining her former composure. Though it did not escape Seth's attention that she tried to hide her still red face from him. "Yes I am perfectly alright. I am sorry for making you think otherwise."

"Okay…"

"Anyway… And Raz… Didn't say anything else?"

"No, not really. At least nothing relating to what you asked about."

"Okay…" Tara responded as she ceased trying to hide her face, but still kept her eyes away from Seth as she seemingly stared off into space. "When… Raz brought me back… How… What… What was his disposition?"

"I don't know what that word means?"

"How did he act?" That question legitimately confused Seth, as not only was he not sure how to even begin to answer that question, but he couldn't for the life of him come up with a reason why Tara would even ask that question in the first place. It took him a few short moments to actually think of something to say as he racked his brain for words, all the while Tara continued to stare off into space as if the entire rest of the world around her had ceased to be.

"He-" Before Seth could say any more the sound of someone knocking on their hotel room door cut him off and also caused Tara to immediately curl away as she brought both of her hands back to her face. Seth, knowing that there wasn't really anything he could do for her right now except answer the door, did just that as he stood up, walked over towards the door, and opened it up before Tara could tell him otherwise. To his great surprise, there, on the other side of the door, leaning against the side of the door frame with an elbow was none other than Raz.

"Hey," Raz immediately said to Seth with a wave of his hand the instant he saw him.

"Oh…" Seth let out instinctively. "Hello, Raz. We were just talking about you."

"Raz!" Tara shouted at the top of her lungs as soon as his name hit her ears.

"Oh, really," Raz responded with his usual smirk as he pushed himself off of the door frame and stood up properly. "Only good things I hope. Can I come in?"

"Sure," Seth answered without thinking as he stepped out of the entryway to the room. Before Tara could speak even a single word in protest Raz was already in the room with them and Seth had closed the door behind him. Tara's eyes instantly locked on his as an expression that Seth recognized as apprehension crossed her face, which she had very quickly uncovered in an attempt to appear more normal.

"H... H... Hi... Raz," Tara hesitantly let out.

"Hey, Tara," Raz calmly responded to her. "How you feeling?"

"Um... Um..." Tara hesitantly responded as her face very quickly turned red. "A... Alright. I mean, I-"

"She said that she had a hangover when she woke up," Seth spoke up from behind Raz as he walked back over and sat on his bed.

"Wait, really?" Raz let out, seeming more than a little surprised to hear that. "You seriously have a hangover after last night?"

"I..." Tara began, but then suddenly stopped herself as she realized the exact situation that she was now in. Before either Seth or Raz could notice anything, she dropped eye contact with Raz and brought one of her hands back to her forehead. "Unfortunately, yes, and it has been bothering me since I woke up so I would appreciate it if you did not make any sudden noises." Seeming well more than a little confused, Raz looked over to Seth, who only responded with a shrug. In truth, Seth believed that Raz likely understood more about what was going on than he did at the moment.

"I'm sorry..." Raz then hesitantly responded to Tara.

"It is quite alright," Tara answered as she slowly regained her composure again and looked up at him from behind her hand. "And thank you for bringing me back here last night. Seth was just telling me about it."

"You're... You're welcome," Raz hesitantly answered as he scratched the back of his head. As he did, Seth thought that he could see a hint of red on his face as well.

"So, um... now that that is out of the way," Tara continued as she removed her head from her hands again so she could properly look more directly at Raz. "What brings you back so soon?"

"A few things actually," Raz responded as he suddenly regained his composure as well. "First off, I wanted to swing by to see how you were doing after last night, and from the look of things I'm glad I did."

"Th... Thank you," Tara responded hesitantly, but still somehow politely.

"The second is that I came here to pass along a message." As soon as he had finished speaking Raz reached into one of his pockets and pulled out a folded up piece of paper, which he then proceeded to hand over to Tara. "And I was going to say that I hope you haven't eaten breakfast already, but from the look of things it looks like I don't really need to." Silence dominated the room for the next full minute as Tara read what was on the paper that Raz had handed to her. Seth was almost certain, however, that whatever was on it wasn't that long of a message, and that Tara had already read it and was just sitting still in shock. Something that she seemed to have been doing a lot of recently.

"What does it say, Tara?" Seth then proceeded to ask with that exact thought process in mind. It was only after he had actually spoken that Tara lowered the paper from her eyes and looked over towards him. The look on Tara's face was a wide eyed expression of shock, which was exactly what he had expected to see.

"This..." Tara began. "This says that Filia wants to invite all of us to brunch in the Suntop District."

"What's brunch?" Seth immediately asked.

"It's when you have breakfast around lunchtime," Raz answered before Tara could. Seth wanted to ask why people would have a name for something like that, but then he realized what time it currently was and that neither he nor Tara had actually eaten any breakfast yet. So it didn't seem as strange to him when he thought of it like that. "But yeah, earlier this morning a messenger stopped by our hotel room and dropped that off."

"And then he told you to pass it along to us?" Seth asked.

"No," Raz politely answered. "Filly asked me to do that in the letter. Can't have her sending a message to two plebs, lest her mother find out about it and shoot down the invitation before it even sees the light of day. Sending it to another noble born though, no problem at all. Nicole's not gonna ask any questions about that. At least not before the message gets to me."

"What's a pleb?" Seth then immediately asked, as for some bizarre reason that word made him feel as if he had just been insulted.

"It's short for plebian," Raz answered. "It basically means a poor person or someone who isn't a noble." Seth was about to open his mouth to ask something else, but Raz cut him off before he could. "And before you ask, yes it is an insult and yes that is exactly what Nicole thinks of the both of you."

"So… so…" Tara finally spoke up. "Princess Filia is inviting us to brunch?"

"Yes," Raz answered again.

"Why?" That question caused Raz to instantly burst out laughing.

"Oh, I don't know," Raz answered after a few seconds once he had calmed himself back down enough. "Maybe it's because she had so much fun yesterday spending time with the two of you that she wants to do it again at least once before she has to leave."

"Leave where?" Seth then asked without thinking. Instead of answering immediately Raz kept silent for a few moments after Seth had asked that, as if he was confused by the question.

"Back home of course," Raz eventually answered. "To Sol." Suddenly it hit Seth as he remembered that nearly every person who had been associated with Filia, including Raz and Tara, had mentioned that place at least once. He even recalled that both Raz and Tara had mentioned that place on more than one occasion back in Canaan.

"And where is that?" Seth asked, now genuinely curious.

"Oh, far from here," Raz answered before bringing a hand to his chin. "I'd say about… three or four days' ride... maybe."

"Exactly four days, actually," Tara chimed in once Raz had finished speaking as she handed him back the letter.

"When does she want to meet us?" Seth then asked next.

"Not long from now, actually," Raz answered him. "And judging by the state of dress the two of you are in you might wanna hoof it you wanna get there on time."

"Wait!" Tara suddenly exclaimed once she realized the direction this conversation was heading. "Wait wait wait… I do not think we have agr-"

"I'll get ready as quickly as I can," Seth interrupted before Tara could finish.

"Great!" Raz chimed back in before Tara could say anything. "I'll wait for you downstairs. You'll actually need to show up with me this time or they won't let you in. So I'll be standing by. See you two in a few minutes." Then with that said, as suddenly as he had come, Raz suddenly left as he walked out the door and shut it behind him.

Once he was gone Seth walked over to his suitcase and began rummaging through it for clothes that weren't the ones he was already wearing.

"Seth, what are you doing?" Tara asked, seemingly forgetting completely about her hangover as she stood up from her bed and walked directly over towards him.

"Getting some new clothes," he answered without looking at her. "You know, like you taught me to. Since I can't wear the same clothes every day."

"I see that," Tara responded, now sounding more than a little annoyed. "But why are you getting out new clothes? We have not agreed to anything, so you do not-"

"Because I want to go," Seth answered before she could finish, as he had a relatively good idea of where she was going to go with that statement.

"But why?" Tara then asked. That question felt like a sting to Seth, and he wasn't sure why. So rather than responding immediately he quietly took out a new pair of pants, socks, and a shirt and placed them onto his bed before standing up and turning around to properly face Tara. While Tara may have been serious before, that persona suddenly dropped when she saw the look on Seth's face as he unintentionally glared at her.

"Because it took her a whole day longer than us to get here and she wants to see us," he answered. Tara wanted to respond to that by asking him what that had to do with anything, but any words she could think of died in her throat as she stared into his red eyes, which he had not yet had the chance to hide with magic now that the morning had come. Through sheer force of will she opened her mouth to say at least something in response, but when she did Seth suddenly spoke over her. "If it took her four days to get here that means she spent four whole days on the road with nothing to do going to a place she didn't even want to go to. Now she's here and wants to see us before she has to leave, which when she does it's going to take her another four whole days to get back to wherever Sol is. So if we don't see her now that means that if she wants to see any of us again then either she will have to travel for a whole week to get to us in Cannan or we'll have to travel for a week to get to her. I don't want to put her through that. Not if I don't have to." Tara could only stare wide eyed as the conviction and resolve in Seth's voice settled in her head. In truth it intimidated her quite a bit.

Before Tara could say anything to him or even process another thought, as quickly as he had turned to face her, Seth turned back around and began to unbutton his shirt. While he could have phrased what he wanted to say much better, Tara could understand that this was something that he cared about, though she for the life of her could not even begin to understand why. Especially after he had run out on them yesterday to chase Vivian. She continued to watch him get dressed for the next full minute as she ran through the list of things she had planned to do today, and upon doing so realized that not only were all of them second to meeting a princess, but the schedule that she had planned for herself had been thrown off somewhat by the fact that the postmaster had been arrested. So really, she had no good excuses not to attend.

With no other idea of what she could do, Tara let out a loud sigh as she resigned herself to her fate. Again.

"Give me a few minutes," Tara said to Seth as she walked back towards her own bed and opened her suitcase. She then began the slightly longer process of getting dressed and making herself look as presentable as possible given the circumstances. As she did though, Tara couldn't help but wonder to herself exactly how much control she still had over her life. What's more, if she ever had control, then at what point did she begin to lose it. Too many big or life changing events had happened to her as of late for her not to at least wonder.

A full fifteen minutes had passed before both Seth and Tara were satisfied enough with their appearances that they decided to head downstairs to the hotel lobby. To be more exact, Seth was satisfied with his appearance early on. Tara took quite a bit longer before she felt comfortable enough to stand in the presence of royalty. If she had her way she would at least put on a nice dress, but unfortunately she hadn't packed any dresses for this trip because she had not expected to encounter a situation in which she would need one. When they had arrived at the hotel lobby they were quick to spot Raz, as he was leaning on the front desk chatting away with the receptionist, who to their surprise was giggling at him.

"I appreciate the attempt, I really do. You're certainly clever with your words," she said to him. "But I'm already spoken for and we already have plans for later."

"Really? Ah crap..." Raz responded with obvious mock disappointment. As he did, out of the corner of his eye he caught the sight of both Seth and Tara by the stairs. "Well when you see him later be sure to remind him how truly blessed he is that someone as cute as you gets to stand by his side."

"Thank you," she responded with another giggle, though both Seth and Tara could tell it was fake. "I will be sure to do just that." Then with a smirk and one last wink Raz left her as he walked over to meet Seth and Tara.

"You two certainly took your time," Raz said as he walked up to the two of them.

"She said that she needed more time because she needed to look presentable," Seth responded without thinking as he pointed at Tara.

"Seth!" Tara let out as her face instantly turned red from embarrassment.

"What?" Seth replied immediately. "That's what you said." Before Tara could respond to him Raz suddenly burst out laughing.

"Really?" He let out once he had calmed down enough. "What did you think you needed to look presentable for? It's not like we're going to meet Queen Faust, just my cousin." Tara opened her mouth to respond to what he had said, but before she could Raz suddenly held up his hand. "And before you say anything, no one else is going to care and Nicole won't even notice what you look like. So it really doesn't matter. Besides, you look great anyway. So you got nothing to worry about." While Tara had a carefully chosen response that she wanted to say to him, that last remark threw her off as she suddenly forgot all of the words that she wanted to say and her face became even redder than it was before.

"Oh... um..." was all she was able to stammer out before she quickly shook her head and recomposed herself. "Thank... you." Raz was about to respond, and Seth could see that he was, but before he could he suddenly stopped as he found himself lost in Tara's eyes and her smiling face. A few quick moments later Raz instead relaxed his gaze and let his smirk fall into a more comfortable smile as he held eye contact with her.

"If I might interject," the familiar voice of Daedalus spoke up as he suddenly walked into the lobby from somewhere. "We are already running late as it is, so do the two of you plan on gawking at each other all day or are we going to get going at some point? Not that it matters to me, you can keep gawking at each other if you want. I just need to know what we're doing so that I can know precisely to what extent I need to be involved."

"Good morning, Daedalus," Seth said to him as soon as he saw him.

"Hello, Seth," Daedalus politely responded back to him with a nod. "And it's technically not morning anymore, so you don't need to say that."

"Oh…" Seth let out as the logic of that statement slowly sunk into his head. In truth he said it without thinking because that was usually what he said to people after he woke up and he never once really thought about it. "Thank you."

"You're quite welcome," Daedalus responded before returning his attention back to Raz and Tara. "So what are we doing, if anything?"

"Daedalus," Tara politely said to him with a nod, though there was noticeably much less energy in her voice than when she had addressed Raz. "Am I safe in assuming that you were invited to brunch along with us?"

"Not officially," Daedalus responded rather bluntly. "Though none of this is official when you think about it for more than five seconds. No, I am attending this so-called brunch date with you all purely of my own initiative. Not that I had much choice in the matter in the first place?"

"Why is that?" Seth asked without thinking the instant Daedalus had stopped speaking.

"Well…" Daedalus began as he looked between all of them. "When a certain dumbass I know is invited to a gathering with very, very high profile individuals, let's just say I would prefer to be close by in case I need to mitigate any damage."

"What kind of damage would you need to be there to mitigate?" Seth then asked. Before Daedalus had a chance to even open his mouth to respond, however, Raz suddenly stepped in between him and Seth.

"Anyway!" Raz let out rather loudly. "Daedalus is right, we are running a little late so we might as well get going." Then, before anyone could say anything more he spun around on his heel and began walking towards the door. "The sooner we get there the less likely we are to miss them." Seth, Tara, and Daedalus could do nothing but stand and watch as Raz walked away from them as if he had just dodged a rock being thrown at his head. Raz had almost reached the door by the time any of them had said anything.

"Why do I have a bad feeling about this?" Tara asked aloud.

"Because your brain actually functions properly," Daedalus quickly answered. "Unlike some people's."

The walk to the Suntop District took a much shorter amount of time than it did the last time Seth had gone there. At first it bothered him, but then he remembered that last time he and Raz had been secretly following Tara, and because of that they were taking great pains to not be seen, which involved a lot of hiding and waiting. Without doing any of that it quickly made sense to him why it would take a shorter amount of time to get there if they were just walking.

What was even stranger to him, however, was that the entire way there not one of them had said anything. Tara and Daedalus he could understand. Daedalus was always quiet and Tara didn't seem to have much of anything to say as of late, but Raz was uncharacteristically quiet. He did, however, notice Raz occasionally glance in Tara's direction when she didn't appear to be looking, though Seth wasn't sure if he was being quiet because of that or if it was simply because no one else was saying anything. Before he could contemplate that any further, however, they had reached the archway that separated the district they stood in from the Suntop District.

"What's up!" Raz shouted at the two guards with a knowing nod, but the only response he got from both of them was a very angry glare as they let them all pass through without any questions. The intense look in their eyes made both Seth and Tara nervous. Daedalus, however, did not appear to be fazed by it in the slightest.

The contrast between the rest of the city and the Suntop District was just as jarring as it had been the first time they had come here. With all of the different color buildings and plant life surrounding them Seth still wasn't sure if they had somehow stepped into an entirely different city altogether. The strangest thing about it though, was that even though all of the buildings appeared different and none of them were beige, they all still looked the same to him. Thankfully both Raz and Daedalus seemed to know where they were going.

Eventually they were led to a completely white building surrounded by a metal fence that had many, many different plants growing all over it, as if the plants were part of the fence itself. Seth could discern that it was some type of restaurant, though much more extravagant than any of the ones he had ever been in before, as not only were there tables set up outside where many different patrons were eating and chatting the day away, but as they grew closer he could see that where the entrance was, most of the front of the building was actually made of glass, and beyond the glass Seth could see more tables inside and yet more people at those tables. At first glance this restaurant appeared to only be a single story in height, but upon closer inspection Seth could see that there was indeed another level to it that didn't encompass the whole roof. What really threw him off about this building, however, was its color. It wasn't that he had any sort of problem with the color white, but the building itself was clearly made of stone, and yet it somehow appeared to be so white in color that he couldn't help but wonder exactly what type of stone was used to make it and where exactly it came from.

Both of these questions went unanswered as Raz led them past the glass doors and into the restaurant itself. Waiting for them on the other side was a thin, but not very tall man wearing a very well made black and white suit. Seth hesitated to call the incredibly small table he stood at a desk, as it was not only so small that it could barely hold two rows of papers, but it was also so tall that he had to stand at it rather than sit. Past the man and his incredibly tiny desk Seth got a better view of the rest of the restaurant itself, and wasn't surprised at all to see that it was very, very well put together. The floors were covered in a very smooth looking maroon carpet, all of the tables were covered with pristine white cloth, and tall glass windows with very finely made, matching maroon drapes were everywhere, as if to allow all of the patrons to see outside without actually having to interact with any of it. Lastly, and most importantly, Seth did not need to look around for longer than two seconds to see that every single one of the patrons in this place were very finely dressed, very well refined, had excellent table manners, and all spoke as if they were more important than everyone else.

"May I help you gentlemen?" the man at the small table said to them as they stood in the entryway. After saying that, however, he quickly looked over every single one of them with what Seth could only describe as a scrutinizing eye, like he was looking for something blatantly wrong with each of them. "Do you, perchance, have a reservation with us?"

"No, we do not," Raz answered before anyone else could speak. "We are actually meeting another party."

"And what party would that be, sir?" the man then asked as he focused his attention squarely on Raz.

"The party of Princess Nicole Solara and Regional Governor Monet," Raz answered without skipping a beat. At his answer, the man at the small desk suddenly fell silent as he narrowed his eyes on Raz like he was trying to threaten him.

"I am sorry sir," he said to Raz. "But there is no party here by that name."

"Yes there is," Raz responded before the man had time to say anything else. "I have it on pretty good authority that they are."

"Even if they were," the man continued. "What makes you believe that they would be expecting you?"

"I can assure you with absolute certainty that we are expected," Raz responded as politely as he could. As he spoke, Seth noticed that next to him Tara was actually shaking, as if she wanted to say something, but was afraid to.

"Why am I here?" he heard Tara say as quietly as she could to herself. "What is going on?" As much as Seth wanted to say something to reassure her, he knew that saying anything right now wouldn't help anyone. In truth he didn't know what Raz was playing at either, but he also knew that his way with words and mindset allowed him to find Tara and meet Filia, so to a degree he felt that he could be trusted. Even with that trust, however, several long moments of silence passed before the man at the desk spoke again.

"Let us assume for a moment that they are here," he began. "Exactly whom is it that I should be telling them that they are supposed to be expecting?"

"Prince Michael Dagon of the royal house of Solara in Sol and Daedalus Olympus the thirteenth, son of Daedalus Olympus the twelfth, the court architect to the Solaran royal family," Raz answered, again without skipping a beat. For a moment the man at the desk looked as if he was about to burst out laughing. Not that Seth could blame him, as everyone else he had told about Raz found it incredibly difficult to believe as well. Instead, however, the man at the desk kept his composure and opened his mouth to speak again. Before he could, however, Raz spoke first and interrupted him. "And yes, we are able to prove we are who we say we are and will do so upon request. Not that it would matter that much to you since for all you know we could be anyone who nicked a family seal or ring, but if you describe us to literally anyone in the party I've described, then they'll be able to confirm who we are, and if you require further proof then we will provide it. Is that sufficient?" As

Raz spoke the look on the man's face slowly changed from a simple threatening glare to someone who was desperately trying to hold back from punching someone.

"Sir…" he began again. "As I told you before. There is no party here by-"

"Look, man, don't bullshit me," Raz calmly interrupted before the man could say anything more. "I know what you're doing and it's not going to work on me. I've been part of this game my whole life. So I know how its rules work. I know they're here. I can assure you that I'm well connected enough to know that for a fact. So as things stand you're left with two options. One, you do your job and tell them that we're here, in which case you won't have to deal with me or any of us cause we won't be your problem anymore. Or two, I can do it myself, save you the trouble." At those words the man at the desk opened his mouth to speak again, but once again Raz cut him off before he could. "And don't even think of telling me that they aren't in that little private area upstairs because if I walk in there and they are then how do you think that's gonna make you look?" Raz finished that sentence with his usual, overconfident smirk adorning his face. The man at the desk, for all intents and purposes, looked as if he were ten seconds away from tearing into Raz.

"It really would be in your best interest to do what my friend here is suggesting," Daedalus then spoke up, again before the man at the desk could even open his mouth to speak. "Of the options currently available to you, only one of them paints you in a positive light, and that's the one where you do your job. If what you have been saying thus far is indeed correct, then you would no doubt make us all look like fools upon your return and we will leave. Which will be worth far more than any words you could possibly say, I assure you. So. Are you going to do your job?" At the conclusion of Daedalus' words, the man at the desk shifted his attention from Raz over to Daedalus, but as Seth knew from experience, even if his facial expression didn't change and he didn't say any words, in his head he no doubt regretted that decision instantly.

What followed were several long, long moments of silence as the man at the desk rapidly shifted his gaze from Raz to Daedalus and then back again several times. While Seth was managing just fine, the same couldn't be said for Tara, whom Seth could see was gripping her hands together incredibly tightly and was shaking even more than before. Unsure of what to do for her in this situation, he opted to simply hold her arm. While the sudden physical contact caused Tara to nearly jump as her attention immediately shifted towards Seth, she calmed down almost as soon as she saw his face. With that, slowly but surely, Tara's fearful shaking began to subside.

All of this, fortunately, did not last much longer than it had to as the man at the desk seemingly gave up on challenging them as he turned around, stepped away from the tiny desk, and walked on into the restaurant proper where he disappeared amidst the sea of patrons and workers that were running from table to table. It was only then that both Seth and Tara felt that they finally had a chance to catch their breath.

"What the hell was that?" Tara immediately let out as she pulled herself away from Seth's arm and took a step closer towards Raz and Daedalus.

"What was what?" Raz responded first, appearing to be legitimately confused.

"No, no, you will not do this to me," Tara answered quickly as she narrowed her eyes directly on him. "You can do it to the maître d' and everybody else that you talk to but not to me. Not ever to me. You know very well what I am talking about so answer me, 'Michael'. What was that? Why did you threaten that poor man?"

"I did no such thing," Raz was quick to respond, as calm as ever.

"Yes you did!" Tara tried to exclaim without shouting, lest she draw even more unwanted attention to herself. "You-"

"Daedalus," Raz interrupted her as he looked over to his friend. "When at any point during that conversation did I threaten the maître d'?"

"You didn't," Daedalus promptly answered. "If you had I would have intervened, but I saw no need to."

"But you…" Tara then very quickly began, only to immediately fall silent as no words reached her mouth. "You-"

"Tara," Daedalus interjected in what he probably believed was a polite manner before she could say any more. "As I am certain you no doubt know just as well as we do. Life is not fair, and not everyone is nice. Because of this, sometimes it becomes necessary to remind people of their place in this unfair world if you want things to go your way. Is it unfair, yes. Is it cruel, maybe, but sometimes it's the only thing that unkind people are willing to listen to. Take Princess Nicole for instance, do you think someone like her will listen to anything else?"

"But-"

"I know what you are going to say," Daedalus interrupted Tara again. "And

I will assuage your fears right now. While this is a privilege that the two of us were lucky to be born with, it is not one that we like to abuse. Or use at all for that matter, but it still sometimes becomes necessary to do so, even for us. That is what separates us from other nobles. They tend to abuse this privilege as if it were some simple right that they have. We don't." Daedalus then paused for a moment to look back over to Raz. "At least that is what we like to believe."

Seth wasn't entirely sure what was going on or exactly what sort of privilege they were talking about, but he could tell that Tara was once again at a loss for words. Something that seemed to be happening more and more often since they all had come to this city. He would have dedicated more time to thinking that through, but before he could his eyes caught the sight of the man at the desk, whom the others had identified for him as the maître d', returning from somewhere towards the back of the restaurant. Trailing behind him was the very familiar, and still very imposing figure of Isaac De La Rosa.

Before Tara, Daedalus, or Raz could say any more the sight of the maître d' returning with Isaac caught their attention as well. While no change was visible in either Raz or Daedalus, the sight of Isaac instantly made Tara stand up straighter as he approached. Before long he was in front of them looking them all over with his cold, piercing gaze. He stopped for slightly longer on Seth than he did any of the others, though this didn't bother Seth at all.

"These are the gentlemen to whom I was referring, my lord," the maître d' said to Isaac with a kind of wicked smile on his face that was not there when he had left. "If you wish I can have them removed from-"

"There is no need," Isaac spoke before the maître d' could finish speaking. "I recognize all four of them. They are who they say they are. And they are expected." That reaction surprised both the maître d' and Tara, though their reactions were very different as Tara's eyes simply went wider than they had been before while the maître d' looked over towards Isaac and seemingly struggled to find the right words to respond to what he had just said.

"My... My lord," the maître d' eventually said to Isaac once he remembered how to speak. "Are you absolutely sure that-"

"Are you questioning the word of the advisor to Queen Faust?" Isaac then said as he blinked, and suddenly instead of a cold, piercing gaze his eyes beheld a death fueled glare that was aimed directly at the maître d'. It took several long seconds before the maître d' was able to find his voice again.

"What… No, no, my Lord. I was-"

"Are you implying that I may be going senile in my old age?" Isaac interrupted again, his death fueled glare seemingly intensifying as he did so.

"What! No, no, of course not my lord!" the maître d' exclaimed to Isaac as he tried to back away, but found his legs unable to move. "It is just that-"

"It is just what?" Isaac interrupted again. This time the maître d' opened his mouth to speak, but no words came out as he found himself unable to respond. Seth even saw him begin to shake where he stood, and with much more intensity than Tara had earlier. "That is what I thought. Now if I am not mistaken, these people are customers in this establishment. So, what is someone in your position supposed to do with customers?" The maître d' remained silent for several seconds longer under Isaac's gaze before he eventually took in a deep breath and steadied himself.

He then pulled out four sheets of paper from what Seth could only assume was a small cabinet behind the desk before looking up at Raz with what was definitely a hate filled glare.

"Right this way please, sirs and madam," he said to all of them as he stepped away from the tiny desk and began to lead them into the restaurant proper. Isaac fell in step behind him as soon as he did, as did Raz and Daedalus. Unsure of what else he was supposed to be doing in this situation, Seth followed behind them all.

"Seth!" Tara let out as she held out a hand to grasp his jacket sleeve, but fell short as he stepped beyond her reach. Seth, however, still felt her touch and turned around to face her.

"Yes, Tara?" Seth said to her, now somewhat worried for her given the way she had been acting. Rather than answer him with words, however, the only sounds that escaped Tara's mouth were incomprehensible, throaty sounds and heavy breathing. This only lasted for a few seconds, however, before she took in a deep breath and looked directly into his eyes. When she did, Seth at first thought that she appeared more relaxed and more in control of herself. Her eyes, however, told a completely different story.

"Nevermind, let's go," she then said before she suddenly walked right past him and caught up with Raz and Daedalus. Momentarily confused, Seth watched her go for a moment before following in step behind her. Her use of a contraction when she spoke did not escape his attention.

Now out of the foyer and in the restaurant proper, the first thing that Seth noticed about this place was that every single person in it was dressed much nicer than he and the rest of his company were. He, Tara, Raz and even Daedalus were all wearing more or less the same type of clothing that they wore most days. By contrast, every single person that Seth could see, men and women, were all wearing something that reminded him of the clothing in the windows of Tabitha's boutique, right down to the minute, extraneous details that he felt only he would notice. So great was this contrast in fact, that they all drew stares from several tables as the patron's eyes followed them to their unknown destination. A few of them even loudly, and rudely, began to ask questions about who all of them were, why they were allowed in, and what they were doing with the personal advisor to Queen Faust of all people. The only one among them, however, that seemed bothered by any of this was Tara, as she appeared to be making every effort to make herself look as small and unnoticeable as possible.

"Thanks for the save, Isaac," Raz said rather loudly, seemingly oblivious to all of the stares that they were getting. "Honestly wasn't sure if you would come through or not."

"Do not thank me yet," Isaac responded without looking at him. "I merely got you in the door. Everything that happens from here on is on you, and I will not be the one to pull you out of whatever fire you set."

"Good to know," Raz responded without a care. "Thanks for the encouraging words." Isaac didn't respond to that as instead his eyes glanced past him and directly at Daedalus.

"Daedalus," Isaac said with a nod. "It is good to see you."

"Likewise, Lord De La Rosa," Daedalus replied with a nod of his own. Both of them fell silent after that as the maître d' led them through a door and to Seth's surprise, into the restaurant's kitchen, where he saw all manner of men and women in identical looking white uniforms preparing all sorts of deliciously smelling dishes. Like in the restaurant proper, the assembled group garnered many stares from the restaurant's staff, though no one in here dared say anything, most likely due to their new company in Isaac De La Rosa. As quickly as they had entered, however, the maître d' led them all through the kitchen towards a door that, to Seth at least, appeared to be little more than a broom closet.

The maître d' then produced a key from somewhere on his person and unlocked the door for them. Once it was open, on the other side Seth saw not a broom closet, but instead an immaculate wooden spiral staircase that led upwards toward a second level. The maître d' then stepped to the side and politely held the door open for them as one by one, starting with Isaac, they all entered the room and began to ascend the spiral staircase. Seth entered the room last, behind Tara, which allowed him to see the maître d' enter after him, upon which he then proceeded to lock the door behind him. The idea of being stuck somewhere behind a locked door didn't exactly sit well with Seth, as it reminded him too much of when the four of them all met with Vito Smeraldo so long ago. Alas, everyone else didn't appear to be bothered by it, so he kept those thoughts to himself.

With Isaac leading the way now, the assembled group ascended the staircase single file, whereupon they reached a set of equally immaculate looking wooden double doors. Without hesitating Isaac pushed the doors open for them and stepped inside.

"My lady," Isaac began as he entered. "Our other guests have arrived."

"Isaac, we didn't invite any other-" the voice of Nicole spoke up, but then immediately ceased once she saw who had stepped into the room behind Isaac, upon which her eyes instantly narrowed on Raz. As Seth was the last person in the room, he did not get to see it immediately, but when he did he needed to blink a few times to make sure that what he was seeing was actually real.

The room he found himself in was just under half the size of the restaurant proper on the floor below and was covered in a fine maroon carpet. Unlike downstairs, where there were many tables, here there was instead a single, very long table that looked as if it could seat twenty people, perhaps more if said people were willing to sit closer together, and was made out of a very fine dark wood. What was odd to Seth about it though, was that the table itself was very, very shiny, and he did not know wood to be shiny. Directly across from where he stood, the wall opposite him was made up of a long, single window that led out to a small balcony and offered a lovely view of the surrounding Suntop district. Seated at this long table, Seth was not surprised to see Nicole and Filia, though the man he had seen before in the regional governor's office where he had met them was also there, along with a dark haired woman he did not recognize.

"You..." Nicole didn't quite speak, as the word seemed to ooze out of her mouth like venom as her eyes focused directly on Raz.

"Yes, me," Raz responded with his usual, overconfident smirk adorning his face as he performed a sort of two fingered salute in Nicole's direction. "It's good to see you too, auntie."

"Raz!" Filia shouted as she suddenly leapt from her chair and ran all the way around the table directly towards him. Like before she ran directly into Raz's arms, upon which he scooped her up into a great big hug, lifted her off of her feet, and spun her around once before setting her back down. "I knew you'd make it."

"Did you ever have any doubt?" Raz responded to her with his smirk still adorning his face.

"What in the name of Solaris do you think you're doing here?" Nicole then asked from her chair, her eyes still deadly focused on Raz.

"We were invited," Raz responded without looking at her. Before Nicole could respond to that comment, however, Raz beat her to the punch again. "That is to say, because I know you are going to ask, Daedalus and I were invited. They are our plus ones. There isn't any problem with that, is there?"

"I'm sorry to interrupt but," the man that Seth recognized as the man from the regional governor's office interjected. "Who exactly are you?"

"Oh, I'm sorry," Raz answered as he took a few steps away from Filia. "We met briefly yesterday, but you were busy so we didn't get the chance for introductions." Raz then paused for a brief moment and performed the same bowing gesture that Seth had seen him do yesterday. "Prince Michael Frederick Dagon of Sol, son of Mara of the house of the Solaran royal family and dear cousin to princesses Filia and Nicole Solara, at your service." Raz then paused for another brief moment to stand back up straight. "My friend here is Daedalus Olympus the thirteenth, son of Lord Daedalus Olympus the twelfth, court architect to the Solaran crown and also of Sol. And these two are Seth and Tara. They are not of noble birth, but they are good friends and they are also our plus ones. I hope that is acceptable." Nicole attempted to open her mouth to speak again, but once again Raz cut her off. "And if there is any doubt at all in your mind as to the validity of any of our identities, I am sure that our good friend Lord De La Rosa here will be able to rid you of them. He is, after all, the advisor to Queen Faust herself and as such speaks with her authority. So if you cannot trust him on such matters then who can you trust?"

The instant that last word had left Raz's lips, the sound of hands violently hitting a wooden surface took everyone's attention away from him as everyone turned to see princess Nicole, now standing and with both of her hands on the long wooden table. Silence reigned over the room for several long moments as she glared very intently at Raz. However, once those few moments had passed and Nicole realized that all eyes were on her, as quickly as she had stood up she recomposed herself, lifted her hands from the table, and took in a very deep breath.

"Governor Monet," Nicole began with a very calm, controlled voice. "It was to my understanding that this was to be a private brunch. If you were to let in anyone who claimed to be invited regardless of who they were, well… That would certainly put the reputation of this establishment at risk, but yours may fall along with it. After all, it was you who recommended this place to us. Specifically for its discretion, if I recall. Many things are said about our family, but one thing that I can assure you is true, we never forget." Silence took the room again as a sinister looking, toothy smile crossed Nicole's face. Both Seth and Raz could see Filia glaring back at her mother with as much intensity as Nicole herself had to Raz earlier, and for a moment it seemed as if Nicole really would get her way.

"Oh, what's the harm?" the woman who sat next to the regional governor suddenly spoke up. "They were let up here, by Lord De La Rosa no less, and your daughter clearly knows them so there must be at least some validity to their claims. Not only that, but I know that at least one of them is who they say they are." As she spoke that last part she turned her head to look directly at Daedalus, which caused him to raise an eyebrow.

"Apologies, ma'am, but you appear to have me at a disadvantage," Daedalus said to her as politely as he could. "Have we met before?"

"No, we haven't," the woman was quick to respond. "But I have met your father. Years ago, when we visited the capital. I must say, you are the spitting image of him."

"That is very kind of you to say," Daedalus responded politely and with a slight bow of his head. "Thank you." After that little exchange all attention shifted back to Nicole as she, despite how calm everyone knew she was trying to be, had resumed her glaring, only now it was directed at Daedalus.

"Well, if there is no harm in it," the regional governor then spoke up with a smile as he stood up from his chair. "It isn't as if we are holding a secret political meeting here. Just a small gathering of friendly faces, and more friendly faces are always welcome. Especially if they are family." As he spoke he walked around the table towards Raz and held out his hand. "Please forgive the delayed introduction. Hubert Monet, regional governor of Dis and the surrounding frontier cities, and it is a pleasure to make your acquaintance."

"Likewise," Raz responded as he shook the man's hand. "As hellish as it can be out here it's good to know that someone like you is watching out for all of us." After shaking his hand the regional governor then moved over to Daedalus, who only silently nodded as he shook his hand as well. Once that exchange had ended the regional governor looked past Raz to see Seth and Tara. While Seth was the same as ever, Tara still seemed to be making every attempt to make herself appear as small and unnoticeable as possible.

"Oh come now, there's no reason to be shy," the regional governor then said as he stepped around Raz towards the two of them. "Just because you weren't born as fortunate as some of us doesn't mean that you're not welcome. Please, treat yourselves as my guests, and besides, I would not be where I am today if I did not take delight in meeting those whom I am sworn to serve." Unsure of what specifically he was supposed to say to this man, Seth defaulted to what Tara had taught him to do for anyone.

"It's nice to meet you too," Seth said to the regional governor as politely as he could before holding out his hand. "My name is Seth."

"Seth…" the regional governor responded as he looked him over and raised an eyebrow. "That is certainly an interesting name."

"I know," Seth responded. "I've been told that before."

Chapter 18

It didn't take long after all of the introductions had been made for all of them to find places at the long table. Filia had taken a seat next to Raz, as Seth had expected her too. Much to his surprise, however, she had invited him to sit on the opposite side of her. Tara had then taken a place next to him, and Daedalus was seated next to her. Nicole, however, had opted to move from the place where she had previously sat and instead took a chair on the opposite side of the table from them, directly across from Seth in fact. Isaac sat to her right, with the regional governor and his wife seated to her left. Why Nicole had sat in front of him Seth could not even begin to guess, especially since she appeared to be making every effort not to look at him.

Almost as soon as they had taken their seats some rather young looking waitresses entered the room and placed a few small plates of freshly sliced bread in front of them. Another followed up with small sticks of butter for each of them as well as a few incredibly small bowls of what, to Seth, looked to be an incredibly weird, multi-colored substance that didn't look quite solid, but clearly wasn't liquid either.

In an attempt to distract himself from the multi-colored things in front of him, Seth instead looked at the short menu that had been placed at all of their seats by the maître d' before he had left. He tried to at least, but once again hit a mental wall as while it was written in a language he could both understand and read, he couldn't actually tell what any of the food items on it were. Even skimming the brief descriptions of what was in each of them gave him little idea of what they actually were and what they would look like once put in front of him.

"Anything catching your eye, Seth?" Filia suddenly asked from right next to him. Hearing her voice again so suddenly while he was trying to figure something out nearly caused him to jump out of his seat in fright. Thankfully, however, his self control kept that instinct in check.

"I don't even know what any of this stuff is," Seth answered calmly once he had gotten over the initial shock. "So no, not really."

"Of course you wouldn't know," Nicole spoke up in what she probably thought was a whisper, but because she sat directly across from him Seth was able to hear her clearly.

"I know that I don't know," Seth said to her. "I've never been here before, so how could I possibly know what kind of foods they serve here?" For reasons unknown to him, that response caused Nicole to instantly glare at him.

"I could recommend something if you're having trouble," Filia spoke up again, effectively breaking the tension.

"Please do," Seth quickly answered as he handed his menu over to her. "I don't see how I could pick something myself if I don't even know what it is. I've never even heard of some of these foods before. I mean, what is a creepy?"

Filia was confused at first at what he was talking about, but once she saw exactly where Seth was pointing to on his menu she couldn't help but let out a giggle. Much to the apparent ire of her mother. The younger princess, however, couldn't help it as she now found his question and pronunciation of the word to be oddly adorable.

"I think you mean 'crêpe'?" Filia then said once she had settled down.

"If that's what it's called then... I guess. I still can't find where exactly it tells me what a crêpe is," Seth answered her, which only caused Filia to let out another, louder giggle followed by a soft smile towards Seth.

"So," the regional governor then spoke up, his eyes on Raz. "I must say the two of you seem awfully close." As he spoke he pointed back and forth between Raz and Filia. "You said that your name was Michael Frederick Dagon, did you not? I'm sorry but your name is not one that I know so-"

"It's alright," Raz interrupted the regional governor as he leaned back in his chair. "And I'm not at all surprised that you haven't heard of me. My family doesn't like to talk about me much since-"

"You should visit us in Sol sometime," Nicole interrupted Raz as she captured the attention of both the regional governor and his wife. "Our family gatherings are abundant with stories of Prince Michael and his rise to fame and glory." She then paused for a moment as she took a sip from her water. When she finished, however, she wore a devious look in her eyes as her lips slowly curled into a smirk reminiscent of the one Raz often wore. "As well as his subsequent and sudden fall from our good graces thereafter." The room then instantly fell silent as all eyes fell on Raz. To Seth's surprise, however, Filia's eyes went not to Raz, but to her mother as she shot her a death fueled glare that Nicole either didn't notice or didn't care about. Eventually a sound did break the silence, but it didn't come from Raz as everyone's eyes slowly shifted over towards Daedalus, who had begun to laugh to himself.

"It's funny how you choose to speak in such ways to the man who is the only reason that you, your mother, and your daughter are all still alive today," Daedalus said once he knew he had everyone's attention before taking a sip of his own water. To the surprise of no one the look on Nicole's face quickly shifted from that of an overconfident smirk to her own death fueled glare.

"And who are you to-"

"Who am I to what?" Daedalus interrupted Nicole before she could get any more words out. "It's true that I wasn't there, but you were. You witnessed the entire spectacle firsthand." Daedalus then paused for another moment as his lips slowly formed into his own smirk. "Perhaps you would like to regale that glorious tale to governor Monet and his lovely wife. I'm sure they would love to hear every detail of it."

"I'm sorry, but…" the governor's wife then spoke up. "I must admit that my curiosity is getting the better of me. What tale do you speak of? What exactly happened?"

"Oh, it is a grand and glorious tale full of all the things you would expect from the capital. Valor, compassion, friendship, betrayal, and one lone Solaran knight's drive to put everything on the line, including his own life, for the sake of his family and country," Daedalus answered before taking another sip from his water. "As much as I would love to regale you with said tale, however, my lady, I only know as much as the other Solaran knights tell. If you truly wish to hear it it would behoove you to ask Lady Nicole, or preferably, Lord De La Rosa. I'm certain that as the personal advisor to Queen Faust, he not only knows every minute detail, but has committed all of them to memory if only to be better prepared in the event that something like it were to ever happen again."

At that moment all conversation stopped as all eyes fell on Isaac, including Tara's, who previously had not appeared to have been paying much attention to anything. Unlike everyone else in the room, however, Isaac did not seem fazed at all by all of the attention he was getting as he sat quietly in his chair not looking back at anyone. As the silence continued, however, and it became clear that everyone really was waiting for him to speak up, Isaac let out a soft sigh. As intimidating as he was, Seth did have to admit that he was impressed by his apparent ability to somehow know who was staring at him and what they were thinking without even looking.

"As entertaining as such a tale would be," Isaac began. "It is, unfortunately, not a pleasant table conversation. Not in the slightest. To answer the question that I am sure was on your mind, however. The answer is yes. Prince Michael really is of royal blood. He is Princess Nicole and Filia's first cousin by way of his mother."

"Interesting..." the regional governor spoke up again as he returned his attention back to Raz. "Out of curiosity then, who exactly is your mother? I know you mentioned her by name in your introduction, but I'll admit to not necessarily listening as your claim seemed unbelievable. So, I must apologize if it seems as if I am being rude, it is only because you do have me at something of a disadvantage since-"

"Oh no offense taken. Not at all," Raz responded with a pleasant looking smile as he leaned back in his chair again. "And don't worry about offending me. I can handle more than a few harsh words, and to answer your question my mother is Princess Mara Solara."

"Ah yes, Princess Mara," the regional governor then said, seeming intrigued. "I must admit I've never met her personally, but I have heard... many positive things about her from my brother-in-law."

"Oh, who's your brother-in-law then?" Raz then asked without thinking. "We might know him." Before the regional governor could answer, his wife spoke up for him.

"Quinn Nebe," she answered with obvious pride in her voice. "The current headmaster of the Solarian University of Magic in Sol, as well as a member of the Queen's royal court, much like Lord De La Rosa here."

"Wait, Professor Nebe is now the headmaster?" Tara suddenly spoke up, seeming more than a little surprised and taken aback by this new information.

"Yes, he was promoted about a year and a half ago when the previous headmaster finally retired," the regional governor's wife answered. "Though from the way you speak it sounds as if you know my brother, Miss Tara."

"He was one of my professors when I attended," Tara sheepishly admitted.

"Oh? So you're also an alumni of the university?" The governor's wife then immediately asked, the shock in her voice obvious to all of them. Before Tara had another chance to speak, however, the governor's wife turned her attention back to Raz. "And I thought you said that she was a commoner."

"Katie," Governor Monat said to his wife in a hushed tone.

"What?" Raz responded. "You saying that commoners can't attend the university of magic?"

"It is okay, Raz," Tara spoke up as she looked directly at him before returning her attention back to the governor's wife. "And he spoke true. I am not a noblewoman. My brother and I were given scholarships because of our latent talent for the art of magic. He is actually a teaching assistant there now."

"Oh? Well I suppose that is impressive in its own right," Katie responded as all of the excitement that was previously in her voice evaporated before she took a sip of her own water. Tara, who obviously noticed this, tried her best to not look insulted, which only resulted in raised eyebrows and a very fake looking smile from her. Daedalus, being the first to notice this, shot a quick glare to the governor's wife.

"I think it best that we decide what we would like to order," he spoke up. "We've kept the staff waiting long enough."

"Well that depends," Nicole then spoke up as her knife-like glare shot itself back in Seth's direction. "Is he done being taught what basic breakfasts are by my daughter?" As she spoke she pointed to Seth, who now had Filia looking over his shoulder telling him what each menu item he didn't know was. "Hey!" Nicole then shouted as she began snapping her fingers repeatedly to grab the attention of both Seth and Filia.

Not as instantaneously as Nicole would have preferred, the two of them looked up from the menu at the snapping princess. As they were no longer focused on what they were talking about, they only just now realized that they had not heard a single word that anyone else had said in the past few minutes.

"Yes?" Seth responded calmly.

"Have you decided on anything or are we going to keep waiting on the glacial pace of your decision making skills?" Nicole didn't so much ask as she did spit out, as if the mere act of talking to Seth was grating to her. Seth, however, not understanding what the word 'glacial' meant, looked back to the menu.

"I guess I'll take an omelette," Seth answered. "Since I at least recognize what that is." Nicole appeared slightly annoyed at that response, but held her tongue. Following Seth, each person at the table then told the waitresses that had been summoned by Governor Monet what they wanted. Following that their menus were collected, and as they were Governor Monet looked over towards Seth.

"Since it seems to be the running theme right now, what about you?" The governor then said to Seth.

"What about me?" Seth responded.

"I'm simply curious," Governor Monet answered. "You seem to be good acquaintances with at least two members of the royal family. Prince Michael said that you were not of noble birth, but that does not necessarily mean that you aren't noteworthy. I suppose what I am really asking is, do you have any family that any of us might recognize? Whether they be from Sol or the frontier, it doesn't matter. Though if they are from the frontier then I might be interested in meeting them." As innocent as that question was, and Seth knew perfectly well that it was an innocent question, the mere thought of an answer sprung to mind images of every monster he had ever seen. One after the other, every single monster he had ever fought or encountered, including Cain, flashed through his mind before ending on the smiling face of Lilim.

"No," Seth responded as calmly as he could. "Well... not that I know of at least."

"Not that you know of?" Katie piped in, seeming curious, or at least pretending to be.

"He has amnesia," Filia answered for him before Seth could answer himself.

"Really?" Katie piped up, now seeming as if she were genuinely interested.

"Yes, poor guy," Filia continued. "I can't possibly imagine what it's like to be wiped of everything, even my own family. He must be so lonely and they must be missing him and-"

"Not really." Seth interrupted, which caused Filia to instantly stop.

"Not really? Why's that?" Filia then quickly asked before anyone else could say anything. The look on her face was a strange mixture of confusion and concern. As much as he wanted to, however, Seth could not answer that question immediately. He tried to think of something, anything that would go along with the amnesia cover story, but wouldn't be a flat out lie that he would have to remember later. Thankfully after a few quick moments of thinking this through, an answer came to him. He wasn't sure at all how good of an answer it would be, but he couldn't come up with anything else and he could see that everyone's eyes were on him.

"Because..." Seth eventually began with a sigh. "Because I've been like this for more than a few months now and... I've accepted it. I don't really care about wha... who I was. Because this is my life now, and if I'm no longer who I'm supposed to be then well... I think I'm okay with that." Before he had even finished speaking Seth saw Nicole roll her eyes in front of him.

     'Great,' the older princess thought to herself. *'Pretentious bullshit that any noble who thinks they're a philosopher could have come up with in their sleep.'* The younger princess on the other hand, had a much different reaction as her eyes instantly grew wide, as if she were only just now seeing Seth as a little bit more than the confused amnesiac that she thought he had been when they met yesterday. Now that she could see that there was more going on with him than what was apparent on the surface level she couldn't help herself as her face began to turn slightly pink. Despite her reaction, however, part of her grew even more curious, as she couldn't help but want to see how much more there was to unwrap with this enigma of a man currently sitting beside her.

     After their meals had been brought to them and they had started eating nothing that interesting happened, at least nothing that interesting to Seth. After the last conversation they had had with him had finished, Princess Nicole and Governor Monet moved on to more mundane topics like politics and the current going ons of this region that had been routinely referred to as "the frontier". Seth remained quiet for all of those discussions not because he didn't have anything to say, but because he couldn't actually follow what they were talking about. Even with the newfound knowledge he had gained in the past seven months of new words, idioms, and how some words could have multiple meanings, he still couldn't follow any conversation they had regarding certain topics and frequently found himself getting lost as they introduced even more new words to his vocabulary such as "decree", "authorization", and "execution". This was in addition to the fact that much of this conversation was based on knowledge of rules and laws from a far away city that Seth did not know anything about or have any frame of reference for.

     At least next to him Filia was still making an effort to see that he wasn't entirely left out. Rather than help him understand what the others were talking about, however, she instead kept finding ways to distract them both from those conversations so that they wouldn't have to hear them. This annoyed Seth a little bit since while he knew that he couldn't understand much of what they were saying right now, he was committing the words and phrases they had used to memory so that he could ask Tara about them later. Despite that though, he still went along with all of her distractions when it became more obvious to him that the distractions were more for herself than they were for him. That, and of course he did not want to be rude to her.

"So, Seth," Filia began as she was finishing the last of what was on her plate. "Just curious. What's your favorite color?" To Seth that seemed like a completely random and bizarre question to ask, as he couldn't think of any situation where such a thing would actually matter. Not only that, but because he had never thought of it until now he didn't really have an answer for her. At least he didn't until he glanced down at the shirt he was wearing, which he only just now noticed was one of those shirts that Tabitha had given him that was meant to be "nicer" than the shirts he usually wore. Given his present company he was glad he had decided to bring it to Dis with him.

"This color," he responded as he held up a bit of his shirt for Filia. She only looked at it for a single second, however, before nodding.

"Purple, nice," she then said to him. "How very patriotic of you."

"I don't know what that word means," Seth immediately responded, which caused Filia to let out another giggle.

"Don't worry, it's a compliment," she explained as she set her fork down. Before Seth could ask exactly what "patriotic" meant and how it could be a compliment, however, Filia continued to speak. "Purple's nice, but I'm more partial to orange myself." As she spoke she showed off a bit of her dress to him, which he had seen before since it was the same one, or at least very, very similar, to the one she had worn yesterday. Given who she was, however, it would not have surprised him if it turned out that she owned multiple variations of the same dress in the same way he owned multiple purple shirts. "I think it goes really well with my hair and compliments my figure perfectly." Before Seth could even think of a response she suddenly leaned in closer towards him so that her face was very, very close to his. "Don't you agree?" Without any real way to answer that question, as he had no idea at all what the correct thing to say was, all Seth could do was stare blankly back at her and maintain eye contact. For what seemed like a long time all he was able to do was stare into Filia's bright, blue eyes as she stared back into his.

During that entire exchange, and indeed most of brunch, Lord Isaac De La Rosa had remained eerily silent. Occasionally he would glance, or more often than not glare, in Nicole's direction whenever she made a rude comment, but he never spoke up. Instead his focus appeared to be almost entirely on Seth, but more specifically on Filia's reactions to him and how close she kept getting whenever she wanted to speak to him. He could see the look on her face perfectly well. The guise of genuine intrigue that was betrayed by flushed cheeks that signaled the beginnings of desire. While it may have been a seemingly innocent desire for knowledge about the man currently sitting next to her as opposed to anything more base, Isaac knew all too well how one desire was able to pave the way for others.

What kept him from speaking up, however, were Seth's responses to Filia whenever she spoke to him. While he was polite, that much could be said for certain, he wasn't actively reciprocating any of her advances or even acknowledging them. While Isaac couldn't be certain whether this was because of Seth's aforementioned amnesia, the fact that he very well could be that dense, or that he was genuinely uninterested, Isaac knew enough about people to recognize basic flirting when he saw it, and Seth was not doing that. Basic flirting would honestly have been preferable to Isaac because at least that he could read, but there wasn't any of that going on in Seth's actions or responses. Isaac even considered the possibility that Seth had a preference for men rather than women, but that idea was shot down quickly when he saw that Seth's demeanor wasn't that much different when he spoke to Raz or Daedalus. Even excusing the fact that he likely was behaving differently because he was in a room full of nobles didn't help Isaac's interpretation, as Seth simply treated everyone who spoke to him in the same manner, as if status did not matter to him. Or more likely he still did not entirely understand the concept. Not that it mattered, with all that Isaac had seen he was able to make his analysis and come to a sound conclusion.

"I must say, this was quite wonderful," Katie said to no one in particular as she, her husband, and Nicole all stood up from their chairs.

"I… actually must admit," Tara then spoke up as well. "Everything here is absolutely delicious. Whomever the chefs are, they must have really outdone themselves."

"Meh," Raz responded as he leaned back in his chair and put his hands behind his head. "I've had better." The instant he had finished speaking, however, as quick as lighting Daedalus smacked him in the nose with the back of his fist.

"Ow…" Raz let out as he touched his nose to see if it was bleeding. Thankfully Daedalus didn't hit him that hard. "What the… hell man. What was that for?"

"Don't insult a restaurant while you're still in it, you moron," Daedalus answered without even looking at him. "Not only is it uncouth, but if any of the staff hears you, and then subsequently recognizes you in the future then they'll know that they have the go ahead to stick their dick in your food."

"Humph, it's nice to see that at least one of you has some idea of what manners are," Nicole butted into their conversation with a smirk on her face that looked strikingly similar to the one Raz often made.

"See…" Daedalus was quick to respond as he gestured towards Nicole. "Even she, of all people, understands what I'm talking about."

"Whatever you say, man," Raz then said after he finished rubbing his nose before standing up from his own chair.

Seeing the direction that everyone else seemed to be going in, Seth stood up from his chair as well. As if the two of them had been waiting for him to do so, on both sides of him both Tara and Filia stood up from their chairs at the same time he had.

"I'm glad you were all able to come," Filia said to him rather than Raz once they were on their feet. "I was really getting worried that I was going to have to suffer through another boring new year while everyone else got to have fun, but now I don't have to."

"Seth, if I may please, a word," another voice suddenly interjected before Seth even had the chance to think of an appropriate response for Filia. It didn't take him long at all to find the source of it, as only one person he knew of spoke with that type of accent. Looking past Filia, Seth was able to see none other than Isaac De La Rosa standing over in the corner of the room, away from everyone else. His cold, unblinking gaze focused directly on him, as if his words were not so much a request, but an order. Unsure of what the correct thing to do was, Seth looked back to Filia, only to see her roll her eyes and let out an obnoxiously loud groan.

"You should just do what he says," Filia said to him with an obvious amount of annoyance in her voice. "He's much, much more likely to leave you alone later if you do." The way in which she phrased that drew a little concern from Seth, but as if she could see it, Filia let out another chuckle and slapped him on the arm. "Oh don't worry about him. I know he looks scary but he's harmless. Really." Despite her assurance, Seth did not feel entirely convinced as he glanced back towards Isaac's unchanging face.

"Okay then…" Seth apprehensively replied to Filia as he stepped around her towards Isaac. "I'll be right back." Behind him, as he walked away from her he could see Filia striking up a conversation with Tara. He didn't get much of a chance to hear what they were saying though, as within a few quick steps he stood in the corner of the room with Isaac. Even standing directly in front of him, Isaac's face did not change as he kept up his cold, unfeeling gaze on Seth and never broke eye contact with him. For a while Isaac simply stayed silent and stared at Seth, and as a result Seth began to wonder if his face was just frozen the way it was. After a few more silent moments, however, it soon became obvious that Isaac wasn't going to start the conversation, so Seth knew that he needed to take the initiative.

"You wanted to have a word with me," Seth began, unsure of what else to say.

"I did," Isaac then finally spoke as he relaxed his gaze somewhat and let his arms fall to his sides. "I wish to apologize." In an instant Seth went from being apprehensive to confused as he couldn't help but raise an eyebrow.

"What for?" he couldn't help but ask. "I don't remember you doing anything to me." To Seth's further confusion, Isaac's initial response was to let out a chuckle himself before his lips curled into a rather sinister looking smile of his own. The sound of his laugh did not sound like anything Seth had ever heard before, as it didn't sound kind or pleasant even in the slightest degree. If there was a way to laugh without being happy, then Seth had to imagine that this was what it would sound like.

"You are correct, I did not," Isaac eventually said once his laughter had died down. "Regardless, I still wish to apologize to you. When we first met I was a little more than… let us just say apprehensive, towards you. Do not take it personally, for you did not do anything wrong. For many years, long before I held the position of advisor to Queen Faust, I was the royal spymaster." While Seth was sure that must have been an important position, he had absolutely no idea what a "spy" was, let alone how one could be a master of it. As such he committed the term to memory so that he could hopefully ask about it later. "After years of grueling work in that position, I will admit that I tend to get more than a little paranoid when meeting new faces. As such, I could not help but feel suspicious of you and your motives simply because I did not know you. However, after getting to know you... I can safely say that you are not one for me to be concerned about. Again, do not take it personally, the fault was entirely my own and stemmed from years of experience telling me to be wary of absolutely everyone that I meet. So with that said, I ask for your forgiveness." As he finished speaking Isaac held out his hand to Seth.

"Th... That's okay. I forgive you." Seth hesitantly responded as he took Isaac's hand, not out of nervousness or apprehension, but because he was genuinely surprised that this conversation took the direction it had and he needed a moment to fully wrap his brain around it. As confused as Seth may have been before, however, his confusion increased immensely when he watched Isaac's eyes suddenly widen to the limits that his eyes would allow, as if he had just seen something that shook him to his core. "What's wrong?" Seth then asked, worried that he may have messed something up with this man.

"Oh, um..." Isaac briefly stammered as his face instantly returned to how it was before, as if that moment of shock had never happened. "Nothing. Nothing is wrong." As Isaac spoke he let go of Seth's hand, but then as he did he brought up his opposite hand and waved it in front of Seth's face before placing it on his shoulder. "You enjoy the rest of your day now."

"Isaac, are you coming!" the voice of Nicole suddenly called out from the doorway, and at the sound of it both Seth and Isaac turned to see her pouting face.

"I am sorry to say, my lady, but I am afraid I will not be joining you at the theater," Isaac responded politely to her. "There are some urgent matters I must attend to before I do. So I will be joining you later." Nicole's initial response to that was to raise an eyebrow, as if that was not the answer she had expected him to give and that fact alone irritated her.

"Urgent matters?" she then said. "What sort of urgent matters?"

"Oh, trifling things," Isaac responded in his usual calm, yet polite tone. "Nothing that the princesses need be concerned with. You go on ahead and enjoy the theater. I shall reconvene with you later. You will not even realize that I am gone." Then, before Nicole, Seth, or anyone else had the chance to say anything to him, with a snap of his fingers and a flash of orange light, Isaac was gone.

"Where did he go?" Seth immediately asked, having not expected him to do that at all.

"Ah, he just teleported," Filia answered as she walked up next to him. "He does that sometimes. Best not to worry about it."

"I know what teleporting is, I've seen people do it. I was just asking where he went," Seth clarified as he quickly turned his head and made eye contact with Filia, who for some reason appeared to find his reaction amusing as she let out a giggle before shrugging her shoulders.

"Don't know," she responded. "That's the thing about teleporting. It lets you go wherever you want to in the blink of an eye. Literally anywhere. One second you're standing here and then the next, you're somewhere else." Then as she finished speaking Filia snapped her fingers in front of his face. "Literally like that." Seth did not respond to her immediately as he held eye contact with her, which she seemed more than happy to keep with him as well. After a few short seconds of this, however, his eyes drifted back over to the spot where Isaac had previously stood.

"I wish I could do that," he said aloud to himself.

"Wait!" The voice of Raz suddenly and loudly exclaimed from the other side of the room immediately after Seth had finished speaking. "You don't know how to teleport?"

"No," Seth responded plainly. "No one ever taught me how."

Chapter 19

Seth would have been lying to everyone if he told them that he wasn't more than thrilled to leave that restaurant. It wasn't because the food they had served them was bad, far from it, he had been served one of the best omelettes he had ever tasted, but there was something about the restaurant itself that bothered him immensely. What made it worse was that he couldn't put his finger on exactly why that was. Perhaps it was because the majority of the serving staff made as little effort as possible to talk to him, instead preferring to speak to Nicole, Governor Monet, or Katie if anyone needed anything. At first Seth thought that was because they were all uninvited guests, which made sense to him, but then he saw them speaking to Daedalus without any issues, so he knew that it couldn't have been that. It could have been because of all the stares that he and his group had received from all the other restaurant patrons and serving staff when they had entered and left, as if they were less people and more things that they didn't get to see often enough. It could have been how outrageously expensive the food was, but as soon as Seth made a comment about that Filia told him not to worry about it and that the crown would be paying for everything. Whatever it was, it felt like a real breath of fresh air to him when he stepped back outside.

"So, Seth," Filia suddenly piped up while Seth was lost in his thoughts. "What did you think of the food?"

"It was… okay," Seth answered hesitantly, though the source of his hesitation was less about him being nervous, which he wasn't at all, and more about the fact that he himself did not know what to think of the restaurant for a number of reasons. So as far as he knew he couldn't really give an opinion of it. The fact that there were more royal guards in metal armor surrounding them all than there were yesterday didn't bother him in the least either. The only thing that bothered him about them was the fact that he did not actually see any of them until they had left the restaurant, so he couldn't help but wonder where they were while they were inside or where they had come from.

"I sense a 'but' coming," Filia responded to him with a strange looking smile on her face as she leaned in closer to him.

"A what?" Seth asked, genuinely confused, as the way in which she said those words made absolutely no sense to him.

"A but," Filia repeated. "You know. It was okay but…"

"But what?" Seth then asked without thinking.

"I don't know," Filia answered with a shrug. "That's for you to fill in."

"Fill in with what?" Seth asked without thinking again. Instead of giving him an answer, however, Filia just stared blankly back at him with her pleasant looking smile adorning her face for a few long seconds before she turned her attention over to Raz.

"Is he always like this?" she asked him.

"If I say yes," Raz began as he directed his full attention towards her with a smirk on his face. "Will that change your opinion of him?" Seth couldn't help but look between the two of them for an answer that he was sure was there. Why had Filia asked him that question? Where was this conversation going? What was all this talk of opinions? With no answers from either of them Seth instead looked to Tara. Tara, however, seemed even more lost in her own world than usual and as such was of no help to him at all.

"So…" Nicole then spoke up, effectively erasing whatever tension was in the air. "Is this the last we will see of your newfound friends today Filia, or must we endure their presence at the theater as well?"

"What's a theater?" Seth then immediately asked as soon as Nicole had finished speaking. The instant he had, however, as quick as one could blink, Nicole spun to look directly at him. The expression on her face was a strange mixture of the same death fueled glare she had been wearing for the majority of brunch and a look of complete and utter disbelief.

"You don't know what a theater is!" Filia then exclaimed rather loudly as her eyes went wide with disbelief as well.

"No," Seth answered. "This is the first time I've ever heard anybody use that word." After taking a few quick seconds to process that answer, Seth could only watch as Filia's lips twisted into a bright, toothy smile.

"And I thought today was going to be boring," she said as she suddenly grabbed Seth by the arm, which almost made Seth instinctively pull away, but he held himself back. "Now you have to come with us, Seth. Sure I could explain what a theater is, but I think it would be better if we showed you. No explanation I can give would do it justice. Trust me, you're in for a real treat."

"I am sorry, but…" Tara finally spoke up for the first time since leaving the restaurant. "What is this about a theater?"

"I would like to know this as well," Raz then added. "Care to explain yourself, Filly?" To even Seth's surprise, Filia initially answered that question by laughing. Unlike all of the other times she had laughed, however, Seth could tell that this time it was because she had very suddenly grown nervous.

"Well, umm... it's actually... um..." Filia stammered out as her laughter slowly came to a stop. Her bizarre behavior was enough to cause Raz to narrow his eyes at her.

"Filly, just spit it out," Raz said to her as they all stopped walking. "You know you can't lie to me. You're not that good, yet. So come on. Out with it." Ahead of them Seth noticed that Nicole, Governor Monet, and Katie had apparently not noticed that they had stopped and were continuing to walk on ahead of them. When Nicole eventually looked back and noticed how far they all were behind them, however, Seth saw her roll her eyes before turning to say something to Governor Monet and Katie, upon which they all stopped and turned their eyes towards them.

"I... I..." Filia began to answer, though it was clear that she was still struggling to get words out. After a few more seconds of this, however, Filia's eyes drifted towards the ground in front of her as she let go of Seth's arm and slumped her shoulders. "I was worried that if I told you what we were doing after brunch you wouldn't come."

"And why would you think that?" Raz then immediately asked.

"Because..." Filia hesitantly began again. "Because I know what you like and what you think is fun. So I know that you must think that going to the theater to see the same thing every year is as boring as I do. So I thought that... Maybe... Maybe if I just invited you to brunch then you would come and then once you were here I could... Maybe tell you about it afterwards... And since you were already here hanging out with me you wouldn't say no."

"And what would have stopped me from simply leaving before you even had the chance to tell me any of this?" Raz then asked as soon as Filia had finished speaking.

"I... I..." Filia stammered out as her words seemingly died in her throat. "Nothing probably."

"If the theater is boring then why do you want us to go to it with you?" Seth then piped back up without considering what he was asking, which caused all eyes to suddenly turn back to him. The expressions on Raz and Tara's faces appeared more or less unchanged, though Seth did notice that Filia seemed much, much more worried than she was before, as if she were desperately trying to keep herself from pleading.

"If I may," Daedalus suddenly interjected before anyone else had the chance to. "The issue here, Seth, is not that the theater is boring. It isn't. It is that Lady Filia believes it to be boring and as such, she assumed that we would all think that it is boring as well?"

"But why would we think that?" Seth then asked. "If I've never even heard of a theater before how could I think it's boring?"

"No doubt it's due to our association with her cousin," Daedalus answered.

"Not to worry though," Raz then spoke up, his demeanor instantly switching back to what it had been before. "There's an easy solution to this." After saying that Raz adopted a more relaxed posture and a much more pleasant looking smile as he looked down at Filia. "Ask me if I want to go?"

"What?" Filia exclaimed, now more confused than worried.

"You sent me a letter this morning asking me if I wanted to meet you for brunch," Raz began to clarify. "And I did. Now you want me to do something else with you. So, ask me to do it. Ask me if I want to go to the theater with you?" Despite how simple Raz's request seemed, Filia instantly became more noticeably nervous as she looked at Daedalus, who gave no reaction whatsoever to her, then to Tara, who just shrugged her shoulders. With nothing from either of them Filia then turned to Seth, who only stared back at her, unblinking, with his large, brown eyes because he didn't have an answer to give her either. After a few long moments of this, Filia took in a deep breath before returning her attention back to Raz.

"Raz," she began. "Can you... Can you and your friends please come to the theater with me? I know it won't be boring with all of you there." Before responding Raz chose to show some teeth with his smile.

"Do you even need to ask?" Raz answered her. The instant those words reached her ears Filia's expression perked up instantly as her eyes went wide and she opened her mouth in excitement. Before she could say anything, however, Raz's hand was already on her head and ruffling her very well groomed hair. "If it's you of course I'll go. To tell you the truth I don't even remember the last time I've been in a theater of any kind."

"Nor I," Daedalus interjected. "If anything this will be a nice change of pace." Hearing that, Filia began to laugh again as she pushed Raz's hand away from her.

"It literally hasn't changed at all since then I assure you," Filia said to Raz as she took a moment to fix her hair. Once she was done with that she quickly turned back around to face Seth again. "You'll come too, won't you Seth?" Before Seth could answer Filia suddenly reached out and grabbed both of his hands. "Please please please say that you will. You'll have fun. I know you will. And if you don't, then at least you can say that you had a new experience, right? Isn't that worth it?" Rather startled by Filia's insistence and the sudden physical contact, Seth looked past her to Raz and Daedalus. Daedalus, as was usual for him, gave no reaction while Raz only shrugged. As much as Seth wanted to look over to Tara as well, given how she had been acting for most of the day, something told him that he was going to get even less of an answer from her. So, with only that to go off of, Seth came up with an answer.

"Sure," Seth answered, upon which Filia's face instantly lit up again. "I'll go. I suppose I should see a theater for myself before I decide whether or not it's f-" Before he could say any more or do anything else Filia suddenly jumped up and threw her arms around his neck in a great big hug.

"Thank you thank you thank you so much Seth!" Filia exclaimed as loud as she could to him. "You have no idea how much of my day you've made! Really!" Still somewhat in shock by the fact that she had hugged him. All Seth could do was hug her back, as he knew that he wouldn't get any answers regarding what to do from anyone around him this time.

"Y... You're welcome," Seth hesitantly said in response. Almost as soon as those words left his mouth, Filia let him go.

"Alright, we should get going then," she then said to the assembled group. "The theater isn't going to wait for us and neither will my mother. In fact I'm surprised she's waited for us this long. So come on. Onwards!" Then, having said that, she grabbed Seth by the hand again and pulled him along with her as she raced back towards her mother.

"Alright then..." Seth said to no one in particular as he let himself be pulled along. Daedalus was quick to follow behind them, as was Tara. Before Tara could get very far, however, she suddenly felt a hand on her shoulder. The instant she felt it she quickly turned her head to see Raz, the kind smile and pleasant expression that had adorned his face before now gone.

"Before we catch up to them…" Raz began as he removed his hand from her shoulder. "Can… Can I ask you something?" From the look on his face, Tara began to worry that it might be something serious.

"Of course," she answered as she turned to face him properly. "What is wrong?"

"Oh, nothing's wrong," Raz answered as he broke eye contact with her. "It's just… There's something I've been meaning to ask you, but it just never seemed like a good time." Raz then paused for a short moment as he made eye contact with her again. "Last night… I know things got pretty crazy and we all had quite a few drinks but... Do you… remember anything… about last night? Y- You can be honest with me. I won't mind. Really. I'm just curious." That question hit Tara harder than she initially realized, as she momentarily found herself unable to breathe. Once that moment had passed, however, she frantically searched her thoughts for an answer. Not necessarily for a correct answer, but just an answer, as none were coming to her. After a few short seconds, however, one did.

"No," she answered him as a somber expression took her face as well. "I wish I could tell you something different, I really do, but the truth is that I do not remember anything." Despite her giving an answer to his question, silence lingered between the two of them as neither one of them dared speak. While it lasted for only a few seconds, for the two of them it felt much, much longer. Eventually it was broken, however, by Raz letting out a deep breath before his lips curled back into a pleasant looking smile once again.

"Alright," he said to her. "Thank you for being honest with me." Then, before Tara had a chance to say anything else to him, Raz turned and started to make his way back towards Filia and the rest of the assembled company. It took Tara a few long moments for her to comprehend exactly what had just happened before she could follow after them.

In the area surrounding the Suntop District of Dis, an area affectionately referred to as "the commons", nearly every city street was bustling with activity. All around residents of the city and tourists alike were enjoying the first official day of the new year, as well as the first official day of the new year's festival. Indeed, so much was happening everywhere that most did not even notice when a well dressed and well put together older gentleman suddenly appeared in the center of one of these streets with a flash of orange light. Those that did notice gave the gentleman a wide berth, as while many had absolutely no idea who he was, they all could tell that he must have been at least someone important given his manner of dress and the fact that he could use magic. Isaac De La Rosa on the other hand, did not spare a single moment's thought to any of these people or give any of them a cursory glance as he made his way forward with his attention firmly focused in front of him. As he walked he couldn't help but replay the last few seconds he had just experienced over and over again in his mind, hoping again and again that he was wrong, or that his eyes had somehow deceived him.

Not even ten seconds ago he was standing in a nice restaurant in the Suntop District having brunch with his lady, Nicole of the royal house of Solara, the regional governor, his wife, and some guests that Nicole's daughter had seen fit to invite. It was there that he had spoken with one of these guests, a man of common birth that went by the name Seth, and at the conclusion of their conversation they had shaken hands. What Seth did not know that Isaac did, however, was that the instant their hands had touched, Isaac saw something. Something that even now after having just seen it, he still could not believe it.

Throughout his many years as spymaster for the Solaran crown, Isaac had often, even to the point of it becoming a habit for him, cast a spell that dispelled all magic on or around an individual whenever he shook said individual's hand. It was a safety measure he had come up with that in the past had helped him catch assassins and spies disguised as diplomats on more occasions than he would have liked to admit. Over the years he had become so good at doing this that he had even managed to reduce the loud, often obnoxious "crack" noise that often accompanied the dispelling of magic to something much quieter that brought to mind the sound that one would hear when making contact with static electricity. A sound most wouldn't notice, let alone pay any attention to. He had done this often enough that even today, as Queen Faust's personal advisor, he still maintained the habit on the off chance that the current spymaster missed something. It did not happen often, but it did still happen.

Most of the time this wasn't a big deal. More often than not nothing would happen regardless of whether or not the individual in question was a mage. There had been one instance in the past wherein he had accidently dispelled an illusion on a prominent female mage that she had been using to hide a rather horrific scar on her face, but that incident had been resolved quickly and nothing had ever come of it. Save for the fact that he knew one more secret about one more person. In a similar vein, when Isaac had dispelled the magic around Seth, he could only look on in paralyzing terror as the man's eyes that had before been a chocolaty brown color instantly changed to a very particular shade of red. The kind that reminded most, if not all who saw it of blood.

Before making his exit Isaac had chosen to reapply the illusion over Seth's eyes so as not to draw suspicion. He was thankful in that regard that no one had either questioned or found it suspicious in the slightest when he had to wave his hand in front of Seth's face to do that, but that left him with another problem that he needed to solve sooner rather than later. Preferably immediately. Now that he was away from everyone it gave him a chance to think, but despite that his mind refused to remain calm as his thoughts ran rampant like a stampeding herd of wild horses as he replayed the image of Seth's eyes over and over again in his mind's eye.

'*What the fuck!*' he screamed in his mind. '*Those eyes! Those fucking eyes! How? The only way he can have eyes that color is if Seth is a monster. How in the name of Solaris is that even possible? I know monsters can look like anything, but what are even the chances that one could appear even remotely similar to a human, let alone act and talk like one? And his eyes… He hid them with an illusion spell. The only way that can be possible is if he knows how to use magic. How is that possible? Magic is supposed to be a gift that only humans can use. Not only that, but somehow he's managed to squirm his way into the social circle of Prince Michael and now possibly even Filia. If anyone were to fall for such a ruse it would be Michael, but I did not give the man enough credit. Coming up with that amnesia story in order to cover up his lack of basic knowledge. Simple, but effective. I cannot even begin to imagine how long he has been playing at this, but if he managed to make his way all the way here and get close to Nicole and Filia, then truly he must think of himself as some sort of master of deception. If so, then he has no idea who he is fucking with. I have taken down much more powerful and much more clever people than someone like him before. Monster or no, this should be easy. It should be, right?'*

In the midst of all those thoughts Isaac forced himself to stop thinking for a moment as he closed his eyes and shook his head clear of anything distracting. This drew some attention from the people surrounding him, but he paid no attention to them as he kept walking forward.

'*Calm down, Isaac,'* he continued to himself. '*This is no time to start panicking. You know this. You need to come up with a plan. To begin with, what exactly could Seth's purpose be in all of this? What does he hope to gain by getting close to the royal family? Assassination? Espionage? Subterfuge? No, it can't be anything that complex. That would imply that monsters are smart enough to come up with complex, multi-phase plans. Even if I were to assume that he is, that does not automatically give other monsters the ability to do so just by virtue of him existing. They are all merely wild beasts with no desires other than to spill the blood of anything that isn't them. They have no desire for power and certainly they cannot comprehend politics. Whatever his intentions might be, however, part of it involves getting close to the royal family. He did not act at the restaurant, and he did not act when he was alone with Filia yesterday, which means that whatever his plan must be, he has not yet reached the culmination of it. If this is the case, then I must act before he does. Though I cannot do it myself. He knows who I am and is likely keeping an eye on me too. Even with my position, were I to be caught I would have a hard time convincing those he has fooled into believing me. No, better he dies first and the illusion fades before I reveal anything. If at all.'*

As that last thought ran through his head, out of the corner of his eye down the road from where he stood he spotted one particular building that was unique from all the others surrounding it. Upon walking closer he saw that it was the headquarters of the Futura Collegium Aureum monster hunting guild. The sight of it caused Isaac's lips to curl up into a sinister looking smirk.

'*I'll give you credit, Seth. If that really is your name,'* Isaac thought to himself. '*You may have even fooled me for a moment there, but you picked the wrong city for a monster like yourself to enact whatever plan you have.'* As soon as he finished that thought, with another flash of orange light Isaac had disappeared again.

The walk to the theater had been a quick one, and not much conversation had followed after their initial one about what a theater was. Although more than a few times Nicole made it a point to tell Filia to stop clinging to Seth. Something that Filia, being completely mindful of her duties as a princess, did her absolute best to ignore. In truth, however, even Seth himself had begun to wonder why exactly Filia had stayed so close to him since even before they had left the restaurant. He had only known her for a day and already she had made more physical contact with him than most people he had ever known.

The theater itself, when they had reached it, was easily one of the largest buildings Seth had ever seen up until that point, second only to the capitol building that he had been in not even a day earlier. It was large, wide, consisted primarily of thick, gray stone, few, if any windows, and had very tall, very thick wooden double doors that stood ajar to everyone who passed by, as if to signal to everyone that it was open. While everything appeared to be stone on the outside, almost everything on the inside seemed to be made of beautifully carved wood and all of the floors were lined with bright red carpeting. Upon entering the assembled group was again approached by a man in a finely dressed suit, who after being rather rudely told by Nicole who they all were and what their expectations were, led them all through another set of doors and up several flights of stairs.

Eventually the stairs led them all to a long hallway where the man in the suit then led them to a door that opened up into a balcony with several comfortable looking chairs on it. That was where Nicole, Governor Monet and Katie were to be seated. As soon as they had arrived there Nicole then instructed the man in the suit to take Filia, Raz, and the rest of the assembled party somewhere else. Everyone agreed to this without a second thought, as it was the unanimous opinion of everyone, except for Tara, who had remained uncharacteristically silent, that they did not want to sit anywhere near Nicole. As such, the man in the suit led them back through the hallway to a completely different, yet exactly the same looking balcony with three identical chairs set up. After arriving there the man in the suit informed them that two more chairs would be brought up for them and that they should remain patient, which no one argued against. Seth saw no reason at all to argue against that anyway, as the man in the suit was only doing his job.

As they waited for the extra chairs to be brought to them, Seth took a few moments to get a better look at the view this balcony offered him, and his initial impression was that of immense disappointment. At least at first. Looking down from the balcony all he saw were rows upon rows of chairs, nearly all of which were not nearly as well put together as the ones that were on this balcony. Seth also saw a few more balconies as well once he looked up from directly beneath him. Every single one of the chairs he saw, whether they were on the floor or on one of the many balconies, all faced the same direction, but when Seth looked in that direction the only thing he saw was an absolutely massive crimson curtain which at the moment, was closed. The curtain itself took up nearly the entire space of the wall, which was both taller and wider than the average house in Canaan, which in turn made Seth wonder exactly how much work had been done to sew and put together a curtain of that size. He would have contemplated that further had the man in the suit not returned with two additional chairs for them as well as two additional people to carry them for him.

It was at that point that Seth noticed below that other people were beginning to enter the theater and take their seats. As such, the others in his group more or less decided for him that they should follow suit. After taking a few moments to move the now five chairs around the balcony so that they could all sit comfortably, Raz and Daedalus ended up insisting that they take the two spare chairs, which left the three remaining and more comfortable looking chairs for Filia, Seth and Tara, who all sat in that order.

"You're gonna enjoy this, I know you are," Filia said to Seth as she moved her seat so that she could be closer to him, something that Seth found odd because they were already sitting next to each other.

"Let him watch it first," Raz, who sat on the opposite side of Filia, spoke up. "He might end up thinking it's as boring as you do."

"I'm sorry, but what am I supposed to be watching?" Seth then asked, upon which both Filia and Raz couldn't help but laugh to themselves.

"Just look down towards the stage," Raz answered once he had calmed down. "You'll see what we're talking about soon enough."

"What's a stage?" Seth then immediately asked, upon which both Filia and Raz instantly fell silent and just stared with wide eyed expressions of shock at him for several very long seconds. Raz, however, was much quicker to recover from this than Filia was.

"Alright," he eventually spoke up again. "You see that huge ass curtain at the back of the room."

"Yes," Seth answered with some obvious sarcasm. At least he tried to make it obvious. It was his first time doing so. While the giggling at his expense was bad enough, he found it strange that Raz was asking him if he could see a curtain that was literally as big as the wall it was covering. So of course he could see it.

"Keep your eyes on that," Raz answered, seemingly oblivious to Seth's attempt at sarcasm. "Trust me, it will all make sense eventually." Seth decided right then that he wouldn't ask anymore questions of anyone while they were here, since it was obvious that they weren't going to answer any of them. Frustrated for only a moment, Seth resounded himself to getting comfortable in his chair while he waited to be presented with whatever they were here to show him.

A little under an hour of waiting had gone by, but eventually Seth did notice that the seats below them were slowly beginning to fill up, and before long most if not all of those seats had been filled. It was then that the light in the whole theater suddenly became very, very dim. Seth, however, couldn't tell exactly what the cause of it was, and that fact worried him slightly.

"It's starting," Filia said to him as that was happening in an excited tone.

"What's star-" Before Seth could even finish asking that question the sound of trumpets blaring from somewhere he could not see cut him off. The fact that all of the lights had suddenly gone out and the equally sudden appearance of phantom trumpets really set Seth on edge, and as a result he felt that he should be on guard. Despite that, however, no one around him appeared to feel like that, not even Tara. With that in mind, despite what his instincts were telling him he forced himself to relax. What would have made all of this more bearable for him would be if someone had told him exactly what was happening so that he didn't have to worry about it. Alas, no one appeared even remotely willing to grant him that courtesy. Without any other recourse and no explanations, Seth decided to follow the lead of his friends as he re-focused his attention back to the curtain just as the trumpets began to die down.

To Seth's ire, the sound of the phantom trumpets blared out two more times before anything else happened. At the conclusion of the third time, however, as if on cue someone wearing the oddest set of clothes Seth had ever seen in his entire short life stepped out from behind the curtain. To start with, from the very silly looking hat he wore all the way down to his shoes that for some reason curled upwards at the tips, every single article of clothing this man wore was covered in vertical stripes that were colored purple, orange and white in that order. Even when he crossed his hands in front of him the sleeves of his outfit still somehow lined up with the rest of his outfit's vertical color pattern. The bizarre looking cap he wore appeared to be made of cloth, like the rest of his outfit, but it consisted of six points, three on each side, that curled upwards almost like fingers and featured a small golden bell at the end of each of the points. The cap, of course, retained the same color palette as the rest of his outfit. Another bizarre thing about this man that stood out to Seth was his face. Seth had seen his fair share of pale people before, including himself, but this man's skin appeared to be literally as white as a piece of paper. Seth was about to ask someone about this, but before he could he noticed a few spots around the man's neck that appeared to be a more natural flesh color. Seeing that made it click in Seth's head that this man's face wasn't unnaturally pale, but it was instead covered in white makeup. This, however, only caused Seth to start questioning why this man had painted his face like that in the first place. As this bizarre looking man stepped out onto the stage a light from somewhere on the ceiling shined down on him as he began to speak.

"Ladies, gentlemen, and esteemed guests," he began in a deep, yet practiced voice. "On behalf of the theatrical community of Dis, as well as those of other such communities throughout the Solaran Empire. It is our esteemed pleasure to welcome all of you to this year's retelling of how our world came to be. A story that has been told time and time again throughout not only the history of our great Solaran Empire, but indeed the known world. It is a story of love, and loss. Of hope, and horror. Of survival, and sacrifice. Of rising to the greatest of heights humanity has ever known, only to fall so far back to our earth. More important than any of those, however, it is our story. For it is because of these events that took place so long ago that we are able to tell this tale again and again. Ladies and gentlemen, it is our immense pleasure to present to you. The story of the Rise and Fall of Solaris." As the man finished speaking the sound of a low drum roll began to kick in and the sound of the phantom trumpets returned to accompany them as the immense curtain the man emerged from slowly began to open. Slowly, as if with practiced steps, the man walked along towards the left of the stage as he maintained a very specific distance between himself and the edge of the curtain.

Once the curtain was opened Seth could only watch wide eyed as he beheld a scene of many, many, many tall buildings. He could tell that it was a painted picture, but the scale of it was beyond anything he could imagine someone putting in the time and effort into creating. What's more, upon a more careful inspection of the scene in front of him, he saw that the background was only painted a light blue color to match the sky. The buildings appeared to be painted on a series of wooden cutouts that gave the illusion of a three dimensional space. The buildings themselves were almost tall enough to reach the height of the ceiling, and from the way they were painted appeared to be made out of smooth, seemingly seamless stone and many, many, many panes of glass. Some of the buildings appeared to be only made of glass in fact. Seth could only guess that these buildings, whatever they were, were meant to be much taller than how they were portrayed on stage, but that gave him no indication at all of exactly how tall they were meant to be. From the top left corner of the room a bright light lit up that served the dual purpose of emulating the sun as well as lighting up the stage for all to see. All the while another, different light still shined on the oddly dressed man as he stood on the far left side of the stage and continued his speech.

"Our story begins before time. Long before any of us can remember or recount," the oddly dressed man spoke. "Back then, the world belonged to humanity. It was our home. Like good neighbors we shared it with each other, and in turn through humanity's collected efforts we grew to master our world. Thanks to this nothing was beyond our grasp. None wanted for anything. No illness was beyond our ability to cure it. We were even able to create edifices so tall that they touched the sky. Truly it seemed that humanity had achieved everything once thought impossible." The oddly dressed narrator then gave an intentional pause to let all of those words sink in. Seeing the image of the tall buildings in front of him, Seth couldn't help but wonder if all of what this man had said was really true. "Until one day. A day like any other. All of it was taken from us."

Then, before the narrator spoke again, the sound of drums suddenly blared up in a single, loud "BOOM" as all of the lights in the theater instantly went dark. All of this was so abrupt and so jarring that it actually caused Seth to instinctively grip the arms of his chair tighter. Before he could even comprehend what had just happened, however, the sound of the drums came back again, and with them the lights came back on, albeit much, much dimmer than before. Now able to see again, Seth beheld an entirely different scene than what was in front of him mere moments ago.

While the city of tall buildings remained, now interspersed between the layers of painted buildings were paintings of flames. Seth could also see that what little light was illuminating the room was actually coming from between the layers of the painted buildings and the flames, as if to give the illusion that the flames themselves were generating the light despite not being real. Accompanying this new image were the sounds of something crackling, again as if to make the flames seem more real and lifelike. The biggest and most important change to the scene, however, was that where once the light that represented the sun had been now hung this incredibly large thing that was suspended from the ceiling.

Even with all of the words he knew, Seth could not even begin to rightly describe the thing he was looking at. It appeared to him like a giant, black ball with a single large, blood red eye in its center. A chill ran down Seth's spine as the color of this thing's eye was instantly familiar to him. Coming off of this black ball with the red eye were many, many appendages of varying sizes that reminded Seth of fingers, but didn't move at all like fingers. Whereas fingers had very well defined points of articulation, the movements of the things's appendages were more fluid and seemed to be able to move whichever way they chose. Even in ways that were impossible for fingers. Their movements actually reminded Seth of a wet noodle. Lining every single one of these appendages in neat, organized rows were more blood red eyes of varying sizes that grew smaller and smaller as they reached the tips. Despite clearly being made of cloth and other materials that Seth recognized, what scared Seth the most about this thing was that it was somehow able to move, as its noodle-like appendages moved whichever way they chose as if the entire thing was suspended in water. Not only that but several of its eyes, including the one in the center, even blinked.

"From the heavens descended Chaos," the voice of the strangely dressed narrator continued despite the fact that he could no longer be seen. "A being of immense power and might whose size was so great that its mere presence blotted out the light of the sun. None knew where it came from. None knew why it chose to come to our home. What it wanted, however, that we were able to gleam." Again, the voice of the strangely dressed narrator paused to let his words sink in, though Seth was only barely able to pay attention as all of his focus was on this thing that was suspended above the city. "Jealous of all that we were, and angered by all that we had accomplished, Chaos desired only one thing. To destroy everything that lived on our home and take it for itself. To fulfill this task, like the god that had created us, Chaos created monsters." Then, as the narrator finished speaking, Seth watched as what looked like droplets of water began to fall from the thing hanging from the ceiling, only he knew that they weren't meant to be droplets of water.

"Buildings that touched the sky, really?" Raz spoke up rather loudly as this was happening. "Is that even possible?"

"It most certainly is not," Daedalus answered. "To touch the sky you would need supports able to hold up more than the entire weight of Sol, and even then you wouldn't get close enough."

Some time later, after he had managed to collect everything that he needed to, Isaac reappeared. This time directly in front of the guild hall. Without hesitation Isaac then stepped into the establishment. The instant he did, however, he was met with a cacophony of different noises, mostly in celebration of the new year as many of the guild's current and prospective members ate, drank, danced to the music that was being played by a visiting musician, talked to each other about their recent and favorite hunts, and were simply merry. Everywhere Isaac looked the guild hall was packed to capacity with all sorts of people, and nearly all of them wore their respective bracelets which he knew signified their rank. It was so loud in fact that Isaac could barely hear himself think, but that was okay for right now. He had a better idea now of what he needed to do. His appearance also drew quite a few stares from the guild's respective patrons, but this was attention he was used to, so it did not bother him in the slightest.

"Excuse me, sir," a voice suddenly spoke up from behind him in a patronizing tone before Isaac had even reached the bar. "Are you lost? You seem to have wandered into the wrong establishment. This is a pretty exclusive club we got here. Not just anyone is allowed in here this time of year." Without saying anything Isaac turned his head to see the source of the voice, a dark skinned man wearing a mustard yellow coat. Most importantly, however, the bracelet he wore was gold. Seeing this, Isaac's lips curled into a smile as he turned around fully to face the man properly.

"No," Isaac answered him. "I am not lost. I am exactly where I want to be."

As Isaac spoke he stood up as straight as he could and slipped his hands into his pockets, if only to show that he was not intimidated. "I came here looking to hire someone for a very specific job. A monster hunting job. One that is going to require the most skilled gold ranked member of this guild. You wouldn't happen to know where I could find this person, would you?" Hearing this the man in the mustard yellow coat's lips curled into a very egotistical smile of his own.

"That depends," he answered. "What sort of job and how much is it paying? No one in this guild works for free, you know. Hard working monster hunters like us need to eat too, you know." Isaac then began to laugh at that loud enough for the man to hear him over the celebrating crowd.

"I am very well aware of this," Isaac responded to the man. "I would not have come here if I did not. What sort of self respecting man do you take me for? To answer the first part of your question, however, it is, as I said, a monster hunting job. To answer the second." Isaac then stopped talking and reached into his coat, upon which he pulled out a small brown pouch. In full view of the man in the yellow coat, Isaac then reached into it and pulled out a single coin, which he then flipped up into the air. Before it could fall past his eyes the man in the yellow coat snatched it from the air, whereupon he then proceeded to examine it. To his surprise, which he could not hide at all from Isaac, the coin he held was not copper or silver, but gold. Isaac's smile widened a little bit as he saw that reaction from him. "There is more where that came from. Half up front and half upon completion of the job. To whomever accepts the job of course, but as I stated I do not want just anyone." As Isaac spoke he slipped the pouch back into his coat where it disappeared from view. "Any one of you could wear a bracelet of any color and kill a monster. I do not want just anyone. I need the most skilled gold ranking member this guild has to offer. You can keep the coin I gave you. Let us call it a down payment for you helping me to find this person." Hearing all of this, the man in the yellow coat's egotistical smile widened considerably.

"Well," he began as he slipped the gold coin into his pocket. "If that really is the sort of man you're looking for, sir. I can safely say that I don't need to help you find him. Because you're talking to him." Hearing that answer, Isaac looked this person up and down as he silently judged him. His manner of dress was odd for his profession, he had to admit, and he saw no weapons on him of any kind, but he forgave that as he knew that today was not a day for weapons or violence. At least it was not intended to be. Isaac could see, however, that this man at the very least had what he needed.

"Well… If that is indeed the case," Isaac then began as he visibly glanced at all the revelry surrounding them. "Perhaps we should discuss this in a more… private location."

"There's an alleyway behind the building we can use," the man in the yellow coat answered him. "No one will bother us there."

"Very well then," Isaac responded with a nod. "Lead the way mister…"

"Booth," the man in yellow answered. "Arthur Booth."

Seth then spent the next couple of hours watching the story of how Chaos created monsters, how they and it destroyed anything and everything that humanity held dear, and how the idea of mercy didn't even seem to exist to them as they killed and killed and killed. The story itself was very familiar to him, as Tara had explained it to him in the library at one point. Having it explained to him and watching it all happen in front of him, however, were two completely different things. Seth knew that nothing that was happening on the stage was real of course, that much was obvious from a glance, but seeing this story portrayed in this manner made him ask all kinds of questions to himself. Questions that he dared not voice aloud.

According to the play, Chaos and all monsters were merciless beasts that knew neither mercy nor reason, and all they did was kill anything and everything that lived until there was nothing left to kill. Then when there was nothing left they simply moved on to somewhere else to find more things to kill. While every single monster Seth had ever seen seemed to fit in this category, the idea that monsters were incapable of mercy or reason did not sit right with him. If that was true then what was he? He had shown mercy before, many times in fact, at least he believed that he had. In thinking about all of this his thoughts returned once again to Lilim. While Seth knew that she hated humans, he also knew that she had to be at least somewhat capable of reason. After all, she had chosen to speak to him when by her own admission she could have beaten him to death if she had so wished. Along with the fact that she didn't lay a finger on Agatha or Vivian. This play seemed to heavily imply that monsters were not even capable of that.

Eventually, after the play had moved on from the initial introduction of Chaos, the monsters it created, as well as the destruction they all had caused, it began to gain some focus as the character Solaris entered the story, here portrayed as a strikingly handsome, yet lithe young man with red hair similar to Filia's. His story began with his early life, being but a child not even ten years of age when Chaos came to the world as monsters of all shapes, sizes and varieties rampaged through his home village killing everyone and everything they saw in increasingly violent and horrific ways. Not a single member of his family was saved from this, with Solaris himself only surviving by the grace of a kind neighbor who grabbed him and ran from the village as he watched his family and everyone he knew get torn apart in front of him. The way the story portrayed it, seeing all of this carnage firsthand was understandably the single most horrific experience of the young Solaris' life. Though Seth knew for certain that the way the play portrayed these people dying on stage wasn't nearly as horrific or brutal as it would have been in real life. Mostly due to the fact that people's deaths were usually nothing more than the actors falling over and all the monsters within the play were either actors wearing all black and wooden masks or puppets who's qualities varied between each of them. None of which were even close to the level craftsmanship of that of the Chaos puppet that loomed over the stage during the entire play like a hungry vulture.

From there the story of the play moved on to Solaris' life as a teen and then a young adult as he moved from place to place, village to village, sanctuary to sanctuary, only to see them all eventually torn down and destroyed one after the other. It seemed as if no matter where Solaris went the people there were simply doomed to die, as was the cruel hand dealt to them by fate. Eventually, by the time he was a young adult he began to learn the art of magic and to Seth's great surprise, Solaris did not actually invent magic. Rather, according to the play it was an ancient, lost art long since forgotten by humanity that a group of desperate refugees and scholars rediscovered in an attempt to find some new way to combat the hordes of monsters that were beating on their door literally every day. To their great surprise it worked, and as such they began to travel the world in order to teach their art to as many people as they could. Even with this newfound knowledge, however, it was obvious that humanity was fighting a losing battle, as for every monster that they had managed to successfully kill with magic, Chaos simply made ten more.

It was one of these scholars who eventually found Solaris in an underground sanctuary that was supposedly safe from monsters, though from Seth's own experience he knew for certain that this would not be the case for long. It was also here that the play introduced another important character, a young woman with dark hair by the name of Orianna, who met Solaris when the scholar had gathered as many people in the community as possible so that he could teach them all magic. As time went on it became obvious that out of everyone the scholar taught, Solaris and Orianna were the most gifted, though Solaris was clearly the more talented of the two of them. Nevertheless through the study of magic the two of them began to grow closer and closer.

What was strange to Seth, though, was that Filia seemed oddly invested in this part of the story. To the point that at some point during it she scooted closer to Seth before slowly leaning towards him and resting her head against his shoulder. Seth initially was not only greatly confused as to why she was doing this, but also very uncomfortable with this action, both physically from the weight of her head and emotionally from this sudden sign of affection being given to him by someone he had only just met yesterday. Despite this he didn't speak up about it. Part of him wanted to, but the rest of him kept telling himself that it would have been rude to make a scene of it. So he just let the princess continue to use him as a pillow.

Eventually, however, as with every place that Solaris called home, disaster struck as a group of monsters that were able to burrow into the earth found this supposedly impervious sanctuary and began to attack it. Thanks to the combined efforts of Solaris, Orianna, and their mentor, however, they were able to repel the attack long enough for most of the community to escape while the three of them stayed behind to fight the monsters. In the end their mentor ended up paying the ultimate price for all of their lives, however, as he was swallowed whole by a gigantic worm-like monster. His last act being to take the worm-monster out with him so that Solaris and Orianna could escape as well.

It was at this point that things began to take a turn for Solaris, as all of the death and suffering he had experienced over the course of his life began to take its toll, and the only person to hear his cries was Orianna.

"All of this... What is the point of all of this?" Solaris asked. "All this suffering... All this dying? What is the point of it all if there isn't even an end to any of it?"

"But what can we do?" Orianna then asked in response. "We know how to fight them now, don't we? If we know how to fight them then we can protect ourselves, right? Isn't that what matters? Isn't that enough?"

"No," Solaris responded without even looking at her. "No it isn't. There has to be more to life than just this. What's the point of living if these... things will just kill us tomorrow. Or the next day, or a week, or a month from now, or whenever they want. What's the point of living if we have to live every second of our lives in fear that monsters will appear and slaughter us like lambs?"

"We can hide from them," Orianna was quick to answer. "There must be some place out there, somewhere, where they can't find us. We'll find it. Make something for us there, bring others. We can-"

"It won't work," Solaris interrupted before she could say any more. "We thought we were safe from them before, remember, and look how that turned out for us. You know as well as I do, Orianna. Nowhere is safe from them. It doesn't matter where we go or what we do, or how much new magic we learn. They will never stop hunting us. That is all they know."

"Then what do you suggest that we do?" Orianna said in turn rather forcefully. "We can't just fight them. No matter how many of them we kill, more will just keep coming. Even if we were to somehow kill every single monster on earth, Chaos would only make more. There's no point in fighting. Nothing will change and all that waits for anyone down that road is death. If we can't run and fighting is pointless, then what are we to do?"

"Who ever said that there was no point in fighting?" Solaris shot back, clearly angry, but doing his best to keep himself under control. "Those so-called scholars who discovered this power. All they ever said was that it was the answer to everything, that it was the power we needed to finally take the world back for ourselves. Even our master went on and on like that whenever we questioned him about it. I know you remember this. You questioned him far more than I did." Solaris then paused for a few seconds as his eyes slowly drifted up towards the sky, though it was obvious to everyone watching exactly where his attention was. "Maybe they were right. Maybe it is the only power we need to defeat them. If that's true then the problem isn't the monsters. It's us. We have this awesome power now, and what do we do with it? Run, hide, and take down anything that follows us like cornered rats. How is any of that different from what we were doing before? The way we fight these things has changed, that much is certain. Perhaps it's time we changed with it."

"Solaris, what are you saying?" Orianna then asked as she walked up next to him and put a hand on his shoulder.

"I'm saying that we aren't doing enough," Solaris answered without looking at her as he balled both of his hands into fists. "We can fight them now, sure, but you said so yourself. What's the point in fighting them if no matter how many we kill that... thing, will simply make more. We've been fighting the monsters for so long that we're too afraid to confront the true source of this calamity." As those words left his mouth Seth watched as Orianna suddenly pulled her hand away from Solaris and took a tentative step back, as if aghast by what he had just said.

"You... You..." she stammered. "You can't seriously be suggesting-"

"That we kill Chaos," Solaris interrupted her without taking his eyes off of the thing hanging from the ceiling. "Yes. Yes I am." Silence reigned for many, many long seconds after those words left Solaris' mouth. While it was obviously because Orianna was shocked beyond belief at what he had just suggested, Seth couldn't help but feel that the pause was more for the audience than the characters.

"You... Can't be..." Orianna eventually spoke again after those long moments had passed, but Solaris did not respond to her at all. Instead he chose to keep his gaze glued up towards the ceiling in perpetual contempt for the thing hanging from said ceiling. "You... You really are, aren't you?"

"Why wouldn't I be!" Solaris then finally responded rather forcefully as he tore his attention away from the thing hanging from the ceiling and looked directly at her again. "Monsters only exist because that thing made them! The only reason we all live in constant fear of dying is because that thing came to our home! Every atrocity that we have ever suffered for our entire lives is all the fault of that thing in the sky! Yes, we can fight now, but why should we only use this power to fight monsters who will only be replaced as soon as we kill them when we should be using it to fight that thing!" As Solaris spoke he kept pointing up towards the thing hanging from the ceiling. "Our master told us before that some spells are so powerful they can bury entire cities! If that's really true then at the very least they should be able to make that thing flinch!"

"But you'll die!" Orianna then shouted back at Solaris, upon which another few seconds of silence followed for the obvious benefit of the audience. "Remember what our master told us. Even with magic, you cannot create something from nothing. It's impossible. All that energy and power has to come from somewhere.

When you light a fire it comes from a spark. When you use magic it comes from within. Even if you were to hit Chaos with something that powerful, then-"

"That is a risk I am more than willing to take," Solaris interrupted again, this time with a much calmer tone of voice. After saying that though, he turned away from Orianna and directed his gaze back up towards the thing hanging from the ceiling again. "We risk our lives every single day fighting monsters, fighting each other, fighting just to survive this hell that that thing made our home into. If we're willing to risk our lives for all of those reasons, then why won't people risk their lives doing something that actually matters. If it's because they're afraid then forget them. I'll do it myself."

"But you'll-"

"But I'll what?" Solaris interrupted again as he turned back to look at Orianna. "Die? I know. You said so before and I can hear perfectly well. But what does it matter if I die? I'm but one man, and if my death means that others don't have to live every single day of their lives in fear of that thing or its spawn then I'll gladly give it. I wouldn't even hesitate. Not if it means that you and everyone else will still be here after I'm gone." As that line left Solaris' mouth the sound of string instruments such as violins and cellos began to blare out from somewhere that Seth could not see. After a few short moments of letting the audience take in their sound Solaris began to sing.

"What is a life?" Solaris sang to the audience. "What is one life? What does one-"

"How do we even know that was what Solaris and Orianna even looked like?" Raz then suddenly asked aloud. "Actually, better question. How do we know that Orianna even existed? She's not mentioned in any of the scriptures."

"Religious propaganda my friend," Daedalus answered. "Obviously there are holes in the story of Solaris' life, and where there are holes somebody will do their damndest to fill them if it removes any facts that they find inconvenient or twists the story to suit their needs. Which is probably why this play shoehorned in that six minute long ballad about how Solaris fucked once. Though I don't need to explain such things to you. Out of everyone here who would know more about filling holes than you."

"Haha very funny," Raz responded with an air of obvious sarcasm and a roll of his eyes. "Though if that's true then how much of this story do you think was made up?"

"Perhaps all of it was made up," Daedalus answered without skipping a beat. "Perhaps there was no Solaris and Chaos simply exploded on his own."

"That's not true!" Filia shouted rather loudly, though thankfully not loud enough to disturb the people around them. "We know that Solaris existed."

"Oh," Daedalus then responded as he looked in Filia's direction with a wide grin on his face. "And how exactly is it that you are so certain of that, my lady?"

In an alleyway behind the Futura Collegium Aureum guild hall, the man claiming to be the best gold ranked monster hunter in the guild was having a hard time keeping silent. As he couldn't help but laugh at the story that had just been regaled to him.

"Do you honestly expect me to believe any of what you just said?" Arthur Booth asked as he came down from his laughter. "I mean credit where credit is due, that was a very entertaining story and it was very cool how you showed me that illusory image of what he looks like, but really. Come on. Do you really expect me to believe that there's a monster walking around this city? This city of all places? That looks and acts exactly like a human? Well enough to pass for one even, and was able to fool even you?"

"I am very well aware of how far-fetched all of this sounds," Isaac answered him with a deathly serious look on his face. "I myself would be questioning it if our roles were reversed, but I know what I saw. At this very moment, hiding under all of our noses is a wolf among sheep." Despite his answer Arthur still appeared skeptical as he took in a very long, very deep breath to keep himself from laughing out loud again.

"Look…" Arthur began in a very condescending tone. "If you really want a man dead you don't need to make up that ridiculous story. There's enough shady people in this city that I'm certain you could find an actual assassin if you look hard enough. Especially someone like you since you know, you got the coin and you got the connections. In fact…" Arthur then paused for a moment as he took a step closer towards Isaac and his lips curled into a smirk. "It makes me wonder why you're here asking me to take care of this little problem for you. Surely someone as important as you could find an actual assassin a lot quicker than you could find a monster hunter. So with that in mind, why are you here? Why exactly do you need me to take care of your dirty work for you?" As Arthur finished speaking he kept the smirk on his face, if only because he thought it made him appear clever. Arthur did not need to be as close as he was, however, for Isaac to smell the pungent scent of arrogance wafting off of him. He actually reminded Isaac of many of the people he knew back in Sol. People he had been forced to deal with since the day he was born and as such, knew exactly how to deal with them.

"You are correct, in one aspect," Isaac said to Arthur without breaking eye contact as he crossed his arms in front of his chest. "It would be easy for me to find an assassin if I really wanted one. All I would have to do is send the right message to the right person and I would be speaking to them within the hour." Isaac deliberately paused at that moment so that he could see Arthur's reaction. When he gave none, Isaac took that as a cue to continue. "However, this task would not be suited for any such assassin. Assassins, you see, hunt men, and my quarry, as I have already explained to you, is not a man, but a monster. As such, a monster problem requires a monster solution. Hence why I am here, speaking to you." Isaac deliberately paused again at that moment, but all he got from Arthur was a scoff, exactly as he had been expecting. Before continuing Isaac uncrossed his arms in order to make himself look slightly less intimidating as his lips curled into his own smirk to match Arthur's. "You are, however, incorrect in another, more important aspect." As he finished speaking Isaac then turned around and began to slowly walk out of the alley. "I do not need you to solve this problem for me. Someone like you, who obviously does not believe he can handle a single monster that just so happens to look like a human would clearly be a waste of my valuable time and money. Now if you will excuse me, I am going to head back inside the guild hall to find someone more capable who will not let something as simple as a monster's appearance intimidate him. I am more than certain that there are plenty of hunters in there today who would absolutely love an endorsement from someone so close to Queen Faust. Come to think of it, after I explain the situation to my Queen, knowing her and how much she loves her daughter and granddaughter I am certain that she would see the hunter who saved her granddaughter as nothing less than a national hero. Perhaps she may even consider-"

"Wait!" Arthur's voice suddenly shouted from behind Isaac just before he was able to turn the corner to leave the alley, which was shortly followed by quick footsteps. Isaac couldn't help but briefly smile to himself as the hunter reacted exactly as he had hoped he would. He did his best to conceal his smile and adopt a much more serious expression as he turned back around to properly face Arthur as he caught up with him. "You say I would get an endorsement if I work for you. That true?" Hearing that, Isaac smiled again as he suddenly adopted a more pleasant tone. Or at least he pretended to.

"Of course," Isaac responded to the hunter. "I always make sure that the people who work for me are well taken care of. Ask any one of them."

"And the national hero thing?" Arthur then asked, exactly as Isaac knew he would.

"Oh, that," Isaac answered, pretending as if it was not that big of a deal. "Unfortunately, if I may speak true. It is not within my power to grant such a title. That honor belongs to my lady Queen Faust, and only her. That being said, however, when I explain to her the story of how a monster that looks like a human somehow got very close to her beloved granddaughter, and how she was saved by a lone monster hunter who put absolutely everything on the line to serve his crown and country using the skills that his upbringing and training had blessed him with, I think that she will be willing to be at least a little generous. If nothing else, you will still get a substantial amount of coin, as promised, as well as recognition from many, many other important people in the capital. Along with-" Before Isaac could say any more Arthur held up a single finger and silenced him.

"You can stop talking, old man," Arthur said to him. As much as Isaac hated being referred to that way, the way in which the monster hunter had said it made him visibly smile. "I only have one more question for you. Where do I find this monster?"

As Seth sat and watched the rest of the play he couldn't help but wonder to himself what the actual battle between Solaris and Chaos must have looked like, because the way in which it was portrayed on stage left quite a bit to be desired. True to the story that Tara had told him, after traveling what was known of the world with Orianna for some time and learning all that he could about magic, without any hesitation or doubt Solaris flew into the sky to challenge Chaos all by himself. He didn't ask anyone to help him, not even Orianna, he just did it. What's more, the entire battle was set to a series of loud drum beats that practically shook the entire theater.

Their fight supposedly lasted for days, though as Seth imagined it was difficult to portray something like that on a stage like this, with only subtle changes in light on the background being the only indication that time was passing. Also, with the lack of any real magic, at least what Seth assumed was a lack of real magic, most of the fight amounted to the man playing Solaris being held up by ropes to simulate him flying and throwing glowing balls of something Seth couldn't recognize or identify at the thing hanging from the ceiling that was supposed to be Chaos. Very few, if any of Solaris' attacks had any effect on it, however, so in one last desperate attempt to do something Solaris let out a scream that Seth assumed was supposed to sound heroic as he flew directly at Chaos. The instant the two of them collided, the thing hanging from the ceiling suddenly spit apart like an egg as an incredibly bright light suddenly burst forth from the spot where the two of them had been. It was so bright that Seth had to momentarily shield his eyes as the light lit up the entire theater like a sun. After the light had faded both Solaris and Chaos were nowhere to be seen.

Once that explosive scene had ended the scene then shifted to somewhere back on the ground where Orianna was looking up towards the sky where Chaos had been, completely and utterly speechless at the spectacle she had just witnessed, though there was definitely a hint of sadness in her expression, as if a knife had been plunged into her chest. As she stared upwards, from the dark, cloudy abyss that had been the sky for the entire play, a single beam of light began to shine down upon her. A beam of light that was then followed by another, and then another, until finally the clouds parted and light on the ceiling that was meant to be the sun, which hadn't been seen since the first act, returned. It was only once the sun had made its return that Orianna began to speak.

"You did it…" she spoke aloud, though on the stage no one was around to hear her. "You… you actually did it." As those words left her mouth she suddenly fell to her knees, and then shortly afterwards she fell forward as she tore her eyes away from the sky, her hands and arms only barely supporting her. It was then that she began to make crying noises, though Seth was too far away to see if she was actually crying. "You foolish, foolish man, you actually saved us, but at what cost. At what cost..." She then spent several more moments crying to let those words really sink in before continuing. "I told you this would happen. I told you what would happen to you if you did something like that, but you did it anyway. You... You..." It was at that point that Orianna broke down fully and began to openly sob on the stage as she attempted to bury her face as far into herself as she could.

As Orianna wept on the stage a soft choir began to sing out from somewhere. Between that, all of the music, and the sound effects, it was beginning to bother Seth that he still didn't know where any of these sounds were coming from. Yet, despite that, the choir grew and grew in volume until it was only barely louder than Orianna's sobs. Eventually, after a few, long seconds of sobbing had passed, Orianna suddenly ceased her sobbing.

"But you were right," Orianna then said as she slowly brought herself back to her feet. "In the end... You really were right. We could have defeated Chaos, we had the power within us all this time. All it took... was for someone to be brave enough to go through with it. Someone... Someone like you." Orianna then paused for another moment to let the audience take in her words as the melody of the choir began to change slightly. "What is done is done. We cannot change what has happened. You taught me that. Because of you, Chaos is gone, and so our nightmare ends. Because of you, we don't need to live in a world ruled by monsters. Because of you, we are all still here... Yes... We are all still here." It was then that Orianna slowly turned her attention back up towards the sky. "You may be gone from this world, Solaris, but you haven't left us. No we, all of humanity, owe everything that we have now to you. For it is because of you that we are all still here. We will never forget you, Solaris. Not ever. I will make sure of that. I will tell your story again and again and as many times as need be until all have heard it. And Solaris..." Before continuing Orianna took a moment to place her right hand over her stomach. "You may be gone, but a part of you will remain with us forever."

It was at that moment that the choir suddenly picked up in volume as all of the previously dead and alive characters came back out onto the stage to stare up into the light of the sun with Orianna. For a second it confused Seth greatly why all of the characters who had died during the play were there as well, but he quickly realized after Solaris and Orianna's mentor came out on stage with them that it was meant to be symbolic. Before long, all of the characters who had been in the play were on the stage. All except for Solaris.

"And so," the oddly dressed man with the painted face who had narrated the entire play spoke as he stepped out onto the stage next to Orianna. "Solaris sacrificed himself to save humanity from Chaos. There was no body to bury, no song to sing, and nothing to mourn, but the memory of the man he was and the great deed that he alone accomplished remains with us to this day. For it is because of his sacrifice that we are able to tell his story again, and again, and again, and as many times as need be so that all may hear his story. The story of a man who put others before himself, who rose to such great heights amidst so much tragedy, who even gave his dying breath, so that we could live. And while many monsters still roam the world, and even today there is still much, much work that needs to be done for us, humanity, to rise back to the heights we once achieved, it is because of the sacrifice of Solaris that we have the chance to do so. For it is because of Solaris, and the sacrifice he made for all of us, that we are all still here."

As the man finished speaking the choir began to slowly die down as the light from the ceiling slowly faded along with it. Then, once the light was gone, the curtain began to close. Once it had closed completely everyone throughout the theater suddenly stood up from their chairs and began to clap as loud as they could. Filia and Tara were among them as well, and even Raz and Daedalus, who had spent the entire play commenting on what was happening and making glib remarks wherever they could, were standing and clapping. Unsure of what else to do, Seth rose from his seat and began to clap as well. As he did the curtain suddenly opened up one more time as the light from the ceiling lit up the stage. It was then that everyone who had been in the play, even Solaris and all of the people who had portrayed the monsters, stepped out and all took one practiced bow in unison.

With that done the curtain then closed one more time, and with it, the rousing applause began to quiet. All Seth could do was fall back into his chair and stare wide eyed at the empty stage and the large curtain covering it.

"So, Seth," Filia spoke up once the theater had quieted down. "What did you think of it?"

"I have several questions," was the only thing Seth could say in response.

Chapter 20

Seth felt his stomach rumble as he stepped outside of the theater, which greatly surprised him since he felt that he had just eaten not too long ago. To make sure of this he glanced upwards to the sky so that he could check the position of the sun. Much to his utter amazement and shock, the sun was not at all where he thought it should have been and the sky itself was beginning to take on a more orange tone.

"How... long were we in there?" Seth asked aloud as he kept his eyes on the sky.

"What, in the theater?" Raz was quick to respond as he and Filia walked up next to him. "I'd say... about five... five and a half hours. Maybe six since that intermission was a little long."

"Five hours!" Seth let out as he instantly dropped his eyes from the sky and spun around to face them properly. "Why were we in there for five hours?"

"Because that's how long the play was," Filia answered as she struggled to hold back a laugh because of that remark. "I thought that would have been obvious."

"Then why was the play five hours long?" Seth then immediately asked without waiting for anyone else to speak.

"Because that's how long whoever wrote it wanted it to be," Filia again answered with some hesitation. As she spoke her voice showed more apprehension and her face was quick to follow suit, as if she were for some reason afraid that her answer was not good enough for Seth. This was a look that Tara definitely recognized, as it signaled to her the moment when most people became unsure what to say to Seth because of all the questions he asked. What surprised her the most, however, was that it had taken Filia this long to show it. "I don't really know why, actually. Writing has never been one of my strong suits, so I don't really know how these things get decided."

"That one was actually short by comparison to others I've seen," Daedalus spoke up as he descended the steps of the theater to meet them. His words caused Seth to instantly forget about Raz and Filia.

"What!" Seth practically screamed as he spun to face Daedalus.

"Oh yes," Daedalus responded with the brimming confidence of one who knew exactly what he was talking about and was more than happy to share. "There's actually one that's so long that it has to be performed in segments over a period of five days. I have yet to see it myself but I have heard good things."

"So," the now familiar voice of Nicole Solara interrupted Seth before he could ask Daedalus what the name of that play was and why someone was insane enough to make it that long. As if responding to some unspoken command, all attention fell on her as all of them turned to see her descending the steps with Governor Monet and Katie. "Now that your mind has been sufficiently blown by the theater, is there somewhere else you would have us take you. Perhaps to see a street musician perform on the corner so that you can hear music for the first time, or to see one of the many sculptures in this district so that you can learn what art is."

"I know what those are," Seth was quick to respond before anyone else could.

"Oh really," Nicole replied as she pretended to act surprised. "I never would have guessed."

"I mean the play had moments where the characters were singing for some reason. So you should have at least figured that I knew what music was, or were you not paying attention?"

"As amusing as I'm sure it is for you to keep insulting the mentally deficient," Raz spoke up before Nicole could as he stepped between her and Seth. "We would all very much appreciate it if you stopped it now, please. I'm sure our present company finds it very offensive." As Raz spoke he gestured towards Governor Monet and his wife, both of whom were still at the sides of Princess Nicole, who narrowed her eyes at Raz.

"And you really think I care what others think?" Nicole then said, each of her words dripping with venom as they left her mouth.

"Lesson number eight," Raz then answered without skipping a beat as he took a few steps closer towards Nicole. "What is spoken about an individual is a reflection of how the world perceives that individual. Whether they be spoken aloud or in private, one must always be mindful of what others say. For if ignored they will only hurt you in time." By the time Raz had finished speaking he had walked far enough ahead of the others that he now stood directly in front of Nicole on the steps to the theater. "Yours words, Auntie, not mine, remember?" As Raz finished speaking, the familiar looking, cocky smirk that he usually wore fully adorned his face. Nicole, for her part, appeared as if she were attempting to contain an explosion within herself as she kept her eyes locked on Raz. It was so much that from where

Seth stood he could see her hands ball up into fists. For a moment Seth was worried that Nicole may actually strike him.

"I disappear for only a few hours and what do my eyes behold when I return?" The familiar voice of Isaac De La Rosa cut through the tension like a hot knife through butter as all of the assembled party turned to see him approaching the theater with his hands behind his back, a look of stern disappointment on his face, and his cold, piercing eyes staring directly at Raz and Nicole. "Do I need to repeat what I said to the two of you in Governor Monet's office? I sincerely hope not. You both know much I despise repeating myself."

"No," Raz was quick to respond despite the tension as he took a step back from Nicole, turned to Isaac, and then held up both of his hands as if to show that he wasn't doing anything with them. "Everything's fine here. Just a minor disagreement is all. Nothing at all to worry about. Right Nicole?" Despite how sincere Raz made it sound, the only response he got from Nicole was a very audible growl in his direction. So audible in fact that both Governor Monet and his wife took a step back away from her, something that went completely unnoticed by Nicole herself.

"Where've you been, Isaac?" Filia then spoke up as she stepped out ahead of the group in her own attempt to diffuse the situation. "You missed the whole play. I thought you liked these sorts of things."

"I do," Isaac quickly responded as he instantly switched back to his more polite demeanor before walking the rest of the way to the group. "But sometimes one's duties do not offer the luxury of enjoying plays. That is why I enjoy them as much as I do, for I rarely get to see one."

"And where exactly did your duties take you such that you needed to be gone all day?" Filia then asked. "And on the first day of the new year of all days." Despite how clear Filia's question was Isaac's first response was to offer a warm looking smile to her before placing his hand on her head.

"Oh, nowhere that you need to concern yourself with," Isaac said to Filia as he ruffled her hair in a similar manner to Raz. Something that Filia appeared to like equally as much when it came from Isaac. "Perhaps when you are older I may choose to burden you with the truth of all that my duties entail, but not today. Not on the first day of the new year of all days."

"So what happens now?" Seth asked once he felt that it was alright for him to speak up again.

"Now we leave," Nicole answered before anyone else could say anything as she walked away from Raz and over towards Isaac and Filia, her guards following her every step, though strangely Governor Monet and his wife remained where they were. Once she was around more familiar company Nicole turned around to properly face everyone, though mostly Seth's group. "As interesting as it was spending the day with all of you, I'm afraid that it's now time for us to take our leave. I'm sure that all of you have other places to be, as do we. So for now I will bid you all adieu, and if we ever do see each other again I hope that our next meeting is just as pleasant." Though she appeared to be sincere when she spoke those words aloud, from her eyes Seth could tell that she was faking it for the sake of appearances. "Come Filia, we-"

"No," Filia responded calmly before Nicole could utter another word.

"Filia…" Nicole responded in turn with ice in her eyes. "Don't ma-"

"I know what you're going to say," Filia interrupted her mother before she could finish. "And it's not going to work." She then crossed her arms across her chest and spoke in her best impersonation of Isaac. "Do I need to repeat what I said to you in Governor Monet's office? I sincerely hope not. You know how much I despise repeating myself." Before Nicole could open her mouth to speak again Filia beat her to the punch as she turned her attention to Isaac. "Isaac, I'm going to be taking a few of the guards as I will be spending the rest of the evening with my cousin. Unlike last night, however, I promise that I will return in a timely manner before it gets too dark. On this you have my word, and as I am certain you know, as a princess of the Solaran Empire, my word is my bond." Isaac seemed to consider Filia's words for several, long, drawn out seconds before Nicole was able to speak up again.

"This is ridiculous," Nicole said to no one in particular. "Isaac, plea-"

"You two," Isaac interrupted her as he snapped his fingers and pointed to two of the guards that were with Nicole. "You stay with Princess Filia. You know what I expect of you. Don't let her out of your sight and don't let anyone other than them get close to her. Understood?"

"Understood, my lord," both of the guards responded in unison as they both slapped a gauntleted fist to their chests and bowed their heads to him.

"Issac!" Nicole shouted the instant she had the opportunity to. "What do you thi-"

"You really should just quit while you're ahead, mom," Filia interrupted again before Nicole could say anymore. "Whatever you're thinking of saying or doing, I'll tell you right now it's not going to work. The decision has already been made so just relax and accept your minor defeat with the dignity afforded to us as members of the Solaran Royal family."

"Filia…" Nicole spat out, though it sounded more as if she were grinding her teeth together rather than saying her daughter's name.

"As often as I am inclined to disagree with members of your family," Daedalus then interjected as he walked up next to Filia. The look on his face was that of a confident grin, as if he had Nicole exactly where he wanted her. "This is one of those rare instances where I find myself agreeing with your daughter, my lady."

"You…" Nicole let out as she shifted her gaze over to Daedalus, and again her voice sounded more akin to grinding her teeth together rather than speaking.

"Me what?" Daedalus responded without even blinking. Before Nicole could open her mouth to say another word, Daedalus beat her to it. "I'll save you the trouble and a lot of pain from the migraine you'll no doubt receive from continuing to pointlessly argue. As much as it no doubt physically pains you to believe it, there are such things as battles you cannot win, and this, my lady, is one of them. So respectfully, my lady. Just stop. Listen to the words of your mother's advisor, go on your merry way, and just stop. Continuing to argue will get you nothing." Silence dominated the space between Nicole, Isaac, Filia and Daedalus as Nicole seemed to be having a silent stare down with all three of them. All the while Daedalus, Filia and even Isaac refused to budge at all. Like before it was Nicole who eventually broke that silence.

"We will have words later," Nicole said to Daedalus, each of her words practically dripping with venom as she spoke them before returning her gaze back to her daughter. "Especially with you, young lady. Do not think I will forget this."

"Ooh I'm so scared," Filia responded as she held up her hands and pretended to back away from her mother, but then stopped mid step and broke out laughing. That outburst seemed to be the last straw for Nicole, as the instant her daughter's laughter hit her ears she spun around and began to stomp away from the group as quickly as she could without running. Her royal guards kept pace with her the whole way.

"It would be best if I remained with her," Isaac said as he watched her leave. "As difficult as I am sure it may be to believe, she does tend to avoid saying or doing things that she will later regret when I am around."

"Yes, that probably would be for the best," Daedalus agreed. Before leaving, however, Isaac turned to properly face them all.

"Gentlemen," he said as politely as he could to all of them, though Seth did notice that his eyes lingered slightly longer on him than everyone else before turning to Tara. "Lady Schäfer." With that said he then returned his attention back to Filia one last time. "As you so eloquently said, my lady. You gave your word that you would return in a timely manner before it gets dark. As a lady of your station I expect you to honor it." Then with that said he turned around and began to start off after Nicole. "To the spirit and to the letter." The instant he started walking all of the remaining royal guards except for the two Isaac had ordered to stay behind followed after and kept pace with him. As they all watched them walk away Governor Monet and his wife took the opportunity to enter their field of vision.

"Well..." Governor Monet began. "I cannot speak for them, but I will say that I greatly enjoyed your company." He focused his attention more on Raz than any of the others as he spoke. "You all are... a very interesting lot." That remark caused Raz's lips to curl up into a smirk again.

"It's okay, you can say it," Raz responded, much to the immense confusion of the regional governor.

"I'm sorry wha-"

"I know that we're all degenerates and scoundrels," Raz answered before the governor could say any more. "And maybe a few other creative words for good measure. It's okay, I've heard them all. So don't feel that you have to withhold them just to be polite. I won't judge." Raz's response actually shook Governor Monet somewhat, as he began to stumble over his words with no real idea of what to say after that. His wife, however, simply began to laugh.

"Such words may describe you perfectly well," Daedalus spoke up rather loudly from where he stood. "But the rest of us still very much try as hard as we can to be upstanding citizens of this region of the empire."

"Whatever words you use to describe yourselves," Katie interjected once Daedalus had finished. "I will say that I found all of your company to be very, very entertaining. It's not often we get to meet people who have such interesting things to say. Especially about their own families."

"What can I say," Raz responded with a shrug. "I speak my mind and I'm not afraid of who might hear it." That answer caused Katie to laugh a little bit more.

"Well do be careful then," she said to Raz. "One day that might get you into trouble."

"Oh, it has," Raz was quick to respond. "I've just gotten better at getting out of-"

"It was our pleasure to be in your company, my lady," Daedalus interrupted as he stepped up next to Raz and bowed his head slightly. "And we hope that the two of you enjoy the rest of your new year."

"Well, at least one of you is a real gentleman," Katie then said as she shifted her attention to Daedalus.

"Given the present company, someone has to be," Daedalus responded with a smile.

"Well, I am afraid we must be off," Governor Monet then spoke up. "Whatever you may think of her, Nicole was right about one thing. We do have places that we'd rather be on a day like today. So I'm afraid we must bid you adieu as well. Oh, and Daedalus."

"Yes," Daedalus responded with a raised eyebrow.

"I may have some work for you," Governor Monet said with a knowing grin. "Your address is in…"

"Canaan," Daedalus answered before he could. "It's a small town between here and Taurus. Shouldn't be too difficult to find on a map."

"I'll be sure to find it then," Governor Monet responded as he shook Daedalus' hand. "You'll hear from me soon."

"I look forward to it," Daedalus responded in turn.

"To the rest of you," Governor Monet then addressed the group. "I hope you all enjoy your new year and I do hope that our paths cross again."

"Thanks, me too," Raz responded first.

"Th… thank you for having us," Tara spoke up once she had found the will to speak again.

"Thank you," was all Seth could say to them. Once all of them had spoken Princess Filia waited a moment before addressing them herself.

"We would like to wish you the best of years as well," Filia began with a bow of her head. "Your generosity and hospitality will be spoken of highly in the courts in Sol."

"We'll speak highly of you here in Dis as well," Katie then said to Filia before she and Governor Monet turned and took their leave. With them gone, all that was left was them and the two royal guards that had been assigned to Princess Filia.

"So…" Seth eventually spoke up. "What do we do now?"

"Well…" Filia began. "The way I see it, I still owe you guys for yesterday so… I know it seems like we just ate, but allow me to treat you to dinner."

"And where exactly do you plan on taking us?" Raz interjected. "I wasn't aware that you knew of any good places to eat in this city. Especially since you were so eager to have us show you around yesterday." Filia's initial response to that was to mimic Raz's smirk before answering him.

"My whole life doesn't revolve around you and mom you know," Filia answered confidently. "There's this nice little place close to where we're staying that serves amazing roasts. A bit fancy, but I swear to Solaris everything there actually is really good."

"It's not expensive is it?" Raz was quick to ask as he dropped his smile.

"A little," Filia answered. "But we're on the crown's dime so you don't have to worry about that. Hell, order everything if you want to. Order the most expensive bottle of wine they have. Order every drink that has alcohol in it." She then paused for a second and leaned in closer to Raz's face to whisper. "And if it irks my mom then what reason is there not to." Upon hearing that the smirk returned to Raz's face. Seeing them like this, it was clear to Seth just how closely related they were, as aside from the multitude of differences between them their smirks were nearly identical.

"Well since you're so confident then, you lead the way, my lady," Raz said to her, making sure to place obvious emphasis on the last two words in an attempt at sarcasm. No one other than Filia found it particularly funny, however, as she had to keep herself from laughing too loudly.

"Well, onwards then!" Filia then declared as she took a few steps forward and began to lead them in the opposite direction of where her mother and Governor Monet had gone. "Don't fall too far behind now, you hear!" Raz let out a quiet laugh as he quickly caught up with her. The two royal guards flanking both of their sides.

Just around the corner of one of the buildings near the theater, a dark skinned man in a mustard yellow coat kept his eyes fixed on the entourage that Princess Filia Solara of the royal Solaran family had with her, his attention focused squarely on one of them in particular.

'*So that's that Seth guy?*' Arthur thought to himself as he took in Seth's lithe, yet strangely intimidating looking form. '*Doesn't look like much to me, though if that geezer wasn't bullshitting me then that's probably part of his cover. His hair looks close enough I'll give him that. Can't see the eyes though. Need to get closer for that.*' As he ran through those thoughts he watched as the assorted group, along with the two royal guards, began to walk away from the theater at her declaration of "Onwards then!" Before following them Arthur took a moment to check through his pockets before pulling out a small glass vial. As he looked at the vial in his hand he contemplated the words that his strange employer had said to him when he had given it to him.

The sack of coins felt more than a little hefty in Arthur's hand as Isaac handed it to him. Already he felt proud of himself for scoring such a high profile job. Assuming he pulled it off of course, which he had no doubt that he would, then the path to a very bright and prosperous future lay ahead of him. Especially when he considered that he would no longer have to prove that he was the best because everyone would know it. That thought alone was enough to get him motivated.

"Thank you for your patronage, kind sir," Arthur said to Isaac as he pocketed the sack full of coins. "By sunup tomorrow they'll be one less monster in the world for you to worry about."

"Before you go," Isaac spoke up before Arthur could leave, after which he then reached into his pocket again and produced a small glass vial, which he then handed to Arthur. "A little something to make your task that much easier. Consider it a gift from me to you." Arthur took it without a second thought before proceeding to examine it. The vial itself was small, not much larger than one of his fingers, and inside was a thick, viscous liquid that looked to be yellow in color, though the shade of yellow that it was was so dark that Arthur doubted he knew the proper name for its color. It actually reminded him of urine somewhat, if said urine came from a man who had been eating extremely unhealthily. Seeing it, Arthur couldn't help but laugh.

"What is this, poison?" Arthur asked without thinking.

"Yes, actually," Isaac responded with a completely straight face. Arthur didn't even need to look at his face after he had said that to know that he was deadly serious, and the implications of that caused the smug grin he was wearing on his face to instantly drop. "I would advise against breaking that. It is quite potent."

"What is this then?" Arthur asked with obvious suspicion, again without even thinking about it. "Grey Rot?"

"Would you believe me if I told you that it was?" Isaac was quick to answer, again with a completely straight face. Considering that he had already taken the money, Arthur knew better than to ask any more questions. Especially from someone like Isaac. So with that in mind he reluctantly pocketed the bottle of poison. "Do be careful with it. Even an amount as small as the head of a pin is fatal if it enters the bloodstream. One prick from a blade coated with that and human or monster, it will not be waking up again." Then, having said that, Isaac turned and began to walk out of the alley before Arthur could say anything else to him. "Good luck, mister Booth. I look forward to hearing of your success."

"Hey, wai-" Before Arthur could even finish speaking that word, with a sudden flash of orange light, Isaac was gone. Now alone in the alleyway behind the guild hall, Arthur could only stand and contemplate exactly what he had gotten himself into.

Seeing Princess Filia and her entourage begin to walk away, Arthur quickly slipped the vial of poison back into one of his more secure pockets before leaving the corner of the building to follow them. He made sure to maintain enough distance between them so that they would not notice him, but he made no effort to hide himself to avoid looking too conspicuous.

'If I'm gonna do this,' Arthur continued with his thoughts. 'Then I need to wait for a moment when he's alone. Fucking Solaris this would be so much easier if Princess Filia and those two Solaris damned guards weren't with them.' Despite the presence of the guards, however, Arthur continued to tail them from a safe distance.

Fortunately for him, however, they all appeared to be so engrossed in the conversations they were having with each other that none of them bothered to look behind them. Along with that, many passersby were more focused on the fact that they were seeing the princess in public than the man in the mustard yellow coat following them. All in all not a single person gave so much of a passing glance at Arthur, or so he believed.

'*You know, this might be easier than I thought,*' Arthur couldn't help but think to himself as he watched them. '*I still need to wait for a moment when he's alone though.*'

"Arthur!" A joyous sounding voice suddenly called out from seemingly nowhere and snapped Arthur out of his thoughts. Momentarily startled, Arthur quickly looked to his left only to be instantly taken aback as a tall, lithe, blonde man wearing a greenish-blue shirt, tan slacks, and a bronze bracelet around his wrist similar to the gold one that he wore ran up and enveloped him in a great big hug. "Where ya been? I haven't seen ya since last night." Arthur's momentary confusion as to what was happening passed quickly as he soon realized exactly what was going on and who had hugged him, and that realization caused a brilliant, yet devious new idea to pop into his head as he let out a smile and returned the embrace.

"You seem a bit more affectionate than usual," Arthur said as he hugged the man back. Thankfully while he was doing this he could still see the group he was following, and in particular Seth out of the corner of his eye. "Did you miss me that much or did you get an early start celebrating the new year?"

"Mayyyybe a little bit of both," the man responded. The faint smell of alcohol on his breath told Arthur that he indeed had begun celebrating early. "I mean, I at least expected you to stick around for breakfast." As he spoke the man pulled away from the hug and put on a fake pouting face that Arthur couldn't help but find incredibly adorable. It reminded him of a puppy.

"Oh, trust me Ben," Arthur began. "I wanted to, I really did, but it's kind of hard when you disappear so early in the morning without a word." At those words the man, Ben, put on an overly dramatic, wide eyed face and let out an obviously fake gasp. As quickly as he had done that, however, he dropped it and put on a more genuine looking smile instead.

"Fine, you got me there," Ben responded. "But I still think you owe me for doing the same to me yesterday."

"Hey," Arthur responded with his own obvious sarcasm. "It's not my fault that my meeting with the big three was at ten and you normally sleep until eleven." After saying that Arthur subtly glanced back over towards his target, only to see them getting farther and farther away from him. Thankfully he could still see them now, though he could tell if he didn't catch up with them soon that wouldn't last long. "But since you feel that I owe you, why don't you join me. I'll admit I don't know what I could possibly do to repay you, but I'm sure we'll come across something."

Instead of answering with words Ben gleefully huddled up closer to Arthur and almost began to snuggle into his chest, but stopped himself once he realized that they were still in public. Arthur, seeing that, wrapped his arm around Ben as the two of them then began to walk through the streets of the Suntop District, though subtly in the direction of Princess Filia and Seth.

The entire time Arthur kept his eyes on his target like a starving falcon as he and Ben kept walking. Never once did Arthur's target group, and Seth in particular, leave his sight. Even when he had to make eye contact with Ben in order to talk to him, Arthur always kept them in his peripheral vision at least so that he could keep at least one eye on them at all times. This did mean that a few times whenever he had to speak to Ben he either needed to suddenly pull him closer so that he didn't have to turn his head completely or in one instance actually physically turn him around so that he could keep both him and Seth in his field of vision at once. Thankfully Ben never questioned any of these sudden, spontaneous physical acts. In fact, he seemed to think that they were all Arthur's way of showing affection and as such went along with them whenever Arthur had to move him. This served Arthur quite well for a number of reasons, but mainly it served as a way to distract Ben from what he was really doing here. It also served to distract Ben from the fact that Arthur had absolutely no idea where they were going.

"You know," Ben eventually spoke up. "I don't think ya ever answered my first question. Where've ya been? I thought for certain I'd see ya at the guild hall with everyone else, but ya weren't there."

"Oh I had to step out for a bit," Arthur quickly answered. "Something came up, but it's nothing you need to worry about. So let's just focus on the now since the now is what's important."

"Alright, if you say so," Ben responded, apparently convinced. "But that does make sense. When I went there to find ya that skinny guy, I think his name was

Chris, said that he saw ya leave, but that was it. He also said that he didn't know if ya came back in or not, but before I could ask him any more he started rambling about this one monster he fought that he said looked like a rat but was the size of a house."

"Was he drunk?" Arthur then immediately asked.

"Yes," Ben was equally quick to answer. "Yes he was, actually, but he was also the only one there that said he saw ya. Everyone else was either busy doing something else, too drunk to pay any attention to me, or just straight up ignored me because I'm new." Arthur couldn't help but laugh at what he was hearing.

"Don't take anything that guy says at face value," Arthur advised. "There are actual bags of manure that are full of less shit than him. Hell, I wouldn't be surprised if he ever tried to convince someone that Chaos had somehow come back and that he had single handedly killed it by stabbing it in one of its gigantic eyes. Of course no one was there to witness this miraculous act and anyone who was probably died valiantly in battle so that one of them, aka him, could secure victory. So naturally we'd all have to take his word for it." That response caused Ben to let out several loud giggles despite his best attempts to stop himself from doing so.

"Yeah…" Ben eventually said once he had calmed himself down enough. "I do know his reputation."

"As for everyone else, fuck em," Arthur then continued. "Their heads are all too far up their own asses for any of 'em to give you a chance. They'll all see though. Give 'em time and a few monster heads and they'll be talking to you about how badass you are before long. Then when they start buying you drinks and wanting to be your friend you can say 'Sorry, but I don't have time for you cause Arthur's waiting for me.' Let 'em see how they like it." As soon as he had finished speaking Arthur subtly diverted his attention back to Filia and Seth. It was then that he saw the group walk into a building that had a rich, meaty aroma coming from it. Just smelling it made Arthur a little hungry, and that gave him an idea.

"Say, Ben," Arthur then began as he slowly turned to properly face his lover, which he could now do since he no longer needed to keep Seth in his line of sight. "I still owe you for skipping out on breakfast, right? You hungry?"

"Well, that depends," Ben responded as he put on a rather sly looking smile and moved as close as he could to Arthur's face without actually touching it. "What for?" Arthur could only barely keep himself from making a scene by bursting out laughing from that remark.

"Just regular food, sorry to disappoint you," Arthur answered. Before Ben had the chance to put on the pouty face that he knew he would, however, Arthur suddenly closed the remaining distance between them and rubbed his forehead against Ben's. "Though that's no reason to say that we can't have both. I still owe you after all." Arthur did not need to see Ben's face to know that he was smiling at that. In fact, he could practically feel his anticipation through his forehead. "So what do you say? Regular food now, something else later."

"Lead the way," Ben answered in the smoothest, most inviting of voices that he could muster. Arthur did not need to be asked twice as he led Ben to the restaurant where Filia, Seth and the rest of their group had entered. When Ben saw it, however, his eyes went wide and he momentarily lost his breath.

"A restaurant in this district?" he asked, sounding apprehensive. "Isn't that a little pricey?"

"What can I say," Arthur was quick to respond. "It's a brand new year, I got quite a bit of extra coinage from my most recent job, and I still owe you. So I feel like splurging a little bit. Besides…" Arthur then paused for a moment and poked Ben on the nose. "If it's for you it's worth it."

"Weeelllll if you insist."

"I do," Arthur responded as he suddenly pulled Ben in closer to him for a great big hug, which Ben was all too eager to reciprocate. "Now come on, let's go enjoy ourselves." With all of that said Arthur very quickly pulled Ben into the restaurant with him. To Ben, Arthur knew that he must have figured that this was just a way of showing affection, and it was okay to let him think that. In actuality, however, Arthur knew that just because he knew where his target was didn't mean that he could not potentially lose him. So he wanted to move as quickly as he could.

So without even stopping to see what the name of the restaurant was or what it specialized in, the two of them entered. Once they were inside, however, it became clear that Ben's initial assessment of this place being more than a little expensive was more than certainly correct. Just from the entrance Arthur could see that all of the walls were lined with marble and a series of intricately designed marble pillars ran the length of the restaurant, effectively separating one side from the other and giving the impression that this place was more of a temple than a restaurant. On the ceiling hung an immaculate glass chandelier which reflected the light from a series of candles settled into it so beautifully that it gave the appearance that there were stars on the ceiling even though it was bright on the inside. Lastly, on the opposite side of the restaurant from where the two of them stood was a stage where a quartet of violinists were playing a beautiful, yet calming symphonic tune. It was upon seeing all of this that Arthur instantly became glad that Isaac had paid him in advance, and in gold no less.

It was enough that Arthur became almost certain that he could hear his coin purse crying just from the appearance of this place. Part of him hoped that he could somehow convince Isaac to reimburse him for this as a business expense, though knowing what he did of those noble types from Sol, that did not seem likely to happen at all.

"Good evening gentlemen," the maître d', a man in a perfectly contrasting black and white suit with hair slicked back with so much oil that it practically shone in the light from the chandelier, said to them as they approached the front desk. For a moment Arthur was shocked to see him there, as his attention was so focused on what this place looked like that he hadn't seen him when he walked in. "Do you have a reservation?"

'*Fuck!* Arthur couldn't help but mentally scream at himself. This was a roadblock that he honestly did not see coming when he took this job. Though given who his target's apartment company was he couldn't help but feel like a little bit of an idiot for not thinking of this. "Well… Unfortunately, no," Arthur began as he stepped away from Ben and walked closer to the desk that the maître d' stood at, whereupon he propped his elbow on it to give him support as he put on his best and most convincing smile. "This was more of a spur of the moment thing if I am being perfectly honest. Since it's the new year my partner and I wanted to do something a bit more to celebrate than just get drunk." As he finished speaking he very subtly reached into his coin purse and withdrew three gold coins, which he then placed on the front desk in such a way that the maître d' could see them, but not Ben. "I'm sure you understand."

A few long, awkward seconds of silence passed as the maître d' stared back at Arthur with an unblinking, unchanging face without saying a word. After those seconds had passed the maître d' shifted his attention over to Ben, who had remained where he was, but clearly looked more confused than anything. Seeing that, he diverted his attention back to Arthur, who kept up his smile. Without saying anything or breaking eye contact the maître d' then silently placed a gloved hand on the gold coins and slipped them into his pocket.

"Luckily for you, sir," the maître d' said to Arthur as he pulled out two pieces of parchment from somewhere behind the desk. "We still have a few open tables. Follow me, please."

'*Oh thank Solaris!* Arthur mentally screamed to himself as he let out a breath that he didn't even realize he had been holding in. '*I wasn't sure at all if that would work!* While those thoughts raced through his head, outwardly he did his best to keep the act going as he kept up his pleasant and confident smile before holding out his arm in anticipation for Ben to grab it, which he did. The maître d' did not appear to notice any of this as he kept walking forward without looking back. It was enough that Arthur and Ben needed to run a few steps in order to catch up with him.

"Wow," Ben let out as he looked around the restaurant, then at Arthur. "How did you pull that off?"

'*Good question, I wish I knew!* Arthur mentally screamed at himself as he began to laugh in lieu of an answer. Thankfully Ben chose not to press the issue further as he laughed along with him.

Eventually the maître d' led them to their table. Given the layout of this restaurant it wasn't the most ideal spot for Arthur's purposes, but then again, he did have to bribe the maître d' to even let them in. So he supposed he had to take what he could get. A quick glance around the whole restaurant, however, showed him that he had a direct line of sight to where Princess Filia was sitting, as she and her entourage had taken up one of the more premium, corner tables. Despite that they were incredibly easy to spot, as the two royal guards in their silver armor stood out like blood on grass amidst this place's more common patrons and staff. More importantly, however, he had an unobstructed view of his target, who had taken a seat directly next to Filia. The sight of that made him somewhat nervous, but he didn't change any of the steps that he knew he needed to take in order to get this done.

"Here you are, gentlemen," the maître d' said to the two of them as he placed the two parchments on the table for them. "A waitress will be here soon with complimentary bread and water. We hope that you have a lovely evening." Then, having said that, the maître d' turned on his heel and began to walk in the opposite direction from whence they had come.

With all of that said and done Arthur pulled out one of the chairs and, like the gentleman he imagined himself to be, motioned for Ben to sit in it. Ben could only let out an eager smile as he took his seat. That done, Arthur took the seat across from him. What he didn't tell Ben, however, was that the placement of their seats was intentional. From where he sat Arthur could not only keep eye contact with his lover when he needed to, but just past Ben's head he had an unobstructed view of Seth. From what he could see now, he sat in between the princess and another, brown haired woman who was definitely a commoner, as she looked more out of place here than any of the others did. Currently Seth kept looking between the two of them and showing them his menu as if he had no idea what anything on it was. He had absolutely no idea who the other two gentlemen at the table were, but they didn't matter to him.

Seeing as how he needed to play the waiting game now, Arthur took a moment to look over the menu that the maître d' had given him. To his great surprise this place specialized in exotic meats, or at the very least meats that could not normally be acquired in this region. This didn't bother him at all, but this fact made him increasingly anxious to look over the prices. Thankfully everything on the menu fell within his price range, but only because of the advanced payment he had received from Isaac. Seeing that, he definitely made a mental note to ask Isaac if he could write this off as a business expense the next time he saw him.

"So, um…" Ben suddenly spoke up. "I don't think I ever got a chance to ask you this yesterday due to both of us being a little…"

"Busy," Arthur finished for him since it was obvious to him that Ben was struggling to come up with the correct word to finish that sentence with.

"Yeah, that," Ben continued. "How… did your meeting with the big three go?"

"Meh, it wasn't much," Arthur responded with a shrug. "All it was was pretty much them going 'Hey, you did a really good job this year. Here's the number of reported monsters you killed, here's the list of all of the good things people are saying about you, and here's a list of all the ways you could do better even if it isn't much.' Honestly, it was more or less what I expected after reaching the rank of gold. I mean, it's not like they can promote me any higher. Unless of course one of them suddenly drops dead and they haven't already picked someone out to replace them." That last remark caused Ben to let out another laugh.

"I can easily imagine Ingrid dying from having an aneurysm because she yelled too much," he said once his laughter had died down.

"How about you?" Arthur then asked, genuinely interested. "You've had your meeting too, right? I honestly forgot. Sorry."

"Oh, it's alright. I know we've both been busy," Ben replied. "And no, not yet. Mine is in two days. Though I don't expect much. If I'm being honest I don't think I have enough experience yet to be brought up to silver. I mean, I know I've killed my fair share of monsters, but I also know that there are other bronze ranks in the guild who have killed more than I have. So I'm not hoping for much." Before Arthur could respond to what he felt was an absolutely absurd way of thinking, a young woman wearing an outfit similar to the maître d' suddenly arrived at their table with a basket full of slices of bread and a pitcher of water, which she then used to fill the two empty glasses that had already been placed on the table.

"Good evening, gentlemen," she said as she filled their glasses. "Could I interest you in anything to drink to start with or have you already decided what it is you want?"

"Actually, yes," Arthur quickly answered before Ben could say anything. "What's the freshest bottle of wine you have right now?"

"Well, sir..." the waitress began, but then stopped herself as she clearly needed to take a second to think of an answer to that question, but tried to hide it on her face. "We do have-"

"Actually, I don't really care what it is," Arthur interrupted before she could finish. "Just bring it to us. Preferably sooner rather than later. Chop chop." Arthur emphasized his point by clapping twice to his last two words. Doing her best to stay professional, the waitress simply bowed her head.

"As you wish, sir," she said to him before turning around and walking to another part of the restaurant.

"Arthur..." Ben let out, his eyes wide and mouth agape at the action his lover had just taken. "You didn't have to do anything like that. What if it's really expensive."

"I didn't," Arthur responded as he set down his menu and stared directly into his lover's eyes as he put on the most charming smile that he physically could. "But I wanted to." Ben tried to open his mouth to speak again, but Arthur held up a hand and cut him off. "Let's just say I'm feeling very generous. Don't ask why, don't worry about it, and don't complain. Just let it be." As Arthur spoke he took a quick glance past Ben to see what Seth was up to, only to see the entire table erupt in laughter while he simply sat still with an even more confused look on his face than before, as if he didn't understand whatever joke had been told at all.

"W... Wow," Ben eventually spoke up once he found his breath again. "This... The fancy restaurant, the free bread and water, and now the wine. Honestly, if it wasn't for the fact that all of this was clearly improvised, or the fact that we've been together for what? Three... four months now, I'd almost think you were planning on proposing to me." After he finished speaking Ben took a sip of water to calm his nerves. Across from him, however, hearing what his lover had just said made Arthur's heart momentarily skip a beat, but thankfully he managed to keep his composure.

"Sorry," he said with a laugh. "I may be generous, but I'm not that generous." As he finished speaking he too felt the need to take a sip from his water. "Tell you what. Let's do this again next year. See where it goes. You never know."

"Well now," Ben said as he leaned in closer to Arthur. "Now that you said it, I might just have to hold you to it."

All things considered, there were far worse positions for Arthur to be in. If there was one thing he had learned, and had been stressed to him more than anything in his time as a monster hunter, it was patience. Sometimes monsters didn't always appear where he hoped they would. Sometimes he had to go searching for them. There was even one instance where he had injured a monster in battle and it decided to be smart and run away. It took him almost a full two days to track it down and finish it off. In all of those instances, however, he had never once had to sit still and wait for something very specific to happen, and now that he had to it was making him want to tear the flesh off of his own head.

Enough time had passed that he and Ben had not only ordered, but eaten roughly half of their respective dinners. As delicious as it was, however, it wasn't enough to distract Arthur from the fact that Seth had not moved a single centimeter away from the group he was with since he had come in. All throughout dinner Arthur kept periodically looking over to his table to see what he was doing, and to his frustration nothing much had happened beyond them getting their own meals, which pissed off Arthur slightly as they were able to get this incredibly large spread of all different kinds of meats as well as all different kinds of sides. Though he supposed the only reason that they could afford any of that was because they were on the crown's dime and not their own. It was at times like these that he truly envied the nobility of this country.

There was one thing that caught his attention, however, and that was that Filia appeared to move closer and closer to Seth as the night had gone on to the point that they were practically touching. Since it was slow going it wasn't noticeable at first, but once the realization hit him that Filia was sitting much closer to Seth than she had when they first arrived here made Arthur worry that his opportunity would never come. At least not while they were here, which in effect meant that he may have come in and spent all of this money here for no reason.

Salvation came, however, when he saw Seth stand up from his seat, whereupon he said something to the rest of his group before Princess Filia answered by pointing somewhere towards the back of the restaurant. Arthur couldn't exactly see where that led to from where he was sitting, but Seth began to walk in that direction as soon as he had gotten his answer. Ever cautious, Arthur waited a few more seconds to chew and swallow the food that was still in his mouth before standing up himself.

"Sorry, beautiful," Arthur said to Ben as he got to his feet. "But I'm afraid I must excuse myself for a moment."

"Why, where are you going?" Ben immediately asked as soon as Arthur had finished speaking. In response to that Arthur began to laugh.

"There are some things, beautiful," Arthur began. "That no matter how strong or rich a man might become, he cannot wait for." At first Ben became worried, but then before he could say anything to respond a look of realization came across his face as he realized how needlessly worrisome he had been as he began to laugh again.

"You know, if you really just needed to take a piss you could have said so," Ben eventually responded once he had calmed down.

"It's funnier to see your reaction," Arthur responded in turn with a wink before he spun on his heel and began to walk in the same direction that Seth had. Thankfully that little exchange had allowed enough time to pass where he didn't appear to be immediately suspicious in following him. At least that was what Arthur had hoped. Seth didn't stay in his view for very long, however, as he reached a point in the back of the restaurant where he suddenly turned a corner and walked into a hallway that seemed deliberately placed so as not to draw attention. When Arthur turned the corner, however, Seth was nowhere to be seen at all.

There was little need for Arthur to worry, however, as the corridor he now found himself in did not appear to be very long, a little over three meters maybe, and all there was to see in it were two identical looking doors on opposite sides of the corridor. The doors themselves did not appear to be too special, but engraved in very fancy letters on one of them was the word "Men" and on the other in equally fancy lettering was the word "Women". Seeing that, Arthur couldn't help but smirk to himself a little bit, if only because he had guessed correctly where Seth was going. So without any hesitation he entered the men's lavatory.

To Arthur's slight surprise the door to the men's lavatory didn't make a sound when he opened it. The possibility that the hinges had recently been oiled crossed Arthur's mind, though he didn't dwell on that beyond that single thought. If anything, that fact only helped serve his purpose even more.

Unlike the rest of the restaurant, the men's lavatory didn't boast anything fancy. There were sparse, if any decorations of any kind, with a few simple wash basins lining the wall to the left while a long, stone urinal wall lined the first half of the right wall while the second half boasted four identical stalls. Immediately upon entering Arthur spotted his target at the urinal wall, and a quick glance around the lavatory told him that no one else was in here. What's more, the so-called monster named Seth was apparently so focused on himself that he didn't even notice Arthur enter. Arthur couldn't help but silently thank whomever recently oiled the door's hinges for that minor blessing. With all of this in mind, Arthur remained casual as he strolled past Seth into one of the stalls at the back.

Once inside Arthur closed the stall door, but not completely. He knew that if what he was going to do had any chance of succeeding, then that door needed to open either quickly or quietly. Preferably the latter. Regardless, once he was seemingly alone he let out a breath that he hadn't realized he had been holding in and tried to force himself to relax.

'*Gotta make this quick,* Arthur thought to himself as he quickly bent down and removed one of his hidden knives from the well concealed sheath in his left boot. That done, he placed the knife in his mouth. He would need both hands for what he needed to do next. With that in mind he then reached into one of the pockets in his coat and pulled out a single leather glove, which he then proceeded to put on his left hand. He then reached into a different pocket in his coat and pulled out a handkerchief and the small vial of poison that Isaac had given him. Quickly, but carefully, Arthur then proceeded to, while holding the handkerchief in his gloved hand, remove the cap from the bottle and pour some, but not all of its contents into the handkerchief. That done he quickly capped and pocketed the vial before removing the knife from his mouth, upon which he proceeded to wipe up and down the blade with the handkerchief to apply the poison. Upon finishing Arthur took a moment to look at the blade in his hand. Just holding it made him nervous, as he knew that simply touching it now would likely be lethal, and yet his employer had expected him to use it.

Arthur's attention was brought back to the moment by the sound of running water from one of the wash basins. Shifting his brain back into work mode, he quickly tossed the handkerchief into the toilet behind him and gave it a quick flush in order to give the illusion that nothing was out of the ordinary. That done, he then slowly opened the stall door and peeked out to see Seth standing at one of the wash basins scrubbing his hands clean. Though he knew that he wouldn't remain there for long.

'*Okay, this should be simple enough,* Arthur thought to himself as he sized up his target. '*Stab him, drag him into one of the stalls, drop the murder weapon into the toilet, get back to Ben, finish our meal and our evening, pay, leave, and hopefully that'll be before anyone notices how long he's been gone.* Steeling himself, Arthur quietly left the stall and, with footsteps as quiet as a mouse, snuck up behind the man, no, monster that was his target.

Once he was directly behind him Arthur moved as quick as lightning as his free hand went over Seth's mouth and the other plunged the poisoned knife into Seth's side just under his ribs. The instant he did that, however, he immediately felt that something was wrong. He had stabbed enough monsters over the course of his lifetime for him to instinctively know when his blade had connected with his foe, and this time was no different. He knew that his blade had made contact with his target, he knew that it had penetrated his flesh, if only just barely, but that was where it ended. As he tried to plunge the rest of his knife into Seth's side, he suddenly found the arm that held it unable to move. Instinctively he tried to pull his arm back, but it refused to budge then too.

Immediately Arthur looked down to see what the problem was, only to see that someone else's hand had grabbed him by his wrist. Following the length of the arm attached to the hand, Arthur soon made eye contact with its owner, a young man who appeared to be roughly the same age as Seth with shoulder length brown hair and bright, piercing green eyes. A knowing smirk was spread across this man's face as he held eye contact with Arthur.

"Heya," was all this man said to him.

Before Seth even had a chance to break free from his unknown assailant's grasp, Raz was already upon him as he punched the man in the face before following up with a backhanded strike across the other side of his face. Before the man had any chance to recover a loud cracking noise echoed throughout the men's lavatory as Raz hit him with one more solid punch to his jaw. The impact of that strike was enough to knock the man free of Raz's grasp and off of his feet as he stumbled a few meters backwards before hitting the wall of the stalls behind him.

The man writhed in pain for a few short seconds before he began to prop himself onto his elbows. Acting automatically, Seth spun around and opened his hand to throw lighting at him the second he tried to stand up. The instant he made the motions to do so, however, he suddenly felt all the motion of his body cease as he felt a single, all encompassing pulse run throughout his whole body. It felt to him almost like a heartbeat, except much stronger, so much so that he physically felt pain when it happened. In that moment of hesitation, with a flash of green light Raz suddenly appeared directly in front of the strange man and kicked him in the head as he tried to stand. With that last hit the man's body went limp as slumped back against the stall wall, his knife falling from his grasp as his hand hit the floor.

Without thinking Seth opened his mouth to ask who the hell this man was and what the hell had happened, but when he did, instead of words all that came out of his mouth was the sound of coughing. That sound instantly drew the attention of Raz, who turned his eyes to see Seth as he instinctively brought his hand up to cover his mouth like Tara had taught him. When Seth pulled his hand away, however, his eyes went wide as he saw blood in his palm. Now more worried than confused, Seth looked up to Raz only to see him stare back at him with his eyes wider than the dinner plates they had been eating off of earlier, as if he didn't even need to see the blood to know what had happened.

Unconsciously in that moment Seth took a single step towards Raz, but the instant he did the pulse from before returned, only much stronger than last time. Before Seth even had time to properly form a thought about what was happening to him his legs suddenly became limp, as if they no longer had the strength to support his body and as a result he fell forward onto the lavatory floor mid step. He was able to catch himself before his face hit the solid stone floor of the lavatory, but all concerns about his face were mitigated as he was suddenly hit with another, much more intense coughing fit. Instinctively he brought up both of his hands to cover his mouth as he coughed more and more. When his coughing fit ended a sudden surge of something liquid ejected from his mouth and seeped through his fingers onto the floor. When Seth pulled his hands away from his mouth he saw that they were absolutely covered in a mixture of blood and everything he had just eaten. What was worse, for an instant his vision went blurry as he saw his two bloody hands merge into one before then splitting into four.

"Oh shit, oh fuck, oh fucking shit," Raz let out as he took a few tentative steps away from Seth. Before Seth could ask him why he would do that now, another stream of blood violently erupted from his mouth as another coughing fit began. The instant that happened Seth felt his whole body suddenly become as weak as his legs as he became unable to support his own weight and fell onto the lavatory floor in a pool of his own blood and vomit. "I'm gonna get you help, okay Seth! Just don't die on me!" The instant that last word left Raz's mouth, with another flash of green light he was gone, leaving Seth alone in the lavatory with his unknown assailant.

Unable to do anything except lay there on the lavatory floor as he began to cough up more blood and vomit, Seth began to slowly look towards the man who had done this to him. Even that simple act, however, was difficult for him as his vision began to go in and out with each coughing fit, and even then his vision was becoming incredibly blurry as he kept seeing two of everything. Despite all of that, however, he was able to get a good enough look at the visage of the man who had attacked him in his few moments of clarity. Even as he was he couldn't help but wonder why this strange, dark skinned man wearing an obnoxiously yellow coat would want to hurt him like this. He had never seen him before and he had no idea at all who he was, so it made no sense to him in the slightest why this man would do something like this to him. It wasn't until his eyes fell upon the man's right wrist in one of his few remaining moments of clarity that he found his answer.

Adorning the dark skinned man's right wrist was a golden bracelet with a very familiar looking symbol on it. The symbol was of a shield with an hourglass on the front of it and two crossed swords behind it. It was a symbol that Seth was very, very familiar with, as he had seen it many times before. It was the symbol of Vivian's monster hunting guild. Before Seth could even think of contemplating the implications of what that may have meant, with another coughing fit everything in front of him became black as his vision left him.

Chapter 21

The music that had begun to play in the restaurant now was something that, to most, would evoke sensations of relaxation and contentment. To Princess Filia Solara of the Solaran royal family, however, the elegant and relaxing sounds coming from the instruments may as well have been white noise. It wasn't just the music though, indeed this whole place reminded her of her home city of Sol. She knew that it wasn't entirely the restaurant's fault, as lots of businesses in every city tried their damndest to recreate the feeling of being in Sol, usually at the expense of whatever made said business great in the first place. After all, Sol was such a happening place and everybody wanted to experience it, at least according to her mother. While the idea of that made Filia wish that perhaps her own city should take lessons from the businesses that did things like that, she did have to admit that there were several things from Sol that she was glad businesses like these had copied. Especially things like higher quality standards for food and coffee that was actually tasty.

There were only two things that this restaurant did, however, that did set it apart from other places like it for her. The first was that while this place did attempt to emulate the atmosphere and style that existed in Sol, the food that it served was actually prepared using local methods and ingredients, which resulted in some rather unique tastes that could not be found in Sol. The second was that she actually had friends here with whom she could enjoy all of this with, something that she did not have at all in Sol. While she knew that her friends weren't actually part of the restaurant, it was enough to make a major difference for her, and that was enough. Even with those differences, however, part of her still wished that something exciting would happen. Something that would either give her something to fondly remember or royally piss her mother off. Both were acceptable in her book.

She got her wish when her cousin, Raz, suddenly appeared at their table with a flash of green light.

"Seth just got stabbed!" Raz blurted out before Filia, Tara, or Daedalus even had any chance to say anything to him. There was a very, very brief moment wherein Filia suddenly felt her stomach drop as the exact meaning of the words Raz had just used hit her brain, and all she wanted to do was scream. As much as she wanted to, however, it was Tara who beat her to that particular punch.

"What!" Tara shouted at the top of her lungs as she stood up from her seat like lightning. "What did you just say!"

"Someone just attacked him while he was in the restroom!" Raz quickly responded. "I managed to knock him out but... Agh I don't have time to explain any of this! Daedalus, take Filia home! Tara, you stay here! I'm going to get the city guard so we-"

"No!" Filia spoke up in a tone that was so vastly different from how she usually spoke as she, also like lightning, stood up from her chair and slammed both of her hands onto the table hard enough to nearly topple over everyone's drinks. Before Raz, or anyone could say even a single word to her much less anything in response, Filia turned her attention to one of her two guards. "You! Run as fast as you can and go get the city guard to arrest this man! You're a member of the crown's royal guard and you actually look like a respectable knight so they're more likely to listen to you than my slubby looking cousin!"

"With all due respect, my lady," the guard in question responded in as calm a voice as he could manage given the situation. "We were specifically ordered to-"

"I only need one of you to protect me!" Filia quickly fired back loud enough for most of the restaurant to hear. "Now get going! That's an order and if you refuse to obey me I swear to Solaris I'll make you regret the day you chose to become one of my family's knights! Is that clear!"

"Yes, your highness," the guard in question quickly responded before running out of the restaurant as quickly as he could manage in his heavy armor.

"You!" Filia then quickly spoke up again before anyone could realize what was happening as she pointed directly at Raz. "Teleport to the city's hospital! Tell them what happened! Get a doctor here as quickly as you can! Teleport one back with you if you have to!" As amazed and somewhat terrified as Raz was of Filia's newfound behavior, he didn't say a single word to her in response as he suddenly disappeared from where he stood with another flash of green light. "You!" Filia then spoke up again as she directed her attention to Daedalus. "Run to the bathroom and see what happened! I want you to be the one who gives the report to the city guard when they get here!" Daedalus did not need to hear another word from her as he immediately leapt up from his chair and ran in the direction of the bathroom as soon as she had finished speaking. With him gone, that only left Tara at the table with her.

With her mind still running at several thousand kilometers per second, Filia instantly turned her attention to Tara once Daedalus had gone. When she did, however, all she saw was the look of complete and abject horror that was on Tara's face as her eyes stared directly back into Filia's for answers. It was only after seeing her that the grim reality of the situation truly began to dawn on Filia as she subconsciously began to breathe much, much faster than she had been before and the commanding presence she had possessed began to fade like mist from boiling water. Here she was, in a restaurant where a friend of hers had just been stabbed, and even after barking out orders to everyone like she had just done, she still had absolutely no idea whether or not they would even amount to anything. For all she knew Seth could already be dead.

The thought of that potentially being true caused all of the blood to rush from Filia's face as she suddenly felt lightheaded, which combined with her quickened breathing caused her to simultaneously feel as if all of the breath in her body had left her. That, further combined with the crushing weight of reality made her feel as if her legs and feet could no longer support her weight as she began to sway. Eventually, it was difficult for her to tell how quickly it had happened, it all became too much for her as she began to fall forward. Before she could hit anything, however, she was suddenly stopped when someone caught her. Looking up she found herself staring back into the horrified, yet desperate face of Tara.

Unsure of what else she could do, Filia reached up and wrapped her arms around Tara in an attempt to hold her close. Tara, as if sensing what Filia was trying to do, pulled her in closer so that it would be easier for her. Within Tara's arms everything around Filia seemed to melt away, but the horror of what had just happened and the anxiety of knowing that there may be nothing she could do remained. At some point during this Filia began to uncontrollably shiver in Tara's arms.

Across the restaurant Daedalus threw open the men's lavatory door as quickly as he could and was subsequently greeted by the sight of both Seth and his unknown assailant on the bathroom floor. Seth lay face down in a growing puddle of his own bloody vomit while his assailant leaned back on one of the bathroom stalls with no visible wounds other than the obvious ones given to him by Raz. With the sight as it was, it would have been obvious to anyone what had happened.

"Jesus Christ," were the only words able to escape Daedalus' lips.

Thanks to the advantage of being able to teleport, Raz had arrived back at the restaurant with a doctor in tow relatively quickly. Their arrival was shortly followed by that of the city guard, which in turn was followed by additional help from the city's hospital. The city guardsmen were quick to take in the scene and listen to the reports given to them by both Daedalus and Raz, who had been the first on the scene. While that was happening the medical team was allowed the space to do their work, which since time was of the essence they did with the utmost urgency. The scene had since drawn the attention of every patron in the restaurant and before too long, in full view of all of them, Seth was carried out on a stretcher by two people wearing the white garb of hospital workers.

Tara felt her heart instantly sink into her stomach when she saw Seth, his face and clothes still covered in his own blood, being carried past her on a stretcher. While at first glance this sight wouldn't have been that much different from the state he was in after the first monster attack in Canaan or when he and Raz were brought back from the desert by Agatha and Daedalus, Tara could tell just from one look that this time was very different. Those times Seth had been physically injured, and while he may have recovered quickly, he always did. This time, however, while he was still covered in his own blood, Tara couldn't see any visible wounds on him. Worse still, from where she stood she couldn't tell if he was breathing or not.

Without thinking Tara tried to take off running towards Seth to see if he was really okay, but before she could get very far she was suddenly stopped by Filia's one remaining guard, who held out his armored arm in front of her. Confused, Tara looked to him to ask why he had stopped her, but before she could she watched as Filia's guard simply shook his head. There were many things that Tara wanted to do at that moment. She wanted to scream, she wanted to push past him and run towards Seth anyway, she wanted to punch him in what little of his face she could see through his helmet for daring to stop her, but when she drew her attention back towards Seth she could only watch in despair as the medical staff carrying him reached the door. As she watched her chance to catch up to him getting away from her before her eyes, she realized something. Even if she had caught up to him, what could she do? Right now he was being carried away by people that she knew were trained medical professionals. People who knew what they were doing and were taking him to a place where he would get the help he needed.

Even if Tara had insisted on going with them, she knew that she would only be getting in their way. Not only that, but even if she made up a good enough excuse to go with him so that she could prevent anyone from discovering the truth about him, even if she wanted to, there likely wouldn't be anything she could do to prevent it. She had dealt with Andrea enough times to learn that the hard way. At this point the best she could hope for was to let the trained medical professionals do their jobs and see Seth in the hospital afterwards. So with all of that in mind, as much as she didn't want to, as much as she wanted to push through Filia's guard anyway, as she watched Seth leave the building she took a step back and stayed where she was. Seeing this, Filia's guard gave her a brief look of acknowledgement, as if he understood, before lowering his arm.

With that out of the way, Seth and the line of emergency medics were soon followed by eight city guardsmen, two of which were carrying an unconscious dark skinned man wearing an obnoxiously yellow coat between them, his hands bound in shackles. Less than a single second after she saw him Tara felt the air around her suddenly become much colder, reminding her of a winter day in Sol. Confused, Tara looked back over towards Filia, whose eyes were deadlocked on the man while a look of barely contained rage was plastered across her face. At first it seemed as if Tara would get no answers from her, but then out of her peripheral vision she noticed one of the untouched glasses of water on their table begin to frost over without explanation. The sound of someone running brought her attention back to the scene in front of her as Tara saw a very young looking, blonde man attempt to rush over towards the city guardsmen carrying the unconscious man in the yellow coat, only to be stopped by two more of them before he could approach.

"Sir, we're going to need you to stay back," Tara heard one of the guardsmen say to him. "This is official business. Please remain calm and do not interfere."

"B... B-But that's my boyfriend!" the blonde man then shouted at the guardsman in turn. At this the guardsman in question narrowed his eyes at the blonde man, though from where Tara stood it appeared to be more out of disgust for their apparent relationship than contempt.

"Well, sir," the guardsman began. "Your boyfriend is apparently guilty of the attempted murder of a friend of the Solaran royal family."

"I..." the blonde man began, but then stopped as the full weight of what had just been said to him hit him like a hammer to the face. "W… What?"

"So unless you want us to arrest you as well," the city guardsman continued as he took advantage of the blonde man's dumbfounded silence. "I would recommend that you back off and let us do our jobs. You understand, fairy?"

"C… Can I at least come with?" the blonde man then tried to say. "If only to know what happened so I-"

"Not until our job is done," the guardsman interrupted him, now looking more pissed than disgusted. "Then maybe, maybe you'll be allowed to visit him. So unless you really want to join him in a cell I'll ask you only one more time. Back off."

As that conversation was happening Tara took the opportunity to get a good, solid look at the man who had attacked Seth, if only so that she could commit his face and form to memory. His face, his clothes, his sense of style, with what little time she knew that she had she examined it all and mentally cataloged all of it. As she did this, however, her eyes caught one small detail about him that made her heart instantly sink further down into her feet. Around his right wrist was a golden bracelet that bore a very, very familiar looking symbol on it. Before she could gleam any more details, however, the conversation between the guardsman and the blonde man finished and the guardsmen had resumed hauling him out of the building. The blonde man meanwhile, remained where he stood, still completely dumbfounded at what had just transpired as the guardsmen left the restaurant with the culprit.

After all of that was over and done with Raz, Daedalus, and both of Filia's royal guardsmen eventually all reconvened at their original table. Though after all that had transpired none of them were willing to sit down.

"Okay, I know what you all are thinking," Raz spoke up first as he placed his hands on the table. "But more than likely we're not gonna see him today. Between how severe his condition seemed, the fact that the hospital staff have to, you know, do their jobs and save his life, how long it's gonna take him to recover, and the time of day, visiting hours are gonna be over long before he's fit to see anyone."

"So what then?" Filia spoke up rather loudly. "You're saying that we have to wait until morning to find out if he's even okay? Screw that noise. I'm a princess, they'll make an exception for me so-"

"No, you're going back to your mom," Raz interrupted before she could say any more. Filia almost did not seem to hear Raz immediately, as it took a few solid seconds for what Raz had said to process through her brain. Once it had, however, her eyes instantaneously went as wide as their dinner plates and she had to fight to keep her mouth from hanging open so that she could at least appear somewhat normal. Even with that, however, her disbelief in what she had just heard was obvious to everyone. For a few silent seconds it appeared as if Filia was too dumbfounded to even respond, but then, to the surprise of everyone, Filia suddenly broke that silence as she burst out laughing.

"You... You must be joking," Filia said, though no one else was laughing. "Why in the actual hell would I go back to her right now? She's probably just going to-"

"Your mother will probably have all of our heads on pikes by the end of the week if we didn't return you to her after an incident like this," Daedalus spoke up without even looking at her. Filia without waiting opened her mouth to respond to that, but Daedalus held up his hand and beat her to the punch. "I know what you're going to say, and believe me, as much as I despise every member of your family, I still think that it's best that you return to her and let us handle things from here."

"But-"

"No buts," Daedalus cut off Filia again, this time with a glare. "Or did your mother simply never teach you to listen to your elders."

"You two are only, like, what! Five years older than me!" Filia shouted at him loud enough for everyone remaining in the restaurant to hear. She would have said more, and she certainly appeared as if she intended to, but her words were cut off again by the sudden feeling of someone grasping her shoulder. Upon turning to see who it was, Filia's eyes beheld the face of her cousin, Raz. Before she could say anything else, much less comprehend how he had managed to sneak up on her like that, Raz suddenly pulled her in as close as he could to him and wrapped his arms around her in a protective, loving embrace.

There were many things that Filia wanted to say, many things that she wanted to do, and there were even more things that she wanted to shout at the top of her lungs so that she could make absolutely sure that everyone heard them. In the arms of her cousin, however, all of that was instantly forgotten. The things she wanted to say, do, and scream, all of them were gone from her mind as she fell into the embrace of her cousin. With those tangible thoughts gone from her mind, however, her raw emotions soon welled in to fill the void. First among those emotions was rage. At first her rage was directed towards the man who had done this to Seth as she imagined all of the different ways she would see him suffer for this, but then that suddenly transitioned into rage against her two guards who were so focused on protecting her that they hadn't bothered to protect any of her friends. That in turn transitioned into rage directed against her mother for not caring as much about the people she was supposed to eventually rule over as much as she claimed she did, and by extension for not doing enough for them. Once that avenue had expired, however, that only left her to feel rage against herself for failing to stop the man who had done this with her own hands, or for not seeing him in the first place, or for being so oblivious to what was happening around her that she didn't even bother to do anything at all.

Eventually her rage gave way to doubt, self pity, sadness, but more than any of that, what Filia felt like an overwhelming sandstorm was fear. Unlike her rage or sadness, which she could direct to a specific person or thing that she could blame for why she was feeling the way she did, Filia's fear stemmed from all of the things that she did not know, and that was what ate away at her insides like a ravenous beast. She did not know if Seth would be alright or not, she did not know if he was even alive right now, she did not know how or why this had happened in the first place, she did not even know why he had been the target of an attempted murder when both she and her cousin were right there in the same building. Eventually all of the things that she did not know began to outweigh the things that she did, and in turn the weight of it all began to break her down. Before long she did not even know why she was doing any of what she was doing or why any of it even mattered, and with that thought the facade of control she had built up around herself began to crumble. With that gone, and without a reason to hold back or even care, Filia did the only thing that she knew she really could do. Without even a second's thought she wrapped her arms around Raz, pulled him in as close to her as she could, and began to cry into his chest.

Raz, for his part, held Filia as close as he could and let her cry for as long as she needed. They had all already made enough of a scene as it was, so the idea of continuing to make a scene began to matter less and less to him the longer this went on. What did not escape his attention, however, was how cold to the touch Filia was when he had hugged her. He ignored it at first because he knew that she needed him at that moment, but once the moment had passed and Filia had begun to cry, he quickly became aware of how cold she literally was. It felt less like he was hugging a person and more like hugging a block of ice that was shaped like a person. Much like a block of ice, however, the longer he had held onto it the more it began to warm up and melt. He knew that it had to be magic, no other explanation made any kind of sense to him, and a quick glance over towards her side of the table confirmed it for him.

Where Filia had previously been sitting when all of this had happened, Raz saw that her recently refilled glass of water now contained not water, but a frozen block of ice perfectly shaped to fit the glass. As if the water itself had completely frozen over in the short time they had been talking about all of this. Not only that, but it wasn't only her glass of water that was like this. Indeed every liquid in every glass on their table was now frozen.

'*That's new,*' Raz couldn't help but think to himself as Filia continued to cry in his arms. '*Last time I saw her she couldn't do any more than levitate small objects or snuff out a light. I wonder what this is. I'll have to ask her about it later after things calm down.*'

"I know, Filly, I know," Raz then said aloud as he held Filia as close to him as he could. "I know what you're feeling right now. Believe me, I do. We're all worried about him, you know that, but there really is nothing else we can do for him right now. We've done everything that we can. The rest is up to him." His words did not calm down Filia immediately, but after a little over a full minute of sobbing Filia's breathing began to slow and while she didn't look any better than she had before, she at least looked more as if she were in control of herself now. Even with that, however, some tears still continued to stream down her face. "Now, let's get you back to your mom."

The instant those words had left his mouth, Filia's fury returned with a vengeance as Raz suddenly felt her body become ice cold again.

"No!" Filia shouted at the top of her lungs as more tears streamed down her face, though with how cold she had suddenly become Raz could see bits of steam begin to rise up from where the warm tears touched her cold skin. "If I go back to her now I'll have to tell her what happened, and if I do that then she probably won't let me go outside for the rest of the festival! That's not fair! It isn't fair! I…" Filia's words began to choke in her mouth as she spoke them, but after a few more tears ran down her cheeks she eventually forced them out. "I want to stay with you…" Raz was silent for a few moments before he closed his eyes and let out a sigh as he ignored the fact that his fingers had begun to feel more like icicles the longer he kept his hands on Filia.

"I see," Raz eventually said as he opened his eyes back up. "So you're that determined to stay by my side no matter what?" Filia only responded with a nod. "Then it's settled." Raz then felt Filia's body begin to warm up again as for a moment, the tears stopped streaming from her face and her lips curled into a smile. As she did that Raz pulled her close into another hug, which she eagerly accepted as he turned to address Tara and Daedalus. "I'm going to go see my aunt." The instant those words hit her ears Filia's eyes shot back open. "I'll see-"

"Are you fucking serious!" Filia shouted before Raz could finish speaking as she violently pushed him away from her. "Don't think you can outsmart me like that! I'll have yo-"

"For fucks sake will you please stop acting like a petulant child for five minutes and do the smart thing!" Daedalus suddenly snapped as he punched their table hard enough to knock over every single drink on it. Fortunately, because all of them were frozen, nothing was really spilled. "We've made enough of a scene already and your incessant whining isn't helping. If you're really worried that much about Seth's well being then the absolute least you can do for him is worry about your own long enough to at least find out if he's alive or not. If that isn't what he would want from you then tell me right now what he would actually want since you know him so well." Filia very much wanted to shout back at Daedalus for what he had just said to her, she wanted to lay into him with words that she knew would cut just as deeply. However, she found herself unable to, and the simple reason for that was because she could not come up with a proper response to what he had said. Out of all of the words that she knew, of all of the phrases, insults, and counters that she knew she could say, with all that had happened in the past hour none of them were coming to mind. That fact made her far angrier than anything else he or Raz could have said to her.

Daedalus and Tara left the restaurant no more than a few minutes after Raz had left with Filia. True to his word, if she was that insistent on staying by his side then it was only fitting that he be the one to escort her back to where she belonged. Not only that, but everyone agreed that it would be better to let them have at least a few minutes together before they were inevitably separated. That, however, left Tara and Daedalus to return on their own.

Initially the two of them walked in silence for most of the way. It seemed appropriate, as tensions were still high and all that needed to be said had been said. Even under normal circumstances the two of them had little reason to speak to each other, so there was little reason for them to do so now as well. After the two of them had left the Suntop District, however, despite his intention to give her the space that he knew she needed, Daedalus couldn't help but notice how Tara was more or less operating without thinking. After watching her for no more than a few seconds it became increasingly obvious to him that Tara was only barely paying attention to where she was going as well, instead seemingly relying on him to tell her where to go as she simply followed his lead. Eventually his concern for her began to overwhelm his desire to let her have her space.

"I... know it is not my place to say," Daedalus began, with Tara only barely paying any attention to him. "But as difficult as it may be for you to believe, I do sometimes worry about people. So in the interest of your well being, how are you holding up, Miss Schäfer?"

"Oh!" Tara let out as if she had only just now become aware of the fact that Daedalus was there. "I... uh..." As hard as it was for her, Tara tried to find the words for an appropriate response to his question. After all, she knew perfectly well that it was a legitimate question to ask after what they had just experienced. That being said, to her right now the endeavor was as futile as trying to track down an extinct creature. One look at Daedalus' face, however, while his seemingly unchanging expression remained, told her that it was okay for her to take her time. Tara knew now that if Daedalus wanted something then he would say so without holding back. So if he really, really wanted an answer from her right now he would get it out of her. With that in mind Tara stopped, took in several deep breaths to clear her head, and then took another few seconds to collect her thoughts before trying again.

"I do not know," she began. "I just... I... I do not know what to do. I mean... I know it is pointless to say that I did not expect this to happen. None of us did. But... I... I could not tell how badly he was hurt. I could not tell if he was breathing. I…" Whatever words Tara was going to say died in her throat as she paused for a few more seconds. Daedalus, all the while, remained silent and let her speak at her own pace. "I… I keep thinking about what happens if he does not make it. I… I… I know I should not think like that but… I… cannot help myself. I do not know what I would do. It would be like when Mister Leroy died, but much, much worse so-"

"I'm sorry," Daedalus interrupted. "But if I may ask, who is Mister Leroy?" That question made Tara stop where she stood as she turned to face Daedalus. She looked at him as if he had asked something he should have already known the answer to, and seemingly was offended that he did not know. However, that only lasted for a single second before she thought better of it and resumed walking.

"I… I am sorry," Tara eventually answered. "I had forgotten that I was already in charge of the library when you and Raz first moved to Canaan. Mister Leroy was the man who ran the library before me. After I had first moved to Canaan I worked as his assistant for six months but…" Tara then paused again, as Daedalus could tell that she was recalling a painful memory. "One day I came into work to find him completely still in his bed. He had passed away in his sleep. If I am being honest though, I was not exactly shocked or surprised when it happened. After all, he was almost eighty."

"And that was when you took over the library?" Daedalus asked.

"I had to," Tara was quick to answer. "I… Well, I was already his assistant, and I did most of the work around the library anyway considering how old he was." Tara, despite all that was happening and what she was saying actually let out a slight chuckle as she recalled those memories, something that did not go unnoticed by Daedalus. "Though I did have to buy a new bed. I uh… Well, I was not exactly comfortable with the idea of sleeping in the same bed that my boss had died in."

"I can imagine most people wouldn't be," Daedalus was quick to respond.

"Then I got Florence to help make the library feel less empty when nobody was around," Tara continued, seemingly oblivious to Daedalus' remark. "Something that I still to this day do not regret doing simply because his presence seems to melt away all the stress I manage to accumulate throughout the day. No matter what-" Tara stopped herself mid sentence when she realized what she was about to say, but then instantly thought better of it. "Well, most of the time anyway. Plus, visitors tend to like him, especially the children. I mean, the only person who does not like him is… well…"

"Seth," Daedalus guessed rather quickly, though in truth it was because he could tell in which direction their conversation seemed to be headed.

"Yes," Tara answered, and then fell silent again immediately after doing so. Just the mere mention of his name was enough to conjure up the image of him being carried out of the restaurant on a stretcher again, and that in turn led her to remember all of the other times that Seth had been injured. It was only after thinking about it now that Tara realized that Seth spent a considerable amount of time in bed due to injuries. That in turn led to some uncomfortably dark thoughts about why this was the case, and whether she herself was somehow to blame for any of it. In the end what Tara realized was that her life had become infinitely more complicated since she had let Seth into her life. "Can… Can I be honest with you Daedalus?"

"Are you implying that you haven't been before?" Daedalus was quick to respond. Despite how harsh he may have sounded when he said it, Tara at this point felt that she had known him long enough to know better. As a result she could not help but give a small smile at that remark.

"Telling you all of this," she began. "Reminiscing about what things used to be like. I… I cannot help but think about how different everything has become in these past few months. Taking in someone like Seth… which somehow led to me getting the chance to both meet and dine with members of the Solaran royal family, and even…" The words that Tara wanted to say seemingly died in her throat as she tried to speak them. However, with enough mental strength and willpower Tara was able to overcome that mental barrier, though the time in which it took her to do so did not go unnoticed by Daedalus. "Even… d… d-dance with one of them. All things that I never would have even dreamed were possible during my old life in Sol. Now though… Taking over a library and getting a cat feels like a completely different lifetime."

"If I may," Daedalus suddenly interjected, which caught Tara off guard somewhat. "Raz mentioned to me after our time in the theater that you had no memory of last night. However, what you said just now implies otherwise. So out of simple curiosity, which is it?" Even before Daedalus had finished speaking, the implications of his words caused Tara's face to instantly turn redder than a strawberry.

"I… I… Well, I…" Tara tried to speak, but the more she tried the more her words seemed to suddenly die in her throat before they could reach her mouth, and this time no amount of mental strength or willpower was enough to overcome it. "Well, you see… The thing is…" It was at that moment, however, when Tara directed her eyes back in front of her so that she could pay better attention to where she was going and not to Daedalus that she saw the plaza where the moon pool was located. "Ithinkweshouldgoourownseparatewaysnow. Ourhotelsareindifferentdirectionsanyways." Then, before she could say any more or Daedalus could make any move to stop her, Tara quickly began to walk as fast as she could without breaking into a run away from Daedalus.

Now alone, Daedalus only watched in silence as he couldn't help but raise an eyebrow at the sudden radical shift in personality from the normally apprehensive scholar.

'*Very well,*' he thought to himself. '*I'll just leave that be until it somehow becomes my problem.*' With that settled Daedalus then simply continued on his own not so merry way towards the place where he and Raz were staying.

Once Tara had reached what she believed was a comfortable distance away from Daedalus, and had actually walked quite some distance past her hotel without realizing it in the process, she eventually began to slow down and catch her breath.

'*What was that reaction!*' she mentally screamed at herself. '*Now he definitely knows that I was lying before and-*' Tara's thoughts instantly stopped once she realized the further implications of what that meant. '*Oh no…. Oh no oh no oh no oh no oh please Solaris no he's going to tell Raz isn't he! Oh please Solaris help me please please please! Oh no this is bad this is very bad…*' As those thoughts ran through her head Tara began to walk forward without paying any attention at all to where she was actually going. '*What am I even supposed to say to him the next time I see him now? "Sorry I only just now realized that I like being around you now that I know that you are royalty." Am I really that shallow? Oh Solaris, why is this happening to m-*' Tara's thoughts instantly screeched to a halt when around the corner of the building in front of her a certain, very familiar looking curly haired woman came out pulling a cart full of various miscellaneous pieces of junk behind her.

"Hi Tara!" Agatha gleefully, and somewhat loudly greeted her as she came around the corner. Once she saw the crestfallen look on Tara's face, however, she immediately knew that something was not right. "Is... Is something wrong?" At first Tara considered not telling her, but only a few seconds after considering this did she realize that not only would that be more than a little cruel to her, but that one way or another she would find out on her own anyway if she did not tell her now. All it would take was one look to see that Seth was not with them before she would put the pieces together. With this in mind Tara decided that, as difficult as it was, it would really be better if Agatha had heard it from her first.

"S- Seth..." Tara tried to speak, but even now it was difficult for her to admit that it had happened to herself let alone say aloud to someone else. "He is in the hospital. I do not know if he is okay." It did not even take a second after hearing that for Agatha to drop the handles of her cart and rush over to Tara.

"What happened!" Agatha immediately asked a bit more forcefully than she had intended to as she grabbed Tara by her arms. Tara, however, did not appear to notice or even care.

"Well..." Tara began, though it was still difficult for her to say all of this aloud. "He... Daedalus... Raz, and his cousin Filia-"

"You mean the princess?" Agatha interrupted.

"How... How do you know about that?" Tara couldn't help but ask.

"Seth told me yesterday," Agatha answered quickly.

"O... kay..." Tara responded as she tried to wrap her head around when Seth could have possibly told her that, but then after realizing that asking that would only lead to numerous questions that she didn't really care to know the answers to at the current moment, she gave it up and went back to explaining what had happened. "Anyway, as I was saying, as... As thanks for entertaining her yesterday Princess Filia invited all of us to spend the day with her family in the Suntop District. It... It started out nice enough. She took us to brunch, then to the theater to see-"

"But what happened to Seth!" Agatha asked again rather forcefully. While ordinarily Tara would have admonished her for that using that tone of voice, now she did not have it in her, and Agatha's outburst did force her to admit to herself that she was still trying her best to avoid the issue.

"We..." Tara tried to begin again, but the words became more difficult for her to speak aloud the closer she got to describing the actual event. "After the play we went to see had ended we all went out for a very nice dinner. Princess Filia insisted… At some point during it… Seth… He… He left to use the lavatory. Not long after he had left Raz did too. The next thing we all knew…" Tara felt herself choke on her own words as she tried to speak them aloud, but upon looking into Agatha's pleading eyes she did her best to force herself to speak. "R… R… Raz suddenly teleported back to the table saying that Seth had been stabbed." Just saying that out loud right now was as difficult for her as she had imagined it would be, not unlike throwing up rocks. However, now that it had been said, explaining the rest was something that she suddenly found much easier. "Then he went to go get a doctor and Princess Filia sent one of her guards to get the city guard and… and… the next time I saw him he was… being carried out on a stretcher."

It took many long seconds for Agatha to process everything she had just heard, if only because of the fact that part of that entailed the fact that she had to accept that what Tara had just told her had actually happened. It was a scenario which she herself never thought would have been possible hours ago, and yet, this was the world in which they were now living in. For a moment it became difficult for Agatha to breathe as she mentally ran through all of Tara's words again, as if doing so would give her some glimmer of hope. As she did, however, one detail about Tara's story stood out to her, something that Tara had left out, and that was enough to snap her back to reality and regain control of her breathing again.

"What about the guy that did that to him!" Agatha then asked. "What happened to him! Please tell me they got him!"

"Th… They did, actually," Tara answered, as she found that talking had suddenly become easier for her now that she had been forced to say what had happened. "They dragged him out of there shortly after Seth."

"Who was he?" Agatha couldn't help but immediately ask, now more angry than concerned as she knew that Seth was in as capable of hands as he could get given the situation.

"I d… I do not know," Tara answered. "I have never seen anyone like him before."

"What did he look like?" Agatha then quickly asked.

"He… He…" Tara began as she tried her best to recall the memory again. As painful as it was for her, part of her knew why Agatha was asking these questions, so she did not want to leave her with nothing. In her position Tara knew that she would more than certainly be asking these same questions. "He had really dark skin… wore this ugly yellow coat and-" It was only as Tara was saying all of this out loud that she remembered the one detail about him that stood out to her more than any other. However, she was unsure of whether or not she wanted to tell Agatha about that last detail. One look into Agatha's eyes, however, eyes that burned with the fire and fury of Solaris himself, told her that if she did not tell her this now then Agatha would certainly make sure that she regretted it later. For a moment Tara felt as if she were caught between a rock and a hard place as she was unsure of whom she wanted to betray. In the end it was her own fear that got the better of her as she made a decision, but did so without thinking at all of what would come of it. "He wore a bracelet. It was gold. Not just gold in color, but made of actual gold, and it had the emblem of the Futura Collegium Aureum monster hunting guild on it."

Agatha suddenly felt light headed as those words reached her ears. For a second she could swear that she actually felt her heart literally sink into her stomach as she took a few tentative steps back from Tara. The implications of what she had just been told gave rise to many, many possibilities within her mind, and few, if any of them, were good.

"You… You don't think…" Agatha was only barely able to speak when she eventually found her voice.

"I am not sure," Tara was quick to answer this time. "But if she did, then who knows how many other people she has told." Saying that aloud caused one more frightening possibility to run through Tara's mind. "Oh no… Oh Solaris no, what if someone sneaks into the hospital to finish the job or-"

"Well is someone there to watch over him?" Agatha asked before Tara could even finish that thought. Despite how simple a question it was, however, Tara actually needed to think for a few seconds to come up with a proper answer to that question. The reason for this was because in truth she did not actually know the answer herself.

"I… I am not sure," Tara eventually answered. "Raz told us that we likely would not be able to see him until tomorrow morning."

"Could that be a lie?" Agatha was quick to ask as soon as Tara had finished speaking. "Maybe Raz is in on it. He almost killed Seth once you know. Was seconds away from doing it too. Maybe he's pissed that he never got a chance to finish the job."

"That can't be!" Tara shouted without meaning to, which caused Agatha to first take another step back, then raise an eyebrow at her. When she saw how Agatha was looking at her after her outburst Tara instinctively looked away from her and refused to meet her gaze. "I... I mean that does not even make any sense. Wh... Why would he even bother to save Seth's life if that was what he wanted? Also... Raz... does not seem to be the type of person who does things subtly." For a moment it appeared as if Agatha didn't believe her, as she still appeared to be on edge at the mention of his name. After a few moments though, Agatha had relaxed a little bit.

"I'll just have to take your word on that one," Agatha eventually responded. "I don't think the man's ever said any more than two words to me. Not for lack of trying mind you, but then again even royalty falls flat at the sight of what I got." Agatha let out a half-hearted chuckle as she finished speaking in an abysmally poor attempt to lighten the mood, but when she saw Tara's still unchanged expression she knew that she needed to change her approach. With that in mind Agatha let out a sigh as she walked over next to Tara and put her arm around her. "I'm sorry about that, it wasn't called for, but listen, you've had a long day. Take it from me, walking around aimlessly and moping about what happened or what could have happened isn't going to change anything or make any of it better. So get some sleep. It might not make you feel better, but at least it'll help clear your head somewhat, and hey, if what Raz said was true then you should be able to see him tomorrow. What reason would they have to stop you then? Oh, he needs his rest, well he can certainly still get that while you're in the room with him. Out of everyone I know you're probably the only one with enough common sense to actually let an injured person get some rest when they need it."

Hearing that actually did make Tara feel at least a little bit better. Enough to make her briefly smile.

"Th... Thank you," Tara then said as she quickly wiped a tear away from her eye before Agatha had a chance to see it.

"You want me to walk you back to your hotel?" Agatha offered.

"No, no, that is okay," Tara answered as she gently pushed away from Agatha's embrace. "I just uh... I still need to be alone."

"It's okay, I understand," Agatha replied as she took a step away from Tara so that she could have her space. "Just get some sleep. I know it might be hard right now, but you'll thank me in the morning."

"I will... try," Tara hesitantly responded, not because she did not want to, but because despite Agatha's insistence she genuinely was not sure if she could sleep at all right now even if she wanted to. "A... and... Thank you."

"No problemo," Agatha was quick to respond as she put on her own smile in another attempt to lighten the mood. "It's what I do." Tara did not say anything to that as she turned around and headed back in the direction of her hotel.

Agatha had opted to stay and watch Tara walk away for a little while, if only to see whether or not she did genuinely need her help and wasn't just being polite. Once it became clear that Tara did not and was on her own merry way, Agatha returned to her cart and began to pull it the rest of the way back to where she was staying. As she did so, however, her brow furrowed as her eyes locked ahead of her with a newfound determination, and more than anything else, unfiltered rage as she knew what she had to do now. Whether or not it was the smart or right thing to do she did not know, but she did know that it was something that she had to do.

"Oh thank Solaris you're here!" Nicole, for lack of a better word, exploded as Raz and Filia walked through the door to their place of residence within Dis. Before either of them had a chance to even think of anything to say in response, Nicole had suddenly rushed over as quickly as she could and embraced her daughter in a hug tight enough that one might have thought that she was attempting to suffocate her daughter. "Are you okay? Are you hurt? I knew sending you out into this city with only two guards was a bad idea. He didn't get too close to you, did he?"

While it was obvious to both of them how much Nicole had been concerned for her daughter's well being, Filia couldn't help but look to her cousin for help as she tried her best to avoid being smothered by her mother's bosom. Raz, however, only raised an eyebrow in genuine confusion. In truth he was more surprised that Nicole wasn't screaming her head off at either of them, especially given how disrespectful both of them had acted towards her since they had reunited in this city. Of course he wasn't about to say any of that out loud, but it was at the forefront of his mind.

"M... Mom, I'm fine," Filia tried to speak as she attempted to push herself out of her mother's overpowering embrace. Thankfully after a few moments of this

Nicole appeared to realize what was going on and slightly released her protective grip on her daughter. "I'm fine, mom, as you can clearly see. So I-"

"I don't want you going anywhere else in this city without either me, Isaac, or enough guards to surround you in every direction!" Nicole then promptly interrupted as she squeezed Filia's shoulders so hard that Filia could swear that she was trying to crush them. "Do you understand!"

"Doesn't that-"

"Do you understand!" Nicole interrupted again, this time much louder as she dug her fingernails into Filia's shoulders. If she were squeezing any harder Filia had little doubt that she would draw blood. However, with this being the situation she was in now, she knew that only one thing would satisfy her mother as she took in a deep breath and then let it out.

"I understand, mother," Filia responded with a weak voice. That seemed to satisfy Nicole as she finally let go of her. However, now free of her grasp, it soon became clear to all present that Filia had no intention of remaining silent. "But even still, doesn't that seem like a bit too much? I said I was fine, and you're not blind so you know that I am. So why are you being so paranoid? It wasn't even me who was at-"

"But what if it wasn't," Nicole was quick to interrupt again. "A boy you had just met yesterday being assaulted by some scoundrel is unfortunate, yes, but if it were to happen to you, the future ruler of our great empire… That would be a tragedy."

"Good to see how much you really care for your subjects, your majesty," Raz spoke up. The instant he did, however, Nicole shifted her attention over to him as she shot him a death fueled glare. Raz, unintimidated, just leaned against the wall with his arms crossed. "How do you even know about what happened anyways?"

"Luckily for you the knight that you sent to gather the local city guard was a fledgling mage and sent a message directly to me as he was running," Nicole answered as each word she spoke bore more venom than the last. "Granted in his haste he left out quite a few details that made it unclear to me exactly who the victim was, but that hardly matters now. Besides, shouldn't you be heading back to wherever it is you're staying right now, Michael?"

"Maybe," Raz responded with a shrug. "But I wanted to make sure that Filly didn't do anything rash or stupid when she got here." That statement earned him another glare, this time from Filia, though knowing her as he did Raz had expected a response like that. With both Filia and Nicole glaring at him at the same time like this, however, Raz only now realized how uncannily similar the two of them could be at times. Despite being glared at for completely different reasons the looks in the eyes of both the mother and the daughter were nearly identical.

"I commend your intuition, Michael," the stern, yet soothing voice of Isaac spoke up as he entered the room. "It was insight like that that helped you put that fool Cecil behind bars, after all." Even though Raz knew that Isaac was complimenting him, he couldn't help but grimace at the mention of that particular name.

"So let me guess," Raz then said as he shot his own glare at Isaac. "You know everything already, don't you."

"But of course," Isaac responded with a smile, though when he did so it looked more like a smirk. "Though I cannot help but wonder…" As Isaac spoke he walked into the room proper and headed directly towards Raz. "Call it… professional curiosity. How exactly did this individual get so close to a member of your party in the first place? While I trust the royal Solaran knights to protect Princess Filia from anything with their own lives, you were there too, were you not? And nothing gets past you, does it not?"

"If you know everything already then you should know that he didn't," Raz shot back at him.

"That may be," Isaac responded, undeterred. "But he was still able to severely injure your friend Seth, enough to put him in the hospital. If he was able to do that, then Solaris knows what else he could have done. Or what his purpose was in doing so."

"If you don't know that then you're in the same boat as the rest of us," Raz responded as he pushed himself off of the wall.

"Well, he does have amnesia, does he not?" Nicole then spoke up. "Maybe it was someone from his past life. Perhaps he owes someone money."

"Perhaps," Isaac said as he brought a hand to his chin in thought. He was silent for only a few short seconds before he began to speak again, however. "But regardless, if this individual was able to get as close as he did to someone in the company of a member of the royal family, one has to wonder exactly what this individual's intentions were, and how much more harm he could have done to any one of you." The room fell silent again for another few moments as no one was sure exactly how to respond to that. With that being the atmosphere of the room, Isaac was quick to seize the opportunity to take command of the situation. "This bears investigation. Perhaps I should speak to this individual before he is potentially put to death for attempted murder. If anyone in this city should be able to drag answers out of someone like this, it is the former royal spymaster. Or perhaps the current one, if he was here in my place."

"Are you sure, Isaac?" Filia asked as she raised an eyebrow in a mixture of both surprise and confusion. "Isn't this a vacation for you too?" Isaac couldn't help but let out a hearty laugh at that question.

"My lady," he began once his laughter had died down. "I have not taken a vacation since before your mother was born."

"That sounds… incredibly stressful," Filia couldn't help but respond.

"Are you worried that I will go grey?" Isaac jokingly asked. "There is no need for you to worry about me, my lady, for it is my job to worry about all of you. Now, it is my recommendation that you all get some rest. You after all, my lady, have just endured a more than stressful past few hours. So the best thing for you right now is to get some sleep." As he spoke Isaac walked over and placed a hand on Filia's shoulder. "Trust me, my lady, I know that sleep is the last thing you want right now, but I speak from experience on this. You will feel better in the morning." Despite his seemingly comforting words, Filia was still a little apprehensive about the idea of going to sleep now. Isaac, however, was again quick to seize the opportunity. "If you do not believe me then I am sure your beloved cousin will vouch for me on this one." As he spoke Isaac shifted his eyes over towards Raz, as did Filia. Raz, however, remained completely silent. "Now if you all will excuse me," Isaac then said as he removed his hand from Filia's shoulder and made his way past her and Raz towards the door. "There is a certain scoundrel that I need to interrogate." Before Filia, Raz, or Nicole could say anything else to him, much less stop him, Isaac was already out the door.

Once outside, and out of view of everyone else, Isaac's demeanor suddenly shifted as he furrowed his brow and began to walk much quicker and with more of a purpose to his steps.

"Necesito arreglar esta mierda," he muttered under his breath as he walked on through the night towards the city guard station.

Chapter 22

When Vivian opened her eyes she found herself standing in a place that was very familiar to her. One that she recognized instantly, as it was where she had spent the first eighteen years of her life. Her father's farm. Under any normal circumstance Vivian would have relished the chance to see this place again, if only for its nostalgic comforts and the feeling of simply being in a place that she could call her home. Something that she rarely, if ever, felt anywhere else. This time, however, there were several things that were off about this residence that made it clear to her that it wasn't exactly the same as it was the last time she had seen it, which gave her a growing sense of uneasiness.

To begin with, the house, which she had always remembered being a simple, single story home fit for herself, her father, and her mother when she was still alive, now boasted many, many more floors as the once simple farmhouse now reached so far up into the sky that Vivian could no longer see the top. Indeed there now seemed to be hundreds, nay, thousands of floors that stretched all the way up into a cloudless, oddly rust colored sky. Not only that, but while the house was never in the best of shapes, as there always seemed to be something that needed fixing whenever she visited, now all of the seemingly infinite floors of the house appeared to be completely dilapidated. The wood that made up its walls had long since rotted and was more than likely infested with termites. What little paint was left on it had long since been peeled away by the passage of time, leaving only a few spots of white. Finally each and every window, of which there were now many due to the vastly increased height of the house, now appeared to be either boarded up or completely smashed in.

For the life of her Vivian couldn't come up with a single reason as to how or why this tower of tetanus was possibly standing, as it appeared as if it would fall over like a literal house of cards if one were to so much as breathe upon it. It was only then that she took notice of the fields that surrounded this abominable tower. Much like how she remembered them, there were many rows of crops, but like the tower of a house in front of her they all appeared to be in some state of intense decay. Every single plant was dried up to the point that they were either simply dead or had long since rotted away into dust, unfit for even rats.

Unconsciously Vivian then blinked, and upon opening her eyes again she saw standing across from her a woman who looked almost exactly like herself. This woman, however, appeared to be quite a few years older than her, her hair was much longer, and adorning her left wrist was a golden bracelet for her guild while a silver wedding ring adorned her ring finger on the same hand. This woman didn't appear to notice Vivian at all. However, this did not stop Vivian from calling out to her, her heart seemingly skipping a beat as she did so. However, not a single sound escaped her throat. More than vexed by this, Vivian attempted to shout at her again, this time much louder, only to meet the same result. Again and again Vivian screamed, but no matter how hard or how loudly she tried, it seemed as if the world itself did not want her to call out to this woman whom Vivian had not seen in nearly twenty years.

Again Vivian blinked, and when she opened her eyes this time a creature resembling a chameleon with a hard, glossy exoskeleton not unlike an insect, a dozen and a half beatty red eyes that looked as if they were simply thrown onto the thing's face without any regard for their actual placement, and a long, segmented tail that extended out six meters behind it and ended with a sharp, bladed hook that continuously dripped with an acidic green liquid from its tip that sizzled against the dirt with each drop that piddled down upon it, stood directly across from the older woman. Much like the woman herself, this monstrosity was something that had been permanently etched into Vivian's memory for exactly as long as the woman herself had been. Knowing fully well what was about to happen next, and refusing to let history repeat itself, Vivian without thinking immediately rushed forward to push the woman out of the way of this chameleon monstrosity, only to find herself completely unable to move even a single centimeter before suddenly feeling a sharp pain in her arms, legs, and around her neck. Naturally confused, Vivian glanced down towards her right wrist to see a silver wire wrapped firmly around it, which dug further into her skin the more she struggled. Once she saw that it did not take her long to realize that similar wires were also wrapped around her other wrist, both of her upper arms, ankles, thighs, and neck. Vivian struggled as much as she could to break free of the wires, but every movement she made only caused them to constrict tighter, which in turn sent wave after wave of pain throughout her body as the wires dug further into her skin. It was enough to make her want to scream out in pain, but when she tried to not a peep came out of her as she felt the wire around her neck suddenly constrict much, much tighter than all of the others had. Enough to draw quite a bit of blood from her. It was only then that Vivian realized that if she struggled any harder, it was incredibly likely that that wire in particular would cut right through her neck and cause her to bleed to death.

Before she could make any other attempt to struggle further or attempt to call out to the woman again, Vivian suddenly felt herself get yanked backwards by the wires, forcing her to look away from both the woman and the chameleon monster before the sound of the woman's scream hit her ears. Before she even had a chance to contemplate what had just happened to her the wires suddenly released their hold on her as Vivian found herself dropped face first into the ground below. As quickly as she could she pushed herself back onto her feet, expecting to see the older woman again. However, neither the woman nor the monster were anywhere to be seen, and along with them the tower that was her former home had also vanished from her sight. What she did see, however, was a sight that shook her so much that she didn't believe she could make a sound even if she wanted to.

In front of her now was something that for all intents and purposes appeared to be a tree that had an oddly colored mixture of peach and brown tones. A closer look, however, revealed to Vivian that this tree was not made of bark, as she saw that it was covered in pores. Not only that, but most if not all of those pores appeared to be oozing a sort of viscous red liquid, and it was then that Vivian finally saw the hair, eyes, and teeth that poked out from various parts of this flesh covered tree to create patterns that resembled grotesque parodies of the faces of men, women, and children that, much to Vivian's horror, were all slowly moving as if they were moaning in agony yet were unable to make any noise at all. The horrific realization of exactly what this tree was made of caused Vivian's stomach to turn in a way that she didn't think was possible as she had to fight the urge to throw up where she stood. Despite that, however, she found herself quite literally unable to look away as she found herself unable to move again. As she was forced to continue staring at this flesh covered tree she noticed that its branches were made up of hundreds of human arms, many of which were seemingly reaching out and grabbing at nothing. It was upon noticing this, however, that Vivian saw that nine of these arm branches were holding the wires that held her in place, and it was only then that Vivian further realized that the wires had not let her go, but had merely relaxed their grip on her for a moment so that she could see this.

More important and prominent than the human arms or the wires, however, was that sitting among the arm branches, as they appeared to form a sort of makeshift throne for him, was a man whose form was mostly silhouetted in shadows. What Vivian could see of him, however, was that he possessed black hair and wore predominantly purple. The one feature he possessed, however, that Vivian found herself unable to look away from were his piercing, blood red eyes. Eyes that she could see were filled with nothing but loathing and contempt for her as he stared down at her from on high. After only a few seconds of this the man opened his mouth to speak, but like with Vivian and the flesh covered tree, no sound came out. This did not seem to faze him at all, however, as at the conclusion of whatever he was saying he slowly raised his hand and snapped his fingers. Unlike everything else in this place that attempted to make a sound, however, the sound of his snapping fingers was more akin to a thunderclap as the sheer intensity of it caused what felt like the whole world to shake. Vivian, unable to cover her ears, could only stand completely helpless as an intense, throbbing pain not unlike a hammer suddenly hit her head, which soon faded and was then replaced by an intense ringing in her ears that rather than slowly dissipate, began to grow louder and louder in volume the longer it went on.

As this was happening more of the arm branches from the flesh covered tree began to grab onto the wires that held Vivian and pull on them in a manner not unlike dock workers pulling a ship into harbor. As this happened all of the wires that were wrapped all around Vivian's body began to tighten much, much harder than they had before, and this time they did not stop as each wire cut further and further into her flesh. Vivian let out another soundless scream as she struggled against the wires, but like before her struggling only caused them to tighten much quicker. Any thoughts that she may have had of the woman or the chameleon monster from before were now gone from her mind, as all that she cared about now was her own survival.

However, as hard as she tried, she soon began to feel the strength in her body fading as she lost more and more blood, and with that it soon became very difficult for her to breathe as the wire around her neck made even that a challenge for her. The only thing that she could do was stare back up into the man's uncaring crimson eyes. As she did Vivian then realized that the wires had merely been restraining her before, but now, much like the man sitting in the tree, whatever force that was holding her there no longer seemed to care about whether or not she lived as the wires began to pull on her limbs hard enough to rip them from their sockets if they kept going. With the reality that she might very well die here dawning on her, a multitude of emotions ran through Vivian, but chief among them was not rage, hatred, or even sorrow.

Instead what Vivian felt more than anything else was guilt, and as she felt the last of her life being taken from her by the wire at her neck she looked back up to the man in the tree as she tried to speak one last thing to him. The only thing that she could think of to say that might make him stop. Of course, like before, no sound came out when she tried, and it was only after doing it that Vivian realized exactly how pointless her last action truly was.

The sound of a sudden, repeated, and incredibly loud banging against the door to her room caused Vivian's eyes to snap open. The instant she found herself able to move she sat straight up and brought a hand to her neck as she took in several deep breaths, but nothing was there. The sudden movement, however, forced Vivian to realize exactly how much her head was pounding as she could not help but let out a loud groan as she brought her hand up to her face. The memory of what her mind had conjured slowly began to fade away until nothing but a vague blur remained of it. However, the incredibly loud banging noise that was doing absolutely no favors for her aching head was quickly causing her to forget all of it entirely as she began to focus on the here and now.

"What!" she shouted at the top of her lungs in the hope that her obvious anger would make the pounding against her door stop.

"Vivian! Let me in!" the high pitched voice of Agatha shouted from the other side of the door. "We need to talk! Now!"

"Fuck off!" Vivian shouted back to her without any hesitation. "It's too early for this!"

"It's ten o'clock!"

"So!"

"So open this fucking door before I go get either the city guard or your guild involved!" That was enough to catch Vivian's attention. Of all of the threats Agatha could have made, that specific one was enough to rouse both Vivian's attention and curiosity enough to find out exactly what she wanted. If only to potentially save her own skin.

"Fine! Just give me a fucking minute!" Vivian then shouted back as she begrudgingly pulled herself out of her bed. Whether or not she was doing so on purpose, as Vivian didn't have either the time nor the available brain cells to decide, but as if to intentionally spite Agatha she took her sweet time putting herself together as she very slowly looked around her room for a pair of pants before finding one lying about on the floor not far from her bed. She was relatively certain that they were the same pants she had worn yesterday, but she was both too tired and too annoyed right now to care about minor details like that. Thankfully she still had on the shirt she had worn yesterday, as she had gone to bed in it. So between the shirt and pants that she had worn the day before Vivian considered herself at least presentable enough to open the door.

Still taking her time, Vivian dragged her feet over towards the door to her room and unlocked it. Thankfully Agatha had since ceased relentlessly pounding upon it, which did actually make her head feel somewhat better. Once the door was open Vivian was treated to the sight of Agatha's extremely disgruntled face before she suddenly shoved Vivian aside and stormed into the room before Vivian had any chance to say anything to her at all, much less in protest to her barging in. What she did have a chance to see, however, was that Agatha had come here alone, and that despite her threats no one from either the city guard nor her guild were out there with her.

"Okay..." Vivian said as she took a moment to wipe away the remaining crust from her eyes before closing the door. "What the actual fuck is this about?"

"Seth got stabbed yesterday," Agatha quickly answered. Vivian's eyes went a little wide upon hearing that, but other than that she showed almost no reaction to what Agatha had said at all.

"Wow, sucks to be him," Vivian responded as she crossed her arms and leaned against the door. "But I don't see how that's my problem. You know as well as I do that this city's full of degen-"

"The man that did it was wearing a gold bracelet with the emblem of the Futura Collegium Aureum monster hunting guild on it," Agatha interrupted. Hearing that caused Vivian's eyes to snap open wide and whatever breath was in her lungs to instantly leave her as she realized the exact direction this conversation was heading. "Now tell me, Vivian. Why would a gold ranked hunter from your guild go and attack Seth completely unprompted and unprovoked? I mean, you're pretty much the closest thing to an expert on that exact activity so surely you must have some kind of answer for me."

"Wha… What are you accusing me of exactly?" Vivian stammered as she was only barely able to wrap her head around all of this new information.

"Vivian…" Agatha then said as she cast an accusatory glare at the woman in question. "Look me in the eye and don't lie to me. Did you tell anyone in your guild about Seth's… lineage?"

"Is that what we're calling it now?" Vivian answered with an obvious groan and a roll of her eyes, neither of which resounded well with Agatha. Seeing that, Vivian cast her own glare back at Agatha as if to challenge her before giving her real answer. "No. No I didn't. I never said anything to anyone in my fucking guild. So I don't fucking know how or why he got stabbed, but if you ask me that creep definitely deserved it." The instant those words reached her ears Agatha took two steps closer to Vivian as she folded her hands into fists. Vivian, however, did not back down as she stayed right where she was against the door and matched Agatha's glare with her own. There were at least ten things that Agatha wanted to do to Vivian just for saying what she had, but the better part of her mind held her back. For all of her faults Agatha knew that an actual fight against Vivian was one that she definitely could not win, and she knew that Vivian knew that too.

"What… What exactly happened between the two of you two days ago?" Agatha then asked.

"What?"

"The other day Seth came across my stand and started venting to me about how upset he was about everything," Agatha began. "He's well aware that most of you are only playing nice by the way, though considering how sure he was of how much you in particular must hate him it sounds like you're pretty fucking terrible at it."

"Oh, what, now he's going around telling everyone that I'm the asshole in this situation!" Vivian let out, now very visibly angry as she pushed herself off of the door so that she could stand up straight. "Well fuck him then! I was just trying to grab a few drinks so that I could forget about exactly how shitty my day was, but then he came waltzing on in and fucking refused to stop bugging me no matter what I said. It pissed me off so much that I ended up listing out nearly every shitty day I've ever had to him. Nearly all of which included things like fucking him, and some of which included him himself. Then after hearing all of that he tried to give me that 'I'll do whatever I can to help' bullshit, so then I tried to break his hand because who the fuck does he think he is thinking he can fucking touch me. Then when that didn't work I just told him to fuck off. That was all that happened and if you don't believe me then ask the fucking bartender. She was there. She saw the whole fucking thing. She'll tell you exactly what I did. So there, now you know. Are you fucking happy?" It took Agatha many long seconds to process everything that Vivian had just said to her, mostly because of the fact that Vivian had just blatantly told her something that she had suspected happened, but was unsure if she wanted to believe it. After hearing what Vivian had just said, however, she knew that she had to face the facts.

"So you assaulted him… for caring about you?" Agatha forced herself to ask.

"Is your brain still filled with all the spunk you sucked down the night of the festival!" Vivian snapped in Agatha's face after she asked that. "You know what he is, Agatha! They don't have feelings! They don't care about anything or anyone! They're just beasts that only live to slaughter us like fucking pigs! You guys were already asking a lot from me not to kill him! Now you're here trying to guilt trip me because I told him what for the day before someone from my guild stabbed him! I wouldn't fucking care if he was human! Fucking hell! I swear the way all of you have been acting lately it's like you motherfuckers wouldn't be happy unless fucking Solaris himself came back to fucking life so that he can give Seth a handjob while priaising him as the best fucking guy in the world and we should all be his fucking friend!" Trying her best not to actually picture the visual that Vivian had just put into her head, Agatha in that moment could almost literally feel herself beginning to lose whatever sympathy she may have had left for Vivian as she couldn't help but ball up her hand into a fist. Like before she had to fight the urge to punch Vivian in the face for what she just said, and like before she managed to hold herself back, but even she had to admit to herself how much more difficult that was to do this time.

"It's called empathy you fucking cunt," Agatha responded in the most controlled voice she could manage, though each of her words still dripped with venom. "It's a basic human emotion, and from what you just told me you're apparently less human than he is because he has it and you don't." Vivian couldn't help but take a few steps closer to Agatha and narrow her eyes at her for that insult.

"Are you really, really going to try and convince me that a literal fucking monster is less heartless than me?" Vivian asked. "Who the actual fuck do you think you are that y-"

"Honestly," Agatha interrupted. "I think that I'm the best, if not only, friend that you have right now, and given what he told me the other day I think Seth is convinced that I'm also his only real friend right now too."

"Good for y-"

"Shut up you bitch I wasn't finished!" Agatha shouted, unafraid, into Vivian's face before taking in a deep breath to calm herself before continuing. "Look, just listen to me. I'm not saying that you should completely forget about what he is, and I'm not saying that he hasn't done anything wrong either. What I am saying is, he's in a dark place right now, one that I don't think I can get him out of, and this whole situation certainly isn't helping. Fucking hell, if he hears that it was a member of your guild that attacked him and comes to the same assumption that Tara and I did, I'm certain that it'll completely destroy whatever misguided faith he still has left in you. Do you really want that?"

"Why would I care?" Vivian asked as if the whole issue was less about what it was and more about a petty theft that happened to someone that neither of them knew. Still fighting the urge to punch Vivian in the face, Agatha instead simply glared at Vivian for a few long seconds before she brought both of her balled fists up to her face and let out an incredibly loud groan in a fit of furious frustration.

"Look," Agatha then said once she had calmed herself down. "I'm not going to force you to do anything. I know that I physically can't, but I also know what I've seen with my own two eyes."

"What does-"

"I'm an archeologist, Vivian," Agatha interrupted again. "To some degree it is literally my job to make interpretations based on the things I see, and from what I saw of you a few months back I could tell that you were much, much happier when he was a regular part of your life. Hell, everyone else in Canaan noticed it too considering how many of them asked me if I knew whether or not the two of you were-"

"If we were what?" Vivian cut Agatha off while continuing to glare at her as if she were just daring her to finish that sentence. In truth, however, Vivian did not actually have any idea at all what Agatha was getting at, but did not want to show that.

"You know what, fuck you," Agatha eventually responded. "I'll just let you figure that one out yourself. But anyways, like it or not, when you were training him he was certainly a, if not the most, positive thing in your life at that point. Which considering all of the shit you've been through is saying a lot. Trust me, I've heard you drunkenly pour your heart out to me more than enough times to know how much you hate certain dates." Vivian's eyes went wide as the implications of what Agatha had just said rattled through her brain. Considering how many times Vivian knew that the two of them had gone drinking together in the time they had known each other, the idea that Agatha might know something, especially about "specific dates" made Vivian feel something she hadn't truly felt in a long time. It made her feel weak.

"I... have?" Vivian stammered out while still trying to sound tough, but she knew after she had spoken how badly she had failed at that.

"You're a sad drunk, you know that, Vivian?" Agatha said once she had seen Vivian's reaction. "Honestly, I'm surprised that you really don't remember even a single night that we've drank together, but that must be the case if that's your reaction." It was in that instant that Vivian went from feeling weak to helpless at the realization that Agatha really could see right through her. "But that's not important right now. What I'm saying is that I think that you of all people need something positive in your life so that you don't keep wallowing in your own misery and not do a single fucking thing about it. So please, talk to him. Not just for him, but for yourself as well. Before you add something else to that long list of things that you regret."

Vivian had something that she wanted to say to her for that. Something snarky yet threatening enough that it would get her to shut up and leave the room. However, before she could actually say anything, images of Seth flashed through her mind, and the instant they did she had forgotten every word that she wanted to say. From the time she had first seen him helping Tara around the library, to the times that they had had lunch together while they were on a break from training, to the training itself. All of those memories were actually somewhat pleasant for Vivian to think about. However, now they were all tainted by the fact that as she pictured them in her mind she found it impossible to picture Seth without his eyes bearing the distinct blood red color of monsters. It was enough to make Vivian clench both of her hands into fists as if she were preparing to throw a punch, and for a moment she actually considered it. After several long seconds of silently staring back at Agatha, who still stood as confidently as ever where she was, however, the energy that she needed to do so suddenly left her.

"Ag…" Vivian tried to speak, though it was amazing to her how hard it actually was to force herself to do so at that moment. "C… Can you please leave?" At first Agatha didn't say anything in response, and because of that Vivian began to fear that she no longer trusted her enough to leave her alone. After a few more silent seconds, however, Agatha let out a sigh as she finally, finally broke eye contact with Vivian.

"Okay," Agatha eventually said. "Just… Don't do anything rash, okay?" Then with that said, Agatha walked past Vivian and opened the door to leave. Before she actually did, however, she turned back to look at her one more time. "If I run into any of the others I'll tell them that you're just as confused as we are." Then finally, with that said, Agatha closed the door behind her as Vivian heard her footsteps begin to grow quieter and quieter as she walked farther away.

Once she knew that Agatha was gone, the image of Seth smiling gently at her flashed through her mind one more time, but still bearing the eyes of the beasts she hated. The instant that image appeared in her head, Vivian could not help herself as she screamed as loud as she could, then spun around and punched the wall next to her door as hard as she could. She instantly regretted doing so, however, as her fist went through the wall and pain shot through her hand like a hornet's sting. Slowly Vivian pulled her hand back out, and when she did she saw that it was covered in blood from the splinters of wood that had pierced her skin. The color reminded her of Seth as the image of his gently smiling face flashed through her mind one more time.

"Fuck," was the only thing that she could say.

Chapter 23

It was a quiet night in Dis' Suntop District jail, something that under most normal circumstances would be a good thing, and by all accounts it was. For Pierre, however, who sat at the jailhouse's front desk at this late hour, it was the sort of night that made him pine for something more. Not that he desperately wished for something more to happen, for he knew very well the dangers of such a wish in a place like this, but something that did not involve any of the prisoners would be a nice enough change of pace for him. Earlier in the evening prior to sunset some of the local guardsmen had brought in a man belonging to, of all things, the Futura Collegium Aureum monster hunting guild who had attempted to assassinate someone in the company of the visiting Princess Filia Solara. That was something he wished he could have been there to see, but unfortunately somebody had to keep watch over the jail. It was a thankless task, but Pierre knew that somebody had to do it, even if all that he had to do right now was sit back and read the latest entry in the Wanderer series.

Right now that person from the monster hunting guild was being interrogated in his cell, but given what Pierre had heard from the people that were coming from back there, he wasn't saying a damn thing. Part of him wanted to go back there and see what he could do to assist, but the better part of him knew that he likely wouldn't be of much help. Still, getting his turn to knock the guy senseless for trying to pull something like he had would have been satisfying enough.

In the midst of all those thoughts, however, the door to the jail suddenly opened and in walked a tall, darker skinned man wearing a very finely made white suit with gold trim.

"Can I help you?" Pierre asked as he closed his book and turned in his chair to properly face the man.

"I certainly hope you can," the finely dressed man answered as he held out his closed fist towards him as if it was important. It took a second for Pierre to understand what exactly was happening, but once he did he couldn't help but feel like a fool as his eyes drifted towards the closed fist and saw on it a solid gold ring that bore the image of a stylized "S" that was made almost entirely of ruby, which with the light hit it at just the right angle to make it glisten like fire. It was an emblem that Pierre had seen enough times to be more than familiar with what it was.

It was the emblem of the royal house of Solara.

"My lord!" Pierre only barely managed to say without stammering as he jumped out of his chair and stood at attention as quickly as he could. "I am so terribly sorry. I-"

"Spare me your apologies," the well dressed man interrupted Pierre as he pulled his hand back. "I have neither the time nor the inclination to care about such things right now. My name is Isaac De La Rosa, advisor to her majesty Queen Faust of Sol. I am here regarding the incident that took place in Gustav's a few hours ago."

"Of course, of course," Pierre responded as he grabbed his ring of keys from somewhere beneath the desk. "Am I to assume then that you wish to speak with the would-be assassin in question?"

"You assume correctly," Isaac responded as Pierre began to lead him away from the desk and down a corridor that both of them knew would lead to the cells. "Where is he now?"

"In one of our special cells in the back. Away from the other prisoners," Pierre answered as he led Isaac to where he wanted to go. "The captain's interrogating right now, though so far he hasn't gotten much out of him on account of the fact that he apparently no longer has a functioning jaw. I'm not even kidding either, that guy who caught him didn't just break his jaw, he completely dislocated it. Not only that but if you ask me I think he might also have a fractured skull since he was a little delirious when he eventually woke up. The captain's still trying to get what he can from him though. Though from what I understand he still refuses to say anything. The captain was even courteous enough to have some sheets of parchment and a quill brought to him, but he won't touch 'em. He won't even tell us his name, which is pointless cause all we need to do is check with his guild. At least one of the bean counters there should be able to tell us who he is."

"His guild?" Isaac spoke up as if he didn't already know.

"Oh you don't know already?" Pierre responded, apparently surprised to hear that Isaac supposedly did not already know that. "Our would-be assassin is a member of the Futura Collegium Aureum monster hunting guild here in Dis. Wears one of their bracelets, a gold one in fact. I'm no monster hunter myself but I know they don't just hand those out. Does a piss poor job of hiding it too. If I didn't know any better I'd say he wanted it to be seen." While Pierre had no way of knowing what was going on in Isaac's head, if he did then he would have heard him curse both himself and the man they were talking about for the sole fact that they were all here right now in the first place.

Once that conversation had finished, however, both Isaac and Pierre had reached a sturdy looking wooden door at the end of the corridor, upon which Pierre produced one of the many keys from his ring of keys and unlocked it for them. Beyond the door was a not exactly well lit staircase going down. As Pierre took a moment to lock the door back up after they had passed beyond it, Isaac subtly took a moment to take note of where Pierre put the ring of keys on his person after he had finished. Not that he expected that he would need that ring of keys, but for someone of his position it was always good to know things. After Isaac had seen what he wanted, the two of them began to descend the stairs, and before long the two of them found themselves in yet another corridor. This time, however, the entire right wall of the corridor appeared to be made up of nothing but iron bars.

It was difficult to tell at first glance exactly how many cells were in this corridor, but Isaac's own common sense told him that it couldn't have been too many. After all, this was only the Suntop District's city guard station, not a full prison. That, according to what Isaac knew of this region, was farther out in the desert away from this city or any of the neighboring towns. Isaac's common sense also told him that the person he was here to see was not in any of these cells, but he knew that he would be seeing him soon regardless.

"Ey, ey! You there!" an unfamiliar voice called out to Isaac as he passed by one of the cells. When he turned his head to see, Isaac beheld the visage of a man with long dark hair and a matching short beard, though the odd thing about him was that the only thing he was wearing was a pair of pants. He also possessed a black eye that looked to be very, very recent. "You look important. Any chance you could find it in you to talk some sense into these degenerates and get me out of here? I swear I'm not in here for murdering anyone or anything like that. Hell, what they put me in here for is barely even a crime. So do you have it in you to help out a man in need?" Seemingly ignoring him, Isaac instead returned his attention to Pierre.

"Who is this?" Isaac asked the guardsman as he pointed to the man in the cell.

"Oh, him," Pierre responded immediately. "We caught him out by the moon pool in the common district the first day of the festival trying to impersonate a city guardsman and using that to extort money from some of the visiting vendors.

Dumbass' luck ran out though when he tried to extort sexual favors from one of the prettier ones and got himself knocked out in a single punch by some big motherfucker who happened to be in her employ."

"I did not get knocked out in a single punch!" the man in the cell shouted as soon as Pierre had finished speaking.

"So you admit then that you tried to extort sexual favors from someone under the guise of a city guardsman?" Isaac then immediately asked. The man in the cell then shut his mouth and stayed quiet once he realized his mistake. Once he had him silenced, Isaac's eyes then drifted over to the cell next to his, whereupon he saw sleeping on the cot in the cell with his back to them a tall, muscular man with short, blonde hair. Seeing these two and hearing the story from Pierre made something click in Isaac's head as a newfound realization quickly struck him. However, he knew that he would need to confirm it. "And who is this?"

"That…" Pierre began once he saw whom Isaac was talking about. "That there's the motherfucker who punched him. Says he's a farm hand for some woman in a podunk town to the southwest of here. Though if you ask me-"

"Was the name of that podunk town Canaan by any chance?" Isaac then immediately asked once he had heard enough, upon which Pierre's eyes went wide with obvious surprise.

"Yes, actually," Pierre answered. "How did you know?"

"That is not your concern," Isaac answered as he returned his attention to the man in the other cell. "Now wake him up."

"Why do you-" Pierre began, but then stopped himself once he realized that asking too many questions of this man would likely be a very bad idea. "Alright then, it's your time." With that said Pierre then produced a steel rod from his belt and ran it back and forth along the bars of the big man's cell. "Ey, big guy! Get your ass up! You got a visitor!" The reaction from the big man in the cell was immediate as he sat up from the cot in his cell and looked over to see who was there. After making eye contact with Isaac, Dean let out a yawn before standing up, stretching out his arms for a moment, and then walking over towards the cell door so that he could properly speak to him. He then took a moment to look Isaac up and down, as if sizing him up. Isaac, for his part, remained silent and let the big man do as he pleased, as he had no reason to be intimidated by him.

"Who are you?" Dean eventually asked. "Do I know you?"

"No, we have never met," Isaac answered as calmly as ever. "But I am the man who can either get you out of this cell right now or make sure you rot in here forever depending on what you say to me right now. Do you understand me?" Dean, to his credit, remained more in control of himself than most other people Isaac had given that speech to over the years as all he did was let his eyes go wide for only a single moment before silently contemplating each of Isaac's words. Next to Isaac, Pierre had a similar reaction, though like before his lack of a response was more out of fear than contemplation.

"Yes..." Dean eventually responded, seemingly unsure of what else to say.

"Good," Isaac quickly responded in turn as he crossed his arms across his chest. "Now if you would, please. In your own words. Tell me exactly why you are in here, and please do tell the truth. I unfortunately do not have neither the time, nor the patience for bullshit and there are plenty of other, better things I could be doing. So please, for your own sake. Be honest." Again Dean needed to take a few seconds to comprehend exactly what was happening before he said anything.

"Okay..." the farm hand eventually spoke up before taking a few more short seconds to think of exactly what to say. "Well... It was before the first night of the festival... We had just finished setting up our stand when this guy wearing city guard armor walked up to my boss and told her that she needed to pay her fair dues to the city guard for the privilege of being allowed to set up a stand here in the city. My boss, though, knew he was lying so she refused to give him any money, but then he said that if she wasn't willing to give him money then he'd be willing to accept payment in other ways. My boss, of course, refused that too and told him to leave. He didn't take kindly to that though, and told her that one way or another he was gonna get what was his. My boss ain't afraid of no one though, so she, in her own way, told him to go away again, but after hearing that he got forceful and put his hands on her. Now, I grew up with three little sisters, and I wouldn't let some creep do that to them. So that's when I decided that I'd had enough of what that son of a bitch was saying so I punched him in the face. That's all there is to it, really. After that happened the real city guard showed up and took us both away. I didn't do anything after that."

Isaac took only a moment to consider Dean's words. In his years as the royal spymaster he had heard all manner of stories from people with iron bars between him and them, many of them excuses if not outright lies. Even to this day it amazed him what people would say to get themselves out from behind bars. Very few of them, however, were willing or able to admit what they had done, and while most of those who were only did so either out of arrogance or ignorance, that did not appear to be the case for the big man in the cell here. Because parsing out the truth was the main job of a spymaster, it was a skill that Isaac had honed and become more than proficient at over the years. To the degree that he to this day scared many of the other nobles in Sol due to how good he was at it. It was thanks to those skills that Isaac was able to tell that this man, despite the odds seemingly being against him, chose not to lie and instead admitted to what he had done. If only due to the fact that he had a justifiable reason for doing so. Something that Isaac could sympathize with.

"Am I to assume that what this man is saying matches up with your report?" Isaac then asked Pierre. Pierre, who had not been expecting to be involved in this conversation, needed to take a few quick seconds to put all of his thoughts in order. Something that he tried not to let Isaac catch onto.

"Y-yes, that sounds about right," Pierre answered. "Though there are quite a few more steps in between that is more or less how it happened." Isaac did not appear to show any response to this as he kept his eyes on the large man in the cell, and several more seconds passed afterwards wherein he did not say anything at all. It was enough that Pierre felt that he needed to let out a cough in order to properly get Isaac's attention. "M-my lord. If you wish I ca-" Before Pierre could say anything more he was suddenly cut off when Isaac held up a single finger in a manner that, due to Pierre's years of experience in the city guard and dealing with nobles of all varieties and degrees of importance, he knew well enough to know that he should keep his mouth shut. Despite this, Isaac remained silent in obvious contemplation and seemingly refused to say anything to anyone or even make a sound for several long, long seconds. That was until eventually he reached a decision, something that both Pierre and the man in the cell could see when it happened even before he spoke a single word.

"Get him out of there," Isaac said to Pierre. "His report of the incident in question is the same as your own, along with one that was told to me by a witness to these events, one Princess Filia Solara. While I honestly did not think much of it at the time, I believe it is obvious enough to everyone here what happened so keeping him here does little more than waste everyone's time. Especially when we all know that you are just going to release him later." Pierre, more than a little surprised to hear this from Isaac of all people, needed to take another few seconds to himself to process what he had just heard, and this time he couldn't hide it from Isaac.

"M-my lord," Pierre eventually responded. "Are you real-"

"Yes, I am really sure," Isaac interrupted. "Now are you going to do what I say or am I going to need to persuade you?" While Isaac's words sounded harmless enough, Pierre's years as a city guardsman had made him well aware of exactly what Isaac meant with the use of the word "persuade".

"M-my lord," Pierre repeated before he found himself able to continue. "Releasing a prisoner isn't something I can just do. I need to at the very least get approval from the captain and-"

"Then get approval from your captain and have him give all the orders he needs to and sign whatever paperwork is required to get this man released, but until that happens the very least you can do is let him out of this cell," Isaac interrupted again. Pierre had something that he wanted to say in response to that, but one look into Isaac's cold, seemingly unfeeling eyes told him that it really would be better for him to simply stay quiet. "If he decides to run then no doubt you will have the excuse you need to keep him locked in a cell like this for the rest of his natural life if you so decide. Assuming of course that you are able to apprehend him again, but I have more than enough confidence in the city guard of Dis to believe that you are capable of accomplishing such a task. After all, you have done a more than admirable job in ensuring that the visiting members of the Solaran royal family remain safe. Now are you going to let him out of this cell or not? I know that you have that ring of keys, so I know that at the very least is within your power."

This time Pierre chose not to argue or make any gesture that could be interpreted as arguing as he pulled the ring of keys from his belt and stepped around Isaac towards the cell door, upon which Isaac took a few steps back in order to give him the space that he needed. Within seconds the lock on Dean's cell was undone, upon which Pierre promptly opened it and stepped aside so that Dean could leave.

The big man in the cell, naturally, hesitated as he took a few seconds to process that all of this was actually happening. That his cell was actually being opened for him and that he was actually being told that it was okay for him to leave, all thanks to a man he had never seen before and likely would never see again. It was another reaction that Isaac was familiar with thanks to his years of experience as the royal spymaster. With that in mind, the only thing that worried him about this situation now was whether or not Dean would see this as some sort of trick and decide to remain within his cell, as in his experience most people in this situation often saw tricks where there weren't any. Thankfully, however, after a few short seconds of contemplation Dean eventually did decide to step out of the cell.

"Alright, stay close and don't try anything stupid," Pierre said to Dean once he was out. "If you do then you're going to wish we left you in that cell."

"Oh come the fuck on, really!" the voice of the long haired man from the next cell over shouted as all of this was happening. "You're letting him out but not me! I didn't even do anything! He's the one who attacked me!"

"Now, I believe you were leading me somewhere," Isaac then said to Pierre while completely ignoring the screaming long haired man.

"Oh, um… Yes, my lord, of course. Right this way please," Pierre quickly responded before casting one last glare at the big man he had just released. Dean showed no reaction to it at all as he looked to Isaac for answers. Isaac, however, only returned his gaze for a single second before looking away from him and following Pierre towards his real destination. Unsure of what else to do, Dean followed closely behind them.

"Don't you walk away from me!" the man with the long hair shouted again as they all began to walk away from him. "I have rights too! I'll make sure everyone knows about this injustice! Everyone will know about how I was being repressed!" Despite how loud he was shouting, Isaac, nor Pierre, nor the big man from the other cell said a single word in response or even acknowledgement to him as they all went on their way. None of them even bothered to look back towards his cell as they walked.

After a few more short seconds of walking, and more incessant screaming from the long haired man in the other cell, the now trio finally reached their destination. A large, metal door at the end of the corridor with all of the cells. Pierre was quick to open it and beyond it they beheld another, shorter, horizontal corridor with three more metal doors in it, one of which was opened with two other members of the city guard standing outside of it.

"Just so you know," a deep sounding voice from beyond the open door began. "This is normally the point where I'd start removing your fingernails until you give me the answer I need. But seeing as how you kind of need your fingers to give me any kind of answer, I'm going to spare you that pain. You do still have toenails though, and despite the fact that your punk ass is keeping me here much later than I would prefer, I am a patient man." It was at that point that Isaac seemingly forgot about Pierre and walked over towards the open door on his own, ignoring the two guards standing beside it as well.

"You stay right there," Pierre quickly said to Dean as he saw this happening. "And don't try anything stupid."

"As effective as that may be," Isaac began as he tried to step past the two guards and into the room beyond them, which he now saw was a stone room consisting of a single cell with bars separating the would-be assassin from the Captain of the city guard in this district, whom Isaac now saw to be older gentleman with dark, yet graying hair, a matching pencil thin mustache, and a darker skin tone like Isaac himself. However, as soon as Isaac had tried to step through the metal doorway into the cell, both of the guards standing by it quickly stepped in front of him and put their hands on the swords they wore at their hips. Isaac, however, remained undeterred. "There are far simpler methods of coercing information out of someone. Even if they are unable to speak."

Having heard this the Captain turned from the cell to see who had just come to disturb his interrogation, and at that moment locked eyes with Isaac.

"Who the hell are you?" the Captain was quick to ask. In lieu of any kind of verbal answer, Isaac instead held up his hand to show him the ring that he had shown to Pierre when he first arrived here. Unlike Pierre, the captain did not need a second to realize what the ring meant and instantly recognized both it and its significance, as Isaac saw for himself when his eyes momentarily went wide before giving a quick nod to his two subordinates at the door. Upon which both of them removed their hands from their swords and stepped out of Isaac's way.

"My lord," the captain then said to Isaac as he completely turned his attention away from Arthur and turned to properly face Isaac. "Allow me to apologize for-"

"Spare me your apologies and your pleasantries," Isaac interrupted as he stepped past the two guardsmen without a second thought. "I have neither the time nor patience for such superfluous things right now." As soon as he entered the solitary cell and Arthur saw Isaac, however, the beginnings of a smile began to form at the corner of his lips. Isaac, however, despite being able to clearly see it, ignored it completely. "Have you managed to get anything useful out of him thus far?"

"Sadly no," the captain answered after letting out a rather loud sigh. As much as he did not want to admit that to Isaac, he knew better than to lie to someone like him. "Broken jaw aside, he hasn't given us a damn thing. We even gave him some parchment and a quill so that he could give us some answers that way, but he hasn't even touched them. He hasn't tried to threaten us with them either. I know you're thinking that's ridiculous, but I've seen it happen. People can get clever with improvised weapons."

"Oh, believe me," Isaac was quick to respond. "I have seen more than my fair share of improvised weapons. Some of which were directed at myself." As Isaac said that his eyes narrowed on the would-be assassin in the cell. The effect was immediate as the attempted murderer took a step back from him. "All of those incidents went about as well as you would expect."

"Not that I mean any disrespect, my lord," the captain then began. "But unless you have a way to either read this man's mind or force him to write something down for us, I don't really see how much help you are going to be to us here." Isaac appeared to contemplate this for a moment as he brought a hand to his chin. There were a few other things that the captain wanted to say, as Isaac could tell just from the look on his face. However, Isaac also found it relieving that this particular city guardsman captain knew well enough to keep his mouth shut for the time being. In truth, however, Isaac wasn't actually thinking of anything, he simply wanted everyone to think that he was for their own sense of security.

"I may actually have something for this," Isaac eventually said after several long seconds. "When I was younger I was tasked with interrogating a wanted fugitive whose tongue had been removed before we had managed to capture him. Apparently someone other than us wasn't exactly fond of the things he had to say. Regardless, he may have been robbed of his ability to speak, but he still possessed his ability to give answers, and I was able to get every answer I needed out of him in the end. So if I can make a man without a tongue speak, then I should be able to make a man with a broken jaw sing." That remark caused one of the two guardsmen at the door to suddenly break out into laughter. One quick, soul piercing glare from both Isaac and the Captain, however, returned him to his former quiet state.

"So," The captain then spoke up as both he and Isaac returned their attention back to Arthur. "Am I to assume then that you want us to let you talk to him. Alone I'm guessing. That's how your types like to do it, isn't it?"

"Your types?" Isaac responded with obvious venom in his voice as his eyes drifted over in the Captain's direction. To Isaac's surprise, however, despite how upfront and polite the captain had been up until this point and despite the remark he had just made, he did not waver at all as he just stared right back at Isaac.

"Yes," the captain responded without even a second's hesitation. "You know, you lordly types. You always like to make everything your business. Not that I mean any offense to you, my lord, but if you were literally anyone other than who you are I would be telling you as politely as I can to sit your ass down and wait your turn so that we can do our jobs. I've been the captain of this district for a long time, my lord. So I've seen all manner of lords, ladies, wealthy merchants, and spoiled manchildren who thought they could come in here and try to take a prisoner from us, as if it was their right to do so." The captain then took a moment to pause as he redirected his attention back to Arthur. "The case of this mongrel here though, I understand, is unique in that it transcends our little district here in Dis. After all, this mongrel had the balls to attack someone associated with the Solaran royal family. So we knew that someone like you was bound to show up eventually. That's why I told Pierre there to bring you to see me as soon as you arrived."

Having heard all of that, Isaac did have more than a few things he wanted to say to the captain about his choice of words. However, in this instance he couldn't bring himself to do so, as with a few short sentences this captain of the city guard here in the Suntop district had shown him that not only was he smart enough to know what his place actually was in the wider world, but that he wasn't about to bend over backwards for anybody either. In a way it reminded Isaac of himself when he was younger, though he would never admit so out loud. Not only that, but despite his choice of words this captain was smart enough to know what Isaac wanted before he even got here and was prepared to give it to him. Very few people that he had ever dealt with had thought that far ahead.

"So do you want us to give you fifteen minutes alone with this mongrel?" The Captain then continued before Isaac could speak. "Because in this instance I'm-"

"Make it ten," Isaac interrupted before the captain could finish his sentence. "Although I am certain that I will have everything that we both need from him in five, let us just agree on ten to be safe." The captain, whom Isaac could tell from his eyes hated being interrupted as much as he did, remained silent for a few short seconds before responding.

"Very well," the captain eventually said. "I'll leave a few of my guardsmen outside. Just i-"

"There is no need," Isaac was quick to interrupt again, much to the ire of the captain. "You did thoroughly search him before questioning him, did you not?" Again, the captain kept silent for a few long seconds to let his frustration simmer before answering.

"Of course we did," the captain answered. "We're not morons. We even searched his clothes for hidden pockets, of which we actually found quite a few, though most of them were filled with knives. One in particular though, held a small bag of not silver or copper, but gold. Apparently whomever put him up to this really wanted that sorry son of a bitch dead and was willing to pay in advance. Must suck to be that guy right now. All that gold and it all went to nothing. If I were him I'd probably be so pissed that I'd start breaking everything I own." It took everything Isaac had after hearing that to keep himself under control, if only because of the fact that the captain was absolutely right. "But to answer your question, yes, we searched him. So unless he's either hiding something in his stomach or so far up his ass that he's in danger of choking on it, I'd say we cleaned him of pretty much everything. Although if he is hiding something in his stomach it'll be mighty difficult for him to cough it up now since his mouth only barely works."

"If that is indeed the case," Isaac continued once he was certain that the captain had finished speaking. "Then I will not be needing any assistance or any of your guardsmen to stand by and watch over me. I have had more than my fair share of interactions with dangerous individuals over the course of both my life and occupation. Many of whom have tried to kill me, even while I was alone in a room with them. Seeing as how I am here and they are not, I will leave it to you to imagine what exactly happened to them." While Isaac was saying all of this to the captain his eyes never left the would-be assassin in the cell, as if his words were more meant for him than the captain. Seeing Arthur's eyes widen for a split second upon hearing them was all the confirmation Isaac needed to see that his words had their intended effect. The captain, however, remained silent for a few more short seconds as he considered Isaac's words. Thankfully those few short seconds were all that he needed for that.

"Under normal circumstances I would argue with you on that one," the captain began. "Or at the very least try to remind you of how unsafe such an endeavor would be. However, I can tell from the way you speak that you are used to such things, and that this would be far from your first time alone in a room with a dangerous criminal. So in light of that I will grant you your request."

"Thank you, Cap-"

"That being said," the captain interrupted Isaac this time. "I will have four of my guardsmen standing by in the hall outside. You know, just in case you change your mind and do need backup." As annoyed as Isaac was that he had been interrupted this time, the fact that he had knowingly done the same thing more than once to the captain kept him from speaking up about it. Such an action now would be pointless anyway. He had already gotten what he wanted.

"That is acceptable," Isaac responded as politely as he could. "Even I am not so arrogant as to believe that I can plan for everything, and even without any kind of weapon or magic some individuals have the potential to cause great harm. So I do appreciate your concern."

"That is good to hear," the captain then said after letting out a sigh. "It's also good to see that you actually understand the severity of the situation at hand and don't argue. I'll be honest, you're much easier to work with than most other nobles I've had to deal with. Thank Solaris for that."

"I am not like most nobles," Isaac responded as he pulled his attention away from the would-be assassin in the cell so that he could address the captain properly. "Most nobles... Actually no, I will be honest with you, all nobles are concerned only with their own self interest. I may be part of a noble house now, but I was not born into nobility. So unlike them I understand the concept of serving others. That is why I am here, after all."

"Good to hear," the captain was quick to respond. "I will leave you to it then. If you need something don't hesitate to scream. The walls here are thick but they aren't soundproof. They'll be able to hear you outside." With that having been said the captain then turned and began to leave the cell.

"If you are in need of something to do while you wait for me," Isaac spoke up before the captain could leave. "Perhaps you can see what you can do about getting the gentleman outside released. Your man, Pierre I believe his name was, knows all the relevant details." Hearing that caused the captain to stop dead in his tracks as he turned to cast one last glare back as Isaac.

"This isn't going to be one of those things that'll give me a migraine is it?"

the captain then asked with a deadly serious look on his face.

"That I cannot answer," Isaac responded without even looking at him. "Because I do not know what gives you migraines. I will, however, have something for you by the time you are finished with that, and if I do not, then I will be in the process of getting it. That I can assure you." The captain, again, needed to take a moment to consider Isaac's words before he could come up with a proper response.

"Let's see then if you're more than just your words," the captain then said. "I'd like to think that the Solaran royal family employs people who are the absolute best at what they do, but I've been wrong before." Before Isaac could respond the captain was out the door as the two other guardsmen in the room followed him out. The last one to leave shut the door behind him as he walked out, leaving Isaac and Arthur finally alone.

Despite them being alone now, Isaac remained silent for over a full minute as he just stared at Arthur, as if he were trying to pick him apart for truths and false truths without actually saying anything. Arthur simply stayed silent and let Isaac stare at him. Not that he could do much of anything else. There were things he could have done, even said if he really wanted to, but he knew better than to say or do anything with Isaac in the room. After the minute of silence passed, Isaac finally made a sound in the form of taking in and letting out a very, very deep breath as he closed his eyes in an attempt to forcibly relax himself.

"And so here we are," Isaac began. "Funny how things turn out, is it not?" Momentarily confused by his words, Arthur simply backed towards the wall opposite the bars and leaned against it before crossing his arms, as if to say without words how much he actually cared to pay attention to what Isaac was saying right now. Isaac, however, did not appear to care. "Although I suppose to some people this is not really funny at all, now is it? In fact, I would wager that some certain individuals, including yourself no doubt, do not find a single thing funny about this whole situation." Hearing that was apparently enough to royally piss off Arthur as he narrowed his eyes at Isaac, though he wisely kept himself from making any sounds. "One such person, I am certain, is your employer." As Isaac said those words, he, as if to mock him, narrowed his own eyes at Arthur. When he did something appeared to click into place in Arthur's mind as his eyes slowly went wide and, despite his best efforts, Isaac could see that he was beginning to sweat.

"Because of course you have an employer," Isaac continued as he broke his gaze away from Arthur and began to pace around the limited space he had. "You, after all, tried to assassinate someone who is closely associated with the Solaran royal family. Sure, you may have had your own reasons, but I do not care what they are. Nobody has the stones to just do what you did." Isaac then stopped pacing for a second and brought a hand to his chin in mock thought. "I wonder what he must be thinking right now. No doubt word of your failure has already reached him, so he, assuming it is a he of course, must be very angry. Though both you and I know that to someone with both the resolve and the funds to hire an assassin to murder an associate of the royal family, angry is an understatement." Isaac then glanced back over in Arthur's direction and saw that while he was still attempting to play it cool, the sweat on his forehead was becoming more and more visible. "I can only speculate of course, but if I were him, after breaking something in a fit of rage I would obsessively try to come up with ways to keep you silent. Because the knowledge that if you were to say or even do anything, even unintentionally, even if you are unable to speak, that would connect you back to me... That is simply a risk I cannot afford to take. If only for my own peace of mind and sanity." Isaac fell silent after saying that so that he could see the reaction of Arthur. As he had expected to see, while outwardly he was still trying to play it cool, Arthur was fidgeting quite a bit more than he had been before, though he made obvious attempts to hide it.

"Then again..." Isaac continued as he began to pace around the room again. "Silencing you would be too predictable, and killing your own pawns is no way to ensure loyalty." As Isaac spoke those words, as he had predicted, Arthur showed great intrigue and interest as he stopped fidgeting and began to just listen. "No, to ensure loyalty one must be supportive to one's subordinates, something that includes helping them out when they face times of crisis. After all, someone you pay to do a job is only loyal to you for the duration of the job. Someone whose life you save is loyal to you for at the very least the foreseeable future." Isaac watched as Arthur began to more visibly relax in his cell as his lips curled up into the closest thing to a smirk one can make with a broken jaw. "With that in mind, I am sure that your employer may be working tirelessly to think of a way to get you out of this predicament. After all, you made a mistake, and you know what that makes you? Human. Just like me, just like the city guardsmen, and just like the fool that knocked you out." Hearing that, Arthur chuckled to himself somewhat, though even that was difficult to do with a broken jaw, as he had to stop almost immediately after doing so because of the pain. With that reaction Isaac couldn't help but let a smirk crawl across his own face.

"Unfortunately, because I do not know your employer, I cannot say for certain whether or not he, or she, is at this very moment coming up with a way to either silence you or rescue you. However, I can tell you one thing that I know for certain about him," Isaac then said as he stopped pacing and placed his hands on the bars that separated him from Arthur, upon which with a single finger, he beckoned him to come closer. Arthur got the message instantly as he walked up to the bars directly in front of Isaac and propped his arms on them so that he could lean against them like he had the wall. With them as close as they were, however, Isaac still beckoned him closer so that he could whisper something to him. Without any hesitation the monster hunter complied, and within seconds he was close enough to Isaac that were it not for the bars, they could practically touch each other. It was only then that Isaac spoke with a whisper so quiet that even as close as they were, Arthur could only barely hear it. "More than anything, he absolutely hates loose ends."

Before Isaac had even finished speaking Arthur suddenly felt a prick in his arm, as if he had been stung. Looking to see, he saw that between two of Isaac's fingers was a small blade no longer or thicker than a sewing needle. While that in and of itself wasn't anything to sweat over, the full implications of being stabbed by a blade like that, by Isaac of all people, soon ran through Arthur's head like a stampede as his eyes suddenly became wider than dinner plates. Before he could even do anything to react, however, Isaac's left hand suddenly reached through the bars and grabbed him by his mouth while his right went around his neck.

"Help! Help!" Isaac then shouted at the top of his lungs as Arthur struggled in his grasp. Despite all his efforts, however, Isaac's grip was like iron, and he never budged even a single centimeter despite the immense efforts of Arthur to break free of him. Even hitting Isaac's arms to knock them away produced no results, as Isaac showed barely any reaction at all to any pain. "Somebody help!" The instant Isaac had finished shouting, the four city guardsmen who had been stationed outside suddenly rushed into the cell, upon which Isaac turned his head to address them. "One of his teeth was fake! It contained a poison capsule!" As soon as he had finished speaking Arthur reached through the bars himself and punched Isaac in the face, but even that produced no results as Isaac still maintained his grip on him.

Having seen and heard all that they needed to, the four guardsmen went to work as one of them produced a ring of keys to unlock the cell, two of them rushed to the sides of Isaac and grabbed Arthur's arms to prevent him from hurting any of them, and the fourth one ran back outside to get the captain.

"Do not bite down you son of a whore! Do not fucking bite down!" Isaac shouted at the monster hunter as the one guardsman unlocked his cell. "I will get answers out of you yet! Who sent you! Who fucking sent you!" As soon as Isaac had finished asking that question, however, blood suddenly spewed from between Isaac's fingers as Arthur began to convulse in his grasp.

At the same time, the guardsman with the keys had unlocked the cell door and immediately rushed inside, upon which he ran up behind Arthur and pushed him into the bars so that he could not move. That done he grabbed Arthur by his right arm, and as he did the guardsman holding that arm released it and moved to assist him as he pinned that arm behind Arthur's back. As soon as they were done with the first arm the two guardsmen in the cell then proceeded to pin Arthur's other arm behind his back. As all of this was happening the monster hunter began to convulse more and more in their grasp, so much so in fact that the three guardsmen began to worry that he would become more of a risk to himself than to any of them.

With another great cough from the would-be assassin Isaac found his hand suddenly drenched in more blood as he watched Arthur's eyes begin to roll back into his head. Seeing that, Isaac consciously loosened his grip on Arthur's mouth and let go of his neck. The instant he no longer had hold of him the guardsmen in the cell tore him away from Isaac and pinned him to the floor of his cell. Before either of them could say or do anything, however, with another great cough Arthur suddenly expelled a large quantity of blood from his mouth.

Isaac only silently watched as the guardsmen in the cell did their best to keep Arthur pinned where he was, even if they, like Isaac, knew already that it was too late for him. Even if he wasn't dead now, he would be in a few minutes, so everything they were doing now was pointless, and yet despite that Isaac couldn't bring himself to show any emotion whatsoever, much less empathy. Throughout his long life he had seen more than his fair share of people dying in front of him, and if he had his way he knew that this would not be his last. As such, as he barely knew him, nothing could bring him to feel anything at all for this monster hunter who was now dying painfully in a prison cell. Some blood began to drip from the hand that had previously been over Arthur's mouth, but Isaac barely noticed this, as the sensation of blood on his hands was nothing new to him either.

Just before Arthur could finish convulsing the fourth guardsman returned to the cell with the captain in tow, only for the two of them to watch with Isaac as the attempted murderer fell still on the floor of his cell with one more great cough followed by even more blood violently expelling from his mouth.

"What happened?" the captain asked without taking his eyes off of the freshly dead body in his cell. "Will somebody tell me what the fuck just happened!"

Chapter 24

When Seth opened his eyes his vision was incredibly blurry. So much so in fact that he could hardly see anything in front of him at all, only the color white. Unlike the past few times when this had happened to him, however, the blurriness did not go away, at least not as quickly as it had in the past. More than a little annoyed that this was happening to him yet again, Seth closed his eyes and stayed that way for several long seconds to see if that would help. He had learned since the last time this had happened to him that blinking typically helped to clear one's vision. When he opened his eyes again, however, the blurriness remained, as did the color white. Now more frustrated than annoyed, Seth couldn't help but let out a groan, but when he did his voice sounded much weaker than he meant it to, as if he didn't have the strength to even groan properly. The thought of that made his frustration turn to anger as he subconsciously ground his teeth together. That, however, only served to make his head hurt and before long the darkness had overtaken him again as his eyes closed.

The next time Seth opened his eyes his vision was, much to his immense ire, still blurry. However, most of it appeared to have cleared up as in a brief moment of clarity he could see that he was staring up at a smooth, white ceiling. Before he had a chance to think about what that meant for him, however, the sound of voices that he did not recognize distracted him from all other thoughts. He tried to turn his head in the direction they were coming from to see who they belonged to, but the mere act of doing so made both his head and neck hurt, as if the muscles in them were so stiff that they refused to move. With this in mind, Seth decided to try to lift his arm to test this theory. When he did so he instantly regretted it as a surge of pain shot through all the muscles in his arm as they seemingly refused to move. It was so much that Seth couldn't help but let out another, louder groan before letting his arm fall back down to where it was. What made this worse for him was that because of the angle he was looking at he couldn't actually see or even tell how far he had moved his arm.

The sound of him groaning, however, had apparently garnered some attention from the people that he could hear as he soon heard footsteps coming in his direction. Before long the face of someone that he did indeed not recognize entered Seth's vision. His visage was blurry at first, but after blinking a few more times Seth had a moment to see him clearly. The visage of the man he beheld was of an older, bespectacled man with a square jawline and sharp features. His short, dark, unruly hair and full beard only added to the apparent harshness of his appearance. Seeing him, Seth tried to ask where he was, but when he did so all that came out of his mouth was another groan, as if he hadn't had water for days. A feeling that he knew all too well.

"Easy there, son, easy," the strange man said to him with a voice that was surprisingly calm given his appearance. "Don't try to talk. In fact, don't even try to move. You're lucky to be alive. The best thing you can do for yourself right now is rest." Despite that sounding like good advice, Seth couldn't help but ignore it as there were still several burning questions on his mind that he needed answered. Preferably right now. Like before, however, when he tried to ask them all that came out of his mouth was a groan. "To answer the questions you're no doubt trying to ask," the strange bearded man then said as he looked over Seth and even looked directly into his eyes, which made him incredibly nervous. "You're in the hospital in the Suntop District of Dis. You were poisoned. Some friends of yours got you help. In many ways you're incredibly lucky, son. Most who succumb to a poison like this die within minutes, but thankfully only a small amount entered your bloodstream and our paramedics rushed you here before too much damage could be done. Truly you must be blessed by Solaris to even be awake right now."

While he obviously meant well by what he said, the truth was that those words could not have been any farther from what Seth truly felt at that moment. Blessed was certainly not the word he would have chosen for how he felt right now. With only some of the questions he had answered, no ability to speak, no ability to move, and absolutely no other idea of what to do now, Seth resigned himself to following the advice of this strange man that he assumed was a doctor as he closed his eyes again and was lulled back into sleep.

Eventually Seth did open his eyes again, and when he did his vision had cleared enough for him to be able to make out the details of the ceiling. Not that there were many to see, but the fact that he could see them was a huge improvement for him. Just to see if he could, he tried to lift his arm again. Much to his relief it didn't hurt anymore, but he still felt incredibly weak, as if he didn't possess the strength nor the energy to lift it at all. It was only then that he noticed that he was breathing rather heavily, as if he had run as fast as he could around the whole city without stopping and had yet to fully catch his breath. Still, at least he was breathing as opposed to coughing, and it didn't hurt him to breathe, so that was okay in his mind. For a moment Seth contemplated going back to sleep, if only so that the next time he woke up he would not feel as drained as he did now and therefore would at least have the energy to move. Those thoughts were kicked out of his head as soon as they came, however, as he felt that he had slept enough. Nevermind the fact that it didn't make any sense to him at all how he could be so out of breath when all he had been doing for who knew how long was sleeping.

So with nothing else to do and no desire at all to go back to sleep, Seth just stared up at the ceiling and carefully thought through everything he knew of that had led him to this point. He, Tara, Raz, and Daedalus had all been invited to brunch by Filia, that much he remembered. Then after that they went to the theater, then to this very fancy restaurant where he had something called a roast for the first time, then he needed to use the restroom, and while he was in there someone had attacked him. Then after that the next thing he knew, he had fallen over and was coughing up blood. That much he remembered just fine.

The man he had seen before, whom Seth assumed to be a doctor, told him that he had been poisoned. That was a word he had never heard before, but if what he had experienced was being poisoned, then he knew for certain that there was no way it could mean anything good. The man who did this to him, the last thing Seth remembered about him before it happened was feeling as if he had been poked in the side by something sharp. It didn't even hurt him that much, it was more of an annoyance than a hindrance, barely worth his attention at all. Thinking back on it, Seth did remember that he had a knife, and if that was what poked him that more than likely meant that he meant to sink it in much deeper than he had. Obviously with the intent to do him harm. Still, if being poisoned meant that something so little could hurt so much, then what did that mean about the type of person who used it. All of that, however, didn't matter to Seth as much as who that man was.

He may have never seen him before or known anything about him, but that bracelet he wore, he would recognize it anywhere. It was different in color to the one that Vivian wore, but it was still the same. He had seen Vivian's enough times to know that for a fact. If the person who did this to him wore a bracelet like that, that could only mean that he was part of Vivian's monster hunting guild. If that was true, then Seth could reasonably guess that the reason he had attacked Seth was because he knew what he was and was just doing his job. The one part of this that he struggled to put together was how that could be.

There were only a small handful of people who knew the truth about him, and while all of them were currently in this city, none of them to his knowledge had ever revealed the truth. Tara would never do so just because of her personality. Raz and Daedalus had plenty of chances to do so even before coming here, so why they would have waited this long made no sense at all to Seth. Agatha liked to get drunk and was known for being a bit of a gossiper, sure, but even at her worst Seth felt that she could maintain some level of secrecy. She had for this long, anyway. That left only one remaining suspect, the obvious one, and the idea that it was her was one that Seth did not want to entertain. Despite that, however, the longer he lay there staring up at the blank ceiling with nothing else to do or think about, the more he realized that as much as it hurt him, he had to.

Ever since he had told her the truth their relationship had been rocky to say the least, and it had only gotten worse as time went on. When he had first told her, she tried to kill him without a second thought, and ever since then she had gone out of her way not to talk to or even have anything to do with him if she could. Then there was their last meeting, one that was very much still fresh in Seth's mind.

Vivian had never been one to lie to him, in fact Seth believed that she found it incredibly difficult to tell a lie due to her tendency to shout out whatever was on her mind regardless of the circumstances. That was when she was sober, however. Being drunk not only made this aspect of her worse, but seemingly emboldened her to the point where she saw any consequence of her words less as something to avoid and more of a challenge that she had to meet. This often led to disastrous results, as Seth knew, and their last meeting had been no different. If she had something to do with what had happened to him, however, then Seth had to believe that what she said to him that day went much deeper than a few hurtful words. Much deeper than he wanted to believe.

He knew that Vivian had a hatred of monsters, that much was obvious. In fact, most of the people Seth knew had a hatred of monsters. He didn't need any explanation as to why that was, he had seen their handiwork enough times to know that all of their hatred was justified. He even understood the reasons why she hated him. That said, there was one part of this that didn't make any sense at all to Seth no matter how many times he thought it over. If he was to believe that Vivian was capable of betraying him like this, then why would she send someone else from her guild to kill him instead of doing it herself?

As little sense as that made to Seth, however, the more he kept thinking through it and the more reasons he concocted in his mind for why Vivian would have someone else from her guild do this for her, the more enraged Seth became at her with each new thought. Before long the idea that it had to be Vivian began to make the most sense to him regardless of whatever her reasoning was, and the idea of that made his teeth hurt as he subconsciously began to grind them together in his rage. There was still Raz, Daedalus, Tara and Agatha of course, but the reasons why they wouldn't try to kill him like this made more sense to him than the reasons why they potentially would, especially regarding Raz since Seth knew that he could have at any point just killed him himself and suffer no consequences for it. Seth also knew that he was certainly capable of it. Especially given what Seth knew about him now. Attempting to kill someone like this did seem like something that Tara would do, and there was still a chance that Agatha may have inadvertently blurted something out while drunk, but given that it was someone from Vivian's guild that ended up doing the deed this whole ordeal screamed to Seth that even if it wasn't Vivian she still must have known about it and did nothing to stop it. The thought of that hurt him more than the poisoned blade itself and any of the other reasons he came up with for why she would do this to him.

So there he lay, alone again, in a hospital bed again, left to stare up at the ceiling and do nothing but stew in his own thoughts again. The more thoughts came, however, the more of them eventually led back to Vivian, and the more he thought of her the more the potential reasons he had previously thought of regarding why she would do this to him began to make more and more sense to him. In time his thoughts became less about the reasons and more about Vivian herself. Through this a new wave of emotions flowed through Seth that he normally didn't associate with the redheaded monster hunter, but now he couldn't help himself even if he wanted to.

Rage, pain, betrayal, blind ignorance, those were only a few of the feelings he could name that the image of her face conjured up now. It was enough to make him bite down on his teeth so hard that he actually drew blood, yet he didn't even feel the pain.

Eventually the poison, the reasons why, even his friends, all of them began to fade one by one from Seth's mind until all that was left were his raw, unfiltered emotions. From the first time he saw her in the desert to the last time he saw her in The Tipsy Rabbit, Seth replayed every memory he had of her in his mind, and each new one only served to make him angrier and angrier until all that was left was just the anger. At some point during this Seth began to pass out again, but this time he made no attempt to keep himself awake when it did.

When Seth eventually opened his eyes again the room was slightly darker and had taken on a more orange-ish hue. This immediately told Seth several things. The first and most obvious was that whatever day it was, it would be getting dark soon. What it also told him, however, was that the room he was in had a window, and a window large enough to let in enough light to illuminate the whole room at that. It also told him that he had been here for much longer than he had been initially aware. Not that he was that aware in the first place, but his perception of time had apparently been off with the few lucid moments of consciousness he had. The last, and seemingly most important thing this told him, however, was that if this place had a window then it might be relatively easy to leave.

With all of that in mind Seth decided, for the first time since waking up here, to take an actual look around the room he was currently in. When he turned his head left and right he expected to see more hospital beds like in Andrea's clinic back in Canaan. However, this did not appear to be the case this time as in both directions all he saw was a plain, white wall. To his right he also saw a simple wooden dresser against the far wall and an identical looking nightstand next to his bed. On the nightstand was a purple and orange glass vase with white, bell-like flowers in it. It was only after he saw them that their smell hit his nose, and the instant it did he felt himself instinctively recoil and immediately turn to look in the opposite direction. Despite looking pretty, the only word he could think of to describe their scent was rancid.

To his left he saw only a featureless wall with nothing on, against, or even in front of it. He did see, however, that the window that was letting in the light was in that direction. The window itself wasn't on the wall he was looking at, per se, but rather on the wall behind his bed. It just happened to be situated to the left of his bed. Unfortunately, the angle he was looking in didn't allow him to see outside of the window, so he couldn't get that much of a feel for what time of day it actually was, which greatly disappointed him as he would have liked to know that. Seeing that, however, with slightly more effort than he initially thought it would take, Seth craned his neck upwards so that he could see what was directly in front of him. To his surprise he saw yet another wall with a door on it slightly off center from where his bed was.

The revelation that he had his own private room was not one that Seth was prepared for, but now that he could see it he felt a sense of immense relief wash over him, as if he no longer needed to worry about something that would have weighed him down. In a sense that was very true, for what he felt that he needed to do now the idea that he would have privacy for it was certainly an immense weight off his shoulders. With that established Seth set his mind to the next task that he needed to accomplish. Moving.

Like before Seth started out small by seeing if he could lift his arm. While there was still some pain it had lessened considerably, to the point that it felt less like actual pain to him and more like a stiff muscle. Feeling that, Seth decided that it would be best not to move too quickly, as he knew that would likely be problematic for him. Regardless, with that accomplished, Seth then set about moving his other arm. Again, he did so slowly as he moved his hands beneath the blanket so that they were able to touch each other, upon which he then clasped his fingers over each just to see if he could. The act of doing that strained him somewhat, as even his fingers felt stiff, but it was nothing that he couldn't handle. As long as he kept moving slowly the brief pain he was experiencing felt more like an annoyance than anything else.

With all of that done Seth then steeled himself for what he needed to do next, and for that he knew that he would need to move extra slowly lest he really hurt himself. First, he removed the covers from his bed before slowly turning himself so that he could get out of it. The muscles in his arms strained quite a bit when he tried to push himself up, but Seth was able to fight through it by gritting his teeth. The real shock came to him, however, when his bare feet touched the cold floor and he instantly recoiled back. The sudden drop in temperature was not something he had been expecting, but after experiencing it once he steeled his nerves again and slowly lowered his feet to the floor.

Even with all of that done, however, the most difficult part was still to come as Seth struggled to stand. At first his legs ached from the immense strain of keeping his body upright. So much so in fact that Seth needed to hold himself up on his bed lest he fall over. Even with stiff muscles, however, the pain of just standing in the state he was in was almost too much for him to bear as he grit his teeth together harder than before to fight the pain. After a few seconds, however, the pain lessened as a groan escaped his lips. Unsure of what else to do at this point, Seth simply stayed where he was until the pain lessened a bit more, which after a few more seconds it did. Regardless, Seth was not about to take chances now as he waited for a little while longer until the pain had subsided completely.

Once that had happened, Seth slowly removed his hands from the bed and stood up properly on his own. While he was able to stand, it took a surprising amount of effort for him to do so, so he knew that he couldn't afford to waste any more time. Being careful not to move too quickly, Seth took a single step forward. The sheer amount of effort that was required to keep himself upright now almost made him fall over as he did so, but he caught himself at the last second. It was only then when he looked down at himself to see what had happened that he noticed that all of his clothes were gone and had been replaced with a simple white gown. Knowing that that was an issue he could address later, Seth steeled his nerves again as he took another step forward, and then another, and then another until he reached the window.

Unsurprisingly it took a bit more effort than Seth first thought it would to pull the window open, but he managed to do it without seriously hurting himself. A stiff breeze of warm, night air hit Seth in the face as he looked out the window to see that the sun was indeed setting, as it had since passed behind some of the buildings in the distance. Unfortunately for him, he could not tell at all where in this city he was, as none of the buildings surrounding the hospital looked familiar to him. He could tell, however, by their polished stone, and in most cases elaborate construction, that he was indeed still in the Suntop District of Dis. The number of buildings like this all together in one place was more of a shock to Seth than anything else. Before he had assumed that the few buildings he had seen in the Suntop District before were all unique, and that all of the other buildings in this district simply looked like the buildings in the Common District. His current view, however, was making him question that assumption.

Not that that mattered to him anyway, there was something far more important that he needed to do now besides stare at the view. Despite knowing what he needed to do, however, he still hesitated, as he couldn't help but question if this was really the right decision to make. Remembering the events of the past few hours before he had arrived here, however, was all that it took to make him realize that the decision had already been made for him, and that if he did not do this now he more than likely would not have another chance later.

"Cain…" Seth eventually spoke. His voice was much quieter than he had intended it to be, but then he remembered that he had been in a hospital bed recovering for who knew how long. So with that in mind Seth took in a few deep breaths before trying again. "Cain, are you there?" No response came from anywhere. "Cain… Cain…" Still no response. For a moment Seth considered calling out to the creature in question as loud as he could, but then instantly thought better of it before opening his mouth, as he knew that doing so would raise too many questions that he would have to eventually answer. "Cain, where are you? You said not to worry if I couldn't see you. That you'd hear me wherever I was. So where are you?" Again, the only response Seth received was the sound of the wind passing by. "I want to talk. Cain… Please…" Despite his continued pleas, the only response he received was still silence as he watched the last of the sun disappear behind the buildings.

A sudden feeling of emptiness welled up within Seth as he stood there at the window, seemingly defeated yet again. Here he was, surrounded on all sides by people he knew were his enemies, betrayed by the people he thought were his friends, and now even that bat creature was nowhere to be seen or heard. Just thinking about all of it made Seth feel light headed, as if that was enough to knock him off of his feet again. With all of that work done for nothing, Seth closed the window and slowly made his way back to his bed with his head hung low. As he crawled back into it, however, a greater sense of concern than he had ever felt before washed over him. In that moment he realized that whatever was going to happen, he would need to take action soon lest he befall a fate worse than his current one. He could only hope that he had the chance to act before anyone else did.

That was the last thought that went through his head before his vision faded into darkness once more.

The sound of something tapping woke Seth almost instantly. When he opened his eyes, however, everything was still pitch black, which told him that it was currently nighttime. While he waited for his eyes to adjust to the darkness the sound of the tapping continued. At first it sounded like simple tapping to him. However, upon listening more closely he realized that it was the sound of someone tapping on glass. What's more, given how loud it was, it had to be really close to him. Those two realizations hitting Seth at once made his eyes instantly shoot open completely as he threw the covers off of his bed.

The act of doing that, however, made his arm suddenly hurt, which in turn made him remember that he still needed to take things slow for now. Keeping that in mind, Seth slowly lifted himself from his bed again and made his way over towards the window. By the time he had reached the window his eyes had adjusted well enough to the darkness, and thanks to that his eyes beheld on the other side of the window, tapping a wing against the glass, a large, bat-like creature with proportionally large, piercing blood red eyes and enormous pointed ears. When it saw him the bat stopped tapping as its lips curled up into a wide, toothy grin filled with sharp looking teeth.

Immediately Seth threw open the window, and as he did the bat-like monster flapped its wings and took to the air to avoid the moving pane of glass before flying back forward and perching itself on the open window like a bird. Because of its size the tips of its ears touched the top of the open window.

"Hi," the bat-like monster known as Cain said to Seth in his familiar nasally voice as he flashed another sharp toothed grin.

"Cain…" Seth responded as if on instinct rather than any desire to actually say anything. "You're… here."

"Well of course I'm here," Cain responded with a smile. "You called for me."

"Why… Why didn't you come earlier?" Seth couldn't help but ask.

"Well I'm sorry," Cain replied with a roll of his large eyes. "Not all of us are as... I suppose in this instance it would be blessed, as you are with your appearance." Seth was about to ask him what he meant, but before any words could come out of his mouth he instantly realized what he was talking about as he glanced down at himself.

"Oh…" he couldn't help but let out.

"I mean if I flew around this city in broad daylight what do you think would happen?" Cain then continued.

"I'm sorry," Seth said as his eyes fell towards the floor.

"Oh don't be," Cain responded with a wave of his wing. "You're still young. I get it. All of us go through a period of self discovery before we become enlightened to our true purpose. That is of course, assuming we don't get killed." Cain then began laughing to himself as he brought a wing over to cover his mouth, which after what Seth had gone through he couldn't help but find irritating. Cain, however, appeared to notice this as he stared back up at Seth, upon which he ceased his laughter. "I'm sorry." he said to Seth in what sounded like an apologetic tone. Seth felt that he should tell him that it was alright, but he wasn't sure if he wanted to. "So, since you called me here I assume it's for a good reason."

"I…" Seth began, but then stopped himself. While he knew that he really had no one else to turn to right now, part of him still wasn't sure if this was the right thing to do. Sure, he had no reason to trust any of his so-called friends anymore, but that didn't necessarily mean he had any reason to trust whom he was turning to either. In remembering his friends, however, the image of Vivian's face popped into his head again, and that was enough to steel his nerves and make him realize that he had to do this. "I want to talk to Lilim."

"Really!" Cain let out, seeming excited. "You want to talk to mistress! That's good! Good good good! So you've decided to join us then?"

"No!" Seth quickly responded once he saw how excitable Cain was becoming. "I… I just want to talk to her. That's all." Cain tilted his head to the side as he stared up at Seth with an expression that reminded him of the "head in the clouds" confused stare that he often gave to people. Sometimes unintentionally. At least to him it appeared how his supposed friends had described it to him in the past.

"You just want to talk to mistress?" Cain then eventually said, his confusion evident in his voice as well.

"Yes," Seth answered. "That's not a problem is it?"

"Oh, no no," Cain responded quickly. "Not at all."

"Okay…" Seth let out, though the way in which Cain answered him concerned him somewhat. "So can you take me to her?"

"Of course," Cain answered as his ears perked back up. "But…"

"But…" Seth repeated with obvious apprehension in his voice.

"Mistress is outside of the city," Cain continued. "So we're going to need to get you outside of the city if you want to speak with her."

"Oh…" Seth let out again as he immediately understood the problem.

"What's wrong?" Cain asked, seeing his concern.

"That… might be a problem," Seth answered as his eyes diverted away from Cain.

"Why?" Cain then asked.

"I can't just leave the city," Seth answered.

"Why not?"

"People will notice if I'm gone."

"What is people?"

"Other humans?"

"Oh," Cain said in understanding. "So why is that a bad thing?"

"Because if people notice that I'm gone they'll come looking for me."

"Oh, I see what the problem is," Cain then said as he nodded in what appeared to Seth at least, to be understanding. "If the other humans notice that you're gone they'll come looking for you, and if they find you they'll try to kill you again." While that wasn't quite the line of logic Seth was thinking of when he said that, he didn't have it in him to correct Cain since he was mostly right. Cain then brought a wing to his chin in thought. "So if I'm understanding this right. If you leave and people know you're gone, they'll come looking for you, but if you leave and they don't know you're gone, then they won't come looking for you and everything should be okay."

"That… sounds about right," Seth hesitantly answered.

"Well that's an easy fix," Cain let out upon hearing that as his lips curled into another toothy smile. "All we have to do is sneak you out of the city before anyone knows you're gone and then by the time they do, you'll already be with mistress."

"Okay…" Seth responded. That logic did make sense to him somewhat. "How exactly are we going to do that though?"

"Well lets see…" Cain said as he brought a wing back to his chin. "Mistress said that you could use magic like her. Is that right?"

"Yes," Seth answered.

"Can you teleport?" Cain then asked.

"No," Seth answered without any hesitation.

"Oh, well then that is going to be a problem?"

"Can't she just come and get me?" Seth asked. "She did it before?"

"No," Cain answered as soon as Seth had finished speaking. "Pulling you out of a small town and taking you a short distance was easy at the time, but mistress is much farther than that now and she doesn't know exactly where you are. So she can't do that again."

"Why not?" Seth couldn't help but ask, to which Cain shrugged his wings in place of his shoulders.

"I don't know," Cain answered. "I can't do magic so I don't understand how it works. You'll have to ask mistress when you see her." There were many questions Seth wanted to ask about that, but he thought better of it before he actually did, especially since Cain had just admitted that he wouldn't be able to give him any actual answers.

"So what can we do?" Seth then asked without thinking, upon which Cain silently brought a wing back to his chin again. After a few short seconds of this, however, Seth watched as Cain leaned backwards out of the window to see what was outside. Seth did his best to follow his gaze, but he couldn't see what specifically he was looking at.

"What can you do?" Cain asked as he stopped leaning out the window and directed his full attention back towards Seth. Before Seth could ask him to clarify what he meant though, Cain appeared to see his confusion. "With magic." Hearing that Seth immediately understood where he was going with this.

"Not much," Seth admitted nervously as the realization that this whole endeavor might be futile without magic hit him, and he did not want to feel like dead weight.

"Oh come now," Cain chipped in. "Anything you can do is something.

Don't be discouraged. I mean look at me." Cain then paused for a moment to flare out his wings so that Seth could see all of him. "Anything you can do with magic would be more than I can do. So come on. Out with it."

"Okay…" Seth hesitantly responded. In a way he couldn't help but feel that he was being pressured, but he wasn't sure if that was a bad thing in this instance. "I can… I can throw lightning at things."

"That's good," Cain replied with a nod. "What else?"

"Recently I learned how to move objects that are light enough by thinking about it," Seth then added.

"Okay, that's good too," Cain interjected with another, more fervent nod. "I have absolutely no idea what that could be useful for, but it's good to know that you can do that."

"I can create weapons," Seth continued. "Well, a w-"

"I've seen a lot of magic users do that," Cain interjected before Seth could say any more. "Come on, boy, think bigger. You must be able to do something that's really interesting. Something that you're proud of."

"I…" Seth began, but stopped himself before saying any more. In truth, there was one more thing he knew that he could do, but he wasn't sure if it fit the bill for what Cain was asking from him. "I… can pull rocks up from the ground."

"Ah, so you're a geomancer then," Cain responded as his ears suddenly twitched, seemingly in anticipation. "That… actually sounds incredibly useful. Maybe-"

"A geo-what?" Seth interjected without thinking.

"Don't worry about it," Cain was quick to respond. "It's just a word, you can find out what it means later. No need to think too hard about it."

"Okay…" Seth responded in turn, not really satisfied with that answer. "So do you have a plan now?" Cain remained silent for several long seconds before giving any kind of answer to that question.

"Maybe…" was all Cain said as he leaned back out the window to peek outside again. "Maybe… Maybe I do… Yes… Yes, actually, I think I can work with this."

"Okay, so what do we do?" Seth couldn't help but ask eagerly.

"Well…" Cain began as he took a moment to think carefully about what he wanted to say. "The first thing you are going to need to do is be patient. If we're going to get you out of here then we're going to need to do it right the first time because we might not get a second chance, and that means making sure that you get out of here quietly and that absolutely no one sees you."

"And how are we going to do that?" Seth asked, now more impatient than eager to get an answer. Cain, however, appeared to sense this and looked up at him with a skeptical look in his eyes for several long, silent seconds before actually saying anything.

"Before I tell you what I have in mind, Seth, I need to know one thing," Cain then said as he narrowed his eyes on Seth. "Do you trust me?" Seth actually needed to take a second to stop and think about how he was going to answer that question as soon as he had heard it. As simple a question as it was, Seth had learned enough by now to know that answers to questions like these carried weight. That would have been bad enough if a human were asking him this as opposed to a monster. Not only that, but depending on his answer he would be throwing in his lot with monsters even after all that had happened in Canaan. Seth's hesitation did not go unnoticed by Cain, however, as Seth watched the bat-monster narrow his eyes even further as he seemingly stared not at him, but through him. That was a look that Seth had seen before too many times from Vivian.

"Yes," Seth answered with as straight of a face as he could manage given the circumstances.

"Great!" Cain responded excitedly as he instantly switched back to his normally cheerful demeanor. This seemingly instantaneous shift in personality greatly disturbed Seth, but he knew that he was in no position now to ask about it. "Then what I need you to do is to wait here for one more day." Upon hearing that Seth instantly felt a sudden, almost uncontrollable urge to reach out, grab Cain by his neck, and strangle the life out of him with both hands.

"W... Why?" Seth spoke with a very audible growl in his voice as he grit his teeth together in an attempt to prevent himself from doing anything stupid. Cain appeared to notice Seth's aggression, as Seth watched his eyes quickly shift to one of his shaking hands before looking back up into his eyes, but he showed no reaction to it whatsoever.

"You just said that you trusted me, didn't you?" Cain then asked as his toothy grin returned to his face.

"Well..." Seth struggled to speak over his rising anger. "Yes... but-"

"But what?" Cain interrupted. "You said that you trust me. So trust me. Trust that if I say I will get you out of here, I will. Trust that when I say that I care for your well being, I really do. Trust that when I say that I need some time to figure out how best to get you out of here that I speak the truth, but if you can't trust any of those, then trust mistress. Trust that despite how everything seems, she really, truly does care for you more than anyone in the world and that she would burn this entire city to the ground if it meant saving you." Something broke within Seth's mind as those last words passed through his ears. Even if Cain would not mention her by name, he knew enough to conjure up the image of Lilim's smiling face upon the mention of her. What really broke Seth, however, was the knowledge that he knew what Cain was saying about her was true. She had said as much to him in the past and had already saved him once, so he had no doubts at all about whether or not what he was saying about her was true. "Or if you can't trust that, then trust that mistress will literally bite my head off if I fail to keep you safe."

"I trust you," Seth said as soon as Cain had finished speaking that last part. After the words left his mouth he did feel himself actually begin to relax, and it was only once he had that he realized that all of his muscles suddenly felt much tenser after that outburst from him. It was as if the mere act of being angry was physically hurting him.

"Good!" Cain exclaimed as his familiar chipper demeanor returned. "So now that that's settled, you just stay here and stay cozy. You're going to need your strength when we get out of here since you're probably gonna need to do a lot of running. So some more rest would do you good. Especially since you can barely stand right now." For a moment Seth forgot to breathe as that statement passed through his head. He had hoped that he wouldn't be that obvious to Cain, yet despite that he still saw right through him. "So I'll come back around say… midnight tomorrow night. Be ready to go then."

"How will I know when it's midnight?" Seth asked.

"When I come to get you it will be midnight, so don't worry about that," Cain answered with a smile.

"Okay, but what am I supposed to do until then?" Seth then asked as the reality of what Cain was asking him to do sank in. Staying here in this place carried a lot of risks, and while Seth did not need to be told that, the idea of all of those potential risks hitting him at once was beginning to make him feel very, very uneasy.

"Get creative," Cain answered without skipping a beat. "You've survived this long living amongst the humans, so you must know how to deal with them. Pretend you're still sleeping. Say that everything still hurts and that you can't move. Say that you just don't feel like talking, but most important of all, more than anything, if any of them give you any food, don't eat it. Throw it away, hide it if you have to, but don't eat it. Same goes for drinks too, in fact those can be even worse than food. So avoid them at all costs." While there were questions that Seth wanted to ask about that, at this point he had given up asking questions and began to accept that Cain did in fact know what he was talking about. Even if he wanted to doubt it, which he very much did, he simply did not have it in him anymore to do so.

"Alright," Seth eventually said as his eyes fell down towards the floor. Cain, however, saw this as he dropped down from the window and onto the floor so that Seth could properly look at him.

"Don't worry, Seth," Cain said to him as he waddled forwards a little bit so that he could be in Seth's view. "I'll come for you. I promise I will, and to prove it I'll even shake on it. You know, like the humans do." Then with that said Cain held up his right wing towards Seth. As he did this he put on another smile, though it wasn't one of his usual toothy grins. This time his lips were closed, and because of that his smile appeared at the very least to be more genuine. Seth had absolutely no idea at all if the bat-monster in front of him was actually being genuine or not, however, but without saying anything he relented and gently shook his wing. This seemed to satisfy the bat-monster enough as he nodded back at him before pulling his wing away. "Sit tight and stay alive, brother. We're all waiting for you." Then, before Seth could properly respond to him or even say anything, Cain suddenly flapped his wings, took to the air, and flew through the window, whereupon his black visage blended in perfectly with the night sky and he vanished from sight.

With him gone all Seth could do was stand where he was and reflect on the decision he had just made. Something tugged at his insides as he did this, but he wasn't sure if it was guilt, regret, anxiety, or something else entirely. The one thing that he did know, however, was that he had already made the decision. So there was no going back on it now. Of course he could if he wanted to since he still had to wait one more day, but he wasn't sure whether or not he did want to.

The day passed by Seth relatively quickly, and yet at the same time it seemed to take an arduously long time to actually end. It was quick because he did spend most of the day sleeping, or at least pretending to sleep, and it was long because despite his best efforts there were times when he couldn't keep his eyes closed no matter how much he willed it. It was a feeling he was more than familiar with after all the time he had spent in Andrea's clinic back in Canaan, that he had gotten enough sleep and was just tired of sleeping. The idea of being tired of sleeping was something that confused him greatly, as even now it didn't make any sense to him at all how that could even be possible. Regardless, during those times he did the only thing that he knew he could do, stare up at the ceiling.

To pass the time Seth slowly tried to move each of his limbs one by one, at least when there wasn't anyone else in the room with him. The good news was that the extra hours of sleep really did seem to be doing wonders for him, as when he initially woke up in what he thought was the morning his limbs hurt him much less than they had the previous night. As the day went on he continually tried again whenever he had a chance, and before long he hardly noticed any pain at all whenever he moved. It wasn't as if the pain had completely gone away yet, but it was enough that he hardly noticed it at all.

Whenever someone did enter his room he instantly ceased everything he was doing and closed his eyes so that he could pretend to sleep. Because of this he never saw the faces of the doctor or any of the nurses that came to examine him. Not that he particularly cared what they looked like, but he could still feel it every time they poked and prodded different parts of his body for reasons he could not comprehend. Of course he remembered to reapply the illusion over his eyes so that they would not see what they really looked like, and thankfully they never looked too closely at his eyes. Sometimes when they came in they would leave him a tray of food, which usually consisted of a piece of fruit, a sandwich, and something to drink. Seth, however, keeping Cain's advice in mind, as soon as they left him alone he went back to the one window in the room and threw the food out of it, but kept the tray and dishes so that they would think he had eaten everything. This, unfortunately, had the side effect of causing Seth to become really, really hungry as the day went on, but he knew that he could survive at least a day without food if it meant living.

Privately though, he couldn't help but wonder where his clothes were. The hospital gown that he found himself in when he woke up was certainly comfortable, sure, but part of him did wish that he at the very least knew where his actual clothes were. Plus, the gown was white, a color he was not particularly fond of. Regardless, despite the hunger, lack of clothes, and inconvenient disturbances from the doctor and nurses whenever they came to examine him, the day eventually did pass into night, and it was then that Seth began to grow impatient. What certainly didn't help was that he had no real way to tell what time it was in his room, no way of knowing for certain whether or not Cain would stay true to his word, and no desire whatsoever to go back to sleep, as he had been sleeping all day and was honestly growing irritated with it. It had even reached the point where Seth had begun to question whether or not Cain would even return at all.

Thankfully his patience was rewarded when the sound of light tapping against glass hit his ears. Immediately he threw the covers aside as he leapt from his bed and ran over towards the window where the large red eyes and smiling face of Cain were waiting for him. Seth did not waste any time at all opening the window for him.

"My my, someone is eager," Cain said to Seth as he hung from the top of the window by his wings.

"You have no idea," Seth was quick to respond. "So do you have a way to get me out of here?"

"I do," Cain answered with a nod.

"Okay then, let's go," Seth quickly said in turn. "Where do we-"

"Easy there, brother, easy," Cain interrupted as he held up a single wing in an attempt to calm Seth down. Amazingly, as he did this he was able to stay hanging from the top of the window with only one wing. "I know you're itching to get out of this place. I would be too if I was in your position, but if we're going to do this then we need to do it right, and that means we need to be smart."

"Okay," Seth acknowledged as he tried to calm himself down. "So what do we do?"

"Well…" Cain began. "The first thing you're gonna need to do is crawl through this window. After that you're going to need to stick to the shadows and listen carefully to everything I say. Can you do that for me?"

"Of course," Seth responded quickly, though the speed of his response made Cain narrow his eyes at Seth as he dropped his smile.

"I mean it, Seth," Cain said to him. "Once you're out of this building I really am going to need you to listen carefully to everything I say. Everything I say. If we mess this up the consequences will be grave for us both. They'll kill me, but you… If you're lucky they'll just send you right back here. Sure they might not kill you then, or the next day, or even the day after, but eventually they will. You know that, I know you do. So once you crawl out of this window, if I say to do something, do it. If I say to stop, you stop. If I say to turn back, then do it. No questions. No hesitation. Just do what I say. Do you understand?" The sudden shift in tone of his voice made Seth nervous, as the realization hit him that maybe he did not know Cain as well as he thought he did. Despite that, however, he could not fault Cain's logic. Even if part of him wanted to.

"I understand," Seth answered, this time in a much calmer manner.

"Great," Cain responded as his familiar smile instantly returned to his face. "Let's not waste any time then." As soon as he had finished speaking Cain let go of the window and flew straight upwards. To where Seth could not see, but he did know what he needed to do next.

Looking out the window, Seth could see that it was an at least three meter drop to the ground below. Upon seeing that he couldn't help but curse himself for not checking this earlier when there was daylight. However, he also knew that he had come too far to back out now. So without hesitation Seth crawled through the open window and leapt down to the ground below. It was then that Seth was suddenly very, very thankful to Cain for making him wait an extra day, since because of that he had more time to heal and as such it no longer hurt when he moved. Because of that the impact of his feet hitting the ground hurt much, much less than he knew it could have. It was still enough, however, that Seth had to grit his teeth together in order to keep himself from screaming.

Once the pain had passed Seth took a moment to look around. Unfortunately, in doing so a sense of dread immediately filled him as he could not see Cain anywhere.

"Psst," the sound of Cain's voice hit Seth's ears like an arrow as he instantly looked to both his left, then his right to see if he could find where Cain was. It was only after Seth had looked in both directions, however, that he remembered that Cain had wings, whereupon he looked up and saw him sitting on the corner of the hospital roof. As soon as he and Seth made eye contact Cain raised one of his wings and waved at Seth as if he were waving a hand. Before Seth had the chance to wave back, since part of him believed that was what Cain wanted him to do, Cain suddenly flapped both of his wings and flew straight up out of Seth's view. Seth tried to follow him with his eyes, but Cain was faster than he had expected him to be and before Seth had the chance to look too far up a sudden and unexpected weight landed on his left shoulder. When Seth turned his head to see what it was, centimeters away from his face was the toothy, smiling face of Cain staring directly back at him.

Instinctively Seth swung his arm to knock him off, but before he could hit him Cain flapped his wings again and flew up off of Seth's shoulder. Following the flapping noises with his ears this time, Seth looked ahead of him and saw Cain land on the ground less than a meter in front of him.

"Oh come on, what was that for?" Cain asked, appearing to be shocked, disappointed, and a little hurt. Though Seth could tell that he wasn't being genuine.

"Don't do that, please," Seth answered as he took a moment to collect himself.

"Why not?" Cain then asked with a very exaggerated tilt of his head. "I thought humans liked having birds on their shoulders."

"One, I'm not a human. Two, you're not a bird. And three, animals don't like me at all," Seth responded as he shot Cain a glare. He then watched as Cain opened his toothy maw to respond to him, but then paused as he took a few seconds to think about the answer Seth had given him.

"Touché," Cain eventually said as he pointed one wing towards Seth. "Anyway, let me explain how this is going to work." At that, Seth set aside all of the choice words he had for Cain at the moment and focused completely on him. As much as he did want to say them to him, he knew that now wasn't the time. "I'm going to be your eyes and ears for you as you make your way through this city, and before you ask that means I'm going to be telling you where to go. So keep your eyes up and keep them on me. When you see me fly from one building to the next move to where I'm going and stay as close to me as you can, but make sure you stay out of sight. In fact, that is the name of the game, Seth. Wherever I lead you make sure absolutely no one sees you. I cannot-"

"I know," Seth interrupted the talking bat-monster. "You said that enough times already, and I get it. No one can see me and I understand perfectly well why. So you don't need to tell me again." Cain only stared wide eyed up at Seth for several long seconds before continuing.

"Okay…" Cain eventually let out before shaking his head. "So then, as I was saying. Keep out of sight, but keep your eyes on me. If you see me do this." As Cain spoke he held out one of his wings as far as he could. "It means that there's someone coming and that you need to stop and hide. Don't worry if you can't see me from your hiding spot. When it's safe to go I'll make this sound." Cain then proceeded to emit a single, high pitched squeaking sound from his mouth. It was surprisingly loud, enough to make Seth want to cover his ears, but he quickly realized that it was likely like that because Cain would be farther away from him when he was leading him through the city. So it needed to be loud. "That means that it's safe to go again. Now, this last part is really important. If you hear me make this sound." At that Cain proceeded to make three of those high pitched squeaking noises in rapid succession. Again Seth resisted the urge to cover his ears, but only barely. "That means that someone's spotted me and I need to fly away. When that happens, like before I need you to hide, but when you do you must stay absolutely put until I come and get you. If I can't find you I'll land on a rooftop somewhere nearby and make that noise again to let you know that it's safe to come out. Once I see you though we'll need to move fast because there's no telling whether or not they'll come back again. Don't you worry about me. I've survived as long as I have because I've gotten rather exceptional at avoiding humans. And don't worry about me finding you. I may not be big, like some of our other brothers, but I have impeccable hearing and eyesight. Even at night. Not to brag or anything, but I can find a fly in a pitch black room. So I'll come get you. Don't worry. Now, Seth. Did you understand all of that?"

"Yes," Seth answered immediately after Cain had finished speaking, which appeared to surprise the bat-monster as he stopped smiling and his eyes went wide, as if he didn't quite believe Seth.

"Alright," Cain then said as he took another second to recompose himself. "Let's not waste anymore time then. Don't fall too far behind." Immediately after saying those last few words, without waiting for a response from Seth and with one great flap of his wings Cain took off into the air and flew up above the roof of the hospital. Doing as he was told, Seth followed Cain with his eyes until he saw him land on the corner of the roof of a building across the way from where he stood. Not far from him was another alleyway between two of the buildings in the Suntop

District. Since he had received no signals from him telling him otherwise, Seth immediately took off running and went straight for that alleyway.

Chapter 25

Vivian stumbled into the wall of a nearby building as she made her way through the city at night. Under normal circumstances she would never find herself going in the direction she was now, but the world is an infinitely interesting place and she knew better than anyone that sometimes things happen in it that are beyond the control of regular, mortal, squishy humans. More than that though it was late, she had just been thrown out of another tavern, whether it was her second or third she didn't remember, and she had nowhere else to go because she didn't want to go back to her room. Going there would mean sleeping, sleeping would mean dreaming, and dreaming would mean thinking of things that she would much rather not think about. So here she was, alone, out in the middle of the city of Dis at night, going to a place she never normally would in a million years.

"Halt!" The sound of someone who was obviously a member of the city guard caught her attention before she could actually see him. It was only when she stood still for a moment and allowed her vision to temporarily right itself that she was actually able to see who was addressing her. "What business do you have in the Suntop District?"

"That's…" Vivian began, but then stopped herself as she needed to take a second to think of what she wanted to say. "That's… actually none of your fucking buisiness." Hearing that answer, the two city guardsmen who stood at the gate to the Suntop District simply looked at each other for a moment before returning their attention to Vivian. With one look both of them were easily able to see what was going on with her. Even at this late hour.

"Well, regardless," the guardsman who had been speaking before began. "Entry into the Suntop District is closed for tonight so you-"

"Hey… hey… hey…" Vivian began as she stumbled over in his general direction. "I… I know you're just doing your job being a guardsman and all. A… After all it's what you d… do… right? You're a guardsman… so you g… guard." By that point Vivian was now face to face with the one guardsman who was speaking to her. "But I've got someone I n… need to see. So if you would please… g… g… get out of my fucking way." The other guardsman reached for his sword as Vivian kept talking, but as she finished the guardsman she was talking to subtly held up a hand to stop him.

"Ma'am, if you would please," the guardsman began. "Go home. It's obvious to anyone that you're drunk and even if you weren't we still wouldn't let you through. Entry into the Suntop District is forbidden after a certain hour, festival or no. I would explain to you why that is but it's obvious that you're not in a frame of mind to listen so please turn around and go home or-"

"Or... what!" Vivian snapped back at him. "Y... You asked what my business was, so I... I told you. Even... e... even after I told you it wasn't your fucking buisiness. So g... get out of my fucking way or-"

"Or what?" the guardsman interrupted as he narrowed his eyes on her. As he did the other guardsman put his hand back on his sword and took a few steps closer to the two of them. The sound of his boots did not escape Vivian's attention. Despite being drunk, Vivian felt her body on instinct tense up, like it knew what was coming. It was a feeling that she was more than familiar with, a feeling that she in fact relished.

"Yo... you... you sure you wanna do this?" Vivian asked as her eyes darted between the two guardsmen.

"What's gonna happen if we do?" the guardsman that she had been speaking to responded as he put his own hand on the hilt of his sword. Vivian was more than ready to act, in fact, in her current state of mind, part of her was looking forward to it. If nothing else she knew it would help work out some stress.

"The fuck are you doing here?" a familiar voice to all of them suddenly spoke up from seemingly nowhere. Instantly Vivian spun around to see who it was, an action she instantly regretted as it made her feel a little woozy, but even with her impaired vision she could recognize the smug form of Raz as he walked out from the shadows of the street behind her.

"Oh, it's you," the guardsman talking to Vivian then said as he saw Raz approach. He didn't relax his grip on his sword, but his attention was now on him as opposed to Vivian.

"Yeah, it is," Raz said as he stopped a few meters away from them. "Sorry, I don't remember either of your names."

"We never gave you our names," the other guardsman answered.

"Wha... what am I doing here? Wha... what the f... fuck do you think you're doing here?" Vivian then interjected before Raz could respond to what the guardsman had said. Before Raz could answer her question, however, the guardsman who had been talking to her spoke up first.

"Do you know this woman?" the guardsman asked Raz. There were a few short seconds of silence before Raz answered as he and Vivian held eye contact. As Vivian did with everyone, she tried to pierce through Raz with her glare, but in the state she was currently in her glare was about as effective as being pierced by a toothpick.

"Yes, actually I do," Raz answered as he returned his attention back to the two guardsmen. "She works for me."

"Works for you!" Vivian shouted at him the instant those words left his mouth. "S... Since when did I ever-"

"Okay fine," Raz interjected before Vivian could finish, his attention still on the two guardsmen more than Vivian. "She works with me, not for me. Like anyone else who takes pride in their skills she's kind of a bitch like that. Look, I know what this looks like and I know you guys are just doing your jobs, but incredibly, incredibly long story short, after the incident at Gustav's last night my family decided that it would be a good idea to hire some extra, local security. I brought her on because I've worked with her in the past and well, despite how she acts she is very, very good at what she does." Raz then paused for a moment and noticed the other guardsman with his hand still on his sword. "You can take your hand off the sword by the way. Even drunk she can still kick both your asses." The guardsman in question was hesitant to do as Raz said, as any sane man would be, but after a few seconds of seeing that Vivian was in fact, much calmer now than she had been when she arrived, he did so.

"Pussy," Vivian said under her breath as she saw that. Thankfully he did not hear her.

"So with all of that said," Raz continued as if nothing out of the ordinary was happening. "Mind letting us through please?"

"I thought you were staying somewhere back that way," the second guardsman then said before pointing back in the direction from which both Raz and Vivian had come from.

"Who told you that?" Raz was quick to retort. The second guardsman opened his mouth to respond, but was cut off by the first guardsman.

"It doesn't matter!" the first guardsman shouted before quickly recomposing himself. "Sir, as we were just explaining to your family's employee, entry into the

Suntop District after a certain hour is forbidden. That's always been the rule, yes, but after that incident at Gustav's that you mentioned the powers that be want to be certain that all of us are following that rule exactly as it is written. So regardless of whatever business the both of you have beyond this point it will have to wait until morning. The only reason either of us would let you through now would be if one of you had a-"

Before the guardsman could even finish his sentence Raz suddenly produced from his left side pocket something that looked, to Vivian at least, like a simple leather badge. Burned onto it was the seal of a ring of fire, and inside of the ring were a series of perfectly set rectangles made to resemble a wall. It was a seal that Vivian was more than familiar with, having come to this city many times before, and as such she recognized it instantly as the seal of the city guard of Dis. That being said, however, she had never seen anyone carry anything like what Raz was in possession of before, so the fact that somehow by simply holding it he was able to make the guardsman in front of her to shut up completely stunned her.

"This is what you were going to say we needed, right?" Raz then proceeded to ask without any change in expression on his face. Even his smug looking smirk was not there, as if he really did know how serious this was.

"Let me see that!" the second guardsman exclaimed rather loudly as he held out his hand. Seeing no apparent problem with this, Raz complied as he walked over to the guardsman and handed the leather seal to him, much to Vivian's continued shock. Once the guardsman had it Vivian saw that the leather seal was, in fact, something that was folded in half, as the guardsman unfolded it like a book so that he could presumably read whatever was inside. While the only reaction that Vivian could see from him was his eyes suddenly going wide, she somehow knew that this, whatever it was, was exactly what she needed. A fact that caused her to descend further into shock as her brain struggled to come up with any rational explanation for why someone like Raz would have something like this.

"It's legitimate," the second guardsman eventually said to the first as he looked over to him. "It even has the seals of both the captain of the guard and the Solaran royal family."

'*The fuck, what now!*' Vivian mentally screamed to herself as those words hit her ears. Even in her drunken state she was still able to pick up on those words and imply their meaning, which in turn only raised even more questions from her.

"You sure?" the first guardsman then asked.

"I wouldn't lie about something like this," the second guardsman answered as he then folded the leather seal back up and handed it back to Raz.

"So now that that's settled," Raz spoke up as he put the leather badge back into his pocket. "May we get through please. I've made it a point to check up on my family more often since the incident at Gustav's and I'd very much like to keep to it. After all, we wouldn't want something else to happen to them so soon after that, now would we?"

"What about her then?" the second guardsman asked as he gestured with his head towards Vivian. "I'm going to assume she doesn't have a pass. If she did then she would have had the common sense to show it by now. So mister 'whatever the fuck your name is', what do you suggest we do about her?" Raz then turned and locked eyes with Vivian. Vivian, who usually had some type of witty and insulting comeback for situations like this, suddenly found herself at a loss for words as so much had happened within the span of the past thirty seconds that she had not expected, nor could understand at the moment. The only thing she could do right now was stare back at him and try not to appear as shocked as she truly was, though she knew that she was failing at that too.

"I said that she's with me, didn't I?" Raz then answered. "And I'm here now, aren't I? So she comes with me."

"That's not-"

"Shall I tell my family that you are denying them the extra protection they need right now simply because of your strict adherence to your orders?" Raz quickly interrupted the first guardsman as he shifted his gaze back over towards him and narrowed his eyes like an angry wolf. Something that even scared Vivian for a brief second. A few short seconds of silence passed before the first guardsman let out a loud groan that Vivian recognized as one of sheer defeat.

"The two of you may pass," the first guardsman eventually said as he looked away from Raz. "But don't let her do anything stupid." Despite the better part of her brain knowing that she should keep her mouth shut right now, Vivian couldn't help but let out a very audible growl at that statement. "You may be alright in our eyes, but I know trouble when I see it, and this one..." He then paused for a brief second as he pointed at Vivian. "Is nothing but trouble."

"That's why my family hired her," Raz responded with a smirk, which made

Vivian let out another growl upon seeing it. She wasn't aware before of exactly how much his smirking face could piss her off, but now that she did she couldn't get it out of her head. "Sometimes trouble breeds skill, and what we need right now isn't another schmuck who can hold a sword, but someone who's actually skilled with one." Raz then paused for another few seconds and looked between the two guardsmen, who now had both of their intense, hate fueled glares focused directly on him instead of Vivian. "I see the way you're looking at me. Don't worry, if she does do something she isn't supposed to I'll knock her out and drag her by her hair back to you myself. I may bend the rules on occasion, but I don't break them."

"Oh, so she can kick our asses even while she's obviously so drunk that she can barely stand, but you'll be just fine?" the second guardsman then said with obvious sarcasm in his voice. Raz, however, did not appear to be fazed by this.

"I didn't say it would be easy," Raz responded with another smirk before walking past the two guardsmen and into the Suntop District. Afterwards he then stopped and looked back at Vivian. "You coming?" There were many, many things that Vivian wanted to both say and do to both Raz and the two guardsmen right now, but even in her drunken state of mind she had enough common sense remaining to remember what she really wanted, which was to get through this archway and into the Suntop District. If the only way to get that right now was to follow Raz through and pretend to be his hired lapdog, then there really was nothing else she could do at the moment. That, and despite what Raz had said on her behalf Vivian wasn't entirely sure herself if she could beat these two guardsmen right now, but more than that she really, really did not want to end up in prison. So with all of that in mind she did the only thing she knew that she could, let out another loud growl as she stomped past the two guardsmen and into the Suntop District behind Raz.

Vivian tried her best not to sway, at least until she was out of view of the two guardsmen, but she failed at that almost immediately as she nearly tripped over her own two feet just before reaching Raz. While she managed to catch herself before she fell on her face, she knew that the damage had already been done as she was still well within the view of the two guardsmen. Raz, however, did not appear to care as he turned back around and continued on his way now that she was close enough to him. Once Vivian saw that she quickly pulled herself back together and kept in step with him.

The two of them did not say a single word to each other for a long time after that, and while Vivian knew that there were likely plenty of reasons for why Raz would not talk to her, she was also aware that they were still well within the hearing range of the two guardsmen at the archway behind them. So like Raz she kept her mouth shut, especially after she had already embarrassed herself enough in front of the two guardsmen and now technically owed Raz for getting her out of that jam and getting her through. A fact that irritated her not only because she never asked for his help, but because she truly had no idea why he did it. Eventually, however, after periodically checking behind her more than once Vivian saw that the two of them had walked far enough away from the archway that Vivian felt comfortable speaking again.

"S... so hey, um..." Vivian began. "N... not that I d... don't appreciate your help or anything... but why the f... fuck were you even here? A... and who the fuck is your f... family that you can-" Before Vivian could even finish that question, and before she could even react, Raz suddenly grabbed her by both her neck and shoulder, dragged her into a nearby alleyway between two fancy looking buildings, and then slammed her into the wall of the building so hard that it probably would have concussed her were she not used to taking hits like this.

Vivian, however, being the experienced monster hunter that she was, had fought things that were much bigger and could hit a lot harder than Raz, so being slammed against a stone wall was not something that was new to her. As such, Vivian retaliated immediately as she swiftly kneed Raz in the crotch and pushed him away from her. As tough as Raz was, the pain from such a blow appeared to be too much even for him as he fell onto his back and let out several moans in pain. Vivian, however, was not done as she walked around towards Raz's front and gave him a kick to his head. To Vivian's shock and surprise, however, despite appearing to be in intense pain Raz was able to catch her leg before it could connect.

Before Vivian could even realize what had happened she suddenly lost her balance as she fell over backwards and Raz, from his apparent fetal position on the ground, swiftly rolled on top of her. Vivian was quick to throw a punch once Raz's face came into view. However, Raz caught her fist before she could hit him. Undeterred, Vivian threw another punch at him, but Raz caught that one too before he then grabbed both of her wrists with one hand and pinned them to the ground above her head. As he did so, however, his head moved down with the rest of him and thus closer to Vivian's face, which allowed her to attempt to headbut him.

Unfortunately for Vivian, however, in her drunken state she had misjudged the distance between her head and Raz's, so she ended up hitting nothing but air. Raz, however, seeing what she had tried to do, headbutted her in turn so hard that it actually knocked Vivian's head backwards, which in turn caused it to hit the solid ground beneath it. The combination of her head being hit twice in rapid succession like that and the immense amount of alcohol remaining in her system caused Vivian's vision to suddenly become even more blurry than it had been before as she found herself barely able to see two centimeters in front of her. So much so in fact that despite how close it was, she could only barely see Raz's face. Not only that, but she felt as if she could barely move, and not just because she was pinned to the ground.

"You... really think I haven't been kicked in the nuts before?" Raz then spoke up. His voice sounded far away to her, but Vivian could make out his words well enough. "I've dated girls that were just as tough as you, and not all of them took the breakups that well."

"F... fuck... you," Vivian was only barely able to respond.

"As much as I'd like to, I don't think I'll be able to for awhile since you, you know, fucking hit me there," Raz responded in turn. Vivian would have responded with some kind of witty comeback, but between the now excruciating pain in her head and everything else that was happening, she had lost the will to come up with one. "Now, before I drag you kicking and screaming by your hair back to those two guards at the gate, I'm going to ask you one question, and for fucking Solaris' sake you better have a good answer. Why shouldn't I?" Raz then paused for a moment to let that question sink in, but Vivian gave him no response whatsoever. After all that had happened with him recently, her silence irritated Raz so much that without a second's thought he held his free hand a few centimeters in front of her face and lit it on fire. "Listen, bitch. I've seen you fight. I know you think you're tough as shit, but so do a lot of people, and that doesn't make any of them special. Lots of tough people thought they could beat me, and none of them succeeded. I could kill you right here and it would be no skin off my back, but instead I've risked both mine and my family's good name to get you in here, even after that friend of yours tried to kill our mutual red eyed friend. Yeah, I know about that. I have eyes and a brain, and I can put together that two people who wear the exact same guild bracelet probably know each other. So after all of that, after everything that you've said and done, tell me right fucking now why, oh why, should I not just drag you back to the gate and see that you're thrown into a cell along with him?"

"I h... had nothing to do with that you f... fucking dumbass!" Vivian shouted in his face despite the fire. "For fucks s... sake! Didn't A... Agatha clear that up with you b... bastards!"

"I haven't seen Agatha since we got to this city," Raz responded without breaking eye contact. "And even if I had, do you really think that would be enough to suddenly make me believe anything you say?"

"Alright fine d... dickless!" Vivian then said without lowering her voice. "If I... I... I wanted Seth dead then why would I do it in this stupid r... r... roundabout way! You really think I would let some f... fucking Joe take the credit for th... that! A f... fucking monster that looks human enough to blend into a s... small town or even a city! That's something that people've n... never seen before. They'll r... remember the one who kills that!"

"So that's why you're here then, is it?" Raz asked in response as he moved his flaming hand closer to her face. "Asleep in a hospital with no one around him but blankets and the darkness of the night. Sounds like easy pickings."

"What!" Vivian couldn't help but shout in shock as her eyes suddenly went wide, something that Raz saw as he raised an eyebrow. "N... N... No! That t... thought never even crossed my m... mind!"

"Then why were you trying to get into the district where his hospital is at this time of night, after visiting hours ended hours ago?" Raz then asked as he stared past the fire on his hand and directly into Vivian's eyes.

"I... I... well uh... I..." Vivian stammered as she tried in vain to come up with the right words to say to the person currently on top of her and holding a flaming hand in front of her face. She knew that her current lack of ability to form words was not helping her case at all, but the truth was that she had absolutely no idea at all what to say. Part of her doubted that there was anything at all that she could say to Raz in order to get him to let her go, much less believe what she had to say. Much like most of the people that lived in Canaan, she did not know Raz as well as she knew she should have, but she did know that much like her, whenever he set his mind to something he got shit done.

It was in that moment that a strange, almost unexplainable new feeling completely enveloped Vivian as if she had suddenly been doused with water. A feeling that for all intents and purposes was foreign to her, yet she knew what it was all the same. As she stared past the flames on Raz's hand and into his eyes, it felt to her as if she were staring into a void, and that brought her back to the dream that she so desperately wanted to forget. The fear of seeing it again was what made her realize that what she was feeling right now, while wide awake and fully cognizant of everything that was going on, was indeed fear. The fear itself was nothing new to her, but the fear that she could potentially die right here and now, while being pinned to the ground by a man she only barely knew while he held a flaming hand in front of her face, the idea of dying by that flaming hand right now of all times was too much for her to bear. It wasn't the fear of dying that got to her, however, as she had long since come to terms with her own mortality after all the things she had seen over the course of her life, but the fear of regret, of all of the things left undone and unsaid, the things that she knew would be left behind if she did die right now, that was what truly terrified her in a way she had never known was possible before.

She could fight her way out of this, the thought did cross her mind and she had no doubts at all that she could. She could easily overpower Raz, kick him to the curb, and then run away if she wanted to. At least that was what she believed. However, she also knew that that would not end well for her. At best she would run around the Suntop District for a little while before being picked up by either the city guard or Raz, who would no doubt chase her, and then she would be in the exact situation that Raz had helped her avoid.

More importantly, however, she had lived with the idea of being afraid for so long that she knew it wouldn't just go away if she did that. So knowing that she frantically racked her brain for something, anything that could make the fear she was now feeling go away. After only a second of this a solution did present itself to her, but she didn't know if she wanted to act on it. Doing so would mean doing something that she never, ever normally did, not for anyone, not even Seth. Yet staring ahead of her at the flaming hand and Raz's death-like glare beyond it, she knew that she did not have the time nor the luxury of thinking of alternative solutions. So with that in mind, Vivian steeled herself and took in a breath so deep that to her, it felt as if she were literally swallowing her pride.

"A... Agatha..." Vivian hesitantly began. "D... did a pretty good job of making me feel like a piece of shit, okay. So... I... I was thinking about... t... trying to talk to h... him... to see... i... if he even wanted to talk to me after our last c...

conversation."

"At this time of night?" Raz immediately rebuked as soon as Vivian had finished speaking.

"I... I don't fucking know!" Vivian screamed back at him. "I... I... I didn't think this through!"

"Clearly," Raz responded without any change in either his tone of voice or his expression.

"W... Well what about you then, f... fucktard!" Vivian shouted back at him. "W... What the fuck are you doing out here this late at n... night! Huh! What's your e... excuse since you're so fucking c... clever!"

"Couldn't sleep," Raz answered, as calm as ever. "So I figured I'd stay out a little longer and grab a few more drinks myself, then who should I see walking in this direction?"

"Bullshit!" Vivian immediately screamed back at him the instant he had finished speaking.

"It's the truth," Raz responded in turn. "Not up to me whether or not you believe it."

"Well then, as long as I'm being f... fucking interrogated, w... why don't you let me ask you a question then, huh," Vivian shot back at him, this time without raising her voice. "Why... Oh f... fucking why, are you of all p... people so f... fucking worried about him? D... Didn't he almost kill you? It doesn't make any f... fucking sense."

"That's complicated, and I doubt someone like you would understand," Raz answered as plainly as ever and without any hesitation. Vivian, however, couldn't help but let out an audible growl at that indirect insult. "But since you asked nicely I'll tell you. To put it simply, as potentially dangerous as he may be, he's not a threat, and I doubt he ever will be." Vivian, despite being pinned to the ground, couldn't help but tilt her head in obvious confusion at what Raz had just said to her. Seeing that, Raz closed his free hand and put out the flames on it before pulling it away from Vivian's face. "Listen, while I don't doubt that you've been in a bar fight or two, most of your experience is in fighting monsters. Only monsters. I was a soldier, Vivian. A soldier in the Solaran army. I've fought both men and monsters. Both on, and sometimes off the battlefield, and while I'm not arrogant enough to assume that I can speak for your experiences, I've seen just as much shit as you have. So let me tell you this. The fighting, the screaming, the pain, the loss of life, the look in your enemy's eyes when you know they have the intent to kill you, it's all the same. You don't need red eyes, black scales, claws, or teeth to be a monster."

"I... I know that you f... fucking prick," Vivian responded. "And th... that's not an answer. Seth isn't even-"

"Bitch, did you not hear what I just said," Raz interrupted Vivian as he suddenly narrowed his eyes at her. While his flaming hand was no longer in front of her face, with that look Vivian knew that all it would take was a second for it to come back. "What even is a monster? It's just a term we use to describe something that scares us. Those things that Chaos created to kill us, Seth might be related to them, but he's hardly a monster. When I fought him that night in the desert I saw a lot of things in his eyes. Anger, sadness, anguish, fear, betrayal, but no intent to kill. I know what you're going to say, so before you do let me first say shut the fuck up, and second let me remind you that I've fought just as many humans as I have monsters. I know a killing intent when I see one, and I didn't see it in Seth's eyes that night. I don't know whether it's because of all the time he's spent living with Tara, whether he has some kind of monster brain damage, or whether he really, really was just born the way he is, but he really is just shitty at being a monster."

"H... H... How could you know that?" Vivian then asked once Raz had finished speaking. "How could you p... possibly know that! How do you know he won't just wake up one day and decide to finish the job he started that night in the desert! How do you know that he won't just snap one day and decide that all of us are easy pickings! H... How do you know that any of what you're s... saying is true! I... I... If you really have fought as m... many monsters as I h... have, then you must know what they're l... like! So h... h... how could you possibly know a... any of that!"

"I don't," Raz answered rather quickly, much to Vivian's surprise. "I really don't. But I have a friend who's a much, much better judge of character than I will ever be, and he believes in him. So I will too, and for me that's enough. Like I said, I doubt someone like you would understand." That last comment really, really pissed Vivian off to no end. More than anything right now she wanted to get one of her hands free and break Raz's nose just for saying it. However, when she tried she found that his grip was like iron, and that even after all of this he still would not let her go. Since she couldn't punch him, and perhaps due to all of the alcohol still remaining in her system as well as all of the things she had already said to him, her mind began to contemplate the reasons why that comment pissed her off.

After only one silent second of this, however, it dawned on her that it was because Raz had assumed that she completely lacked a sense of empathy, and as such couldn't possibly understand why other people thought or did what they did. She opened her mouth to scream at Raz again, if only to say that he was wrong, a fucking asshole for saying that, and that she really, really was capable of empathizing with other's feelings, but she stopped herself before any words could leave her mouth. Instead, that thought led her back to her earlier conversation with Agatha, the one that had started this whole mess for her. Agatha had said the exact same thing to her, only more directly. Hearing that now from two different people, and both in regard to the same person, someone who wasn't even human in her eyes, it forced Vivian to ask herself whether or not what they were saying really was true. In an attempt to answer this, she scoured her memory for every possible interaction she had with most of the people she knew, except she then remembered something else that Agatha had said. How she apparently didn't remember half of the things she said or did while she was drunk. That in turn, led her to remember her meeting with her three guild masters, why they had refused to promote her, and the exact words she had used in her defense of them. All of them came back to something else Agatha had said to her, something that she didn't think about then, but came back in full force now.

'*It's called empathy you fucking cunt. It's a basic human emotion, and from what you just told me you're apparently less human than he is because he has it and you don't.*' Vivian's first instinct was to deny this like she had before, but she found it harder to do so when even her own recollection of her memories was flawed and the parts that she did remember only supported that conclusion. That in turn led her back to Seth, the reason for all of this and the reason she was here. She, willingly this time, thought back to every time the two of them had interacted, and not just the times they had talked, but all of the times they had been in the same room or place and she had watched him do things. As much of an incompetent moron as she knew Seth could be, he was also a nice guy and all of the actions she had seen him take supported that. He had even willingly joined the town watch after the "mistake" she had made. Thinking of that immediately made Vivian do a double take in her own mind as she reached a stunning realization. She had just admitted, in her own mind and not out loud, but even that was enough to shake her, that a monster was indeed capable of empathy.

If that was true, then was what Agatha had said also true, that a monster was more capable of empathy than she was? She honestly did not know the answer. She wanted to say that it wasn't, she wanted to scream it, but if she did then she knew that she would never lose the feeling that she was lying to herself. She had never done that to herself about anything, even her own mother's death, as much as it haunted her, so why would she do it here? Her mind was so caught up in all of these questions and thoughts of Seth that she didn't notice when a single tear fell from her eye and ran down her cheek.

"Y… You keep calling m… me a bitch," Vivian eventually said to Raz. "I… If it's enough for you to t… trust someone else's opinion of someone over y… your own, then isn't it e… enough for you to a… accept that I k… know that I'm a b… bitch and that I s… sometimes feel shitty about the things I say and want to a… apologize. I… Isn't that enough? Y… Your reason for trusting him is the s… stupidest thing I've ever heard. So isn't it e… enough that my reason for w… wanting to s… see him isn't that much better than yours. I… Isn't that e… enough?" A long moment of silence followed as Raz didn't respond to Vivian's question. In that time another tear fell from Vivian's eyes as she feared that what she had said wasn't enough to get through to him. It was all she had, and the fear that all she had still wasn't enough began to eat away at her more than her fear of regret. Part of her wanted to pray, but somehow she knew that it wouldn't do her any good.

"We'll see," Raz eventually responded before he let go of Vivian's hands and stood up. Vivian, unable to believe what she had just seen, needed to take a few seconds to process what had just happened as Raz stood over her. For a few solid seconds she really was convinced that he would not let her go, that he really would kill her, or at least turn her in to the city guard. Neither of those things happened though, and before she could even begin to ask herself why that was, Raz reached down and offered a hand to help her up. "Now do you want to see him or not?"

For a second Vivian debated not taking it as she sat up from the ground. However, she realized as soon as that thought had occurred to her that she had already lost her pride, and that nobody else was around to see this, so it wasn't as if taking his hand or not was any kind of big deal. So without hesitation she took Raz's hand and he helped her up.

"H… How can you even s… stand right now?" Vivian couldn't help but ask as she pulled herself back onto her feet. "I… I know I hit you pretty g… good."

"Like I said," Raz answered. "I've been kicked in the nuts before. Like any type of pain you eventually just learn to deal with it." There were at least fifty more questions that Vivian wanted to ask about that alone, but before she could Raz turned around and started walking out of the alleyway. "Come on, I'll take you to where he is."

"B… But I thought you s… said that visiting hours were o… over!" Vivian said rather loudly as she quickly caught up with him.

"For normal people, yes," Raz answered. "But my family has connections. I can get you in." Hearing that triggered something in Vivian's mind as she suddenly remembered their earlier conversation at the gate, and how Raz had pulled something that appeared to Vivian, quite literally out of his ass, that had allowed them to just walk on in here without any questions.

"Wait!" Vivian couldn't help but shout knowing that. "Who the actual f… fuck is your fam-"

"I'll tell you when you're sober," Raz answered before she could finish as he simply kept on walking with Vivian close behind. Right as Vivian caught up to him, however, Raz suddenly stumbled and almost fell over, but caught himself at the last second. A closer look, however, revealed to Vivian that Raz's legs were shaking due to her kick from earlier making sure that not everything was in its original place, and in fact had been that way since before he first stood up. While she still wasn't entirely sure how he could keep himself standing right now, Vivian couldn't help but let out a rather loud snicker upon seeing that.

Neither Raz nor Vivian said anything else to each other during their walk to the hospital. For Vivian, it was because she felt that she had said enough already and didn't want to potentially embarrass herself any further than she already had. For Raz, however, it was because he simply had nothing to say to her and was instead keeping more of an eye on her to see what she would do. That said, Raz was being true to what he had said earlier and was leading her in the direction of the hospital where he knew Seth was sleeping. The combination of their previous conversation and the walk here had sobered Vivian up somewhat, and that was the reason that as soon as they were within sight of the hospital an odd sight caught her eye.

The instant she saw it Vivian quickly grabbed Raz by the shoulder and pulled him behind the nearest building that she could see, out of sight of the hospital. The instant Raz's back hit the wall of the building he grabbed Vivian's hand to pull it off of him, but before he could Vivian suddenly brought a finger to her lips. Raz understood the message immediately as he relaxed his grip on Vivian's arm, and in turn she let go of him. Once she had she quietly pointed back out into the street close to the hospital. At first Raz didn't see anything, but then after a few silent seconds a certain, very familiar looking black haired individual wearing a hospital gown ran out from behind one of the buildings near the hospital before darting into an alleyway in between two more buildings.

"Where do you think he's going?" Vivian asked as she saw that happen.

"No idea," Raz answered before returning his attention back to her. "You wanna follow him?"

"Maybe," Vivian answered. "If only to see whether or not your theory holds up."

Chapter 26

Without slowing down for even a second Cain flew from the roof of one building to the next in rapid succession while from the ground Seth followed closely behind him every step of the way. It actually amazed Seth how Cain always seemed to know where he was even though he never once saw him turn to look and see if he was still following him or not, and Seth would have seen it if he had since he made sure to keep at least one eye on him at all times. Even in the few instances where Cain had flown too far ahead of him he still took a few seconds to find a perch on one of the nearby rooftops and wait for Seth to catch up as he darted from alleyway to alleyway. It was as if Cain somehow always knew exactly where he was despite never actually looking at him.

Seth chose not to question that right now as he darted from one building to the next, hiding himself in the shadows every chance he got even if he didn't see anyone around. He already knew that what he was doing now was against everything Tara and his other human associates had taught him, so he knew that he couldn't afford to be caught. With that in mind he didn't want to take any more risks than necessary. Thankfully for him moving through the Suntop District at this time of night was easy as there was hardly anyone around. There was only one instance wherein Seth saw Cain hold up his wing to signal him to stop, upon which he abruptly stopped where he was and flattened himself against the nearest wall in the shadows between two buildings in an effort to make himself appear as small as possible. He couldn't see what was happening, nor did he have any indication at all of what was actually going on, but he did hear the distant voices of some people walking by even if they were too far away to make out exactly what they were saying. Almost as soon as he heard them though, they were gone, and shortly afterwards he heard the familiar high pitched squeak of Cain which told him that it was safe to move again.

From there things proceeded smoothly and without incident. That was until they had reached one of the archways that functioned as the main gateways into the Suntop District. It wasn't the same archway he had been through previously, Seth could tell that much, but it did look remarkably similar. More important, however, was the fact that even at this time of night a pair of city guard members were standing vigilant at it. Seth could only guess that if there ever was a time to sneak through the archway for any reason, night would be it, hence why they had to still be there.

When Seth saw them he froze against the building he was currently next to as he tried to stay hidden. The route was easy to see, yes, but as far as Seth could see there was no way around the two guardsmen. What's more, Cain hadn't advanced any further either, as he remained perched on the rooftop directly above him. Cain appeared to sense fear, however, as when Seth turned to look up at him he saw Cain staring directly down at him with his pair of wide, red eyes. Their eyes only stayed locked for a second, however, as Cain soon flew straight up into the air before circling around once and landing in the alleyway next to Seth.

"Okay, here is what we are going to do," Cain whispered to him. "I'm going to cause a distraction to get them to move away from the gate. Once they do, just run for it. Get past them and hide somewhere until everything is clear. I'll find you once it is, so don't worry about that."

"What are you going to-"

"Atatat," Cain interrupted Seth as he tried to whisper to him what he thought was a basic question. "Don't worry about it. Don't even think about it. I've lived this long, remember. I'll be fine. Just get through the gate. I'll take care of the rest." Then, before Seth had a chance to say anything else, much less object, Cain spread his wings and took to the sky again. Seth tried to follow him with his eyes, but as soon as he was above the buildings Cain made a hard right and disappeared from Seth's view. More than a little frustrated, Seth let out a quiet growl as he returned his attention to the archway.

At first nothing appeared to happen. Everything stayed quiet and the two guardsmen stood at their posts without saying much of anything. After almost a full minute of silence Seth began to worry that Cain had left him, and he quietly cursed himself for putting his trust into a creature like him. Then, suddenly, before Seth had a chance to reflect any harder on those emotions, the familiar sound of Cain's high pitched squeaking hit his ears as he heard it in rapid succession three times. Before he could register where the sound was coming from, his eyes went back to the archway he was supposed to be watching, whereupon he watched Cain quickly fly in front of the two city guardsmen before continuing off to the left.

"The fuck was that!" One of the guardsmen asked as his attention was immediately drawn to Cain.

"Why are you asking me!" The other one responded as the two of them momentarily left their posts to follow Cain. Seeing his chance, and not thinking about Cain like he had asked him to, Seth wasted no time as he made a mad dash through the archway before diving in between two buildings and taking cover in the shadows once again.

"Where did it go!" Seth then heard one of the two city guardsmen ask aloud. He could tell he was shouting, and going by how loud his voice was it didn't seem as if he was that far away from him.

"I don't know, I lost it," the other guardsman responded much more calmly.

"Do you think we should report it?" Seth then heard the first guardsman ask in what sounded like an attempt to be calm as well, but being as close as he was Seth could tell from the way in which he spoke that he was very likely still shaking in his boots.

"Nah," the second guardsman eventually responded in a much, much calmer manner. "I don't think it was a monster, and even if it was it didn't look that big. So I doubt it will hurt anyone. Just have your crossbow ready in case it comes back."

After that the only thing Seth heard was the sound of their footsteps as they walked back to their posts. While Seth knew it was a risk, he decided to poke his head out a little bit to see what they were doing. Indeed he saw them return to the places they had been standing before, though he also saw one of them walk behind the wall for a few short seconds. When he came back he had a pair of crossbows with him, one of which he handed to the other guardsman.

"Psst," Seth then suddenly heard from behind him. Instinctively he quickly spun around to see who it was with his fist poised to strike, but he didn't see anybody. "Down here." With that second outburst Seth then looked down to see the smiling face of Cain staring up at him. Seeing him Seth couldn't help but silently curse himself for not expecting him to do something like that, especially since he knew fully what kind of monster he was. Seth in turn opened his mouth to say something, but before he could actually speak Cain held up one of his wings to his lips, as if he were making the motion to be quiet. After doing that Cain pointed with his wing behind Seth towards the two city guardsmen, who by that point had returned to standing at attention with their crossbows, which Seth could now see were loaded and ready to use.

Returning his attention back to Cain, Seth watched as he, without saying anything, motioned for him to follow with his wing before taking to the sky again. Amazingly, despite obviously flapping his wings to do so, while that action did make some noise it was not nearly as much as Seth would have expected from a creature of his size and wingspan. Cain had said before that he had lived as long as he had by being good at avoiding humans, and based on what he had seen Seth could only assume that meant that he was good at keeping quiet.

From there things seemed to get much, much easier for Seth as darting between buildings became so much easier for him simply because of the fact that all of the buildings were much closer together in the districts outside of the Suntop District. There were a few more times than Seth would have preferred when Cain had to signal for him to stop because someone was coming, but not one ever saw either of them nor did they get any indication that they were there. With a more densely packed area of the city Seth could only guess that there were more people about even at this late hour.

What surprised Seth more than anything else was how Cain seemed to know exactly where he was going at all times. Sure, he was higher up so he had the added advantage of being able to see above the roofs of all of these buildings, but Seth imagined that even up there all of the buildings here would still look exactly the same to him. Cain, however, did not appear to have that problem as he always knew which building to run to next and which route to take. Even in places where there appeared to be multiple ways forward Cain was resolute and did not hesitate even for a single second. What's more, no one ever appeared to spot him regardless of where he flew.

It was enough to make Seth wonder if the real reason Cain had told him to wait one more day before doing this was so that he could figure out this route beforehand. Even if that were the case, however, Seth imagined that it must not have been easy at all since all of the buildings here looked alike to him and looking at them from above likely would not have changed that. It made Seth question whether or not he had somehow underestimated Cain, or at least had not given him enough credit for the things that he said he could do, yet even with that Seth couldn't help but feel more than a little worried about one gigantic obstacle that he knew they would have to eventually pass through. After passing between a few more buildings Seth and Cain eventually found themselves staring directly at it.

It had taken them a while to get there, but eventually both Seth and Cain had arrived at the edge of the city of Dis and now found themselves staring directly at the enormous wall that kept the city safe from both monsters and the outside elements. To Seth's great disappointment, the only remaining thing that stood between them and their escape was a section of the wall. There was no gate, no guards, and absolutely no way through for Seth. It was this sight that made Seth instantly take back all of the thoughts he had about underestimating Cain, for he now saw that he really did have absolutely no idea where he was going. There was no possible way that Cain could have led him here on purpose. At least that was what any sane person would think as far as Seth surmised.

"Well... Cain..." Seth tried to say quietly, but even still his voice came out with a bit of a very audible growl to it. "What am I supposed to do now?" Despite how simple the question was Cain's initial reaction was to look back at Seth with a confused expression on his face.

"Well I would have thought that would have been obvious," Cain responded as if nothing was wrong. "You're supposed to climb this wall." A moment suddenly passed wherein Seth forgot to breathe as the implications of what Cain had just said sank in, and it was then that Seth realized that his initial impression of Cain had been right after all. He did know the exact route through this city, he did know exactly where he was going and where he was leading Seth, and had in fact led him here on purpose. And now, with all of that, Cain expected him to somehow climb up a perfectly smooth wall. Seth couldn't even begin to guess exactly how tall this wall was, but he could only barely see the top from where he was standing.

"And how exactly..." Seth began, doing his absolute best not to shout, though the growl that was present in his voice before was still there. "Am I supposed to do that?"

"You're a geomancer aren't you?" Cain quickly answered without skipping a beat. "You can move the earth. You told me you could, back in the hospital. Remember?"

"Well, yes but-"

"But what then?" Cain interrupted before Seth could say any more. "You said that you could move the earth with your magic. The stones that make up this wall come from the earth. So you should be able to move them." There was something that Seth wanted to say in response to that, but before he could his eyes instinctively returned to the wall in an effort to see what Cain was talking about.

Surely enough, as Seth could see, as impressive as the wall surrounding this city was, it was not one solid mass of stone like he had imagined it was. He had never noticed before since there was hardly a need for him to pay any attention at all to the wall surrounding the city, but upon closer inspection of it he could see that the wall was in fact made up of many, many, many large stones that were all cut into perfect rectangles and stuck together with materials that Seth could not recognize. Seeing this Seth couldn't help but wonder how something this massive could be put together, though he assumed that it likely had something to do with magic.

That didn't change the fact that Cain somehow expected Seth to pull these large, rectangular stones out from the wall with his magic and use them to climb it. Looking at its construction, Seth wasn't even sure if he could do that, but even if he could he would still have to use them to climb all the way up to the top of the wall. Falling from only a few meters hurt quite a bit, that much he knew, so he didn't even want to think about what would happen if he messed this up.

"Are... Are you serious?" Seth asked, his fears making themselves known in his voice in the form of minor stutters despite his best attempt to hide them. Cain did not answer Seth's question immediately, rather when Seth looked down at him and saw him drop his smile before narrowing his eyes up at him, Seth could tell that this little monster was indeed being absolutely serious. Much to his horror.

"You said you wanted to talk to mistress," the tone of Cain's voice was markedly different from the one he usually spoke with, even when he was being serious. "You had to know what that entailed, didn't you?" Before Seth could speak up to ask Cain what he was talking about, Cain interrupted him and continued speaking. "You knew that mistress wasn't in this city. You knew that other humans, even your friends, would stop you if you tried to leave. You knew that going to see her wouldn't be anywhere near as simple or as pleasant as just walking out of the gate. You know just as well as any of us what humans do to our kind, so you know what will happen if they see you with me, or if one of them happens to see your eyes. So knowing all of that, you must have known that getting out of this city would not have been easy. You must have known that it wouldn't be anything like a simple midnight stroll where I took care of everything for you and all you had to do was follow behind me like a good boy. And you certainly must have known that if this was something that you really, really wanted then you were going to have to put some actual effort into getting it." Those words hit Seth harder than he wanted to admit, even to himself. While it was true that he certainly did not expect anything like a simple midnight stroll, he certainly wasn't expecting something like this either, and here Cain was expecting him to just climb this wall without considering the possible consequences of falling off.

"Oh but I don't need to tell you any of this," Cain then continued before Seth had the opportunity to even think of a proper response. "Because of course you already know all of it. Why would you come all this way with me if you didn't? Why would you sneak out of a human hospital without telling any of your so-called human friends and run half way across this human city, sneak past many armed humans along the way, and make your way all the way here if you didn't know any of that? So if you knew all of that you must have been prepared to do something like climb the wall to escape or run out into the desert with no water or supplies. So since you know all of that I'll just wait for you up top. I'd recommend you start climbing soon though, there's no telling who else might be out at this hour. Oh, and be careful of how much noise you make. There may not be many humans here now, but this is a human city, so they are everywhere and they may be inclined to investigate strange noises. I know I would." Then, before Seth could utter even a single word in response to anything he had said, Cain spread his wings and took off straight upwards towards the top of the wall.

Seth wanted to shout after him. Every part of his conscience screamed at him to do it, but he held himself back the instant he realized that Cain was right. Even at this late hour in the pitch black darkness of the night, there were still more people awake in this city than Seth had anticipated, so shouting up to a large bat-like creature was bound to get attention he didn't want. It was only then, as he stood there, alone, in the silence of the midnight sky that Seth truly realized the magnitude of what he was asking from Cain. He wanted to punch himself in the face for being so stupid and emotional when he had asked Cain to take him to Lilim, because at the time he didn't consider at all that he would have to do anything like this. Those thoughts, along with the ones that followed, caused a shiver to run down Seth's spine. A shiver that soon progressed throughout his entire body until he couldn't help but shake where he stood.

He considered for a moment turning back, going back to the hospital and waiting for his friends to come and get him. Then he thought back to the incident in the restaurant, and the monster hunter guild bracelet his assailant wore, and in doing so he realized that going back would not be safe for him at all. If anything, going back to his so-called friends would be a death sentence for him, since one of them had already betrayed him and he knew that all Raz needed was an excuse to finish what he started back in the desert outside of Canaan. Even without counting them, Seth knew that all it would take was one mistake on his part, one person to accidentally see his eyes for this whole incident to repeat itself. With all of that in mind Seth returned his attention to the top of the wall. He could no longer see Cain, but somehow he knew that he was being true to what he had said and was up there waiting for him.

So, stuck between choosing to go back to his human friends and living every day of his life in fear of getting killed for what he was and climbing up an impossibly high wall to reach the one person who might be able to help him, Seth did the only thing that he knew he could do. He gritted his teeth together as tight as he could and fought back the urge to scream, yet even still a feral growl escaped his lips as he closed both his fists as tightly as he could in an attempt to stop himself from shaking. This done, Seth slowly looked down and returned his attention to the section of the wall that was directly in front of him. He could clearly see the stone blocks that the wall was made of, as well as the fact that there were a whole lot of them all stuck together. So, rather than figuring out how he could move many of them at once, he set his mind to something much simpler as he took in a single, deep breath and held his hand out towards one of them.

At first nothing happened, even when he focused his magic and felt the presence of the stone in his mind, the thing simply refused to move. Frustrated, Seth poured more power behind what he was doing, yet it still wouldn't move. On the third attempt, with even more power behind his intent, he felt the stone block shift before it suddenly shot out from the wall a good fifteen centimeters before it stopped. Seeing that happen, Seth immediately ceased what he was doing and let out a breath he hadn't even realized he had been holding in as he examined what he had just done. Effectively the stone block was still stuck in the wall, but he had managed to pull it out slightly. The act of doing that, however, brought two immediate problems to the forefront of Seth's mind. One, moving just that one block required much more effort than he had anticipated it would, and if he was to climb to the top then he would need to be careful about which blocks he moved. Two, despite his best efforts, moving that one block created quite a bit of noise, and while he saw nor heard anyone around him react to that noise, he knew that it would be only a matter of time before someone did, especially if he had to keep doing this.

With that in mind, Seth decided not to waste any more time as he went over to the block he had pulled out from the wall and climbed on top of it. To his relief it was able to support his weight. However, there was barely enough room for his feet to move, so much so that he had to press his back against the wall itself to prevent himself from falling over, and this was just the first block he had to climb up. Already the prospect of climbing up the rest of this wall made him lightheaded as he couldn't help but look over the edge of the block he was standing on and imagine what the ground would look like from the top of the wall. Steeling his resolve, and set in the fact that he had already made his decision, Seth grit his teeth together one more time as he held out one hand and set about the task of pulling one more block out from the wall, this one no more than two meters above him. As before it took some effort, but eventually he was able to get it. The amount of noise it made while doing so, however, reminded Seth that if he was going to keep doing this, he would need to be quicker.

Without even taking a second to really think about what he was doing, Seth reached up, grabbed the edge of the second block he had pulled out from the wall, and pulled himself up and onto it. The space between the wall and the edge of this block was a little bit less than half a meter, but Seth also knew that he was thinner than most people, so for his purposes the distance sufficed. What it didn't do, however, was take away the sense of imminent dread that Seth felt when he climbed up onto it and knew that he would need to keep doing this. Before he had a chance to contemplate that further, however, the sound of footsteps and muffled voices nearby caused his heart to suddenly stop within his chest.

Immediately Seth pressed himself against the wall in an effort to make himself appear as small as possible as he kept his ears open for any noise. Indeed his ears did pick up the sounds of footsteps nearby as well as some voices. However, they were too far away for him to hear anything they were saying and before long they were gone. Despite the return to silence it took more than a few long seconds for Seth to catch his breath as it dawned on him exactly how badly that could have gone for him. Without thinking he then looked down again. The ground was still a relatively safe distance from where he stood, but as soon as he laid eyes on it he immediately closed them and shook his head to get himself back on track. That done he then held out his hand once again and set about the task of pulling out one more stone block from the wall.

It had taken more time than he would have preferred, and more than once Seth needed to suddenly stop as the sound of people hit his ears, but they always passed by without coming anywhere close to where he was. Truth be told, the number of people that were out even at this time of night scared him even more than what he was currently doing. The height had become easier for him to deal with the higher he had gone, if only because he had figured out a new way to cope with it after the fifth block he had pulled out from the wall. Instead of pressing his back against the wall to move, and as such forcing him to look out, he instead turned around so that he was pressing his stomach against the wall so that he was forced to look at the stone wall directly in front of him. It wasn't much to see, but it was certainly preferable to looking down, something he hadn't done since that fifth block. That didn't make any part of this process any easier, however, especially since he still needed to fight the urge to look down every time he climbed up onto a new block, but it kept him going.

He was unsure of exactly how much time had passed since he had started doing this, but after he had pulled himself up onto the next stone block he was surprised when he looked up to see that he wasn't that far from the top. From what he could see the top wasn't any more than ten meters above where he was. Unfortunately, what this also did was make him curious about exactly how far he had come up since he had stopped paying attention. Without thinking about it or even realizing what he was doing, Seth's eyes drifted downwards to see what was there. What he saw made all of the air instantly leave his lungs as he expected to see the ground, but he didn't, at least not immediately. Indeed the ground where he had stood before was there, but it was so far beneath him that it looked like a speck of dust compared to the surrounding buildings.

That sight made Seth instantly press himself against the wall stomach first as he desperately reached out with both of his hands for something to grab onto, only to find nothing but smooth stone. All the while he needed to force himself to breathe, as he had suddenly forgotten how to do it automatically. Yet, despite each breath, he did not feel any air enter his lungs and he did not feel any more at ease than he did before. Even when he closed his eyes he could still see the image of the ground he had just seen in his mind's eye, as if it was permanently burned into it.

"Hey, did you hear something?" Seth suddenly heard a voice he did not recognize say not from below him, but from above. It only took a single second after hearing it for Seth to remember exactly where he was and where the voice was coming from, and with that in mind he instantly stopped breathing.

"No. What are you talking about?" another voice responded.

"It sounded like someone breathing," the first voice then said.

"Was it you?" the second voice asked in turn.

"I'd think I'd know if it was me, man. Wait, was it you?"

"What makes you think I'd know?"

"Well I'd like to think that you'd know when you're breathing too. Otherwise you might need to see a doctor."

"Well maybe it was then, I don't know."

"Well was it or not?"

"I don't fucking know. Do you still hear it?" The two of them then stopped talking as Seth assumed that they had taken a moment to look around. Now aware of what they were listening for, Seth stopped breathing and pressed himself against the wall as much as he could in an attempt to make himself appear as flat as possible. He knew that this wouldn't do much of anything if they did decide to look down, but it was the only thing that he could do.

Despite only seconds passing it felt to Seth like days as he stayed perfectly still against the wall who knew how many meters above the ground, not moving and not breathing. Even though the night was cold he couldn't help but sweat as the all encompassing fear of everything around him began to take over his every waking thought. More than once he imagined himself either slipping or making one misstep and falling off of the stone block he was currently standing on, and each time it made him want to scream. He shunted those thoughts from his head as soon as they appeared out of fear of them actually coming true. At least that, however, was something he had direct control over, unlike the two people directly above him.

"You know what, no, I don't," the first voice eventually said. The instant he heard that a sense of relief passed over Seth, though he fought the urge to take a breath.

"Maybe you were just imagining things," the second voice then responded before Seth heard the sound of footsteps moving away from him. There were a few tense seconds of silence before the first voice spoke again.

"Hmm… you know, you're probably right," the first voice said, and Seth could tell by how much softer it sounded that its owner was indeed moving farther away from him.

"Wait, you're agreeing with me?" The second voice then said in response to that remark.

"Of course," the first voice answered. "If you're right, why wouldn't I agree with you?" They kept on talking after that, but their voices became harder and harder to hear as they moved farther away. Just to be safe, however, Seth closed his eyes and counted to thirty. In a way the counting also helped to calm him down since it gave him something to concentrate on other than what was ahead of or below him.

After thirty seconds had passed, without hesitating, for he knew that he would be too scared to move if he did, Seth held out his arm again and pulled out one more stone block above him. Once he had it out far enough, without looking down again Seth reached up and pulled himself up onto it. Once he was on it he didn't waste any more time as he reached up and pulled out one last stone block. By this point his arms were beginning to become sore from the effort required to keep pulling himself up onto these stone blocks. However, Seth grit his teeth and fought through that pain as he pulled himself up onto that one last stone block. Then, with that done, he looked up and saw the top of the wall within reach.

Without thinking about it Seth leapt from that last stone block and grabbed the edge of the wall. His arms felt as if they were screaming at him to stop because of the pain they were in, but Seth knew that he couldn't afford to stop, not yet. So, with one last intense burst of effort, Seth pulled himself straight up with all of the strength he had left in him, whereupon he rolled over the stone blocks that served as the guard railing for the wall and fell two meters onto the stone walkway. The impact with the ground actually did hurt him quite a bit, but Seth for the life of him could not bring himself to care as he laid on his back looking up at the star filled night sky above him. Every second of which was spaced out by long, deep breaths as Seth took the chance to replenish all of the air that had left his lungs on the climb up.

As he lay there in silence he began to physically feel his heartbeat begin to slow just a little bit with each breath he took. With that feeling, here at the top of the wall, Seth couldn't help but feel a sense of pride and accomplishment for himself as he stared up at the night sky thinking that now, just for right now, he had made it. He still had a ways to go, he knew, and he knew that the way would be filled with more challenges like this one. He also knew that said challenges would no doubt seem just as insurmountable as the wall was, but right now he felt that he could afford to give himself the luxury of self-congratulations for conquering this one obstacle. Perhaps the ones he would no doubt face in the future would not seem as insurmountable to him with the knowledge that he had accomplished this.

A little over ten seconds of self reflection was all Seth was able to get before the lovely image of the starry night sky was suddenly obfuscated by a pair of large, round, red eyes attached to a bat-like face with a wide, sharp toothed grin.

"I see you finally made it up here," Cain said with a smile as he stood over Seth's head and looked down directly into his eyes. "But I knew you could do it. Always did." Seth couldn't help but let out a groan as he attempted to sit up, if only so he could get Cain's face away from his. His breath smelled awful, like he had been eating nothing but rotten meat and garbage.

"Is that true?" Seth asked with some amount of obvious sarcasm in his voice as he scooted himself around to properly face the bat-like creature. He didn't stand, he simply turned himself around while remaining in a sitting position.

"Of course," Cain answered rather quickly, and with an even wider smile than before. "I never had any doubt in you, kid. Believe me." Despite how sincere he seemed, Seth was extremely hesitant to believe anything he was saying. With all of that said, however, Seth took one last deep breath and stood back up, and as soon as he did he was treated with the view of the city skyline. Even at this late hour Seth was simply amazed at how much of the city he could still see. He almost regretted that he hadn't tried this during the daytime so that he could see the city in more detail. As it was he could mostly see the tops of all the buildings while the finer details of the city were lost in the darkness and shadows. As interesting as it was, however, Seth knew that he couldn't afford to spend too long staring at it. So with that in mind Seth turned around to take a look at whatever awaited him on the other side of the wall. What he saw made his heart sink into his chest.

Seth had seen the desert enough times to know exactly how endless it felt just from staring at it. What amazed him was how quickly he could forget something like that after the relatively short amount of time he had spent in a big city like Dis.

Whereas Dis was packed beyond the brim with buildings, people, and things that were happening, the surrounding desert outside of Dis was little more than a seemingly endless void of sand and heat. The darkness of the night only drove that point further home for Seth as it made that void appear even more endless than it already was. While he knew that he couldn't see Canaan anywhere in that void, he couldn't help but wonder if the direction he was looking in was even the direction Canaan was in. That revelation only made his heart sink into his chest further when he realized that even if he was able to get down from this wall, he would still need to make his way through that endless void of sand with no water and only the hospital gown he was still wearing. He knew that Cain had said something to that effect earlier, but he had barely paid any attention to it at the time due to how angry with him he was at that moment.

"Wha... What do... do we do now?" Seth hesitantly asked, unsure if Cain was even listening to him. Any doubts he may have had about that were put to rest when Seth heard him flap his wings before landing on the outer railing of the wall to the left of him.

"Well..." Cain began as he scratched the side of his face with his wing. "If you didn't like climbing up the wall to get here then you're certainly going to hate this part."

"I don't care anymore," Seth said without thinking as a response. Though when he did so he felt as if his voice was not his own, as if whomever had spoken instead of him really did not care at all what happened to him from this point on. "Just tell me." Despite the fact that Seth knew that Cain was listening to him this time, he did not respond immediately. Instead he simply stared directly at him like he was surprised to hear him say that. Due to his size, standing on the stone guard railing of the wall put him almost perfectly at eye level with Seth, so it was easier for him to hold eye contact with him while speaking.

"Very well," Cain then eventually said as he returned his attention to the desert. "You need to jump." The instant those words reached his ears Seth could swear that he felt his heart literally stop for only a single second as his brain took a few more solid seconds to process what it had just heard, and then ultimately reject it because there was no way it could have been what he had actually said.

"You..." Seth began, though between the feeling of being unable to breathe and the fact that he still hadn't completely processed what he had just heard Cain say

a second ago, he found it difficult to say any more. "You… want me to do what?"
Upon completing that sentence Cain turned to face Seth directly as he narrowed his
eyes at him.

"Listen, I know what you must be thinking and I know what you want to
say," Cain responded to him. "But think about this. If I wanted you hurt or even
killed there would have been many, many, many easier ways of doing it than this. For
mother's sake I saw at least twenty good opportunities to do that on the way here. So
just tru-" Before Cain could finish his sentence, Seth watched as his right ear
suddenly twitched, and with it his eyes suddenly became as wide as dinner plates.
Before Seth had the chance to say anything in response to him, another sound hit his
ears first.

"Are you certain you heard something?" a voice that sounded distinctly like
the second of the two city guardsmen Seth had heard earlier spoke aloud. As soon as
he had finished speaking Seth heard the first one respond to him, but he sounded as if
he were intentionally speaking quietly, so Seth could not make out what he was
saying. Still, hearing them in the first place forced Seth to stop for the moment in
order to better pay attention. Surely enough, it may have been faint and quite a ways
away, but he could clearly hear the sounds of footsteps coming in his and Cain's
direction.

Returning his attention back to Cain, Seth saw that the look on his face had
changed again. This time, however, he wasn't smiling or scowling. Instead the look
on Cain's face betrayed genuine concern, something that Seth was genuinely
surprised to see from him.

"Listen, Seth," Cain quickly spoke much more quietly than before. "I know
why you're hesitant. I would be too if I were made like you, but you have to trust
me. The last thing I want is to see you come to harm, and not just because Mistress
will tear my wings off and my eyes out if I let that happen. I've seen too many of our
kind fall to humans not because they weren't strong enough, but because they didn't
understand enough to survive. I don't want to see that happen again tonight, not to
you. So please, just trust me. Please." Then, before Seth could even think of any kind
of response to him, Cain spread his wings and took off into the night sky above him.

"Come on man, what do you even think we're gonna find?" the voice of the
second guardsman spoke up before Seth could even look to see where Cain went.

"I don't know, just be quiet," the voice of the first guardsman answered before both of them fell into silence, though when he listened carefully Seth could still hear the distinct sound of their footsteps hitting the stone. Worse still, the sounds of their footsteps were becoming louder and louder with every step they took. Seth did not even need to think to know that they would soon be close enough to see him.

So alone again, Seth found himself between two seemingly impossible choices as he looked out into the endless desert in front of him, and then back to the city of Dis behind him. On one hand, there was the paper thin hope of salvation for him in the form of Lilim, who no doubt would have the answers he wanted. On the other, there was the seemingly comfortable life he had always known. Comfortable, except for the fact that every waking second he had to worry about what would happen if somebody found out what he was, something that had already happened to him twice. All the while the sounds of the footsteps continued to grow louder and louder as they grew closer. Part of him debated hiding and waiting for the two guardsmen to pass, but the only place he could think of to hide was down on the side of the wall he had just climbed up, and he did not want to face that again. One way or another, he knew that he would have to make a choice and he had to make it now.

Stuck between a city of humans that no matter what perspective he looked at it with spelled certain death for him and the bottom of a wall that led into an endless desert that also spelled certain death for him, Seth took in a deep breath, steeled his resolve, and made the only decision he knew that he could. Without thinking or second guessing his decision lest he be seen, Seth climbed up onto the railing of the outer wall, closed his eyes tightly, and leapt off of it. He no longer heard the sounds of the approaching footsteps or even the sound of his own breathing, all there was for him to hear was the sound of the wind rushing past him. He dared not open his eyes, for he did not want to see the fast approaching sand that he knew would eventually kill him.

With the darkness surrounding him and the feeling of the wind rushing past his face, a kind of serenity washed over Seth that he had never felt before as he felt himself relax. For reasons he could not comprehend, the knowledge that everything would be over soon made him feel content. If everything did end, then he would no longer need to worry about anything, and those who still may have been his friends would no longer need to worry about him. Those thoughts made him feel at peace, a feeling that until now he wasn't sure he had ever truly known before. Those feelings of peace and serenity only lasted for a few, short seconds, however, as Seth abruptly came to a sudden stop when he hit something. As soon as it happened Seth knew that something was not right, as not only was he aware that he was still alive, but the feeling beneath his fingers and toes didn't feel anything at all like sand. Instead it felt more like fur.

Upon opening his eyes Seth saw that he hadn't hit the ground, but rather had landed on the back of an enormous flying creature, the features of which he couldn't exactly make out as he was on top of it. Instinctively Seth looked behind him to see if the wall of Dis was still there. When he looked, however, he saw that the wall was indeed behind him, but was somehow moving, as all of the blocks that made up the wall were rushing past him as if the wall itself was spinning. Upon seeing that Seth instantly became aware of how fast this creature was moving as he watched it circle around what felt like most of the wall around the city at an insane speed. With that knowledge Seth immediately grabbed onto the fur on the back of this flying creature as hard as he could to prevent himself from flying off, and as soon as he did he watched as the flying creature suddenly broke away from the wall surrounding Dis before gaining altitude and flying upwards into the night sky.

Looking back Seth could only watch as the city of Dis began to shrink into the distance behind him. He wasn't sure at all exactly how fast this creature was flying, but it must have been much faster than a horse for the city to shrink behind him that quickly. As soon as that thought came, however, the flying creature began to level out and slow its speed to something a bit more manageable. Before long the wind hitting Seth's face began to bother him less and less, to the point where he hardly noticed it anymore. Along with the wind Seth felt his heartbeat begin to slow as well as he finally, finally felt that he could actually relax. As impossible as it had seemed when he had started, he really had made it out of the city of Dis and no longer needed to worry about being chased.

Now that he had a clear head, possibly for the first time since leaving the hospital, Seth took a few seconds to take in his surroundings as well as figure out what in the actual hell was going on. He wasn't scared anymore, that much he knew for certain. Even if he wanted to be scared he couldn't bring himself to feel that way anymore, at least not right now. That didn't mean, however, that his natural curiosity wasn't getting the better of him and that his need for answers wasn't overwhelming any chance of fear. His common sense, however, remained perfectly intact.

To start with, Seth looked down at the gigantic, furry creature beneath him and was surprised to see that it wasn't as big as he had initially believed it to be. Its body was just a little bit over three and a half meters in length, and turned out to be perfectly spherical. On both of its sides were massive, black feathered wings that were well over twice the length of its body each, and despite their occasional flap to keep the thing aloft, neither wing made a sound when they moved. The black fur on its back where Seth sat was not like any animal Seth had ever felt either. Instead of feeling smooth, like hair, this thing's fur felt far more coarse, and actually itched his skin quite a bit the more he touched and dug into it. Given its black fur, wings, and its odd shape, Seth could only come to one conclusion as to what this thing was as he slowly crawled forwards and looked over the front of its body in order to see its face, which he could not initially see because of the creature's odd shape. When he looked down to see its face, however, he nearly leapt back in panic as he did not see a face, but instead a single, massive red eyeball that took up the entire space where its face would be.

As if sensing what he was doing, the red eyeball suddenly glanced up to look directly at Seth. Its sudden movement caused Seth to actually panic as he instantly backed away, but the creature did not appear to mind his sudden movement as it just flew on. It was only when Seth had touched the back of this creature and began to slide downwards that he became fully conscious of the fact that he really was riding on top of an eyeball with wings, and that due to its spherical shape he did not have nearly as much room to move around as he had first thought. After taking a few deep breaths to calm himself again, Seth decided to do something that he knew was stupid, but he also knew that it would keep bothering him if he didn't do it. So, his curiosity getting the better of him, Seth slowly, while keeping his hands firmly grasping the eyeball monster's fur, moved over towards the back left edge of it just past its wing and looked straight down.

Surely enough, he saw the desert sand below him, but because of how it seemingly went on forever and how dark it was, Seth had no way of actually telling how high up he and this creature were. He was able to tell, of course, that he was much higher up than when he was on the wall, and that fact made his heart stop as he froze in place and instinctively gripped the eyeball monster's fur that much tighter. Before he could contemplate that any further, however, the sound of another set of flapping wings coming from directly behind him suddenly hit his ears as he instantly turned his head to see what it was. To his immense surprise his eyes beheld the bat-like form of Cain as he appeared to be only barely keeping pace with the giant, flying eyeball. Forcing himself to relax just a little bit more, Seth pulled away from the edge of the flying eyeball monster so that he could sit comfortably in the center, at least as comfortably as he could be on top of a giant, flying, almost perfectly spherical eyeball with coarse fur. As he did so he watched as Cain veered towards him before eventually getting close enough to land on top of the flying eyeball monster himself, which he did as he touched down directly in front of Seth.

"Ah, there we go," Cain said as he let out an immense sigh of what sounded to Seth like exhaustion before turning around to face Seth properly, his toothy grin having returned to his face. Thanks to his much smaller frame he could move around much easier on the eyeball-monster's back than Seth could. "See, Seth. I told you that you could trust me."

"Wha... What is this thing?" Seth couldn't help but ask now that he had someone to talk to again.

"Oh, him?" Cain responded cheerfully as he looked down at the eyeball-monster beneath them. "You don't have to worry about the big guy. He's harmless. At least to you and me. He's taking us to Mistress." As Cain spoke he spun back around and sat himself comfortably in Seth's lap, something that Seth was not exactly comfortable with himself, but he made no effort to stop him. "Oh, and sorry, but the big guy's not exactly gifted like you or me. So he won't respond if you try to talk to him."

"But... What is he?" Seth again couldn't help but ask once he felt comfortable speaking again. To which Cain looked directly up at him like a cat would. The expression on his face was one that Seth was innately familiar with. Pure confusion.

"What do you mean what is he?" Cain asked. "He's a monster, like you and me."

"Yeah, I know that," Seth responded. "But what is he? Like what kind of creature is he?" Cain immediately opened his mouth to answer Seth's question, but when he did no words came out. A quick moment of silence passed before Cain looked away from Seth and out in front of them as he appeared to contemplate Seth's question.

"I don't actually know," Cain eventually responded. "I've never really thought about it, to be honest." That answer told Seth a lot more than he intended to know about not just Cain, but monsters in general. While with humans they rarely, if ever, seemed to have any answers that satisfied his many, many questions, if Cain didn't know at all what kind of creature another monster was, then perhaps the monsters didn't have any more answers than humans. That fact made Seth suddenly feel uneasy about this whole endeavor to see Lilim, though he knew that it was far, far too late to back out of it now.

Seth was unsure of exactly how long he had been sitting on the back of this flying eyeball-monster, but he knew that it couldn't have been any more than a couple of hours. Two and a half at most. Cain had stopped talking after their last conversation, perhaps out of some ill conceived notion that in the silence Seth would relax and enjoy the view. Neither of those things happened, as Seth found himself unable to truly relax in any way, shape, or form since leaving Dis. It wasn't because of the fact that Cain stubbornly refused to move from his position in Seth's lap, or the fact that he was flying at all, or even the fact that he wasn't sure at all where this thing was taking him. He had made his peace with all three of those facts once things had settled for them upon leaving the city of Dis, and the abundance of fur on the eyeball-monster's body allowed both some level of comfort as well as something he could grab onto in those moments when he felt unsafe. Something that had been happening more and more as their flight went on.

True to what Cain had said earlier, the giant, flying eyeball-monster never made any attempts to communicate with either of them, whether they be in the form of grunts, growls, or some other sound Seth had not yet considered. In fact, the flying eyeball-monster hadn't made any sounds at all for the entire duration of the flight. Even the occasional flaps of its wings only made at best a minimal amount of sound given their size. It was enough to make Seth wonder whether or not being silent was somehow this thing's speciality despite its shape and size. That, combined with how silent he knew Cain was, gave Seth an eerie feeling that these two may have been watching him for much, much longer than he had originally believed.

The true source of his discomfort, however, lay in the newfound insecurities he now had with himself regarding his decision. He didn't regret leaving Dis, at least he didn't think he did, but he couldn't help but wonder exactly what was to become of him now that he had come all the way out here. What would Lilim say when he told her what had happened to him? What would his life be like from here on out if he decided to stay with her? What would she say about any of his friends if he ever saw them again? Would he see them again? These were all questions he did not know the answers to, and part of him doubted that Lilim would know the answers too. Despite his best efforts not to think about them too hard, all of them and more found ways to crawl back into his head over the course of their long, long flight. What made it even worse for him was knowing that he would likely find out the answers to all of these questions somewhere down the line, but he wasn't sure if he would like the answers.

All of these thoughts were interrupted when he suddenly felt the flying eyeball-monster begin to list to their left. Instinctively Seth grabbed two handfuls of fur from the eyeball-monster's back to prevent himself from falling off, but that didn't seem to be necessary as the eyeball-monster didn't lean too far to its left. Despite that, however, Seth was not about to take any more chances as he held onto the eyeball-monster's back for dear life. As if in direct contrast to Seth, the instant this happened Cain's smile suddenly returned wider than ever, to the point where Seth thought that his lips might tear from the strain of it.

"We're here!" Cain let out as he looked directly up at Seth with obvious elation in his voice. "I'll see you on the ground. I need to tell Mistress that you've arrived." Then, before Seth could ask him what he was talking about or where they even were, from his position in Seth's lap Cain suddenly spread his wings and took off straight up into the night sky before flying towards his left away from the eyeball monster and diving straight down to the desert sands below. Seth followed him with his eyes as he watched him dive, and what he saw took so much of his breath away that he nearly let go of the tufts of fur on the eyeball-monster's back.

Instead of the endless ocean of desert sands that he had expected to see, the ground below matched the night sky above in that all Seth saw of it was a vast expanse of black amidst the desert sands like a pool of water. Looking at it closer made Seth realize that not only was the eyeball-monster circling this expanse of black, but that the expanse itself was not a singular thing. Instead it was a gathering of many, many, many different monsters. From his position in the sky Seth counted hundreds of them, more than hundreds even, possibly reaching a number that he did not even know. Then he remembered that monsters came in all shapes and sizes ranging from giant ones like the deer skulled one he had fought in Canaan to smaller ones like Cain, and that in turn led him to realize that there might potentially be more monsters in this gathering than he could see. That in and of itself was terrifying, but the fact that the eyeball-monster was rapidly descending towards it as it flew in its circular path caused Seth to start shivering uncontrollably despite the temperature not being that cold.

His shivering went unnoticed by the flying eyeball-monster as it circled around the immense gathering of monsters. With each pass it descended further and further towards it, and the closer it got to all of them, the faster Seth felt his heart begin to beat. The sight of just one of these creatures signaled an incoming fight to Seth. Walking into a gathering of this many of them made him worried that they were all going to tear him apart the literal instant they saw him. He even saw some of them look up towards him and the flying eyeball-monster as they descended further towards them. The sight of them making eye contact with him even from this distance made his heart stop in his chest more than once as he couldn't shake the feeling that they were looking directly at him, which considering how close they were coming to the ground now, he knew that they probably were. As they grew closer Seth could even see that some of them had wings of their own, meaning that if they wanted they could very easily fly up and tear him from the eyeball-monster's back with little effort, but none of them did.

Eventually, as Seth could only barely tell what was going on around him as his attention was more focused on the approaching gathering of monsters than the ground, but with a sudden, almost grinding halt, the flying eyeball-monster stopped in its tracks as it made contact with the ground at the edge of the gathering of monsters. From where it stood now, with its size Seth now saw that he was eye level with some of the larger monsters at this gathering, but to his horror he also saw that some of them were much, much larger than the height of both him and the eyeball monster together. One monster with armor plated scales even appeared to be taller than the capitol building that Seth had seen in Dis. With his attention still on all of the assembled monsters that he could see, all of whom were still staring directly at him, Seth didn't notice when the eyeball monster held out its left wing to the ground and leaned so far to its left that Seth almost slid off of it. Instinctively he grabbed tighter onto the tufts of fur on its back as he nearly fell off, but after pulling himself together and actually taking a look at the position the flying eyeball monster had taken, it became clear to him that its intent was for him to slide down its wing and onto the sand below.

As clear as the eyeball monster's intentions were, Seth wasn't sure at all if he even wanted to get off of it, as doing so would leave him standing on the desert sand, alone, surrounded by many different monsters, all of whom were still staring at him like predators eyeing up a potential meal. Despite that, however, every single one of the monsters that he could see remained perfectly still where they were, and none of them made any advances of any kind towards him or the eyeball monster. Not only that, but Seth knew that if he were to look down at the eyeball monster's face he would see it looking back up at him with a very confused expression, at least as much as one could accomplish with only a single eye, as it wondered why he wasn't sliding off of it like it wanted. So with that in mind, and knowing that he had already come this far, despite the soul crushing terror of seeing so many monsters in one place Seth obliged to what the eyeball monster obviously wanted and slid down its wing towards the sand, if only in fear that it would somehow attempt to forcefully remove him if he did not comply.

The instant Seth's bare feet touched the desert sand a series of memories flooded back into his mind of the first day he had woken up in the desert, and how the sand beneath his feet felt then. Memories that were instantly forgotten when he looked straight ahead and saw the gathering of monsters all still staring at him. The instant his eyes met all of theirs a wave of paralyzing, soul crushing terror washed through Seth as he felt like a mouse being eyed up by a group of hungry cats. Even more so now since he was no longer on the back of the flying eyeball-monster and therefore had to look up to meet most of their gazes. Before he even had a chance to react, much less change his mind, the eyeball-monster retracted its wing and shook its entire body to clear any unwanted sand from its fur and feathers. It was only then that Seth noticed that this massive, round monster stood on only a single leg that reminded Seth of a hawk's talon, or at least something that belonged on a large bird of prey. The eyeball-monster's leg muscles, however, were much thicker than they would have been on a normal bird, presumably to compensate for the fact that it only had a single leg as opposed to two or four like most creatures Seth had seen.

Because it was obvious to Seth now that the flying eyeball-monster was not going to let him back onto its back much less fly him away from here, Seth turned back to face the gathering of monsters. To his horror, none of them had taken their eyes off of him. He couldn't even tell if any of them had blinked. However, they still had not made any sort of moves to get closer to him, much less attack him. Exactly why none of them were attacking him was beyond him. He had killed enough of these creatures to know that he had certainly not earned any favors from them. If anything the fact that they weren't attacking him made the soul rending fear that was skulking through him more all encompassing.

Before he had a moment to contemplate that any further, however, Seth was suddenly and rather violently shoved forward so that he fell face first into the sand. After quickly brushing the sand out of his face and spitting out the few bits that had made it into his mouth, Seth looked back to see the flying eyeball-monster with its wing extended in his direction. Seeming indifferent to his plight, the winged eyeball monstrosity simply retracted its wing and returned to its former standing position, though Seth somehow knew that if it could turn to face him so that it could glare at him like the others it would. Returning his attention forward, to his further horror Seth saw that the eyeball monster's wing had actually pushed him a few meters farther than he thought it had, as he now found himself right at the feet of this gathering of monsters.

As much as he wanted to stay where he was, as much he wanted to stay face down on the sand and not stand up so that he would have at least some pathetic excuse not to further approach them, it soon dawned on Seth that if the violent shove from the eyeball monster was any indication, he did not have a choice. Thinking back, of all the times he had considered turning back in Dis, the time to truly turn back from this had long, long since passed. That time would have been before he had jumped from the wall back in Dis. Now he had made his choice, and whether he wanted to or not he would have to follow through on it. Before he could make that choice, however, his eyes caught a glimpse of movement within the gathering of monsters. That sight was followed by one that Seth had never expected to see from creatures like this. With their eyes still on him, Seth watched as the monsters that stood directly in front of him began to take a few steps back from each other. For some of them it was more difficult to do than others because of their vast differences in sizes, but when they had finished Seth saw that they had formed a sort of pathway towards the center of their gathering.

With nowhere else to look Seth's eyes were drawn down the path that the monsters had created. What he saw at the end of that path, however, made him feel as if his heart had stopped completely dead in its tracks as he suddenly felt tense all over his body. At the other end of the path walking directly towards him was the silhouette of another human. At least it appeared human, but Seth knew better. It's gaunt, yet feminie frame, it's unnatural height that he could see even from a distance, it's wild, unkempt hair that looked as if it had never been properly combed or taken care of ever, and the flimsy dress that it wore all told Seth exactly who and what this thing was. What's more, he could see that she wasn't just walking towards him, she appeared to be walking as fast as she could without breaking into a run.

The sight of her took away all of the fear within Seth as he suddenly felt his heartbeat return and his limbs become less rigid. It was only then that Seth remembered that he could move as he slowly pushed himself back upright into a standing position. Once he was up he returned his attention to the woman shaped figure approaching him, and it was then that its silhouette began to break and he could see her eyes. Her blood red eyes. Her eyes were soon followed by her face, and then by the rest of her as she walked out from the crowd of monsters and stood directly in front of him. It had been some time since he had seen her outside of his imagination and dreams, but now, amongst this gathering of hundreds upon hundreds of monsters, Seth found himself staring up into the face and eyes of Lilim.

The look on her face when she saw him was one that Seth couldn't place, at least not immediately. At first she appeared shocked just from the sight of him, but then the shock began to fade as the look in her eyes began to soften and her lips began to curl up into a smile. It wasn't a sinister or even a happy smile, however. Instead, from what Seth could see she appeared to be genuinely relieved. Much like the way he had felt when staring at the immense gathering of monsters, it was as if the sight of him put her at ease, and because of that she knew that she no longer had to worry anymore. It was a sight that Seth had become more than familiar with during his time in Canaan, as he had seen it multiple times on Tara whenever he had woken up in Andrea's clinic or returned from doing something dangerous. It was a look that, to him, told him without words that everything was going to be alright now.

"Lilim-" Seth said to her, but before he could say any more, with a speed he couldn't even fathom both of her arms had wrapped around his neck and pulled him in so close to her that Seth could hardly see. The next thing he knew Lilim's grip on him had suddenly become much, much tighter, as if she were attempting to pull him in as close to her as possible. She wasn't hurting him, and Seth didn't feel any discomfort whatsoever in the way he was being held by her. Her actions confused him immensely, but only for a moment as he realized what the exact way she was holding him was meant to be. She wasn't hurting him, she was hugging him, and hugging him so tightly that it was obvious to Seth that she had no intention of letting him go. If he could see her face, he knew that the expression on it would be one of immense joy.

That fact, if only that fact, made Seth feel that he could really, and truly relax as he no longer had anything to worry about. It soon dawned on him that he wasn't even sure when the last time he truly felt like this was. Since he had woken up in Canaan after his fight with Raz? Since he had left Canaan? Since he had decided to talk to Cain? Since he had left Dis? Regardless of whenever it was, none that mattered to him anymore as he let out possibly the first, real deep breath he had taken in a long time and returned Lilim's hug.

Chapter 27

Seth didn't know exactly how long he and Lilim remained in each other's embrace, but the truth was that he did not really care. It didn't fully occur to him until after she had already hugged him, but despite all appearances he truly felt safe here. No one here wanted him dead, no one here was looking for an excuse to kill him, and no one here was only pretending to be his friend so that they might avoid his potential wrath. It wasn't exactly what he wanted, nor was it what he had expected, but the mere fact that all of those things were true was overwhelming to him. It was so surreal, just knowing all of that made him feel lighter, as if a great weight had literally been lifted off his shoulders. Something that Seth had heard others say before but had always assumed that its meaning was more figurative than literal. Now though, knowing that he really, truly was safe, even if only for a few moments, was enough to break the dam that kept back all of the emotions that Seth had been holding back since his fight in the desert with Raz.

With nothing to hold back the tidal wave of emotions that violently washed over him, Seth did something that he had not done in a long time, but could not keep himself from doing it now even if he wanted to. He cried. He didn't know why his first response to all of this was to cry. Tara and everyone else had told him that crying was what people did when they felt sad, but Seth didn't feel sad about any of this. Not even a little bit. As confusing as it was for him though, Seth was unable to bring himself to stop as he unconsciously tightened his grip on Lilim. In response Lilim tightened her own grip on him as she pulled him as close to her as she physically could. With that done she remained still and let Seth cry for as long as he needed to. As long as she was there to accept his tears, she was happy too. For more reasons than Seth could ever know.

Eventually, however, the tears began to dry and the violent tidal wave of emotions that hit Seth began to settle. As such he began to slowly pull away from Lilim, who resisted at first, but then let him go after another few long seconds. This had the unintended side effect of making Seth feel incredibly small, however, as Lilim towered over him with her almost inhuman height when she fully stood up in front of him. As intimidated as Seth may have been by her height, however, the joy fueled smile that was plastered on her face took away any doubts that he may have had in his mind about her.

Now that the moment for hugs and reunions had passed, Seth's mind shifted back into focus as he remembered why he was here in the first place. He opened his mouth to speak to her, but before he could say anything Lilim spoke first.

"Now, Seth, as much as I want to say that it's good to see you, and believe me, it is. You have no idea how happy I am to see you right now. But if you're here and you're wearing..." Lilim had to pause for a moment as her eyes did a quick once over of the hospital gown that Seth was still wearing. Seth, who instantly realized what she was doing, became more than a little embarrassed as he remembered that it was literally the only thing he was wearing. "Whatever that thing is, I'm going to assume that something happened. Something bad. Am I right?"

"Y-Yes," Seth hesitantly responded as his eyes fell down to look at his feet. As glad as he was to be here, it still felt odd for him to talk to monsters. "I was with my-" Seth immediately stopped himself as he realized that he was about to call the people he knew his friends. The fact that that might not have been true may have been important, but Seth wasn't sure how Lilim would take to the idea of him calling a group of humans his friends. Especially after all that had happened recently. "Some of the humans from Canaan and... and I was stabbed in the side by a monster hunter. I had never seen him before, but... that doesn't really matter. It makes sense for someone like him to attack me if he knew what I was, but... f-for that to happen s-someone must have t-told him and..." As Seth spoke his words gradually became more and more jumbled and less coherent, as if the mere memory of that event was a source of physical pain for him. It was so much that Seth unconsciously balled his hands into fists as he tried his best to not break down crying again in front of all of these monsters. Before that could happen, however, Seth suddenly felt Lilim place both of her hands on his shoulders.

"As much as I would love to say that I told you so," Lilim said to him in as soothing a voice as she could manage. "I think that doing so would be pointless, now that you already know. How could you not after experiencing something so horrible. What you need to know right now though is that everything is going to be okay. You're safe now. Your big sister is here to protect you."

"Big sister?" Seth couldn't help but say, as he vaguely remembered Lilim using that term to describe herself the first time they had met.

"Why not?" Lilim was quick to respond as she let go of Seth's shoulders, took a few steps back from him, and then stretched her arms out to her sides as she motioned to all of the monsters surrounding them. "I mean after all, we're all related to each other in some way or another since we all come from the same place. Some of us are just older than others. So why can't I be your big sister?"

"We all come from the same place..." Seth repeated. "You mean Chaos?" Lilim didn't respond to Seth immediately after hearing that, but after a few seconds a light chuckle crossed her lips, which worried Seth because he was now afraid that he might have said something that he shouldn't have.

"Ah yes," Lilim eventually said after her chuckling had died down. "That lazy name that the humans gave mother. Never was a fan of it myself. But yes, we all came from mother, so we're all one big, happy family! Aren't we!" Lilim's enthusiasm was not met by a single one of the many, many monsters behind her. A good chunk of which still had their eyes fixated on Seth as if they were just waiting for an excuse to eat him. "That actually reminds me. I want to try something. I hope you don't mind, but I really am curious." Before Seth even had a chance to answer whether or not he minded, Lilim suddenly spun around to face the army of monsters and cupped her hands around her mouth. "Hey ladies! Any one of you remember this guy popping out of you a couple of months ago!" Seth wasn't at all embarrassed by what she had said, but he felt as if he should be. If only because he felt that Tara and some of the other humans he knew would be if a question like that had been asked about them. None of the monsters, however, responded to Lilim's question in any way. Most simply stood in place while others looked at each other, appearing to be as confused by the question as Seth was. "Well, that's a shame."

"Umm... Thank you for trying... I think," Seth said in response to that, unsure of what else to say. When Lilim didn't say anything to him in response, Seth took that as his chance to ask the one, all encompassing question that had been on his mind ever since the second he had arrived here. "Um... Lilim, if you don't mind me asking-"

"I don't mind. Go ahead, ask away," Lilim joyfully interrupted as she spun back around to properly face him, much to his annoyance. He decided not to let that bother him, however, as he did not want to be rude to her. Not here anyway.

"What's with all these monsters?" Seth asked. "I've heard about groups of monsters, but I didn't think they were this big. Why are there so many? As far as I can remember I've never heard of, much less seen, so many of th... us, all in one place." Lilim's initial response to his question was made not with words, but with her lips as they curled up into a very wide, very wicked looking smile. While Seth had seen Lilim smile before, the fact that she did so immediately after he had asked that particular question was unsettling to him, and he did not know why.

"Oh, them," Lilim eventually answered as she pointed back to the army of monsters behind her. "That's simple. We're going to do what mother always intended for us to do." Hearing that made all the feelings of relief and happiness that Seth had felt before evaporate like water on a hot day as he almost literally felt his heart sink into the deepest pit of his stomach.

"W-What exactly d-do you mean by that?" Seth then asked without thinking.

"Oh, Seth, don't be coy," Lilim answered with a laugh as she slapped her hands onto his shoulders again. "I know you know what I mean." While Seth was certain that Lilim had expected some kind of verbal response from him, he did not give her one. There were a few reasons for that, the fact that he genuinely could not come up with any sort of response to what she had just said being only one of them. A more important reason, however, was that he needed a few seconds to mentally digest the implications of her exact words. In truth, Seth had expected something like this. After all, if he was a monster and he was going to associate himself with other monsters, then they would expect him to kill some humans. This many monsters, however, and the idea that they were all going to march around and destroy everything that was in their path, was unsettling to him in ways that he could not properly describe. He imagined the city of Dis, all of the people he had seen living there, and the idea of that many people being slaughtered like pigs at the claws and teeth of this many monsters almost made him throw up in his mouth. Thankfully he did not actually do that, but he was certain that Lilim had seen some kind of reaction from him, as the smile she wore began to fade as quickly as it had appeared.

"I should have figured," Lilim muttered to herself as she removed her hands from Seth's shoulders. While he could hear perfectly well what she had said, the look on her face when she did so was one that Seth could not place. It looked to him like a mixture of anger, disappointment, and sadness. At least as far as he could tell. "Listen, Seth. You've lived with humans for what, seven months now, more or less. I'm certain that in that time they must have told you all about Solaris and how he was the human that blew himself up in order to slay our dear mother." Seth's mind immediately flashed back to several moments from the play he had seen with Filia,

Raz, Tara, and Daedalus before he had been stabbed. That play's depiction of Solaris' life was more or less in line with what everyone had told Seth about him even if it did leave quite a bit to be desired. "Well, to the north of here is the capital of this wretched country, a city called Sol. It's where Solaris' descendants have been peacefully living and ruling over the people of this country for hundreds of years. A place that they believe is safe from us, but more than that, it's a monument meant to mock us. A fortress made up of humanity's cruelty and hubris."

"I… don't know what hubris means," Seth sheepishly spoke up as he realized that Lilim's anger had been growing with every sentence that she spoke.

"Let me explain it this way," Lilim began. "A long, long time ago, I was told an old human story. One that predated the arrival of our mother by thousands of years, of a boy named Icarus. He and his father were imprisoned on an island by a cruel and unjust king. So in order to escape Icarus' father made them wings out of wax and feathers. Something that wouldn't ever work in real life, but human stories are stupid like that. Anyways, Icarus' father warned him that even though their bullshit wax and feather wings allowed them to fly, not to fly too close to the sun. Otherwise the wax that held their wings together would melt and he would fall. Icarus, being a little shit, ignored his father's warnings and flew as high as he could because he felt empowered by his newfound ability to fly, and you know what happened when he did?" While Seth felt that the answer to that question was obvious, before he even had a chance to say anything much less answer her, Lilim continued without waiting for him. "The heat of the sun melted the wax holding his wings together and he plummeted to a watery, bone crushing death into the ocean below. That is what hubris is, Seth. Arrogance. The belief that you're invincible. The idea that nothing is going to go wrong simply because you're you. Humanity has been flying closer and closer to the sun with every day, every week, every month, every year that they haven't been wiped out. So it's time to send them crashing into the ocean where they belong. Starting with the city that they believe is safest from us." Seth wanted to say something, but before he could Lilim suddenly shot him a glare so intense that it made him instantly shiver where he stood. "I know what you're going to say, and yes. It has to be Sol. I will not accept anything less. I need that city to be reduced to nothing more than ash and embers beneath my feet!"

As she shouted that last sentence to him Seth saw something in her blood red eyes. Something that he had seen before, but could not place where. Hearing

Lilim yell, however, brought to mind his last encounter with Vivian, and that was when it clicked into place for him. The look in Lilim's eyes, it was the exact same type of look that Vivian gave him whenever she talked about how much she hated monsters.

"I... you... y..." Seth tried to speak, but found himself unable to put together a coherent sentence as the full implications of Lilim's words ran through his head. "You are... To Sol? Will you-" Seth's babbling was interrupted by Lilim as she suddenly dropped her glare and burst out laughing hysterically.

"It's okay, I know," Lilim said through her laughter as she put a hand on Seth's shoulder again. "I know this is a lot to take in. Especially since you were still living among the humans until a few hours ago." Lilim looked as if she was about to say more, but before she could her eyes suddenly went wide. Seth wanted to ask her what was wrong, but before he could she suddenly slapped herself on the forehead. "That reminds me! I can't believe that I almost forgot about that! Dear mother, I'm so embarrassed!" She then paused for a few more seconds to laugh some more. "I have something for you, Seth. A gift." Before Seth could even think, much less ask her what she was talking about, Lilim suddenly disappeared in a flash of red light. While he was absolutely terrified of saying it to her face, he was beginning to find her constant interruptions of him more than a little annoying.

As quickly as she had disappeared, however, Lilim soon reappeared with something that was about the size of a small coin purse in her hand. It looked, to Seth at least, like a piece of white fabric that appeared to have been torn from someone's clothing and was wrapped around something as sort of a makeshift bag. Seth couldn't tell exactly what it was or supposed to be, but Lilim, her joy fueled smile back with a vengeance, held it out to him as if she were eager for him to take it from her.

Unsure of what else he even could do at this moment, Seth hesitantly took the gift from Lilim. Only when it was in his hand, however, did Seth notice that the string that tied the makeshift bag together wasn't made of rope or leather, but rather twisted together strands of dark hair that wasn't the same shade as Lilim's. Now with even more hesitation than before, Seth slowly untied the string of hair, only for it to fall to the sand at his feet once he did so, as it was not actually connected to the bag in any way. With nothing keeping the makeshift bag closed, what Seth saw when it fell open greatly confused him at first. It appeared to be a pair of mostly white orbs that had red crack-like patterns that connected to these pinkish-red strands coming out from the back of both of the orbs. It was only when one of the orbs rolled around in the fabric due to Seth's handling of it that he finally noticed that the front of one of them had a single, small black circle in what he assumed to be the center with a wide ring of brown surrounding it. It took Seth a few seconds for his brain to process exactly what these were, but when it did his blood instantly froze where he stood. Inside of this makeshift bag were someone's eyes.

"Surprise!" Lilim shouted before Seth was able to fully bring himself back to reality after what he had just seen. "They're the eyes of that guy you didn't like! What was his name? John, Jimmy, Jerome…" She then stopped for a second as she directed her attention towards the flying eyeball-monster. "Ey, you're the one that brought him to me, you remember his name?" The eyeball-monster's only response to that question was to very slowly blink. "Eh, it doesn't matter."

"J… J-Joseph?" Seth finally managed to spit out once he had regained his ability to speak.

"Sure!" Lilim immediately responded. "If you say so. So how do you like it, Sethy? I bet you love it! If even half of what I've been told about that pushover was true I know I wou-"

"Are you insane!" Seth shouted at her as he dropped her "gift" onto the sand below. "Why would you think I would like this!"

"Well, our mutual batty friend, you call him Cain," Lilim began to answer. "Cute name by the way, saw you talking to him that one night before you left that town of yours. He said that you told him 'the wrong town watch member died that night'." When Lilim quoted Seth she deepened her voice to do an impression of him, which greatly disturbed Seth because of how uncannily close it sounded to his actual voice.

"I… I was just mad at him!" Seth shouted at Lilim in response. "He was harassing me because I beat him in a poker game and then admitted that he intentionally left a friend of mine to die! I wasn't thinking when I said that!" Seth was about to say something else, but then stopped when something more important occurred to him. "W… Where's the rest of him?"

"Well, if you're acting like this to the parts that I saved for you, you probably wouldn't have liked to see what we did to the rest of him," Lilim responded as if she were talking about the weather or how nice someone's clothes looked.

"Though I don't even see what the problem is here."

"Just because he was rude to me doesn't mean I wanted him dead!" Seth shouted at her in turn. Lilim's response to what he had said, however, was to stare at him as if he had spoken gibberish. Like before this greatly disturbed Seth because while he could tell that she was obviously confused, the specific look of confusion that she wore on her face was nearly identical to what others had described to him as the look he wore whenever he was confused. Which was often.

"Why are you getting this upset over someone you hated?" Lilim then asked, and from the tone of her voice Seth was now absolutely sure that she genuinely did want an answer to that question because she did not know it already. "Are you going to act like this when we get to Sol?"

"What?"

"What do you mean what? You came here of your own volition and chose to leave the humans behind. You're here now and I've filled you in on what brought about this great big family reunion of ours. And now that you are here and know all of that, you're going to be fighting alongside us, aren't you? Why would you come here if you had any other choice?"

"I-" Seth began, but stopped when he realized that he didn't really have an answer for that question. Yes, he wanted to come here so that he could talk to Lilim and be safe from other humans who may have wanted to kill him, but it only now occurred to him that he never once thought of what would happen or what he would do beyond that. Like his words to Joseph he had made that decision in the heat of the moment, and in doing so had completely neglected to think about the future. Only now was he beginning to regret both of those things. "I... wanted advice. I wanted someone to help me that I knew for certain wouldn't lie to me."

"And I haven't," Lilim was quick to respond.

"I know!" Seth continued. "But that isn't the issue here! I came to you for help and you gave me eyes!" As he said that out loud though, another thought suddenly occurred to him. One that built upon all of the other things that he had suddenly realized since he had arrived here. If Lilim did this to Joseph, someone that he barely knew, because of one comment that he had made in the heat of the moment without thinking about it, what would she do to the people he actually cared about? The friends he spent time with, the people back in Canaan, the people in Sol, where he knew that Filia, Raz, Daedalus, and Tara were all from. Not only them, but despite everything even Vivian still came to his mind when thinking about this. Lilim did say that she was going directly to Sol, a city full of people Seth did not know and likely never would, but given all of the things that Seth had learned about monsters in the time he had been alive, as well as all of the things that Lilim had said to him in the short time they had talked, one thing was becoming more and more clear to Seth the longer they did talk. She would not stop with Sol.

Seth initially had come here to escape his fear of being killed and all of the pain that came with it. Now, however, in light of all he had just learned, he now understood that in running from one fear he had encountered another that was so much larger, and so much scarier than he could have ever imagined. Yes, he was a monster and he knew perfectly well that monsters killed humans, but the idea of killing enough humans to fill a city, including humans that he cared about despite everything, and then moving on to another place to do it all again unsettled him to such a degree that he could not even comprehend it. Then the thought occurred to him, if this gathering here was enough monsters to kill every single human in what Lilim had said was the most impenetrable city in the world, what would they do to a small town like Canaan? It was at that realization that Seth fully accepted that he had made a mistake, and that he had no one at all to blame for it but himself.

"I…" Seth began as he balled his hands into fists and put on as brave a face as he could. "I can't let you do this. I'll… I'll stop you." Silence reigned over the next several seconds as Lilim at first didn't give any kind of response whatsoever to what Seth had said to her, but then suddenly burst out laughing again as if she had just heard the funniest joke in the world. Unlike before, however, her laughter was like a howl that echoed loudly throughout the vast, endless desert they were all in. Seth even felt a chill run up his spine as he heard what sounded like several of the monsters behind her attempting to join in her laughter with mixed results. Lilim's laughter continued for several long, long seconds before she eventually slowed down and drew her attention fully back to Seth. The joy fueled smile that she wore before returning with a vengeance as she did.

"Ah, Seth," she began once she had calmed herself down somewhat. "I know you're young, but don't be stupid. You're surrounded by more of your brethren than you can count. Nearly all of which I had to beat into submission to get them to follow me. Do you really think that you can do that to me? And even if you could, I think it's far more likely that one of your brothers or sisters behind me here would immediately challenge you to a fight afterwards instead of following you. Are you really going to try and risk having to fight every single one of us?" Seth looked out at the army of monsters behind Lilim as she motioned towards them with both hands. While he could pick out individual ones here or there, in truth there were so many of them that they all blended together like an obsidian sky filled with ruby stars. If he really was going to do what he said he would though, he knew that he couldn't let that intimidate him. So with that in mind, he returned his attention back to Lilim, took a deep breath, and then spawned a sword in his right hand with his magic. Seeing that, Lilim closed her eyes and let out a sigh. A sigh that Seth recognized as a sigh of disappointment.

　　"Well, if you really wanna do this," Lilim said as she moved her head from side to side and then cracked her knuckles. "It looks like your big sister is going to have to discipline you."

　　Despite the overwhelming feeling of dread in his chest, Seth forced himself to stop hesitating as he swung his blade at Lilim. Lilim, however, despite clearly seeing the attack coming, didn't move even a centimeter from where she was standing. Then, just before the edge of his sword could touch her, Seth's body very suddenly felt incredibly heavy as his sword faded back into mist and the arm that held it dropped to his side as if something was pulling on it. His arm was quickly followed by the rest of him as he collapsed onto the ground and was forcibly pushed into the warm embrace of sleep.

　　A smile crawled across Lilim's face as she beheld the sleeping form of Seth. Even with his humanoid appearance, the way he appeared now while sleeping on the sand brought to her mind the image of a sleeping baby. Part of her even wanted to pick him up and carry him all the way north towards Sol. As much as she wanted to, however, she also knew that he hadn't yet learned his lesson. So with that in mind Lilim lifted one of her legs so high up that it was practically vertical to the rest of her body and her foot was even above her head. Her foot only remained there for a second, however, before like lightning she dropped it into Seth's ribs, upon which a very audible cracking noise rang throughout the desert.

　　Seth's eyes instantly shot back open as the sudden sensation of stabbing pain erupted from his side. Instinctively he tried to scream, but when he did so he felt all of the air in his lungs escape from him as he began to rapidly cough. With both hands holding his side where he had been kicked, Seth rolled onto his back to see

Lilim towering over him with the same foot raised over her head again. Thinking quickly, Seth managed to roll away from Lilim just before her foot could come down where his throat was. He was able to roll up onto his knees. However, in doing so he had to roll over the side of him that Lilim had hit, and this caused another sudden burst of pain to erupt from his wound. This in turn caused him to instinctively wince in pain for a moment as he closed his eyes just before he could pull himself back up. As a result, when Seth opened his eyes back up to look where Lilim was, she was no longer there. While he assumed that she could have teleported, the fact that he did not see her do it was troubling for him.

As soon as that thought entered his head, out of the corner of Seth's eye he caught the sight of a sudden flash of red light coming from behind him. Before he could even turn to look, Lilim hit him in the back of his head with a thin, metal club that had a sort of ovalular bulge at the end of it. The impact from that blow almost knocked Seth face first onto the sand, but he managed to catch himself before he could fall completely. Seth could only let out a growl to fight through the intense pain coming from his now throbbing head as the blood from his newly opened wound began to soak through his hair. Before he could even properly react, much less push himself up, Lilim hit him with the club again with a shot to his back, which knocked him fully onto the sand as Seth let out a scream of pain. Lilim was not done, however, as she then rained down blow after blow upon Seth's prone form with her metal club.

"So sorry that I have to do this. I really am," Lilim said in between strikes. "But you need to learn your place!" Lilim then raised her club high over her head with both hands and brought it down hard on Seth's shoulder blade as he tried to push himself back up again. Not content with that, Lilim then kept relentlessly raining down blow after blow upon Seth until he ceased to move. Just before Seth began to feel the now all too familiar sensations of slipping back into unconsciousness, however, Lilim stopped. Confused, Seth turned his head to see Lilim still standing over him with her metal club held high as the two of them locked eyes. However, rather than strike him again, Seth watched as Lilim's club vanished from her hand as it dissipated into red mist.

Seth's momentary relief did not last long, however, as Lilim then bent down and with one of her long, branch-like arms, grabbed him by his hair and lifted him up from the sand so that they could look into each other's eyes properly. As winded as

Seth was, and even at her mercy, he still found enough energy within him to let out a scream as he swung at Lilim. However, it was for naught as Lilim swatted his pathetic attempt of a strike away from her with her free hand before it could even get close to her.

"Please, Seth," Lilim then began in a calm and genuinely apologetic tone of voice. "Before I have to make it even worse for you. Believe me, I can. Please just stop. Stop trying to fight me. You won't win. It's not like you have anywhere else to go anyway." Seth tried to speak, but when he did instead of words he let out a violent cough as blood flew from his mouth before falling onto the sand between them. When it was over he looked back into Lilim's eyes with the sharpest glare he could manage.

"I refuse," Seth responded with a weak voice before he then thrust his other hand directly into her face and shot a bolt of lighting from his fingertips. Lilim, however, only tilted her head slightly to her right to avoid it. That done, Lilim closed her eyes and let out what Seth recognized as an annoyed sigh, but with a very audible, inhuman sounding growl at the end much like what Seth did whenever he was angry. Before Seth had a chance to contemplate what that might have meant, however, Lilim grabbed a handful of the hair on the back of his head and slammed his face into the sand beneath him, forcing some of it into his eyes, nose and mouth. Not only that, but the impact from the blow was so sudden and so strong that Seth momentarily became dizzy, and as such was unable to figure out which directions were up and down, much less push himself back up.

With Seth at her mercy, Lilim let go of Seth's hair and then, without moving from where she was, reached over to grab one of his ankles. Once she had him, and with one hand at that, Lilim stood back up to her full height and lifted the still blinded and confused Seth up off the sand by only his one ankle. With Seth in hand Lilim looked around and noticed something in the distance, her sadistic smile returning to her face as a twisted, new idea came into her mind.

Seth was only vaguely aware of exactly what was happening to him, but he was aware enough to know that he was being held upside down. The instant that realization came to him, however, his vision suddenly began to speed up as he watched the night sky begin to move in circles around him, the stars in the night sky appearing to look more like fireflies in a tornado as he picked up more and more speed. Before Seth could even fully realize what was happening to him Lilim suddenly let go of his ankle and threw him. With all of the momentum that had been built up from swinging him around like a boulder attached to a rope Seth went flying in a direction that, for all he knew, was away from the army of monsters.

Before Seth had any kind of a chance to clear his head, work out exactly what was happening to him, or even think at all, any and all thought processes he may have had were swiftly and suddenly interrupted when he slammed into something so hard that it both knocked the wind out of him and made him cough up more blood, though he only barely felt that when it happened. At first he thought that he must have been thrown into some rocks, for what other than rocks could hurt that much when thrown into them. As Seth fell forward back onto the sand, however, he began to roll downwards as if he were on a hill as more sand began to slide down with him and bury him slightly. Very confused and in a lot of pain, Seth slowly, for nearly every single muscle in his body now screamed in agonizing pain when he tried to move them, so much so in fact that he wanted to scream, but no sound escaped his throat when he did so, looked back up at what he had been thrown into and was shocked to see that it was in fact a sand dune. This confused Seth to no end because as far as he was aware, sand was soft. It was nothing more than many, many, many tiny rocks all collected together in one place, and the most it had ever done to him in the past was burn his feet when it was too hot. Yet the pain was real, his breath was still gone, and the indentation in the dune as well as the runoffs where the sand fell when he hit it were all there. How something that he knew to be soft was able to hurt him so much when he was thrown into it he had absolutely no idea. Indeed it even hurt his brain just trying to think about it right now.

Seth never had a chance to get an answer to that question as in the time it took for all of that to run through his head, another sudden flash of red light caught his attention from the corner of his eye and he instinctively looked directly above him to see Lilim squatting over him. She wasn't doing anything. She wasn't smiling. She didn't even appear to be angry. She was just squatting over and looking down at him as if she were examining a corpse. Seth wanted to pick himself up and at least try to fight back, but every muscle and bone in his body kept screaming at him that it was too much. He even attempted to get his hands underneath him so that he could push himself back onto his feet, but he only managed to push himself a few centimeters off of the ground before the weight of his own body became too much for him and he collapsed onto the sand again. Seeing this, an expression that Seth recognized as desperation began to slowly form first in Lilim's eyes before encompassing the rest of her face. He had seen expressions like it enough times when Tara had shown them to him, but whether or not Lilim was being genuine he could not tell.

"Please, Seth. I'm begging you at this point," Lilim said to him. Her desperation was in her voice as well as her eyes, which gave some credence to the idea that she was being at least partially genuine. "I don't want to keep hurting you. You need to understand that what I'm doing to you is only a fraction of what humans will do to you. A fraction of what they have already done to you. I can protect you. All of us can protect you. And one by one, city by city, human by human, we can wipe them all out. We can fulfill the purpose that mother gave us and cleanse this world of all life that isn't us. Then, and only then will it be truly safe for our kind. Why wouldn't you want that? Because of a handful of humans that you've decided to give some attachment to? One day they'll be gone and then you will have nothing but a world that wants you dead solely because of the color of your eyes. Trust me, I know what I'm talking about. I know you probably don't believe me, but you should. Because it's true. I've been watching their kind for longer than you've been alive. Longer than anyone you know has been alive. So believe me when I tell you that beyond what you've seen of them, they really don't get any better. They just get worse. So much worse. So please, please Seth. Use that common sense that I know you have and make what is obviously the right decision here. If only for your own self preservation. Please, Seth. Don't make me hurt you any more than I already have." As she finished speaking Lilim held out one of her hands towards Seth.

For a moment Seth considered taking it, if only to end the pain. In truth, part of him knew that Lilim was right. He was more than willing to admit that he really did know only a small handful of humans, but how many was that compared to so many others? There were more people in the city of Dis than he had ever seen in his entire short life, and if there were more cities than just Dis, then how many humans were there in this world? He couldn't even begin to fathom the answer, but he did know that of that number, the vast majority of them held similar opinions of his kind to Vivian, and for good reason. However, before he could make the choice of whether or not to take Lilim's hand, the choice was made for him as he watched Lilim's eyes suddenly go wide.

Before Seth even had a chance to touch her hand, Lilim leapt away from him just as a massive column of fire suddenly burst up from the sand surrounding him in the form of a twister and began to envelop him completely. Lilim landed a little over a few meters away from Seth as she watched the twister made of fire shoot its way into the sky. A flash of pain in the hand that she had held out to Seth momentarily distracted her, however, as she couldn't help but instinctively grit her teeth. When she held up her hand to see what had happened, she beheld the pink, red, and charcoal black colors of terrible burns, and as such it pained her to even move her fingers. She also saw that the reds surrounding the burns, however, were rapidly beginning to turn pink again as the pain slowly began to fade.

With a loud growl of frustration Lilim returned her attention back to the column of fire. While the fire itself resembled a twister in shape, it was not perfectly smooth, as there were some gaps in parts of it, which allowed Lilim to see a human man with long, brown hair standing inside of it with Seth. Their eyes met for only a brief second and a look of recognition crossed Lilim's face as she let out another very loud growl. Before she could do anything else, however, the fire twister suddenly burst outward like an explosion. Instinctively Lilim held out her arms in front of her to protect herself, but luckily for her she was far enough away from the explosion that all she felt was the intense heat from the fire as it momentarily got uncomfortably close to her. After the flames had dissipated neither Seth nor the brown haired human were anywhere to be seen.

With Seth now gone Lilim simply stood where she was and stared at the still glowing glass that permeated the ground where the fire had been. An intense mixture of confusion, rage, and sadness filled her head as she loudly ground her teeth together in frustration and anger. Her attention was suddenly taken away from all of that, however, the instant she felt something land on her right shoulder. With a quick turn of her head her blood red eyes beheld her scout, the bat-monster that Seth had named Cain. The bat-monster didn't say anything to her at first as he simply stared back at her with an almost pleading look upon his face. Seeing that, Lilim gradually came to her senses and took in a very, very deep breath.

"Mistress," Cain spoke to her. "Do you wish for me, and perhaps some of the others, to go look for him and bring him back again?" Before answering Lilim looked back down at her burned hand, which was already looking much better as a good majority of the black portions were considerably smaller than they were before.

"Oh, I would love that," Lilim answered as she dropped her hand back to her side. "But no. If Seth is truly as foolish as he chose to be tonight, then the only thing we can do for him now is let it bite him in the ass. He won't learn otherwise."

As Seth came out from a very unexpected teleport he looked over to Raz, only to watch him fall forwards as he collapsed face first onto the sand where he stood. Without him there to support him Seth followed suit as he hit the sand, then rolled away from him as he landed on his back. As dark as the night sky was, it quickly began to grow even darker in Seth's eyes as the all too familiar feeling of losing consciousness began to take hold of him again. Just before it could turn completely black, however, someone with short, red hair entered into his field of vision. That was the last thing he saw before his vision went completely black.

"Wake up you fucking son of a bitch!" Seth then suddenly heard a very familiar voice shout at him before the sharp sting of a slap to his face forced his eyes to shoot back open. If the red hair, familiar sounding voice, and the burning smell of alcohol breath wasn't enough, the angry as all hell face that he saw when he looked forward told him everything he needed to know about whom he was talking to. Part of him didn't even want to believe that it was really her, yet the evidence was right there in front of him. Seeing him awake, Vivian just stared at him for several very, very long seconds as she took in many deep, heavy breaths. The smell of alcohol invaded Seth's nostrils every time she did. "You... You don't have any fucking idea how badly I want to kick your ass right now you fucking dumbass. Maybe I should." As Vivian spoke her voice almost sounded like a growl, not too different from earlier when Lilim had spoken to him like that. Hearing that made Seth flinch, as he fully expected her to make due on her threat. However, much to Seth's surprise, Vivian instead began to relax a little bit and let out what sounded to him like a relieved sigh. "But that tall bitch beat me to it, and given the reason she did I don't see the fucking point."

It was at that moment that Seth became aware that Vivian was holding him by the front of his hospital gown, which was only barely intact after his fight with Lilim. However, the only reason he noticed that at all was because he suddenly felt a trembling sensation on his chest. When he glanced downwards to see, he saw that Vivian's hands were shaking. Seeing that Seth quickly looked back up into Vivian's eyes, and when he did he saw something that he hadn't noticed before due to the shock of seeing her here. Her eyes were twitching, as if she were trying to look everywhere at once and yet was still trying to focus on him. Not only that, but while he had seen her take in deep breaths, her breathing hadn't slowed, as the smell of alcohol never left after she had finished speaking.

It took Seth a few seconds to put all of these pieces together, but when he did it almost made him believe that he wasn't really looking at Vivian. The shaking hands, the twitching eyes, the rapid breathing, these were all things that Seth had seen people do before, but never Vivian. He had seen Tara do all of these things plenty of times before, and as such he knew exactly what they all meant. Vivian was afraid.

Before he had a chance to mentally process that any further Vivian suddenly let him go of him and stood up before offering him her hand. Given what she had just said to him, as well as what had happened in their last encounter, Seth was hesitant to take it as he just stared at it in confusion.

"Why are you here?" he asked her with a very weak sounding voice. "You're the o-"

"If you're gonna accuse me of the same bullshit that Agatha and Raz did, then shut the fuck up and take my fucking hand, okay," Vivian interupted in a sort of commanding tone that Seth couldn't help but listen to. When he did reach for her hand he was relieved to see that she didn't do anything to him other than pull him up to his feet. Even with her help, however, he found it difficult to stand as his legs struggled to hold him up. He did manage, however, if only through sheer force of will.

Now that he was back on his feet again, Seth looked around to see where he was, but didn't see much of anything due to the dark of the night and the endless surrounding desert. If it weren't for the fact that he couldn't see the army of monsters anywhere he would have sworn that they were standing in the exact same place as before. What he did see less than a few meters away from him, however, was Raz, who unlike him was laying on his back with both of his hands pressed against his head as if he had been hit with some kind of hammer. Not only that, but he was drenched in sweat as if someone had just dumped a bucket of water on him and was in the process of taking several very deep breaths as if he were trying his best not to throw up.

"Are... you okay?" Seth couldn't help but ask him.

"O-oh yeah... I'm... f-fine," Raz answered in between his dry heaves without removing his hands from his eyes. "U-used... a lot of... m-magic... j-just to get here. S-saving... your ass... u-used the last of it. S-so... I-I'm tapped."

"Oh so now you're gonna be just like everyone else for the next several hours," Vivian then said with obvious sarcasm in her voice. "What a nightmare."

"F-fuck... y-you," was all Raz was able to say in response.

"As much as I'd like to," Vivian then said with a snicker as a smirk crossed her lips. "I don't think you'll be able to for a while."

"Nah..." Raz responded with a weak laugh as he removed one of his hands from his eyes. "It looks as if... you have other plans... anyway." As Raz finished speaking his lips curled into his own overconfident smirk. At first Vivian didn't understand what he was getting at until Seth's legs gave out and he stumbled forward. Fortunately he was able to catch himself before he could fall completely, but in doing so he dragged Vivian with him, which in turn led Vivian to realize that neither she nor Seth had let go of each other's hands the entire time since she had helped him up. Once that realization struck her she quickly let go and pulled her hand away from him. Seth didn't understand what that was about, but a part of him felt a twinge of disappointment in the fact that she had done that. Before he could dwell on it, however, Vivian suddenly pointed at him.

"Don't even begin to think that you're off the fucking hook you fuckwad!" Vivian then said to him rather loudly. "You escape from your hospital room in the middle of the night, meet up with a literal fucking army of monsters, then we have to save your fucking ass and now we're in the middle of the fucking desert at night with no fucking idea which way the city is!"

"It's... that way," Raz interjected as he finally sat up, though he still looked incredibly pale and clearly needed some more time to get back up to one hundred percent. As he spoke he pointed somewhere off to his right. A direction that at least to Seth and Vivian, seemed to come straight out of his ass. "That flying eyeball... only flew in a single direction... and kept punching it." As much as Seth wanted to ask why Raz had chosen to use those particular words, he wisely kept his mouth shut. There were, after all, much more pressing matters that needed to be addressed first. "So... knowing that and... using the stars... for guidance. I have a pretty damn good idea of which way... we traveled. So I'm pretty sure... I can get us back."

"Oh, and how is it exactly that you are so certain of that, dickless?" Vivian couldn't help but immediately ask with obvious sarcasm, which caused Raz to start laughing again.

"I'm not," Raz answered after a few good seconds of weak laughter. "Nothing is... ever certain. But do you have any better ideas?" Vivian's only answer to that question was silence as her eyes darted between Raz and Seth, which again caused Raz to burst out laughing. "It's amazing how much you claim to be such an expert monster hunter... yet... you know astonishingly little about... surviving out here. Did all of your training consist of hitting things... and not much else?"

"You better watch what you sa-"

"Before you start with your... threats," Raz interrupted as he held up a hand. "Let me... just say that if I really am the only one that can get us back then... kicking my ass wouldn't exactly be wise. Now would it?" Vivian's only response to that was, again, to fall silent, which in turn caused Raz's smirk to widen. "Yeah... That's what I thought. Let me also remind you that I'm tapped out of magic, he just got his ass handed to him by some tall bitch who leads an army of monsters, oh, and there's an army of monsters that's still out there. So unless you wanna pick up the slack miss 'professional monster hunter', if anything finds us we're fucked. I... should probably also mention that it will take us a few hours at least to get back to Dis... and since we left in a hurry we have no water. So if I were you I'd save your energy and vent your frustrations out on the next abomination of nature that we see. In the meantime... I suggest that as soon as some of us are able we start walking. We only got so many hours until daylight and while it's not the best idea, given our current predicament it's better than walking in the sun."

"Great," was all Vivian could say in response before she then spun back around to face Seth, put her face only a few centimeters from his, and shot him a death fueled glare that was not unlike an angry mother wolf protecting her newborn cubs. "So that means we have a few hours for you to explain to us exactly what in the actual fuck is going on here. And you better answer any follow up questions that we have. Got it?"

"Umm... yes," was the only thing that Seth felt that he could respond with, albeit with obvious anxiety in his voice as he tried to back away from Vivian without actually moving.

"First thing's first then," Vivian then said. "Who the fuck is that woman?"

While Seth was hesitant to answer that question, he knew that he couldn't avoid it forever now. So with that in mind he took a second for himself, took in a deep breath, steeled his nerves, and tried to think of exactly where the best place to begin would be. After only a second of thinking about it, however, the answer became obvious.

"Her name is Lilim," Seth began.

Made in the USA
Las Vegas, NV
25 February 2025

18661727R00322